For Cheryl,

THE FIRES OF EUROPE

All the best to a fellow Huguenot!

Phyllis Harrison

THE FIRES OF EUROPE

A Novel

Phyllis Harrison

iUniverse, Inc.

New York Lincoln Shanghai

The Fires of Europe

Copyright © 2007 by Phyllis Harrison

iUniverse books may be ordered through booksellers or by contacting:

iUniverse
2021 Pine Lake Road, Suite 100
Lincoln, NE 68512
www.iuniverse.com
1-800-Authors (1-800-288-4677)

Because of the dynamic nature of the Internet, any Web addresses or links contained in this book may have changed since publication and may no longer be valid.

Certain characters in this work are historical figures, and certain events portrayed did take place. However, this is a work of fiction. All of the other characters, names, and events as well as all places, incidents, organizations, and dialogue in this novel are either the products of the author's imagination or are used fictitiously.

ISBN: 978-0-595-44349-9 (pbk)
ISBN: 978-0-595-88678-4 (ebk)

Printed in the United States of America

Rouen, France, Spring 1640

Giles looked beyond his father, out over the water, to the ships coming in. There was a fair breeze today and so the sails remained very full until the scurrying men on board either dropped the sheets onto the deck or hauled them in, depending on the size and type of the vessel and how quickly they were approaching their destination. Their quick motions were accompanied by assorted creaking and clanking sounds that traveled over to his ears across the water and Gilles watched as the ships glided in to the docks the rest of the way, guided by rudder or oar. Gilles' eyes strayed but he kept his head in the direction of his father's voice so he would look like he was paying attention and he hoped that his face didn't betray how bored he really was. It was yet another day of his father telling him about the finer points of the family business, the minutely finer points of the business. Gilles held out the hope that the men working on the docks would lose their footing, slip and drop something in the water, themselves included, just to create a diversion for him, at least for a little while, but they were too practiced and it was a rare occurrence.

He had accompanied his father occasionally since he was four years old and it used to be much more fun than this. After fifteen years, what more could there possibly be to learn about the trade business? Gilles wished that he could be out on one of the boats, wandering around as he used to do, eavesdropping on the crew's lewd gossip as they loaded or unloaded the cargo, maybe tasting some of the forbidden liquor that was sometimes offered to him by the coarse men who worked under the captains while his father did whatever it was that he did. Gilles hadn't known or cared how his father spent his time and he still didn't know. He tried to wait patiently for his father to move on to the next ship. How could the old man make an interesting subject so dull?

It hadn't been so bad when his older brother was still alive and the three of them went out on the rounds but that was a lifetime ago, his brother's lifetime. Gilles reminded himself that it had been last spring, nearly a year now, that his brother had been taken from them. The pink and white apple blossom petals fluttered over from the orchard nearby, just as they had a year ago and Gilles watched the wind take them up from the land and disburse them over to the water. Perhaps in the same way, his brother's spirit had floated up to heaven after he had died. It would be so good just to fly away on the wind, to go with the currents and end up in a different place, any place, far away from here. If Gilles had one wish, just one wish ... but his father's voice broke into these thoughts.

"Gilles, be wary of trade with the Spanish traders. The honest Spaniard hasn't been born yet. The English claim to be our allies as well but none of them has any integrity, none at all. They are rogues, pirates, and so it is best to avoid the English routes, even to save sailing time. They are not successful at their own trade so they must make a living by preying on others. Scavengers and crows they are! You don't have to worry yourself about the Habsburg's so-called sailors, though. There isn't a sailor in the Holy Roman Empire who knows how to sail at all, and if they *do* manage to get a boat on the water, they can't catch our fast ships anyway. Try to speak with any new crew members on my ships who don't look like they are French. Find out who they are and where they come from."

Gilles just nodded assent to his father. He usually got along well with most of the sailors, better than his father in fact. He was a strong and hard worker, not above offering to lend a hand when it was needed and he did know a great deal about trade even though he was still very young. Although he had never sailed far beyond his home port of Rouen, he couldn't avoid knowing about it; just being present at the dinner table exposed him to more information about the family business than many sailors accumulated in a lifetime. With the death of Gilles' older brother, Gilles freedom had come to an end; Now Gilles was his father's heir and future business partner, accompanying him to the ships and business offices in Rouen and Havre while the senior Msr. Montroville personally oversaw all of the business for the family's accounts. Jean Louis Montroville was not a man to trust the running of his business to anyone else, especially not to any hired accountants.

In the past, Gilles had always amused himself with whatever interested him at the moment. He always reappeared just in time for his father and brother to collect him for the next stop. Msr. Montroville had decided, and not without some urgency on his part after his oldest son's death, that it was time for Gilles to learn everything there was to know about the business; after all, Jean Montroville was now approaching forty-five and getting on in years. The boy had to get serious and truly learn everything about it if he was to run this large an operation. Who knew how many more years a man had left on this earth?

"Ask the captain about repairs after each trip, Gilles, and check on them! A good captain knows enough to make the repairs, of course, but the fact that you *asked* him will keep his respect for you; it will also keep the ship from spending too much time in port making all the repairs at once on the little things that add up to bigger things. Sometimes they think they make more profit for you by *not* taking the time out for repairs or spending no money on them, but they are mistaken!"

"Yes, Father."

"I lost an entire week one time on a rotted deck that should simply have been sealed in time! It wasn't until a sailor fell through and died that I knew about it. Be assured, that captain no longer works for me. A rotted deck! The idiot told me that the ship could still sail fine but the crew *couldn't even get to the sails!* Stupidity! Ask, always ask them."

"Yes, Father."

Gilles had started his formal education with a clergyman teacher his father had retained for him. A brilliant, if somewhat quick-tempered, young Father Isaac Jogues of the Jesuit Order had swept into the boy's life with his brown robes and his brusque manner only to discover something that he and his young pupil had in common: a gift for languages. Father Jogues told Jean Montroville that the boy had a good mind and was proficient enough in accounts but that his real talent was with languages. By the time he was eight years old, Gilles had a solid working knowledge of French, English, and Latin and at the docks the boy had learned even more, colorful and useful words in several other languages, none of which he would never be able to use in front of his father.

The young Jesuit priest was a fine teacher but he longed to save souls. His greatest desire was to convert all of the savages they had discovered in the new world. Sometimes Gilles could get Father Jogues to tell him stories about New France, the newly claimed continent across the sea, diverting the course of studies for a few brief moments. After a time though, diversion was no longer the objective: Gilles's imagination had truly been captivated by his tutor's stories.

It was finally the offer of advancement that took the priest away from Gilles though, not to the new world, but to Paris for further studies and Gilles' next tutor was not nearly as gifted a teacher as Father Jogues had been, completely without his predecessor's wit or winning personality. The new tutor emphasized geography and music and complained to Jean Montroville that the boy did not work as hard as he might. The tutor, whose claim to excellence was that he had actually attended the university at Leiden as he loftily told Jean Montroville frequently, believed fervently that this laziness needed to be beaten out of Gilles if he was ever going to live up to his potential. Gilles was only too aware, though, that he was very big for his age and he suspected that his new teacher was afraid to attempt physical punishment without getting his father's permission and perhaps his help, as well. The long hot summer days passed while Gilles added long columns of numbers for practice and this time sorely tempted Gilles to test his physical strength against the intruder. Only the fear of his father's anger kept him from doing something to act on this recurring impulse. Instead of a confrontation, Gilles feigned interest in attending the university some day, using this as his new diversionary tactic with the newcomer.

The new teacher tried to keep Gilles from reading any more of the literature books left behind by Father Jogues by reporting the wasted time to Gilles' father. The tutor felt that if the boy *really* wanted to learn a language, it should be Greek to study the classics, but Jean Montroville drew the line at having Gilles taught such a frivolous thing. He felt that the tutor did not emphasize enough the math that Gilles would need for the accounting side of the business. Further education for Gilles at a university was totally out of the question, even if Gilles *had* actually been interested, a complete waste of time and money to Jean Montroville's way of thinking. Msr. Montroville could buy any teacher, any tutor in the world that he wanted as he believed that his son should learn from the best, but in his own humble opinion, Jean Montroville *was* the best and any teacher was only preparing his son in the most basic way for his real education that was to follow.

Msr. Montroville informed Gilles that it was now time to get more of a practical education anyway and so the disagreeable tutor now worked only with Gilles' younger brother, Charles, any and all physical punishments allowed, and Gilles sometimes listened with pleasure, especially on hot summer days when the windows were opened and the sound of the switch and his brother's reactive yelps reached his ears from the direction of the cottage classroom. Charles studied whatever the tutor wanted him to study and Jean Montroville was not too concerned with the curriculum of his third son as he now put his full efforts into finishing Gilles' education in the practical knowledge of trade. Jean Montroville had discovered that there was an unexpected benefit of taking Gilles with him on the rounds.

"Gilles! Come here! The captain tells me this *German* sailor knows some English and he is the only one who can tell us about the origin of this cargo. What is he trying to say?"

Jean Montroville emphasized the word German as he gave his son a meaningful look.

Through some back and forth, some gestures and questions, Gilles nodded his comprehension. "What did you want to know, Father?"

"First tell me what he said!" Jean Montroville demanded.

The ragged sailor was grinning at Gilles and gesturing at Jean Montroville as he pointed at himself and rambled on in his native tongue.

"Something about him being very helpful to us," Gilles replied uncertainly.

"Yes, yes, of course, but where the devil did the wheat come from and can he get more for us?" Msr. Montroville asked impatiently, pointing to the sacks.

After some more communication between Gilles and the sailor while Jean Montroville waited impatiently, Gilles turned back to his father.

"He said it's bulgur wheat. It was bound for the Netherlands but something happened. I didn't understand all of what he said. He speaks a peculiar German dialect."

"Well, can he get us *more*? A lot more?"

Jean Montroville looked the sailor over. He probably *had* stolen it from somewhere and probably *couldn't* get any more but if there was any possibility, trade in the stuff would make a nice addition to Jean Montroville's income if he could find a steady supply. The commodity was in short supply in France and so it had great value locally but the Netherlands had plenty of it and probably wouldn't miss it if the shipment never arrived.

Gilles gestured as he asked, mixing English with a few German and Dutch words he had learned. The sailor puzzled at first, then nodded and smiled in a sideways, mincing kind of way as he replied.

Jean Montroville didn't need the answer translated: *His* language skills had more to do with the unspoken language and they were keen.

"I thought so! Stolen. Well, all right. If they can get more of it without creating any legal difficulties for me, I'll buy whatever they can bring to me, just as long as it is not wet of course."

The foreign sailor tried to curry the senior Msr. Montroville's favor by smiling and saying something in German to the older man but Jean Montroville had already dismissed him with a wave of his hand.

"What the devil is he trying to say? I can't understand that babbling!"

Jean Montroville put his arm around his son in a fatherly sort of way, a way that Gilles was generally unaccustomed to, and he led the boy a short distance away from the sailor and the captain. In a low voice he said to Gilles, "Let me explain to you about stolen goods, Gilles: *Never, never*, steal from your trading partners. We have many partners: the sailors, the captains, the buyers, the warehousemen. *Never* steal from them because it will come back to you. But if some commodity just happens to come into your possession … eh? Eh?" Jean Montroville grinned and tapped his son on the chest, then turned back to the captain and the German sailor who had been standing there trying not to look like they were straining to hear the conversation between father and son.

"Unload the wheat *here,* for sale in France, Captain. Fill in the available cargo space with salt; they always seem to need more of that for all the damned salted fish they send out of Amsterdam."

The captain nodded assent.

"Did you get that mast fixed yet?" Jean Montroville challenged the captain.

"Yes, sir, I knew you would ask me that. I had it fixed yesterday. Would you like to go over to see it?"

"I will look at it when you return but see to it that I get the repair bill in my hand before you leave. I can't anger my repairmen by making them wait for their money."

"Oui, Monsieur."

Jean Montroville said to his son as they walked away, "Check *just* often enough so that they don't lie to you about making the repairs and be sure that you inspect the quality of the work. Soon you will learn which captains can be trusted and which can't, but continue to inspect the repairs from time to time, eh? And be sure to inspect it when the ship is empty; you can't see damage if our cargo is covering it up."

Jean Montroville was enjoying his new role as teacher to his son and he jumped in with an energy that only someone who truly relished his vocation for the past twenty five years could. He divulged all of his secrets and tricks for success and he swelled with visible pride whenever the boy picked up on some obscure point of trade. Today Msr. Montroville continued his lecture on the subject of stolen goods, started yesterday, and told his son how to find out if the captains had brought all the cargo in to port or were withholding cargo to sell on the side, cheating on the trades. As he talked on and on he punctuated his speech with "Isn't that right, Gilles?" and "You know this, Gilles?" His eyes probed his son's relentlessly to make sure that the boy was listening.

"Yes, Father," Gilles would answer dutifully and he tried to appear attentive, if not interested. Gilles distracted himself by rearranging the lace on his cuffs until his father stopped talking and glared at him, until Gilles' attention returned to his father.

Jean Montroville might have been the way he was because his family had lost almost everything except their title before he married his wife. Her family did not have the lineage of the Montrovilles but they *did* have a gift for making friends and for making money. Jean Montroville certainly believed that his wife's family had not watched their accounts as closely as they might have and so had let way too much of the profit that might have been theirs slip away but he was happy that Gilles had inherited many of his mother's beneficial traits. If he could simply impress upon the boy the importance of watching the financial details, the family fortune would surely take care of itself, just as long as the next years of war were no worse for the country and the business than the last six years had been.

"Empty cargo areas, the crew stalling to keep you from boarding the ship after it has reached port, people hanging around who don't seem to belong there but who appear know the crew ... Are you listening to me Gilles?"

"Yes, Father, Sir, I am listening!"

"These all seem like *little, insignificant* things, they *want* you to think that, but if you see a pattern, be on your guard! They will steal you blind if you let them! And *never, never* allow them to become friendly with the accountants of the business. An alliance between two of them can wipe out a family's fortune in no time at all! Look for unusual cargo, cargo that is not ours, on board. Did they put into a port where they were not supposed to be? Favorable winds and very good sailing time may hide this additional stop but some of our goods may have been traded for something that the sailors want for themselves. Collect *all* of the receipts and when you get them, *look* at them and make sure the right mark is on there. If the mark is not what it should be, it could be that a bottom portion of the receipt has been cut off, altered or forged. *Illegible* receipts are a concern too. They *never* get so wet in storms that they cannot be read if they were stored properly, not unless the ship went down completely!"

"Yes, Father."

"These are not *only* important for our own profit but the King keeps a close watch on the taxes he gets. *Little things, little things*, but they will make sense to you if you look for the pattern!"

Sadly for Gilles, this would probably be the most interesting part of the lessons for today. Gilles could only look forward to more grueling hours later at the accountant's and bookkeeper's dark little offices, poring over their long columns of figures before they could take a break and go home for midday dinner.

"*Columns*, Gilles, *Columns!*" his father would say all the while they were at the bookkeepers. At least when he was outside, Gilles could see the things his father was pointing out on the ship and he could see the activity on the docks and around the warehouses.

Gilles sighed. It was going to be another long day. Was there no end in sight?

Running footsteps interrupted the lesson today though.

"Monsieur Montroville, you are a man of God! Save me, don't let them take me!" The man flung himself at Jean Montroville's feet and clung to his ankles, nearly tripping him and causing him to fall over on top of the beggar.

Gilles recognized the man from town, one on speaking terms with his family in the market but otherwise not very well known by them.

"For *God's sake*, please help me!" the man cried, tightening his grip around Jean Montroville's legs. "Don't let them hang me! I'm innocent!" the man whimpered.

Four of the king's soldiers pushed their way through the mid morning crowds gathering on the nearby dock, many of whom were now staring at the man curled up at Jean Montroville's feet. Kneeling down swiftly, two of the powerful soldiers easily peeled the man's fingers and arms from Jean Montroville's ankles.

"If you're innocent, the courts will bear this out," the captain said to the man. "Sorry to have disturbed you, Msr. Montroville."

The captain of the group swept his hat off and bowed while the other three warriors dragged the sobbing man away.

Jean Montroville said nothing at all about the incident, didn't even acknowledge that anything out of the ordinary had just happened but continued to walk along the quay, talking to Gilles about something that had happened to him once, something that had to do with trade and theft but Gilles was no longer listening. He was shaken down to his core by the incident and he wanted to ask his father who the man was and what he had done, what crime he had committed. Before Gilles could think of a way to ask the question, a way that would not annoy his father, Msr. Montroville called out a greeting.

"Bonjour, mon pere!"

"Good Morning, Msr. Montroville, bonjour Gilles."

The priest dipped his head in return as did the other four priests who followed closely behind him. His dark robes billowed in the breeze and the oversized silver cross on his chest glinted a blinding light from the sun directly into Gilles' eyes. The clergyman's hat stayed perched on his head, but just barely. The breeze threatened to take that away at any time and Gilles waited to see if it would sail off among the confetti of apple blossoms that was now sprinkled across the surface of the water. The priest reached up and held his hat in place with his left hand as he spoke to Jean Montroville.

"I did not see Gilles in services last Sunday."

He was a fat man with bulging eyes and made by anyone else, the remark might have been taken for a kindly inquiry. Msr. Montroville responded with diplomacy.

"I am sure that you just missed him in the crowd, Father. I believe that he *was* running late for one of the services and did not want to disturb your service by taking our usual seat in the front."

"Ah, oui?" The priest pulled his lips back over his teeth into the shape of a smile. "I have not been invited to your home in some time, Msr. Montroville," the priest went on, "but it may be time for me to perform some weddings soon, eh?" He looked directly at Gilles as he spoke.

"An oversight. Father, we have been so very, very busy with the spring trade. Forgive us, we shall send someone around for you this very week."

Jean Montroville smiled courteously but Gilles still had said nothing and found himself glaring at the priest. Gilles rearranged his face as quickly as he could. He had enough difficulty staying in his father's good graces without anyone else creating more difficulties for him. He had only missed one service, having fallen asleep on his bed after the big midday meal.

"Gilles, have you nothing to say? Perhaps you can practice your Latin when the Good Father comes over," Msr. Montroville said. "Unfortunately I myself do not have this gift, but Gilles ..."

"Yes, I look forward to it," Gilles replied dutifully, delivering the words in just the way his father had made him practice this all-purpose phrase but he had interrupted his father and the sentence hung there, limp and without life in the morning air. Gilles hoped that it didn't sound as empty to the priest and to his father as it did to himself. One talent that Gilles did not possess, had never had, was lying, not even to the extent of masking the expression on his face or hiding it, even when it came to a friendly wager over cards.

"What brings you to the docks today, Father?" Jean Montroville asked, changing the subject.

"We are just taking in some air," the priest replied, smiling at his followers, before allowing his eyes to travel over the moorings and the ships.

Gilles wondered what he was really up to, watching the docks so closely. He was certain that the man had no love of the out of doors and was more often to be found smelling of wine and exiting one of the brothels in town, "saving souls" or "on an errand" as he would offer in explanation when their paths crossed. The man of God said nothing more though; he bade them good day, made the sign of the cross as a farewell blessing and moved off along the docks, his flock following along behind him like young spring ducklings.

"What is the matter with you?" Jean Montroville asked through gritted teeth when the priest was out of earshot. He gripped his son's upper arm. "Don't you realize how important it is to keep the damned church happy? We could lose *everything*, including our lives! He is a powerful man with great connections! Why can't you be more like Charles and make a better impression?"

"Because Charles always tells people *only* what they want to hear. He is a polished *liar* and I am not."

Gilles had no sooner said this when Msr. Montroville squeezed his son's arm painfully. He did not often hit his son in public as he did not wish the talk of the town to be centered around this, but he was getting frustrated with his son. Although Gilles was now as tall as he was, Jean Montroville pulled Gilles aside, still gripping his son's arm tightly. In a low and slow but unmistakably angry voice that also seemed to Gilles to hide a certain amount of panic, Msr. Montroville spoke in Gilles' ear.

"Appearance is *everything*, Gilles. For God's sake, for *all of our sakes*, do not let the Cardinal's huntsmen think for a *single moment* that you are *not* in every way a good Catholic. Suspicion of collusion with the treasonous Huguenots can put us all in very serious trouble and do this *very* quickly. You saw what happened here not a half hour past?"

The law of the land actually promised religious freedom, even to the stiff-necked Protestants who were unwilling to bow to anyone but in truth, enforcement of it varied from week to week with the winds of politics. When any one of them dared to speak of the promised freedoms, which was only rarely and only in very closed and very trusted circles such as immediate family, someone always whispered that it was not the King, who could be trusted, but that the true ruler of France, the one to be feared the most was actually the church's powerful Cardinal Richelieu, although he was supposed to be a mere advisor to the King. The Cardinal had declared himself to be the Protestant's champion and friend, and he was, at least when it suited his purposes. At other times he used his leverage to pry loose some of the power and money from the tight fists of the noble families that had accumulated too much of either commodity, riches that might have been shared more generously with the King and with his inner circle of friends. Richelieu had used whatever means he could, including laws and including shame, reproaching the nobles publicly for being so selfish and unchristian, for not loving their country enough to help alleviate their country's growing expenses of the war, for not contributing to the great projects that had been started to honor the King and for not understanding the need for the requisite magnificent trappings of government that were most certainly expected from the greatest civilization in all of the world.

Jean Montroville did not care at all about religion except as it affected his own business and he was not unhappy that the King and Cardinal Richelieu were far away from Rouen. Msr. Montroville was many things but above all, he was a very practical man and if worshiping sheep had been good for his business and future prosperity, then that is what he would have done.

Father and son walked on together toward the offices of the company accountants and for a time Jean Montroville was silent. As they traveled along the filthy streets, avoiding the hazards of animal and human excrement, Gilles took stock of all of his own thoughts about the puzzle that was religion. His mother seemed to have a deep faith that he could not fathom at all but he didn't feel comfortable enough with his mother to ask her about it or to discuss it in general with her.

If Gilles still had access to his best friend, Claude, he might have been the person that Gilles would ask. The isolation of the family estate had always been difficult for Gilles and during his childhood, Claude had been his sanity's salvation. Claude's family lived on the adjoining estate and they were wealthy enough that Jean Montroville had no objections to Gilles spending time with him but suddenly, at the age of twelve, Claude was sent away to join the church and live with the priests, studying at the Chateau de Gaillon with other young priests of great intellect. Never once had Gilles heard Claude mention the church until the day that he told Gilles of his joining. Claude had given no whys or wherefores, simply that he was joining tomorrow and that was that.

Gilles and Claude had seen each other nearly every day when they were growing up but they never got to see each other now except briefly during church services when Claude came in with the procession on Sundays and sat down with the other priests in their own private section of the cathedral. The two friends never got to exchange more than a greeting now and that was only in passing as Claude filed in, surrounded by the other priests, never breaking step, and then leaving in the procession as well. Gilles had never even had the opportunity to ask if the church was truly his friend's calling or if it had been Claude's father's decision, but the novitiate period was short and it seemed to Gilles that he saw a growing sadness in his friend's eyes, a resignation to life rather than the spark of joy and mischievousness that used to be there.

"Another one of God's mysteries," Gilles thought angrily.

Although his father probably kept much of life's unpleasantness from him, Gilles had seen and heard enough in his life already to make him cynical, if not openly disgusted and it all seemed to lead back to the church or at least to Cardinal Richelieu who simply did as he pleased, and took whatever he pleased from anyone who had something that he wanted. It seemed that no one could or would stop him, not the King or even the King's mother who was at first Richelieu's champion and then the only one under the heavens to stand up to him.

No, it was definitely safer to stay on the side of the church, where the power was, and Jean Montroville knew this. In his younger son, Charles, he had an ally who also understood that it was not so important what thoughts you had, only what thoughts you shared with the world. One's inner self could be kept hidden and one's thoughts could not be taken away. Gilles' stubbornness was frequently a problem and a source of trouble for his father.

"My own cross to bear!" Msr. Montroville would say out loud sometimes as if supplicating the heavens. "Who sent this child to me, God or the Devil?"

Jean Montroville must have been thinking along these very lines today for he let out a sigh that sounded like one of resignation to Gilles.

"Come along, Gilles, let's go on board the Marianne and I'll show you something else that I've been meaning to."

His father led the way up the gang plank onto the little ship. Gilles sighed too and followed his father, wondering if it had been God's design or simply an accident of birth that had shackled them together, a father so vastly different in temperament and interests from his own son.

He may not have been the son that his father wanted either but Gilles had to appreciate his own creativity and ability to make up new games to pass the time that he was forced to spend with his father each day. Count the sails. Look at the girls. Chip the wood off the dock with his toe. How many sailors per ship? How many ships in port? How many sailors total? He did make it to all of the church services on time on the following Sunday. Claude was there, of course, and Gilles realized now that he missed his old friend terribly. They used to ride their horses all over the countryside and sometimes they would talk about their future conquests and dreams. Now that both of them were reaching maturity, now that it was time for those dreams to start coming to fruition, Claude was not there to share them with Gilles.

Gilles did manage to have a civil visit with the priest when he came to dinner during the week. It was a pleasant visit if one could call watching a viper without blinking for four hours pleasant. Gilles was guarded in what he said, what he did, and even what he thought in case his face might get him into any more trouble. Monsieur Montroville took pains to lead them all in the long version of dinner prayers before, during and after the meal. He had asked the priest to lead the prayers but either due to respect for Jean Montroville's being the master of the household or perhaps a desire to see how thoroughly he knew and practiced them, the priest insisted that his host say *all* of the prayers. Gilles did get to practice his conversational Latin although there was a good amount of church-related discourse: It was difficult to carry on a conversation in Latin without noting sections of the services that were pertinent to the subject. Charles joined in with his beginner's grasp of the language and Gilles was impressed that his little brother had learned so much. No one ever said as much aloud but everyone knew that Charles was not, and never would be, the student that Gilles was.

After the meal the priest dabbed his large lips delicately with one of the linen napkins, turned to Jean Montroville and said, "You have two fine sons and one with a wonderful proclivity toward those things that the church loves. Would you not give one of your sons to God's service?"

Gilles shuddered at the thought and for a moment he felt the fear that his father might answer with some politely positive remark. His father only smiled and changed the subject, much to Gilles' relief.

Thinking that the polite inquiry by Msr. Montroville regarding the increasing number of daily church services was based on a true interest, the priest was happy to expound on the great need for more guidance in the community.

"A good shepherd does not let his flock stray at all where they would be vulnerable to wolves," the priest said and repeated the phrase in Latin, looking over at Gilles as he spoke. "Any deviation from the one path, *any* deviation at all, leads us to stumble and fall over the precipice into damnation. These are dangerous times for our souls and we must not allow *any* deviant behavior, in ourselves or in others in our community lest the seed of sloth take root and grow into an evil tree."

Gilles did his best to suppress an outright laugh at the mélange of metaphor and wondered how much longer their guest would stay but to his relief, the priest excused himself for the night after he had finished his second helping of dessert and his third glass of brandy.

"I have two executions tomorrow. It's my duty to go and pray for their souls, you know," he said with a smile as he left.

Gilles wondered if one of the executions was the man who had pleaded earlier in the week for his father to save him from the hangman or if it was one of the other townspeople who had been rumored to have been arrested.

The lessons from Gilles' father continued on Monday with Jean Montroville's take on the ongoing war and what it meant for the future of the shipping business.

"There is talk of agreements and peace! That will mean much *more* trade with the Netherlands, England, Denmark and Sweden, *great* opportunity for *great* profit!"

His eyes held excitement and Gilles wished that he could feel that way about anything to do with the family business. Although he tried to learn all that his father wanted him to, it was still under the best of circumstances, only a pleasant pastime and that was only when his father was not around. Gilles made a serious effort to learn the accounting side even though it bored him to tears and he even found that he had a certain talent for it, or so they told him.

His father was pleased with Gilles' progress, too, and perhaps for this reason, as a reward for his son, he told Gilles to pack his things, that he was going on a voyage to the Netherlands on the next trade ship out. Gilles couldn't believe that it was true, that he would finally be getting a chance to escape the drudgery of lessons for a time but his father told him that it had all been arranged with Captain LeBlanc. The little trade ship would take them out to Havre where they would transfer the goods to one of Jean Montroville's larger ships going to Amsterdam with a full cargo of spirits and other trade items from both the Rouen and Havre warehouses.

"*Never* sail a half-empty ship, Gilles. It's a waste of time and money. Fill it up! *Someone* will trade something for something else. The Dutch have more money than they will ever need from their plundering of the rest of the world and with the end of the war in sight, we will be sending more ships there. We will build two new ships, bigger ships, to bring back more of their guilders."

Gilles could barely sleep until the ship set sail but she was in port for another full day until repairs were made to a cracked mast and local goods were loaded. Bottles of wine and mead were loaded along with casks of cider, sherry, Calvados, and Claret to fill the hold of the little ship.

The morning of the voyage was full of fog and Gilles thought that it might be dark and cloudy all day long when he first woke up. His father was already eating when Gilles went down for his breakfast but the rest of the family was nowhere in sight. Gilles rode with his father in the carriage down to the docks, the mist from the fields rising still around them on either side of the road until they entered the closely packed houses that defined the town. The family watchdog, Wolf, followed behind the carriage at a trot, and the port was already busy with activity despite the early hour. Jean Montroville pulled Gilles aside before he let him get out of the carriage.

"It is good to learn all that you can about the family business," he said. "A fool who doesn't know the business well will be unable to realize any profit from even the best business. I know the business as well as anyone can know it and yet *someone* is stealing from me on this route. I believe that the authorities in Amsterdam can be trusted: The Netherlanders are an efficient, meticulous and watchful bunch so it *must* be someone else along the way and I want you to try to find out who it can be. Be very careful though, they will keep you from telling me if they suspect that you are watching them. Captain LeBlanc has his eyes open for the thieves and will watch out for you, too. It *is* time that you learned some of the harsher realities of this business though, Gilles, and if I didn't think you were up to the job, I would not be sending you."

This was heartening and worrisome news all at once. Gilles was pleased that his father trusted him with such a mission and had faith that he could discover something but he had also heard of the sailors who disappeared sometimes during such activities. Gilles had listened with fascinated horror as these stories were told on the docks and the ships as the sailors talked among themselves.

Then the thought occurred to Gilles that perhaps there was really no thief at all, that this was just some test of his father's for him and that was why Jean Montroville felt that his young son and heir was safe enough to be sent alone. If there was any theft, probably it was so inconsequential that it would not be life-threatening; after all, his father had been known to visit the kitchen on a regular basis to count the silverware and the wine cellars to count the wine bottles. This thought reassured him and Gilles thought to himself, *"It's a minor matter, if anything at all. It will be nothing to worry about."*

He said nothing though, just nodded to his father and then gathered up his canvas bag of clothing. He was to be treated like one of the crew on this trip and so he only took clothing he thought suitable for such work. He did tuck some extra money into a hidden pocket of his shirt, not a lot of money, but enough so that he would have some, just in case he needed it.

His father went over to supervise the loading of the barrels of spirits and to take a final count on the shipment. Jean Montroville was not so concerned with the other goods, the dry goods and food stuffs to be taken in trade, but the alcohol was by far the most valuable commodity as well as the most vulnerable to theft. Gilles saw him uncork one of the barrels at random and smell it.

"Ah, non!" Gilles thought, *"He is checking to see if it really is alcohol or if someone has switched it for a barrel of water. Now the crew will certainly see me as a spy, an agent of my father's."*

Gilles turned up the collar on his cloak although he did not really feel that cold in spite of the dampness of the morning. He made exaggerated movements of bending over and examining his bag although there was nothing that needed examining there. He wondered if he should try to slip quietly onto the ship or stay behind and try to blend in with the activity on the dock until it was time to leave.

"You're young Gilles, is that right? Come along, then."

The voice arrived in the fog before the person did and Gilles thought that it might be the captain of the ship, Captain LeBlanc, until he had a better look at the young man who called out to him. He was not much older than Gilles, too young and too slight to be the captain of anything, somewhat darker in complexion, like a Spaniard, but with features so refined, and dark eyes so intelligent that Gilles was certain, even without the excellent French accent, that he was indeed a Frenchman and a Frenchman with impeccable family lines.

"I'm Jean Durie and you can stick with me throughout the trip if you'd like. I'll help you with your bag and show you the sleeping quarters. You can go back and say goodbye to your papa after that."

Durie seemed too short to be a sailor but he was deceptively strong, grabbing Gilles' bag and flinging it over his empty shoulder, his own bag over his other shoulder, not even breaking stride as he headed toward the ship.

"I can take my own bag!" Gilles shouted after him.

That would be all that he would need, for the crew to see someone acting as his personal manservant. Gilles had started out with the hope that he would fit in with the crew and they would surely lose all respect for him and hate him immediately if they saw someone carrying his bag on board for him.

"Fine."

Durie swung the bag down again to the ground but his pace barely slowed so Gilles had to scurry to pick it up and then follow after him. Gilles wondered who this young man was as they bounced up the planks onto the deck, and then climbed down the steps into the little vessel's hold where Jean Durie pointed out into the darkness. "Quarters" had been a grand choice of words. There was barely enough room for a man to crawl over the loaded cargo without banging his head on the underside of the upper deck.

"Is there room for everyone to sleep here?" Gilles asked as his eyes adjusted to the darkness.

"Non. If they get to sleep at all, it will be up on the deck but it's only a couple of days out and your father feels they can certainly go without sleep for that long. I'll leave my things here with you if you don't mind, though: I'd like for my clothing to stay dry if that is at all possible. Listen, don't leave *anything* here that you don't want to lose! They're a good crew on this ship but they'll steal you blind just the same; that's the way it is with sailors. You probably won't be resting very much anyway. It's a short trip over with a very minimal crew, even after we leave Havre, and we'll need every man on board working, both going out and coming back. You wouldn't think there would be that much to do but there are always repairs to be made and things to be kept up, as well as the sails and tiller to work and underwater hazards to avoid. I haven't seen the trade ship yet that sails with enough hands though, let alone any extra. Meaning no disrespect to your father, the merchants won't waste the space or take on any additional weight from men when they can pack more goods onto it."

Jean Durie didn't talk like a sailor but he did seem to know a lot about sailing. Gilles had a good ear for accents as well as for languages and Durie's accent fascinated him. It was not exactly a local accent, more like Havre's, but it had something else laced through it, too, a peculiar, exotic kind of quality to some of the words. Gilles wondered who he was and where he was from but he would have to listen to Jean Durie talk some more until he figured it out.

Gilles left his bag down in the little dark space and returned to the upper deck behind Durie. The morning light was just starting to comb through the fog, sending small beams of lighter gray through the mist as they emerged from below deck. It was still not light enough to get a very good look at the features of Durie's face, especially when he never stood still long enough for Gilles to get a good look at him. He seemed familiar to Gilles somehow but Gilles was not sure if he knew Durie or not: Perhaps he had seen him around town or in Sunday services. Gilles wondered if Jean's comment about stealing meant that he knew something about the thefts or about Gilles' mission. Jean Durie had already known Gilles' name, indicating some link to Jean Montroville or to the captain. Was Durie there as a bodyguard, a baby-sitter, or just another voyager?

Gilles started down the planks to leave the ship so he could say a farewell to his father, when he met a burley sailor coming up at the same time, rolling a heavy cask of brandy up the planks.

"Out of the way you dumb oaf!" the sailor yelled at Gilles. "Don't you know anything at all about ships?"

He was very big and very dirty-looking, menacing in his demeanor. His bloodshot blue eyes glared challenge at Gilles and blond stubble from his scarred and crudely shaved head stuck out from beneath the dark and moth-holed woolen cap that was perched on the back of his head. Gilles moved quickly out of the way, back onto the deck of the ship, but indignation quickly overcame him. The sailors *always* made way for the Montrovilles, the owners of the ships. Gilles' first impulse was to rebuke the man and to inform him that he was not to address a Montroville in that tone, but Gilles' desire to blend in with the crew tempered his response today. He was not sure how many of the sailors knew who he was or why he was there. Maybe all of them knew.

As the sailor passed by to get the keg down to the hold, Gilles believed that he heard the sailor cursing at him under his breath *"Damned nuisance child! Petit Marquis!"* but he was not sure; it might all have been in his imagination. The sailor continued on, lowering the barrel into the hold by rope as other sailors passed Gilles by, struggling to keep their balance as they made their way up to the boat deck with some smaller casks of special cognac under each arm.

Gilles recognized some of the other sailors but not the mean one. Captain LeBlanc had been in his father's employ for some time and Gilles had heard that he was his father's best captain but even so, the crews changed often and there were new sailors on every trip. Seafaring was no occupation for an old man or a man who loved life too much, as too many things happened on the most routine of voyages: Men were swept overboard, killed or crippled by falling sails and crushed in the holds when cargo came loose during storms, not to mention the perils of battles with hardened sea thieves and plain old everyday food poisoning. You could always tell the men who were at sea for too many years as they always got skin diseases and then lost all of their teeth as well. Often these minor health distractions led to major infections and more serious complications including death eventually. Every sailor always said that he was only going to be at sea for a few years, just long enough to make sufficient money to buy a farm. They all said that, but for whatever reason, most of them died before they purchased so much as a handful of tillable earth.

Gilles *had* hoped to blend in with the crew a little more than he seemed to be doing now. When the planks were cleared of the cargo and sailors for a few moments, he made his way back down to his father.

"Remember what I told you and stay close to Captain LeBlanc, Gilles."

"Oui, Monsieur," he answered his father obediently.

Fear briefly passed through Gilles but he reminded himself that he wouldn't have any rounds to go on for a while and *just maybe* there would be some greater adventure. At the very least he would get to travel, even if it was just a little and for a short time. Gilles embraced his father and went back up onboard the ship, being careful to travel behind a line of sailors going up with the very last of the cargo. He could hear some voices from the sailors that were not speaking French, speaking Dutch probably, or perhaps German. Gilles understood some words here and there and he listened attentively. He wasn't sure what he should be doing next when Captain LeBlanc greeted him.

"Welcome aboard, Gilles! I'll be a little busy getting this freighter going and convincing enough of the crew to go on from Havre with us but I trust that you can entertain yourself?" He clapped Gilles on the shoulder in a friendly way.

"Bien sur," Gilles assured him, grateful that the captain was treating him just like any other crewmember.

The captain strode off to the far end of the boat and Gilles watched him go. LeBlanc was all that a captain should be: a large and strong man, friendly and pleasant but very knowledgeable and very tough in business. Gilles wondered briefly what his own life might have been like now if the captain had been his father.

Gilles looked over and saw that the difficult and boring man who had sired him was now checking on something in the small accounts book that he always carried in his left breast pocket over his heart. Maybe Gilles was finally old enough now that he had a choice. Maybe now he could *become* a man like the men that he so admired, a man like the one who now stood at the bow of the ship directing the crew to make the final preparations for casting off and pulling up the anchors.

Gilles heard his father yell a final something to one of the deck hands and then he saw the old man tuck the little book back into his pocket before he strode back to his carriage, climbing in without a single look back. Gilles thought that his father might at least look up one last time and wave to him but Jean Montroville was busy with whatever had occupied his mind during the last few minutes. The Montroville carriage moved forward, back up the road to the estate, followed once again by Wolf traveling at his usual leisurely trot behind.

"Well, I'm a big boy, I don't need my Papa to wave good-bye to me," Gilles thought. He turned around and saw that the planks were already moved and the lines were coming up. The ropes creaked and buzzed against other wood parts and some of the sailors grunted with their efforts. Gilles stayed out of the way until the well-rehearsed crew had the boat headed up the river and out toward the sea.

"Boy, come over here and grab this line!" someone yelled to him.

Gilles smiled to himself. He was going to like being just another one of the crew.

They kept him busy for the rest of the voyage. Gilles helped out with most of the work on the ship and his hands hurt from the ropes by the end of the first day. They were bright red and throbbed and there were new blisters on his palms as well as at the base of his fingers. He thought that he worked hard at home in the fields but the rough sea ropes were a new experience to his hands and were not at all like the smooth leather reins he was accustomed to gripping on a ride through the fields or even the softer barn ropes. Gilles looked around for something cold to put on them and the cool salt water helped at first until some of his blisters broke open. The salt in his open wounds was a new experience too, an experience in pain.

At Havre they changed ships and after the cargo from the Marianne was transferred to the more sea-worthy Lyon, additional cargo was hauled on board. Jean Montroville had talked sometimes about moving *all* of the family shipping operations to Havre, especially when staying in Rouen seemed to be less than cost-effective, but the family home was in Rouen, had always been in Rouen, where their ancestors had lived since Roman times and even long before that, ostensibly on the same piece of land. Besides the issue of comfort though, Jean Montroville liked the anonymity of the countryside. The important ports on the coast came more frequently under the King's watchful eyes and Richelieu's eyes as well, too often for a businessman to develop any permanent sense of financial security there. Gilles wondered if the boat would sink with all of the extra weight but he didn't give voice to his thoughts. Surely the captain and crew knew what they were doing or Msr. Montroville wouldn't trust them as he did.

Jean Durie said little to Gilles during the journey and talked with the crew for most of the voyage. Gilles never saw him go below at all but he did see Jean sharing ale with the men and conversing with the captain. Gilles amused himself when he wasn't helping the crew and the entire journey was bliss, passing uneventfully except for Gilles' missing stockings. His boot hose had disappeared from the top of his sack of clothing and Gilles did not discover who took them, although he kept his eyes open for the remainder of the journey after he made the discovery. The theft made him angry as they were warm and clean and with them gone, Gilles had to wear the same damp and dirty stockings until they reached Amsterdam. Most of the men on the boat wore no shoes or stockings at all and though Gilles continued to look for his hose on every man that *did* have shoes on, he never caught so much as a glimpse of them.

The theft aside, the crew treated him well enough. They were not overly hard on him and no one mentioned his father at all but Gilles was quite sure by this time that they all knew who he was. The sailors did not defer to him though, and so it made for a comfortable trip. The captain told Gilles that they would be staying just one night in Amsterdam and then head back to France in the morning with trade goods from the far corners of the earth. Gilles had seen the bright fabrics from the Far East, exotic spices that smelled like no flower or fruit known in Rouen, exquisite Ming China, shiny black lacquered bowls and dried fruits from lands far from the civilized world of Europe. The Lyon might not have stayed even this long under ordinary circumstances, as time that was wasted in resting, even just overnight, was time that was not spent profitably in moving goods and making money, but Captain LeBlanc told him that it would probably be dark when they got in to port. The city of Amsterdam closed her outer harbor to keep everyone safe from marauders but it also prevented the larger ships from loading and unloading goods after dark.

They made better time than expected though it was nearly sundown when Gilles got his first glimpse of Amsterdam. The city lay beyond a forest of ship's masts and flags that moved with the waves in the light breeze coming in off the sea. Windmills over on the land added to the moving picture in front of him and the effect was quite disorienting. In the fast-approaching dusk, Gilles could see the buildings that were mostly three stories high and packed in tightly next to each other like bottles of wine in their cases. Up ahead he could see the Dutch officials making ready the harbor booms to close the port for the night to what-ever dangers lurked out in the sea as the ship sailed forward through the Ij.

There was no letting up in the efforts of the crew to bring the ship into the harbor as soon as possible; if anything there was a redoubling of work to beat the sun's descent below the horizon and to make it into port before the city officials finished and left for their homes.

They sailed past the outer ring of boats, perhaps faster than was advisable, and received angry stares from some of the men on board the anchored boats. The ship passed by another ring of boats and then within sight of some pillories at the edge of the land. Gilles did not know what they were at first until he saw a second crow come down and land on one. The rags that once had been clothing fluttered in the wind and it seemed to Gilles that the remainder of the bones and flesh on the body left a faint smell on the twilight breeze. The bodies hung, each one like Christ on the cross, their lives not measuring up to what the judgment of man thought they should have been. Jean Durie had just walked across the deck to speak with Gilles when he saw the objects of his young companion's stare.

"You wouldn't have seen the scaffolds before," Jean said apologetically. "The Netherlanders take a very dim view of illegal activities. They kill you a few times for each crime you are convicted of, just to make sure that you are really, really, dead. Usually they garrote you in the square first before your peers, then they leave you out here as a reminder to other newcomers who may have the mistaken idea that being caught at committing a crime is not so much to be concerned about. It works too: There's very little crime here, except for what the officials choose to ignore."

Gilles said nothing as they passed by but he felt nausea as he noted that one of the bodies had the remains of a dress on it. Some solid food or strong drink perhaps might have settled his empty stomach but now he had no appetite for either.

On the captain's orders, the boat made a fast turn, the remainder of the sails were quickly hauled in, and the crew dropped anchors stopping neatly in the exact place the captain had selected. Captain LeBlanc hailed a small launch boat in the harbor that they had nearly swamped with water after they just barely avoided running over it completely.

"You there! Boatman! Help my crew unload a few of these containers and take these three men with you. We'll pay you extra if you make it to the Waag before it closes!"

The ferryman moved to help, not at great speed as Gilles would have expected if he was excited by the captain's offer, but he was an older man and probably had already had a very long day and many such proposals.

"There have been recent reports of pirates lurking in the outer harbor and if you can meet up with Msr. Montroville's Amsterdam agent and take some of the more expensive spirits to the Waag, then I won't have to worry about leaving them on board over night," Captain LeBlanc explained to Gilles and Jean.

Gilles climbed down the ladder after Jean Durie and the captain's man, into the small boat where they attempted to hold it close to the Lyon while casks of sherry and claret were lowered in with them. The ferryman bailed out water taken on board from the Lyon's fast approach and Gilles was soon certain that the tiny vessel would sink beneath the water from the weight. Not long after Gilles made this assessment, the ferry captain did insist that he would take on no more. They made for the land but it was very slow going with the great weight in the boat. They made it into the inner harbor just as the booms came out, the last vessel into the city that night.

"I don't see any agent here to receive our shipment," Jean noted when they pulled up to the pier. "They were supposed to be expecting us today. Maybe he got tired of waiting though, and just went home."

This confirmed what Gilles had suspected all along, that Jean Durie was in fact working for Jean Montroville and was the person who would *really* be doing the investigation work. Gilles wondered if the missing Dutch agent was one of the things he should tell his father about. Gilles really didn't know what he was supposed to be doing now and he tried to remember what his father had been talking about with him for the previous few weeks. Counting barrels. Sniffing at the wine casks. Measuring lumber. Nothing in his memory seemed very helpful or applicable to his current situation. Maybe if he had paid closer attention to his father …

Jean Durie seemed to sense his confusion and helped Gilles by explaining a little about the timeline of the process, something that his father had never taken the time to do in an organized way that would help Gilles make any sense out of it.

"All of the goods unloaded from our ship have to be checked against the bill of lading made before she sailed. Our shipments are weighed and taxed on arrival over at the Waag, the weigh house, and that information will go to the customs house accountants for taxation. What we can get unloaded tonight can be weighed, taxed and then sent on to the warehouses this evening, our warehouse that we use here if we have not already sold the commodity ahead of time on paper, their warehouse if we have a contract from someone already to buy the goods. If the Waag is already closed, the goods that we already unloaded from the ship will have to be left on the dock under a guard's care over night until it opens in the morning."

Jean squinted out over the western horizon and shook his head. "By now the Waag will be closed though, so Chastain here will have to watch the goods tonight."

"Will we stay and keep watch too?" Gilles asked him.

"No need, he is reliable and usually sober."

"Cart your goods for you?" A ragged young man with a rickety cart offered his services.

"Nee, nee, go away. We have no need of a cart man." Jean Durie dismissed him.

"I can cart them *anywhere*, or I can watch them overnight for you so you can go for a meal and some sleep. I'm experienced!" the young man persisted.

"Not tonight, go away," Jean replied.

"Well *I'm* not unloading this for you and I'll need my boat in the morning. You need to empty my boat so I can go home now!" the ferryman interjected.

"Of course! We don't want to inconvenience you since you provided such excellent service! What is your name? Can you help us again tomorrow?" Jean Durie handed the ferryman a gold coin. Gilles wasn't so interested in the ferryman; he was looking the beggar over.

He was about his own age he guessed, and likely strong enough to haul goods competently if the pathetic cart he dragged behind him held up to the job. The cart had obviously been made of salvaged materials with one wheel being a different size than its partner. The young man's dress seemed similarly to be made up of a conglomeration of someone else's discarded articles. He did not remove his hat at all, an impudent gesture for one who was hoping to curry favor and gain employment, to Gilles' way of thinking.

"All right then, you there, you can unload the cargo here for us. We don't need to have it taken anywhere tonight, though."

Jean Durie gave the beggar a gold coin too and the young man started to work, lifting the boxes and tipping his head up enough to reveal in the twilight a firm and determined mouth, a straight if somewhat elongated nose, and intense dark eyes just under the brim of his hat. The ferryman, in a better state of humor than he had been previously, lifted a few boxes as well and Jean gave him another gold coin. He even gave Chastain a coin while he had his money out. The three men, the ferry captain and the beggar finished unloading the boat, following Jean Durie's directions as to where and how to stack the goods. When they were finished, the ferryman checked his moorings a last time, bid them good evening, and went up the street. The young stranger also melted into the darkness of the streets of Amsterdam, only the fading sound of his cart reporting on his progress as he went.

"Eh bien, allons-y!" Jean said to Gilles. "I usually stay at an inn near the water when I'm here on business. It's nothing fancy but it's clean and the food is good, a favorite of the East and West India Company men, too, although many of them have become so rich from trade that they could certainly afford much better. You can come along too if you'd like, unless you have other plans."

Gilles had no other plans. He hadn't really stopped to consider what he would do or where he would spend the night and his father had told him nothing about where he should stay. He had vaguely supposed that he would be sleeping on the deck of the ship but since he had no way back to the ship for the night, he accepted Jean Durie's offer.

Gilles and Jean set off, passing through the winding streets along the water and on into Amsterdam's back streets, their canvas bags slung over their shoulders. As they walked on into the dusk, Gilles observed that the Dutch buildings had a number of features that were not generally found at home in Rouen. There were steps and stoops leading up to entrances on a main floor, sometimes with a basement shop down below that level. Pulleys were built into recessed openings in the outside walls near the roof on many of the buildings and seeing him looking up there, Jean explained to Gilles that they were for hoisting goods up and storing them on the third story. The fronts of the buildings were usually narrow and sometimes they had little bay windows. Here and there were tiny patches of dirt in the front of the structures, some with bricks corralling carefully tended flowers, often times encircling tulip leaves that were now just past their bloom. Where there was no greenery, the spaces were rarely abandoned to the creations of nature; they were still decorated with non-living ornament, stone and brick pavers or tiles. In the rapidly fading light Gilles could still just make out the windmills in the distance, still moving the sea back from the land, grinding the flour, doing all the work that the Netherlanders had discovered that the wind could do and do it far more efficiently than any man or animal could. There were canals, too, little arms of water that went everywhere along the streets and Gilles saw more bridges during their short walk than he could easily count. Jean Durie pointed out a drawbridge, a magnificent piece of modern machinery with a balancing beam that allowed a portion of the bridge to be raised, permitting boats with masts taller than the bridges to sail on through.

Even at this late hour, there were still merchants in the streets and at any given time during their walk to the inn Gilles could hear at least two languages being spoken and one of them was not always Dutch.

"The only place in the world where more languages are spoken in one place is in the new world, New Amsterdam! Now watch your pockets," Jean said to Gilles. "They'll pick them clean here before you know it."

Gilles touched his hidden pocket and was reassured to feel that his coins were still there. Amsterdam *was* an interesting place but what impressed him the most about Amsterdam were the women. At home there were a few that hung around the docks but here there were all kinds of women of all ages running to and fro, even at this late hour. Many of them looked respectable and Gilles noted with approval that some of them were quite pretty. Most of them were properly dressed with their caps in place, their necklines high and their hemlines low but a few showed a little more neck than Gilles was accustomed to seeing. Instead of just standing around to talk and smile at the sailors as they did at home though, most of these women seemed to be in too much of a rush to slow down and talk with anyone, men or women. They all hurried along, some openly holding hands with men, much to Gilles' surprise and amazement.

Gilles had to make an effort to keep up with his companion's shorter but faster legs. The pace of the city was contagious.

"Is everyone always in this much of a hurry?" he asked.

"Of course, there are fortunes to be made that won't wait! There are goods to move and this city runs on trade and speculation!"

"Speculation?"

Gilles had heard his father use the term but he didn't understand how it applied to the frantic activity that he saw all around him.

"Mais oui! There is an active trade market here and these people *adore* the sport of it, not *just* the trading and purchase of commodities but buying and selling things, just on paper too, even things they have *never even set eyes on*, have no knowledge of! A few years ago there was a great market built completely around tulip bulbs and it was the stupidest thing you could imagine, the prices that they were getting for one pretty tulip's bulb, the striped *'Bizarres'* as they called them. These tulip bulbs were not even planted, not even blooming! Sight unseen they would buy them! The bulbs sold for as much as a good horse or *even more* sometimes. Some criminals made money selling ignorant fortune seekers onions or leeks and I think everyone was relieved when *that* nonsense came to an end. This year it is spices that they speculate in. They will buy the promise, just the promise, of a shipload of spices from the orient or the Brazil colonies! Next year it will be something else, probably the beaver pelts that are now gaining value so fast in the market. Speculation is the national religion of the Netherlands."

Gilles was wondering if he could find something as common as a tulip bulb to make his own fortune if the buyers in Amsterdam had so much extra money in their pockets that they were eager to throw away. His father must have heard of these incredible things and perhaps that was the reason why Msr. Montroville was *so* determined to take part in the trade with the Netherlands although there were long lists of legal obstacles and new taxes every year that the King decreed for anyone wishing to trade with the stubbornly independent Dutchmen. Jean Montroville willingly, even eagerly, sent his ships to the Netherlands and his taxes to the French king, knowing two things: that there were great fortunes to be made here and that there were severe penalties for not sharing enough of that revenue with the king. Flowers that could make a man's fortune and pretty women moving those fortunes around the streets! It was another world completely and it made Gilles dizzy to think about it.

Even without the cue of language, Gilles was acutely aware that not all of the people they passed on the streets had been born in this country. There were all kinds of people from different places dressed in a variety of ways. They poured into the streets from the alleys, human tributaries into a stream of multi-colored humanity, and they moved along the streets, swirling eddies of color and sound. Gilles tuned his ear to the different sounds of just the clothing and shoes alone. There were taps and clacks of shoes and swishes and crickles of fabric, even some jingles and clangs of jewelry coming from the men as well as the women. The tables and booths that lined the streets held anything imaginable for sale as well as the unimaginable and were only now being packed up for the night. Gilles saw one table of goods presided over by a man with one arm. The man had two cages of goldfinches as well as a few large squawking birds with feathers so colorful and bright that they hurt Gilles' eyes just to look at them. The man also had a monkey chained to the table and was calling out to passers-by to come and buy his creatures and his wares. Gilles had heard of monkeys but he hadn't quite believed that they really existed until now and it was difficult for him to take his eyes away from the small energetic creature. He wondered how the man moved his goods around or how he had even captured them at all when he only had the one arm to work with.

The buildings were jammed even more closely together as they neared the square and Gilles noted with surprise that there were few wooden buildings here, that nearly every building was made of stone. Jean made a sudden turn from the crowd, pulling Gilles along with him, up the steps and into the inn through a narrow doorway. The streets were noisy enough but Gilles was nearly deafened by the roar of activity inside the tavern room. A blond girl who looked to be about his own age was directing all the traffic, to the tables, to the rooms upstairs, to places in the city that desperate people were still trying to locate before nightfall. They lined up in front of her and she directed the roughest looking boat crews as well as the finest gentlemen in every direction, explaining in precise detail to each one where and how they needed to proceed. Wisps of her blond hair escaped her white cap and piercing blue eyes accompanied an efficient if somewhat cold smile.

"Close your mouth, Gilles," said Jean with a grin. "That's Elsje. She's one of a kind and you'll see her here as well as on the streets tomorrow. She seems to run half of the city as well as her father's inn! Her mother died when she was young and they say she just took over. She has four younger ones that she looks after, too."

Gilles could do nothing but stare. His own mother was a commanding sort of person, too, but he could not see her dealing with the rough crowd that young Elsje was handling with ease. It made no difference at all to her who they were or what their problem was. She dispatched them all with efficiency and moved on to the next crisis that needed her. The kitchen staff obviously depended on her as well and had some crisis going on in there tonight because a young maid came scurrying out from the back with a worried look on her face. Elsje quickly took care of one last man in the dining room and then disappeared back into the kitchen area to see what needed her attention there.

"We'll need to get some sleep tonight," Jean said. "I know you'd like to see the city but tomorrow we need to get up and get going very early."

Jean pushed through the crowds to a small table in the back, with Gilles hanging on to his pocket and following closely along behind him so that he wouldn't get robbed or lost in the crowd. Jean exchanged a few words in Nederlands with the men at the table and they offered him their table as they stood up to put their cloaks on.

"How did you do *that*?" Gilles asked him.

Jean didn't answer. He just smiled mysteriously and pointed to the other chair. Elsje had reappeared with two mugs of ale in hand and she came over to their table.

"It's so good to see you again, Jean! Sorry the food is a little slow in coming out tonight." She pushed a lock of blond hair back up under her cap. "We were so busy today that we ran out and I had to make *more*. It should be done soon though, so while you are waiting, have some ale. I'll get this table cleaned up for you."

"Dank u. We'll be fine here. We're not in a very big hurry tonight."

After she had set the mugs down, she said to Gilles "I'm Elsje", wiped her right hand on her apron and then offered it to him.

Gilles shook her hand and remained staring at her, not knowing what else to say. He had never known a woman that shook hands. "Gilles," he offered his name to her, at last remembering a remnant of his manners.

Her Netherlands speech seemed softer to Gilles than the others that he had heard today. She spoke with Jean and Gilles followed the conversation in her language as best he could, picking up the general meaning. After she had returned to the kitchen, Jean turned to Gilles.

"Well, what do you think of Amsterdam so far?"

Gilles wondered if everything he said was going to make it back to his father's ears and so he chose a vague and social reply.

"It's like nothing I have ever seen before," he replied truthfully.

Jean Durie grinned at him. Gilles now realized that he was hungry and thirsty and he quickly emptied the first mug of ale to fill his empty stomach even though he would have preferred wine. Elsje was prompt in bringing over a second mug. Gilles was used to drinking all kinds of wine ever since he was a small child but he had greatly underestimated the potency of the Netherlands ale. He heard Jean Durie talking on and on to him as they waited for their food, saying something about the Netherlands' struggle for independence, their hatred of the occupying Spaniards, and the role that the Oost-Indie Compagnie and the Westindische Campagnie or WIC as they called it, played in the conflict between the countries.

Gilles felt very comfortable, very warm and suddenly very sleepy but he did go outside to relieve himself before he got too drunk and before it got too dark. He returned to the table just as Elsje was setting the plates of food down in front of them. Gilles said a quick prayer over his food even though his supper companion had already started to eat. Gilles was suddenly aware that he was in an entire country that was missing Catholics and so he very clandestinely crossed himself after his prayer and before he started his meal.

Gilles watched Elsje's comings and goings throughout the meal. People continued to stop her to ask for help and somehow she managed to continue with her work, clearing tables and bringing food, all the time solving the problems and challenges of those who sought her out for her help and advice. Her bread was very good, steaming hot, golden and sweet, melting in his mouth as the butter had melted on the bread and the food was simple but tasted very good and more importantly, it filled his belly. It was so very pleasant in the smoky tavern room that Gilles thought he could stay there for a very, very long time and be content just to eat and drink and watch the frantic activity and variety of patrons.

They were very nearly finished with their dinner when there was a commotion outside in the streets. One man walked to the door and leaned outside to see what was going on. He turned back into the tavern room and shouted "Fire! There is fire on the docks!"

Nearly everyone who had been inside the room ran out, leaving their unfinished dinners or drinks, a crush squeezing through the doorway and pushing others as if the fire was not outside at a distance but inside the inn itself. Many of their livelihoods were tied up with the boats and they were not about to sit around finishing dinner while their fortunes escaped into the heavens with the smoke.

"Come on!" Jean urged, pulling at Gilles' arm. Gilles grabbed his cloak and they were running out the door and up the street with the rest of the city, back in the direction of the docks. There was a smoky smell in the air as they approached the docks, a smell that was different from the smell of the fireplaces and the cooking fires; a heavy sweet smell. It was not like the acrid smell that hung over Rouen on occasions when executions by burning took place, but there *was* something familiar about the smoke. Gilles' heart began to register panic as the crowd continued to run toward the place where they had first set foot on Amsterdam's shore.

Somehow Gilles knew, even before he saw it with his own eyes that it was *their* cargo, their sweet-smelling alcohol that was burning. A large crowd had gathered to watch the fire and Jean and Gilles had to push their way through to get closer.

A few men were throwing buckets of sea water on the flames in a vain attempt to extinguish the fire. In the small, limited area of the dock there was not much room for many people and so there was little to be done to help those who already had buckets. The burning pile of casks blazed up to the heavens as did the ferry boat that had brought them and their goods over from the ship earlier in the evening. The flame's light illuminated the Montroville markings on one of the containers and the flames burned with an intensity that could only mean that the spirits were now fueling the fire to an even greater heat and intensity. Explosions of the heated containers released even more alcohol, sending bits of the flaming wooden containers into the night sky as the spectators scurried back away from the blaze with shrieks of panic at the noise and intense higher flames. The fire fighters backed away from the heat and the explosions too, unable and unwilling to do any more.

Jean Durie held him back by the arm although Gilles had no intention at all of trying to fight the fire. Along with the flames, black smoke also billowed up from the settling pile of burning cargo. One cask at the base of the fire retained its shape even after it burned, glowing orange in the inferno, transformed from a wooden object into a creation of glowing coals.

Gilles felt sick. How was he going to explain this to his father? He should have stayed there with the cargo and not followed Jean Durie to the inn. Some of the debris had fallen or been pushed into the water, perhaps in an attempt to save the docking platform from catching on fire. This debris floated away, hissing and steaming as it carried hot embers out over the waves toward the open sea. Gilles looked around at the crowd. They were mostly curiosity seekers. Where was Chastain, their guard?

The fire could do no more damage as it was contained in the area with the burning dock and ship. The end of the dock attached to the land was soaked with water and other ships that had been nearby, with the exception of the ferry boat, had been moved away to a safer distance.

Jean Durie had been engaged in conversation a slight distance away with some people who looked to be the port's officials and he rejoined Gilles.

"The authorities wanted to know *why* the goods were on the dock, where they should not have been, and who was responsible for watching our goods. They wanted to levy a fine on us but I convinced them not to. Everyone *always* leaves their goods and they don't generally enforce that regulation."

"Are we in trouble?" Gilles asked.

"It's all right, I took care of it. Come along now," Jean said to Gilles, "There is nothing more we can do here in the dark. You and I will return to count our losses at first light."

On the way back to the inn, Jean explained to Gilles that the city of Amsterdam had a special fear of fire due to the great blazes that had nearly destroyed the city at least twice before. Jean pointed out that all of the new buildings going up were stone and that there were very few wooden buildings to be seen anywhere.

When they arrived back at the inn Gilles was relieved to find that his clothing was still there and had not been stolen. He was tired and ready for sleep now. In spite of the evening's excitement, the intensity of the night's events as well as the fatigue of the journey had exhausted him. Elsje was in an agitated state herself, as many of the patrons who had been eating and ran out to the fire had neglected to come back to settle their accounts. She already knew all the details about the fire though, and told them that a passerby had seen the goods stacked on the dock earlier in the evening with no watchman in sight.

"Perhaps someone tapped out their tobacco pipe there," she suggested to Jean. Gilles understood enough of her language to know what Elsje was saying and Jean answered something like "Perhaps" but Gilles thought that it was a doubtful explanation.

"I hope that you find your accommodations acceptable," Elsje said to Gilles in passable French.

Gilles did not sleep well at all as the large room where they slept was full of strangers and strange noises. Individual rooms had all been taken and so they had no option but to accept the hospitality of the "community room". The "bed" was nothing like his at home, simply a place on the floor among other strangers, the hay bedding not even as good as Gilles' tapestry floor coverings at home. Gilles used his bag of clothing as a pillow and fell asleep fairly quickly but his sleep was disturbed throughout the night by a recurring image of his father's angry face, no words accompanying the vision, just his angry face. This peculiar dream was interspersed with images of the burning cargo and the smell of the smoke that still clung to his hair and clothes. Gilles finally gave up on getting any more sleep in the early hours of the morning and went to see if he could find some food. He left Jean Durie behind, stepping carefully over all of the snoring men, bringing his bag of clothing with him and going down alone to the tavern room.

The room was empty of patrons but Elsje was there already, lighting the wall lanterns to disperse the early morning darkness. Didn't she ever sleep? Gilles sat down in the corner at the table they had occupied the night before. A prosperous-looking gentleman, perhaps a merchant, came into the room behind Gilles and asked Elsje about something. Elsje gave an answer, patted the man's arm in friendly dismissal and then went over to Gilles' table.

"You're awake early. Are you hungry?" she asked him in French.

He replied in French, "You can speak Neerlandais. I learn quickly."

She smiled so he assumed that she understood what he said. She named some foods that were available for breakfast but none of them were familiar to him although they might have been foods that he knew in France by a different name. None of it even sounded good this morning and he wondered if he had been so hungry last night that even the strange Dutch food had tasted good. Perhaps he had had too much ale last night or perhaps it was the memory of the fire that was ruining his appetite this morning.

"Bring me what you like, you know what is good," he replied.

Elsje shrugged and disappeared into the kitchen.

A few other men came into the dining room and Gilles wondered what kind of business they were conducting here. One of them sat down to eat and the others just settled unpaid accounts from the previous night before leaving. A dark complexioned man wearing a bright yellow costume and turban entered the front door of the inn. The other customer stared at him and Gilles was curious as well.

Elsje was not uncomfortable with the man in the least, asking him if she could help him after she walked over. The man appeared surprised to see her and more than a little uncomfortable but he asked her something in what even Gilles could hear was an oddly accented Neerlandais. Elsje drew a map of something in her palm with her index finger and explained to the man twice how to get to the street that he asked about. The turbaned man couldn't seem to stop staring at her but finally he thanked her, bowed a little, and left.

Another blond girl came into the dining room from the kitchen and Elsje barked some instructions to her. There was enough of a resemblance for Gilles to surmise that she was Elsje's sister. Gilles tried to listen to all of Elsje's conversations to learn what he could of the language while he waited for her to bring him his breakfast.

"There you are!" Jean joined him, looking very sleepy himself. "I wondered if you'd been spirited away during the night although there is little chance in *that* room."

"I couldn't sleep very well."

"Was it the accommodations or the cargo?"

"Both."

"Ah."

Elsje brought them some cheese, fruit, heavy dark bread and some ale. She smiled at Gilles and he smiled back at her before she returned to the kitchen. Jean saw the exchange, smiled to himself, and shook his head in amusement as he broke a piece of the bread but he said nothing to his young companion.

"Tryntje!" Jean called over to Elsje's sister. "Hebt u boter?"

Elsje's sister called out an affirmation before she turned and went into the kitchen. Gilles said a quick and silent prayer over the food, crossed himself as unobtrusively as he could manage with his head down and his hand barely moving further than a six inch diameter of the sign but when he had finished, still he felt the warmth of color moving up to his face as he raised his eyes and reached for the bread. Durie had said nothing, done nothing, to make him feel this way but either he was not a Catholic or he did not reveal any outward indications of his faith here in this foreign place. Gilles admonished himself to relax and to do the same in the future. He decided to ask some questions to see if Jean Durie knew more about the trip's purpose since it did not appear likely that the subject was going to come up in idle conversation.

"Do you know my father very well?" Gilles asked him.

Jean looked a little startled at the sudden question. "Somewhat. I have worked with him several times and he knows that I know this route and his agents. He hires me to advise him on some matters of trade sometimes."

Gilles was surprised that his father would listen to *anyone*, let alone trust someone who was so young. What magic did this man Durie possess?

"What did he tell you about why I was sent on this trip?" Gilles asked him.

"To get experience and to understand the workings of the business," Jean replied. His answer flattered Gilles but it volunteered no new information. "Why do you ask?"

"No special reason," Gilles replied.

He would leave the subject alone for the moment. Durie was either not trusted enough to be told about the thefts or was a very skillful diplomat. Perhaps Durie was a person his father suspected of collusion if not the actual thief of their goods.

"Then am I to understand that you have you gained some understanding and some experience?" Jean asked.

"I suppose I have," Gilles said and it was certainly a painful truth. He had learned that their trade goods had to be watched every step of the way and that their custody was not to be routinely left to others. In short, Gilles had learned that trust was a valuable commodity, more precious than Spanish gold pieces and was not to be handed out indiscriminately.

Tryntje brought a round dish of golden butter and set it down in front of Jean Durie with a smile and an explanation about something. From Jean's reaction and reply, Gilles thought it might be something that she had made herself especially for him. Tryntje's main distinguishing physical feature besides an over-abundance of blonde hair that wouldn't stay under her cap was a radiantly beautiful face. She was by far the more beautiful of the sisters but to Gilles, Elsje was much more interesting. Now that he had eaten a little of the bread and berries and had some ale, Gilles was feeling a little bit more like his old self again in spite of being tired. Elsje brought them the rest of their food from the kitchen and she shooed Tryntje away from the table. Gilles couldn't decide just what it was on the plate but it looked like some concoction that had eggs, cheese, meat and vegetables all cooked up together.

"Dank u, Elsje" Gilles said, wondering if he was brave enough to taste it while she was still standing there.

She asked, "It's a French dish, yes?" and then left again as abruptly as before.

"Always in a hurry, that one," Jean said, looking after her. He picked up a spoon and portioned himself a bite. "Try the food, you don't seem too willing, but trust me, she's a great cook, even if she's a little *too* creative sometimes."

"She has an odd idea of what French cooking is. She cooks all this?" Gilles asked, lifting part of it up with his knife and sniffing at it.

"Well, with kitchen help, of course, but she oversees everything and could do it all herself if she didn't have so much else to do. If she was my daughter I wouldn't let her be that way, out with the men all the time and such. Old Hendrick can't control her though. She's even more headstrong than most of the Netherlands women and that *is* saying a lot! She's old enough now that she should be putting her efforts toward completing a trousseau."

The suggestion made Gilles nearly choke on his bread with laughter. The thought of Elsje demurely sitting in a chair by the window with needle and thread in hand, waiting for a suitor struck him as very funny.

Jean Durie gave him an annoyed look and said, "Well, *French* women aren't like that, thank God, and it's not the way women *should* be." He took a bite of the bread.

"You aren't married yet and you must be *at least* twenty-five." Gilles couldn't resist needling him.

"Twenty-three, and there is a lady, not that it's any of *your* concern," Jean replied sharply.

"I didn't mean to offend you," Gilles said. He *was* just a little pleased that he had irked his unflappable companion, though.

"I'm not offended at all. You don't find her *attractive,* do you?" Jean was more amused than annoyed now. "*Elsje?*"

It would do no good for Gilles to deny what his face had probably already told his companion. "The French girls bore me. They are just silly creatures who are interested in nothing more than to continue their frenzy of buying expensive clothes and going to parties. They are only interested in my money and position and besides, they all look sickly to me. She looks … *healthy*, yes, healthy."

Jean disagreed heartily. "Are you *blind* Gilles? The Nederlands girls are all too heavy! It's all that heavy food they eat and not enough wine for their digestion! They all weigh more than a plow horse in their old age! I, for one, am looking forward to a lovely French wife and a future life of leisure, a wonderfully boring life; I hope to just collect money for my services and to enjoy my home, my wife, books, and music."

"Not me!" said Gilles. "I will probably *die* of boredom. There is nothing I can look forward to in a marriage to one of them." "*And not much to look forward to in the business either,*" he wanted to add, but he didn't, afraid that the comment would find the way back to his father's ears. He sighed.

"If you don't know what there is to look forward to with a wife, then you *are* in for a nice surprise" said Jean with a sly smile.

"Besides *that*," Gilles said, coloring slightly. "*Any* woman will do for that. I want someone interesting, not someone I want to avoid in the daylight or have simply as a reliable escort for my dinner parties."

Jean shook his head in amusement and just continued eating, making no reply.

"Elsje isn't fat anyway; she has nice, round curves." Gilles appraised her as she bent over a nearby table.

As if overhearing this, Elsje looked over and called "Did you men need something else?"

Jean waived his hand and answered, "Niets meer, dank u."

Gilles dropped his knife on the floor and bent down to retrieve it.

"Come on up, Gilles, she's gone away now and she won't see your red face," said Jean, smothering a laugh. "Enough looking at the girls! We need to get going; anyway, the sun is already starting to come up. We need to unload what's left of the cargo and get the ship loaded up again for the return trip."

"I'll see you next time," Elsje told them after they settled their account with her. "Come back again soon."

"Ja, next time" Gilles replied in her language.

"Your Dutch is coming along fine, Gilles, we'll make a trader out of you yet!" Jean laughed as they went out into the Amsterdam morning.

The smell of the burning casks was still in the air although anyone else besides Gilles might not have noticed it with the morning cook fires burning and the shipyard's tar pots going. When they returned to the scene of the previous night's fire, Gilles saw that most of the landing was gone; a stump of charred boards was all that remained, the area cordoned off from where the remainder of it had burned and then the twisted wreckage sank down into the water. All that was left behind of the launch boat that had brought them over from the Lyon was a rope still tied stubbornly to the ship's blackened bow that poked up through the water, flotsam floating on a tether, an indicator pointing up to the heavens in either supplication or accusation. The casks that had fueled the fire were long since gone.

"There is nothing of the casks left to look at!" Gilles exclaimed to Jean Durie.

"I can see that," Jean replied and in a quieter voice he added, "and so we have no way of knowing if all of what was here burned or if some of it was taken *before* the fire."

The owner of the launch and Captain LeBlanc were already there, surveying the scene as well. Gilles didn't know what to do or say and so he followed Jean Durie's lead.

"How much of the cargo was lost?" Durie asked the captain.

"Everything of what we brought over, the one load last night," LeBlanc replied. "Unfortunately it was the one part that we wanted least to lose."

"And where was the watchman, Chastain, when the fire started? We have not seen him at all."

"He stayed at his post! A woman came and they were having a little ... ahem ... *companionship*, when she hit him over the head with a bottle and took his money. They found him tied up just over there this morning. It's a good thing the fire didn't go any further than it did or he would have been burned to death! As it is he has singed hair and burns all over his body from bits of burning ash that blew over and fell on top of him. He had a night of terror."

"*Tied up*? By *one* woman? And there is no way of finding the woman I suppose? I'd like to talk with her about what happened to our shipment ..."

Jean turned to the man who had owned the launch next. "Was she all you had?"

"Ja, *everything* I had!" The old man was close to tears.

"Has the captain here compensated you?"

"Nee."

"*Compensate him*?! I'm not giving him any money! It was an accident and his own fault if he didn't keep a closer eye on his own ship! Besides, I don't *have* any money to give him!" LeBlanc objected.

"And I spent what I had on our room and meals. Do you have any money Gilles?"

"Yes but …"

"How much do you have? Show me!"

At Durie's insistence Gilles reluctantly pulled the money out of his inside pocket, meaning to hold some of it back but the coins all came out together. Jean took the money from Gilles' hand and started to count it out but before he had finished, he handed the entire fistful over to the man.

"We are sorry that we have no more to give you but I trust this can get you started with a new boat?"

"Ja! Bless you!"

The man's face at last gave way to tears, tears of relief, while Captain LeBlanc looked on uncomfortably and Gilles tried to control his temper. Durie had no right to take his money and so far nothing at all had been said to him about repayment.

"If I had the money …" LeBlanc began.

"There's no more to discuss," Jean replied, dismissing LeBlanc's feeble attempt to match his generosity.

Gilles was furious. It was a goodly sum of money and since it was not Gilles' fault that the old man had lost his ferryboat, then Gilles saw no reason why he should have to part with his own money to pay for it.

"Come along now, Gilles," Jean Durie said. "It's all part of the cost of doing business and we can't spend any more time on this. What's done is done. We need to get the other goods unloaded and landed safely, then load the Netherlands goods on board and head back. We have no more time to waste."

Their local agent, missing the day before, now joined the group and asked them what had happened. He said that he had heard about the fire but had not heard that it was the Montroville shipment that had been lost. As De La Houssaye was introduced to Gilles, he clucked in sympathy and then dispatched a boy to go round up cart men and wagons, both from the warehouses and from the ranks of the free agents to move all of the cargo from the French ship into the Dutch economy. Gilles still fumed about his personal loss of money but he *was* somewhat relieved that Jean Durie had not offered to compensate anyone for the destroyed dock. He wondered about their agent, whether he had anything to do with the fire and he also wondered about the vagrant with the odd cart who had been there the day before, the one who had not returned. Surely he would be here looking for more work unless he had something to do with the fire and was in hiding.

The sailors loaded the rest of the Montroville goods from the ship onto the ferry boats, and after the cart men who arrived were vouched for as being honest men by either the agent or by Jean Durie, they were permitted to offload the goods from the boats onto the wagons. After the cargo was weighed and taxed at the Waag, the officials confirmed the receipt on the Montroville documents, signed the papers and handed them back to Captain LeBlanc.

"Other captains are paying their taxes here. Why don't we have to give them any money now?" Gilles asked Jean.

"Your father has an account in good standing here. He pays monthly so we don't *have to* pay as we go." Jean gave him a smug smile.

When they arrived back at the quay from the warehouse, goods were already being stacked there under the direction of De La Houssaye. There was such a great quantity for them to bring back to France that Gilles was quite certain it wasn't all going to fit on the boat. When Gilles voiced his concerns quietly to Jean Durie, the reply was a loud laugh.

"It will all fit even if we have to stack it up to the top of the main mast!"

Gilles and Jean counted crates, barrels and boxes as the ferries took cargo out and loaded the ship back up. Gilles was certain that he could see it sinking ever lower in the water with each boatload of goods that was hauled aboard. Jean Durie made odd notations, both words and symbols in a little book like the one Gilles' father carried and Gilles wondered if he should obtain such a book for himself. The book, a small vial of ink and a small nail that served as a quill came from inside a leather pouch that hung from Durie's belt and Gilles wondered what else Jean carried in the little bag.

Although every man in the crew appeared to be working as hard and as quickly as he could, far harder and faster than Gilles ever could have managed, it was nearly midday by the time they were finished loading the ship. Gilles wanted to have his midday dinner first but Jean shook his head and told him that they would have to make do with the ship's fare as they had lost too much time already due to the distraction of the fire. Durie compared his count of goods with the agent's and with Captain LeBlanc's, and satisfied that the quantities counted all matched, Jean put his little book away in his pouch and stepped into the launch that would carry them out to the ship with the captain. Gilles climbed in behind him and sat down but before Captain LeBlanc stepped into the boat, a man caught him by the arm and led him a short distance away to where they engaged in a lively discussion on the dock. Gilles couldn't hear the words but the man appeared to be quite angry.

Jean Durie called over, "May I be of any assistance?"

"Just a personal matter, nothing for you to be concerned about!" Captain LeBlanc answered stiffly.

"What is that about?" Gilles quietly asked Jean. "Our goods?"

"It's probably more of a personal nature. I've never seen that man before and besides, I'm quite sure that the good captain doesn't live the life of a monk when he is here. Laissez les bon temps roulle!" Jean smirked at Gilles. "But you can learn from his example! Make sure the lady isn't already married before you spend any time with her."

The man talking to the captain finally snorted like an angry bull and turned on his heel when he left. He did not look satisfied at all about the outcome. Captain LeBlanc looked sheepish but his only explanation to Gilles and Jean as he joined his companions in the boat was that there had been a simple misunderstanding.

While they rowed out into the harbor, Gilles thought about what and how he was going to tell his father. Perhaps someone had only set a few of the casks on fire to confuse how much had actually been burned. Gilles remembered the burning pile and thought that it was lucky that more of the docks and more of the ships didn't go up in flames with all of the alcohol burning, or was there that much alcohol in the fire at all? Perhaps it had been completely drained from the casks before the fire was set.

The ship had been loaded nearly up to the upper deck with very little space left below. Some of the goods were on the deck, secured to the masts to avoid having the payload shift too much during any high seas even though it looked like there would be good sailing weather. The anchors came up and the great ship, low in the water, slowly moved off toward France.

When they were clear of the harbor and underway, Captain LeBlanc called Gilles up to his tiny room.

"You were probably wondering what the discussion was about on the docks before we left, eh? Msr. Van Ness claims that he did not receive ten casks of claret that he was promised. I told him that we apologize but they were all burned up in the fire."

"Is he an unreasonable man?" Gilles asked, trying to get more information without tipping the captain off to his father's suspicions. Gilles did wonder why Jean Durie had not been summoned to the captain's quarters as well.

The captain grinned and scratched his beard as he replied.

"Who can say what is reasonable and what is not? I think he is being *most* unreasonable in this case."

"Is Msr. Van Ness a new account then?" Gilles asked, hoping his interest appeared to be polite conversation.

"On my route he is," LeBlanc replied. "Of course, I do not know what problems *other* captains may have had with him in the past."

The captain excused himself then, saying that he needed to go and check on a torn sail. Gilles could see that he was being dismissed, even if it was in a diplomatic way and as he climbed back down to the main deck he felt a depression settling into his mind like a morning fog. His chance to prove himself to his father had come and gone and he had failed. He would tell his father about the fire as well as the missing agent, the angry customer, and the missing watchman but he did not want to think about how that conversation would go right now. They had lost a lot of his father's money.

The return trip passed too quickly. Gilles put his energies as well as his back and hands into helping the crew. The men grew comfortable enough with him to teasingly ask him how he had spent *his* night in Amsterdam. They tried to shock Gilles by telling him stories, each trying to outdo the other with more and more explicit and fantastic details of their exploits with drink and the women of Amsterdam but Gilles doubted that they could have been so busy all night long and still be on their feet. He enjoyed their improbable stories though and pushed away the certainty of returning to the daily rounds and his father. Gilles wished that he could turn the ship around so that he could go back to the adventures in Amsterdam that he never got to have.

Gilles could make out his father already standing there, arms folded in front of him, waiting for the little ship to come in. As always, Wolf sat at attention behind him. Someone had obviously sighted the ship along the way up river and had notified Msr. Montroville of her return, just ever so slightly behind schedule. Gilles decided that a proactive approach was needed if he was going to avoid a very long series of lectures on his mistakes. He ran off the ship first and stayed by the planks to count the goods as they were unloaded. He needed to at least give the impression that he had been working hard, doing his job. Jean Durie was beside him, counting as well and Gilles could feel, rather than see, his father approach him.

"An uneventful trip I trust?" Jean Montroville asked as Gilles continued counting.

"Non, Father," Gilles replied, "But the return trip was somewhat better."

Glancing over his shoulder, Gilles saw now that his father was in the company of one of his accountants. The numbers man had even set up a little table, complete with ink and paper right there on the quay.

"What's all this?" Captain LeBlanc asked with an uncertain smile, as he strolled down the ramp and handed his paperwork over to Msr. Montroville.

Jean Montroville was all diplomacy and confiance as he replied.

"The damned warehousemen just *never* seem to get the counts right, LeBlanc! I need to get rid of someone, preferably today, and I hope that this is the shipment that will tell me which one of them is unable to count as well as even a small child."

"Shall I stay to help you then?" the captain offered.

"There is no need for that; go ahead and get yourself something to eat. We'll be done here in a few hours."

Having been left with no choice in the matter, the captain inclined his head slightly in acquiescence and took his leave. They stood where they were until the captain was gone from sight, but when he was gone Jean Montroville dropped his nonchalant stance and strode up the planks to board the ship. The sailors who were still offloading the cargo deferred to him of course and waited for Jean Montroville to come aboard before they continued carrying their heavy goods down, balancing them gracefully for a few moments on their broad shoulders, against the small of their backs or grasping them firmly beneath arms with muscles of wire. Gilles followed his father, leaving Jean Durie to continue the counting at the foot of the planks. Gilles was not at all sure what he should be doing next but his father seemed to know.

Msr. Montroville looked around at every part of the ship, even inside the captain's quarters but still Gilles had no idea what he was looking for. Msr. Montroville even tapped with his knuckles and heel on some of the inner partitions and the floor, peering closely at all of the lower decks too, at times from very peculiar angles.

"Father …?" Gilles began.

"Shhh! Later!" his father replied.

He said nothing at all out loud, not even lecturing Gilles as was his custom, but eventually he had covered every bit of the ship before he disembarked again, not even checking the payload at all.

While the rest of the cargo was unloaded, Jean Montroville stood in one spot, his hands clasped behind his back for the entire time overlooking the operation, only the plume in his hat moving ever so slightly when the breeze would pick up for a few moments before dying down again. The sailors, who had at first given the accountant and Jean Durie a glare or two, avoided any eye contact at all with the Montroville party and remained quiet and subdued until they had silently finished their work. One by one they slipped away as the very last loads of the cargo were loaded and hauled off. The accountant handed Msr. Montroville a paper with final counts on it and packed up his things, table and all, into his carriage before he climbed in and it rolled away.

"Durie, join us for dinner tonight," Msr. Montroville said, his invitation more of a command than a request.

"I need to take some time to clean up first, but it would be my pleasure," Jean Durie accepted.

"Do you need a ride back?"

"Non, I'm just a few streets away. I can go faster on foot than by carriage but thank you for the offer."

Msr. Montroville and Gilles climbed into their own carriage that had been standing at the ready. The driver climbed in and gave the reins a snap before the experienced horses started rolling the carriage up the road toward home.

"You look like a common sailor," Jean Montroville said to his son, folding all of the papers together with a neat crease and then cramming them into his breast pocket, the one where he kept his little book of numbers.

"I would hope so Father, I've tried to blend in with the crew," Gilles replied.

He told his father about the fire and the last minute discussion on the dock between Captain LeBlanc and Van Ness. Gilles tried to be matter of fact, in the manner that he knew his father liked to have things presented, but he also presented his own actions in the most favorable light possible to make it clear that he had tried his best to watch over the family cargo. Gilles was relieved and a little surprised that his father looked thoughtful and not angry though he said nothing when Gilles had finished his recounting of events.

"I want to go back to Amsterdam, Father" Gilles said, rather more suddenly than he had planned to say it. "I will have a better idea of what to look for next time."

Msr. Montroville waived his hand to dismiss the idea. "Non, non, too dangerous! It is pretty much on the other end that the problem exists, I have been sure of that for some time. The cargo all goes out and makes it to Amsterdam but not all of it gets to the buyers. I will hire people there to find out what is going on; you will stay here with me."

"I want to go, Father, I let you down and I will do better!" Gilles pleaded.

"You've done fine for a boy. The fire was obviously an attempt to cover a theft. We just need to find out who set it and then we will have our thief or at least his accomplices. I will have the names of every sailor, every warehouseman, and every buyer on that trip and I will find out who it is. I will make an example of them so that the world will know that they cannot steal from Jean Montroville!"

Gilles knew enough to let the matter drop for the moment but he had already decided that he was going to have his way this time; he would get back to Amsterdam to find out who took them for fools and stole from his family. He knew better than to say anything to his father for the rest of the ride, though.

When he arrived at home he went directly up to his room to wash up, ignoring his sister's teasing.

"You smell like a sailor! Wolf smells better than you do!" she laughed, pointing at a stain on the front of his shirt.

Even in his room there was no peace for him. His brother Charles ignored the closed door and wandered in while Gilles was still washing up at the basin.

"How was it? What was it like?" he wanted to know.

"I liked it. I want to go back." Gilles replied, scratching the stubble on his chin.

"Ugh, all that dirt, the smelly sailors, great crowds of heathens … I've heard how awful Amsterdam is. Except for the women …" Charles grinned at him, waiting for a response, hoping to hear something juicy.

Gilles smiled a sarcastic smile back at him. Kind words were just wasted on his mean-spirited younger brother. He had only come in to find out if Gilles had had the opportunity …

When Gilles finally was cleaned up and dressed in good clothes, he ran a comb through his hair but dismissed the attentions of the servant who usually shaved his father every day and when Gilles needed it, shaved him as well. Gilles' mother wouldn't like it but he wanted to keep the stubble for now, a souvenir of his first business trip and journey as a partner in the family business. When Gilles descended the stairs, he could already see Jean Durie in the reception room, eating a small cake from the three levels of cakes set out on a great silver tray. Durie looked up and grinned at Gilles who was struck by the humor as well, of each of them looking so very different in their regular clothes. Lace and colorful brocade had replaced their gray linen and broadcloth.

"Did you have your clothing burned too?" Jean called out to him.

Msr. Montroville invited Jean Durie into his study and for the first time in his life, Gilles was allowed to go in as well. He tried not to stare at all of the things he saw, all of the things he had never seen except in brief glimpses from the hallway as he had passed a briefly opened door: portraits of the family, many leather bound books of different sizes, the great desk, crystal bottles and decanters with glasses on top of an oak cabinet, even an ornate clock.

"Would you like a drink?" Msr. Montroville offered his guest.

"Brandy is fine," Jean replied.

"I'll have the same," Gilles said and wondered if his father would send him back outside in the hall or just refuse to pour it for him but still allow him stay. To his surprise though, his father poured him the drink and handed it to him. It was at that moment that Gilles knew he was there as a businessman, no longer just his father's child. His father seemed almost pleased at this, too, in spite of the matter that brought them there, but at last there was something about his father's business that Gilles found interesting, even intriguing. Perhaps it could even be the beginning of a better relationship between father and son.

"There was no problem with the shipment of goods that went out. Even the goods counted at Havre matched the bill of lading," Jean Durie opened the meeting. "This was the first time that there was a loss of goods due to hazard, though. Whenever a loss has occurred before, the discrepancy was picked up at the warehouse. We have been checking there, too, but it has happened at more than one warehouse. If the warehouseman already signed for it, we have maintained that it was not our concern, it was not our loss, but we do not want the reputation of shorting people on promised goods. One of the cart people bringing it to the warehouses *could* be the thief. This time there was only Gilles and I on shore with Chastain and given his injuries from the fire, I would find his involvement most unexpected. I should have stayed with the goods until morning I suppose, and made sure that they got out safely," Jean Durie summarized, ending with appeasement.

"Non, non, it's not your job, Durie," Msr. Montroville said. "Is it possible that the same man owns *all* of the warehouses that are involved? What about LeBlanc? He is looking more and more like either a fool or a thief. He's no accountant but he has to make sure that all the cargo gets there! Steering a ship is only a small part of a trade captain's job. What was the cargo doing sitting on the docks, anyway? It should have been loaded onto a wagon and taken straight away to the weigh house and then on to the purchasers!"

"It was late and the customs houses were closing. LeBlanc got the goods to Amsterdam all right but he thought he might make it to customs just in time with the one load, relieving himself of the responsibility of the cargo that was most dear or at least save some effort in the morning," Jean Durie volunteered. "Chastain has always been honest and reliable and he is the man that *I* would choose myself to guard our merchandise. Amsterdam is as safe a port as there can be in the world."

Gilles held his tongue.

"Then the damned idiot should have left the goods on the ship where they were safe! If I take it out of his pay, he'll check first next time to see if the offices are closed for the night; that is if I don't have him hanged first as a thief!"

Gilles shrank from his father's anger but Durie was unperturbed as usual.

"The captain informed me that there had been recent reports of marauders or *pirates* in the outer harbor at night and perhaps this was his reasoning for rushing to beat the closing of the harbor. It may even be possible that some of these thieves slipped into the city at night." Jean Durie took another sip of the brandy and said nothing more, waiting for the next question or observation from Msr. Montroville.

"Well, we will have to come up with another way to find out. We'll hold the shipments of claret back for a time and make sure that there will be some demand for it by the time I send more. We'll send Captain LeBlanc again in a few weeks with a shipment of claret and see what we find out; by then we'll be ready in Amsterdam."

The business at hand concluded, Msr. Montroville gestured to Gilles to open the door for them and as he did so, Charles was standing there on the other side.

"Ah, good, I was just coming to let you know that supper is ready," Charles said.

"Don't we have servants for that?" Gilles muttered under his breath. He didn't know why he should be surprised at Charles' eavesdropping.

Any discussion of the matter of the thefts was over for the evening as the meal would have several guests in attendance in addition to Jean Durie. The Junots were there, much to Gilles' annoyance. It was unfortunate that a day that had gone so well had to end with them seated across the table. They were lovely people with a lovely daughter and were invited to dinner and seated next to Gilles far too often. Gilles often had the feeling that he was the only one in the room that did not have his marriage and life to Marie Junot all planned out. When they were in attendance, Gilles could never just finish dinner and go upstairs as he sometimes could; he would be expected to walk with her through the rose gardens afterwards.

"Good Evening, Jean, Good Evening, Gilles." Msr. Junot greeted them, looking at Jean Durie and obviously wondering who he was. "You are late in getting out of your study and to your supper this evening. We have already been urged to start this wonderful first course."

"We just had to finish some *family* business," Msr. Montroville said, emphasizing the word "family". "Let me introduce Jean Durie who has been working with Gilles lately."

"Ah, Gilles has finally been taking a hand in the business? That *is* good news," Msr. Junot said, his curiosity apparently appeased by the explanation. He peered closely at Jean Durie and then stole a glance at his wife before he asked his daughter, "Did you hear that, Marie? Gilles is *working* in the family business."

"Yes, Father."

Marie didn't look up at all until her mother cleared her throat.

"Yes, Father," Marie said in a louder voice. She smiled obligingly at Gilles before her gaze dropped back to her food.

Msr. Junot was a sometime business associate of his father's but Gilles knew that Junot was not as indispensable as he believed himself to be. His major value was in his political connections and in his personal friendship with Richelieu in spite of what could have been serious differences in philosophy with the cardinal; for this reason many people were wary of Msr. Junot and did not speak very freely with him although he was always invited to every social function, both major and minor. Jean Montroville waived his lace-cuffed hand to dismiss the earlier discussion and said, "Let's not discuss the problems of business just for tonight! Let's just enjoy our meal. I should just go into some other line of work altogether; I should become a simple vintner, checking my wine and my vines each day."

That picture brought comic relief and a smile to more than a few faces around the table. It was a standing joke that Gilles' father refused to give up on growing wine grapes although he had yet to produce anything more than a general consensus that the area was better suited for cattle than for growing grapes. Gilles' father asked Jean Durie to say the dinner prayers for the newcomers and when they had finished and crossed themselves, the servants brought their first course. Conversation warmed up and turned to the unusually warm weather that had come so early this year. Dinner was excellent as always but tonight Gilles thought about the simple tavern food he had in Amsterdam and remembered his time there as he looked across the table at Marie Junot.

"It's just as I told Jean," he thought, *"she's too pale with that powder on her face, she looks like a ghost, she's too thin and she can't even think for herself without a servant to do it for her."*

He felt somewhat ashamed of himself, being so hard on the girl. It was not her fault, after all. She glanced up and saw Gilles looking at her, smiled an uncertain smile back at him and quickly lowered her eyes again. Gilles noticed that his father was smiling at him now, too. He really had to let his family know, and let them know soon, that he had no intention of marrying this girl. She was no more than a child. They could just find someone else for him who might be more attractive. There were plenty of girls available for an alliance with his family. He would just pick the best one out, the one that interested him the most.

Near the end of the main course he became aware that his father was watching him intently. After cognac and dessert, Jean Montroville proposed a walk in the gardens as he always did when there was good weather. Jean Durie excused himself, thanking them for the repast and saying that he was tired. Some of the Montrovilles' other guests accepted the alternate offer of the reception room, preferring the warmth of the fireplace and more cognac to the cool night air and roses.

"I will see Jean Durie out," Gilles offered and was gone before his father could stop him. It was really not a necessary duty as the servants not only saw to every guest's cloak and hat but also provided escorts to the carriages with a lantern or a loaned carriage itself from the stables if necessary. When they reached the foyer, Gilles said to Jean, "I need to speak with you in private. Where can I find you tomorrow?"

"I have offices on Water Street if you want to come by. Do you want to hire me?" He smiled at the boy.

"I wanted to ask you something."

"You can ask me now if you'd like."

"No, I'll go to your offices tomorrow. Tomorrow is better." Gilles bid Jean a good night and then he rejoined the others.

"You are very quiet tonight, Gilles" his father noted.

"Just tired, Father," Gilles replied.

"Gilles went on business for me to Amsterdam," Msr. Montroville offered.

"Ah!" the Junots both exclaimed together.

"Gilles, let's show Marie the new roses," Jean Montroville urged.

Obediently Gilles took Marie's arm and led her out the door and up the walk to the newly planted area. He said nothing to her. He couldn't think of anything at all to say this evening. The roses had not taken root yet and the buds on the bushes were not opening; in fact most of them looked like they were turning brown and ready to die. His father had gone to a lot of expense to have the bushes shipped to Rouen.

Marie's shoes were not made for outside paths and she slipped. Impulsively Gilles caught her elbow and she smiled up at him in gratitude. Gilles did not dislike Marie, he didn't even know her and he tried but he couldn't seem to feel anything for her at all. Elsje's face flashed through his mind without being summoned, and she was laughing. It was a good feeling to remember Amsterdam. The memory of freedom left a smile on his face but to his chagrin he noticed that Marie had seen the smile and was smiling back.

"Slow down, Gilles!" his father called out to them from behind. "Not all of us are as tall or as young as you."

"Of course," Gilles answered dutifully. He had hoped to finish the walk as quickly as possible and to go to sleep but now he had to put each foot in front of the other, measuring his steps, slowing his progress and drawing out a night that had already been too long. It was an effort to get through the rest of the evening without falling asleep on his feet, forcing himself to stroll leisurely through the roses.

The time did come when at long last he could say goodbye came and he gratefully and enthusiastically kissed Marie's hand as well as her mother's. He felt that he had done very well this evening given how tired he was and he bid them all a polite good night. He was more than ready to go to his own comfortable bed and dream of the sea but his mother stopped him.

"Gilles, if you please, a word with you, in my sitting room."

"Now what?" he wondered, as he followed her up the stairs and down the hall to her rooms. His mother didn't often take the time to speak with him. It was not so much a lack of affection that kept her from her children but too many tasks that kept Mme. Montroville busy running the household and organizing social activities to help the family business. She was just too busy most of the time for her children.

"Gilles, sit down."

She motioned to a chair. She did not sit down with him and that was not a good sign.

"Gilles, we all have duties to perform, responsibilities. You are fast becoming a young man and if your father has not spoken to you of these things before, I must do so. Our first responsibility is to the church and to our King," she began.

"Another lecture on the virtues of the Catholic Church," he thought. *"I can just tell her I will be sure to attend church more often and then maybe I can go to bed."*

Gilles thought this might be easy after all but why did she have to start this now when he was so tired?

"… But we also have other responsibilities," she continued. "It must be so for the preservation of our fortunes. I remove what distractions I can from your father's life. I direct the menus and hire our household help," she continued, as she rearranged some things on the fireplace mantle, with her back to Gilles. "I bring information to your father as to the needs and progress of the household and I maintain our social ties with people who are important to the business." She turned back around to Gilles. "I also look for opportunities, alliances that may be important, that will help us to increase our wealth and to avoid any political difficulties.…"

Her voice trailed off. She finally sat down in a pink upholstered chair across from Gilles but she leaned forward and clasped her hands. "When I met your father, I knew that we were already promised to each other. Both of our families had much to gain from the arrangement and you can see that we have prospered greatly because of it. Your father and I are very good together and have been blessed by the Almighty with children to carry on our family business. There was no discussion of the matter between us, it was all arranged and when we first met, it was a time to get to know each other just a little. Getting acquainted with each other more was something that we would do over the rest of our lives. Any difficulties or unpleasantness between your father and I might have caused problems for our own fathers' businesses and so we made certain that it would not happen. It is *your* responsibility to learn about the business *and* to take a wife who will solidify our interests and take up her share of the responsibilities that are so heavy in running a large household. Some of the newly successful families, *les bourgeois*, suggest that a child might choose their own mate from anyone in their circle but clearly such a matter is too important to be left to chance or to those with less experience in such matters but I promise you, Gilles, that you and Marie will grow close over time, too." Madame Montroville paused to make sure that her son was paying attention and to see if she would get any hint of cooperation from her son.

Gilles calmed himself for a moment and then started to speak very slowly.

"I am not a child, Maman. I am learning the business and I want very much to help Father more. I want you both to be pleased with my progress."

"And so we are, as far as that goes, Gilles," she replied, "but it is too much to expect you to do it all by yourself. I have spoken with your father about this. You will need to have help and it is time that you took a wife so that she can learn about the workings of our household while I am still around. She will have to take up her share of the social obligations as well as to bring new contacts to us. We have many fine business and social contacts, some with lovely daughters, but

Marie Junot would be an excellent match for you. Her father has the contacts and although she is young, she already helps her mother run *their* household. You would have close friends at the palace, too."

Gilles tried to picture sharing a bottle of wine with the king but that was an image that would not come to him at all except as a joke.

His mother spoke again. "The Junots are agreeable to a marriage when she turns fourteen in a few months. I believe that she is quite fond of you already, which is always a happy surprise in a good match."

"Does everyone have this worked out except me?!" Gilles was on his feet now. The irritations of the day, the liquor he had consumed during the evening and the exhaustion from the trip caught up with him and his temper flared.

"Gilles, I meant to wait a few days to talk with you about this but you seemed very reserved toward Marie this evening and you must not throw away your future due to some mood you are having."

"This is not a 'mood'; this is the rest of my life!" Gilles stated emphatically.

"Exactly, Gilles, and ours too, which is why you need to accept God's gracious gifts and your share of the responsibility. You also need to avoid the temptations of the world and have your mind *fully* on your work. It is not a time for you to have too many diversions. Idle minds …"

Gilles calmed himself and said determinedly, "Maman, I am *very* tired. I will be very nice to Marie when I see her again but tonight I need some rest."

"Then it is settled?" his mother asked him with a smile. The iron hand in the velvet glove again. She wouldn't let him rest until he agreed with her.

"It is settled that I am tired and cannot carry on with this conversation tonight," he said to her. "Good night, Maman."

He was probably in trouble now. His mother would speak with his father. As desperately as he wanted sleep, it was a sleep that came to him filled with angry dreams. He had a recollection of shouting at someone but he was not sure who it was and there was a vague image of tapestries at the palace and walking through great halls. As morning broke he was still tired but feeling somewhat calmer, even more accepting.

Perhaps his mother was right. Everyone had to get married sometime and his parents had already been married at his age. His mother had moved into the house at the age of sixteen and his grandparents had set about educating her as to her duties. He could not let his father and mother down. Who would they depend on to carry on the family business if not him? Charles? That was laughable. Someone had to oversee the future fortunes of his sisters, too, if they were unmarried and his parents were not around. It was selfish to throw away every-thing that his family had worked so hard to accumulate for centuries just for his own selfish desires and entertainment. What was to be gained? He was off sailing around the world when there was work to be done. His father was getting old before his eyes and suffered the humiliation of theft of his goods.

Gilles sighed and ran his hands over his face. Marie was not so bad. She prob-ably would make a good wife and was not so very unpleasant to look at. He didn't want his parents to be disappointed in him. He would work harder to understand the books and to learn all about his father's business, marry Marie as soon as possible and get that out of the way, just as soon as he got back from his next trip to Amsterdam and discovered who the thief was. He had to talk to Jean Durie as soon as possible and find out when they might go again, how he might proceed and succeed on his quest. When he had proved himself to his father, then perhaps he could have more of a role in directing his own life and how much traveling he could do. It was a goal worth working toward.

Msr. Montroville rose at an early hour considering the late dinner the night before. Madame Montroville was already in the dining room finishing her breakfast. It never took her long as she never ate more than some fruit and with no one to talk to except the servants, it took even less time.

"You are up early Msr. Montroville," she said to her husband.

"I need to catch up from taking off early for the dinner yesterday," he replied.

"Then you won't be taking Gilles with you today?" she asked.

"No, let the boy sleep, I'm sure he's exhausted from his trip and dinner last night," he said, pulling up his chair and shaking out his napkin.

"Gilles has already been gone for some time. He said he wanted to go riding but would be back shortly to accompany you."

"Riding! There is work to be done and the boy is off on pleasure rides? Send him to me when he gets in, I guess he's had enough rest! I can't wait; I need to be going right after breakfast."

Gilles had not wanted to drag a carriage with him or the servants to report to his father where he was going. Gilles would tell his father the truth if he asked but it would be easier if there were no questions. He had hoped to go and be back before his father woke up. Water Street was not very hard to find; it was a short street off one of the main streets near the water. Gilles had passed by there many times but had no occasion to turn up the street until today. The little street was quite busy already as the people who lived and worked here had to be up earlier than those whose lives included late dinner parties. Gilles passed the office once before reaching the end of the street and realizing that he must have missed it. He turned around and carefully read all of the proprietor's signs on both sides of the street. A tiny office tucked between two larger ones had small gold lettering in the corner of a window. It simply said "J. Durie".

"He must be newly starting out and without much business yet," Gilles thought. He tied his horse outside and went up to the door. It was not locked and a bell attached to the door jingled as he walked in. The furnishings were very spare and there were absolutely no personal touches of any kind. There were no curtains, no paintings, no floor coverings, and nothing on the walls at all. There was just the desk, two chairs, and a table with ink and some papers neatly piled on it. Jean Durie came out of a back room that was behind a curtain and had obviously slept there last night. He was dressed in different clothes but unshaven this morning and slightly disheveled.

"Ah, I see you found me. Sit down, Gilles, have a seat."

Gilles sat in one of the chairs in front of the desk but Jean pulled up the other one instead of sitting behind the desk. Jean ran his hands through his hair, trying to contain or at least influence the tangle. Gilles never would have guessed that Durie's hair would be so naturally unruly. It surely said something about his grooming efforts that he was able to train the mane of hair.

"What's on your mind that you couldn't say in front of your Papa?" Durie smiled at Gilles from behind sleepy eyes.

"My father wants me to learn his business," Gilles started, still not sure of exactly what he was going to say. "I just want to show him that I am capable of handling the family business."

Jean nodded sympathetically and smiled as if this amused him, but said nothing.

"I know I have a great deal to learn about many other parts of the business but I want to solve this particular problem for my father to help him out," Gilles continued.

"So far I see nothing wrong with that but I do not see what this has to do with me and why it needed to be discussed so early in the morning. Go tell your father this, Gilles, and I'm sure he will understand. He does listen, you know," Jean said, now running his hand over his chin to assess what grooming was needed there.

"I have told my father that I want to return to Amsterdam but he won't listen to me! He probably thinks it is too dangerous but there is nothing I can do for him here."

"Gilles, your father is getting agents together there to take care of the matter. The people who are stealing from him obviously know you and they know me by now. Our being there will do nothing except to make them more cautious and to endanger us," Jean replied.

"Then you are not going back to Amsterdam and will let them handle the matter?"

"Ah, I always have business that takes me there, although I like to go in better style than as a deck hand! I may go back another time, after your father's agents are in place, but as you can see, I do have a business here to run."

Gilles resisted the temptation to ask exactly what that business was. He continued with his plea. "You and I need to go to Amsterdam together. I can help there and I will stay out of the way. You can just tell me what to do and I can help you! You only need to convince my father that I should go with you."

Jean said nothing but ran his hands through his hair again. Gilles went on talking although he asked all that he had come to ask. If he continued to talk for long enough, Jean Durie might at some point give in and agree to help him.

"All you have to do is to ask my father that I help you out. You won't regret it!"

"All right, if that's all you had to ask me, you've asked. Now go home and let me get my day started," Jean said, but not without some good humor.

"You will ask him?"

"I will ask. I don't know if he will agree, but I will ask. I don't really know if going there will do us any good, though. It seems like a waste of time to me and probably does to your father, too. Are you sure there isn't another reason you want to return there?"

Gilles didn't answer his last question but thanked Jean for his promise and left. He returned home as quickly as he could, attempting to arrive before his father woke up but he realized that he had missed that deadline when he got there. His mother sent him back out to find his father and he did, at one of the accounting offices on a street adjoining Water Street. His father was annoyed at Gilles' being late and Gilles was annoyed that he had completed an entire circuit of the town, wasting time and tiring his horse.

"Pressing business Gilles?" his father asked caustically, not really expecting an answer. Msr. Montroville returned his attention to the accounts they had been going over and discussed a supply problem they were having with getting enough suitable white oak for some of the spirit barrels. One of the accountants had the misfortune to mention that another type of wood might do just as well and Jean Montroville lost his temper for the second time that day. Gilles stayed attentive and waited until they had left the office together. He stopped his father for a moment, hoping that his father's temper had subsided.

"I went to see Jean Durie this morning," Gilles said, deciding to tell his father before any assumptions were made as to where he had been or what he had been doing. "I believe that I can be of great help to you if Jean and I return to Amsterdam and discover where the difficulties lie there. Before you answer, Father, please listen to me. I need this chance to show you that I can handle things and that I am as concerned as you are with the profitability of that route and with the future of our business."

The speech sounded good to Gilles and he was certain that he had hit all the highlights of his father's concerns and objections.

Jean Montroville only shook his head and said nothing as he climbed into the carriage. Gilles hitched his horse to the back of the carriage and resentfully he got in with his father. He said nothing more for the rest of the day and was quiet even through dinner. If Jean Montroville even noticed his son's silence, he said nothing and showed not the least sign that he cared. It went on this way for the next week although Gilles followed his father dutifully, saying little and offering nothing. All day long he listened to his father's teaching while thinking up new schemes to talk his father into letting him go back on the next trade ship to Amsterdam, only to discard the ideas that he came up with before he got up the courage to present them.

The big news of the week was that a large business and lands belonging to a prominent family were seized by the King's men. It had been suspected for some time that they were not good Catholics and had more than just Huguenot sympathies, that they were in fact plotting to overthrow the King. When a Protestant service was discovered during the night in one of the outbuildings, the family was detained inside their house. After a few hours, the father and his three sons, looking much the worse for wear, were taken into custody. A rare bargain was struck though and after a few days the family was allowed to pack up some of their personal belongings, although the neighborhood rumors had it that this did not include any money, jewelry, or valuables, not even family heirlooms, and they were escorted to a ship that was sailing for the Netherlands.

This family had been in the trade business also, a competitor to Jean Montroville, and if they had been put out of business by an act of nature or a bad decision, Msr. Montroville might have rejoiced and opened bottles of his best wine to celebrate. Instead, Gilles heard his father mutter "I'm probably next" when they heard the news and that was the last time it was mentioned.

There were those among the University-educated and upper classes who had begun to question the dictatorial attitude and power of the church over every detail of everyone's life but as long as there was relative peace and stability in the country and enough to eat, most were content to allow the clergy to do as they pleased: It was of no great concern to them. Gilles wondered if half of the country really was plotting to overthrow the King as Cardinal Richelieu had insisted. How could this be so? The King was loved by many but the Cardinal was hated although no one would publicly admit to this: It would be seen as a sign of great disloyalty to France. Richelieu seemed to have as much power as God himself, much more than the King, certainly. One man being led to his death on the gallows in the square shouted that Richelieu was not the soul of the church, that the cardinal was the embodiment of evil but they silenced him even before he was hanged, still unconscious, those words being his last. All of the recent past bloodshed, perhaps even of some innocent people, all of the guarantees and promises made by the church and the King for religious tolerance, none of it made any difference. It was even whispered in the kitchens that there were nobles who lived in such fear that their own servants might turn them in for reasons real or invented that they had those servants killed outright as a preventative measure. After all, servants were much more easily replaced than family fortunes. It was just another concern that Jean Montroville had to add to the list of his growing troubles: Taxes to support the war, someone stealing on the Netherlands route, worry about his oldest son and heir and now the church coming to take it all if they didn't cheerfully pay enough in taxes or show enough humility.

With all that was going on, Jean Montroville really had little time to worry about what was going through his son's head. Gilles was showing up, accompanying him every day, and not creating a nuisance. What more could a father ask? Some enthusiasm perhaps, some real interest. The boy seemed to genuinely want to help in the Netherlands but it was getting more dangerous even on that route. There were rumors of thieves and pirates prowling the seas looking for lone ships and cargos to seize. Jean Montroville should never have risked his son by sending Gilles the first time. The boy seemed eager to return though and either did not understand the dangers or maybe he had been pursuing other idle interests while there, the women or the gaming houses. Msr. Montroville was not so much worried about these pastimes with Gilles, though. Gilles' interests and passions seemed to lie more with just going off on some adventure or other. Jean Montroville had not liked the yoke any better when he was a youth but he had adjusted and he was certain that Gilles would adjust too. Gilles just needed to be married to settle himself down and to look more to business for his excitement, his challenges, and his adventures.

Jean Montroville had his people in place in the Netherlands by the end of the month. They were reliable people and he felt fortunate in finding them, confident that they would quickly discover who was stealing his shipments of spirits. Two of the men would go on the boat from Havre and four would be waiting in the Netherlands to follow the goods. Jean Durie would be sent along to tie up a few loose ends on the other side as far as the accounting and on some shipping tax issues that were not clear regarding furs coming from the colonies in the Americas. Jean Montroville sent for Jean Durie and ordered a large shipment of Claret to go out the following Tuesday along with bales of wool, the first straw-berry wine of the year, and the usual items of trade. Things were moving forward.

Jean Durie was always able to accommodate Jean Montroville. How could he say "non" to one so powerful and one so stubborn? He knew the temperament well. It was just easier to rearrange his schedule than to try to negotiate a different day. He knew what Msr. Montroville wanted and had been expecting to hear from him when he was summoned. Gilles was just coming into the house as Jean Durie arrived and he asked, "Is it on again, then Jean?"

"That's what I'm here to find out. My guess is yes," Durie replied.

This time Gilles was not invited into the room with Jean and his father. They were not in there for more than ten minutes when the door opened again and Jean Durie left, closing the door behind him. Gilles waited for him in the front hall.

"Did you ask him about me?"

"I *did* ask but he's not willing to send you along. I leave Tuesday for two weeks. Maybe you'd better let the subject drop for now, Gilles." Jean patted his shoulder.

Gilles said goodbye to Jean Durie, and then went directly to his father's study. He knocked on the door and called out, "Father, may I have a word with you?"

"Enter!" Msr. Montroville called. He motioned Gilles to come in but he didn't even look up from his papers.

"Father."

"Yes, yes, Gilles, what is it? I have much to do today, *we* have much to do today!"

"Father, I want to go with Jean Durie and to help him discover who is stealing from you on the Netherlands route. I feel that I need to go and do this for you."

His father looked up at him impatiently.

"Gilles, we have already discussed this. You need to continue your education with me here and it is time to send investigators to do the work that they do best. It is not always necessary to do one's *own* work, just to hire good people. Besides, it is too dangerous to risk my heir. The matter is closed. Be back here in half an hour, we will be going out to check the warehouses today." He waived Gilles off and had his nose buried deeply in his papers again before he had even finished the sentence. "Close the door."

Again Gilles knew that it was of no use to argue and so he left. He might have been angry that his father had not even listened to him but he had expected as much and now determination had replaced his anger. He was outside kicking a rock along toward the stables when he was summoned back to his father's study. Jean Montroville was just finishing up reading whatever it was in those papers that held his interest so closely. The papers were then shoved into a folder and his father rose from the desk, took up his coat from the hook on the wall and put it on.

"Come along Gilles, the day is getting old," was all that he said. Perhaps he didn't even remember hearing Gilles' earlier request.

They went to several of the warehouses and talked to the people who oversaw them. Jean Montroville tried never to give anyone any warning that he was coming and often it was amusing for Gilles to see people scurrying here and there when they appeared, sometimes trying to hide spirits or an ongoing card game, once even a woman. At other times Gilles pitied them as they struggled with things that they were trying to work on, not needing the additional distraction of Jean Montroville's showing up unannounced.

Infrequently, Gilles saw other business owners like his father on the streets. It was often with some amusement that they regarded Msr. Montroville, accompanied by his son, his papers and his dog, conducting his own business personally and not leaving it up to professional business managers. Those businessmen were content to let others run their businesses for them so they could concentrate on making more contacts and more deals or just spending their time and their profits. Mostly it was good-natured ribbing but sometimes Gilles had the feeling that they were laughing at his father.

Let them laugh, no one could turn a profit like Jean Montroville. An old family legend centered around the time that Jean Montroville had purchased an entire boatload of spoiled lemons while his competitors shook their heads in disbelief. He put every cook in the house to work making a recipe for lemon sauce, bottling it in his wine bottles and trading it or sending it out for sale in distant markets at an inflated price. People still came around, years later, asking if they might pay any price, any price at all, for the wonderful sauce they had once had, Montroville's Citron Sauce. Jean Montroville had not continued the venture, whether it was due to a slim profit margin, too much effort, or just the fact that he had already proved his point that he could make anything, even spoiled lemons, profitable.

The warehouses were secure this morning but a leak was noted in one of the roofs. Msr. Montroville ordered it to be fixed at once and told them that any spoilage due to the leak would be taken out of their pay and out of their hides. The storage seemed otherwise in order and Gilles took note of the orderly stacks of goods as his father went on with his observations and teachings of what to look for, what to observe. Even going to the warehouses was better than going to the stale little accounting offices.

The accounting offices were sometimes located in part of a private home and sometimes in a self-contained office. Since Jean Montroville didn't trust them either, he had many different accountants for many different things and changed them often, sometimes for no reason. Just keeping track of which ones were doing what was hard work in itself. Some were located near the water, but all of them were dull, more or less, in different degrees. They were just gray buildings filled with gray men to Gilles. Gilles much preferred going to see the ships or checking the wine cellars although the cellars could be dull also if his father decided to start counting bottles. How could a man find so many details to check and make what should be fun absolute torture? At times Gilles could see himself running the business in the future. He wouldn't re-check the locks on the doors each time he went in and out, each and every week, though. He wouldn't check all of the account books every single day. Gilles suspected that his father did some things mostly for show, to impress his people with his thoroughness.

Sunday came around again and Gilles accompanied his sisters to church. Charles left for church before them and said he would meet the family in their usual seats but Gilles did not see him there. This morning's sermon was on the duty of all to protect the King and the Church and to be on guard against tolerating any differences that would lead to weakening their chances of salvation. When mention was made of the One Who Is All-Powerful, Gilles couldn't help but wonder if the reference was to Cardinal Richelieu or to God. When he was leaving the first service, his friend Claude was waiting for him in the vestibule. Gilles didn't even have the chance to ask why he was there alone when Claude threw his arms around him.

"Gilles, my oldest friend, I have not seen you for so long!"

The enthusiasm of this greeting took Gilles by surprise. As they embraced, Claude whispered to Gilles "Midnight tonight by the old cottage!"

Gilles saw no one around him except for the crowds of people leaving. He wanted to ask Claude outright what he meant but Claude had already started to walk away, his hands clasped in prayer, his dark robes swaying as he walked.

"You look well, too," Gilles called after him, unable to think quickly of anything else to say.

This was not true as he had never seen Claude look so pale. If Gilles had to make a professional diagnosis, he would have said that his friend's soul was sick. He was overjoyed just to hear a word from his old friend, but he wondered why the sudden need to see him alone when they had not spoken in years. Gilles looked around but he did not see the one priest in particular that seemed constantly by Claude's side.

Midnight.

Only Huguenots went out at that hour, Huguenots or prostitutes and their customers.

Gilles tried to sleep between services so that he would not be so tired that night. He wondered about Claude all day and when he looked over at him during afternoon services, Claude would not make eye contact with him.

Gilles was still tired after supper. It had been a very long week. When he retired to his bedroom, he took his cloak with him and remained standing or sitting to avoid falling asleep. He wrote a little bit, thinking that he might write his reasons down for going to Amsterdam to present to his father but mostly he covered the paper with scratchings and ramblings that he ended up throwing in the trash. At last he decided that it was time to go out to meet Claude or close enough to it. The noises in the house had been quiet for some time and he walked slowly across the creaking floor, closing his chamber door and moving across the hall next to the wall where the floors were quieter. He used the back stairway, went out the servant's entrance and walked over the grass to the street because it was quieter than walking up the noisy cobble and gravel drive that would no doubt alert Wolf. Just up the street and down an overgrown lane was a fallen-in cottage where years ago the boys used to play. Back during those days it was a fort, a ship, a castle, a stable full of fast horses but not in such disrepair then as it was now. Sheep grazed around it by day now and Gilles was just barely able to get inside the front door as part of the roof had collapsed in the center. The sheep would give no alarm now; they were in their pens at night, safely away from the wolves that sometimes still came down into the town at night.

"Gilles."

Claude was waiting for him. He moved out of the shadows, as silently a cat, and Gilles felt suddenly loud and clumsy. Had his friend had so much practice moving soundlessly around?

"Are you all right my friend?" Gilles asked Claude, embracing him. The response was cool.

"I am well enough," he replied. "I have come to warn you and your father to be careful. There are those who watch all that you say and do and report it to others. It is not a safe thing to be too prosperous now, as my parents can well tell you."

Gilles knew that Claude's parents had made a sizable donation of lands and money when Claude had joined the church but was not exactly sure what Claude meant.

"I must be going now, I will be missed," Claude said, "That is all I have to say."

"Missed? Surely you can stay a few hours and they will not miss you until morning! We have so much to talk about! I miss our conversations, Claude."

"I will be missed and I often think about you, Gilles my friend, but I have no news to tell you. Each day is the same with my life."

"Just stay for a little time, can't you?"

"I must go now, Gilles. Go with God's blessing. He watches over all of us."

Claude walked silently past him and then he was gone. Claude had never kept anything from him before. They shared secrets, even their thoughts. Gilles knew that he would never again have another friendship like that, not with any man and he could not imagine that such a friendship could ever exist with a woman. With Claude gone, a large piece of what was good in his life was gone before he even knew or appreciated what it was; and yet, he would be at peace in leaving all that behind if only he could just have some assurance that Claude was truly all right.

Gilles walked home slowly and stopped to listen often. Could someone be following him even now? It was *possible* but the world seemed to be silent except for occasional breezes that hummed past his ear. Most of the road was very dark, even with the starlight but still he kept to the shadows. Perhaps he was just too nervous and needed some leeches or something to balance his bodily humors. If it was not a serious matter though, why couldn't Claude tell him this simple thing at church? He also wondered how Claude could be missed at night when everyone slept. Surely they didn't stay up all night praying? Gilles walked quietly across the wet grass of the field until he got to the back staircase door. He was startled to see one of the kitchen delivery people standing there.

"Msr. Gilles, what are you doing out so late?" the man asked.

For a moment Gilles was off his guard. "Shhh!" he said with as broad a smile as he could manage. "I don't want my family to know what kind of girl I have to see in the dark of the night. They'll be marrying me off soon and my fun at night will be over!" He winked at the servant, pushed past him and went up the stairs.

The servant just stood there with his mouth still open and Gilles surmised correctly that Msr. Charles seeing a woman would not have surprised anyone, but Msr. Gilles' doing so did.

Gilles slipped into his bed and was barely asleep, it seemed, when one of the servants was calling him to get up. It was Monday morning and his father was waiting for him.

Today was the day that they were going to the docks in preparation for tomorrow's shipment to the Netherlands. Jean Montroville greeted Captain LeBlanc amicably and Gilles noted that some of the non-perishable goods were already being loaded. The spirits would be loaded last, safe for another day in their French warehouses in both ports. A mountain of wool, rolled up in bales like hay, was stacked next to the ship. Gilles saw the big mean sailor pounding something into place on deck with a large wooden mallet and some other members of the crew were splicing ropes. Another man was applying tar to something on the starboard side of the ship and the smell of it filled the air. Other crew members, mere sailors and less useful in doing repairs, were not there yet and would arrive in the morning, just in time for the voyage. Msr. Montroville examined what had been loaded already and made a great show of inspecting every item although Gilles knew that his true concerns were with the spirits coming on board tomorrow. Gilles tried to count every item and made mental notes of the placement and the quantities also.

"Will you be coming with us again, Msr. Gilles?" Captain LeBlanc inquired.

"Non, he is much too busy here with me," Gilles' father answered for him.

"Pity, he was a good sailor, not sick once and helped out more than some of the regular hands!"

"Now do you understand the importance of getting everything unloaded and into the right hands right away?" Msr. Montroville queried, ignoring the captain's friendly chatter.

LeBlanc's smile slipped from his lips. "Respectfully, Msr. Montroville, it was not my fault! I could not get to shore with the outer harbor closed and my duty was to stay with my ship!"

"What burned on the dock then?" Msr. Montroville asked sharply. "Next time keep the cargo *together* and defend it with your *life* if necessary. That is what I am paying you for."

LeBlanc said nothing and Gilles could feel the tension in the air. His father often had that effect on people and it used to bother him but now he was used to it.

"Fine, then," Msr. Montroville dismissed the matter as he always did, "we will have a better trip this time, I am certain of that, yes? I will be back here in the morning."

Gilles yawned and stretched, then thought about Claude's warning the night before. He wondered how much he should tell his father and if there was a way to bring up the subject without his father exploding in anger. Gilles knew that no one was more prompt or fastidious in payment of taxes than his father and Claude had not been at all specific about what the dangers were or who the threats were coming from. Gilles' father surely already knew all that Claude had told Gilles, which wasn't much at all. Gilles never did find a good moment during the day and in the end, it was probably best forgotten: It would be just one more reason for his father to be annoyed.

The following morning a misty rain was falling and the streets were a muddy mess. It would have been a good day to stay inside but Jean Montroville was up early and called immediately for his carriage. He took a leftover dinner roll away with him to eat on his way to the docks, refusing the full breakfast of fruits and saying that he would be back for his meal as soon as his early morning business was concluded. He had to make it to the docks before the casks arrived and were loaded on board. He touched the little accounts book in his pocket to reassure himself that he had remembered it, grabbed his cloak and hat and was on his way just as soon as the carriage pulled up to the front door.

He arrived at the ship just ahead of the claret and other spirits and started the count when he heard Gilles' voice behind him.

"Father."

Msr. Montroville was astonished to see his son standing there behind him.

"You seemed tired yesterday so I thought I would let you sleep late this morning."

"I am going to Amsterdam with Jean Durie," Gilles replied, sounding calmer than he felt, and pulling his heavy canvas bag closer to him.

"Gilles, you will go home now and wait for me there," Mr. Montroville ordered.

"I have to do this. I will be back in two weeks."

"Gilles, your responsibilities are here! Go home right now!" his father snarled.

"Father, you are right. I have not been taking on enough of the responsibilities and that is why I must go now. I will be back in two weeks and you can talk to Msr. Junot about wedding arrangements when I return."

Jean Montroville opened his mouth to say something but closed it again when he heard Gilles mention the Junots. Perhaps it was only now, at this moment in the pouring rain, that he realized he could no longer physically drag his son back home. Gilles was as tall as he, but moreover, he was now as stubborn as his father as well.

Msr. Montroville's expression softened only slightly and he wasted no words.

"Very well. Two weeks. Stick with Durie and do not get into any mischief there; I can't afford to lose another son."

It was as close to a blessing as Gilles was going to get.

The sailors had slowed down in their work and appeared to be listening in on this exchange between father and son.

"What are you standing around for? Get back to work!" Captain LeBlanc shouted as he nervously eyed Msr. Montroville, who was probably taking mental note of the work slowdown and deducting it from his final pay.

Gilles and his father resumed counting the small kegs of claret, and when they had finished, Gilles bid his father good day, picked up his bag, and went aboard without looking back. It was just easier to leave that way. He sought the refuge of the ship's hold and a surprised Jean Durie turned around, his lantern and the list in his hands.

"I was wondering if you were here already or not," Gilles greeted him.

"You've come to see me off, Gilles?" Jean asked, pausing to lift the lantern and check something on the paper.

"Non, I'm going with you. My father said to stick by you and help you."

"He did? A change of heart, eh?" Jean Durie smiled at Gilles and turned back to his counting.

Gilles waited until Jean had finished before he spoke with him again. It wouldn't do to have to recount everything. "Some of those goods have been moved since yesterday," Gilles noted.

"Which ones?" Jean asked, seeming somewhat surprised at Gilles' detection of the change.

"Those in the corner with the bolts of linen were not there yesterday, they were on the other side," Gilles said.

Jean dug through some of the bundles and counted the crates. "Twenty-eight," he said.

"The count is right," Gilles said, looking them over himself.

"Observation is very important sometimes," Jean said. He had satisfied himself that all was as it should be. "… and other times it is not so important. They probably just decided they could fit more cargo in if they rearranged them."

The count finished, Gilles reluctantly followed Jean up on deck. He avoided looking over in the direction of his father. Jean Durie waived farewell to Msr.

Montroville, though, as the sailors secured the last of the cargo below and cast off the lines. The planks came up and the lines were pulled in. The little ship slowly moved forward.

"*Well,*" Gilles thought, "*at least I will get to see a little of the Netherlands before settling into a life of reviewing musty account books.*"

He thought about Marie, another part of the package deal and was somewhat surprised to find that he was getting used to the idea. Maybe it wouldn't be so bad. After all, she wasn't as ugly as Msr. Corbeil's daughter.

Gilles remembered that his father had agents on the ship and he tried to guess which sailors might be the ones that were looking for the thieves. This passed the time on the trip as he looked over each man. He wondered if Captain LeBlanc knew and how he could not know who might be an agent for his father. The captain usually hired all of the crew. Maybe they were regular members of the crew who had now been recruited by Jean Montroville for a second job.

When he wasn't helping the crew, Jean Durie spent much of his time on deck carving a small piece of wood with a short knife. Gilles would have thought that Durie might spend his time reading or in some more intellectual pursuit but Jean seemed to enjoy whatever it was that he was making. Gilles thought it might be a whistle. It was too short for a walking stick. Gilles mainly spent his time looking out over the water. He liked this feeling of freedom and it was the closest thing he could imagine to the flight of a bird. He spent a little time trying to catch up on his lost sleep but he dreamed about Claude and remembered, even in his sleep, that he had not had the chance to speak to his father. Gilles reassured himself of his father's caution in business matters; he would remember to talk to him privately on his return.

They were delayed in leaving Havre and on this trip it was early in the day when they got in to the port. If he thought it was busy in Amsterdam before, Gilles had no idea how much *more* activity there could be in the city during the day. Gilles could see the streets in the distance as they approached land and all he could think of were the swarms of ants he had seen on the broken branches of the apple trees in spring, the attraction of the sweet sap moving the creatures to frenzied levels of activity. Gilles and Jean left with the first ferry, disembarked first and counted each item as it came over from the ship. Captain LeBlanc came with them this time and stood nearby looking annoyed at this. He said nothing to Gilles and Jean but anyone passing by might have been amused by the sight, the three of them standing side by side, going over accounts books in their hands, collectively but individually like some small religious prayer gathering. The cargo was stacked on the shore for a time but the agent was there and very soon the carts arrived to take the goods to the Waag, then on to the warehouses. Jean shook hands with all of the cart men, no matter how dirty their hands were, and introduced himself when he did not know them.

When all of the introductions had been made, and the carts with the claret were loaded, Jean abruptly grabbed Gilles by the elbow and said, "Come along, Gilles, our work here is done." Gilles started to protest that only a small portion of the trade goods had been unloaded but Jean gave him a look that told him not to argue. They started up the street toward the main square but had not gone far when Jean Durie quickly turned a corner, pulling Gilles into a small alley.

"What now?" Gilles asked.

"We wait and see what goes by on the way to the Waag," Jean replied.

They didn't have very long to wait. The wagons that carried the claret went by with their goods and every one of the drivers and wagons was accounted for.

"It looks good so far although we don't know for certain what made it onto the wagons. It's up to the warehouse people now," Jean said.

They stepped out of the alley and continued on to Hendrick's Inn. Elsje was there as usual, and was as busy as ever. She turned around from speaking with a very dark complexioned and raggedly-dressed man. Her frown of concentration turned to a smile when she saw them.

"Welcome back, Msr. Jean and Msr. Gilles," she called out to them.

"Are we too early for midday dinner?" Jean asked Elsje. "We'll be taking two small rooms for two weeks as well if you have them."

"For you, absolutely! Two rooms later and two dinners right now." She went back into the kitchen.

Gilles was immersed in the language around him now and was starting to pick it up more quickly. He thought he understood what was being said, even if he didn't know every one of the words.

"We'll eat now and meet with our people later tonight," Jean said to Gilles. "Tomorrow you will be on your own as I have some of my own business to attend to. I assume you can stay out of trouble for a day?"

Gilles wondered why Jean couldn't take Gilles with him tomorrow to learn more about his business and for a brief moment he wondered if Jean Durie might be part of the theft ring, too, but then the thought crossed his mind that perhaps there was a woman here. Jean had mentioned a woman during his last trip, one in France. This was not to assume that there couldn't be other women here but Jean seemed too serious for that sort of thing. Gilles shrugged. He would not concern himself with it; he would just find something else to do. There was more than enough for him to see and do in this place.

They took as long as they could to finish dinner. Elsje might have thrown them out if Jean had not been such a good customer but she let them sit there and pass the day away, even when all of the other customers had left. Gilles wanted to see the city or to visit the warehouses but Jean insisted that they stay where they were.

"Give the thieves a chance to do whatever it is that they will do. They will probably know that we are sitting here, very comfortable and very visible," Jean said.

They continued drinking ale after they ate and perhaps as a special treat, Elsje brought them something that she called a French pastry. A few people wandered into the room and although Jean didn't look directly at them, Gilles had the sense that he was scrutinizing each person. Elsje disappeared into the kitchen and a young girl with dark hair came out and washed the scarred old tables.

"Exactly what kind of business is it that you do, Jean?" Gilles asked, being curious as well as hoping that conversation would pass the time more quickly.

Jean rubbed his forehead with one finger and said, "Well, I guess if I had a *title*, it might be 'Advisor'. I have studied the law and know the local regulations and customs for most of the countries involved in our trade. I also try to keep up with the difficulties that *might* arise in our business from month to month, even week to week. I have been successful at matching up markets for merchants, and some captains and sailors to crew the boats here and there too ... perhaps a 'facilitator' might be a better word. Oh, and tax laws too, I know about the various tax laws."

"And people pay you for this?" Gilles asked. "You just know this and they pay?"

Jean shrugged. "They know I can do the job and if I don't know, I find out. They give me the money and I work at it until I get the details fixed. My name and my reputation are my credentials."

"Why don't you practice law then?" Gilles asked. "Would it not be easier work?"

"Easier maybe, and more profitable sometimes, but not as interesting. I can't see arguing over trivia all day for a living when there are things that can be ... accomplished. It's too political just dealing with the laws. It's a great waste of time and energy."

Gilles could see that Jean was selecting his words carefully. Again the thought crossed Gilles' mind that Jean could be profiting in some way from the thefts. In his line of work, smuggling would be easy, very easy.

"I thought you said you liked having a predictable life." Gilles smiled at him.

"I like predictability at home. Challenge and variety are what I do for a living."

"How does one train for this and where do you get trained?" Gilles asked, interested now for himself. *"What a wonderful life it would be if I never saw another accounts office again!"* Gilles thought.

Jean shook his head. "Self-training is the only way to do what I do, to know what I know, along with some imagination. I did have some good teachers, men of ideas, especially my father. They just never acted on their thoughts. I *did* and found out that I could make a living at it and a good living as well."

Gilles had never heard Jean mention family before. "Does your father live in Rouen? Do I know him?"

Jean smiled a faint smile and said, "Non. How is that French pastry? Elsje will probably be offended if you don't try it. She prides herself on her cooking, you know."

Gilles didn't want the sweet with his ale and he was not very hungry after his meal. In truth, it didn't look very attractive to him. It looked like a large lump of fried dough with sugar sprinkled on it. At Jean's urging, though, he took a bite of it and immediately contemplated his options for its quick disposal.

Jean didn't even try to hide his laughter. Apparently he had been the victim of Elsje's cooking experiments before. Gilles looked to see if Elsje was nearby and then he quickly slipped out the back door with the bite still in his mouth and the rest of the pastry in his hand. He spit out the bite of pastry and deposited the rest as well behind a clump of withered tulip leaves on his way out to the privy.

When Gilles returned, he was surprised to see that there was a great deal more activity in the room. There were servants rushing table linens through a door to a back room that he hadn't noticed before. Although Gilles couldn't see inside very well, it was obvious that they were setting up tables and taking some pains to set them up in a grand fashion. Several bottles of very good wine went by and Gilles adjusted his chair so he could see inside even better the next time the door opened.

"I didn't see any of that wine here before!" Gilles exclaimed to Jean. "We need to get some of that!"

"I see Hendrick is doing some entertaining tonight," Jean remarked.

"Yes, I am! Welcome back, Durie!"

Gilles turned to see a stout old Netherlander with just enough features similar to Elsje's to know that it was Old Hendrick himself.

Hendrick shook hands heartily with Jean. "I'll have to visit with you more tomorrow, too much to do tonight! Who is your young friend?"

"Msr. Gilles Montroville from Rouen, a friend and associate of mine."

Hendrick shook Gilles' hand vigorously between his two large hands, not mentioning or perhaps not noticing the sticky sugar that was still on Gilles' hand from the discarded pastry. "Prettig kennis met u te maken."

"Prettig kennis met u te maken" Gilles repeated. He hoped the Nederlands phrase was right.

Hendrick's eyes twinkled so Gilles assumed that he had made some grammatical error. He hoped Hendrick hadn't seen him trying to peer inside the back room.

Jean said to Hendrick, "I have business to attend to tomorrow but I would like to at least have an ale with you tomorrow night, if that is possible."

"Not only possible, it is a sure thing!" Hendrick replied and left for the back room. Jean Durie translated for Gilles who had already understood most of what was said.

"I won't translate anymore for you then, since you obviously don't need it." Jean smiled at him.

Men started to come into the inn for supper or drinks after their workday but there had been no sign of Elsje or her sister for the last hour. Three servant girls went quickly from table to table taking orders, bringing drinks and cleaning up. They looked harried, the three having great difficulty in trying to do Elsje's one job. A patron asked one of the girls a question and she shrugged, pointing first one way up the street, then the other way, then finally directed the man to ask another patron. She dropped an entire pitcher of ale and hurriedly mopped up the mess with a broom and her apron. She approached Gilles and Jean, still dripping ale from the hem of her dress, wisps of hair straggling down from her cap.

"Are you going to eat yet?" she asked Gilles. He understood "eat" and he heard the edge in her voice.

"Sure, bring us some supper," Jean replied. The girl was gone before he had finished his sentence.

"You didn't just ask for food, did you?" Gilles asked. "I'm not very hungry yet."

"You might be hungry by the time those three get it out here. They will probably forget us anyway," Jean said. "It just seemed easier to agree with her now; besides, we have nowhere to go yet."

A small company of men came in, wealthy men from the looks of their clothes. They moved around the nucleus of one loud man who had a commanding attitude and a loud demeanor, noticeable even in the short time it took for him to move through the dining room. Gilles turned to ask Jean who they were but Jean was not in his seat. The men were obviously familiar with the inn and proceeded directly to the back room that had been prepared. Just after the men entered and closed the door behind them, Elsje and her sister entered the dining room from the kitchen, on their way to join the company in the back. Both girls wore silk dresses that emphasized physical assets that had not been obvious in the plain dresses and aprons that they usually wore. They did not pause to talk to Gilles or to anyone else as they swept past but before they could reach the door to the back room, regular patrons started to call out to them.

"Elsje! Marry me, my love!" "Tryntje, come away to sea with me!"

Elsje blushed a deep shade of red and grabbed her sister's wrist. Tryntje had slowed down, fully enjoying all the attention she was getting from the men in the tavern. She blew two of them a kiss before Elsje pulled her inside the room, closing the door behind them.

"Busy night indeed for Hendrick," Jean said, pulling up his seat.

"Where did you go? I wanted to ask you about those men!" Gilles said. "Who were they?"

"I haven't been to relieve myself all afternoon, surely I had to get rid of all that ale sometime," Jean replied. "Besides I had the privilege of seeing Stuyvesant and his courtiers on the way in. They always remind me of Clematis on a Hawthorn tree."

"Stuyvesant?"

"Yes, he's between assignments in the New World, I guess. He's a politician mostly, although he fancies himself civilization's greatest-ever soldier, sailor and scholar. He will probably work his way up to Governor General of one of the colonies, if not all of them someday. He's ingratiated himself to everyone who can help his career and angered and irritated many others who would approve the appointments just to have him sent to the farthest ends of the earth. As long as he doesn't foul up our trade there, Brazil is a good place for him, along with all the other greedy fortune-hunters of his ilk."

"Why would anyone want to go to a place like that, so far from civilization?" Gilles asked. "Is it just a stepping stone in his career?"

"Profit, Gilles, profit! They would pay him like a king and he could live as he pleased with the best imported finery there. It's quite tolerable for a time while you put away a tidy fortune to bring back."

"But what about the savages?" Gilles asked. "I've heard stories about the savages ..."

"Well, there is that. They probably aren't any worse to deal with than the English or the Danes though, ha ha! Old Hendrick still has hopes of marrying Elsje off to old Stuyvesant, bad-tempered and obnoxious though he is, or to one of his well-to-do cronies. Hendrick's started looking for husbands for both girls even though they *are* a little young yet. I guess he knows he'd better start early to get Tryntje used to the idea of having just one man and Elsje used to the idea of *any* man at all! Elsje will converse with the men, she's good at that, but I don't think she'll ever get married. She'll be here with Hendrick forever, running things in her mother's stead. I don't think old Stuyvesant will ever get married, either. He's not rich enough for *anyone* to put up with unless they are very desperate and he's too discriminating to settle for less than the best."

Gilles felt pity for Elsje and a kinship with her. She didn't look like she enjoyed private entertaining at all, and like himself, Elsje was stuck working in her father's business. Gilles wondered if she, too, ever wanted to escape.

The servant girl returned with two bowls of food and dropped them in front of Gilles and Jean. Gilles said a quick and silent prayer over the food but decided not to cross himself anymore while he was in Amsterdam. He never saw anyone else cross themselves here and now the gesture made him feel different and uncomfortable.

"Ah, you can tell when Elsje's touch is missing. It's slopped over the side of the plate and it is cold," Jean said, tasting it with his spoon. "When we finish here, we will go out and find our people to see if they have any word on the progress of our shipment. While I'm off on my business tomorrow, I want you to promise me that you won't go out into any out-of-the-way places alone. Stick to busy streets or better yet, stay here."

"I'm not a child," Gilles answered, irritated that Jean was treating him as his father usually did.

"No, you aren't, but at times life can be very cheap to the profiteers. If anything happened to you, I'd have to be the one to tell your father and that's one job I don't want. It would ruin my chances of ever getting business from him again." Jean gave Gilles a half smile.

From time to time they heard roars of laughter coming from the room behind the closed doors as they finished their supper. Gilles couldn't hear much else, even when some more bottles of wine came through and the door opened briefly. When they had finished eating, Jean noted that Elsje hadn't told them where their rooms were yet so he asked one of the servants to keep their things for them until they returned to the inn. Gilles and Jean put on their cloaks and Gilles noted that Jean's cloak was inside out. He wondered if he should mention this to his impeccably-dressed friend who had perhaps not noticed due to the amount of drink he had consumed. Gilles decided that it was not important enough to mention. They traveled up the stone streets and the evening fog had begun to come in off the water. There was a sweet smell of smoke in the air that was becoming familiar to Gilles and Jean noticed it, too

"That is tobacco from the new world colonies. They have it in France, too, but we don't love it the way the Netherlanders do! The new world has goods to trade with us that we didn't even know existed, goods like to-bac-co and Indian wampum money as well as fine beaver pelts."

They passed by the doors to the city orphanage and continued on to a very foul smelling street. Whatever was in the gutter here was worse than what the rest of the city held. There were more people on the streets here, both walking and lying there and more laughter and light pouring out of the buildings, spilling over onto the pavement. They came to a stop outside an establishment with loud music coming from musicians playing inside. The air itself smelled of ale and vomit and there were so many people at the front door that they couldn't even get inside the building.

"Er ... Jean, are we going inside here?" Gilles asked.

"Shhhh."

They stood patiently for a few minutes at the back of the crowd.

"It's a popular place!" Jean shouted to Gilles, and then somewhat quieter to him, "Mind your pockets!"

Gilles had learned quickly about his pockets and was already watching them.

Two women pushed through the crowd and walked up to them.

"Would you look at this, Hendrickje? What fine gentlemen we have here! Buy me a drink, Lover!" said the older one as she buried her face in Jean's neck and pulled at his collar's band ties with one hand.

Gilles tried to keep one hand on his pockets as he fought off the other younger woman with his free hand. Gilles was nearly overcome with the smell of sweat and spices as she hugged and kissed him, playfully biting his ear while she sighed, "Oooh, I do *love* the young ones!"

Gilles hoped that Jean wasn't interested in staying here but he didn't seem to be struggling very much; Jean's woman still had her face buried in his neck. The smell of his female companion was making Gilles nauseous.

Suddenly Jean announced, "You ladies need to leave us alone; we just wanted to have a drink and hear some music!"

"Oh nee, Lover! You come with us and we will hear some fine music!" She threw her arms around his neck again but Jean pushed her away and grabbed Gilles by the arm. "Let's go!"

Jean pushed through the crowd, walking away as briskly as he could, looking annoyed. Gilles didn't say anything to Jean but he wondered how they were going to meet with their contact if they were headed back to the inn already. He could still smell the woman's scent on him and Jean had a smear of rouge on his cheek.

"Jean?"

"Later, Gilles!"

When they reached the inn they went inside and Jean found them a seat at a table facing the door before he spoke to Gilles.

"If you are with me on this job, it is important that no matter what I do or say sometimes, that you go along with me. Is that understood?"

"All right, but what about the contact for our claret and how will we see if it made it to the warehouse?"

"We already did. She told me that the merchandise was all accounted for at the warehouses. I guess our work is done and there was no theft this time."

"Gentlemen, you look like you could use some ale!" Elsje stood over them with a pitcher of ale and some mugs. She still had the silk dress on but with an everyday apron over it and a wet cloth over her arm just below where her lace-edged sleeve was pushed up above her elbow.

"I thought you were still in with the party," Jean said.

She winked at him and replied, "I told my father they needed help out here. Our guests are either asleep from the wine or have moved on to more *entertaining* women up the street."

Gilles wondered if the men were going to the section of the city that they had just come from.

"So you will be staying for a time, for two weeks?" she asked as she set the mugs down and filled them from the pitcher.

"Yes," Jean replied. "Perhaps you can direct Gilles here to something that will occupy his time and keep him out of trouble tomorrow while I take care of some other business."

Elsje smiled at Gilles. "I can do better than that! If you'd like, you can accompany me to the Dam, the market, and see some of the city. It won't be very exciting, probably, but you can find something along the way that might amuse you." She turned to Jean. "Does he understand *any* of what I'm saying?"

Jean grinned at her but Gilles had already replied, "Ja, I understand." He wondered briefly what she would be wearing tomorrow but then he reprimanded himself and thought of Marie. Although many men had women they kept in other cities, he had no wish to be one of them. It took too much time and energy, from what he had seen. As his mother had said, he and Marie would grow close over time.

Being young and not very experienced with women, Gilles thought that relationships must be somewhat like learning to tell the difference between good wines and bad wines, savoring the good wine, growing to prefer the one variety over all the others, sampling it over time, comparing it to others occasionally, but then returning and appreciating it more and more each time.

"Tomorrow, then. I need to take care of breakfast first," Elsje said, smiling at Gilles. She left to fill another empty mug at another table.

"She knows the city as well as she knows the inn," Jean said. "Just stay out of trouble and harm's way, Gilles. Stick to the crowds and I'll be back in the afternoon, just after midday dinner."

For a minute Gilles was tempted to ask again to go with Jean but he just shook his head and had a sip of his ale. Maybe going to the market would be interesting.

"What?" Jean asked, seeing the gesture.

"Rien. I'll be safe as a babe with my nurse. I'll be here waiting for your return."

Jean didn't say much after that. It was as though he was already working out some details of whatever it was that he was doing in the morning. He finished his ale, said goodnight to Gilles, and left to find the way to his room but Gilles was not really tired yet and besides, he could sleep late tomorrow. Gilles watched Elsje escort Jean up the stairs and he thought about how Jean always finished his ale faster. Gilles was used to drinking French wine, not the Netherlands ale, but he was starting to get used to it now, like the idea of marrying Marie. It was getting late and the dining room was getting empty of patrons now.

"Do you mind if I join you?" Elsje asked.

Gilles hadn't heard her walk up to the table.

"Not at all," he answered but he was shocked at a woman just inviting herself to sit down alone with a man. Elsje didn't seem to have coarse habits but her habits were different than what Gilles was accustomed to. He couldn't think of anything to say to her but she was not at a loss for words.

"What is France like?" she asked. "I've never been there but I've heard wonderful things about Paris. Tu me comprends?"

"Ja." Gilles spoke in French but threw in as many Dutch words and phrases as he could remember. "I was in Paris once when I was small but I don't remember much about it. France is ... not like here. There are fewer people, and they are ... qu'est-ce le mot? Serious?"

Elsje laughed at his attempts to come up with the words in her language but it was not an unkind laugh. "Do you mean we worry less and have more fun here?" she repeated the sentence in broken French and smiled at him.

"Yes, something like that. I guess I expected more Spanish soldiers or something, more difficulties here ..." He was still mixing words from both languages and struggling but remembering more than he believed he even knew. The drink helped.

"We do have the occasional soldiers that come through but we just go on with our lives. Their legal claims are not a concern to us. We just ignore their decrees and they have learned that! There are many Spaniards here, some soldiers, but many have left Spain to live a free life in Amsterdam. They gave up on converting us to their ways long ago. You probably didn't understand any of what I just said, did you?"

The gaze from her blue eyes penetrated his as she tried to ascertain how much of what she said was lost on him.

"I understood." Gilles thought of the difficulties at home in France, the people who were losing their lives and their businesses to continue financing the ongoing war and Cardinal Richelieu's excesses. The Spanish probably bled the Netherlands dry, too, and he found it odd that the situation here didn't seem to concern Elsje as much as the situation at home concerned his own countrymen.

"Should I try my French?" Elsje asked, seeing he had not much to say and taking it for lack of comprehension.

"No, I need to practice my Nederlands," Gilles said, as much because it was true as because it hurt his ears to hear how she attempted his own language.

"You are so serious!" she chided him. "Are you always this way?" She made a serious face and passed her hand over it to get her point across to him.

"No," he smiled a little, "things are just difficult, in France, now. I was thinking about that."

"Just right now?"

Elsje smiled at him but he sensed sarcasm behind the smile. There *had* been continuous fighting in Gilles' lifetime and there probably had more or less been some kind of civil strife for two hundred years before that, some of their battles with the same armies that were laying claim to the Netherlands now, but what were armies for and what would soldiers do with themselves if not defend their country?.

Gilles replied, "Well, I am happy to get away from the troubles at home for now."

"I have heard that there are many people being executed there," Elsje said. "Are the French so evil then, that they kill their own people for their very thoughts?"

Gilles frowned and shook his head. "The King and the Church demand loyalty; it is a completely reasonable thing to expect. Do you allow dangerous and treasonous people to live unmolested among you?"

Either she didn't comprehend what he was saying or perhaps she was bored by the discussion, because Elsje didn't answer; she changed the subject. "Tomorrow I can show you some of our city. Can you help me carry some of my parcels back?"

Gilles wondered if he looked weak or like too much of a gentleman to carry packages for a woman and that was why she asked.

"Of course, but don't you have servants for that?" he asked her.

Elsje looked at him with an odd expression but she had no reply to this either.

"We'll see you tomorrow after breakfast then," she said as she got up. "Oh, your room is the second one on the left at the top of the stairs." She held up two fingers and pointed to her left hand. "Your things are over there by the kitchen door. Goedenacht."

Gilles wondered if he had insulted her in some way but all of the people here spoke in a more direct way than he was accustomed to hearing. *"Well, no matter,"* he thought to himself. *"She can find me some diversion tomorrow and I'll amuse myself.* He had another sip of ale and decided that he was getting used to it and starting to like it a little, not unlike the idea of his upcoming marriage. He had had enough to drink for tonight though. *"Night Marie,"* he said to the almost-finished mug of ale and hoisted himself up from the table to go find his bed.

The accommodations were better this time. Gilles' room was a small private room just big enough for a bed and a washstand. Gilles didn't sleep as late as he thought he would although Jean was long since gone when Gilles got downstairs. There was no sign of Elsje yet in the dining room but he thought he heard her voice in the kitchen. Tryntje brought him his breakfast.

"Hebt u brood?" he asked her. He did like Elsje's bread.

"Ja, it's Peter Stuyvesant's *favorite*," she informed him with an air of authority.

Gilles was still in the dining room, trying out some tea, when Elsje finally came in from the kitchen.

Gilles had heard of tea and the tea trade of course, but not many people in France had actually ever had any. It was a peculiar hot beverage but in an interesting sort of way; it was all right.

"Are you ready to go?" Elsje asked, throwing a cloak around herself. She was not wearing the plain dresses he had usually seen her wear but it wasn't the silk either.

"Show me Amsterdam!" he said enthusiastically.

She was halfway to the door before he caught up with her. Gilles opened the door for her and grabbed her elbow as he was accustomed to doing with Marie on their walks. Elsje grinned in surprise and perhaps amusement but said nothing. On the street, together they dove into the flowing crowds for a block before turning right and leaving the throngs that were headed to the marketplace behind them.

"It's the long way but good to see things," Elsje said. "This is a very old church and here are some beautiful homes that belong to some of our richest merchants. They are wonderful, aren't they?"

"There are no beggars here, people who ask for money?" Gilles' asked.

"Ah, beggars! A few. Have you heard the old man who plays the fiddle music? They can beg for a short time here but then they must either find work or leave."

"Many sailors too, from many countries. Are they difficult, troublesome?" Gilles asked as he saw some military sailors in unfamiliar uniform.

"The Danes and the Germans are!" Elsje said. "Our jailers keep busy. They often start fights in the ale houses."

"Many Spanish here, but not all soldiers," Gilles noted as they passed a group of people arguing loudly in Spanish.

"Ah those are the *Marranos*. They are another gift from our Spanish *benefactors*. They mostly live on the other side of the city. There aren't many of them in the trade business yet, although some are working in banking or are helpful in our Brazil colonies. They know the Spanish trade and the language. Many are poor but a few have done very well for themselves. They say many of them are Jews or they were before they were forcibly converted to Catholicism. The Jews here from the northern countries are a different story: They are mostly all like animals; poor, uncultured, and crude. Sometimes we see *Gypsies* here, too. We escort those out of the city right away and brand their flesh if they try to come back in."

"Jews can stay?" Gilles asked in shock.

France's King had tried to expel the Jews for a third time twenty-five years earlier, but they always found their way back into the country, "like rats", Cardinal Richelieu had been heard to remark to a courtier. Only eight years earlier, Gilles had seen three dozen "New Christians" arrested in Rouen but once they were allowed to declare their fidelity to the King and Church and pay a penance, they were released again. He had never heard what became of them.

"Oh yes, the Jews and many French Protestants, too," Elsje said with a patronizing smile. "The only religious group we ever executed here were the troublesome Mennonites although we probably wouldn't do it again today. That was a long time ago."

Gilles said nothing but tried to assimilate all this information. How did they keep track of all the different groups? Did it matter if his father dealt with a Dane as opposed to a Swede in Amsterdam? How could he tell a northern Jew from a Mennonite, a Spaniard from the Portuguese? Would there be any trade dealings with the Marranos if they were becoming active in the Brazil colonies? He was beginning to understand why a man like Jean Durie would be indispensable to his father here. Jean Montroville couldn't hope to keep track of this in every country he traded with. With the different laws and taxes in the different countries, it was overwhelming.

Elsje made a left turn and now in front of them was the huge open market, the Dam. There was a large building that Gilles decided must be the Waag, where imports were weighed and taxed. There was much activity and spirited conversation going on all around the Waag; it was a meeting point for people and a focal point of the activity in the square although other smaller clusters of activity took place around the center stage of the weigh house. Elsje pointed it out although she didn't need to. There were all kinds of vendors in the square and the market activity spilled over into the adjoining streets and alleys. There were goods for immediate consumption, herring and other foods to eat now, and durable goods from near and far, equipment for boats, furniture for houses, live animals and wonders just to look at. The smell of foreign spices hung over the market and added to an already intoxicating effect. Artists on the edge of the square had their canvases set up, comfortably painting on the street with no concern as to the noise and distraction all around them. The pictures they painted were like little windows mirroring the scenes of life in front of them. Gilles looked at some brass lanterns with an unusual pattern of holes punched in them as they passed by. The old man selling them had a brightly-colored cloth wrapped around his head. He had a long robe for a garment and his complexion was dark and deeply etched with lines. Gilles tried not to stare. He had never seen a man dressed in this manner. Elsje didn't seem to notice or even to slow down, so Gilles kept walking, too. She must have been used to seeing such sights.

"There is the Council Hall and the City Exchange. You can change French money to our money, if you need to. We change your money to ours so you can spend all of it here with no problems!" She winked at him.

Gilles took it all in, the towers, the great buildings with arches, and the sculptures.

"A half stuiver for ale. A guilder, a florin note from the bank, is twenty stuivers?" He flashed all of his fingers at Elsje twice.

"You are very good at calculating the cost of ale. Are you as good with other high finance?"

Elsje's eyes held mischief. Gilles understood the joke but he took no offense.

"How much is it for a man and woman to go eat a very good meal?" Gilles asked with a sly glint in his own eye, pointing at Elsje and then himself, making eating motions.

"I don't know about such things. You would have to ask them for yourself."

Smaller ships with less draught crowded the Damrak, the part of the sea that went right up to the Dam on one side. Some of the boats already had been unloaded and were making their way through the crowded waterway back out to the sea. Carts of all sizes and descriptions from tiny carts pulled by dogs to huge wagons pulled by teams of great draft horses took the discharged goods away to the Waag and then on to the warehouses or to the square. In the square, goods were sold for whatever price could be had on the open market if there had been no advance trade agreement, no merchant to purchase the goods ahead of time and have them delivered or stored in a warehouse. A very large and heavy wagon rolled by carrying wood and brick for construction of a building somewhere. In one area, many well-dressed merchants hurried over to buy a printed page, tossing their coins to the man who handed out the pages.

"What is that? Pages from a Bible?"

"Bible? Nee! That's the recent trade publication, papers with the news on trade. Don't you have them in France? So they know prices and harvests in this market and around the world? How can you trade without them?" Elsje looked at him with curiosity.

Much of the traffic was entering the Dam from the noisy Kalverstraat south of the Dam. The very old and ancient alley way had people and horses all trying to get through at once and everyone didn't stop at the Dam; there was even more activity beyond the main square. Gilles and Elsje passed more tables of goods; iron and copper, gleaming furs from the far north and the west, large quantities of grain with small sample bowls set out. Wool, lace, cloth, silk, velvet and furs were all haggled over by women buying for their households and by some men who looked to be tailors buying large quantities for their businesses. Elsje finally led Gilles to a market area that had mostly fresh food and Elsje stopped at one vegetable stand to look over what they had on display. Some people greeted her by name and she either called out a greeting to them or shook hands. Everyone knew Elsje. She picked out four cabbage heads that she liked but she shook her head at the carrots and earth apples.

"We might have had a better selection earlier but I just can't leave my sister to serve breakfast alone. They want too much money for those rotten vegetables, though." Elsje spoke somewhat loudly to Gilles and he wondered if she did this so that the merchant could hear her. "I will have to send someone out early tomorrow to find some better ones." Gilles picked up the two sacks of cabbages, avoiding eye contact with the vendor who was giving them both an angry glare and completely unperturbed, Elsje moved on to look for fruit.

"We do keep a few animals in the back and I have someone who comes by selling milk, flour, eggs and butter, but I need to shop for the vegetables myself. You just never know what the quality or the price will be: It is so dependant on the season and the weather you know. I have to change what I will serve if the vegetables I need are not so good. That is why I am always trying to find new dishes that I can serve."

The apples looked terrible, covered in large part with bruises and worm holes but to Gilles' surprise, Elsje bought two great baskets of them.

"They're from last autumn and they don't look so good but they aren't soft and will do fine in a pie or tart," she explained to Gilles. "I guess that's about all I am going to find here today," Elsje sighed. "Are you tired from carrying these or would you like to go home another way and see more of the city?"

"I can carry them. Seeing more is good," Gilles replied.

"I will carry the apples, then. I had not meant for you to carry *all* of them."

Elsje took the heavy bags from Gilles before he could protest. She tied the two bags to opposite ends of a strip of cloth that hung over her shoulder and she carried them with greater ease on her makeshift yoke than Gilles managed with the cabbages.

As they walked on, Gilles marveled at the sheer variety of people and languages. He saw very tall blond people in unusual costumes and very dark-skinned people wrapped head to toe in some type of garment that he had never seen before. There were slaves whose skin was as black as the shadows of the night and oriental men and women dressed in bright silks with gleaming black braids that trailed from the napes of their necks to the backs of their knees. On this day a murderer was being garroted to death in the square and a crowd had taken a break from their shopping to watch the execution. Elsje wasn't particularly interested, though, having more pressing things to do and so they continued on, leaving the square behind.

The buildings towered up to the sky and blocked the sunlight entirely from some of the streets. The structures stood shoulder to shoulder with no wasted space at all between them. A few buildings were scarcely as wide as a man's arms spread out and Gilles could look straight through some of the open doors to the very back of the building. In one area of the city first floors held offices, the second floors had living quarters and the top floors had warehousing space. Gilles often saw the large door on the third floor opened and the workmen using the pulleys to haul goods up to the top floor. In some of the other houses the people lived on the first floor with all of the upper floors being used for storage of goods. In the next neighborhood they passed, the houses and all three floors were residences for the wealthy families. In any patch of ground that was not paved over or built upon, there were the flowers, always the flowers.

"This is my church," Elsje said as they approached the big old structure. It looked like it was wedged in between buildings and scaled down, almost like a smaller replica of a church when Gilles compared it to the cathedral that he was used to. It was very plain and simple, without statues, without much of any decoration at all. They had stopped for a moment in front of the church steps to get a better grip on their sacks of produce when a strange movement up the street and a familiar figure caught Gilles' eye. Looking over, he saw that it was indeed Jean Durie, walking at the head of a line of ragged men, leading them up the street toward the church and toward where Gilles and Elsje were standing. Jean did not appear to have noticed Gilles yet, and was speaking loudly to the men, almost yelling something in another language, something unintelligible, perhaps urging them on. Elsje heard the commotion and looked up too. Jean continued to speak loudly to the men in the strange language and then suddenly the entire column of men turned the corner before they reached the church. So stunned were they that neither Gilles nor Elsje spoke for a moment.

"Who were those men?" he asked Elsje finally. He couldn't pretend that they had not seen Jean Durie among them.

Elsje shrugged. "I thought you might know. I've never seen him with any Marranos before."

"Did you say that the Marranos were Spanish Jews?"

"Often they are Jews but not always. They could be anyone who is newly converted to follow the Catholic Church. They could be Muslims, Moors, even former Protestants, I suppose. Sometimes the conversion isn't dramatic enough and the Spanish torturers test their faith. Sometimes the Marranos live, sometimes they die, and sometimes they escape and come here. Isn't it true that you torture people in France too?"

There was no hint of malice or accusation. She stated it as though it was a simple fact that everyone knew.

Gilles said nothing for a moment. France was nothing at all like Spain and he took offense at the comparison. He didn't want to think about the Church right now and running into Jean Durie somewhere with his group could make for an uncomfortable stay with him for the next two weeks. They probably weren't going to come back this way if they were going somewhere.

"Can we just sit for a minute, Elsje, or do you need to get back?"

"Do you need a rest?" She asked but she sat down on the church steps for a moment and leaned back against the side wall.

"How do you know about so many things?" Gilles asked her, just to start a conversation.

"Oh, we have people and goods here from *everywhere*; China, India, Persia, even savages from the New World. My father sits and talks with them all in our inn. Do you travel a lot, Gilles?"

"I will be traveling more as I take over more of my father's business."

He said it because he felt defensive but then he reminded himself that he would not be getting out more; he would be stuck at home with Marie when he wasn't reviewing the dreary warehouse accounts.

"How old are you?" Elsje asked suddenly.

"I'll be nineteen soon, why do you ask?"

Elsje laughed a little. "You are *very* young, you just seemed older," she said.

"I'm not so young, I'm old enough to take over my father's business soon and to be married!"

"Married!" Elsje repeated. This seemed to amuse her even more.

"And how old are *you*?" he asked, less than politely, he hoped.

"Older than you," she said. "We generally marry much later here in the Netherlands, both men and women, well into our twenties at least."

"If you wait too long there will be no one left for you to marry!" Gilles retorted, hoping that his comment would bother her.

It didn't seem to bother her though. She made no reply but looked thoughtful as she rearranged the pleats in her dress and then looked out at the passersby traveling just inches away from them.

They both sat in silence for a few seconds more.

"Hm. Well, I need to get back and get dinner started," Elsje said at last, not seeming interested anymore in conversation.

"We haven't been gone that long. Can't you stay for a few more minutes?" Gilles asked, sorry now that he would have no one to talk to and nothing to do until Jean Durie returned to the inn.

"No, but you can stay. Just follow this street and turn left at the artist's big stone house. You'll know it by all the paintings in the downstairs window." Elsje rose and picked up all the bags, Gilles' included.

"I promised to help you with your packages, Elsje, and I will."

Gilles decided that it was no wonder that she had no marriage prospects. She really was very irritating and had no manners or social graces at all.

Gilles wasn't sure what he would do for the next few hours until Jean's return. He thought about going back to the Dam but the thought of running into Jean Durie was daunting. Gilles wasn't sure if he should wait and ask Jean directly about his day's activities, ask him indirectly or just pretend that he had never seen him.

Gilles and Elsje hauled their goods into the kitchen and Elsje directed him to set the sacks down on the kitchen table. The servants and Elsje's sister looked sideways at Gilles and giggled. Elsje gave them all a sharp look. She pulled off her cloak and exchanged it for an apron that was hanging from a peg on the wall. She barked orders to the others and then set to work herself, ladling soup here, fixing a plate there. Gilles had never spent any time at in a kitchen and it held a certain fascination for him with all of the gadgets and procedures. He didn't leave right away but pulled up a stool in the corner. He had nowhere else to go. The other kitchen help still stole looks at him from time to time but Elsje allowed him to stay. He marveled at the efficient order and military precision of the preparations as well as the odd equipment that he had never seen. There were different sizes of little cups, bowls full of little holes, different sizes and kinds of spoons and peculiar wooden paddles.

"Msr. Montroville, I appreciate your help this morning but a gentleman like yourself doesn't need to stay around the kitchens! I can send out some lunch for you in the dining room if you'd like."

"I'd rather stay here." He smiled at her, hoping that he irritated her, at least a little.

"Well, take a plate and go in the back then. You're just in the way here!" she said.

He obediently took up the plate and slice of bread that she handed him and went out the back door. The back stoop faced other stoops that were the backs of buildings facing the next street. The yard was barely big enough to contain the outbuildings, privy, and small garbage pit. It wasn't unpleasant though, as what wind there was today was blowing in the other direction. Gilles realized after he got out there that he wasn't alone. There were two Marrano men huddled next to the wall and when they saw Gilles, they moved further away from him. They did not make eye contact at all but continued eating from their plates of food. Gilles finished his plate and sat there, enjoying the warm sunshine and the day, but keeping one eye on the Marranos. He could hear all of the sounds from the kitchen as Elsje prepared the midday dinner. In a few minutes Elsje came out to retrieve plates and cups from the Marranos as well as from Gilles. The Marranos were looking for more but Elsje shooed them away as if they were stray dogs. The pack of them slipped out of the courtyard and down the narrow alley to the street beyond.

"I hate to do that but most of them can't speak Nederlands and I don't know that much Spanish. If I always feed them, they will just come back and not find food on their own. I feed the newcomers and am sorry that they have to live like animals but what can I do?" Elsje shook her head.

Gilles understood most of what she said. "Are they always old men?" Gilles asked.

"Not as old as they look, and yes, very few women and children make it out." Elsje seemed almost matter of fact about the situation. In France they would probably be rounded up and thrown into one of the prisons if they were lucky. Any undesirables that turned up usually disappeared though, long before they ever became a problem. Few undesirables ever did turn up in France, though.

Elsje opened the lower half of the door with one hand and balanced all the plates on the other. The brown-haired servant who was washing the dirty dishes took them from Elsje.

"Why do they all come here?" Gilles asked, following Elsje inside.

"The Marranos? To be free I suppose. To worship as they choose. Some to spy on us and report back to Spain. We have all kinds of churches and places of worship here. Some will go on to make their fortunes elsewhere, the German States, the New World, the ships that remain on the sea but never stay in one place. Most of them move on eventually. Amsterdam is just too crowded these days even for the Marranos. Now get out of my kitchen, Msr. Gilles, we need room to clean up!"

Gilles wandered back out to the backyard. He had a lot to think about now and that included Marie. He wondered if she had ever cooked. That idea was ridiculous though; what were servants for? There was so much to be done before the wedding. There were agreements to be drawn up, parties with all the required people to invite, housekeeping arrangements to set up. Just showing up for all these things seemed to be a very large commitment of time and trouble. There would be the tailors who needed to do their work, too. Gilles would be measured and pinned and measured again. Things just seemed more complicated than they needed to be. He sighed and looked out at a lone tulip still in bloom growing in Elsje's back lot.

"Life can be simple," he thought, *"You are born, you try to keep yourself alive and fed, and you die. Why does it have to be so complicated?"*

Elsje came to the door and called to him, "Is this how you amuse yourself?"

"Ja," Gilles replied stretching his legs and folding his arms. He looked out at the lone Linden tree that stood in the back, its newly sprouted lopsided green leaves moving slightly in the quiet breeze. Here and there small branches sprouted in a thicket on the trunk where an old branch had broken off and four new ones took the old branch's place.

"I'm sorry that I couldn't spend more time this morning showing you Amsterdam. I wake up with long lists of things that need to be taken care of and go to bed at night with longer lists. There are so many people needing help, a ship to find, and a place to sleep ..." Her voice trailed off. "I am boring you. Please do not think all of us here have bad manners! I just do not have so much time for good manners."

"Or yourself?" Gilles asked

"Myself?" She looked puzzled.

"Yes. Time for yourself. Just to go and see all the ships coming in from all over the world, to sit and talk, to watch the people."

"I have had no time for these things since I was a child."

"It's good to sit. One needs to digest a meal, to listen to music."

"For someone here on business you certainly seem to have a lot of extra time," she said sharply.

"We are waiting for someone to contact us about our business." Gilles had not noticed that her eyes were beautiful before. They had always seemed too cold, too sharp. They had gold flecks in them and a certain light of their own, not just what was reflected.

"I wait for no one, they always seem to wait for me," Elsje sighed. "If I could *just* get my sister to help out a little more ... but she is young yet and her judgment is not that good. She still needs help in finding her way down the stairs in the morning."

"What do you do for fun then, have dinner parties with Msr. Stuyvesant?" Gilles asked. It was true that Elsje wasn't as pretty as Tryntje but she was infinitely more interesting to talk with.

Elsje snorted. "That is *absolutely* not my idea of relaxation. It's the least fun part of our business. You must spend a lot of time at dinner parties, too, but I expect *you* enjoy them all."

"I detest those parties as much as you do. Now, if I could invite *anyone* I wanted, wear anything I wanted, and *do* anything I wanted, that would be an enjoyable party! You probably think we French are all stuffy."

Elsje colored somewhat, confirming his suspicion.

"So, what do you do to relax or have fun?" Gilles persisted.

"Marketing or church, feasts ..."

"Church! That is more of a chore than the tiresome dinner parties!" Gilles exclaimed. "If I never had to see the inside of a church again, I would be *very* happy."

"I suppose you would feel that way." She looked at him again. "You *are* a Catholic, aren't you?"

"Is your church so very different?" Gilles asked. "Are your services so enjoyable?"

"Well, I've never been in a Catholic church so I don't know. All are welcome into our church if you ever wanted to satisfy your curiosity. As long as you aren't afraid you'd burn in hell."

Gilles thought he saw laughter in her eyes and was about to take offense but the light in her eyes was attractive. She didn't seem to laugh very often when she was at work inside the inn.

"What if I did? Tomorrow? Tomorrow is Sunday."

"Well, you would be welcome as long as you didn't keep us waiting. It's enough of a chore getting the little ones and Father ready on time."

"I didn't keep you waiting today, did I? Do you really have four younger brothers and sisters that you take care of, too?"

"Yes, who told you that?" She turned a piercing gaze on him now. "You seem to know a lot about me and I know *nothing* about you."

"That's all I really know. Jean mentioned it because I said that you handled all of your responsibilities well and he said that you had even more responsibilities." Gilles wasn't sure how he would put her back at ease. "I just find you different than the ladies in France," he finished.

"A curiosity? No doubt I am different than your fiancée. We take great pride in being different from the ladies in France although I always have the feeling that the French men are comparing us unfavorably to their women at home. We aren't heathens. If you would like to attend church with our family, you are welcome to join us tomorrow."

"I will do that. My Maman will be happy to hear that I have not missed church as long as I do not tell her what kind of church it is!"

"Well, we leave early. Be in the dining room and don't be late or we leave without you!" Elsje called over her shoulder as she went back into the kitchen.

Tryntje came out to tell Gilles that Jean had returned. He was sitting in the dining room having an ale, acting no differently than usual but he did look very tired.

"Do you like that stuff better than wine?" Gilles asked as he pointed to the mug.

"Today I'll take *anything*, it has been a long day," Jean replied wearily.

"Was your business successful then?" Gilles asked, wondering if Jean would volunteer any information.

"I'd say so, and yours? Were you out with Elsje all morning?"

"We were a little rushed. She had to get back before dinner time."

"Rushed is a good word for it. Elsje is a regular sea storm! Tomorrow I can go with you and show you some of the things that *I* enjoy about the city."

"Can we go in the afternoon? I have something I'm doing in the morning."

"Afternoon it is then."

Jean didn't ask what his morning plans were and Gilles couldn't help but look at Jean in a new way now: Jean knew a strange language that was like nothing Gilles had ever heard before. Gilles also noticed that Jean's face had many features that could be Marrano or was it just the dim light of the inn? What Gilles had taken for color from time spent on the ships may have been Jean Durie's natural coloring. When they were drinking together the night before, Gilles had felt that they were kindred souls but now he was seated across from a stranger. The lack of conversation between them finally induced Gilles to go up to his bed earlier than usual but he slept deeply, slept well until a servant's knock at the door woke him.

"What is it?" he called.

"Elsje says don't be late or she'll leave without you!" The girl called through the closed door.

This startled him because he had been dreaming that he was in a Protestant church and he was holding Elsje's hand. He couldn't remember any more than that but it seemed peculiar to just be holding her hand. There was no talking with her, no prayer or anything at all besides her hand. It had been a nice dream, though. He hurried to get ready, not wanting to be left behind. Only the servants were downstairs when he got there but he managed to get some bread and tea from them. He gulped down the last of it when Elsje came into the room, wearing a dark blue dress today.

"You're going to do this then?" she grinned at him. "I'm sorry, I shouldn't tease. It will be interesting for you, I'm sure."

Gilles did have some vision of damnation far in the back of his mind but he shook off the image. He didn't exactly believe that he would burn for it (as promised by the priests) but he would probably spend some time in purgatory at the very least.

Old Hendrick led the way out of the door and down the street. He said nothing but a half-suppressed smile led Gilles to believe that he was amused by Elsje's talking some French Catholic boy into going inside a reformed church. Elsje was busy herding her younger siblings, like so many stray chickens, into a uniform line behind her father. Tryntje flirted with Gilles all the way to the church although she had not been nearly as friendly last night at suppertime when one of the WIC captains had taken center stage in the dining room. Tryntje was about Gilles' own age he guessed, with not more than a year or two between herself and Elsje. Jennetje was probably about twelve and Corretje and little Hendrick both looked to be about ten years old. Jennetje stayed close by her father but Corretje and Hendrick often slowed down or strayed to look at something in the street or in the house yards that they passed. Elsje would shoo them back into line, admonishing them not to touch that or to hurry and keep up. Through it all Old Hendrick kept walking and let Elsje do the work of keeping everyone apace behind him.

Outside the church, people called out greetings and shook hands with the family as they eyed Gilles curiously. The church was filling up quickly as they walked to their seats near the front. Here there were no seats reserved for the "best" families, the families that had contributed the most money, as there were at home in France and Gilles had to practice vigilance to keep from automatically kneeling and crossing himself several times. This church smelled different than his church at home, mainly because it lacked the incense. It smelled good though, like lemons and hay as well as old fireplace smoke. There were no statues, no pictures, no fantastic glass windows or gilded ornamentation as there were in Gilles' cathedral, only whitewashed walls and dark wood trim to look at. The church that seemed deceptively small on the outside was actually quite large inside and packed to capacity even before the service had started.

The children were herded into their seats by Elsje who sat next to them, followed by Gilles and Hendrick taking the last seat, the aisle seat. The hubbub that characterized the city continued in the church until a hush fell and the service began. Gilles could not remember much about it later except that there was no long procession and that the service centered around the pulpit that was at the heart of the church. He did remember later that it was all in Nederlands with no Latin. He would have understood it *all* in Latin but he did know the biblical references and followed along fairly well. In the sermon there were some references to the Catholic Church that would have offended him if he had more certainty as to the exact meaning of the Nederlands words.

There was a man sitting across the aisle who looked familiar to Gilles and he wondered how many of the sailors, dockworkers, and beggars ever attended this church. These lower classes were not exactly discouraged from attending in France but neither were they encouraged to sit among the good Christians. Gilles tried to look at the man without appearing too obvious about it and once Gilles thought he caught the man looking at him also. His heavy eyebrows seemed familiar and yet Gilles couldn't place him. Perhaps he only looked like someone he knew at home in France. Gilles wished that he could unobtrusively ask Elsje who the man was, but there was no opportunity for that.

After the service people greeted each other outside and under other circumstances Gilles might have thought that this was a nice local custom. As it was, it was unnerving to him: It was one thing to go out in the streets and disappear into a Huguenot church with the safety of the closed doors but to stand outside of it in broad daylight and not be afraid of being seen there was unthinkable in France. It was almost sacrilegious for the Dutch to be so noisy, so loud, and so happy near a church. It did not at all give the proper respect to the priests that they had always declared that God demanded. These people seemed drawn by a wish to be here, not a requirement to attend. It was a strange sensation, good and strange and wicked all at once. Gilles felt as though God's eyes were on him.

Gilles also believed that the entire congregation could see that he was not one of them and that he did not belong here. He was relieved that it was over and now he just wanted to get away from the church and go back to the inn. Unfortunately he could not get away quickly as everyone knew Hendrick and Elsje and everyone wanted to greet them and exchange pleasantries. The familiar looking man from inside the church had vanished into the crowd before he could point him out to Elsje and ask her about him.

"You must come dine with us now, Msr. Montroville," Old Hendrick said, putting a friendly hand on Gilles' shoulder.

"Well, I was going to go out with Msr. Durie after dinner," Gilles replied.

"Nonsense, our Sabbath dinner is a simple affair. We can answer any questions you might have about the service. Bring along Msr. Durie if you like. We haven't had the opportunity to get together yet."

Gilles did not want to bring Jean along and he hoped that Jean would not even see them returning. Sitting through dinner discussing Protestant theology could be somewhat interesting but what might Jean's contribution be if he spent his days with Marranos? The entire world had gone mad on the subject of religion but the Netherlanders alone all seemed quite relaxed about it. Gilles could think of nothing to do to avoid the invitation so he smiled weakly at Hendrick and Elsje. He rather thought that Elsje was enjoying his discomfort and now he wished that he had never accepted her invitation to go to church. Gilles wondered how fast he could eat and leave.

When they arrived back at the inn, they all climbed up to the third floor from the kitchen stairway where Elsje, Hendrick and Tryntje lived. The quarters were spotless and not remarkable but as he had never seen a dwelling like this before, Gilles tried not to be too obvious in looking around. The kitchen and eating area were just inside the door but they had no fireplace here, only a tiled area where food was brought up from the kitchen below and set on a warming box. The other end of the room had two cupboard beds with their curtains drawn and a small area with a curtain around it in one corner. Gilles could see inside the only other room on this floor, a small room sectioned off from the rest that he assumed was Hendrick's bedroom.

The table was set up for three but Elsje and Tryntje quickly had Gilles sitting on one side with Jennetje, Corretje and Tryntje opposite, Elsje and Heintje at the foot of the table and Hendrick at the head of the table.

"Sit, Msr. Montroville, the girls will bring our dinner. And you two also!" Hendrick scowled at the two youngest ones. They immediately sat down and behaved, having learned well that it was best not to try their father's patience. Elsje, Tryntje, and Jennetje brought herring, mussels, bread, butter and an apple pie that Elsje had made from the apples they bought on their shopping trip the day before.

Hendrick led them in a simple prayer of thanks for the food and when he said "Amen", Gilles automatically crossed himself before he remembered not to. No one said anything or appeared to notice except the two little children who stared at Gilles for a few minutes before Hendrick lifted his hand in a threatening gesture and they looked away.

"Thank you for inviting me," Gilles said.

"Eat, young man, you are welcome here. Your Nederlands is not so bad!"

Gilles looked at the little ones and wondered how old Elsje's mother had been when she died and what she died of but this was not the time or place to ask such questions.

The herring was very salty but the mussels, bread and butter were good and the apple tart was better than Gilles hoped, having still remembered the terrible "French" pastry from his last visit. Elsje also brought out shellfish chowder.

"It's my special recipe," she told him.

It spices wafted up on the aroma and Elsje continued, "I'm sure you've not had *anything* like this."

Gilles managed a nervous smile. He gingerly tasted it and was taken by surprise by the hot spicy quality of it. He grabbed his mug of ale and had several swallows. Tryntje grinned broadly at him and the other three children giggled. Elsje looked worried. "It's too spicy for you!"

"No, no, it's fine, it's just … What's in it?" Gilles' eyes watered and one tear ran down his cheek before he stopped it with his finger.

"It's curry powder. I love to cook with all the spices from the east."

"Sorry Montroville, I should have warned you," said Hendrick. "We don't get much good basic food around here anymore; she has to try every spice she finds on all of us in some dish we liked well enough before. If we don't die right away she serves it in the inn. It probably scares off half of our patrons!"

"It's good, really, it's fine." Gilles smiled at Elsje who finally looked somewhat relieved, refilling his ale glass as she gave her father a sharp look.

Tryntje was staring at Gilles and smiling at him. Gilles looked to his hostess, Elsje, who had invited him on this adventure, but she seemed only interested and polite, nothing more. None of the children said much during dinner and Hendrick was happy to have the guest's attention mostly to himself.

"What did you think of our service, Montroville? Have you ever attended Protestant services before?"

Elsje startled at this question from her father but recovered quickly.

"No, I have not. It was very … interesting." He fished around for the words and hoped they were not only grammatically right but also appropriate. Elsje gave a nod of support in his direction and Gilles relaxed just a little.

"I hear that there are many going to such services in France and many more that would go if they were not afraid for their lives and livelihoods there," Hendrick said.

"Father!" Elsje glared at him. "This is not the time to ask our guest …"

"My daughter thinks I should not be so open. My apologies if I have offended you."

"Not at all. Some are offended by the truth but I am not. It is a matter we have yet to resolve in France," Gilles replied.

"Yes, it seems the property of all of the Huguenots ends up in the King's possession sooner or later and the former owners end up here in Amsterdam if they are able to escape the King's fires."

"Father!" Elsje admonished him again. "Gilles did not come to discuss our countries' differences. We are, after all, partners in trade, aren't we?"

"My daughter!" Hendrick waived a fork in her direction. "Always the diplomat! That's all right, Montroville, we have our own problems here. Our leader is so jealous of our own merchants and the city of Amsterdam that he would gladly smash all of our business and trade if he could, just to experience the feeling of a little power! No king in Europe has any great love of Protestants, not Louis in France or Charles in England although they oppose Spain and the Habsburgs. Sweden and Denmark are the only ones with backbone enough to take a stand on the side of a man's free choice of how to worship."

"Well, Sweden and Denmark are no longer in any position to be a threat to Spain so they don't have to fear an attack any time soon, do they?" Gilles observed, somewhat disrespectfully.

"You are here on business then, Msr. Montroville?" Hendrick continued to eat as he talked, occasionally glaring at Corretje and little Hendrick when their noise level approached competing levels.

"Yes, for my father. We have some business we have yet to conclude here."

"Let me know if I can help. I have many contacts in business and trade circles," Hendrick offered.

"Thank you, that's good to know."

Gilles wasn't sure if he could use Hendrick's help at all but he wanted to leave that door open. An extra ally here was always a good thing to have.

"Are you promised to someone, engaged then, Msr. Montroville?" Hendrick asked as he scrutinized some herring, turning one piece over with a fork.

"Father!" Elsje interjected again. "Perhaps Msr. Montroville would rather not discuss his personal life, just something less controversial, like the church or his country's politics!"

Hendrick regarded her briefly and then returned his attention to the herring. "I didn't think it was a sensitive subject."

"I'd like to know if he's engaged." Tryntje spoke up.

Under the withering gaze from her father she turned very red and suddenly got very interested in her apple tart.

"My parents have someone in mind for me." Gilles said.

Elsje looked up at him and Tryntje made a sound like a snicker. Hendrick glared at Tryntje again and she resumed looking at her dessert and poking at it with her spoon. Even the little ones sensed that something interesting was going on and they paid close attention. They had even stopped eating.

"These matters are *arranged* in France and Msr. Montroville is a man of some position, isn't that right?" Hendrick explained to his children, mainly his older children, as he selected the herring he wanted from the platter.

"Oh, do you know my father?" Gilles asked. He suddenly realized that Hendrick's use of the name was referring to himself and not to his father as Msr. Montroville, and he turned red.

"I have heard of him in regards to the wine trade and other spirits but I do not know him *personally*. If you have finished eating, I can offer you some after-dinner tobacco Msr. Montroville. It's very good."

"Er … no thank you."

Gilles was a little curious as he had smelled it around the city but he did not want to appear foolish in not knowing how it was used. It was not a popular thing in France and not the custom in his house or among his father's close associates. Gilles decided that this was not a good time or place to take the risk of looking foolish, even if he might appear to be rude.

Tryntje retrieved the tobacco for her father which he kept on a shelf in an ornate wooden box. The tobacco was a yellowish-brown curled substance that had the appearance of wool shavings or perhaps thin strips of old bark. Hendrick tore off a small piece and stuffed it into his long white clay pipe. While Hendrick prepared the pipe, Tryntje went down the stairs and then returned with a candle and a long piece of straw with which to light the tobacco. The smell was not unpleasant to Gilles but it seemed rather more trouble than it was worth since it kept going out and had to be lit again and again.

"This tobacco is the best and it is from England's Virginia Colony. Trade is on again and off again with them, depending on the mood of the English and how their war is going with Scotland from week to week. It's a good thing we grow our own tobacco here in the Netherlands and some more in New Amsterdam, just in case the supply gets cut off. Did you know the savages in the new world have smoked this for ages and consider it magical? If it cures my gout it will be magical."

Hendrick pushed his chair back to relax, talk with Gilles, and smoke as Elsje and Tryntje started to clear the table.

"The West India Company trades in all kinds of things: Sugar, pearls, wood, ivory, even African workers to keep the trade going in the new world. We'll have to talk about trade later with Msr. Durie." Hendrick nodded at Gilles.

This seemed to be a good time for him to take his leave so Gilles seized the opportunity.

"I'd like that. Right now I must find Msr. Durie but I thank you for all your hospitality. It was an interesting morning."

"Off so soon? Come back and be my guest another time. We will discuss opportunities for trade to the new world, something you will want to get in on.

There are great fortunes being made and most of the rich never even leave their comfortable homes here in Amsterdam! I could put you in with the right people for a small fee. You would be rich!" Hendrick said as he stood up and shook Gilles' hand.

"Thank you, I will consider that." Gilles made his exit.

"Goodbye Msr. Montroville!" Tryntje called after him as he went down the stairs.

Gilles found Jean sitting on the stoop in the back of the inn whittling another piece of wood. Gilles vaguely wondered where Durie got it since every piece of wood in the city seemed to be used right away for building warehouses or ships or buildings.

"You had lunch with the family, eh?" Jean asked him. "You didn't sign any trade agreements did you?" Jean's good humor and energy had returned.

"No, but he did mention it. Does he always have some new proposition?"

"Almost always," Jean said, "Some are good, some are not so good."

"Where are we going today?" Gilles asked.

"Oh, here, there and everywhere. Your father has another ship coming in tomorrow so if you want to send a letter back, you'd better get it written tonight or very early tomorrow."

Jean's tour took them down the street in the direction of the Dam and Jean told Gilles some more about the great fortunes built by the Dutch West India Company.

"More people are starting to settle over in New Amsterdam as they see the opportunities opening up and there is somewhat less hardship there now."

"Hendrick started to tell me about it. They trade in human beings too?" Gilles asked, as they passed a dark man in shackles struggling to carry a wooden crate up the street for an elderly Netherlander.

"Yes there is a slave trade, laborers needed to keep things going I guess, but people can go there to be free, too. There are people who have been freed from the other colonies in the south and half-free African slaves who pay a tax each year and can remain free. With enough money, anything is possible there and making any amount of money is also possible there."

"If it's so wonderful there, then why aren't you going?" Gilles asked him.

"Me? Go to the Americas?" Jean obviously found the suggestion humorous. "I can make my fortune here and marry my lady while living in the comfort of France. I can't see forgoing any of the comforts of home!"

"Hendrick told me about people who are making their fortunes there but have never left this city. It's true then?"

"Yes, true enough. The only difficulty we have is in hanging on to it here and not getting taxed into poverty."

Gilles was shocked at this irreverent statement. It was not a loyal thing for a good Frenchman to say. This brought to mind some of Hendrick's comments at dinner and he had to ask the question.

"Jean, does everyone here see the French as a little crazy?"

Jean thought for a moment before he answered. "I think they see us as people who do not question our King or our laws at all; they may not fully realize that we must always think of the consequences of what we say before we say it. You must admit that we look crazy to others as we alternately make peace, then attack, make treaties and break them with the same countries. Richelieu crushes the Protestants at home to keep them out of power and takes their property but sides with them against the Spanish and Habsburg Catholics! The people of the Netherlands are too busy with trade to have any interest in following all the intrigues of court, the Church and Richelieu. It's far too complicated for most of them to follow. They just don't understand that to us the law, the King and our faith are all one and the same thing."

"I went to a reformed church service with the family this morning."

Jean looked over at him as they walked but he didn't break step. "Why did you do that, just out of curiosity?"

"I'm not really sure why I did it, to tell you the truth. Elsje invited me and I went."

"Although it seems like a safe place here, I would caution you to be discrete, Gilles. The eyes of the French King see far and Richelieu demands strict adherence to the one right path."

Gilles did not reply. He decided that Jean made too much of nothing, just like his father always did.

They walked past the docks and saw ships that had already come in today and some that were on their way in, even though it was Sunday. Such work activity would not have been tolerated at home in France but it seemed to go on here every day, although Gilles learned that there were those too, in Amsterdam, who grumbled about a lack of respect to the church with work being performed every day, even on the Sabbath. There were ships in the port from the Far East that carried pepper, cloves, ginger, porcelain, jewels and silk. There were ships coming in from the Brazil Colonies with all kinds of exotic goods, animals and people and there were English ships arriving to trade tobacco, molasses, animal pelts and sugar from their overseas colonies.

Gilles glimpsed his first savages from the new world but he was somewhat disappointed when Jean pointed them out to him. The man he saw up close was dark with somewhat heavy features and long straight brown hair pulled back in a Chinese braid but he was not fierce and warlike at all. His clothes were made of animal hide and the most colorful thing about him was a leather bag embroidered and decorated with shells that hung at his side. Indeed, there were no feathers to be seen and some of his blond English shipmates were even dressed in the same manner! When the men called to each other in their unloading activities, Gilles was surprised to hear the savage speaking London's English. Gilles tried not to stare but he suddenly realized that this magical world he had been hearing about did indeed exist and was not only very real, but was now spread out before him. The savage worked alongside the English sailors and two more savages appeared from below the deck before Gilles and Jean had passed beyond the ship.

"Some call them "Indians" although they are not from India," Jean whispered to Gilles. "They say there are many kinds, each with their own language and customs, some to be trusted and some not, but all of them liking brightly colored things, alcoholic spirits and tobacco. They trade with us and bring the furs out from the wilderness. Some have learned Nederlands and others speak French that they learned from our settlements in New France. Some are slaves but these men here appear to be free men."

"French?" Gilles couldn't believe it. "Some of them speak French?"

"Some have probably learned German and Swedish, too, since there are a lot of those settlers in New Netherlands!" Jean laughed. "Imagine a savage speaking Swedish!"

"How do you know so much about the New World if you have never been there?"

"Just the trade business. You may not think so now, but it's *very* interesting."

"You make it sound interesting. My father makes the same business dull."

"You would be surprised what a column of figures can tell you, Gilles. It can tell you that a man has no self-control, that he can't stop himself from gambling, that he has a mistress, that he has much more money than he shows on the books. For those who can read the language of accounting, it always tells a story and often a very interesting story."

A very well-dressed man who looked like a noble passed them and greeted Jean.

"Who is that?" Gilles asked, turning to look at him, his eyes wide.

"Joseph D'Acosta. He is a stockholder in the Dutch West India Company. He is going places too, some say, only just started his climb up to the top."

"Will you introduce me to him sometime?" Gilles asked.

"Of course, how rude of me," Jean replied, but Gilles had the feeling that Jean did not want to introduce him for some reason.

"Is that a Spanish name? How did you come to meet him? Was it through the business?" Gilles was full of questions this morning.

"Um-hm, let's take a short cut here, we need to be going north on the next street over."

Jean clearly knew his shortcuts and Gilles was taken aback by what opened up to their view on the next street. It was as though he had been instantly transported back to France. The shops on the street all had French names and the goods appeared to be as fine as any in France. Gilles wondered if there was a pastry shop here and if he might buy one for Elsje so that she could compare and adjust her recipe accordingly. She would probably be offended at the offer, though. Gilles decided that he might come back here and buy one for himself later on in the week.

"These shops are all owned by Frenchmen, Huguenots or Reformees who have left France," Jean told him. "They have many wonderful things here but you must be very careful not to be seen spending too much time here."

"Is all of this caution really necessary?" Gilles asked Jean impatiently.

"Your father may not have told you this, but there are many things that one needs to be careful about. The missing Claret that concerns him may not be a simple matter. There may be more to it than just simple theft," Jean replied. "There could be other things being smuggled on his ships. Our people are checking into that, too."

"Like what?" Gilles asked.

Jean sighed and looked into his eyes. "Like people. Human beings. The King does not just let the Huguenots walk out of France with their money you know, or maybe you don't know, but it's time you learned. They have far too much wealth and influence to just be allowed to leave and continue their lives elsewhere. Other smugglers have been caught shipping people out in hidden compartments on the ships. The stakes are high on both sides with great profits to be made in the trade and severe penalties for those who think they are just helping their fellow human beings. It's a growing problem for the King, one he is determined to put an end to. Richelieu takes such activities as a personal affront to King and country, too."

"And are my father's ships being used for this purpose? Would he be blamed for this and suffer the consequences if it were true, even if he didn't know what was going on?"

Gilles wondered if Jean Durie might be involved in this trade but how could he have smuggled so many Marranos off of one ship? The number he had been seen with was more than one or two, it was more like a dozen. Where had they come from? His father's ships?

"I don't believe they are being used so, but yes, it could cost him dearly," Jean replied.

"Believe so or know so?" Gilles asked pointedly.

"I have checked the ships and can find evidence of no such activity. I have found no hidden compartments or extra containers. Your father is concerned about this also and wants to make sure. We need to stop the ordinary thefts of his goods anyway, although the thieves may be more than ordinary thieves. They might be delivering the spirits and the human cargo for a double payment."

"Who would they be? The captain? The sailors?"

"Gilles! Enough questions! We do not know the answers yet! There appears to be nothing at all unusual about the last shipment because nothing was reported missing. It may be that they know we are watching now and the thefts from your father will stop completely. The ship due to arrive tomorrow has no spirits on board except for some wine and mead. Another one should arrive late in the week or early next week with claret, wine, sherry and cognac. We will see what happens with that one. In the meantime you and I will visit the counting houses here and examine their books and their records of our shipments."

"And will you have more of your own private business to conduct this week?" Gilles asked.

"Probably so," Jean answered, his face betraying no discomfort from the inquiry.

Gilles was starting to feel that he was sitting with the stranger again. If Jean Durie was using the Montroville ships to smuggle Huguenots or Marranos, that might have been the warning that Claude was trying to give him. Gilles' father could lose everything, his life included, if such an operation were to be discovered on his ships. Gilles shuddered at the thought of his father being executed in front of him. Gilles hadn't actually *heard* what the prostitute had whispered in Jean's ear. Perhaps they were in collusion.

Another thought occurred to Gilles now; that his own life could be in danger from this man Durie, this man he had been calling "friend".

Jean and Gilles talked a little while they ate dinner and drank a few ales but it was mainly conversation about Amsterdam and its many wonders and not about the shipping business. They did make plans to go to one of the counting houses in the morning and check on the Montroville accounts. Gilles was very tired as it had been a long day and they had walked a great distance around the city. He was more than ready to go to sleep when he turned in but he had odd dreams that woke him throughout the night. He dreamed that a line of Marranos came into a church with monk's robes on, swinging incense burners that burned tobacco. They were not chanting in Latin but in their own language. Claude came in after them and pointed to something up on the wall where the Virgin's statue was in her niche in the cathedral at home. What adorned the wall now appeared to be one of Jean's carvings. Gilles turned to look for Jean Durie but saw that he had already left the church. Gilles' father sat in their usual pew, not with his family but with all of the sailors from all of his ships. Gilles woke with a feeling of panic in the early morning light, soaked in his own sweat. He didn't want to go back to sleep so he put his pants on and went downstairs even though he still felt tired.

"It was just some bad fish," he told himself, but he was more than happy to put an end to the strange dreams and stay awake for the rest of the day.

After finishing breakfast, Jean and Gilles went out to the counting house to review the Montroville accounts. A light mist was falling from the sky today, dampening everything, including Gilles' spirits. Although some of the buildings and procedures were different than they were in France, the work was pretty much the same. Jean was impressed by his young partner's knowledge of accounting although neither one could find any irregularities in the bookkeeping. It was as Jean Montroville had said: The Netherlanders were precise and meticulous, even scrupulous in maintaining their accounts. They were finished with the review by midday so Gilles went back to the inn alone to eat a midday dinner and to write a letter to his father while Jean went out to his own business. One of the Montroville ships was expected to arrive in Amsterdam sometime today and could carry the letter back to Gilles' father. Gilles couldn't believe that so many days had passed since he had left and that all too soon he would be going back home, back to Marie and back to the counting houses as well. Gilles missed France but at the same time he wished that he never had to go back: It was pleasant here. He would love to be able to just return to Amsterdam whenever he pleased. Perhaps he could work something out with his father so Msr. Montroville would agree to let him come a few times a year.

During his dinner, Gilles noticed for the first time that he had not talked to Elsje at all since the day before. She always seemed to be busy in some other part of the room. He approached her after the mid-day meal and asked if she had some paper, a quill and some ink that he could use to write the letter.

"Of course Msr. Montroville," she replied and hurried off toward the kitchen. Gilles waited patiently for some minutes until at last she returned, deposited all of the requested items in front of him, and sailed off again. Gilles looked around but none of the tables had a surface that he could write on. They were all deeply scarred from countless encounters with patrons.

"Elsje?" He stuck his head inside the kitchen.

"Yes, Msr. Montroville?" She eyed him somewhat impatiently, kneading some bread dough as she spoke.

"Is there a better surface I can use to write on?"

She seemed even more impatient at the silly question and gestured to the area where they kept their record books for who was staying there and who owed what to the inn. It was actually more of a high table than a desk and there weren't any chairs nearby for him to sit on. Gilles decided not to ask Elsje for anything more, just to stand up and write a very short letter. The letter would not take too long anyway, as he didn't have that much to say. Writing the letter was just another way to placate his father.

Where to start with his missive? His goodbye had been rushed and his father may not be thinking kindly about him yet because of the way he had left. He thought that he really should warn his father about what Claude had said but he wasn't sure what to say or how to say it in a letter without alarming him. It *had* been a vague warning anyway. He did want his father to think that he was working hard and working well with Jean Durie, accomplishing *something*, but what could he truthfully say? That Jean was smuggling Marranos only, not Huguenots and not on your ships? Gilles sighed and looked up at the ceiling, trying to come up with some inspiration. Elsje darted past him, gathering up his dinner dishes from the table in the dining room.

There was Marie. He could talk about Marie. His father would like that.

Gilles worked the cork stopper out of the ink bottle and gently chipped off the old ink that had dried on the quill's tip. He dipped it into the blue-black liquid and tested it out on the date line.

He wrote the greeting to his father and told him in the most positive but truthful way that progress was being made on the business they had come for. He did not want to be too specific about how they were proceeding and what they were doing because whoever carried the letter might read it and there was the possibility that it could fall into the wrong hands; also it seemed pitiful to Gilles that all they could do to try and find the stolen spirits was to make contact with a few people who watched the streets and go through some record books. It was no wonder that his father thought Gilles' coming here would be wasted time. He was beginning to think so himself, at least from a business point of view, but he couldn't admit that to his father.

Gilles wrote that Jean and he were working together to achieve their ends and that he hoped it would be a profitable partnership. Gilles noted also that Jean had his own additional business to attend to sometimes but that they both hoped to finish their business in the Netherlands with satisfactory results and would be returning home soon. He thought better of writing the part about Jean's own business later but since Elsje had not given him any more paper and he didn't wish to cross it out, he just left it. It didn't seem too bad, he thought, as he read that part over again. Gilles added that he had a renewed interest in the counting aspect of the business since he had worked with Jean Durie and that he hoped to serve his father here again sometime in addition to keeping up with the books at home. He finally decided to mention Claude's warning in passing by stating that a good friend in France wanted them to be most precise in their bookkeeping and other affairs. Gilles finished by saying that he was ready to assume all of his responsibilities, including marriage, and that at any date agreeable to his father.

He read it over and was satisfied that it was vague enough to pass any smugglers who might read it on the ship but specific enough that his father would understand that they were making good use of their time here. Gilles blew on it until the ink dried and then called for Elsje to see if she had any sealing wax.

She made a grumpy sound and after running a towel briskly over her dough-covered hands, she rummaged around in the back of a drawer until she found an old piece. Apparently Elsje and her father did not do a lot of letter writing. She lit a candle for Gilles from the fire and slamming the candleholder and wax down on his writing table, she returned to her dough without a word to Gilles.

Her mood and demeanor were not lost on him, so when he had finished preparing the letter, he went in to the kitchen to make his apologies.

"I am sorry to put you to this extra work, Elsje. Can I make it up to you by taking you for a walk later?" Gilles asked hopefully.

"Nee, I have too much to do."

"Well, then tomorrow maybe?" he asked.

"I am *always* very busy. Taking the time off before with you was a mistake." She continued to punch and pound and roll the dough.

Gilles shrugged. Women could be so moody. It was no wonder with her though; all she ever did was work. Someone should teach her how to take time off, how to enjoy life. Gilles tucked the letter into his breast pocket and putting his damp cloak and hat back on, he went down to the docks to see if his father's ship had come in yet.

The *Destinie* had just anchored out in the harbor and though it was at a distance, Gilles could see that there was still a great deal of activity all over the ship so she had not been in port long. Small ferry boats had brought over the first two loads from the hold and Jean Durie was already there checking cargo with the captain.

"Is it all in order, Jean?" Gilles asked.

"So far," Durie replied. "We haven't finished the counting yet, though."

Jean appeared to be doing a very thorough job and Gilles now wondered if he was completely mistaken in suspecting Durie of being in league with the thieves or if he was just an excellent actor, very good at appearing to be competent and loyal. Wherever he had been earlier, Jean Durie had quickly received word from someone that the Montroville ship was in port. Gilles and Jean worked together wordlessly, except to compare counts, completing the job in record time.

"You have been very quiet lately, Gilles," Jean observed. "Don't you feel well or is it thoughts of a woman that occupy your mind? I can't bring you home to your father like this if you are sick with the plague."

"I'm well enough and it's not women," Gilles said. "I do have some things on my mind … about the business."

"You do not need to worry yourself, Gilles. That is *my* job and you just signed on as an apprentice when we left port. Things are going as well as can be expected and I see no cause for you to worry right now. I am confident that we will get to the source of the problem eventually but I have to get back to my own business this afternoon"

"Does your own business take you here often?" Gilles asked. "To Amsterdam?"

The question had seemed innocent enough but Jean Durie had perhaps picked up on something in the tone of the question. "When I am here, there is much to do, but I don't *have* to come here often," Jean replied, measuring each word carefully.

"I wrote to my father. Did you have a letter or anything else that you wanted to send to him?" Gilles asked.

"No, I've already sent a letter by way of another ship that was heading to Rouen and the captain promised to have it to him by yesterday. Now we wait for the next ship of your father's that comes in at the end of the week. Captain LeBlanc will be making that run and we will be returning with him, if nothing exciting keeps us here, that is! Give the Destinie's captain your letter then and be quick about it. We will follow this wine to the warehouse today, just to give us something to do but I don't expect we will see anything out of the ordinary."

Gilles handed the letter over to the captain, making his request for delivery. They finished the count, followed the shipment to the Waag and watched as the officials counted and weighed and took the tax money from the agent who was prepared with just the right amount of money. Jean and Gilles went from there directly to the warehouse and were already waiting there when the wagons with the wine pulled up to be unloaded.

"Who are you?" A big burley man snarled at them.

Gilles could smell ale on him and his bloodshot eyes looked ready, even eager, for a fight.

"We are agents for Jean Montroville," Jean Durie replied, "here to check on the wine shipment. Are you the warehouse watchman, the man in charge? We would like to take a count on the wine that has just come off the ship."

"No one told me about any agents or any count, get out of here!" the man shouted at them menacingly.

"Msr. Montroville can have all of his goods redirected to another warehouse if there is no cooperation here and that would not be good for your employer or for you. If we had to, we could talk to the people at the Waag to help us clear this up," Jean said.

"How do I know that you are who you say you are? How do I know you aren't a thief?" the big man said as he looked them over. His watery eyes rolled from Jean to Gilles and then back again.

"Do we really look like thieves?" Gilles asked, as he straightened his collar and his hat.

"Do you have any written orders?" the man asked, still not cooperative but obviously not wanting to involve the officials.

"Just a document stating that I am Jean Montroville's agent," Jean replied as he reached into his breast pocket and handed it over.

"How do I know it's not a forgery?" Scratching his beard, the big man threw a small coin at a ragged boy who had been sitting on some crates on the side of the warehouse. "Go ask the captain, the Destinie!" he bellowed.

The young boy caught the coin like the professional that he was and took off toward the harbor at a run.

"In the meantime you two *gentlemen* can stay out here. No one comes inside *my* warehouse!"

Gilles thought that the man looked a little disappointed that he wasn't going to be able to fight them. The man eyed them briefly again and then looked again at the papers that Jean had handed him. Gilles knew the man could not read but he made an attempt to look like he was scanning the papers; Gilles knew this because at first the papers were upside down but then were quickly turned right side up while the man stared at them. He handed them back to Jean Durie too quickly, before anyone could have taken the time to read them properly.

"They look to be in order, I guess. You still wait!" the big man roared.

"With your permission, may we start counting what is on the wagons?" Jean asked.

The watchman shrugged.

Jean and Gilles counted what was on the wagons, four large wagons in all, pulling a bottle here and there to make sure that it was full and that neither the contents nor the cork stoppers had been tampered with.

The boy returned before they were finished counting and said to the warehouse man, "The captain swears for them. They were there at the ship before they came here."

"We wish to thank you Msr. er … We are attempting to locate some lost cargo," Jean said when they were done, handing the warehouseman a coin.

"I never lose *any* cargo out of *my* warehouse." The big man looked at the coin before he pocketed it and turned to go back into the warehouse. "Bring it in, and make sure *they* didn't take any of it," he called over his shoulder to the men with the carts. The young boy had already scampered off somewhere, probably to buy something with his new found wealth.

"Great manners." Jean grinned at Gilles. "It's all here, though."

As they turned to go Jean said to Gilles, "The last shipment of claret that disappeared came through this warehouse, too. It was worth taking the time to check. Fifty bottles gone, just like that."

A small army of beggars made their way up the street toward them, targeting Jean and Gilles, two lone gentlemen in a sea of workmen that populated the warehouse districts. Jean grabbed Gilles' arm and pulled him quickly up the street and away from the approaching pack.

Jean sighed. "There is more and more of that too, since things aren't as prosperous here as they were just five years ago. At least in Amsterdam they have a place to help poor people, that is, if they are a part of the community and will allow themselves to be helped," he said to Gilles. "Sometimes you see whole families begging for food. They lose their money and then they lose their minds. It is a terrible thing."

Gilles had not noticed the poverty; he saw only prosperity and people hurrying here and there during the day. Of course he saw the beggars but they were everywhere in France and he did not know how good times must have been in Amsterdam before. Those who were still making money did not have the time to stop and notice such things.

"If the warehouseman can't read, how does he know he is not being cheated?" Gilles asked Jean as they headed back to the inn.

"You saw that, eh? You *are* very sharp, young Gilles! Well, they read numbers well enough and the good ones may not know a single letter in a name but they know the signatures well enough to spot a forgery long before anyone else who can read. If they are very big, mean, and sober too, it's nearly a perfect combination of qualifications for someone in that position. Two out of the three isn't bad, though." Jean apparently made reference to the smell of the ale on the warehouseman.

"So you don't think he can be cheated but may be a party to the thefts?"

"I'm convinced it would be the captain at the front end or the warehouse people at the back, maybe both in partnership. The business about the fire on the docks still bothers me, though: They never tried that before." Jean consulted the sky. "I guess it's not too early for supper, is it?"

"I just finished a big dinner but I'll join you for some ale first," Gilles volunteered. He wondered if he should ask Jean about the Marranos. His curiosity was getting the better of him but he was still afraid to trust Jean completely. Gilles still wondered if Claude's warning was about Jean Durie.

Because it was still so early, they found very good seats at the inn.

"Two ales please, Elsje!" Jean called out to her.

She brought them promptly, set them down without a word and then turned on her heel.

"What did you do to her?" Jean asked. "Oh, non! You didn't...."

"What?" Gilles asked. "I thought she was just very busy lately."

"Elsje's *never* so busy that she doesn't have a kind word, for most of us anyway," Jean replied. "You did treat her like a lady the other day, didn't you? You didn't treat her like a servant?"

Gilles flushed with anger. "Of *course* I did! I thought we had a fine time. I had lunch with the family and that was fine ... I think."

He looked over at Elsje and tried to solve the mystery. He reviewed the events and the conversation that he remembered but nothing seemed amiss.

"It was fine." He tried to reassure himself as much as Jean.

"Well, something's changed," Jean said. "Go and tell her we want some supper now. See if she'll talk to you."

Gilles nodded, got up and walked over to her. "Goedenavond Elsje, we're ready for some supper now, if it's ready."

"I'll bring it out right away," she answered and turned to go into the kitchen.

"Wait, Elsje! You seem a little ... upset. I apologize if I said or did anything ..."

"You didn't." She started to leave but Gilles caught her by the elbow.

"Are you certain?"

Old Hendrick entered the room at that moment and he called out to Elsje, "Is there a problem here?"

"No, Father, no problem."

She pulled her elbow away and left in the direction of the kitchen. Gilles turned to go back to his table.

"Msr. Montroville, I will talk with you now," Hendrick said. It was an order, not a request.

"Yes?" Gilles asked.

Hendrick moved closer before he spoke in a low voice to Gilles. "My daughter is a *good* girl. We know that you French do not think it proper for women to work in businesses. She did not understand your customs concerning marriage until I explained them to her. She should *not* have been out alone with a young engaged man. You stay away from my daughter now."

"I meant no disrespect," Gilles started to explain but Hendrick cut him off.

"There is no more for us to discuss."

The old man moved off to talk with some of the West India Company shareholders who had just come in. Gilles felt as though the blood had drained out of him and his hands started to shake.

"What's the matter with *you*? What did the old man say?" Jean asked, taking in Gilles' pale face.

"Rien. Just to stay away from Elsje," Gilles replied. He really didn't feel at all hungry now.

Instead of being sympathetic though, Jean snickered.

"It's not funny!" Gilles said indignantly. "I don't even *like* her!"

"Don't concern yourself about it, Gilles: These Netherlanders are a strange people: They'll take in total strangers and then fight terrible fights with their own family members. They have their own peculiar customs which they are totally rigid about and yet will fight for a stranger's complete freedom to do whatever they want, including ignoring those same customs that they hold so dear! They are terribly concerned with their own morality but have more prostitutes in this city alone than there are in *all of France*. I gave up trying to figure them out long ago. Don't give it another thought, just be pleasant to them both and keep your distance from the girls. Here, just think of it in terms of negotiation guidelines for future trade and all the money to be made from it."

He had finished speaking just as Elsje returned to the table with their dinner.

"Thank you, Elsje." Jean beamed at her.

"You're welcome." She smiled back at Jean but she didn't look at Gilles at all as she set the plates down.

Tryntje brought some fresh bread and butter over. She was not reserved in the least but gave Gilles a big smile and wink and said, "This is for *you*. I know how much you like our bread, Msr. Montroville."

Jean had a pleasant smile for Tryntje, too, and when she had left, he whispered to Gilles, "It's not *Elsje* that Old Hendrick should be worried about: It's that wild younger sister he should keep his eye on! Don't get any ideas or give him the wrong impression about her, either: We need Hendrick's good will for the success of our future trade here. The West India people are here at the inn all the time because it's cheap and it's not too far from the ships. It's a great place to make connections and deals. Just look at who is sitting over there! The Netherlanders think little enough of the French in general, but I have worked *very* hard to convince them that I am one of the few good ones." Jean nodded a greeting to the three well-dressed men who were smiling at him from a table in the other corner. "Are you sure you didn't inadvertently say something suggestive to Elsje? Maybe she's what has you so pre-occupied lately, eh?" Jean gave Gilles a smirk.

"What has me preoccupied is the theft of my father's goods and the trouble my father might have if he is accused of smuggling or not paying taxes," Gilles said irritably as he put his fork down. The utensil wasn't serving much purpose anyway as Gilles was not using it to *eat* his food, only to move it around the plate.

"I see," said Jean, the smile fading from his face. "Perhaps you think I am not working as hard as I might to stop the thefts?" he asked Gilles, "… that I am not earning my pay?"

Gilles' stomach hurt even more now. "I don't know *what* to think," he said truthfully. "I feel like I don't know what is going on." Gilles paused then, saying nothing more at first, wondering if he should bring up the subject of the Marranos that he had seen Jean with. He stared at his food for a moment more while he collected his courage before pushing ahead. "*Oh, why not?*" he thought.

"My father has placed you in a position of trust and you have the means to ruin him, even to forfeit his life if you have already broken that trust."

Gilles' throat started to dry out and he had a sip of ale to help him finish and to steady his nerves. The whole evening was going very badly: First Elsje and Hendrick were upset with him and now there was this very unpleasant discussion with Jean. He couldn't stop himself now, though, he couldn't stop until he had said what he was going to say.

"I have to consider *every* possibility. I don't know what I should say to my father when I get back to France."

"What *you* should say? Do you suspect me of collaboration with the thieves? Is that what you said to him in your letter?" Jean asked, a hard look entering his eyes.

"I *said* that we worked together well but that sometimes you had your own business to attend to, whatever that might be. Does it concern you that I might have said something to him?"

"Do you really think that I might be in league with the thieves?"

"Non. Oui. I don't know."

Gilles was honest. He had said it. He really didn't know.

Their eyes locked, each re-evaluating the other, both angry, neither one backing down. It was undecided for a time who would speak first and which way the future conversation would go, toward a mending of bridges or toward widening the chasm between the two. Gilles could not dismiss the suspicions that were gathering in his mind; they gained substance from his fears and from his malaise at seeing Jean's easy familiarity with the strange Marrano people.

Finally Jean spoke.

"Gilles, right now trust is a commodity that is harder to find than diamonds. It is nearly impossible to convince someone to trust you if they do not already have the inclination to do so. I will stay here and will continue to do my best for your father, no matter what you may decide about me. I won't ask you to trust me; I just ask that we continue to work together as best we can for your father's interests."

"I know what my father's interests are but no one knows anything about *your* interests. No one knows anything about you, your family, or where you come from, do they?" Gilles challenged him, unwilling to make peace yet.

"Your father, my client, has made his usual thorough inquiries; enough to satisfy *him*. I have no obligation or desire to share my private life with *you*."

Gilles wasn't sure what to do with the food on his plate anymore. He certainly didn't feel like eating now but Jean had already finished a good portion of his dinner before he had lost *his* appetite. They were both out of ale though and Elsje brought refills. "Is there something wrong with the food?" she asked them, looking at the plates that had so much food left.

"Nee, it's fine, Elsje. You can take mine away, I'm just not very hungry this evening," Jean said.

"Mine, too," Gilles added.

Silently she removed the plates. When she left, Gilles said to Jean, in an effort to move back into more peaceful waters, "They seemed fine at church on Sunday. I don't know what happened afterwards. Dinner was fine. Hendrick even told me to come by and talk about trade with him."

"That really *wasn't* a good thing to do, Gilles. Don't go back to that church. As I said, the King's eyes extend even to the Netherlands. Regarding Hendrick, I think you'd be surprised at how amicable the man can be when it comes to the subject of trade. We will talk to him and get you back in his good graces. You'll still have to keep your distance from Elsje and Tryntje, though. Try to remember that the Dutch do not share our values and though they are wonderful hosts to everyone, in truth they do not like us very much. Do not *ever* think that they will truly be your friend: We are just too different."

Gilles thought about this for a few moments. Perhaps Jean was right about that.

"We've had a very long day today, Gilles. Tomorrow will look better, it usually does," said Jean and he excused himself for the night.

Gilles sat there, still wondering a hundred things about Jean, including whether or not he could trust him, but those questions would just have to remain unanswered, at least for the time being.

The next morning Jean was already having breakfast with Hendrick when Gilles came into the dining room. Gilles didn't want to sit with Hendrick at all but he felt that he had little choice; he couldn't very well turn around again and leave or take a seat across the room. Jean solved his dilemma by waiving to Gilles in greeting.

"Gilles! We have been making trade deals already while you sleep the day away! Come and join us."

Some rolls, two cups, and a large pot of hot chocolate were in front of the two men. Gilles knew immediately what the chocolate was, although he had never seen it before. For one thing, it looked and smelled different than tea. He sensed that Jean Durie would rather have had tea to drink but Hendrick probably considered the chocolate imported from across the sea a fine treat for his special guests.

At home in France they had heard all about chocolate. The priest wrote entire sermons about chocolate, an evil drink, the devil's own brew. Gilles was very curious about it and looked forward eagerly to trying this sinful drink. He would just go to confession and say several Hail Marys. Elsje was bustling around the dining room but Gilles was careful not to even look in her direction.

"Bring us another cup for my other guest, Elsje," Hendrick called out to her.

Jean didn't seem fond of the tobacco smoke, either, but Gilles was getting used to it and rather liked it; it smelled warm and mysterious to him. Jean leaned back in his chair, out of the smoke, as Hendrick puffed on his pipe. Hendrick jumped right into the subject of trade even before Elsje had returned with the extra cup for Gilles.

"If you invest now, you can make money enough to be rich and stop working while you are still young. I made a small investment five years ago, before anyone else was investing much in New Netherlands, and today I am quite comfortable! I just keep the inn to stay busy and to keep up with new opportunities that come through our door. This is absolutely the best time for you two gentlemen to invest. Most of the risk is already gone but everyone will be in on it in the next few years and the profit will not be as great then."

The old man continued his sales pitch as he poured a cup of chocolate from the pot for Gilles.

"Beaver pelts are the new gold. They say the land north of New Amsterdam is absolutely *covered* with the creatures and the savages bring the finest pelts down from the north where the winters are the coldest and the fur is the thickest. But why am I telling you this? You must know this from your own trade in New France! We need just a little *more* money upfront to pay the savages so they will keep bringing the furs out to us and not make new deals with the Swedes or the English colonies to the east. The English are *always* trying to cut into our trade."

"Isn't that risky, to pay them *first*?" Gilles asked, smelling the chocolate in his cup again after his first taste. It was heavier than tea, odd and sticky on his tongue. "What if they disappear with our money?"

"Well, that depends on which tribe you deal with, so they say. Some of the savages are more reliable than others and there are the different alliances between the French, the English, ourselves, and the different tribes. I can hardly keep them straight, the Lenni Lenape, Maquas, Mahegans and Abenakis and all the others I hear about. The savages often fight among themselves and even pay protection money to the stronger tribes, but a modest investment can just about buy one of their trappers *for life*! There is unimaginable timber, too, and it will only be a matter of time before shipbuilding there becomes a great business. They say the trees are as tall as the sky and as straight as you could ever want. Getting to the timber has been a bit of a problem so far, that and finding skilled shipbuilders to send over. Sometimes it has been hard finding any people at all to settle there, but the West India Company will give you land and money just to get on the boat with a few of your closest friends. It's not even necessary to go there to build a fortune, though. One of our pearl merchants that lives just outside of the city owns a huge tract of land outside Fort Orange that he has *never even seen*. It's just as good as owning his own country! And then there is the tobacco. We grow it here now, of course, but they are growing it in New Amsterdam, too. Some people prefer the English colonies' tobacco. They say it's better due to the warmer weather and longer growing season. Our ships can put into their ports as easily as we trade with France, as long as you pay their tax, of course. Now, you may have heard the rumors that the English might stop us from using their ports soon. That isn't going to happen; we pay them too much now and they need the income. There are risks, of course, I don't want you to think the profit is guaranteed, but the risks are not so great when you see how much people are making and how much they will be making in the future. New Amsterdam will become the next Amsterdam of the new world! We will have twin jewels on opposite sides of the ocean, and with the Brazil colonies adding their wealth to our bounty, the Netherlands will completely dominate both continents if you Frenchmen will excuse my enthusiasm!"

Hendrick relit his pipe with a straw he held over the lantern candle on the table. A great puff of smoke escaped his lips as he sat back to survey their faces. It was obvious that he had a grand vision of the future and of New Netherlands, but Gilles doubted that his vision would ever come to pass. Whenever the subject of trade in the new world had come up at home, his father had just laughed, listing the reasons why it would never be profitable and why the land across the Atlantic would soon be abandoned, due in no small part to the distance and the time it took ships to travel the route. Add in the great cost and likelihood of ships lost and cargo spoiled and it just wasn't worth the trouble, Jean Montroville would sniff, not even for the beaver skins. Gilles wondered if Hendrick was dreaming or if there really were so many men made rich in the short time since they had started the route. Jean's face was unreadable as ever but Gilles was curious.

"How many people are there living in New Amsterdam now?" Gilles asked Hendrick.

"There must be close to five hundred souls there." Hendrick nodded for emphasis.

"*Only* five hundred? I thought there were many more people there than that! That doesn't seem like a very large number, especially when the savages outnumber them." Gilles was shocked. One outbreak of the plague or a minor war and the continent would quickly be cleared of the entire settlement.

"Five hundred rich people are as good as a million poor people anywhere else!" Hendrick replied.

Gilles decided not to even pursue that argument. "How much of an investment do you have to make and when will we see our returns?" he asked Hendrick.

"Ah, a true trader. I like that. Any financial investment will certainly be returned in about six months. The profit is about *five times* the investment right now. Three months over, three months back at most and some time in between for trade until a regular route is established. But there is something you gentlemen might consider trading that has *an even better return* than furs."

Hendrick lit his pipe again, possibly to pause for dramatic effect and the corners of his eyes crinkled in a secretive smile. All kinds of things ran through Gilles' mind before Hendrick leaned forward and spoke again, very softly.

"*Guns.* The *new* currency of the *new* world." Hendrick smiled at them conspiratorially. "The savages are getting plenty of blankets and trinkets but what they are starting to value the most is our weaponry against their enemies. Steel knives have been good but guns! They are mad for guns, I hear."

"Is that a good idea, to give your enemies weapons to use against you?" Gilles noticed that Jean Durie was not saying anything.

"You have a lot of questions, Msr. Montroville, but that is good! They are not all our enemies and besides it wasn't our idea to give them guns. The cursed Swedes started it so now we have to keep pace with them! We have to keep the savages trading with us by having something that they *want* to trade for and to protect the traders that are working with us. If the Susquehanock get all the guns they will soon be sending all the furs in the new world to Sweden! Besides, neither side gives them much ammunition and they haven't figured out how to make it yet so it's more like a big trophy on some savage king's wall. All you have to do is to bring some French guns on one of your trading trips and that will save us the trouble of buying the guns here in the Netherlands. You could just unload them out beyond the harbor, from your boat directly onto a boat headed for New Netherlands. There is no need to bring them through customs and no one on your side ever has to know except the captain and maybe some of the crew. If we don't keep the Maquas happy though, we will lose control of the area north of New Amsterdam."

Hendrick paused to relight his pipe again although he hadn't smoked it since the last time he lit it. He was definitely a good talker.

Jean pulled a handful of money out of his pocket and pushed it across the table to Hendrick. "I expect to see five times this or more in six months," he said with a smile. He had obviously come to breakfast this morning ready to do business.

"I don't have much money with me and I want to think it over first," Gilles volunteered before Hendrick could ask him directly.

"A wise thing." Hendrick nodded, drawing on his pipe. "Talk to people, think it over and of course be prudent, but do not fail to recognize *opportunity,* either, if it is there! You know where to find me when you are ready."

Hendrick counted out Jean's money, shook his hand and called out to Elsje.

"Elsje! Pen and paper to write this man a receipt."

Gilles could not believe that deals were made this way here, so quickly and involving so much money.

"The trade problems sound more like Europe than the new world. Blackmail, bribery, trade problems, one group against another, weapons, does it ever change?" Gilles asked Jean.

Jean laughed. "No, I guess it doesn't."

Elsje brought over the pen, paper and ink. Hendrick wrote out a basic receipt and handed it to Jean, waving it this way and that for the ink to dry. "Here is your receipt, Jean, and it has been a pleasure doing business with you. You'll be a rich man one day soon!"

Jean put the paper down on the table, waiting for the ink to dry completely. "And you will be rich too, one day, Hendrick, if you aren't already with all of your dealings!" Jean laughed again.

Gilles emptied the chocolate from the bottom of the cup. He was waiting for sinful impulses to overtake him as the priests in France had promised with the consumption of the dark, sweet liquid, but so far he felt nothing unusual. Jean Durie picked up the receipt that had fully dried by now, carefully folded it and put it in his inside breast pocket. "Shall we stretch our legs, Gilles, or would you like some more breakfast?"

Gilles still wanted to be away from Hendrick and so he agreed to go outside with Jean. They both shook hands with Hendrick and left the inn.

"You don't have to accompany me if you don't want to, Gilles. I just had to get away from the smell of the smoke and the chocolate. I don't care for either but I see that you enjoyed yours. You'll be taking up a pipe like a Netherlander next!"

Gilles had to smile at the idea. "Do you think it really is a good investment, Jean? You know more about such things than I do but it seemed like you didn't give him a great deal of money."

"I see many people here getting *very* rich," Jean replied. "Of course, as Hendrick said, there are always risks but our risk is our money, not our lives. We can stay here in Europe and become rich ... or not. Perhaps I have just acquired the Netherlanders' love of speculation from visiting so often. It doesn't hurt to bet what you don't mind losing."

"I don't know if the guns are a good idea," Gilles said.

"They are most definitely *not* a good idea! What would happen if one of the King's agents discovered them on your father's ship?" Jean admonished him.

Gilles hadn't even thought of that but Jean was right. Their destination and purpose might not be clear and they could be accused of selling arms to the enemy or even of sedition.

They found themselves strolling through the French area now and Gilles said, "Let me buy a pastry here and see if it is as good as those at home!"

Jean looked around. "All right, but be quick about it, we should not even be here. It is too Protestant."

"Jean you worry too much! The people who live here cannot hide anywhere, this is their home! Do you see spies everywhere?" As soon as Gilles said it though, he remembered the familiar-looking man in the church. He pushed the thought away though, went into a bakery and was back in no time at all with two pastries. He kept one and handed the other to Jean.

"All right, we can leave now," Gilles said. "Mm, this is as good as any at home!"

"Yes, it is very good, we'll just hope it's worth our lives," Jean mumbled.

Jean's mood was better by the time they reached the Dam and they took their time today looking at all the goods from all over the world. Gilles inhaled the scent of the exotic spices and his eyes took in all of the goods. Even the vendors were worth looking at with their different colorings and customs of dress. Gilles spotted Elsje at the end of a row of tables, digging through some onions. He started toward her but Jean grabbed his arm.

"Now what did Old Hendrick say to you? Stop bothering his daughters! You just got that smoothed over and now you want to create difficulties again?"

"I just thought I would be nice, go over and say 'Goedemiddag'."

Jean stood in front of Gilles, blocking his way in case his young companion had other ideas. "Gilles, these Netherlanders are funny people and if she takes offense again, we've lost more than just a place to sleep! I just gave Hendrick a handful of my money!"

Elsje turned in their direction and Gilles thought that she *must* have seen them by now but she made no acknowledgement of their presence and turned back to the vendor.

"You're right: They are peculiar people. I will just pretend that I don't see them."

Jean and Gilles moved off in the opposite direction, away from Elsje. There was so much to see and sample that they didn't even notice the time until the sun was moving down behind the buildings. They had forgotten about dinner and supper completely, having sampled many different kinds of foods including the French pastry. The long week had worn them out and Jean told Gilles that he had some more personal business to attend to the next day. They were both ready for sleep as soon as they returned and there was no ale drinking late into the night tonight.

The next morning Gilles awoke to the sounds of rain, a constant drizzle. Remembering that Jean would be gone for the morning, he brought his coat and hat down to breakfast with a plan to go out somewhere. The rain had to come down from the heavens sometime to keep the crops growing and it came often in the Netherlands even though there had been uncommonly good weather for most of their stay. Gilles didn't feel much like going out in the damp rain but he didn't feel like staying in his tiny room or in the dining room watching Elsje supervise window washing, either. The soot from the fire, the oil lamps, and men smoking tobacco quickly darkened the windows and Elsje, Tryntje and the servants seemed to clean all of the windows on a daily basis. Gilles was finishing his breakfast, trying to decide where he should go and what he should do for the day when Tryntje came over to him and asked, "Can I get you anything more, Msr. Montroville, anything at all?"

"No, thank you, I'm fine."

He tried to smile at her in the same fatherly way that Jean smiled at them, in a dismissive sort of way, but she kept on talking to him. Tryntje annoyed Gilles too, but not in the same way that Elsje did: One sister was too friendly and the other was too cold. Hendrick entered the dining room and for a moment Gilles was worried that the old man would be upset to see one of his daughters talking with him again but today Hendrick appeared not to notice at all. Perhaps it was all right to talk with them as long as it was in the dining room.

Tryntje appeared not to notice her father's presence at all but stood there talking to Gilles about the weather and then about the ships in the harbor. Gilles definitely had to get up and go somewhere just to get away from the babbling girl. He pulled on his coat and hat, bid her good day and walked out, leaving her in mid-sentence, going to no place at all in particular.

He walked by the market but he wasn't in the mood to look at much of anything. Many of the vendors had sail canvas pulled over long pole frames in a futile effort to keep their goods dry. They were not in the mood to talk today or to pass the time; they just wanted someone to buy all of their goods quickly so they could get their money and go home. Gilles made his way around a big puddle as he passed by Elsje's church. He thought briefly of Jean and the Marranos. Were they out here somewhere today? Hardly any time had passed and Gilles just couldn't go back to the inn yet. He wasn't really in the mood to go back to sleep and it wasn't yet dinner time. He doubted that he could keep himself occupied without talking to Elsje or otherwise getting into trouble until Jean returned.

Gilles suddenly realized that he was walking in the direction of the warehouse that he and Jean had visited and he had no wish to be set upon by the pack of beggars that roamed those streets so he decided to take a shortcut, making a quick turn up an alley to go to another street and then head back in the direction from which he had come. Too late he discovered that it was a dead-end alley with no vendors there, just two men involved in what looked to be a private discussion deep in the shadows. In the split second that he realized his mistake, Gilles noticed that one of them had bushy eyebrows and looked a little like the man that he saw in Elsje's church. Gilles turned around to leave right away but then he found himself facing another man, a man whose face he never had the time to see, a man who hit him with a heavy blow to the head that immediately took Gilles down to his knees. He held his arms up over his head and tried to regain his feet but the blows kept coming to his head and then to his stomach where someone's foot was connecting with it. The blows seemed to hurt less eventually and his last thoughts were of the rain coming down harder, hitting him too, along with the men, and sorrow, sorrow that his father would never know what had happened to him.

He didn't awake in purgatory as he expected, but in a comfortable curtained bed. His head, arms and stomach were in pain and he had someone else's long shirt on, a shirt that smelled of tobacco. Gilles groaned before he realized that he had done so out loud. He needed to move the bed curtains so he could see where he was. If they were keeping him prisoner here, he at least wanted to know why they beat him and why they had not killed him yet.

Perhaps they wanted a ransom from his father. He appeared to be all alone here as there was no sound of anyone else nearby. He wouldn't wait for them to come back though; he had to try to escape. If he could make it outside, he could ask for help and then he had a chance of making it back to the inn. He tried to roll to his side but he felt a stabbing pain in his chest and ribs as he moved. He knew then that he couldn't run anywhere but he might be able to creep slowly out to the street. He drew himself up slowly and painfully and reached for the curtains, again with great pain when he stretched his arm out. He managed to draw the curtain back and found himself looking out into Hendrick's dining area. He eased himself back onto the pillow. Either he was safe or Hendrick was in on whatever mischief had befallen him and was just waiting to kill him at the most opportune time; his thoughts on this were not too clear. In either case, it was just not worth the effort to get up and he doubted that he could get his legs to work anyway.

"Are you awake then, Msr. Montroville?" It was Elsje's voice and he wondered if he was hallucinating. "Gilles?"

He decided that he was not hallucinating. "I'm here. I'm not so sure I'm awake," he replied in French. He closed his eyes and wished to be back asleep to avoid the pain.

Elsje pulled the curtain back and the light hurt his eyes. "You need some eel soup," she said.

"No, no soup," he moaned as she gently lifted his head back onto the pillow. "I need a physician."

"One has already seen you, although we don't put a lot of faith in the old man," Elsje replied. Then she was gone again.

While she was gone he tried to rearrange the pillow to get his head back down to go to sleep but he couldn't manage it so he just closed his eyes again. He did not know how long she was gone but before he knew it she was back with some soup that smelled good. Unfortunately his stomach was not interested in the food.

"Where is your father?" he managed in Nederlands this time. "Oh my God, I'm in trouble now."

He didn't see Elsje smile but he heard her say, "It's all right, he knows you are too sick to attempt any indecent actions toward me."

"Let me sleep then," Gilles moaned.

"No, no sleep. You need to wake up. You can rest later when we are sure you are all right. I've seen this sickness before, sometimes after a fight."

"It wasn't a fight. How do you know about fights?" Gilles asked.

"Enough talking. Eat some soup. You will probably be sick but what little you can keep down will help. I'll get you a basin."

"No. I'll stay awake if you really want to torture me, but no soup."

Elsje picked up a cloth and dipped it in the basin of water on the stand next to the bed. A strong smell of vinegar stung his nostrils and his face as she gently pressed it to his head. He noticed that there was some blood on it.

"It's bad?" he asked.

She nodded. "This rosewater and vinegar will help if you have a fever. You don't seem to have much of one now but that may come later."

"I need to talk to Jean Durie. How did I get here?"

"Msr. Durie has not yet returned. Two gentlemen dumped you outside the inn and then left without talking to anyone about you."

"Did he have heavy eye ..." Gilles didn't know the Nederlands word for eyebrows so he gestured.

"I don't know what you are trying to say, but you don't seem to have fever." Elsje felt his forehead around the cuts. "Save your strength. Tryntje will send Msr. Durie up when he gets back here or if we can locate him before that."

Gilles leaned back and closed his eyes.

"Stay awake!" Elsje barked at him and the noise hurt his head.

"Then you have to talk and keep me awake because I haven't the strength," Gilles muttered.

"What should I talk about then?" she asked.

"Anything. The market, the inn. Your father. Why is he so upset with me?"

Elsje rearranged something on the washstand. "He's not upset. He just doesn't want us to become too close. He thinks all Frenchmen have wives at home and mistresses abroad."

"Some do, but not me," Gilles mumbled.

"He is very protective of me," Elsje said by way of explanation.

"He's afraid you will get married and leave him to run the inn alone?"

"You are mistaken in that! He tries to find me a husband but I want to stay here, with him." She felt Gilles' cheeks and forehead again. "Nee, you aren't feverish."

"I've heard Pieter Stuyvesant might make a fine husband for you."

"For someone, I'm sure, but not for me or my sister. He can be very, um, *difficult.*"

"And you aren't difficult?" Gilles turned his head slightly toward her.

Elsje ignored his question. "I will have to see to making supper soon. You must stay awake, though. Perhaps I will send Tryntje up to sit with you when she gets back."

"No! I mean, Jean should return soon." Gilles wasn't sure what else to say.

"You don't like my sister?" Elsje looked at him with wide eyes.

"I like her well enough but perhaps she likes me too much." Gilles hoped that she understood what he was saying and that she wasn't going to get angry. If she did get mad though, she might go away and leave him in peace. There was something good in that, too.

"You flatter yourself too much, young rooster! She is friendly with *everyone.* Sometimes I wish I had her friendly manner." Elsje sighed.

"Perhaps I should try to move back to my own bed now. Why am I up here?" Gilles tried to pull himself up but the pain was back in full force before he could make any further progress.

"No, you will be fine here tonight. Father thought we could all keep an eye on you together if you were up here. Tryntje can sleep with me and you will be better in the morning. I'm going to check on supper preparations now. Promise me you won't fall asleep and will have some soup while I'm gone. I'll leave it here."

She left before he could summon the strength to answer her and Gilles thought that he had just fallen asleep again when Jean Durie strode into the room with Tryntje right behind him.

"Gilles, what happened?"

"I just ..."

"Didn't I tell you to stick to the main streets? What did you get yourself into? How will I explain this to your father? Maybe he won't be able to tell."

Jean quickly settled into the chair that Elsje had dragged next to the bed and holding Gilles' chin turned his head to the other side.

"Ouch! Get away Jean!"

"Well, that won't work. He'll have to know, I guess."

"I need a mirror. Everyone seems so concerned about my face but it hurts the least," Gilles muttered, rubbing his stomach.

"It's not so bad, I've seen worse. What else hurts?" Jean looked him over.

"My ribs and stomach. My arms. Elsje says a doctor already saw me but I don't remember it."

"Are you going to tell me what happened or not?" Jean asked impatiently.

"My head is pounding, Jean. Give me a chance," Gilles pleaded, "or better still, just go away."

"All right. Take your time then and tell me what happened," Jean said, a little more patiently this time.

Gilles told Jean what he could remember which wasn't much and asked him if he had seen a man with bushy eyebrows around. Jean shook his head but Tryntje, forgotten behind Jean, stepped forward and said, "I've seen such a man. He has been here a few times in the past week. I never saw him before and he's not in here every night. He sits in the corner and drinks."

Jean turned to her. "Is he a Netherlander, a Frenchman?"

"I don't know," Tryntje answered.

"Try to think, Tryntje. Was there anything different about him, an accent, clothes?"

She wrinkled her forehead in concentration but said again, "I don't know. All he ever says is 'Ale!' I bring him ale, he gives me money."

She was staring at the opening in Gilles' shirt and suddenly Gilles felt more awake and very uncomfortable. He pulled the shirt edges together. Tryntje didn't look away or blush. Gilles wondered if he dared to fall asleep with Tryntje nearby.

Jean hadn't noticed at all; he was too busy thinking.

"I don't know if the authorities have enough information to find the people who did this to you, Gilles."

"Not that I'm ungrateful, Jean, but why do you think they didn't kill me?" Gilles asked.

"Bodies raise too many questions and missing people that someone will miss raise even more. They obviously didn't want you to die or they would have left you where you were or dumped you at sea. They must have known where to leave you though; they dumped you here," Jean reasoned.

Then Gilles remembered his money. "Tryntje, where are my shirt and coat?"

"Over there, Elsje was going to have them washed out. Shall I bring them to you?"

"Yes, please."

Tryntje brushed his hand with hers when she handed him his clothes. Gilles wished he had the strength to run away but he didn't so he just felt through his clothes. Both jacket and shirt were still damp from the rain and stained with blood and dirt. Gilles still felt the money in the hidden pocket so it was probably not a robbery unless they were unable to find the cache. Gilles was glad that he still had the money but wondered why they didn't search him more thoroughly to relieve him of it. Surely they had enough time. Gilles handed the money to Jean and said, "Watch this for me, all right? Don't spend it all on ale, either."

"He's all right, he's thinking of his money and his sense of humor is returning," Jean said to Tryntje. "Don't you have anything to give him for the pain though? Brandy, anything?"

"The doctor left something, I think he called it quinine, but Elsje told me not to give it to him yet. He wanted to put leeches on him too, but Elsje wouldn't let him do that, either. The doctor got mad at Elsje and said he couldn't help Gilles if ignorant people refused him medical attention. Elsje threw him out then …"

"Jean, please get me something for the pain. My body feels like it fell under a coach."

Jean nodded and stood up to go get Elsje. Tryntje stood staring at Gilles but made no move to go.

"Come along Tryntje," Jean said, taking her elbow and nodding at Gilles.

"Thank you, Jean," Gilles said to the empty room since they had already left before he had a chance to get the words out. He closed his eyes again.

After some discussion between Jean and Elsje, she agreed to give him some of the powder the doctor left for him. She dissolved it in water and Gilles drank it all although it had a bitter taste to it. He fell asleep and did not wake until the next morning. The light was seeping into the room and now he could hear too many sounds that he was not used to hearing. The loudest was snoring, probably from Hendrick in his bedroom across the way, and softer breathing sounds were coming from another part of the room. He heard birds outside on the roof and sounds already coming from the street, a cart passing, two men talking as they walked by and something else that he couldn't identify, a sort of tapping sound.

Gilles had to find a chamber pot or make it to the outhouse but how could he get up? He might be able to make it downstairs today. He had to try. The pain was still there but even in his sleep he was learning how to move so that it did not hurt him as much. His head was definitely better and that helped. Gilles got the curtain pulled over and dragged his legs over the side. The bed made a small noise and he sat on the edge for a minute gathering his strength. There was a sudden rustling on the other side of the room and Elsje appeared with only her under dress on.

"Gilles, what are you doing?" she whispered.

"I need to ... go outside."

He concentrated on getting up again, trying to ignore the pain. He made it to his feet.

"You can use the chamber pot behind the curtain there." She gestured.

"I'd rather go outside and besides, I'm hungry," he whispered back. They were almost eye to eye now and he took a single step forward, testing his strength.

"All right, wait for me to get dressed!" she whispered loudly.

Gilles nodded. He needed her help. "Don't take too long. I can't wait too long."

He had noticed that her hair was longer when it was down than he thought it would be. He could hear her moving around behind the other bed, pulling on an over dress and just for a moment he was not thinking about his pain or his bladder, he was thinking about her getting dressed but even that thought couldn't keep the pain out of his consciousness for more than a few moments. Elsje helped him on with his boots, then grabbed his elbow. Gilles eased forward one step at a time. This close, Elsje smelled like flour and apples.

"It's not too bad if I go slowly," he whispered to her.

They made it down the back stairs, one painful step at a time. Elsje walked him to the back and to the outhouse. There was fog hanging over the city yet although the sun was over the horizon and tried to penetrate it. The mist was cool and damp, sticking to everything including Gilles. He shivered and rubbed his arms to warm them but both activities hurt his stomach and chest too much so he stopped rubbing and tried to will himself to stop shivering.

"Thank you, I can manage from here," Gilles said and pushed open the door.

Elsje made no move to go back to the kitchen.

"You can go back inside now," Gilles called out to her.

"I'll stay here and wait for you," she replied.

"I'd prefer you didn't. I won't fall in." Gilles had stopped and was looking at her now.

"You French are so peculiar! What if your friends who left you this way come back to finish you off? Tryntje said they had been here, at this very inn!"

"And what will you do, thrash them all by yourself?" Gilles smiled in spite of himself. "All right, go over by the building then." He waived her off and stepped inside but he still felt self-conscious.

Because it was so early, it was still rather dark inside and he had to leave the door cracked open to see what he was doing. One hearty fly was already buzzing around and the smell was not a good thing to start the day with. He finally was able to relieve himself after a minute and it took a long time to discharge the contents of his bladder. After he had finished, he gingerly stepped outside and made his way back to Elsje, wiping a spider web from his hand onto his pants.

"Come inside the kitchen, Gilles. I'll get you some water to wash with and some food."

She helped him to sit down at the kitchen table and poured some water into a basin before she set it down in front of him with a cloth. She sliced some bread and cheese for him.

"Now you sit and wait here while I go outside and I'll help you back upstairs when you are done eating," she said to him.

"Don't you want me to stand guard for you?" Gilles asked.

Elsje smiled at this joke but he was serious. What if there were dangerous people lurking around? She was gone outside before he could say anything more. When Elsje returned, she washed her hands and put on an apron from the hook on the back of the door.

"If you have had enough to eat you need to get back up to bed now."

"I could use some more to eat; I'm still hungry."

"That's a good sign! I will be making breakfast soon. Just sit and let that food settle before you try any more."

From under the table Elsje pulled out a board that she set on top of the table. She pulled out a small wooden barrel from under the table next, pried the top off and sprinkled a cup of flour across the board. She picked out a few stones and a dried leaf that had made it into the flour and threw those into the fireplace. At last she reached under the table again and dragged out a large and heavy bucket that was covered with a cloth. The contents proved to be bread dough, rising nearly to the top of the bucket. In one motion she dumped the giant wad of dough onto the board and then started to knead and pound the dough.

Steps on the stairs preceded Tryntje's appearance at the bottom of the back stairway.

"Tryntje! Don't just stand there, make yourself useful! Go see where the dairy-man is, he's late and we need just about everything this morning!" Elsje called out to her.

Tryntje smiled a sleepy smile at Gilles, took a cloak from its hook and went outside.

"You seem very angry with that bread Elsje," Gilles observed.

"You've never seen bread made before, Msr. Montroville? No, I suppose not." She answered her own question. She finished pounding, rolling, and pushing the bread and stuck it back into the bucket, put the board on top of the bucket and then pushed the production back under the table again.

"Where has Tryntje gone *now*? She's no help at all!"

Elsje was out the door again, to the dining room this time. Gilles was still in pain but in spite of this fact, he was still enjoying himself. He had to admit that he liked sitting in the kitchen watching all of the activity. He liked it until Hendrick came down the stairs and into the kitchen, stopping to glare at Gilles.

"Feeling better this morning?" he growled.

"Yes, I should remove myself to the dining room now."

Gilles pushed himself up from the table slowly but caught the look of surprise on Hendrick's face as he did so.

"You *are* hurt," Hendrick said.

"I'll be all right. I'll just go up and change into my own shirt now before breakfast."

Gilles didn't refuse though when Hendrick offered to help him up the stairs and to his room.

"Do you need help with anything?" he asked Gilles.

"No, I can manage, now," Gilles said. "I'll just change out of your shirt to one of mine."

But when he tried, Gilles found that he could not even change his own shirt so Hendrick helped him to get a clean shirt on. Even in the dim light of the room Gilles could see large dark bruises on his chest and stomach. "So that's it," he said.

"You haven't seen them before for yourself?" Hendrick asked.

"No."

Hendrick helped Gilles back down the stairs and into the dining room where Jean was already seated.

"Are you awake already, Gilles?"

"I've been up for some time, Jean!" Gilles bragged, lowering himself slowly into the chair until he dropped the last few inches onto the seat. He thanked

Hendrick for his help and Hendrick went back toward the kitchen, but not without a backwards glance.

"So you will be well enough to return when the ship gets in?" Jean asked.

"Oh, yes, well enough. I won't be helping a lot with the sails though." Gilles managed a weak smile.

"I may go and see if I can find anything out about who did this to you and why," Jean said. "You probably just walked in on someone's illegal business transaction, that's all."

"Well, be careful, they got me in full daylight, in the morning," Gilles replied.

"You are telling *me* to be careful?!"

Elsje flurried out of the kitchen. "You are all right for now, Gilles?"

"Ja, dank u, your father helped me to change my shirt. The one I borrowed from him is a mess though and it will be hard for you to get all the blood out. Sorry."

"That's all right, don't worry yourself about it. Are you gentlemen ready for some real breakfast now?" she asked, maybe not yet totally convinced that Gilles was well enough to be up and around.

"Yes and tea first, thanks," Jean replied as she left. "She better not bring any more of that terrible chocolate stuff," he said to Gilles. "It seems that you have found a way to patch things up with Elsje and her father although you really could have found an *easier* way. You are absolutely more trouble than you are worth, you know."

Traders, merchants and travelers were coming into the dining room now and Gilles was watching for the man with the heavy eyebrows.

"Don't bother Gilles, I doubt that they will show their faces in here even if you *could* recognize them. Tell me what happened again, just one more time."

"It was near the warehouse that we went to and I decided to take a shortcut to avoid the warehouse itself. I turned into the alley but it was not a pass-through. Two men were talking there. It was pretty dark and the only one that I saw clearly was the man with the bushy eyebrows, the one who looked familiar to me. I turned around to leave but there was someone right behind me, someone who hit me. That's all I remember."

"So someone was following you?"

"I suppose so. I hadn't heard anyone. If there wasn't anyone behind me, I would have just turned around and left and that would have been the end of it, I think."

"Can you remember anything else? Were the men holding weapons or trade goods? Was there was nothing else that you remember about them?"

"No." Gilles searched his patchy memory. "There was nothing special about them at all."

"How about the man behind you?" Jean pressed on.

"I never saw him! I assume it was a man and not a beast!"

"And that's all you remember until you woke up here?"

"Yes. I thought I was dead. I dreamed that I was sitting with my Grandmere in her kitchen in Rouen and eating onion soup with her and then I woke up."

"Onion soup?"

"When I was little and not feeling well, she made me her homemade onion soup. She's been dead for many years. I thought I was dead and that she was taking care of me."

"All right, well, that was a trick of the mind due to your injured state, I'm sure. You *will* be able to stay out of trouble today?"

Elsje brought the food and smiled a broad smile at Gilles when she set down the plates. "Are you feeling well enough to eat this?" She touched Gilles' shoulder.

"Well, maybe not," Jean answered his own question after she had left.

Gilles' mind was still not clear and still not quick enough to keep up with regular conversation, let alone Jean's quick wit concerning Elsje.

After breakfast Jean left Gilles behind at the inn again and Gilles didn't feel like attempting the steps up to his room; it was far too much effort just for the reward of lying alone in a dark room. He wasn't very sleepy and as there was no place to sit in front of the inn, he decided that he would sit in the back. He slowly got to his feet and made his way to the kitchen. The bread was baking now and something else that smelled like an apple dessert of some kind was bubbling in a pot over the fire. Elsje thought that fresh air was an excellent idea and she even brought out a chair for him, one with arm rests. With Elsje's help, Gilles lowered himself into the chair, enjoying the morning. The fog was starting to lift and it looked like it would be a beautiful sunny day, a very good day just to sit and appreciate being alive, a gift from the heavens.

"If I had to miss one day here, I'm glad it was a rainy one," he thought.

It had been good to see his Grandmere again, though. He had not realized how much he had missed her although he hadn't really given her a thought in many years. Gilles watched the chickens in the pen flutter, cluck and scold each other; they scratched at the dirt and pecked angrily at the fencing. Three Marranos crept silently around the corner of the building but seeing Gilles sitting there, they started to back away again. As Gilles continued to just sit there though, they proceeded forward again, moving toward Elsje's back door, even more hungry and curious about Gilles than they were fearful.

Gilles no longer feared them. They were less of a threat to him than all of the people in the world who were not Marranos: the French clergy, the drink-crazed sailors, the thieves and pickpockets. Elsje must have seen them approaching or expected them because she opened the door and gave the men bread and some cheese on a plate. Just feet away from Gilles they fell on the food together, starving wild dogs pushing and punching each other, grabbing at it, finishing it off quickly and then holding out their hands to her for more but Elsje shooed them off.

"Why do you give them a plate, Elsje? It hardly seems worth the trouble," Gilles noted as she picked the plate up from the ground and turned back toward the kitchen.

"They have been treated like animals enough. Someone needs to start giving their dignity back to them," she said. "I'd give them utensils too but they always steal them."

Gilles liked this place in the back of the inn. It was peaceful back here with the birds singing in the Linden tree but at the same time he could hear all of the goings on in the kitchen and, if he listened closely enough, of the whole city beyond, too. He had no concerns for his safety in this place but he took some time out to think about the attack. Was it a chance meeting with thieves, a botched robbery, smugglers that he happened upon? Could it have anything to do with the thefts from his father? Was it possible that Jean Durie had hired men to lie in wait for him in a failed attempt to silence Gilles? These questions hurt his head and none of them seemed likely. Gilles decided not to think about anything at all and here in Elsje's back lot, Gilles could do that, he could just *be,* as he could at home when he escaped from his father, out into the freedom fields.

Home.

He would have much to tell his father about when he returned. Gilles reminded himself that he had a wedding to look forward to and his own household to establish. He would live in the old wing, in his grandparents' old apartments but they would surely need some renovations. The entire wing had mostly been used for storage since they died.

Tryntje stepped outside the kitchen door and joined Gilles.

"I trust that you found *my bed* comfortable, Msr. Montroville?" she asked.

"Very good. Thank you for letting me stay there last night," he replied, not too icily but not too warmly, he hoped. He quickly checked to make sure that his shirt was fully closed.

"My sister is doing the marketing right now but I felt that *someone* should check on you, just to make sure that you are feeling all right." She crouched down next to him to look directly into his eyes.

"Where is your father? He has been most helpful and most attentive to me this morning, too."

"He has gone away on some business, and so has Msr. Durie." She put a hand to his forehead. "Nee, no fever that I can feel."

"I'm sorry I'm not feeling up to talking with anyone right now. I will just close my eyes and rest a little and soon I will be fine."

"Do you want me to help you up to your bed?" she asked, standing up and leaning over him. She was just a little too close to him.

"No, I'm fine here," he said.

She put her hands on the arms of his chair and leaned over him even more.

"*You* are a very interesting man, Gilles. May I call you 'Gilles'? I'll bet that you have seen all kinds of places and people. I'd love to hear about some of them, that is, if you aren't too tired, of course."

"Not really, I haven't traveled that much. My stomach is in great pain though, so I think I just need to rest now."

He rubbed his hand across his chest, more to emphasize the pain that clung to him there, but his actions only seemed to interest Tryntje all the more.

"I haven't been *anywhere* in the world and most of what I have seen is here at the inn. Some people that stay here are more interesting than others, of course. *Like you.*"

Gilles wondered what she was going to do next.

"It's very private back here, don't you think?" she asked him.

"People *do* come by from time to time, though," Gilles noted hopefully.

"Not many at this time of day." She smiled at him. "Do you think I'm pretty, Gilles?" she asked. You must have many women who find *you* attractive."

"Not really," he replied, in answer to the latter statement but Tryntje's head shot up with the look of anger that he knew from Elsje's eyes.

"What I meant to say was, that I don't know a lot of women, but you certainly are a lovely *young* girl."

He hoped the last part was grammatically correct in Nederlands and that he hadn't accidentally called her a desirable woman. Gilles looked around as unobtrusively as possible to see if perhaps any Marranos or anyone else might be coming by to rescue him.

"What you need is a nice cup of tea. Why don't I take you upstairs and then fix you some? I could look at your stomach and make that sure it is healing."

"I want to stay here right now. Maybe you could go inside, though, and make me some tea?"

"I could do that," Tryntje said, but she didn't move.

"Don't you have someone that you are promised to Tryntje? Someone who might not be happy that you are here, alone with me?"

"We don't marry so young here. There are some marriage prospects in the distant future but that doesn't mean I can't still be friendly with other interesting people. Father told us that Frenchmen often marry *and* take a mistress here and I find that … interesting."

"Well, this Frenchman doesn't have any mistresses, or even a wife."

"Well, I know that will change. The wife part I mean." She gave him a sly smile. "You don't mean to tell me that you haven't been with a woman? I don't believe that. But that's very interesting, too."

Gilles just sat in his chair clutching his shirt closed. Even if he had any interest in Tryntje, he didn't feel well enough or safe enough to be alone with her in Hendrick's house. Tryntje was a beauty, a star that stood out from the rest of the firmament; it was just her aggressive personality that put Gilles off.

"I … ah, I just have *other* interests …" Gilles began, not having any idea what he was saying or what he was going to say. His head was still not clear enough to think properly about a strategy.

Tryntje straightened up as if someone had thrown a bucket of cold water on her.

"Oh. I see. Maybe I *will* go and get you some tea now."

Suddenly she was gone and Gilles had no idea why she left but he was glad for whatever had just happened, glad to get some peace and quiet.

Tryntje returned with the tea, handed the cup to him and then left without saying anything more. Gilles drank it, idly wondering if Tryntje and Elsje were any odder, any more peculiar, than the rest of their countrymen or if Jean was right about the Netherlanders in general.

Gilles finished the tea and was wondering if he could bend over and set the cup on the ground without feeling too much pain when Jean Durie came through the kitchen door.

"Ah, you are back! Good, then I don't have to get up and bring this into the kitchen," Gilles said.

"I made some inquiries but I didn't find out anything about what happened to you. I think I found the alley and some people have seen a man who fits your description but they don't know who he is or where he lives, and no one can say how you would end up back on Hendrick's doorstep! I trust that you have had a quiet morning?"

"I've just been sitting here but Tryntje won't leave me alone," Gilles complained.

"She's taking very good care of you, I'm sure," Jean said.

"She's taking *too much care of me* and I just need some rest."

"She flirts a lot but she isn't really interested in you; she is far more interested in *me*. What happened then? Where is she now? I didn't interrupt you?" Jean stood there with an amused smile on his face.

"I don't know, she just went away all of a sudden." Gilles peered around Jean to make sure that Tryntje wasn't coming back or listening in.

"I think your imagination plays tricks on you, Gilles."

Gilles sighed. It was too much trouble to explain to Jean. "I need to get up now, anyway. I need to relieve myself."

"Let me help you, Gilles."

As Jean was helping him to his feet, Gilles saw Tryntje peering out the back door at them.

"Strange Netherlanders!" Gilles muttered. He needed to get used to being on his feet, though. He would have to walk some of the way if he didn't want to be carried onto the boat going back to France.

The Lyon was already in port that morning, a day earlier than Jean had been expecting the ship. He told Gilles that he might not have known about her arrival at all, having been distracted by his young companion's misadventures but one of the Amsterdam merchants that he knew mentioned seeing the ship at anchor and asked Jean if there was any more of the wonderful Calvados available for purchase. Gilles decided that he was well enough to walk to the docks and when he stood still, Gilles did not look injured at all to the casual observer except for a deep cut above his right eye that was going to take some time to heal. Gilles shook hands with Captain LeBlanc and then stayed out of the way. He tried counting the goods as they were unloaded from the ferry boats but he knew that his mind was still not functioning well at all. Afterwards he walked slowly back to Hendrick's by himself, letting Jean follow the shipment of spirits out to the Waag alone.

Gilles was a little concerned that Jean might meet with some misfortune and not come back but he returned safely and well before supper time, reporting no difficulties or shortages. Perhaps it was as Jean had told him before, that there might not be any more problems since the thieves would know by now that the

Montroville ships were being watched. Gilles was ready to go back to France although he had been enjoying himself up until his unfortunate encounter in the alley. He missed his family but he missed his own comfortable bed even more. After they had supper, Gilles left Jean at the table and went over to Hendrick to settle his account. He pressed additional investment money into the old man's hand.

"We leave early tomorrow," Gilles told him. "Invest it well for me!"

Gilles felt that even if he lost it all, it was not such a big risk. His father would be giving him more money now that he was taking a more active role in the business and then there was the dowry money from his future wife. Gilles didn't know if or when he could return to collect his profits but someone could always collect it for him if necessary, Jean Durie, or one of his father's captains.

Hendrick took his pipe out of his mouth after he counted the stack of coins. "I'll write a receipt out for you. It's a lot of money; are you sure you want to risk it *all*?"

"I won't need it on the way home," Gilles told him, "There's no place to spend money on a ship unless you gamble with the men and I don't."

Gilles returned to his ale and was talking with Jean about what they would tell Jean Montroville when Elsje brought the receipt over to Gilles at their table.

"You leave tomorrow? When will you return?"

She asked both of them but her eyes lingered on Gilles.

"I don't know, but thank you again for taking such good care of me," Gilles replied.

"Take care of *yourself* and don't go looking for any more trouble," she admonished him with a wink.

"That's what I said to him!" Jean laughed. "Wasted words, Elsje, this one is nothing but trouble!"

When they left in the morning, Elsje gave them each an entire loaf of her bread for the trip. As they sailed out into the open sea, Gilles looked back in the direction of the inn but could not see the building from the ship. He watched all of the activity on the shore until it was too distant to make out any more except for the outline of the buildings and finally, even that receded in the distance in the early morning mists. Jean joined him on the deck with his ever-present knife and piece of wood that always came out of his bag whenever he was bored.

"Where do you always find wood and what are you always making?" Gilles asked.

"Nothing in particular, just passing the time," Jean answered. "Maybe you need something to do?"

"I don't think I could concentrate on it; my mind is somewhere else."

"Well, that's to be expected, you are still healing," Jean said. "I was just upstairs talking with Captain LeBlanc.

"I should have gone with you," Gilles said.

"We didn't talk much about the cargo," Jean said. "Mostly we talked about Rouen. There has been another outbreak of Huguenot fever there."

"*What?*" Gilles asked, hopeful that he was misunderstanding the expression.

"They have seized more lands and executed more people while we were away and now it seems that no one is above suspicion. We just have to attend to our own business though, and we should be all right." Jean brushed some wood shavings off the piece he worked on and then changed the subject back again. "Where is your mind then, Gilles, if not here?"

"At home, I suppose. I will be getting married and will have to do my share of work for the business now. The accounts are so *dull*; I would just like to go to Amsterdam and to other places for my father."

Gilles looked out across the water and let the wind push his hair out of his eyes. England was somewhere over there, in that direction. He had never been to England.

Jean smiled again. "You don't do much when you *are* there, except look for trouble. Could it be that you just have an aversion to doing work?"

This comment from anyone but Jean would have angered Gilles but he knew his friend only chided him. "Perhaps a little. The counting houses are so dreary and dark. It is like being entombed alive." Gilles glumly contemplated his fate.

"But you are happy with the wedding? To Marie Junot, isn't that right?"

"Oui. Did you say that you will be getting married soon too, Jean?"

Jean's eyes suddenly had a light that Gilles had never seen before.

"Oui. To Eleanor St Amand. I would never have believed that I could even hope for such a thing."

Gilles didn't know what to say. He had no such enthusiasm for his own wedding. "I know the name St Amand; you *have* made a very good match, Jean."

"For a facilitator or a clerk, you mean? Oui, for anyone, I suppose. I was able to help her father out of some, er ... *difficulties* last year and he told me to name my price. He was shocked when I asked for his daughter but he's a man of his word."

Gilles recalled that there *was* some trouble with the King over St Amand's loyalty and that the trouble had mysteriously vanished as quickly as it had appeared.

Not only was St Amand saved from execution, he did not even lose much in the way of money or lands.

"*You* did that? You helped Msr. St Amand?"

Gilles looked at Jean with a new respect for his friend. He knew of no one else who had gone up against the King and Richelieu and had won, unless you counted the competitor of Jean Montroville's, the family that was allowed to leave with just their lives.

"It was merely a matter of providing the right records," Jean said modestly but clearly he had reason to be proud of his accomplishment. Not only had he bested the King and Cardinal Richelieu in the courts, but he lived to tell about it, and was even rewarded on top of that.

"Then you have known Mlle. St Amand for some time?" Gilles tried to sound casual but he was interested.

That peculiar light did not fade from Jean's eyes as he answered. "I met her when I first came to Rouen. She was *very* young but she was *so* beautiful! She was too young, really, but I was stricken with passion, losing interest in anyone else. I never had any reason to think that I might one day marry her but if I could not have her, I would stay a single man. When the opportunity came up to work with her father, I talked my way into the position just so that I could be close to her every day."

"She is an obsession with you, then?" Gilles smiled at his friend but the idea terrified him.

"Oui."

Gilles felt that he had to change the subject now. This was a side of his friend that he cold not comprehend and it made him uncomfortable, even perhaps a little queasy to talk about such things. He didn't get the chance right away though: Instead Jean Durie asked him softly, "Have you never *loved* a woman, Gilles?"

"Of course! I have passions for many women. They always start to bore me after a time, though."

Jean only nodded and returned his interest to his woodwork. It was he who changed the subject. "We should have fair weather all the way in, which will make for good time. Your father will no doubt want to meet with us. What you tell him about your mishap is up to you, of course, but I do not think it has anything to do with his business problems and you may not wish to worry him unnecessarily with details. As for the matter of the missing goods, it is one of the two warehousemen or one of the buyers, or both in league with each other, I'm convinced of that, but we need to find out more about each one of them."

"So you don't think it might be the captain or the crew?" Gilles spoke quietly so that the crew would not overhear him.

"Non, and I'll tell you why: You might have wondered why Captain LeBlanc with his considerable skills doesn't own his own ship. He used to have his own merchant ship sailing out of Havre and he also used to drink very heavily. He lost his ship in a card game, *a silly card game*! Your father was generous enough to buy the Lyon and then hire him to sail *his own ship* for five years. At the end of five years, LeBlanc will own his ship again as per the agreement. Your father allows him to trade some other goods and sail some other ships, including the Marianne, to make some extra money, just as long as your father has room for all of his trade goods on each trip and as long as LeBlanc is ready to go when the ship sails again. The captain only has two years left on the contract and would be crazy to get mixed up in smuggling. In addition to being executed or going to jail, he would lose any chance of getting his ship back, *ever*."

Gilles thought this over and Jean was right. LeBlanc would have to be a complete fool to risk so much when he was so close to getting it all back.

"Maybe I can talk your father into sending you back with me to find out about the warehouses and Van Ness, that is unless you are afraid to go. I'm guessing it's the warehouses," Jean offered.

Gilles was grateful that Jean thought enough of him to take him into his confidences and to treat him like an associate instead of a child. "I'll go! If you *could* talk him into letting me go, I'd be in your debt, Jean!"

"Well, it would be only one trip for you out of the accounting offices, I guess. After that you would have to find your own means of escape for the next forty years." Jean winked at him and went back to his wood.

Gilles wondered if his sore stomach would ever feel better. It still ached when he climbed down the ship's stairs. He knew that he couldn't hide the cut on his forehead but he hoped that he might cover up the extent of his other injuries. His mother and father would worry and never let him go anywhere again but after several days of thinking about the incident, Gilles had convinced himself that he had just been in the wrong place at the wrong time. Even if the man with the bushy eyebrows was the same man who frequented the inn and the church, there was no reason to believe that he went to those places just because Gilles did. Amsterdam was such a compact city that people in the trade business simply could not avoid running into each other every day. It made no difference, really: he might never again get to see the Netherlands or any of her people, the good ones or the bad ones.

When he set eyes on it again, his home port looked somehow distant to him, as if he was looking at Rouen through a sailor's lens or at one of the Amsterdam street artist's paintings. Everything was where it should have been but it didn't look real to him at first. It was familiar and strange all at once and Gilles realized that he had been away from his home for the longest time in his life. There was a haze over the city and as they got closer there was the smell of something burning. It wasn't the smell of cooking, tobacco, or even burning rubbish; the smoke had the smell of death in it. Gilles had grown up with the fires and he usually didn't even notice it anymore but being away from home had sharpened all of his senses.

Jean smelled it, too. He had been leaning against the rail and he looked up from his wood carving, now much smaller in size than it had been when they had set sail and surely nearer to completion.

"Ah, a reminder of Hell's furies to greet us! It's good to be home, isn't it? The English burned Saint Joan for us here and now we save them the trouble and burn our own!"

The Montroville coach was waiting for them but there was no sign of Gilles' father. The old driver, his bones stiff with age, laboriously climbed down from the carriage and limped over to Gilles and Jean. He had a message to deliver.

"Msr. Montroville requests that you join him at the house now, unless you have more pressing business, Msr. Durie."

"Not at all," Jean replied.

The driver yelled to a boy at the dock to come and get the two bags that Jean had been carrying, his own and Gilles'. The old servant struggled to drag one bag closer to the luggage rack and ordinarily Gilles would have helped but he wasn't sure whether he *could* pick it up. He finally decided to let the servant take it, as much to spare the old man's pride as to avoid hurting himself any more. Jean climbed into the coach with Gilles following behind closely him. Gilles winced at the continuing pain as he slowly climbed the steps, sometimes moving the wrong way and then experiencing fresh pain, but finally settling as gently as he could into his seat.

"It still hurts, Gilles?" Jean asked, seeing the look on his face.

"Yes, not too bad, but I'd like to be the one to tell my father about it before he sees it for himself."

"All right. I would have liked to freshen up first before seeing your father," Jean said. "These clothes aren't the worst but I do like to dress better for my clients. We'd better not keep your father waiting, though."

"No, he doesn't like to be kept waiting," Gilles agreed.

He wondered if his father would be angry at him still for the way he had left and he also wondered if his father had received the letter that was sent to him from Amsterdam. It seemed a little silly now to have suspicions about Jean Durie. Gilles forgot exactly what he had written but he hoped that he had worded it vaguely enough so that he could explain it to his father if necessary.

The boy tossed Jean Durie's bag onto the rack and the jolt to the rear of the carriage made the team of horses jump. The driver reached up to grab the reins, trying to steady the nervous horses as he yelled to the boy, "Be careful now! If you scare the horses you won't be paid at all!"

The boy mumbled something that no one could hear clearly but he tossed the second bag up the same way. The old servant threw him a coin when the boy was through and then, assured that the horses had calmed down, he went back to secure the bags for the ride home. With another unintelligible curse, the boy sauntered back to the ship, probably in the hopes of finding easier and more lucrative work. The Montroville's servant had a few choice words of his own that he was muttering under his breath as he pulled the straps into place and tied down the bags. The old man at last climbed back up into the driver's seat and they started rolling toward home.

The streets seemed strangely quiet for midday and at first Gilles thought that it must have been a trick of the mind, the change from the constant activity of Amsterdam but Jean commented on it as well.

The carriage bumped up the hill now and soon the house was in sight. The house was quiet as well, with less activity outside today than was usual. Perhaps it was Sunday? Gilles saw the cottage in the distance and then remembered that he needed to tell his father what Claude had told him.

They pulled up to the front door and Jean jumped out first, holding the carriage door for Gilles. Gilles slowly got down, trying not to inflict any more pain on himself than he could. He was moving easier and could do more than he had since the beating but healing was still a slow process. The old servant climbed down and called to one of the younger servant boys to get Msr. Gilles' bag. Gilles and Jean Durie met up with Jean Montroville in the foyer where he was standing with Charles.

"Ah, back at last. Come into my study!" Msr. Montroville took in the cut over Gilles' eye but said nothing about it.

Gilles noted that his father's coat was new and seemed very formal. In just two weeks Gilles had grown comfortable going around Amsterdam in simple shirts, even without his coat on sunny days. They went into Msr. Montrovilles' study and Gilles held the door open for Jean Durie, although not without some effort due to his injuries. While Gilles held the door open, Charles strode in and before Gilles could close his mouth, Charles had poured himself a drink and taken a seat by his father.

"Charles, move yourself and give Msr. Durie that seat," Jean Montroville said, not objecting and indeed, appearing quite comfortable with his younger son's presence in the room. Charles barely held back a smirk that wanted to appear on his face and Gilles was sure that he saw Charles half raise his glass in mock salute to him.

Gilles poured himself a drink to help him deal with the shock of his brother's presence and also to ease his pain. Jean Durie began his report.

"It is not the middlemen, Msr. Montroville. Gilles and I traced the movement of the goods from three shipments now and can find no irregularities there. We checked the counting houses and accounts also. No thefts occurred while we were there this time. We made certain that others who were unknown to anyone except myself also traced the goods and there are two possibilities: One is that the warehousemen at two particular warehouses are taking the goods and the second is that the purchasers are not reporting what they have received accurately. It is not that they do not appreciate your fine wine, I am sure, but that they have more of a financial interest in stealing the claret."

"Was it during these investigations that you were injured Gilles?"

His father turned to him now. While Gilles was grateful that Jean Durie had given Gilles more credit than he deserved for doing the actual work, it probably sounded very dangerous to his father who certainly still saw Gilles as a child.

"Non, Father. Someone tried to rob me but I am fine now."

Jean Montroville grunted. "You will be fine in a few weeks, I'm sure."

Gilles' eyes met Jean Durie's. As always, Jean gave no sign of what was on his mind but Gilles *knew* what his friend was thinking. He was wondering why Gilles didn't tell his father more.

Msr. Montroville continued.

"While you were gone, Charles and I have been visiting our counting houses here and he has proven to be quite useful to me." Jean Montroville smiled at Charles who luxuriated in the rare praise.

Gilles felt as though he had been punched in the stomach again.

"Perhaps *you* could take Charles around sometime too, Jean, and teach him some more things about the business."

"Bien sur!" Jean replied.

The door opened and no one said anything while the servant put down a large tray of cheese, pate, fruit and bread. No one said anything until the servant had left and shut the door behind him. It was good that there was that small interruption because it gave Gilles an opportunity to calm down and to control his anger.

"And what will I be doing if Charles is doing all of the accounts, Father?" Gilles asked as calmly as he could. Inside he was seething that Charles had taken over his place while he was gone.

"Well, the same thing of course! Charles was *absolutely* correct in that I have *two* sons, why should I not have *two* new partners? Charles is very good with the counting house and you appear to have a talent for meeting with people and being my emissary to solve problems. I could never have planned it better! Two sons and two new partners!" Jean Montroville seemed very pleased with this new saying and this new arrangement. Charles was smiling broadly too. Gilles only hoped that his face wasn't relaying too much of what he was feeling.

"Well, if our business here is concluded, get some refreshment and relax a little." Jean Montroville pushed the plate of cheese toward Jean Durie.

"If you have no further need of me, I need to attend to my own business, Msr. Montroville." Jean Durie rose to go.

Jean Montroville nodded acquiescence from across the table. He would not have expected otherwise from Jean Durie. "See Msr. Durie out, Charles, and close the door behind you. Gilles and I have some further matters to discuss."

Charles looked very pleased with these instructions and it was obvious that he expected his father to upbraid Gilles for rushing off and for not obeying his wishes. Charles gave Gilles a final grin on his way out the door which Gilles ignored. How could his father consider taking that *child* into the business now? It would be *years*, if ever, before he grew up and took responsibility for his actions.

When the door had closed solidly again, Jean Montroville turned to his son.

"You are telling me the truth about your injuries?" he asked.

"Oui, Father."

"And Msr. Durie says that you worked hard and well together."

"Oui, Father."

"It was wrong to just go off to the Netherlands when there is so much for you to learn here."

"Oui, Father."

"You are too large to strike anymore but I expect you to remember that *I* am the owner of this business, the senior partner, not just your father, and *I* will say how the business is run, *who* does what, when, and in the end, *who* will inherit my portion of the business. Do I make myself clear?"

"Oui, Father."

"Enough 'Yes, Fathers' and tell me something that I do not know. If you are my ears abroad, then I expect you to act that way."

"You received my letter, Father?" Gilles was almost afraid to bring it up, thinking it would raise questions about Jean Durie but he thought it would be a good starting point.

"No, I did not receive a letter. What was in it?"

"It was just a progress report, as Jean just summarized."

"And all of your time was spent in tracking my goods?"

"Mostly, sir. There was time in between to see some of the port and to learn about the trade going on with the new world."

"There are great opportunities for the Netherlanders there, and many ways to get into trouble, too. Ah Gilles, I was young once, myself, but you must *not* go out at night alone in strange cities. Even harmless-looking women can be trouble."

"Yes, sir. I also had a warning from someone here before I left that we should be very careful about what we say and do. Has there been trouble here?" Gilles wasn't sure if he should ask this question now but he needed to bring it up while he had the time alone with his father and before he forgot again.

Jean Montroville looked startled. "Who said that? There is *always* trouble," he said with disgust, "although there has been no more than usual for *me*. Others have not been so fortunate. That is why I need my sons to be vigilant and to work with me on these matters, not to bicker with each other. You are no longer small children!"

Gilles almost said that it was not *he* who was acting childishly but he held his tongue. "Father?"

"Yes, Gilles?"

"I have made some decisions while I was gone. I *do* wish to do a better job at learning the business and accepting my share of the responsibilities. I would like to go forward with the wedding as soon as possible."

Gilles' speech had exactly the desired effect on his father that he had hoped. All traces of anger and stress fell away from Jean Montroville's face and Gilles saw that it reflected a mixture of pride and relief before he walked over and embraced his son. Gilles thought to himself, *"Do better than that, Charles!"*

"The Junots will be coming to dinner tomorrow night. We had not expected you back until then," Jean Montroville said. "That will give you an opportunity to speak with Marie and I can speak privately with Msr. Junot."

Jean Montroville opened the door to the study and Charles, who was already standing there, looked puzzled at the joyous look on his father's face. Charles scanned Gilles' face which told him nothing except that he had won some type of victory with their father. Jean Montroville rushed out, perhaps to discuss wedding arrangements with his wife and Gilles pushed past Charles without saying anything, as much to drive him crazy as because he had nothing civil to say to his brother. Gilles remembered that he had not seen his mother yet but he could see her later at dinner.

"Well, now I've done it," Gilles thought to himself as he escaped out into the fields. He needed some time alone to think and so he went as quickly as he could away from the house and away from the confusion of life that was contained inside the massive old structure. The western sky was infused with red and in the distance the dark silhouettes of the workers coming home from the vineyards moved in front of the setting sun, exiting the fields in one long, dark line for the night. The field workers greeted Gilles, welcoming him home as they passed him. They were used to young master Gilles being out there, sometimes even working alongside them. "The soul of a farmer!" they often joked among themselves but it was not said in derision; they respected Gilles for it.

Gilles went up to a rail fence and leaned on it, looking out over the vineyards. He grabbed a long stalk of grass growing by the fence and chewed on it.

Married.

Soon he would be married and children would follow soon after. This thought occurred to him for the very first time in his young life.

"When he is born, I'll take my son here and show him the vineyards that will be his when he is older. I will show him how to trim the vines each year and explain to him about the different kinds of blight and the vine's needs. When he is older, I will take him to the sea and maybe I will even take him to the Netherlands and show him that, too."

Gilles' thoughts were frightening and yet heady all at once. To run the business and have a wife and children was not something that he could have envisioned even a few months ago. He told himself that now he was a responsible adult and had even made his first investments in global trade, in the emerging new world with Hendrick; it was already like witnessing a birth. Jean Durie could retrieve his investment for him or Gilles could let it continue to grow by investing more through his emissaries. The possibilities were endless and things looked very bright, if a little large and frightening. He wasn't going to let Charles' new position bother him; after all, Charles was the *least* senior partner. Life was good. How had Jean Durie put it? A wonderfully boring life of plenty? It was all here in front of Gilles now, it was all just beginning.

Dinner that afternoon was a happy affair. It was obvious to Gilles that his father had already had a chance to speak with his mother. She embraced Gilles when she saw him and he was embarrassed by her sudden and unusual demonstrativeness; Jean Montroville and his wife chattered happily over dinner, *like twittering birds*, Gilles thought with some disgust. Even Gilles' sisters were drawn into the good mood. Only Charles and Gilles sat somewhat subdued, Charles because he had no idea what had transpired and Gilles because it was all so overwhelming. After lunch the festive atmosphere persisted and his father took Gilles aside.

"We have much to do and so little time! Aside from the wedding, which will be quite enough to plan, I need to renovate your living quarters. I need to get workmen and I don't think the fireplaces have been used at all for many years. They must be cleaned and inspected, of course. I will need to revise my business affairs. I will draw up documents giving you a fourth of my holdings now so that you can dress and live the way you need to. I don't know what Marie's dowry will be exactly, but be assured, you will be a very rich man!"

Before Gilles had a chance to open his mouth his father was off, looking for the best workmen in the city and people to cart away the old unwanted things that had been stored in the heretofore unused portion of the house. He had never seen his father so happy, except perhaps once four years ago when a very large contract came through and his father made as much money as he generally made in a year on one single trade. Soon word spread and the entire household, right down to the child who peeled potatoes in the kitchen, was off planning his wedding. Gilles simply wanted to go to his room and sleep. It was all very tiring. Gilles had a glass of brandy to ease the ongoing pain in his midsection before he went up to his bed. As he wearily climbed toward his room, Charles called up to him from the foot of the stairs.

"So you are to be married, eh? My brother the landowner!" Charles shouted.

"Yes, Charles, and since you are so skilled at it, you can take account of my holdings." Gilles had an extra charitable smile that he didn't begrudge Charles today.

"That I will, Brother!" Charles responded.

Gilles completed his climb slowly and lowered himself down onto his bed. He could hear a noise like bees throughout the house.

"Everyone must have heard the news by now. They are all getting ready."

He fell asleep quickly and dreamed about riding the long fields from one end to another and they were all *his* fields, every one of them belonged to him.

He didn't wake up until supper time and his mother and father were still happily talking away when he went down the stairs. They continued to talk and plan at the table and the topics went from colors of the new draperies to the smallest wedding details.

"Of course the Junots will want to plan their own wedding but we will certainly have it here in our chapel," Gilles' mother said. "Our gardens are better than theirs, if not bigger."

"Of course," Gilles responded.

If this madness kept up for the next few months, Gilles felt that he would have to find somewhere to go to escape it. He hoped that Jean Durie was having an easier time planning *his* wedding. Gilles wondered if the chatter would continue the following night with the Junots. Perhaps they would have a more sensible outlook on it or take control of the situation so that Gilles would be spared all the details and all of the decisions. Gilles' mother kept starting sentences with "Of course we'll have to …" and Gilles kept responding with "Of course we will." Perhaps life would only return to normal *after* the wedding. It *was* nice to be the center attention, of good attention, for a change.

Gilles still needed a lot of sleep at night. His stomach and chest were turning a yellow green color from the healing bruises and he still felt pain whenever he moved too quickly the wrong way. He grew tired of drinking sweet things to numb the pain and tried some Scots Whisky that helped to ease the pain without making his head as groggy afterwards. He hoped that the cut on his forehead would not be completely repulsive to Marie or to her father. It was a dark red line now but the healing was coming along. He would have to put his injuries in the best possible light and make sure they knew that he was not one to get involved in fights.

Mme. Montroville worked with the servants all day on supper plans and the dining room was decorated with too many flowers when their guests finally arrived. Roses and their scent overwhelmed the house and there was not enough room left to put all of the food on the dinner or side tables. Servants were sent scurrying at the last minute to remove some of blooms to other rooms.

Marie might have had an idea that this would be a special night, too, because she wore a new pink dress that Gilles had never seen before. The color suited her well but the revealing bust line did not make her look like she was a young woman ready to be wed; on the contrary, it made her look like she was a child of no more than ten years old. The idea of touching Marie while she wore that dress, of taking that dress off her, made Gilles feel odd, like he would be doing inappropriate things to a small child. He dismissed his feelings by removing his eyes from her bosom and looking into her eyes as he helped her out of the Junot carriage. She was a pretty young girl and his fate would not be so hard to take. His thoughts strayed from her eyes and he hoped that the rest of her body would be pleasing to him as well. Her dress was tight enough tonight for him to decide that it would be pleasant, if she wore a different dress anyway, and he was ready for the wedding right now if it meant having Marie on their wedding night; the sooner the better.

"Please excuse my appearance, Mlle. Junot. I had a minor mishap while on some business in the Netherlands but I am recovering."

Gilles gestured at his head. He wondered if he should have said anything at all but he thought that it was better to say something before the Junots had mistaken ideas about what might have befallen him and then asked him more direct questions.

Marie almost looked as though she thought Gilles' injury was attractive in a certain way but her parents said nothing. Perhaps Gilles imagined it, but he thought they looked displeased about it. Dinner was pleasant enough, though. Perhaps Gilles stared at Marie for too long because tonight whenever Marie looked at him, often it was with a look of puzzlement on her face but during every previous dinner, Gilles had always had his eyes fixed firmly on his plate and if anyone spoke to him, he generally answered in one-word answers. Tonight he talked, looked all of his dinner companions in the eye, and he addressed most of his conversation to Msr. Junot.

After dessert, Gilles asked Msr. Junot's permission to take Marie for a walk in the garden even before his father made the usual suggestion. Marie's father smiled and heartily accepted for his daughter.

"A walk is just what is needed for our digestion," Msr. Montroville agreed, "but if you have a few minutes, Msr. Junot, perhaps our wives could accompany the young people while you and I have a private word in my study?"

"All right."

Mr. Junot looked slightly puzzled but not very. He had suspected the topic, Gilles was certain of it. Mme. Junot smiled sideways at Gilles' mother as they rose from their chairs and Gilles' mother smiled broadly at her guest in affirmation.

Gilles helped Marie with her chair before the servants had the opportunity. The staff brought the cloaks into the dining room and Gilles put Marie's on, accidentally touching her bare shoulder and noticing as he did so that it was very, very soft.

She looked up into his eyes again and this time Gilles felt a surge of energy run through him. They left the house and started up the path as they always did and the night air was as heavy with the scent of the roses as the dining room. Marie wore perfume, too and at times Gilles caught the scent of it as well. Gilles wanted to put some distance between them and their mothers but he didn't have to work at it tonight: Gilles mother had slowed her pace.

"Let's sit and rest," Gilles said when they reached the bench at the top of the hill. He noticed that his mother, Marie's mother, and his sisters were all taking other bench seats further down the hill. He and Marie looked out over the land in silence and Gilles began to talk to her.

"I'm sorry that I haven't been a very good conversationalist and I suppose that I'm not really that good a one in general." He continued to look out over the gardens and not directly at Marie although he watched her out of the corner of his eye.

She shrugged and smiled to herself as if to reply that it didn't really matter to her.

"I have been taking care of some business for my father but it is time I thought about my future, about *our* future," he corrected.

Marie just nodded, looking a little teary-eyed, Gilles thought. *Wasn't she going to say anything?* This might be difficult if she was not going to help him at all.

"Our parents would be pleased with our union and I believe that it would be a good match, too."

He looked directly at Marie now but she was still not looking at him. Perhaps he was going too fast and he needed to wait for her to take it all in. Just because he had known for three years who he was supposed to marry did not mean that *she* knew: After all, she had only been ten years old when they started having regular dinners together. She couldn't be rejecting him? If that was possible, why did her parents still come to dinner so often? Gilles remained silent to give her a few minutes to collect her thoughts before he continued.

"My father is speaking with your father now. I would hope that you, too, would not find me a bad choice for a husband because it *matters* to me what you think. If you find me objectionable, I will tell my father that I will not obey his wishes and that there will be no marriage."

Marie looked up at him at last. She stammered slightly as she spoke.

"Y-You m-must follow your father's wishes but I am p-pleased to think that it is your idea, t-too. M-m-m-my father takes me to d-dine wu-wu-wu-with Cmt. De Calais t-t-too, w-when his teeth and his g-gout aren't bothering him t-too m-m-m-much."

Gilles had never heard her speak more than a word or two before. He hadn't known that she stuttered. She looked directly at him, smiling with her eyes as well as with her mouth and Gilles was surprised to see the warmth that was there. It was apparent now that Marie already had feelings for Gilles, feelings that were well-hidden by proprietary requirements and her shyness. Gilles felt a measure of pity for her, that she was forced to dine with the fat old Cmt. De Calais. Surely he wasn't her other marriage prospect?

Marie sat with her hands folded on her lap, looking shyly out of the corner of her eye at Gilles. Gilles put his hand down on top of hers, being careful not to let his nearby chaperones see it or to touch any other part of her other than her hand.

"As I said, my father speaks with yours tonight. I look forward to completing the arrangements and I hope it is soon."

He smiled at her and noticed that her breathing was coming somewhat faster. He thought about that and suddenly he wanted them to be married that very evening so that he could take her to their apartments. Her hand was soft and small under his and if he didn't have an audience nearby, he would have been tempted to take more liberties with her. She was to be his wife soon anyway, so why wait for a ceremony and documents to be drawn? Surely the joining of their bodies was enough of a ceremony.

"Blasphemy!" he admonished himself but rebellious thoughts followed. *"I don't care, she is mine ... "*

He gently touched the inside of her wrist and her palm. She pulled her hand away and blushed. This action worried Gilles a little because Catherine, the kitchen maid, never blushed or pulled away when he touched her *anywhere*. If his new wife was not agreeable to his bodily advances he was not sure what he would do. He didn't really want to force himself on her: that would not be very pleasurable. His worry only lasted only a minute.

Marie said, "I w-want to be your w-w-wife soon, t-too. You m-must not make the wait too d-difficult for me by t-t-touching my h-hand that way. The time will c-c-come soon."

She looked up into his eyes before she blushed and looked down again. Gilles was no longer worried. He did not believe that Marie had ever known another man in any way but he did believe that she was more than agreeable for Gilles to be the first. Gilles stood up and walked a few steps away to pick some of the rose blooms for her. He just needed to get away from her for a minute, to cool down until they resumed their walk. She was charmed by his personal gift and rewarded him with a blushing smile.

When Gilles and Marie walked back into the house, their respective fathers were in very good spirits and more alcoholic spirits had obviously been consumed while the two men talked in the study. The two fathers never did make it out to the garden but when the strolling rose fanciers arrived back at the house, the entire household, with the possible exception of Charles, was in a very good humor. The Junot's carriage was brought around and happy wishes for a good night were exchanged. After his guests had left, his father told Gilles that the agreement was signed and in place; only the final details and date needed to be worked out.

Gilles was relieved now that he had made the decision to go ahead and be married. He had some difficulty getting to sleep even though he was tired and he had the strange thought at one point as he dozed off that Marie was next to him in his bed. The smell of her perfume followed him into his dreams.

Jean Montroville met with Msr. Junot twice more over the next week and the house was in even more of an uproar over the wedding than it had been previously. It was decided that they would have an autumn wedding, no sooner than three months ahead, because of all the important guests the Junots had to invite. The wedding was not to be held at the Montroville home and it turned out to be a very good thing as the workmen had started their noisy and messy renovations. Gilles woke to the sound of the workers hammering and sawing and he fell asleep to it too as they kept working by lamplight. When the workers were finished at last, it was still no quieter because new furnishings had started to arrive. When he wasn't out with his father on business, Gilles was busy being measured and measured again for all kinds of new clothing. True to his word, he attempted to do more with his father in the way of the more mundane business chores. Charles did seem to enjoy the business, even the accounting immensely, and if Gilles thought at first that it was only a deception to get into their father's good graces, he was not so sure by the end of each day when Charles' enthusiasm for columns of numbers was still there hours after Gilles' had waned. How Charles could find anything interesting, let alone exciting, about counting houses was beyond Gilles' comprehension and imagination.

The final agreement with Msr. Junot, all details included, had been drawn up for the wedding and the dowry. It was as his father had told him: Gilles was going to be a very rich young man. Gilles found that his father allowed him a little time to escape some of the rounds if his request involved the wedding plans and Gilles took full advantage of this by making excuses to go to the Junot's home to see Marie. The Junots were pleased and amused that he wanted to see his future bride every day. Gilles believed that *this* must be the feeling that Jean Durie had spoken of on the last return trip from Amsterdam; he even went to the finest jewelry merchant in town to buy Marie a wedding gift without being prompted to do so by his mother or his father. He decided on some pearls with gold work and he thought of how lovely they would look on her neck. He was so lost in thought about the pearls that he was barely paying attention to what he was doing when he left the shop until he bumped squarely into Jean Durie out on the street.

"Jean! What brings you out of your dark office today?" Gilles grinned at him.

"I have some routine business nearby."

Jean shifted some papers that he carried under his arm and seemed agitated as he looked up and down the street.

"You *must* come to my wedding. I'm not even sure if my father invited you! That is, if you are not going to be married or away on business yourself then? It will be in the early autumn."

"Well, that sounds good; I will have to check my calendar of course." Jean seemed preoccupied, in a great hurry and very distracted.

"What about *your* wedding? When will it take place? Am I invited?"

"Soon, very soon. Congratulations, Gilles."

"Marie and I are very happy. The date ..."

Jean suddenly interrupted him. "I'm sorry, Gilles. I have to go now. I will talk to you another time and you can let me know the date then." Jean raced up the street still clutching his papers.

Gilles stood looking after him for a time but he was not really so surprised: After all, the frantic wedding activity must be affecting Jean the same way it was affecting his mother and sisters. They had that same harried look but Gilles would not have thought that Jean Durie could be so crazed by mere wedding plans. Gilles wanted Jean to be there at his wedding to Marie because he was probably his best friend since Claude had joined the church. Jean was definitely a better friend than his own brother who would certainly have to be there at his wedding. Gilles would just make sure that an invitation was sent out and he went home wondering if his mother could take care of it or if he needed to talk with the Junots about it.

At home Gilles' father and Charles were not back from their business rounds yet. It still bothered Gilles a little that his brother was taking over his place in the counting houses but once the wedding was over, he would regain his rightful place and would have no more excuses to take him away from going out all day with his father. It was a relief for now not to have to go out with them all the time.

Gilles went up to his room and took out the pearls. They were even lovelier than he thought in the store. He held them up to the light and saw the light move across them. The gold work was very precise, very fine. He carefully put them back into their box and put the box in his pocket. Marie would surely like these. He would put them around her neck himself and feel for himself which was smoother, which was more beautiful, the pearls or her skin. He looked around his room and realized that soon this would no longer be his room. He liked the window looking out over the big tree but soon his view would be of the vineyards, his vineyards. It was as it should be. He should be able to see what was going on every day with his own land as he was waking up and as he was going to sleep. Still, he had slept in this very room since he was a very small child and he would miss it.

He touched the box of pearls in his pocket and then went down the stairs to see if supper would be served soon. It was time but what was keeping his father and brother so late? Why had the servants not come up to get him yet?

As he reached the landing he heard loud voices. His father and Charles had just come in and were not arguing as he thought at first but talking very animatedly.

"But that is no reason not to see us!" Jean Montroville sputtered, in a temper.

"Father, you *know* he has very important clients who cannot be interrupted. Too many wish to see him on the merest whim." Charles was attempting to calm his father down.

"And I am not important? He could spare five minutes to talk to his daughter's future father-in-law! Non, it is an insult! I will *not* be treated this way! I am Jean-Louis Montroville!"

"Father, let us have dinner first and calmly think this over. Then we will send a message to him, worded in a diplomatic way of course ..."

"Bah!" Jean Montroville threw up his arms and marched to the dining room.

Gilles marveled at his brother's influence over their father. He had never had that kind of influence, that much influence, he was certain of that.

"Is it the Junots, Charles?" Gilles asked his brother before they joined their father in the dining room.

"Oui. Father stopped in without letting them know that he was coming. I told him it was a bad idea and that they would be too busy but you know him! Father said, 'They will certainly take time to see me!'"

"Is that *all*? I just that hope we can get through the wedding without a major incident if Father is going to behave like this. Thank you, Charles."

Gilles meant it sincerely. His brother was actually helping him.

Charles smiled and put a hand on Gilles' shoulder. "Pity me, brother! You are the first so he will probably be better behaved for your wedding! Come along then, maybe supper and a few drinks will calm him down."

Gilles was surprised at the friendly gesture. They had always been rivals but perhaps being included in the business was having a good effect on Charles. He could hope.

Msr. Montroville was so angry that he forgot to say dinner prayers before he sat down and took a sip of wine. Charles started the prayers. Gilles knew his brother wouldn't get them right and of course he didn't. Perhaps Charles had forgotten the exact words since he never listened to them, but Charles was good at improvisation and he concluded with "... remember me when you eat and drink."

Gilles had never heard such a mélange before but maybe it was something that his tutor had taught him. Gilles wasn't sure if the prayer was sanctioned by the church but it made no difference; they crossed themselves anyway and started eating their supper.

A strained, angry silence filled the room at first but by the time they got to the second course, Jean Montroville had started to talk. Charles and Gilles agreed with everything their father said at first. He spoke angrily in the beginning but then he started to talk himself out of his anger. By the third course he had reasoned that Charles was probably right and that he should not do anything to jeopardize his eldest son's wedding plans or the future alliance. When dessert arrived, things were almost back to normal. The girls were teasing Gilles and there was pleasant, if subdued conversation between his parents.

It was so normal in fact, that Gilles would always remember that night. He remembered the way the candles threw their shadows when someone entered the room and the slight breezes from the open windows that made the flames and the curtains dance a soft minuet. He would remember how his family was dressed, right down to the smallest details, his sisters' shoes, and the smell of the roses, still in their vases and just starting to wilt all around the house. He remembered which servants were there and which were not and he remembered thinking that the family was going to change forever once he was married. He would have many opportunities to go over each detail again and again. Some scenes are painted permanently in the mind.

They were eating dessert when the servant appeared and told Jean Montroville that there was someone there who needed to speak with him right away.

"They can wait until we are finished," said Msr. Montroville, waving his hand in dismissal.

The servant disappeared but was back again right away, looking pale and distressed. She made a quick curtsey and said something to Jean Montroville so quietly that Gilles could not hear what she had said.

Jean Montroville got up and left the room looking disturbed himself. Gilles' sister who had been next to her father looked pale and was suddenly quiet.

"What is it?" Gilles' mother asked her.

His sister gestured confusion but it was apparent that she had heard more than she was telling. No one else had heard the remark and it had not been resolved in the few moments before four soldiers appeared with Msr. Montroville in the dining room. Gilles thought his sister was going to scream out loud but she stifled the sound in her napkin. His mother stood up, clutching her stomach and looked to her husband. It was clear that she was trying to hide the terror she felt and was mentally casting about for something else that it might be, perhaps a social call or something to do with the important wedding coming up. Jean Montroville made a motion to her to be silent. Gilles was immediately afraid for his father. What could he have done? The soldiers only came to take people, usually to their eventual deaths.

"They have orders to take Gilles," Msr. Montroville said and Gilles felt the color as well as the strength drain from his face and his body.

"Non! Not Gilles!" his mother cried out but quickly Jean Montroville gestured for her to be silent again. She clutched her stomach tighter, tearing at the material with her nails but she complied with her husband and remained silent. Gilles' legs shook as he was escorted, an officer on each side, out to the foyer.

"My cape," Gilles said hoarsely when they got there, although he didn't know why he needed it, habit maybe. It was absurd to worry about a cape. The senior officer nodded and a servant brought it out for him. The servants didn't look directly at Gilles or at the soldiers but did what they were summoned to do and then scurried away quickly.

"I will be in to clear this matter up as soon as I can, Gilles," his father said to him.

Gilles nodded but he said nothing; he was certain that his voice would shake as much as his legs if he tried to say anything out loud.

A mental fog had settled down over Gilles and he couldn't seem to see anything clearly. His vision was fixed straight ahead in the dark foyer, carrying him forward into the future. He was aware of noises behind him and he knew that there were choking sobs coming from his mother. The house was very quiet though and the loudest sound that he heard was the blood pounding in his ears. He put one foot in front of the other to go along with the officers who had no faces, only uniforms. Gilles had no idea if they were individually old or young, friendly or frightening, tall or short. They were just soldiers, all around him.

Someone opened the door and then he was outside. He did notice that it was getting dark. The old servant who had picked him up from the ship held the wagon's horses for the soldiers. Gilles was escorted across the drive, the small stones there crunching rhythmically under his feet. He was vaguely aware of his family who stood at the open front door, behind him now and the distance growing as he walked. He put his foot up on the step and then he was seated on the plank seat in the back of the open wagon. Officers sat on either side of him, officers with daggers in their belts.

"They don't need to arm themselves!" Gilles thought. *"This can't be happening but Father will get it sorted out very soon."*

This affirmation of faith didn't give him as much comfort as he hoped it would. He forced himself to listen to the crunch of the stone under the horse's hooves as they started off and then to the turning of the wheels. Gilles believed that if he stayed focused on the sounds, they would keep him in the here and now and he wanted that very much: He was slightly afraid that if he didn't, he would lose control, just scream and throw himself out of the wagon, running for safety back to his home, either that or laugh out loud and tell the officers that this was a *great* mistake on their part for *he* was Jean Louis Montroville's son.

Another possibility, one that terrified him, was that he might be swallowed up in the darkness of the night and just die somewhere out there, his heart bursting from fear and his body going on to whatever it would be going on to: purgatory and heaven of course, the priests had told him.

The thought struck Gilles that it was a peculiar way to enter paradise, seated in the back of a rickety old army wagon. The officers said nothing and the driver continued driving. The road was dirt now and the ruts were jolting his bones. Gilles suddenly realized that they were going toward the prison and he wanted to scream out loud that they were going the wrong way. He bit his lip to keep from opening his mouth, bit it until he tasted blood.

To the prison. He didn't like to think about that place, much less go near it, even in the light of day. The ghosts of the executed dead and those of the incarcerated living remained there and Gilles was going there during the night, in the dark.

Suddenly he was cold. He pulled his cloak around him more tightly to stop himself from shivering. Would there be a fire where they were taking him? Perhaps there would be and it would more than warm him, it would *consume* him. Gilles wondered if he might beg for a better and faster way to die but the options that he thought of, hanging quartering or disembowelment, were no more appealing. He tried to rescue his composure by reminding himself that he had done *nothing* wrong. No one had named any charges, but was that going to matter at all?

"Nothing to say, Young Montroville?" One of the officers smiled at him, displaying a mouth devoid of many teeth. "Don't worry boy, we'll treat you well. We treat people from families like yours very well. Just be thankful that you don't have a less important family. You are *most* fortunate!" He smiled and laughed.

"Leave him alone," another officer said.

"Well, we'll see if he dies like a boy or like a man then," the toothless soldier said. He didn't say anything more to Gilles though, so the defender must have outranked the toothless one.

The smell of the prison was getting closer now and the wagon had slowed for a moment, then climbed up onto stone paved streets. On the wind there was the smell of garbage and human flesh in various stages of decomposition, both live rotting flesh, decaying dead flesh, and burned flesh. The burial grounds, unmarked pits to hold the human remains that had proved unworthy of burial in sacred ground, surrounded the prison, adding the heavy smell of fungus or mold. Gilles thought, *"I hope they can at least bring my body home to be buried. I would be able to look over my fields if I was buried in the family burial grounds."*

He pushed that thought away though; he had never meant to think it at all and was disturbed that it settled so quickly and so easily into his mind. The wagon drove through the old prison gate, past guards on sentry duty and on to a smaller, dark building adjacent to the main prison building. It stood silhouetted against the sky, with no lights coming from the windows at all except on the lowest of the three floors. It was a tall, stalking creature that was waiting to consume Gilles and any other human being that was unfortunate enough to be brought in to it by its human caretakers.

Gilles wondered what he would be dying for. *"The King? The Church? The truth? I would only like to know why!"* Then he thought angrily, *"I will not die. I will not die!"*

The carriage pulled to a stop and the officers got out first. Gilles felt shaky yet and this feeling was starting to intensify again. His stomach was unsettled, in part from the smell and in part from his fear that he tried to keep swallowing. One officer grabbed Gilles by the arm, helping him and pulling him down out of the wagon all at once. Toothless clamped on to his other side when Gilles reached the ground, just after a jolt of pain went through Gilles' still-recovering midsection. The touch from Toothless had no compassion in it; it was almost gleeful in the harshness of the grip. Gilles was escorted up the steps toward the lights and inside the building. He thought briefly of fighting his way back outside but there were just too many soldiers, and now he was surrounded by many more. They lounged against the walls with their weapons leaned there beside them, some drinking and some laughing. He would surely die at the hands of one of these drunken soldiers if he attempted escape. Gilles would do better to wait and see if his father could straighten things out with the authorities. When they arrived in the room that was their destination, a card game was in progress.

"Ah, Young Montroville." A higher ranking officer got up from the card table and adjusted his shirt sleeves. "You will be happy to know that you will have our *best* accommodations and that you will *not* have to wait very long for your hearing: It's privilege you know. Some are here for months or even years before we can get around to a trial." He addressed the officers who had brought Gilles in. "Take him up, top floor, Poulin's cell."

Gilles realized with another sinking feeling in his stomach that he was familiar with the name. Msr. Poulin had only been executed that week, just after his lands were seized by officers of the king. Gilles had to wonder if it was Msr. Poulin's smell that lingered over the city, like a vengeful ghost, leaving the smell of the fires and his flesh in the air, clinging to everything and everyone. Toothless and the other guard escorted Gilles up narrow stone steps, circular steps that over the years had been worn down by many feet in little depressions near the middle of each step. The lamp that Toothless carried brought with it just enough light so that Gilles could make out each individual step and not trip and fall. The other officers followed closely behind, presumably as an escort to ensure the delivery of such a dangerous criminal. As they climbed upwards, there were little clinking and thunking sounds of the soldier's weaponry that echoed against the claustro-phobic walls, confirming the soldier's armament.

"Perhaps I should have been a murderer," Gilles thought. *"They are often just let go after a time if the courts are too busy."*

He briefly thought about murdering Toothless, just to get a better deal but he reasoned that they would only give him double the penalty, whatever the penalty was and that depended on the still unknown charges. Besides, Gilles wondered how he might manage to kill him. He wondered if he even had the stomach to kill a man.

He didn't know. He was too frightened to consider the idea fully just yet but maybe if he was in here for a long enough time ...

His legs were still shaking and the damp rotting smell as well as the smell of urine intensified. For the first time since his arrest he was able to wonder, if only briefly, what his crimes might be. He had not even been in France very much recently and when he was, he accompanied his father everywhere on business or went out into the fields or the vineyards alone. He had been in all of the church services on every single Sunday that he was here. He *had* been late to one service last Sunday but surely they could not imprison or kill him for that?

At the top floor they turned to the right, the lamplight flickering briefly as they turned the corner. There was a pile of rags or debris of some kind on the floor and Gilles had to step over it to keep from tripping. Gilles wondered where he was going and for an instant he feared that they had just *told* him that they were taking him somewhere and were really going to throw him from the roof.

"An escape attempt," he could hear them solemnly telling his father.

Gilles remembered the stone courtyard below and he shuddered but then he remembered that his father was Jean Montroville and he held tightly to this thought. His father was a *very* important man. He was certainly more important than anyone in this miserable prison and had very important friends and con-tacts. There was Marie too! Gilles had not thought about Marie. He knew that she cared for him and Marie's father was a personal friend of the King's.

Gilles just needed a little patience and he would certainly be freed right away. *Someone* had made a very big mistake and Gilles as going to see to it that all those responsible paid for it! He took a deep breath and straightened up. Toothless saw the action and looked at him strangely but Gilles made no attempt to escape. He could wait.

The cell was behind a heavy wooden door with iron hinges and a sliding bolt. It had a very small hole cut in it for viewing inside or out. The door was already open and his guards pushed Gilles inside. It was too dark to see anything at all so Gilles just stood where he was as they closed the door and then bolted it behind him. Gilles had noted, almost unconsciously, that the cell they passed just before his appeared empty but he thought he heard noises coming from the cell on the far side of the empty cell. The walls were thick stone, though, so he was not sure. Gilles continued standing there for a long time, standing until his eyes began to adjust to the darkness. The first thing that he observed was that there was a small window! He was so happy that he thought for a moment he might cry.

"How bad is one's situation when one is grateful for a window?"

Gilles noticed that the glass was mostly broken out of the window but it didn't matter. There was a chamber pot in one corner and there appeared to be a pile of rags in another.

He caught his breath.

Was there someone in here with him or a body they had not yet removed? His heart started to pound again and he stood where he was until he could stand the unknown no longer. He took one step toward it and then another and another until he was right beside it. There was no sound coming from it. He touched it with his foot and saw then that it was only a mat of straw to sleep on. He thought about his father's barns and the sweet hay that he used to sleep on in there sometimes. Gilles recalled that his sisters used to tease him about that but then he thought, *"They would surely die if they were left in here for a night."* He thought about them now and about his mother, too. He wished he had been able to tell them goodbye, just in case he never got to see their faces again. He thought about dinner, about all the food they had, what everyone was wearing, and what the conversation was.

Nothing appeared to be moving in or on the straw mat so Gilles sat down on it. His eyes detected some movement in the corner near the window and he stood up again very quickly. After a few moments it moved again. Gilles slowly approached the movement and from that and the noise, Gilles was certain that it was a rat. Gilles couldn't imagine why it was there since there probably was no food in here. He kicked at the creature and it scurried away, into a large crack at the corner of the room. Gilles took some of the straw from the bedding and pushed it into the hole quickly. He didn't want to give himself time to think about the rat biting his fingers as he stuffed the straw in. When he had finished, he walked over to the window and paused there to look outside.

It was now dark except for a bright moon and stars but he could see some light in the distance, maybe a bonfire of some sort, and it was difficult for him to determine which direction he was looking in. The dirt, cracks and bubbles in what glass was left in the window didn't allow him to see very much anyway and so he walked back to the straw and sat down on it again. It was going to be a very long night.

"Best accommodations" the officer downstairs had said. Gilles didn't want to think what the other accommodations were like. The officer had also said that it wouldn't be long until the hearing. How long was long? Hours? Days? Weeks? He thought of living here in this cell for weeks and Gilles wasn't sure if he could do it.

"Hearing" was a peculiar name for the proceedings. Who would be listening to what? Would he be hearing what his sentence was for unnamed crimes? Would they hear what he had to say? Gilles pulled his cloak around him. He had to have a plan. His father always said that. Gilles had to calm down and get a plan if he had any hope of surviving this. He did not know if he would survive it at all but he wanted to escape it if he could, if and when the opportunity presented itself, and so he needed a plan.

The first plan was defense, the second would be escape and the last would have to be to accept his own death. He would reason all three of these through and be ready for any of the three outcomes but he would put his energies toward his first two choices, and convince himself of the possibility of his successful defense or escape.

To defend himself he would need to know the charges but he might not know these until the hearing. The hearing could be a very short affair and have a very predictable outcome.

Option two, escape, would probably have to be at the hearing because Gilles could not see himself escaping from the locked cell, especially with the soldiers downstairs. The broken glass in the window might be helpful, though. Despondently, he thought that he would probably not be successful, but his death might be faster and easier if it came during an escape attempt as opposed to during an execution. The glass might come in handy for his last option as well, although he liked neither the idea of cutting himself nor of bleeding to death.

Gilles decided not to think too much about the last two options tonight until he had thought some more about the first, his defense. He was not at all ready to sleep although his body was tired. His mind was active and continually searched for possible charges although it was a puzzle with no clues and no ready solution. Gilles remembered Claude and his warning. Claude's warning was so vague and seemed to be more about his father than himself. Could they have mistakenly taken Gilles instead of his father? Claude's warning reminded him of Jean Durie's warning in Amsterdam. "The King's spies are everywhere," Jean had said. Thinking it over, there was much that could have caused difficulties there if Jean was right: The Protestant church service that he went to, investing in the Dutch West India Company, implication in his father's ships transporting Huguenots and even the theft of goods that had perhaps not had the correct amount of the King's levies paid on them. They could all be considered treasonous acts. There were probably other things that Gilles hadn't even thought of yet, but he hadn't been back from the Netherlands long enough to get into any trouble in France.

The authorities would have to save face as they would certainly not admit to mistakenly arresting Gilles. Who were his accusers? Were they powerful? Were they within the church? There was still hope, though. Some people had been cleared of charges and freed. Gilles remembered the St Amands and wondered if he could get Jean Durie to help him, too. Surely Jean would be able to help him the way he had helped the St Amands. Gilles was starting to feel a little better. He would simply have to get word to his father. He could probably bribe a guard when he saw one. Gilles recalled that he didn't have much money in his pocket but then he remembered the pearls. If he had to give up the beautiful pearls for his freedom, then he would do it.

He put his head down on the straw mattress and prayed before he thought of more plans throughout the rest of the night. His thoughts were somewhere between nightmarish sleep and waking. He thought he heard the rat again during the night but he just rolled over to face away from the hole. His father would surely be able to gain him his freedom in the morning.

When daylight found his cell, Gilles was tired from the mental work of the night before but feeling somewhat more optimistic. There was really nothing he could think of that he had done wrong and certainly they could have no proof of anything that he might have done. As the sun was coming up, he went back over to the window. It was cold in the room for late spring, but the colorful orange and red sunrise cheered him. He could look across the rooftops and he could make out the water beyond. He couldn't see his house from this direction but in a way, seeing it would have made it worse for him. Gilles heard roosters crowing and some other sounds that indicated that the city was waking up. He wondered if anyone was going to come to help him today and when they might do so. He wondered why they had not come to free him during the night and he wondered briefly, too, if everyone had forgotten about him but he knew that his mother had not. In a fleeting dream during the night he had dreamed that his father had come to take him home but he woke up before he found out if permission was granted for that. He hoped that this was not a bad portent. Gilles made use of the chamber pot in the corner. The whole area around it smelled and was stained but he was grateful for any little bit of humanity, no matter how small.

"Maybe this is the 'better' accommodation they spoke of," he thought bitterly.

After a time, two officers came up the stairs and presented him with a bucket of water and a basin for washing. There was no towel but Gilles thought better of asking for one. The soldiers didn't look at him or even acknowledge that he was there. They just put down the bucket and bowl and left, latching the door behind them again. Gilles might have talked to them but he couldn't think fast enough of what to say.

"Maybe this is breakfast. Or the whole day's meals," Gilles thought as he looked at the water. Gilles moved to the door and looked out through the peep hole. He could see only a section of wall outside, and the wall told him nothing. He listened and heard the steps of the two men still going back down the stone stairs to the floor below, and then it grew quiet again except for some rustling noises.

"The rat again?" Gilles wondered but it was in a different direction, outside his cell and down the hall.

"Who is there?" a voice called out in a hoarse whisper from somewhere.

"I am," Gilles answered uncertainly. It felt good to say that though, an affirmation that he was still alive. "I am!" he said louder, with more certainty in his voice.

"Who are you?" the voice came back. "Did you come in last night?"

"I am Gilles, who are you?" Giving too much information might not be a good thing so Gilles kept his facts to himself for the time being.

"Rene DeMaire. I didn't *hear* you come in."

Gilles recognized the name. "Are we the only ones?"

"There's another one. He doesn't speak. How many did you want to be here?"

Gilles felt just a little better now. He wasn't entirely alone. The voice spoke again.

"I'll be leaving soon. I've been in here for three days and they will get me out soon. I've done nothing wrong," Rene said.

"Nor have I," Gilles replied, a little indignantly.

"Well, they have to keep everyone working at some job I guess, even the soldiers. We should be honored that we are their raison d'etre," Rene said.

"Do they ever bring you food?" Gilles' stomach was starting to rumble now.

"Oh yes! They have to keep us alive! They will bring it soon. Just be certain that you look it over well before you bite into it, though."

Gilles wasn't sure if he wanted to know any more details about the food. He wanted to ask Rene about everything and about nothing. He wanted to know all about the routine and what good signs of hope he might look for but he was afraid to find out why Rene was there, afraid that there may have been fewer reasons for arresting him than for arresting Gilles. As long as Gilles could believe that Rene was some kind of criminal and that Gilles was less guilty than his fellow prisoner, it was easier to cling to hope. Gilles calmed himself with this thought as he heard footsteps coming up the stairs again.

Breakfast was a hard biscuit accompanied by some kind of gruel or porridge that was watery. It was served in a wooden bowl with a wooden spoon and again the men who brought it didn't even look at Gilles. They were in a rush to be done with this chore and get back to something more important, not something as trivial as keeping a fellow creature alive. Gilles was sure that these oxen types of men simply did not understand how prominent the Montrovilles were and how much helping one of them could do for their military careers. If the soldiers were always the same ones, then Gilles might be able to bribe them with the pearls. He had to be careful in how he went about it though, or they would just steal them and give him nothing in return

Gilles looked over the food, or what passed for food, and decided that he could eat it; that he would have to eat it or he would stay hungry. He could hear the two soldiers going to Rene's cell and could hear Rene trying to talk with them. They answered a little but it was not a detailed conversation. Gilles heard them go on to another room, the one where the man was that didn't talk. There was no sound of human voices from this delivery and soon the footsteps were coming back toward Gilles' cell and then turned to go down the stairs again.

Gilles recited the blessing, crossed himself, and picked his way through the food that was completely bland and tasteless. He did eat it all even though he wondered if he would be able to hold it down. He thought of the wonderful breakfasts at home that he often skipped and then thought of his room. Just hours ago his room at home had seemed to be inadequate for his needs. Now his room was a palace that he had never appreciated until now.

"If I ever get out of here alive, I will never complain again," Gilles thought. "I will tend my fields and vines, go to church and be the perfect partner for my father."

The thoughts of how good his life would be in his familiar home and business were painful, though.

If.

"When!" he corrected himself. *"I must not lose hope! I will get out of here!"*

"Enjoying your breakfast?" Rene called out to Gilles, interrupting his thoughts.

"I'm tired. I think I will try to sleep," Gilles lied. He didn't want to talk to Rene.

"Yes, it is hard to sleep in here the first night or two," Rene said.

Gilles didn't answer him in the hopes that Rene would just be quiet.

It was getting lighter in the room now. Gilles could see a lot more. If there was one word to describe the room it would be stained. There were great brown stains in the ceiling from where the roof had leaked and loosened the plaster and stains on the outside wall from the rain coming in from the broken window. There were stains from rain, pollen and insects on the window itself and stains on an inside wall that upon closer examination proved to be someone's writing. The writing included a name that meant nothing to Gilles and the declaration "Innocent!" written along with something else that was incomprehensible even though the letters could still be made out. There were stains on the floor and wall around the area of the chamber pot and a large brown stain on the wall behind him that Gilles had taken for a long crack in the wall earlier. If Gilles had to guess he would say that it looked as though someone had been run through with a sword there and the impact and blood left behind had never been removed. The covering on the bed was stained and Gilles wondered if it was sweat from some contagion or just from hot days and fear mingled with other body fluids. The room was most certainly filled with ghosts, if not the spectral kind, then traces of human liquids, past lives that had left something of themselves behind, other men who had lived for a brief time in this same room.

The men who had lived here probably also lived with cold, fear, uncertainty, and the same needs that Gilles had: to use the chamber pot, to look outside, to divine the future. They had been other men who may have wondered about their families, had fathered children, had taken a ship to a distant port too, had a woman like Marie who waited at home for them. Gilles wondered if *any* of them still lived or if they were all dead now.

Gilles took the opportunity offered by the daylight to more closely inspect the bedding and make sure there were no moving bugs. The room appeared to have been empty just long enough that there were no more living bugs and so the rat probably felt free to place an exclusive claim to it. Gilles knew that this was not the case though, as Msr. Poulin had only recently vacated the cell and this life.

Gilles decided to lie down on the bed and try to sleep some more. He dozed off a few times but kept dreaming that there were bugs crawling on him. Finally he decided to just stay awake until his father came for him. He needed something to do to pass the time, though, and so he went over to the window. If only he had a pen and paper or a book. Even wood and a knife for carvings like Jean Durie's would have been a welcome diversion. He could almost see the town's great clock from the window or at least where it should be if he had had an unobstructed view of it beyond the great Oak trees.

This was a different perspective on the city than he was used to. There was movement down below in the courtyard and Gilles could see people there as well as over in the market part of the town, too. The grass was so green and the water was so very blue today, even in the distance, and it had never really occurred to Gilles before that he lived his life every day in a beautiful place as well as one that he loved. He stood watching everything that he could see, leaning this way and that until his fatigued legs grew too tired to stand any more and then he sat on his bedding, just thinking of all of the good things and how he might defend himself when the time came.

The officers came again at dinner time and put some kind of stew in his room. They took away the breakfast dish and again said nothing to Gilles. They moved on to Rene's room and Gilles again heard him trying to make conversation with his jailers.

"Fine China, Gold and Silverwork".

Gilles remembered now what Rene's business was. Gilles' family probably had all of their eating utensils made by Rene's business or at least imported by him. Clearly Rene was well off financially and Gilles wondered why he had not been freed yet. Perhaps he *really was* guilty of something.

The footfalls disappeared down the stairs again, quieting as they receded down to the ground floor and Gilles looked at the food. He was not of a mind to try it yet and his stomach was not so much hungry as pained and recovering from the poor breakfast. Cramps seized his midsection, adding to his discomfort. Gilles folded his cloak and put it on the bed, and then he walked back to the window, hoping that walking would help the pain in his stomach subside if he moved around.

Not long afterwards, footsteps came up the stairs again and Gilles froze. What did they want and who were they coming for? Why were they returning? Could it be his father? Was it time for his hearing? They paused outside Gilles' door and the latch scraped as it slid back.

The door was opened and the last person that Gilles expected to see walked into his cell. The priest, newly elevated to the post of archbishop, walked into the chamber. He was alone, not followed by his usual entourage, but clothed in his finest robes and smiling a great, fatherly smile at Gilles. The door was shut and latched behind him.

"My son!" he greeted Gilles and he held out his arms.

Gilles embraced him, kissed him dutifully on each cheek and then knelt to kiss his ring. At last someone had come to take him home and Gilles didn't care *who* it was; he had never been so happy to see the old bastard in all of his life.

"I have come to help you, Gilles," the priest said with a smile that perhaps was meant to look paternal.

His eyes had an oddly cold but penetrating look to them that did not reassure Gilles but instead made him wary but Gilles listened carefully to what the man had to say.

"I can help you, Gilles. Good, they brought you the water and the wash basin." He nodded at the pitcher. "Your father asked that they bring that for you."

"Is my father outside?" Gilles grew excited. "Or Jean Durie?"

"Neither Msr. Durie nor your father can help you now, Gilles. They are searching Durie's offices as we speak and there is no sign of him and anyway, he is the one who is responsible for your present difficulties. He may be in here already, too. Or in the fires," he added as almost an afterthought, in an oddly calm way, Gilles thought.

From this news and the priest's demeanor, Gilles began to understand how serious the charges against him were. He could not believe that his life could have changed so much, could possibly even be finished. Just days ago it seemed that his wonderful future was just starting. Gilles' first thought was panic and then that he must not be afraid. The archbishop had *said* that he was here to help. Gilles struggled to regain his composure and then impatiently waited for the man of God to speak again.

The priest reached into his pocket and Gilles thought for a moment that he might be pulling out a weapon for him. Instead he pulled out the church's chief weapon, a rosary.

"Your father sent it for you and be sure that they see you using it! If they ask you directly, tell them that you repent and you wish to embrace the church anew. Even if they *don't* ask, tell them that it is so. I have the power and the connections to save you. You do wish the church to save you from the fires of hell, don't you Gilles? You are so young ..." The priest reached out and touched Gilles' hair, holding a strand of it in his fingers for a brief moment. Gilles looked down at the smooth brown beads and knew his father believed him to be close to death if he was sending him a rosary. A vivid picture of the front drive at home came to Gilles' mind for no particular reason and he felt close to tears. He gripped the beads tightly so that they would hurt his fingers but the pain stopped his tears from coming.

"Have you ever seen one of the burnings, Gilles?" the priest asked softly. "It is a terrible thing. The skin turns pink, then red, then it starts to blister. The blisters darken to char, all the time with an outpouring of blood and sweat and terrible screams of agony coming from within the very soul ..."

"You said you were here to help me?" Gilles asked the priest, confusion and fear reigning supreme in his mind, unable to stop hearing the words although he tried to shut them out.

"Let us pray together for the deliverance of your soul, Gilles."

Gilles did not take this for a good sign. Was he administering last rites? The priest knelt and gestured for Gilles to join him. Gilles did not know what the priest wanted but he knew that the priest was his best hope for life. Gilles went quickly to his knees. The priest moved closer to Gilles, close enough so that they touched. They recited the Lord's Prayer and the priest told him to start a rosary.

"Hail Mary ..." Gilles began. The priest rose to his feet and walked around in front of him as Gilles continued uncertainly with the prayer. The priest leaned over and placed both of his hands on Gilles' shoulders. Gilles stopped praying and looked up at the priest.

"I can save your life, Gilles. How grateful would you be if I saved your life?"

Gilles started to shake and he didn't know why. It started with his chin, and traveled to his hands, then to the rest of his body. He was still clutching the first bead.

"Would you be *very* grateful, Gilles?" the priest asked softly.

"Oui, mon pere," Gilles said obediently but a tight feeling was growing in his stomach.

"Would you be grateful enough to show your gratitude to *me* and to stay for the rest of your life in the service of our Lord?"

Gilles' legs were shaking now even though he was still on his knees and he was not sure why.

"Would you?"

"I ... I ..."

The priest touched his hair again.

Gilles suddenly felt like he was going to be sick. He jumped shakily to his feet and made it across the room to the chamber pot, turning his back on the priest momentarily, taking in gulps of air to dry the salt saliva that flooded the floor of his mouth. He rocked back and forth, still holding onto the rosary, breathing in and out deeply until he had regained enough control of his body to turn back to the priest.

With eyes downcast he murmured, "Father, I would be forever grateful to you if you could get my *old life* back for me."

The priest exploded with anger.

"Go to hell! The devil can keep your soul then!"

The priest banged his fleshy fist on the door and very quickly it was unlocked from the other side by the soldiers. The priest stormed out, his robes billowing out behind him like flames dancing in a breeze, and Gilles thought that he saw the guards laughing.

A part of Gilles wanted to throw himself on the floor after the priest and cry out *"Don't let them burn me! In the name of God and humanity, help me!"* but he could not. By the time he found his voice, the lock had already scraped shut and the men were gone, their steps only an echo, one angry stomp leading the way, descending on the stones, followed by the soldier's boots, already far, far down the stairs.

Something inside of Gilles still refused to believe that he would die, not now or ever, but a small part of him had already accepted that his imminent death was inevitable; he was resigned to it and couldn't explain the paradox. He felt like his soul had been splintered into many parts.

Gilles wondered if he would ever see his father or any of his family again. He remembered now what his mother had said when they took him away: "Not Gilles, no, not Gilles!" He knew that he was his mother's favorite and he wondered if his father and brother as well as his sisters had resented her outburst. It almost implied that it was better to take his father or Charles away.

What if Gilles had been nicer to the priest? Would he have been back at home tonight?

"Are you planning your strategy?" Rene's voice intruded on him again. "It's Gilles *Montroville*, isn't it?"

"Yes, Montroville." Gilles couldn't deny it or escape the man's intrusions.

"Got you some water, eh? I have a little that they brought but no basin here!"

"Do you always talk so much, Rene?" Gilles asked impertinently, *"And eaves-drop?"* he wanted to add.

"Yes I do, and I'll tell you why," Rene replied as Gilles rolled his eyes heavenward to express his irritation, "because you build relationships with even your enemies when you talk to them."

"Just what I want, a relationship with Toothless," Gilles muttered.

"I didn't hear all of that," Rene replied, "but 'Toothless' is in a position to help you and you'd be smart to remember that. It's my philosophy in business, too."

Gilles looked at the rosary that was still in his hand and then threw it across the room at the wall. He looked at his dinner but decided that he was still not hungry enough to eat the slop, not yet.

"Better eat to keep your strength up!" Rene called as if he could see and hear everything that Gilles was doing and thinking. Gilles thought that it might even be wise to turn his back to Rene's direction when he used the chamber pot.

Gilles decided not to reply, to just ignore Rene and go back to looking out the window. He did not see any sign of the priest leaving. There must be another courtyard on the other side of the building although Gilles was sure it was the one below him now where they had brought him in last night.

Gilles' thoughts turned to Jean Durie. Was it really true that Jean Durie was the source of Gilles' misfortune?

"No sign of him" the priest had said. Gilles' meeting with Jean had been very short the day before. Had Jean Durie turned Gilles in to the authorities for some unknown crime and then climbed aboard the next ship out? If so, that was a cold thing to do.

What were they looking for in Jean Durie's office?

Gilles' thoughts turned back to his own fate. His father was a very important and powerful man but if he could not do better for Gilles than he had done already, Gilles' fate might already be sealed. Gilles didn't want to think about the possibility of being executed. Perhaps he could get out through the little window in his cell and if there was no better way, throw himself to the ground below. That was not an appealing way to die but fire was worse.

He thought about fighting the guards. There were only two of them that came upstairs but where would he go if he won a fight? Down the stairs seemed the only way out and the lowest floor was full of guards.

Gilles was dimly aware that Rene was saying something and he wondered if the jabbering fool was *still* talking to him. Gilles approached the door and listened. Perhaps Rene had gone mad after only a few days of incarceration.

Rene *was* talking but not to Gilles. Gilles listened carefully and heard enough of the words to know that Rene was praying but it was not a Catholic Church prayer; it was a strange concoction of French phrases that Gilles had never heard before. If Rene insisted on butchering the Church's sanctioned prayers, it was blasphemy and no wonder that he was in here. God was not going to save Rene if he did not speak to the Almighty in the right way.

Gilles was suddenly tired so he rested on the bed. He reminded himself that he would need to conserve his strength for whatever was to come. He drifted off to sleep and dreamed that his father came and freed him. The dream faded and Gilles knew, even in his sleep, that it was only a dream. He rolled over on his other side and dreamed that he was with Marie. They were out in the garden and the smell of the flowers was all around them. Gilles kissed her and pulled her dress off one white shoulder before he woke up.

The annoying part about waking up, apart from the frustration, was that he knew instantly where he was; the cell was starting to become familiar to Gilles. The hour did not seem very much later than it was when he fell asleep. He got to his feet, rubbed his eyes, and looked outside again. There was some activity down in the courtyard but not enough to be of much interest. Some men were unloading some barrels, food and drink supplies probably. It was no wonder that Poulin who was in here before him had taken to writing on the walls with nothing to do and nothing to see all day.

His day had been too long already. Gilles paced from the window to the hole in the door, to the writing on the wall, to the bed. He had not even been in the room for twenty-four hours and the thought of staying here for weeks or months or years was unbearable to him. Gilles thought about the Marranos in Amsterdam. What they had come from, the Spanish and Portuguese prisons and the torture, was certainly as bad or worse than what many of the detainees in France faced. It was no wonder that they seemed more madmen or savages than human beings by the time they escaped or were finally released. Gilles started to have an understanding of his father's fears and peculiarities of habit and for the first time he realized how sheltered his life had been.

Gilles made the decision to set a date: He would stay in here no longer than one week. He would rather die than let them turn him into an animal like the Marranos or a fearful man like his father. Gilles could tell himself that now, but a part of him wondered how brave he would be in a week's time when his deadline was fast approaching. The security of the jail cell might look *good* compared to the heat of a fire on his face or a noose waiting for him on a scaffold. For now though, he told himself that he would mark the days and on the week anniversary of his arrest, he would escape or die. A week was a good amount of time: His physical strength might not hold up much longer than that with the poor quality of food that he was being served and he might not be as certain of his mental facilities after that time, either. One week. He could and would do one week.

Gilles heard church bells outside. He had always heard them, on every day of his life, but today they sounded far away and sad. They were tolling the hour, or a wedding, or a death. Gilles wondered if *his* passing would be marked with the bells when the time came or if he might live long enough to hear his own wedding bells first. Gilles hated the uncertainty of his future. These thoughts kept him occupied until it was supper time. The light was fading by the time he heard the officers coming up from the lower floor.

"Your majesty!" one of them smiled and bowed but it was an ugly, mocking smile.

Gilles saw that dinner was meat, vegetables and bread. He couldn't believe it and touched it first before he put it into his mouth. It was cold but it tasted good and he didn't care if it was poisoned or not; he fell on it ravenously. He had already finished it but was still hungry when he heard the officers leave the last cell and go back down the stairs. Rene's voice assaulted Gilles' ears again.

"Stew again! I'm sure that *they* eat better than this!" Rene sighed loudly. "But still, they feed us *three* times a day and the regular prisoners are only fed once."

Gilles was glad Rene could not see that his food had been different and better but he wondered if Rene could smell it. Gilles didn't know what to say so he just grunted.

"Enjoying yours Montroville? You seem to be eating a lot tonight."

"I didn't eat much dinner earlier," Gilles replied, feeling very guilty.

His father must have found a way to send it to him. If Gilles' father could send better food, he could possibly get him out, too. Gilles started to feel a little better about his situation and he dared to hope that he might be able to put aside his earlier escape plans. He tried to forget about the archbishop's visit too, but he could not. He went over to the corner and picked up the rosary beads from the floor. Perhaps it *had* been good advice. The prayer beads *were* from his father, even if the priest had defiled them by touching them with his grubby hands.

Darkness was falling again and the priest had been the only one to come and see Gilles today but hopefully his father would get him out of this place tomorrow. Gilles put the beads around his neck, daring to hope that his actions would secure divine help and protection. He climbed onto his straw bed, pulled his cloak up over him and was grateful for its familiar feel and smell. He had never given much thought to his clothing before.

He awoke suddenly in the darkness to hear whimpering and the muffled sounds of a struggle. Gilles wasn't sure who or where it was and he was afraid to move, afraid to get out of his bed or to call out. He prayed that they wouldn't come to his cell next and he tried to listen although this was difficult due to the noise of his heart pounding in his chest. He remembered the rosary around his neck and clutched it while he lay there, not praying, just staying still, listening as hard as he could. The sounds seemed farther away than Rene's cell but he could not be sure. As annoying as Rene was, Gilles didn't like the thought of Rene being gone, of his being completely alone in this place. The whimpering escalated into a scream that echoed in someone's throat, a sound that Gilles had sometimes heard at night when a wild animal fell on its prey again and again before the prey was fully dead. There were thumps now and scrapes along with the sound of something being dragged, all the time with the terrible half-human sounds accompanying the activity. The sounds all moved toward Gilles' chamber, then toward the staircase, finally descending with the cries continuing and curses coming from the guards. Gilles believed that he still heard them for some time after he should not have been able to hear them anymore, perhaps crossing the court-yard below and going somewhere else. Gilles was shaking for a long time after-wards but at last he sat up and tiptoed over to the window, the rosary still around his neck and in his hand. He could see nothing out there in the darkness, no lan-terns, no movement at all under the stars and moon. He tiptoed back in the dark-ness, toward the door, his heart still pounding, his ears still listening.

"It's just the two of us now."

Gilles didn't say so but he was relieved to hear Rene's voice.

"There's no reason to creep around so quietly, Montroville. They know you're here and you know you're here."

Gilles felt foolish tiptoeing but somehow he felt safer when he did, as if they might forget that he was there and somehow *not* come for him.

When had they taken him from his home? Was it only two days ago? Gilles remembered his family as they had been then, all sitting at the table, unaware of the future stalking them, coming to steal their peaceful present. Gilles didn't think that it would ever be possible to find that feeling of confidence and peace in his life again.

He paced the room, still quietly but it was not fear that pushed him: It was determination. If he fought off the two soldiers he would go and let Rene out if he could because they would stand a better chance together than Gilles would alone. The soldiers always used the same staircase in their comings and goings so there was probably no other means of escape; Gilles and Rene would just have to go down those stairs and then take their chances. Gilles wouldn't let them take him alive because he wouldn't want to die a slow, lingering death due to infection from a pistol shot or a knife wound. Perhaps if he fought them hard enough, they would kill him outright and not just subdue him.

"Rene!" he called.

"Ah Montroville, are you in a talkative mood at last?"

"How long have you been in here, Rene?" Gilles called out to him.

"Just a couple of days; they will be coming to get me out soon," Rene replied.

Rene had told Gilles the same thing when he *first* came in. He hadn't seen Rene with his own eyes and so Gilles could not judge whether Rene looked like a madman or if he was wearing clothes that had been on him for more than a few days. For all Gilles knew, Rene might have been in his cell for *years* already.

"How do blind men do it? How do they judge people?" Gilles muttered to himself.

"Eh, Montroville?" Rene asked. "What's that?"

"Rien. What takes them so long in getting our hearings?"

"The magistrates are busy with those that they have caught *in the act*. They have nothing on us and so they are trying to prepare cases and find some witnesses to pay to testify against us. That all takes time, you know."

"I hope they empty the chamber pots soon then, if we are to be in here much longer," Gilles remarked, noticing that the smell was becoming difficult to live with.

"I'm sure they will get around to it sometime," Rene replied. Gilles wondered again how long Rene had been in there and how bad it smelled there if they had not emptied his yet.

"This building was not built as a jail, you know," Rene said, perhaps by way of casual conversation.

"Non?" Gilles replied. He didn't really care but he didn't know what else to say.

"Non. It used to be the barracks and that is why the accommodations are spacious but lacking some of the necessities that they have in the real jail. The *real jail* is overflowing and they are very busy keeping the fires going as well. Soon they will have to have *every* man in the King's employ, that is every man who isn't to be executed!"

Rene laughed at his own joke but the words spoken aloud terrified Gilles. He did not want to mention the King out loud for fear that he would worsen his own situation. *"The King's spies are everywhere,"* Jean Durie had told him. Where was Jean now?

Gilles walked back over to the window. He hadn't imagined it: There was definitely smoke in the air. He wondered if it was *the one that didn't talk* who was already burning out there. Perhaps he would talk when he sighted the fires, blazing up, ready for him. He would have talked and then cried, then finally screamed. Maybe the fires *never* stopped. Maybe it was only the wind that sometimes changed direction from time to time. The haze hung over the city again, suspended, a hovering thing stopped in time.

Gilles heard Rene saying something and he moved back toward the door to listen. Was Rene still talking to Gilles? No, Rene was praying again. He was praying loudly enough for all to hear, in the profanity of the people's common language, not in Latin. That alone was reason enough to execute the fool. If Gilles was imprisoned with him it was a good thing and a bad thing: It was bad that the authorities felt that he should be incarcerated with such company, two of a kind, and good that the contrast in their behavior just might be Gilles' salvation.

Was today Sunday? Was Gilles missing church? He would surely burn on earth or in the afterlife, possibly both, if he missed another service without going to confession. Rene suddenly stopped his prayers and Gilles detected the faraway sounds of footfalls coming up the stairs again. They had the slower, deliberate pace that they did when they carried something, when their food arrived. Gilles moved back away from the door before the men opened it. One of the guards set his breakfast down and the other one threw a bundle on the floor at Gilles' feet.

"Clothes for you. Your hearing is scheduled for today, in the afternoon."

They left and locked the door behind them before Gilles could ask what time the hearing would be although it didn't much matter *when*, exactly. Gilles had nowhere to go and no real preparations to make in the meantime. He was glad to be moving forward but frightened about what he would be moving on to.

The guards opened the door and left food for Rene.

"A pretty morning, isn't it gentlemen? A *fine* day," Rene said.

"Yes, a fine day," one of the men answered.

"Is there any word on when my hearing will be?" Rene asked pleasantly.

"Non, no word," came the reply.

Gilles looked at the clothes that he had on, the same clothes that he was wearing when he was detained. They were soiled and rumpled, covered with bits of hay and food stains. They had been lived in for too long to be presentable and he might just throw them out, although he greatly favored the color of the shirt that he had on. His cloak was the least compromised in appearance although it had served him well these past few days, both as a blanket and as a small measure of comfort. When Gilles looked at his cloak, he could see his old life and all of its comings and goings, not his current imprisonment.

The guards had gone now and Rene was back at his door, calling out to Gilles.

"Brought you clothes, eh? Bien! What charges are you answering to, Montro-ville?"

"I don't know," Gilles replied truthfully.

"Don't know? Are you one of the Reformees, too?"

"A Reformee? Non! I don't *know* what they think I have done."

Gilles decided that it was not too early to get dressed. The clean clothes looked inviting and he wanted to be ready whenever they came to get him.

"They will be having my hearing soon, too, I expect," Rene said mat-ter-of-factly.

Gilles wondered if Rene had anyone working for his freedom on the outside. As long as Gilles was locked up, he could be assured that his father was trying to move the heavens to free him as soon as possible. Gilles didn't know what to say to Rene that might be encouraging so he said nothing.

Gilles wished now that he had a mirror in the room. The water was all right for washing up but he could not see how he looked. His hair would probably be all right but he wished that he could shave. His stubble was itching and probably made his face look dirty and disheveled although he could grow a respectable beard if he was so inclined and if he had some more time to grow one. More time in *here*? He certainly did not wish for that.

"Let my fate come to me now," Gilles thought. *"Whatever it is, it will be better than rotting in this place."*

He went over to the window to see if he could see his reflection at all in some of the jagged pieces of glass that hung there. He couldn't make out any details and what he did see did not look like him. The stranger in the reflection seemed older and thinner, grim and pathetic, although there could not be that much of a change in just a few days. Gilles decided that it was a trick of the glass. *"Older and thinner is all right,"* Gilles thought and drew himself up to his full height. *"I am a Montroville and will go where I must with dignity."* He remembered the child that took his first trip to Amsterdam only a short time ago. He was young then but now he had jumped across adulthood and middle age to old age and acceptance that death was lying in wait for him. His clothes fit him loosely so Gilles knew that he must have lost some weight. He used the chamber pot and then decided that he would to wear the rosary *under* his shirt. Wearing it outside might be too obvious a ploy for freedom and it was possible that they might take offense. He would take his cloak with him when they came for him.

Gilles barely paid attention to his midday dinner when it came. He picked at it and knew that he should try to eat more so he could keep up his strength. He was too much on edge to eat a lot, though, so he paced the floor again, thinking of what he might say for his defense. He had worked through most of what he was going to say and what might be good strategies, that is, *if* he had the charges right, *if* he was allowed to talk at all, and *if* they asked him any of the questions that he thought they might ask, when he heard the footsteps coming back for him.

The same two soldiers who had always come at mealtimes opened the door.

"You come with us now," the taller one said.

Gilles said nothing in reply but picked up his cloak and walked out between them. The men did not object to his taking the cloak and Gilles left his dirty clothes behind, even his favorite shirt: He wouldn't have any place to leave them during the hearing. Gilles corrected his posture and walked eagerly toward the stairs. He glimpsed what must have been Rene's door but of course he could not see Rene's face although he could feel Rene looking out at him.

"God be with you, go in faith," Rene half-whispered to him.

"Go left," one of the men behind Gilles barked.

Gilles needed no instructions as he remembered very well how he had come in. He had thought more about the stairs than about anything else since his arrival. The card game was still going on downstairs and Gilles wondered if it was the same card game from days earlier or a new one. He also marveled at how the guards could be so casual. Perhaps they sent innocent young men to their death every day and it was nothing unusual, perhaps today was just like any other day at their work. Gilles was angry then that his life was so insignificant to them; at first he was angry because he was a Montroville, and that the name meant so little, but then he was angry that they would treat any human being in this manner.

When he stepped outside at last, Gilles suddenly remembered how beautiful the outside world was. It was still early in the afternoon, the most beautiful time of the day. Most of all, Gilles would regret not seeing the sunshine and green fields if his hour of death had truly come. Gilles was not sure where he would end up after his execution and he was not sure if they had such things there, even with all of the assurances from the priests. He could smell the acid smell of the oaks in the air and he hoped that he could at least carry that smell with him through eternity: It was the smell of heaven to him.

Suddenly he worried that he might have to face his accusers alone. What if his father was not there or anyone else he knew? He would hope that they gave him the chance to speak, hope that he found the right words to retain his life. Gilles was escorted over to a carriage, shabby but nicer than the wagon that he had arrived in. They pulled away before he had the chance to look up to see where his window had been. He did glimpse more than one window on the top floor as they drove away and he wondered if Rene was watching him now. Probably so.

The ride to the Justice Building was short. To his great shame, Gilles was taken in the front door but thankfully he was spared the humiliation of seeing any neighbors or business associates. He wondered again if he would have the counsel of his father or someone else to plead his case for him and Gilles feared that he was too young and too inexperienced to know how to persuade a judge: He couldn't even persuade his own father on most of the things that were important to him.

The crowds inside the building were coming or going straight forward, to or from the main chambers, but his escorts turned Gilles to the right after they entered the building. Gilles took off his cloak and draped it over his arm as he walked down the quiet side hall. They continued all the way down the hall and entered a door near the very end of the building.

"Perhaps they will decide that it was all a big mistake and send me home," Gilles thought hopefully. Then he remembered that the cemeteries in France were full of men, some of whom had protested right up until the very end that they were honest men and had done nothing wrong. The door opened to admit the small group and Gilles heard the door close behind him again. The magistrate on the bench was a man that Gilles recognized, an important man, but Gilles could not remember if his reputation was for mercy or for cruelty. Gilles had never paid any attention to politics before but now it was the most important thing in his life, the only thing that mattered in his life.

Gilles tried to assess the man's face as he walked forward toward the bench. It was a tired-looking old face but had an air of intelligence about it and Gilles was not sure if this was a good thing or a bad thing. There were five men standing to Gilles' right and they all were less than amiable. Gilles spied his father standing to his left with two men that he did not know and the priest standing alongside his father. The clergyman must have had a change of heart and Gilles hoped that he was going to help him in spite of his refusal to accept his earlier offer.

Gilles could not look long on his father's face until he was turned around to face his judge but in that short time, he clearly saw the worry there.

"Gilles Louis Charles Montroville, this is your name?"

The magistrate started the proceedings in what was obviously a very routine exercise for him.

"Oui, Monsieur." Gilles tried to sound loud and confident but not defiant. His voice sounded weak and high-pitched to his own ears.

"We have allowed you a more private hearing as befits your family's position. You will answer the questions so that there is no need for a more elaborate proceeding, a more public proceeding, is that understood?"

"Oui, Monsieur."

"You are a citizen of Rouen and one of the King's loyal subjects?" The magistrate scanned a paper in front of him that contained many lines of swirling black writing.

"Oui, Monsieur."

"You profess to be a faithful follower of our King and God's own religion, the Catholic Church?"

"Oui, Monsieur." Gilles had decided that for now one word answers appeared to be the safest course. Why was the magistrate asking him such obvious questions?

"And you claim not to have committed treason either against our King or our church?"

"Non, Monsieur."

"And yet you have been observed slipping out at night to secluded places to meet with unknown persons. You have been passing coded messages, traveling to enemy countries, and consorting with enemies of the King.

Gilles felt as though he had been dealt a blow to his stomach. He did not even hear much after the slipping out at night part for now he realized that Claude could be in danger, too. Was it a crime now to leave your house at night?

The magistrate was not finished speaking though. "You have some good friends, even some church officials, and your father, who have pleaded your case and assured me that it must all be some kind of misunderstanding. Only you can answer to these charges now and clear up this matter if this be the case."

Gilles took a deep breath and knew that he had to calm down or his brain would not function. He had to slow things down and control his emotions. It would be all right, he would clear up the misunderstanding. He tried to picture sailing on the ocean to calm himself and then he stared at a spot on the bench. The emotional diversions started to work a little as he felt himself start to relax and actually hear what was being said.

"Oui, Monsieur." He tried to bring his eyes up to look into the magistrate's. Averting his eyes would be taken as a sign of guilt, Gilles feared, even though it made him shake all over to look the man directly in the eyes. The face was hawk-ish, like a bird of prey, and his eyes were very sharp but Gilles saw a spot of lint on the magistrate's wig that he could look at and in doing so, appeared to be looking directly at the judge.

"You have been observed slipping out at night to meet with unknown people in very out-of-the-way places."

Gilles did not want to drag Claude into it so he told the lie that had worked with the servant before. *"Don't let my face show it!"* he prayed.

"I left my home one night, to meet a woman."

Luckily his nervousness was playing well, more like embarrassment or some-thing akin to it and there was a snicker from one of the men in the group on his right.

"And who was this woman?" the magistrate asked.

"I … I would rather not say, Msr. since I am to be married to another soon, I …" Gilles stopped. Was he getting himself into more trouble?

The magistrate's mouth turned up at one corner but quickly resumed its grim set. Gilles hoped that it was an expression of amusement and not a smile of mockery. What name could he give if he was questioned further? Should he make one up? What woman would he take down with him? Gilles also hoped that Marie would forgive him later. He did wonder about the servant that he had seen at his house on the night that he returned from his meeting with Claude. The judge's next question confirmed his suspicions.

"You have been sending coded messages to someone."

The magistrate handed a paper to one of the five men who passed it down the line and then showed it to Gilles. It was flattened now but once it had been very crinkled. It was the page he had drawn on to keep himself awake before he met with Claude that night, a page retrieved from the trash in his room.

"It is nothing. They were only meaningless lines to pass the time before I left for our meeting."

Gilles was comfortable in saying this as it was the truth and he started to relax and look into the magistrate's eyes. Luckily one drawing looked like it *was* in the shape of a woman and one of the men standing next to Gilles' father handed it back to the magistrate, muttering and pointing at it. The Judge looked at it briefly, glared at the five men and tossed it aside.

"So far, so good," Gilles thought.

"You have traveled to other countries and consorted with our country's ene-mies." The magistrate held the paper with the charges out at arm's length to read it and then peered over his nose at Gilles as if daring him to answer that question correctly.

"I went to the Netherlands on business for my father."

Gilles hardly considered anyone that he had met in the Netherlands an enemy of France but if the magistrate believed this, he was not going to argue the point. Gilles wondered if it would help him to say more but he was afraid that he might say too much.

"You attended their churches while there, is this not true?"

"I did attend *one* service, this is so. It was at the insistence of the man whose favor I hoped to cultivate for our business dealings."

Gilles hoped that the small lie about Hendrick would work.

"So you had no wish to go to the *Huguenot* services but would do it for business? Was his daughter helpful in this arrangement?" The magistrate spoke the word 'Huguenot' derisively. His mouth curled up again on one side and the five men on his left sneered in unison.

"Oui."

Gilles didn't know what to say and he hoped that he was saying the right thing to gain his freedom. He hoped that it was safe to agree with their interpretation of things and if he was correct in his assumptions, it appeared to Gilles that the judge was trying to offer him a way out. The idea of Elsje being a form of currency exchange would have been humorous in any other situation. It was as Rene had said; they had no real evidence of *anything* against him.

"You have interests in *many* young women for a man so soon to be married," the magistrate observed acidly.

Gilles said nothing in reply. It was more Charles who had the many interests but Gilles would not argue with the man who held his fate in his hands; this much was the very least that he had learned from his father over the years.

The judge continued. "You have been observed recently in the company of an evil man, in fact you have been observed with him on *several* occasions over the last few months. This man plots with a seditious faction of the Spanish expatriates overseas, smuggling information out on how to overthrow their king and ours. He has gone out of his way to curry favor with highly respected men in positions of honor so that he can obtain even more information to give over to our enemies. Do you deny your association with this spy and traitor?"

"Pardon? Monsieur, I don't understand."

Gilles looked at the magistrate, trying to read his face. What was the question? What was the right answer?

"Do you *deny* knowing one that goes here by the name of Jean Durie?" The magistrate had an impatient look on his face now.

"Non, Msr. He is a business advisor to my father …" Gilles wished he had not said that. Would his father be in trouble now too?

"And what matters does he … *advise* … on?"

The magistrate looked down over his long nose again and searched Gilles' face. The judge's eyes did not blink nor did his robes move. There was movement beside Gilles, slight movement from both of the two councils.

"Trade mostly. Legal matters sometimes. Contacts in countries where we are not familiar with the customs of many people or their ways of doing business."

Gilles stopped talking and examined what he had just said. It seemed all right to him, or was it? He decided not to add any more to this unless he was asked further.

"Your father *with all of his wealth*, connections, and business knowledge has *no* real legal advisors to help him there but depends on this young *advisor*?"

The magistrate had put the paper down now to the side of him and glared at Jean Montroville too.

"My father *does* have other legal advisors but when we are far from our countrymen in France, Msr. Durie has knowledge of things there where our French advisors have less expertise."

Gilles had a very bad feeling about where this was going. He was paddling quickly against the current and hoping that he was not headed into dangerous whirlpools.

"*A fortuitous thing!* And how did he come by *all* this knowledge?"

The magistrate now folded his hands in front of him. The crossed fingers were purple-looking with large veins that protruded over the backs of his hands. A large gold ring with a ruby adorned the index finger of one hand. Gilles tried to focus on the ring for a moment before he moved his eyes back to the magistrate's, before he delivered his answer. He must not falter now. He must get it right.

"From experience with trade, I expect. I don't know for certain." Gilles answered. He would have to watch his answers more carefully now and take more time without seeming to take more time.

"How much do you know of this man? You have been seen at his offices here in Rouen on more than one occasion. Are you not in league with him and also plotting to overthrow the King?"

"Non, Msr. I do *not* know him that well, except as a business associate. I have been to his offices to discuss our business relations on only one occasion that I can recall."

"You spent weeks with this man in a foreign country where there are few others who speak your native language, living with him day and night, and you say you scarcely know him?"

Gilles thought of all the people who spoke French in Amsterdam, the Netherlanders and the Reformees as well as the sailors and was struck by the ridiculousness of this accusation. The magistrate obviously knew nothing of the Netherlands and had already formed an opinion. Gilles formed his words carefully.

"We spoke only of business and women. What other parts of his life there may be, I am not aware." Gilles prayed they would not see this lie for what it was. He really didn't know *exactly* what other parts of his life there were, other than whatever business it was that transpired between Jean Durie and the Marranos. Gilles had never asked about *that*, not directly.

"Was there not money that changed hands between you both and this Hendrick Hendricks in his tavern in the Netherlands?"

Gilles was treading on thin ice. Who had seen money pass between Jean and Hendrick? Working directly with foreigners in order to avoid French taxes was a serious matter. Could anyone have really seen the money he handed to Hendrick when he left? How much of what they had been saying had been overheard? Gilles could not be sure and he did not have the time to think it through.

"You are obviously still under Durie's malevolent influence. Do you still profess yourself to be innocent?"

The magistrate was growing impatient even in the few seconds that Gilles had hesitated.

"I do not know why Msr. Durie handed him money. I handed Msr. Hendrick money to pay my account; for my meals, my room, and my drinks, and I guess Msr. Durie was giving him money for the same."

This seemed to both annoy and quiet the magistrate all at the same time and Gilles did not know if this was a good or bad turn of events. Gilles ventured another line of argument, hoping to end the line of questioning, once and for all.

"Monsieur, if there *was* an evil influence, I was not aware of it or I would certainly have resisted! I am loyal to our king and loyal to our church."

The magistrate had never taken his eyes off him and now Gilles was able to fully return his gaze. It was the truth.

The magistrate suddenly broke eye contact, though and nodded to one of the five. The man left the room by way of another door, a door just behind the judge. Gilles and the magistrate continued their staring contest for long moments.

"You are aware of how serious these charges are?" the magistrate asked Gilles pointedly. "Do you profess then to be an innocent who is unaware of how your conduct could indicate your guilt?"

"Oui, Msr.," Gilles replied meekly.

Charges? The magistrate was down to two at best, his friendship with Jean Durie, whoever or whatever he might be, and possibly tax evasion. How else could Gilles respectfully answer?

The door behind the judge opened again and the man who had left did not return alone but to Gilles' shock, he returned dragging behind him a bloodied and bound Jean Durie. Blood stained all of his clothing, dried brown blood on his torn shirt and coat, fresher red stains on the rest of him. Cuts and bruises covered his face and Gilles realized that Jean had the same clothes on that he had last seen him in. Had he been locked up and beaten for the last few days? Jean Durie had not escaped and it seemed unlikely as well that he had been the *cause* of Gilles' misery if he had been mistreated so badly. This realization brought to Gilles a surge of guilt, that his own detention had certainly been much better than Jean's, and that he had spent all of his time bemoaning the terrible conditions but in fact, he had not suffered any real physical harm.

As usual, Gilles was unable to read anything in Jean's face, even looking beyond the discolorations and swelling. What kind of a man was Jean and what. life had he lived that he could conceal his pain and justifiable anger after such maltreatment?

Gilles was badly shaken, realizing that they could take him off to the same fate next and there was nothing that anyone, even his father, could do to stop it. The magistrate must have seen the change in Gilles' demeanor for he suddenly took on a kindly, almost fatherly, air.

"You know this man and you say that he was hired as a family advisor, Gilles?"

"Oui, Msr."

"And yet you claim that he has not in any way corrupted you?"

"Non, he has not, Msr."

"But you spent time alone with him when you are not conducting business in Amsterdam, is this not so?"

"Oui, sometimes, Msr."

"Discussing women, you told me."

"Oui, Msr."

"And you are unaware of his meeting with Spanish spies or that he contrived to marry into one of the best families in France? He has *ingratiated* himself with this girl's father in order to gain access to important financial information and state secrets that concern the King *himself*. He tried to pass as one of us."

"I'm sorry, I don't understand," Gilles said. What was the magistrate saying?

The judge lost his temper and exclaimed *"This man Durie is a Jew!"*

How could it be so? There were none to speak of in France. Gilles couldn't make sense of Jean Durie at all so he had just left all of his nagging suspicions undisturbed in a dark corner of his mind.

"You are not totally surprised by this then?" the magistrate asked, the sharp edge back in his voice.

"Oui, I *am* surprised, Msr." Gilles tried to look surprised and as if his momentary lack of response was shock. It *was* shock. Gilles' statement and actions were apparently believable because the magistrate seemed somewhat satisfied and more sympathetic toward Gilles as he spoke again.

"I can see that this man has deceived you, too. He has *unnatural* powers of persuasion and we had him examined for the mark of the devil when we took him into custody. It is perhaps not the fault of one as young as you not to have seen the monster for what he truly is."

Gilles was all for saving himself but he was getting the uncomfortable feeling that things were getting worse for Jean even as they were getting better for him, perhaps *because* of him. Even if he was a Jew, Gilles certainly did not want to make it any worse for Jean.

What did they mean by the mark of the devil? He had never seen any marks, even when Jean changed out of his wet shirts at sea. Gilles began to have a queasy feeling in his stomach again. Maybe they wouldn't be sentenced to death; maybe they would only have to serve prison sentences. Gilles hated the thought of going back to his cell but he hated the promise of death or beatings even more.

The Magistrate continued, "We now know that the young woman who was Durie's pawn was not an accomplice, only an innocent victim of his treacherous intentions. Although she has neither been profaned nor soiled by him, Durie's criminal *intent* was there. Jean Durie's sentence has already been pronounced but we are here to decide *your* complicity or lack thereof. I believe that you are *innocent*."

Gilles' heart leapt with joy until the magistrate held up his hand and started speaking again.

Gilles Louis Charles Montroville, you will acknowledge to this court and to God and country that this Jean Durie attempted to enlist your help in his seditious quest by deceiving you as to the nature of his intentions and that he regularly met with Spanish spies in the Netherlands. You will be sent to live for the next few years in the cloisters and if your behavior there is good, you will then be allowed to enter the Chateau de Gaillon where you can rededicate your life and your soul to our Savior."

Gilles fully understood the terms of his acquittal right away: He could save himself by condemning Jean Durie to death and by joining the clergy, probably forever. Gilles thought of the damp darkness of the cathedrals and churches, darker even than the counting houses. He thought of the darkness that had entered his friend Claude's eyes after he had joined the church and he thought of the cowering Marranos. They had not resisted, they had submitted. Gilles' father made a movement that was visible in his peripheral field of vision. His father nodded his head very slowly, just once.

"Do it, boy!" he was saying. *"Do it now!"*

Gilles could also see Jean Durie from the corner of his other eye, standing in front of the five men. His bruised and torn face showed no emotion, no innermost thoughts.

"A death mask," Gilles thought. *"He has already accepted the sentence."*

"Msr. Montroville, we await your decision on the acceptance of our *generous* offer of salvation," the magistrate said irritably, impatiently tapping the finger with the ring on it.

Gilles looked up at the magistrate and swallowed a large lump in his throat. Gilles spoke clearly.

"He has never deceived me."

He was not sure at first that it was his own voice, let alone why he said it. He heard his father gasp and saw something change in Jean Durie's eyes, just for a split second before they returned to their mirrored exteriors. The magistrate's face was quiet rage.

"Take both of them away to the prison, then. They will not have long to wait and they can go to hell together."

The magistrate waved them off with the gold-ringed hand and angrily got up from his seat, annoyed that he had wasted his afternoon by trying to help a boy from a good family who would not accept help. Soldiers grabbed Gilles almost before he finished picking up his cloak. Gilles looked back over their heads and could see his father.

It was a terrible thing, seeing the emotion on his father's face, emotion that he had never witnessed before. Jean Montroville seemed to be asking, *"Why, Gilles? Why?"* Gilles was dragged away before he had any time to communicate anything to his father and in a sense it was more merciful that way because he couldn't explain, not even to himself, what he had just done.

He and Jean Durie were taken outside the back door and put into the wagon that would take them to the main jail. The soldiers shoved them into the wagon and then climbed up to sit across from them. Jean didn't look at Gilles at all but sat quietly next to him, upright with dignity and detachment, saying nothing. His hands were still bound but Gilles' were not and the thought occurred to him that *this* was the time to escape.

Gilles knew that Jean Durie could not escape, not with the injuries and not with the ropes on his hands. *It didn't matter, though.* Gilles needed to try, to save himself and Jean's fate would be the same, regardless of whether Gilles was successful or not. Gilles looked across the guards and beyond them. The wagon was open and he could probably jump off and be gone before they could fire a shot or run after him. It was a distance to the ground. Were his ribs healed enough to make the jump? What if he broke his leg or turned his ankle?

In the end, he didn't know why, but Gilles did not attempt his escape and too soon they were nearing the prison. The trip was not a long one and now thunderstorms were rolling in. The first raindrops fell as they passed the guard house where Gilles had been held earlier. Gilles wondered if Rene could see the wagon going by. Moments later they had arrived at the prison itself. There were no windows in these cells, only small openings that were too small for a man to fit through. The stone building smelled of urine and of something else, something damp and fungus-like. Gilles and Jean were pulled out of the wagon and led inside, down a long stone corridor. The guards removed Jean's bonds at the door of the cell before both men were roughly pushed inside. As Gilles' stood there, his eyes adjusting to the darkness, he could see as well as hear and smell dozens of souls all around him.

One prisoner at the door greeted the guards as a comrade and the guards spoke to him in a friendly manner.

"Here are two more for the fires, Martin. Keep an eye on them for us."

Martin nodded and the guard threw him a small coin and he snapped it up the way that Wolf took food that had been purloined from the kitchen help.

As his eyes adjusted, Gilles saw about forty men, each taking up their spaces against the walls and each staring at the newcomers. One man paced around, arms folded, barely pausing to note their arrival. Another lying in the middle of the floor appeared to be either asleep or dead.

"Welcome to the place of the dead, gentlemen, or the soon to be dead," one man said by way of a welcome. Jean looked around and started walking over toward an open space along the wall.

"Best not be going there, that's Poteet's spot," the welcoming man said.

It was too dark to see the voice's face clearly and Gilles thought the disembodied voice could have come from the heavens or just as easily, from hell.

Another voice called out, "There's room over here; he won't be coming back."

Jean made his way over to the voice, stepping over the dead man and regardless of whether Jean wanted him there or not, Gilles followed, staying as close to Jean Durie as was possible. It was a small space but they both squeezed into it and sat down against the wall.

A man somewhere was coughing, a continual hack that was hard to ignore. Gilles looked over but in the dim light he couldn't see much of the coughing man, either.

"Don't worry, they have a cure for that," the voice next to them said. "What fine clothes you gentlemen have! You're too rich for thieves. Are you Reformees?"

The voice belonged to a man with a long, dark face. The specifics of the face's features were still hard to see in the dim light.

"Non," Gilles said.

Jean said nothing.

"Ah, that's too bad. My name is Villeneuve and I am proud to say that I am a Reformee. I'm pleased to make your acquaintance."

"Don't get him started," the welcoming voice called from across the room, "We'll tolerate no more of that religious rant! If there *really* was a god who cared about us, we wouldn't be here."

The cougher started up again. Gilles' eyes were slowly becoming used to the darkness. The cell looked as though it might have been built for half the number of men that were crowded into it. Only the far corner was empty of men and Gilles saw a shallow trough there. Obviously wastes were collected there and then were swept out through a small opening in the wall from time to time. They were not close to the trough or to the dead man and so their spot was a good one even if it might prove to be difficult to listen to Villeneuve's Huguenot sermons. Maybe Villeneuve wouldn't go on too much about his god but with death hanging over them all, it seemed unlikely that the man would remain silent on the subject for very long. Gilles' assessment was immediately proved correct as Villeneuve spoke again.

"There is indeed a wonderful god who watches over us all. France has been turned into a dung heap by the money changers, not by God," Villeneuve declared. "They guard the doors to their temple, filling their chests with gold and use fear and the power of the Catholic Church to keep everyone in line. If Jesus were here, he would certainly be burned as an agitator, too."

"One more word about your god and I'll break your face open like an egg," a deep voice from the other side of the room promised.

Gilles thought about Villeneuve's assessment. France had some problems right now but on the whole, he could not imagine any place in the world that was better, that is, setting aside his own personal situation at the moment.

"What place could be better than France? The Netherlands?" Gilles asked.

"*The Netherlands*? Ah, non! Paradise on earth! New France! I should *never* have come back to this gutter place of humanity," Villeneuve lamented.

"It's time for an omelet. You won't insult *my* country again."

A large and burley man walked over to them from the corner nearest the door. Even in the dim light, Gilles could see that the big man had a red face that was covered with open sores, the oozing and angry face made all the more menacing with a frame of matted red hair. Along with the anger, he carried a look of eager anticipation and Gilles knew instinctively that this man's principal excitement in life came from his inflicting pain on others. Gilles hoped that it was some other disease and not the fearsome contagion of the pox that drained from the man's face, the face that was now so close to his own. At the first punch, Gilles had already decided that he would run, climbing over Jean Durie if he had to escape that way.

"You have been in the wilderness for too long, Villeneuve, and living like the squirrels, you have *become* a squirrel. You take wild animals to mate with, too, don't you? That is, if you mate with anything at all, you pathetic little man!"

The aggressor bent over his intended victim, hands on his knees, looking directly into Villeneuve's eyes in a taunting way, enjoying the foreplay.

Villeneuve did not turn away though, but returned the gaze.

"You do not scare me, Poteet. All that you know are threats and thievery. It's too bad that you never found *your* way to God."

Villeneuve did not speak as though answering a challenge though, just as if it was a simple fact that everyone should know.

Poteet reached out and grabbed Villeneuve by the neck of his shirt with one of his massive hands. His upper arms were the size of hams and Gilles thought that he should be able to quite easily and quite quickly kill Villeneuve with one hand. What happened next was too fast for Gilles' eyes to follow but somehow Villeneuve had come up to the side of Poteet's arm and hit him in the forehead with a force that send the big man over backwards. Gilles scrambled to safety but looking back, he saw that Poteet had not released Villeneuve's shirt from his fist, and so the two men tumbled over the floor together as the other prisoners moved out of the way. The guards outside the door looked in briefly to satisfy their curiosity but made no effort at all to enter the cell. Fighting was a common enough occurrence and they expected that Poteet would win quickly, at the least within a blow or two. Whether a prisoner died in the prison or in the fires was not really of any importance, anyway: It saved the executioner's fee and the end result was the same.

Poteet regained his feet but in some way Villeneuve managed to trip his attacker, sending him over backwards. The altercation ended up with Villeneuve on top of the big man, his thumbs poking into Poteet's neck just under his jaw line. This had just the desired effect that Villeneuve intended.

"We can finish this now, Poteet, or I will leave you alone to live a while longer. You just stay on *your* side of the room and I will stay on *mine*, eh?"

The wiry Villeneuve pushed Poteet away without extracting any verbal concessions from his adversary. He stood looking at his attacker, not looking threatened at all but somehow reminding Gilles of a snake, calculating his strategy but ready to strike again. Poteet shrugged his clothing back into order and moved away, but he did not take his eyes off Villeneuve.

Everyone else in the room pretended not to notice. They did not know how they would fare against the big man if they had to defend themselves as Villeneuve had done. The cougher hacked again and a few people sniffed. One man got up and walked over to the trough to relieve himself. The tension broken, a few men started to talk together again but no one mentioned what had just happened.

"Is it always this crowded in here?" Gilles asked Villeneuve when he had taken up his place again next to the wiry little fighter.

"I've only been in here for two days," he replied. "They came and took us out sooner but I heard someone outside the door say that the main executioner was ill."

"Nothing serious, I hope," the man across the room said.

"They'll be back for us soon enough," Villeneuve assured them.

"And we will wave goodbye to you, Villeneuve, and listen for your dying screams," Poteet said.

"You lived in New France?" Gilles asked Villeneuve, ignoring Poteet.

"Yes, it is my home. I only returned here because my sister was dying. I didn't get to see her before she died, though."

"Awww!" Poteet interjected from across the room but he was fast losing the small following that he had, those who were beginning to see him for the coward that he was.

"I would have loved to have seen New France just once," Gilles sighed.

"It is something great to see! There are sparkling clean rivers with thundering rifts, overflowing with fish. The land is full of every kind of game you could hope for, birds, rabbit, deer and bear. There is *never* any hunger there because food is so plentiful. There are mountains that go up into the sky and split the clouds, thunder that rolls through the valleys making the sound of a cart rolling along cobbles for a very long way, lightning that breaks on the cliffs over the lakes and rolls down in fiery green wheels into the water …"

Villeneuve was losing himself as well as a few others in the reverie and Gilles had to wonder how much of the story was true and how much was fantasy. Villeneuve certainly could tell a good story.

"Who cares?" Poteet snarled. "What about women? And good wine? There's none of that over there in your wilderness!"

"I'll miss Rouen when I'm gone. I'll miss the smell of the fields here after the rain has stopped and the sun has come out, the scent of the apple blossoms in the spring, the sound of the bees, and the lambs on the hills in the spring," the voice from the welcoming man across the room spoke.

"You must not even *think* that way but trust that God will deliver us! We all have a life that we will miss when we are at last gone, someday far in the future Rapalie, but then we will go to an even *better* place," Villeneuve assured him.

Poteet shot back, "Don't start again, Villeneuve! There is only *one* religion and I applaud them for exterminating your *particular* kind of rat."

Villeneuve was unperturbed. "A true defender of the faith, just like the black robes of the towns in New France; and yet few of them ever set foot outside their woodland palaces to see God's creations or to minister to anyone who might truly need them. They prefer to lie in wait and set upon any unsuspecting person who enters the city looking for help in the hopes of selling them their god, of turning them from their so-called heathen ways. The Church could learn much about fraternity and God from the savages. The King has declared New France to be a purely Catholic territory but that is his own little self-deception."

"My cousin left France and traveled to New Amsterdam with the Dutch," Rapalie offered.

"After I escape this place, I will live outdoors always and will never again live inside a building. I will just take in the smell of the trees and the earth with each breath," Villeneuve said. "The wilderness is my cathedral, my place of worship."

"*Villeneuve,*" Poteet said. "*Villeneuve.*" He repeated the name again and sneered. "*New City*! What is your *real* name? The damned Huguenots are fond of changing their names, playing word games with the meanings of their names, fond of perverting their own names and perverting God's word!"

Villeneuve ignored him still. "Living outside among God's works, done by His own hand, is a glorious thing, Gilles. You can't stand the smell of mankind that abides in the houses when you are used to being outside."

"If I could leave, I would love to visit there," Gilles said. "I would have to see if my wife would go with me, though."

"You are married? What is your wife like?" Rapalie called over, anxious for a different diversion.

"Well, she is not my wife *yet*. We are to be married next month," Gilles replied, "*Were* to be married next month." Sadness crept into the edges of his voice.

Poteet snorted. "Not now you won't be, not unless she likes to have relations with a burnt and headless corpse." He laughed an ugly laugh.

Gilles shuddered at the thought but it brought him back from future fantasy to present reality. He noticed that Jean, who was still beside him, had not uttered a single word since they had left the magistrate's chambers and the hearing. Perhaps now that Gilles knew Jean's secret, Jean would want nothing to do with him. Was Jean more seriously injured than Gilles had realized or was it humiliation that kept him silent? Perhaps Jean blamed Gilles for not testifying well enough to get them both released. It could be that Jean worried about the men in this room, that if they ever found out that he was a Jew, they would kill him on the spot for the simple sport of it. Gilles dared not ask directly about any of these things on the off chance that someone might overhear them. He decided to try to engage Jean Durie in conversation, though.

"How long do you think we'll be in here, Jean? Will we be taken out together?"

"I don't know."

Jean was at least coherent. Gilles admitted to himself that he was glad Jean was here with him. It was not that he wished *either* of them to be here in this place but Gilles was afraid to be alone, afraid to die alone. Did anyone ever outgrow the feeling of wanting to be accompanied by someone through the darkest passages in life? Gilles had never known a time as dark as this one. It had never *occurred* to him before that he would ever experience anything like this in his lifetime.

Supper arrived and the fare was exactly what Gilles had expected: It was the mystery stew again but there was no meat to be found in it, only occasional pieces of bone. The men lined up and were given worn and splintery wooden bowls and spoons that did not look very clean. Poteet was first, of course, and Villeneuve was only two men behind him. They passed each other when Poteet returned with his food. The adversaries' eyes met for a moment but there was no incident. Jean joined the line and received his ration but he set his bowl down without even tasting it when he returned to his seat. Some of the men said no prayers over the food at all but others said the Catholic prayers. If the Reformees wanted to say their own prayers, no one dared to say them aloud except for Villeneuve who said his in French, clearly but quietly. The food was not even as good as the food in Gilles' last prison but Gilles was starving and so he choked it down, giving thanks and also praying that it would not kill him or make him very sick. He tried to be grateful for the sustenance but he found it difficult to say the prayers at all.

"I see Martin got a bigger share and an extra piece of bread," Gilles said quietly to Villeneuve.

"Yes, he was brought in to be burned six months ago but they lost his paperwork, his main accusers all died of the plague, and the executioners forgot about him. Now he tells tales about us to the guards in the hopes that they will forget to burn him, maybe even let him go free one day. They can't do that though: Someone might be out there, sick but recovering, someone who would come and ask for him one day. In the meantime, he collects pieces of silver for all of his betrayals."

"Do they always come in threes when they open the door?" Jean spoke at last and he addressed Villeneuve, nodding in the direction of the guards. He wiped perspiration from his forehead onto his ragged sleeve.

"At dinner, yes. There are armed men outside behind them too. There are more of us than them but no one wants to be the first man to die. Instead we will all go to our deaths in an orderly way, like lambs at Easter time. No one is left here long enough to plan an escape, no one except Martin who would tell the guards anyway."

Villeneuve chewed thoughtfully on some part of the stew, perhaps the gristle or maybe on the tough and stringy beans. Gilles was hopeful now though: If Jean was asking questions and considering his options, things would be all right. Others put their faith in God but Gilles had faith in Jean Durie, that he would find the way out, just as long as he had enough time to study it, to plan it and to execute it.

Jean watched the line of prisoners. Now most of them had their bowls of dinner. Gilles could see him sizing up the situation outside the door although others might believe that Durie was simply daydreaming. Jean's hidden feelings and quiet agendas were obviously longtime characteristics of his, something else that he must have learned in his youngest days. Gilles wondered how a Jew could just pass for a Christian and how Durie could have advanced himself so far in France. Gilles also wondered if there were many others like Jean who walked among them, traveling unknown and unrecognized and if they were all a little unusual, all like Jean: Gilles supposed not on both counts.

When they were finished with their meal, the men brought their empty bowls and spoons over to the door for the guards to collect.

Rapalie noted, "The same fine recipe and *all* the prisons have it."

"How may prisons have you been in?" someone asked him.

"Only two, but happily, I feel sure that this will be the last one."

"Rapalie thinks he is a funny man," Poteet growled.

Gilles could see Jean's eyes travel over the walls. Even the hole behind the trough was viewed but Gilles could see for himself that it was far too small for any man to fit through. There was no escape route other than through the door.

A boy was thrown into the room, handed a bowl of stew and a spoon and told to eat it quickly or he would have nothing until the morning. Gilles felt sorry for him as the boy looked to be no older than fifteen and after a few more minutes of watching him, Gilles discovered that he was blind as well. The boy ate the food quickly without complaint starting and finishing it on the spot where it was handed to him and when he was done, he handed the bowl back to the voices in front of him. He stood where he had landed for some time until one man approached him and helped him over to a seat by the wall. The door closed, the key scraped in the lock and the bolt was thrown on the other side. Jean got up and wandered toward the door, looking like he was simply stretching and exercising his legs.

"I would have liked to have seen the new cities across the ocean," Gilles told Villeneuve again. "Tell me more about them."

Villeneuve told stories similar to the ones Gilles had heard from Hendrick, of the rivers running heavy with fish, the woods filled with game, the wonderful smells and opportunity around every corner. He told of the native people and that some were gentle and some were warlike but that there were many different savages, all speaking different languages, hundreds of languages, hundreds of nations.

"There are towns they are building," Villeneuve continued. "As you go up the river from the ocean, there will be the city they are trying to establish, Quebec, a fortified city on the side of a small mountain. Sometimes you do not even know that you are on a river because it is as wide as the ocean! It will probably be a fine city someday but more suited to bureaucrats than to real businessmen like me."

Gilles tried not to smile. Villeneuve *did* look as though he spent most of his time living in the woods. He was amused that Villeneuve thought of himself as a "businessman."

"The next settlement is Trois Rivieres and the most important one of all, for most of the trade goes through there. The French governors talk about building another settlement soon on the side of a mountain further up, Mount Royal, but that will never amount to much. The St. Laurent River trade comes from the savage lands far to the west and the large lakes around the great Huron Empire. The ships from Europe come in from the east and trade goods come up from the New England colonies to the south over Pitonbowk, or Champlain's Lake as it is sometimes called, and up the North River from the Dutch and English territories to the south. You can stay all year in Trois Rivieres and make a fortune if you are a sharp trader! Anything you need to buy, anything at all, can be found there. I am sure that it will be the greatest city in all of the world one day."

"Is your favorite place Three Rivers, then?" Gilles asked.

"Trois Rivieres? Mais non! I prefer not to see *any* cities at all, though they might be smaller than many in France. I make my home in the Sokoki mountains to the west of Lac Pitonbowk and south of the French settlements. I only go to Trois Rivieres during the spring trading time and then I only stay there for about a week. We catch up on gossip with each other as we sit around the fires."

"What do you do all winter, nothing?" Gilles asked.

"Winter is the busiest time of all! I go out on snow walking shoes to check my trap lines and check on my trees that give us sinzibukwud syrup in the spring. Of course sometimes the storms come across the lakes bringing us snow and always it is higher than the rooftops unless you keep it away. We have to watch the weather when we know that a bad winter is coming and there are years when we don't think we will even make it through alive to the January thaw, let alone to May."

Gilles didn't understand much of what Villeneuve was saying. He didn't want to appear stupid but he did want to understand. Perhaps Villeneuve was exaggerating.

"So you can tell when a bad winter is coming?" Gilles started at the top of his list of questions.

"Of course, yes!" Villeneuve laughed. "The signs are obvious and if the North River freezes across before Christmas, well, you know it will be a hard winter."

"What is the January thaw?"

"It comes every January. Outlanders often think it is spring so we call it 'Fool's Spring'. All the snow starts to melt and the air is so warm that you have to open the flap of your shelter to sleep at night … that is, if the high winds don't take your wigwam completely away for you! It did that to me a few times until I learned how to build it just so."

"What do you do all winter, besides look for food?"

"We visit each other's houses, sit by the fire, tell stories and exchange news from other villages."

Gilles digested this for a moment. It sounded like Villeneuve vastly preferred the company of savages to his own kind.

Villeneuve told a few stories and along the way he mentioned too many savage tribes for Gilles to keep track of them all, the Mohican, Iroquois, Abenaqui, Mic-Mac, Pequot, Huron and Lenni Lenape among them. Villeneuve ended his tales about the lands across the sea and then told Gilles about the sickness of his sister and his wish to see her one last time before her death. She was already dead though when he arrived in France and before he could get on a ship to take him back to the colonial provinces, an old neighbor told the authorities of his arrival.

Gilles was taken aback that Villeneuve wasn't the least bit embarrassed or ashamed that he was a wanted man, both in France and across the sea, for his anti-Church Reformee activities. Villeneuve even admitted that he had interfered with attempts to convert the savages to The Faith and stated unequivocally that the savages should be allowed to keep their *own* beliefs. Villeneuve explained to Gilles that the authorities were generally not quick to go after trouble makers across the sea when there were bigger problems to deal with at home everyday, but with Villeneuve conveniently in France and justice so accessible here, it was quite another story.

Jean Durie, who usually had a great interest in such narratives about the new world, had not been sitting with them but had been slowly walking the periphery of the room. He returned to Gilles and Villeneuve now, his wanderings completed, pulled Gilles and Villeneuve aside and said in a very quiet voice that both men could barely hear, "It must be tomorrow at dinner. For it to work, we will need to organize the others *just* before it happens, in case anyone feels the need to confess to the guards at any time before that. We will need Poteet's help though, and must enlist his cooperation now."

"Why do we need *him*?" Villeneuve asked with noticeable irritation in his voice.

"Because he is a strong man and capable of much diversion. Alone in the woods may be the best way in New France but here in this place we *must* work together."

Villeneuve was quiet for a moment, and then nodded acquiescence to Jean.

"Do you want me to talk to him? He has no grudge against me," Gilles suggested.

"Non. This is the kind of work that I do best. If I have had any kind of training or experience in my life to prepare me for this moment, I need to summon all of my knowledge now to persuade our new best friend to work with us. If we all work together, three, at most, six of us will die and the others will live. I will go first and lead the escape."

"Very noble," Villeneuve said, "but why sacrifice yourself?" he asked suspiciously.

"Nobility has nothing to do with it," Jean said curtly. "My life is finished any way I look at it and I am ready to quit this place no matter where I end up next. I have lost everything that is dear to me and if I can leave someone else with another chance at life on my way out, then that is the choice I make, not to just allow others to be taken if I am to die anyway. Besides, I'm hoping I will live or at least die more quickly."

Jean looked at Gilles briefly for the first time since before their trial but quickly broke eye contact and got up to talk to Poteet before Gilles could say or ask him anything. Gilles had the feeling that Jean was trying to save him, perhaps in repayment for his loyalty at the hearing or perhaps just because they had been friends. Gilles wanted to talk Jean out of the foolish plan but he knew too well that Jean would not be moved from his decision. The only way that Gilles could repay the favor would be to escape and to live.

Gilles tried to pretend that he was not looking at Jean and Poteet but it was difficult. Gilles saw the look of distrust from the corner of Poteet's eye when Jean walked over and then Gilles saw the guarded look that came over his scabbed face. Poteet raised his voice just once until Jean interjected something and then both men lowered their voices. Two men from across the room were watching the exchange between Jean and Poteet with great interest, as was Martin.

"Those two aren't spies?" Gilles asked Villeneuve nervously.

"If they are, they must be paying them a great deal to stay in here like this. Non, more likely they are hoping it is an escape scheme that they can join."

Martin wandered over near Poteet but the big man suddenly got up, sending Martin scurrying away in a panic and nearly causing Gilles to laugh out loud. Gilles pulled his knees up to his chest and rested his arms and head, pretending to rest as he continued to watch Jean out of the corner of his eye. Jean touched Poteet's sleeve and it was at that moment that Gilles knew it was done: Gilles had seen that touch many times before, knew that it was the close to the sale, and that Jean Durie had once again received what he had set out for.

Jean Durie returned to Gilles soon after. "It's done. Poteet will provide the diversion and I will rush the door. We will select three men as backup to me and it will be a fait accompli. We will have to go out the same way we came in, to the right. It seems the surest open route but we don't know how many soldiers with guns are between us and the outside." Jean pushed back a damp and sweaty strand of hair.

"I will be one of the three then," Gilles volunteered.

"And I, too," Villeneuve added quickly.

"Non, you two need to be in the *middle*. Many of the men escaping will need help, especially if they are unfamiliar with the city, and the hope is that they can elude their captors until night falls. *You* know the dark," Jean said to Villeneuve "and *you* know the city," he nodded to Gilles although Gilles wondered if that was his true rationale for wanting him farther back from the front line.

"We need to get some good rest tonight. We will need our wits and energy tomorrow if this is going to work. Heading to the docks after seems the best option," Jean said. "If there are enough of you, you can probably commandeer a ship during the night and then try to make it out into open water before the alarm is raised on the coast. If you are still alive after that, my first choice would be the northeast route to Scotland. If there are no ships in Rouen, find cover in the countryside and travel throughout the night, heading to the western provinces that are more … sympathetic."

Gilles realized now that Jean hadn't decided *absolutely* that the docks were the best alternative and Gilles was somewhat nervous about that small bit of indecisiveness on Jean's part. The King's horsemen on the shore *could* dog them all the way to the ocean even if they managed to stay ahead of them or worse, summon ships to intercept them before they even got there. In fact, the soldiers could hunt them *all* down in no time at all even if anyone managed to make it out of the prison alive. The plan was flawed but it was the only plan they had and with time running out, there was little choice but to put it into action and see what it could do for them to extend their lives.

"Well, there is always tomorrow to work out the details if we manage to live through the entire day and are not taken out to be executed first," Gilles thought.

He took solace in the knowledge that the executions required an audience and did not take place during the night. He only hoped that tomorrow morning the executioner would still be ill and that the authorities would still have no replacement.

They had just settled down to sleep for the night when Martin walked over to them. Gilles worried that he was going to ask about their earlier conversation with Poteet but he had something else in mind.

"You!" he kicked Gilles' foot. "Nice clothes! I'm cold. Give me that cloak under your head."

Gilles sat up, ready to defend his property. "And what if I don't?"

"Then I will call the guard and tell him that you are making trouble and don't need to wait for the executioner."

Gilles felt Jean's hand clamp down his arm. "The poor man is cold, Gilles. Have you no Christian charity? *Give him* your cloak."

Gilles did not want to let go of this last piece of home but at Jean's insistence, reluctantly he handed it over to Martin.

"That's better," Martin grinned. "I'd take your clothes, too, but they wouldn't fit me. Perhaps when they take you to the fires, though, I will exchange my clothes with yours. There is no need to burn up perfectly fine clothes!" Martin snickered as he moved back to his spot by the door, caressing the softness of Gilles' cloak as he went.

Gilles sighed and tried to use his arm for a pillow. All was quiet around him for a few minutes except for the sounds of snoring and deep breathing from the other prisoners but then Jean Durie spoke quietly to Gilles.

"*Why* Gilles? I don't understand; *why* did you not save yourself? Are you *that much* of a fool?"

"Oui," Gilles replied. "Blame yourself for your poor choice of friends."

Gilles tried to sleep but he could see by the light coming from the trough's drain that the sun had not gone down yet and a dozen scenarios played out in his head, many ending with their being shot, run through with a sword, or caught and hanged on the spot. He tried to imagine a successful conclusion but every time he did so, it usually seemed to involve stepping over Jean Durie's lifeless body.

He hadn't been paying attention to it before but now he realized that his skin felt as if hundreds of ants were walking all over it, and had felt like this for at least the last few hours. The sensation was unnerving but since there was nothing he could do about it, he did his best to ignore it. The cougher kept Gilles awake, too, and he was not used to sleeping in a room with so many other men. It did remind him of his first night in Amsterdam, sleeping in the common chamber and this thought cheered him up for a moment. Gilles was sorry that he could not see Amsterdam one more time and sorry that he would probably not be able to say goodbye to his family, no matter what was to happen on the morrow.

Maybe he could stow away on a ship that was going to England, if he made it out: Gilles had heard that they often kidnapped sailors and Gilles could speak enough English to get by. The French wouldn't be looking for him there, but then again, he might not be able to escape from an English sea captain for years to come. If he ever made his way to complete freedom, then maybe he could send for Marie. Ah, Marie.

All of these thoughts and more went through his head but finally exhaustion overtook him as he fell asleep and started to dream. He and Jean were taken by wagon to a hill with crosses on it. The hill was covered with roses, and the thorns tore at Gilles' flesh as he struggled along from the wagon to the cross, a cross that resembled the pillories he had seen in Amsterdam. They were both nailed to the crosses and Gilles marveled that it did not hurt that much although blood ran down his legs, hands and arms. A little boy threw rocks up at him until his mother scolded the child and led him away. Poteet smiled and waved up at them from down below.

"They let thieves go, you know," Poteet informed him, then walked away.

Gilles' mother, sisters, and Marie were there, all dressed in black and weeping at the foot of his cross. Jean was no longer on the cross next to him and his sudden disappearance frightened Gilles. A priest said prayers and then lit fires at the base of each crucifix. The fires glowed like individual candles on the vast altar of the hills, growing in intensity and then consuming everything. Gilles wondered if the blackened and weakened timbers of his cross would crash over first and the fall would kill him or if the framework would hold, burning him to death. He wondered which death would be more painful. A guard with a gun stood at the base of the cross so Gilles thought that perhaps he would just be shot first, the leaden balls tearing hot, jagged holes through his skin, bones, and vital organs.

His family had disappeared now, and Gilles was left completely alone. There was only the fire burning at the foot of his cross but the smell of the smoke grew stronger.

"Hail Mary ..." he began, "blessed art thou ... the hour of our death ..."

His lungs burned and he coughed as he awoke and realized that the smoke was not a dream at all, that the prison cell was filling with smoke.

He shook Jean awake, also coughing in his sleep and together they woke Villeneuve.

"They save themselves the trouble of moving us to the fires!" Villeneuve cried.

Poteet woke up and was immediately alert; he jumped to his feet and ran toward the door, perhaps with the intention of breaking it down, but he had not reached the door yet when it swung open, slamming hard against the stone wall and the top of Martin's head as it did so. Two priests carrying bundles ran inside the cell before any of the detainees regained their senses enough to realize what was happening.

"Gilles Montroville!" one of the priests called out and Gilles knew in an instant that it was his father's voice.

"Over here!"

"Gilles, this way!"

His father and Claude were dressed in the priest's robes and they each carried another robe which they quickly threw over Gilles and Jean in one quick motion, with one hand while dragging them back toward the open door with the other. More of the prisoners were awake and on their feet now, running toward the open door as well. Only Martin sat motionless, propped up against the wall with blood pouring into his eyes from the dripping gash on his head. He held his injured head in both hands as the escaping prisoners either stepped over him or on top of him to get outside to freedom. On his way out, Gilles only paused long enough to kick Martin over and take back his stolen cloak before he pushed out into the hall with the rest of the prisoners, all of them now running and all of them now pushing each other, surging forward toward freedom.

The corridor between the cells was complete confusion with thick smoke on the right, obscuring the path of their planned escape route. In spite of the smoky cloud that lay in front of them, most of the prisoners chose to plunge into the smoke, knowing that there was an unlocked door on the other side of the fire. There were only a few soldiers and guards to be seen, two of them trying to put out flames on their clothing and a few others looking dazed and trying to decide what to do next, but none of them making any attempt to apprehend any of the prisoners. Gilles saw prisoners that he did not recognize and there were far too many of them to be from their cell alone; it was obvious that the escape had been planned and that other cells in the prison had been vacated as well. Some of the escapees brandished small weapons or pulled guns out of the hands of the guards as they dove into the smoke, into the very substance that might have accompanied their death but was now graciously offering cover for their escape into a new beginning.

Gilles and his companions did not follow the men into the smoke, though: Another robed priest stood waiting for them at the corridor and led his four followers in the other direction, to the left, away from the smoky fire. The unknown priest led the way as Jean Montroville held Gilles' elbow and Claude escorted Jean Durie out. Gilles could hear shouts and breaking glass sounds from the mob behind them and although they were walking quickly, they were not running. The five priests moved forward with brisk and deliberate steps, hoods up, faces and hands completely covered by their robes

Another prisoner rushed past them from behind, running up the corridor and pushing them roughly aside. The sound of the footsteps approaching from the rear sent shocks of fear through Gilles but his relief afterwards was short-lived when a single prison guard stepped out of a shadowy doorway in front of them just after the running prisoner had passed through.

"*Stop!*" he ordered the five priests. "Stop in the name of God and King, *stop!*"

The unknown priest who had been leading the way pushed the soldier from their path with ease and then efficiently stabbed him with a long knife that he had been hiding up his sleeve. They wasted no time in committing the murder but continued walking to the end of the hall, around a corner and through an unlocked door to the outside.

A simple wagon that looked like the type priests would use stood there and when they reached the wagon, a man who had been holding the horses there let go of the reins and walked away into the darkness. The five priests climbed up and squeezed onto the bench seats. Large wine casks filled the back of the wagon and even from a distance, Gilles could smell the wine. Gilles believed the casks to be full because he could hear the contents sloshing around as the leading priest, the murdering priest, took up the reins and the wagon moved slowly forward. From inside the prison there were the cries of men and the sounds of boots running on the stone floors but those noises were becoming more distant, not just with their moving away but also due to the prisoners being mostly gone from the building by now.

The big work horses moved the wagon forward at a slow pace and the priests all sat wordlessly as they passed through the prison gate and then through the streets of Rouen, traveling in no particular hurry. Gilles could feel the weight of the barrels and he wondered why they had not brought a faster means of escape.

"Father," Gilles began, as he tried not to cough from all of the smoke that he had inhaled.

"Be quiet!" snarled the driving priest.

They headed toward the docks, crossing a large main street and then turning up a smaller street. It was only a few blocks to the water now. Gilles guessed that it was just before daybreak because the streets were completely empty except for a stray dog rooting through a pile of refuse, a drunken or perhaps dead man lying by the side of the road, and a man and woman in the shadows who surely thought that they would not be seen or heard by anyone on this night, and most especially not by a wagonload of priests.

The wagon pulled up to a stop just before they reached the water and the driving priest croaked, *"Now."*

Jean Montroville and Claude moved over to the barrels and pulled the tops up from two of them that turned out to be empty.

"Get in!" the driver barked at Gilles and Jean Durie.

Gilles still could not see the man's face but it must have been someone that his father trusted so Gilles obediently climbed inside although the fit was tight, even in the great barrel. The smell was overwhelming and he wondered if he would soon be drunk or dead from the fumes. He recalled now that he had once climbed inside a barrel when he was a child but one of his father's workers had yelled at Gilles to get out at once. The worker scolded Gilles and said that people *died* from the fumes if they were inside for very long. Claude threw the priest's robe and Gilles' retrieved cloak in on top of Gilles.

"I can't get in there." Gilles heard Jean Durie's voice, sounding oddly strained. It may have been the cask around Gilles that was distorting the sound.

"There are holes in the bottom and the plug is removable from the inside. You will not suffocate because you will not be in there for very long," Jean Montroville said in a low voice but Gilles noted that his father *did* sound harried.

"I *can't* get in there," Gilles heard Jean Durie say again.

"Get in there or we cut your throat now!" the other priest growled.

Gilles heard the reins drop to the floor of the wagon and saw the unknown priest pull out the blood-covered knife from his sleeve. Gilles had no doubt at all that he would kill Jean as promised for he had already killed one man tonight.

"He is right. You endanger us all. It will not be for very long, Jean," Msr. Montroville said.

"Make no sound if you wish to live, not even a cough! Someone will come for you soon!" the driver priest snarled. "I should never have included the bastard in the bargain!"

Jean moved at last to get into the barrel just as Gilles' father lifted the lid to cover Gilles' cask. Before his father closed the lid down over him, Gilles spoke his last words to him.

"Father, tell Marie I'll be back for her soon."

His father was silent for a moment before he answered.

"You can *never* come back; other arrangements have been made. Be safe, Gilles."

The lid was put on and tapped shut. Gilles found the removable plug and availed himself of the fresh air but it felt as if death itself had descended over him. The black emptiness that surrounded him was capped closed, the sad vintage of more than a century of bitter events. He could hear Jean Durie climbing into the keg beside him and Gilles also heard his father talking to Jean before that lid was clamped down as well.

"You know it was nothing personal? I was only trying to save my son."

"I know."

When both lids were in place, the wagon moved forward again. The fumes inside the cask were overpowering, even with the air hole. Gilles started to feel the comfort of the wine vapors and then he stopped worrying about whether he would survive. Did it matter much? He was to have been executed anyway. Marie was gone. He could never return to his home again, would never see it again. He did have his life but that was *all* that he had now. What had Jean been saying back at the prison?

It makes no difference; my life is over anyway.

The barrels were lifted from the wagon and set down again on the dock. Gilles could see none of this but he heard and felt everything; he was familiar with the activity from the outside and now he realized that he was experiencing it from the *inside*. His crossed ankles hurt from being pressed down against the wood as did his knees. He tried to keep his legs upright and cushion them with his cloak but the keg was designed for wine, not for the comfort of a large person sitting for a long time inside the container. He tried to spare his aching ankles by putting his hands under them but he ended up having his knuckles scraped on the splintery wood. Something in his pocket was digging into his thigh but he was too tightly packed in to shift it away to a better position.

Gilles heard the priest's wagon roll away, presumably taking his father and Claude with it. He heard the sound of approaching men and quickly put the air plug back into place. The barrel was turned on its side and rolled up the bumpy gangplank, making Gilles feel dizzy and sick. He heard the rope as it was tied around his barrel and then the barrel was hoisted up, swung over, and lowered down below the main deck, giving Gilles the feeling that he had briefly left his stomach behind. He made up his mind that he could *not* get sick in here, though: he would surely suffocate from it even if the sound and smell did not lead to his detection, apprehension and eventual execution.

The container came to rest at last with a jolt, somewhere down in the hold of the ship. After a short time, the noise of sailors moved all around the ship but no longer seemed very close to him. He had to remove the plug for some air now or

he was certain that he would die. He wondered if Jean Durie was still next to him
or even near him at all. Gilles panicked when he couldn't immediately locate the
string handle fashioned onto the plug but it had draped up over his knees, probably while he was being rolled along. Gilles pulled the stopper out of the wall of
the container and took his first breath of air in several minutes. Gilles' air hole
was lower than the level of his eyes so he could not see outside at all but he *did*
smell and feel the fresh air. It was just enough to make him wish for more of it,
but it was good to be able to breathe again: He was not going to suffocate after
all.

Gilles could feel the ship moving out toward the sea almost immediately
which was most unusual. Would he be wedged in this barrel, then, for the entire
journey? How long would that be? Where were they going? To England? As miserable as his situation was, Gilles decided that it was better to be uncomfortable
than to be dead. The ship must have been in the harbor, ready to go and just
waiting for them considering all the last minute details that usually kept the ships
in port until after sunrise. As it was, Gilles knew that they were probably sailing
in the darkness as Gilles judged the hour to be still before dawn. There would be
other ships sailing out behind them, and probably not very far behind them.
With all of the shipping activity at that time of day, it was a good plan because
there would be too many ships going out now to stop and search them all.

The lid on his barrel suddenly moved and Gilles' heart leapt with the sound. A
one-eyed man that Gilles presumed and hoped to be a sympathetic captain of the
vessel reached in and pulled him up by his collar, up onto his feet.

"Come with me, quickly! Be silent!" he said in a heavy Netherlands accent.

Gilles started to protest about his friend but the captain was ahead of him,
already pulling the top from another cask with a small pry bar. Jean was lying
very still at the bottom of his container, in fact, in an unconscious heap. The captain swore under his breath as Gilles tried to climb out of his own barrel, having
to expend a great deal of effort to do so successfully because his legs and feet were
shot through with pins and needles and his head felt as though he had been
drinking heavily all night long. The fresh air brought Jean around to consciousness again and the captain helped him out. Gilles held the two priest's robes and
his own cloak in one hand and steadied himself with the other, trying just to keep
his footing due to his physical disorientation and the motion of the ship. This
task was made even more challenging due to the small boat and Gilles' inability
to stand up without cracking his head on the overhead beams.

"This way!" the captain whispered.

He crawled across the top of the cargo, leading them over to a wall just in front of the tiller where he pulled out two wooden pegs. The upper section of the wall fell forward on leather hinges, revealing a small compartment that was about eight feet long by five feet wide and five feet high. Gilles supposed that it was always used for smuggling as he noted that it already had a chamber pot and a burlap bag inside.

The captain helped them in and admonished them, "Be quiet! Not all of my men know that you are aboard and they may discover you if you make any noise! I will come back for you when we reach Amsterdam."

Gilles and Jean climbed into the dark space as the captain quickly replaced the wall and the pegs from the outside. There was very nearly total darkness inside the hidden compartment but it was larger than the containers and it smelled better. Gilles listened as the captain moved across the containers in the hold, then climbed up the few creaking steps back to the top deck of the little vessel. Gilles *did* have the happy thought that if they were to escape to anywhere in the world, Amsterdam was where Gilles wanted to be going.

He had not recognized the captain or the ship. Maybe it was a Dutch ship or maybe Jean knew him. Gilles was quite certain that this was *not* one of his father's ships; surely his father would know that the authorities would be checking every one of those once word of Gilles' escape got out.

Gilles could see a little bit more as his eyes adjusted and as the sun started to come up. Light came down into the space from the hatch and penetrated the thin cracks in their outer wall. Gilles could see now that Jean did not look very well; he looked feverish. His friend had not fared well in the cask and he had not looked good at all when Gilles saw him in the courtroom. Gilles looked inside the burlap bag and discovered two jugs of water, biscuits, dried herring, and dried beef. It might be all that they would have to eat until they reached their destination but Gilles was grateful for it. He spread one of the priest's robes down on the floor for Jean and then fashioned a pillow for him from the other robe. Jean smiled in gratitude and then he put his head down on the pillow immediately.

If he had been in France, Gilles would have already sent for the physician. He seriously worried that Jean might have contracted the pox from Poteet and Gilles prayed that Jean wouldn't die before they reached the Netherlands. What would he do with his friend's body if he had to stay with it in the dark hole until then?

Gilles reminded himself that he might not have to worry about that at all; If it was the pox, Gilles could well be dead himself by the time they reached Amsterdam. They might die together after all. Since Gilles had already been in contact with Jean, it made no difference now if he shared his cloak with his friend. Gilles covered Jean with it and listened for news of their progress coming from the noises around the ship. He heard all of the routine sounds that he *wanted* to hear, the sounds that told him when things were going as expected; the rigging slapping against the wood, the water lapping at regular intervals against the sides. He heard the water rushing under the ship and the men chanting in rhythm as they pulled in or changed the sails and their calm pace as they moved nimbly across the decks securing lines. He heard the silky *shush* of the sails as they filled up with the wind and the clanks and clunks of the hardware against other metal rings and wooden spars. If this had been another time and under other circumstances, Gilles would be up there now, if not helping the crew, then just taking in the fresh air that would became more salty as they approached the ocean. Hopefully the good weather would quickly put distance between the ship and Rouen but they had a long distance to go yet before Gilles could relax.

Jean slept, shivering in his sleep while Gilles prayed. He prayed that there would not be any sounds of the ship being boarded and searched and he also prayed that Jean Durie would not die, cry out, or snore loudly in his sleep today. The authorities would quite probably kill the captain along with them if they were discovered. Jean still shivered, even under the cloak, so Gilles took off his jacket as well and put that over Jean to keep him warm.

He rested his back against the wall and looked at his sleeping friend. What had Jean been through? Gilles had all kinds of time now to catch up on his own thoughts. Jean's face was cut and bruised; his clothes were ripped and bloody. Gilles remembered how Jean always liked to dress in his very best clothes, sometimes changing his clothing several times in a single day.

There was no explanation as to how or why things in his life had taken such an unhappy turn. Was it only bad luck? A curse? What could he have done differently?

The answer was simply nothing at all. Gilles hoped that he and Jean Durie had escaped the fires and would escape death completely. He also hoped that his father would escape punishment for any complicity in his escape: It would be a terrible thing if his father was executed for helping them to escape and then they both died on the voyage to the Netherlands anyway. It was out of his hands now and in the hands of either God or the captain, whoever was now in charge of his future. Gilles was exhausted from his ordeal and felt that he could sleep now, too. He curled up next to his friend and soon he was fast asleep too.

He awoke to the ship pitching and heaving. He could hear excited shouts on the deck far above and the lines sliding across wood at a very rapid pace. The sails were being changed. At first he thought they were being boarded but then Gilles realized that they were in a storm. The jugs of water inside the burlap bag were hurled into Gilles' side and one of them leaked precious water out before Gilles could secure the stopper again. The chamber pot lurched as well, spilling its contents on the floor and on them too. Jean's body nearly left the floor with each great wave and then he woke up, too. It must have still been daytime because Gilles could still see a little in spite of the dark shadows. Some light came down to them from somewhere up above and Gilles thought that perhaps the captain's cabin was up there and the light might be coming from a lantern.

Jean looked around with feverishly wild eyes. "We will die here for certain!" he said to Gilles and then he whispered "Hail Mary, full of grace ..." He never finished the prayer though because abruptly he stopped and started chanting something else. "Yiskadol vyiskadash ..."

Gilles tried to quiet his friend. "We won't die, the ship will bring us safely into Amsterdam," he whispered.

"We will go down and die in this trap, in this oversized coffin! Damn, I can't remember all the words to *either* one ..."

"Hush!" Gilles moved next to his friend and grabbed his upper arm. He was afraid that he heard someone moving outside the compartment. He motioned to the wall and made a gesture for Jean to be quiet.

Jean nodded. He understood that someone might hear him but he was in a panicked state, rocking back and forth silently for a time, silent but still hugging his knees. Gilles had not known this before but now he understood that his friend could not tolerate confined places. Jean had surely been in hell while incarcerated in the prison. Gilles had no assurance that they would not die in the storm either, but he had faith that his father had put him in the care of a good captain, having heard stories since he was a small child of ships that had survived great storms. Gilles was reasonably sure that being found by the sailors would be imminently more of a danger to them than a mere storm. The waves continued to lift the ship up before they slammed it back down into the troughs again and again. Finally they seemed to find a regular rhythm and even though the waves seemed no better than before, they were more regular and more tolerable with their predictability. When they grew too tired to sit up alone any more, Gilles and Jean rested against each other; flesh was a better cushion than the walls but both men were bruised anew from encounters with the floor, walls, and each other inside the shuddering ship.

Sometime later Gilles awoke. He didn't remember falling asleep and the sea was much calmer. It was darker outside because he could see nothing at all. He felt around for Jean and the provisions and he did not have very far to reach in the small and confined space. Jean was asleep on the floor again but he still felt very warm to Gilles' touch; there was absolutely nothing he could do about that. He curled up next to Jean, making sure that his friend was covered up completely to help him sweat out the fever, and he waited for the morning to come.

The space was brighter. The water was moving freely and easily under the boat. Jean still slept. Gilles reached over to feel his forehead but Jean jumped at the touch.

"I didn't mean to wake you," Gilles whispered.

Jean's eye was still swollen but he looked a little bit more like himself now for the first time since their miseries had begun.

"Non, it's all right."

Jean looked around the space while Gilles opened the sack.

"I am almost starved to death. We have biscuits and water here."

He handed his friend a soggy biscuit and one of the jugs. There was a sudden noise at the outer wall and they shrank back against the side of their wooden cave but there was no place to hide, really. The wall came down and to their immediate relief, it was the captain who crouched outside the wall before them.

"Got your food? Gut, gut. Because of the storm I could not check on you until now. All is well with us and there is no sign of trouble, God willing. We hope to make Amsterdam on time. You will stay here until I come back for you and *stay quiet!*"

"Dank u," Gilles said, not knowing what else to say.

The captain shrugged and closed the wall up again.

"Thank you? I would not thank him! I should have died in prison instead of here!" Jean lashed out.

"We are still alive and headed for freedom. The man doesn't even know us and yet he risks his life for us; you could *at least* be grateful."

Gilles took a bite out of the biscuit. It was very hard inside and soggy on the outside but it tasted good to him. He needed some water from his jug to wash it down and he wished that *he* could change the water into wine. He said a silent prayer over the food because he really *was* grateful for the food but he didn't cross himself; it no longer felt comfortable to do so in front of Jean Durie.

"You can be sure that the captain has been paid well and we probably won't live long enough to see freedom, anyway," Jean grumbled.

"We just need to last another few hours." Gilles said. "We can talk quietly."

Gilles sounded like Rene now. Was that what Rene had been trying to do? To get Gilles to take his mind off his troubles? And now Rene was all alone, left to rot and die there, in all probability. At least if Gilles died *here*, he had tasted a small measure of freedom again before his death, he might *not* die by fire, and he had a friend to accompany him to freedom or to be with him as he died. Gilles was astonished to find that there *were* a few things to be thankful for, after all.

"I wonder what the arrangements are in Amsterdam," Gilles mused.

"That is taken care of, I'm sure. The captain will know and if he doesn't, I know a few places."

"We can stay at Hendrick's!" Gilles said, brightening up even more.

"No, we won't be seeing Hendrick. We have to stay far away from any place where we might be recognized and found. They can still bring us back, you know."

Gilles hadn't known. "Where will we go then, should we stay in the city at all?"

"There are places in the city that are hidden and safe. We can stay there until we decide where to go from there." Jean wrapped his arms around his legs and took a deep breath. "I wish we had more air in here."

The air seemed fine to Gilles. "I will bet you whatever money you have, that we will reach Amsterdam earlier than expected." Gilles tried to distract Jean from his discomfort.

"I have no money to bet. They took everything."

Gilles was never even searched during his confinement. He might have had a matchlock concealed on him for all his guards knew.

"I'll bet you then, your first day's wages at whatever job you find, that we will arrive ahead of schedule."

"And how will we even know this?" Jean asked, not sounding at all interested, "how will we know whether we are early or late?"

"We could have the captain settle the wager."

Jean was still not interested.

"All right, then, I will bet you your first day's wages that I can call two out of three coin tosses."

Gilles reached into his pocket for a coin. His hand touched the box with the pearl necklace but he wouldn't think about that now. He shoved the thought of it to the back of his mind and moved forward onto his knees. As he did so, the rosary fell out of his shirt.

Jean looked at it and although his face did not generally show his thoughts, Gilles believed that he had come to know what Jean was thinking, just by what he looked at and by the amount of time that he spent in looking at things.

"Well, I don't need this anymore. Father's good luck charm; I guess it worked." Gilles felt uncomfortable with it on but he worried a little that their current good luck might be broken if he took it off. After a moment of indecision, he decided that it was more uncomfortable to leave it on. He swiftly removed it from his neck and deposited it into his pocket.

"I never knew you to be such a religious man, or a gambling man either, for that matter," Jean observed. "It's peculiar all the different ways that imprisonment and facing death can change a man. Do you have a taste for strong drink and women now, too?"

Gilles saw that Jean had not lost his sense of humor due to these experiences, but the mention of women was not comfortable; both of their losses had been too great and too recent.

"Maybe I could learn to cultivate those," Gilles said.

He spread out the priest's cloak to deaden the noise of the coin when it dropped and then Gilles tossed it. "Two heads, one tail," Gilles whispered. It fell back into his hand, tails. A second toss was heads, as was the third.

"We can always make a living gaming if you don't get us both killed for cheating," Jean said.

They heard footsteps coming down the squeaking steps under the hatch and of a necessity they fell silent until the steps wandered back to the hatch and ascended again.

"All right, now that your first day's wages are mine, what else should we bet?" Gilles said.

"We can bet we will die in this hole and never reach Amsterdam where they seriously know how to play wagering games!" Jean said.

"That's no bet. We'll be fine, and besides, what would I win? I will bet you an excellent French meal in the best French establishment we can find that I can call these next three."

"All right, a good meal." Jean seemed mildly interested in the game now. "I will call two heads and a tail." Jean must have thought that the coin would come up that way every time.

"All right then. I call two tails and a head."

Gilles won the toss again. Jean grabbed the coin away from him and examined it.

"You are cheating somehow."

"How would I do that? It's a regular coin," Gilles replied but now he was smiling.

"All right then, do it again." Jean said.

"Ah, ah, ah! You have to tell me what you are wagering *first*," Gilles teased, clutching the coin to his chest.

"No I don't, just toss it!"

"Yes, yes, you do. It's my coin and we don't play unless we bet something." Gilles insisted.

"All right. I will bet you a gold ring that I win this time and *I* will toss the coin." Jean seemed satisfied with this arrangement.

"And the loser gives the winner a ring? Where will *you* get a gold ring?" Gilles asked.

"Where would *you* get one? I didn't understand there to be any constraints on time for repayment."

"All right then, a gold ring. Call it, Jean."

"Two heads and a tail. Now you call."

"Two tails and a head."

Both of them watched as the coin made its arc and landed back in Jean's hand. Two more tosses and Jean had thrown three heads.

"That is *just* our luck now," Jean said, "There is no winner."

"Then we will just keep tossing until there is a winner. You have to keep trying."

Gilles made the next round of tosses and Jean was the winner.

"You let me win that round," Jean accused his friend.

"How could I do that? Besides, why would I *want* to lose a gold ring? Anyway, I thought you said I was cheating."

"It's a silly game anyway, all this talk of gold and fine restaurants." Jean was looking over at the walls again.

"Well, we could eat all the way to Amsterdam but the food isn't that enjoyable and we would too soon finish it. We need to pass the time *somehow*."

Gilles was right, of course, and Jean might have seen that too if he took the time to think about it but he just sighed.

"Why did you do it, Gilles?" he asked as he shook his head from side to side.

"Are we back to that? I don't *know* why I did it! We are both alive, aren't we? Are you complaining?"

"I feel responsible for your life now, your young life. If *only* you had saved yourself! I will have to live with the burden that you have placed on me for the rest of my life, that your life has been ruined because of your association with me ..."

"I had no time to think of anything better to tell them than the truth. Anyway, I can take care of myself without any help from *you*."

Gilles thought now of all those men in their cells, condemned to death, their lives destroyed forever even if they were eventually released alive, and for what purpose?

For the truth or for lies?

Even if they *were* guilty of their crimes, did it really matter so much when it came to extinguishing a human life, to smashing a family into pieces? All of the great officials of the government and officers of the courts judged and condemned others as easily as they decided what to have for dinner each day. Everything was stripped from the prisoners with the exception of a few remaining choices: to tell the truth or to lie, to fight for their lives or to go quietly to their death.

"Don't you hate Jews too?" Jean asked Gilles, an odd expression on his face.

"I might if I knew any. Are you really one?" Gilles asked, not looking at him but closely examining a dent in the coin.

"They say I am," Jean mumbled.

"You mean you don't know?" Gilles looked up at him in puzzlement.

"It's complicated. Can we talk about something else?"

"I thought you wanted to talk about it. All right then, another toss," Gilles said, more than a little curious now about what Jean meant. "If I lose, I will buy you the best knife I can find for your carvings, and if you lose, you will buy me some good wine, a French pastry, *and* a new suit of clothes."

Jean frowned. "All of that? Well, those are not very extravagant or permanent things, I suppose, but you might forget that I repaid you once you drank the wine, ate the pastry and ruined the clothes.

"Well, I can't think of anything else that I need right now."

"Do you have so much then?" Jean's mouth twisted up in his one-sided smile.

"Non, I have *so little* that I wouldn't know where to start. Perhaps plenty and scarcity are two sides of the same coin."

"I know what I will get for you: a *tomahawk* or a *wampum bag*."

"A *what*?"

"A savage's war axe and a money bag made of shells."

"What would I do with those things?" Gilles was mystified as well as disdainful.

"They are quite interesting things to have and you could have something of the new continent, unless you'd rather have a savage's ceremonial tobacco pipe. You seemed quite interested in that sort of thing while you were talking with Villeneuve."

"I was just trying to keep him off the subject of religion! Well, I guess I could always *trade* those things for a good bottle of wine. I will bet you a gold watch *and* a knife."

"What would I need with a *watch*, Gilles? They are playthings for the wealthy! All you need is the sun or the town clock to get where you are going, give or take an hour."

"Well, other things we have already bet are just as silly."

"Maybe we should bet something more practical then."

"A fast horse perhaps?" Gilles asked.

"Ah! Now you are talking!" Jean agreed.

They passed the time in this way, not speaking about anything that was too important but mainly spending money that they were not sure they would ever have and planning trips to places they might not ever see. In the dark hold it was hard to tell how much time had gone by, whether it was hours or days since they had left Rouen, and there was no possibility of looking out or going up on deck to see the daylight hours passing or to sight land in the distance.

In spite of the fact that there were no more heavy seas or storms, Jean still looked ill and Gilles wondered if his friend still had a fever. Gilles didn't ask; it would be pointless as there was no help for him other than water. Gilles observed no eruptions on Jean's skin and this was a hopeful sign. Very soon Jean tired and fell asleep again and soon thereafter Gilles' eyes were closing, too. Sleep seemed to be a good way to pass the time.

Gilles walked up the drive to the house. The fields were very green today and he noted with interest that there was a strange black horse hitched in front of the house as he went inside. There was no one around, not even a single servant. He went up the stairs and walked in the direction of his old room but he ended up in the other wing, noting that it had already been renovated in a magnificent fashion. Wealthy nobles walked past him in the hall but they didn't talk to him; they didn't even acknowledge Gilles' presence. He stopped in front of a door, knowing that she was inside.

He didn't want to open it but the door swung silently open by itself. Marie sat on the bed, waiting for him, and around her neck were the pearls. A man pushed Gilles aside and walked over to the bed, taking Marie's hand up in his.

Gilles woke up in a sweat with an overwhelming desire to find the man and kill him. Who had taken everything from Gilles, his past and his future? Who had set the plans in motion to bring this curse down on his life and for what reason?

Gilles spent no more time sleeping. It was just easier to keep his thoughts and nightmares farther away when he was awake. He didn't feel like eating either; what he hungered for the most was to put his feet on land and to start living his life again, no matter what kind of a life that would be. The ship transported them between the past and the future, from death to life but it also confined and restrained him until Gilles found it very difficult to wait patiently any longer. Dark day melted into darker night in the dusky hold and only the noises on the deck gave Gilles any clue as to what was going on outside. When Gilles thought that he would go mad, that he could stand it no longer, at last there was a noticeable increase in the activity on the deck above them and he knew that they were headed in to the port.

"It smells bad in here," Gilles said to Jean, noticing it for the first time. "I couldn't help it though, I had to go."

"We both smell bad and a beard doesn't suit you *at all*," Jean whispered.

"Or you," Gilles returned but he was happy that they were approaching their destination without apparent detection, at least so far.

Steps came down the stairs and noises approaching the wall in front of them told them that someone was coming before it opened up once more. Gilles' pulse leapt even though it was only the captain who opened the hidden compartment. He led them out to the barrels again, first closing the wall up behind them, and now Gilles understood fully about why they counted and inspected all of the containers.

Jean eyed his cask and Gilles touched his arm.

"We are there, Jean; Just one last time. To freedom."

Jean nodded in agreement but Gilles saw the look in his eyes.

Gilles climbed into his container quickly, pulling the monk's robe and his cloak in with him and throwing Jean's robe over into his barrel. He was eager to make the last leg of the journey to freedom. The captain wasted no time as he swiftly tapped the lids down into place over their heads. It was all very much like a magic trick: The casks were closed up inside a smelly freighter boat and they would open again to release them into freedom, into a more pleasant future. The footfalls of the sailors above them were quicker now and there was a sudden slowing of the ship's speed. The lines hummed as they were dragged over the deck and one loud crash was accompanied by some cursing and yelling from above their heads. As the ship lurched to a final stop, several sailors moved quickly down the steps into the cargo hold. Some grunts of effort and not a few harsh words were heard in addition to the scrapes and bumps of other containers against theirs as they were moved a short distance across the lower deck, closer to the hatchway.

Gilles heard voices and then a line was knotted around his container. His barrel was hoisted through the air and then set down on the deck of the ship for a few moments while someone did something else with the rope, perhaps tightening the knot. Gilles' keg then traveled through the air again, a longer distance, over to a smaller vessel that would ferry them over to the land. He knew that it was a vessel and not the dock because there was a bobbing and rocking motion that subsided after a few moments but never ceased completely. After a few moments Gilles felt a bump and assumed that it was Jean's container landing next to his. The ropes were removed from the barrels and after that there was the peculiar sensation of being inside the closed barrel on the boat that was still moving up and down on the water.

As they moved toward the shore, Gilles heard two muffled voices outside, coming from the rear of his container. He quietly removed the plug so he could get some air and listen to their conversation. He could hear the sound of the oars and the motion told him that it was a very small boat, not one of the larger ones that generally ferried greater quantities of cargo. Gilles' stomach was queasy from the motion, the smell of the spirits that had taken up residence inside the grain of the barrel, the lack of food in his stomach, and being cooped up with the smell of himself. He tried to breathe slowly to settle his stomach and was forced to breath through his mouth to cut down on the smell.

"… but they pay you well enough, don't they?"

"Usually, but if there are bargains to be had and if they don't pay me enough in currency …"

"What do you have in there this time?"

"Wine, French wine. I don't want it for myself but I know a gentleman who will pay me well for it."

"I don't hear it sloshing around."

"It's the heavy stuff, the thick, syrupy stuff that the French like."

"Ah!"

From the tone in his voice, Gilles surmised that the one oarsman might have had an idea as to what the cargo truly was, but Gilles wasn't taking any chances: Making any noise at all could be a fatal error on his part and Gilles was too close to freedom now to let that happen. He calmed his stomach by listening to more of their conversation and concentrating on what was going on outside. The boat was pushed forward a measured distance through the water with each pull of the oars and then slowed for a moment as the rowers returned the oars to their former position, readying them for the next stroke.

Gilles worried briefly about the barrel falling overboard. What if he drowned before he could free himself from inside the barrel? It might be airtight but what if it leaked, the barrel filling up with water before he could get the top off and escape?

Gilles decided that there was not much that he could do about it except to hit the lid with all of the force he could muster at the first indication of trouble. Before that happened, it was pointless to worry and death would come anyway, or not, as God willed it, and perhaps the barrel would even miraculously float upright if it *did* fall overboard. Gilles wondered if Jean was thinking similar thoughts in his container beside him.

Finally the boat bumped up against a dock and Gilles barely had time to close the air hole before he heard the scrape of the rope against his container again. After the barrel was on the quay though, the containers sat still for a long time and Gilles started to worry again.

"Don't leave me here!"

He wondered if he could free himself when night fell or if the lid had been jammed on too tightly. He didn't know what the delay was but after several minutes more passed, he heard voices speaking in Nederlands and then both casks were hoisted again, this time onto a wagon. Gilles believed that he heard only a single horse, pulling them along at a slow pace through the streets. He removed the side plug again and now he could see the muddy street passing below as his field of vision encompassed the interior of the wagon and what was just over the top of the planked side of the cart. The smell of the spirits made Gilles very drowsy and he must have fallen asleep for a short time because it came as a shock to him when the lid was pried off and cool, fresh air poured down over his head.

"Whew! They smell as though they have spent the night in the drink house!" a stranger's voice exclaimed in Nederlands.

"And they are all yours. Here is a letter," the captain's voice answered.

Gilles attempted to get to his feet but his knees buckled and he thought he might be stuck in the barrel. Someone grabbed him under his arms and only then was he able to pull out one shaky leg at a time so he could at last climb out the rest of the way. It was a major feat accomplished when he finally had both of his feet on the ground.

Jean was being similarly helped out by the captain and the other voice, the voice behind Gilles, said, "You might have arrived in a more dignified way. Was this the best that you could do?"

The fresh air was reviving Gilles quickly but he was still feeling disoriented. The kegs were in an alley with no sign of the cart that had brought them there. Out on the street Gilles could see the buildings across the way and glimpse people as they passed by, hearing bits of Portuguese and Spanish mixed in with the Dutch. The construction of the buildings was definitely Amsterdam, but there was something different about them here. The neighborhood appeared to have some prosperity, even wealth, judging by the furs worn by passers-by, but this place was not at all familiar to him, even after spending two weeks seeing what he thought was the entirety of the city of Amsterdam. The smell of cooking onions and something sweet that Gilles could not identify was drifting out of a window that opened onto the alley.

"I'm sorry I couldn't oblige you by arriving in something more suitable, like a casket," Jean replied tersely to the voice as he first staggered forward, then backward before he finally found his footing. Gilles wondered if he had translated the Nederlands incorrectly but one look at his friend told him that he had not: He had never seen such an angry look on Jean's normally placid face.

"You two get inside."

The stranger pointed the way through a door and gave Gilles' shoulder a rough push in that direction. He put the tops back on the barrels, leaving them outside in the alley pushed up against a wall as the one-eyed captain walked away. Gilles was sorry that he had not had the opportunity to thank the captain for bringing him to safety but he and Jean were quickly ushered through the door and into the kitchen of the onion house.

"Onion soup," Gilles thought and remembered something but then the thought was gone, chased away by the alcohol's spirits that were still dancing in his bloodstream.

They passed through the kitchen and into a small sitting room. The dwelling belonged to a rich man or at least to a very well-to-do man, with all of the tables covered in fine porcelain dishes, silver, and golden bowls full of flowers. Paintings covered the walls but the scenes in them did not look like places in Amsterdam: The cities in the pictures looked like they were far away, in some more exotic place, and the climate looked hot and dusty; much less inviting to Gilles. A very thick book that boasted a silver cover with inset jewels sat on another table, an unusual design or strange writing, perhaps, adorning the front of it. Lace table cloths covered the tables and lace drapes framed the leaded glass casement windows. The sitting room had two large chandeliers made of gold and crystal, one hanging at each end of the room.

"Sit!" the man motioned to velvet cushioned chairs as a servant offered sweet wine and little cakes on a silver tray. Their host tucked a fat envelope into his pocket before he sat down.

Gilles was starting to feel better and he noticed the man's eyes first. The man's eyes were like Jean Durie's but darker and Gilles then took stock of other similarities. The hands were the same too, and some of their gestures as well. The man poured himself a full glass of the wine and poured drinks for Gilles and Jean. Gilles noted that Jean had not lost any of his look of annoyance since the lids had come off the barrels in the alley.

"From one death to another," Gilles thought he heard Jean mumble to himself.

"I could put you back outside for the French to find," the man suggested as he sipped his wine. The suggestion carried no emotional content with it at all. Gilles heard no accent other than Amsterdam Nederlands but the man's style of dress was a little unusual, more Spanish than Dutch, if Gilles had to guess.

Gilles introduced himself since Jean seemed to have forgotten his manners.

"I'm Gilles Montroville," he said, not knowing whether to stand up to embrace the man or to extend a hand to him in the Dutch fashion.

"I'm Dirck," the man replied, offering no last name, no physical contact, and no further information.

Gilles believed that he was sitting with Jean's father but there seemed to be no polite way to confirm this. The cakes were light and sweet and so was the wine. Gilles skipped the prayers and picked up a cake at the man's urging. He tried to stop eating them so quickly but he could have easily eaten them all and emptied the bottle of wine, as well. It was difficult to act civilized in a gentleman's house when one had been so recently starved.

"So they were going to burn you. I told you they would," Dirck said, reaching for another cake.

"It's not a subject that I care to discuss right now." Jean still looked annoyed.

"Of course not. But now you see that I was right all along, and you have no choice but to live here and to join me in my business. Now maybe you will forget about France and about your other life. Here we live like men, not like animals. Here we own property, live as we please, worship as we please, and can be ourselves: No one bothers us here. It's just lucky for you that I could save you."

Jean made a derisive snort. He wasn't talking to Dirck and he wasn't eating. What he *was* doing was drinking a good deal of wine. Gilles wondered if he should mention that Jean needed a physician. He felt a knot starting to grow in his stomach and it grew worse with Dirck's continued haranguing of Jean.

"Change your name and appearance and anything else that you like, but they will *never* let you forget that you are still one of us, even if *you* can forget for a time."

"I don't belong here, either," Jean snapped, finally picking up a little cake and taking an angry bite from it. "Did you forget that my mother is a Catholic?"

"It makes no difference. They will accept you here when you join the community in work and worship, take a wife and have children. Rachel Del Arroyo is still unmarried," Dirck offered.

Jean responded to this by getting up and walking out of the room toward the back of the house where Gilles heard a door slamming shut. Dirck continued to eat his cakes and sip his wine, apparently not even noticing that anything was out of the ordinary; perhaps it was not. Gilles was uncomfortable sitting there alone with Dirck and he felt even greater malaise when he considered leaving the house. If he left here, where would he go?

"I will have some blankets brought out for you and you can sleep in the alcove over there," Dirck gestured. "You will provide your own food after today since you are healthy enough to work and should be able to find work *somewhere;* there are enough jobs for those willing to work hard. Of course you will need to stay around here and not stray over into the Christian side. Don't shave the beard and get rid of those clothes! They are too French-looking."

I can probably find another place to stay soon, too," Gilles volunteered, thinking that this offer might appease his host.

Dirck waived his hand. "No need of that, your father has paid me enough to keep you here and *you* certainly wouldn't know who can be trusted to keep your identity a secret."

"But he didn't send enough money for you to feed me just a little, too?" Gilles thought angrily. He took a deep breath and then reminded himself that for now he had nowhere else to go, no other alternatives.

During his recent brush with death, Gilles had thought of many things that he wanted to do before he died. He didn't think so much of women or of completing some great enduring and timeless accomplishment, but Gilles' greatest desire and need after eating was simply to go outside, to be in a place where he could walk and see the open sky above him. The urge returned to him now and was becoming too strong to ignore for much longer.

"Thank you for your hospitality, Dirck. You will excuse me?"

Dirck looked up at Gilles as if just remembering that he was there or perhaps in surprise at his guest's formality of speech and only nodded. Gilles walked through the kitchen, to the door that opened on the back alley, took a deep breath and then took a giant step outside the walls. As he expected, it was a very good feeling to be outside but to his surprise, it was also a peculiar feeling that was accompanied by anxiety. He stood in the alleyway for a few moments, hoping to feel better but he just could not shake the feeling that he was doing something wrong in being there. Gilles pushed that thought aside though, and shaking his head in wonder at what they had done to him in such a short time, he took one defiant step and then another until he was outside the alley and walking around the building. He stopped when he reached the front of the house where he sat down on the stoep, content for the moment to let the world pass by and to see an unfettered world eddying around him. Dirck came outside after a few moments and handed Gilles a battered old hat.

"If you must go out of doors, put this on, keep it on, and keep it pulled down! Strangers invite questions and if anyone seizes you, I will deny that I know you at all."

Having delivered the hat and his message, Dirck returned inside but Gilles stayed right where he was. Who was going to look for him here, in this place? He examined the hat. It was greasy, ugly, and smelled as though it had belonged to a common laborer. It was not stylish and even looked like it was some sort of servant's cap. Nagging fear made Gilles put it on, though, and he pulled it down as Dirck had instructed.

He relaxed enough to watch the people passing by now. They were mostly darker people than in the rest of the city, some more exotic in appearance than others. A good number of the men had a white fringe sticking out from under their coats and most had untrimmed beards; unfortunate oversights in their grooming on men that otherwise were fastidiously dressed. Some appeared very well-to-do and a few others seemed poor. The women here traveled together in groups more than they did in the rest of the city and men and women did not hold hands or even walk closely together here. Some men strolled by wearing magnificent clothing, furs, gold, jewels and even dainty rosettes on their satin high-heeled shoes.

Gilles sighed, exhaling a week of pain and trying not to allow worries about the future to seep into his consciousness and enjoyment of the moment. What was life going to be like now? Was this it, never to see his home, his room, his family, or his vineyards again? Marie popped into his mind but he quickly pushed her into the dark shadows before he could register any conscious thought about her. There was nothing warm or friendly about this foreign place or these strange people and having to stay here for the rest of his life seemed, as Jean had said, another kind of death. It was still a mystery as to how Gilles had come to be in this place. He could not stay out here in the front of this house forever, could he? He felt pain in his stomach and wondered if it was hunger; he thought not but he wasn't sure what it was. There was a numbness that had overtaken his body and yet at the same time there was a feeling of dull pain that was coming from everywhere.

Gilles decided to walk around the block and see if there were any nearby job prospects. It seemed that if he wanted to eat, he would need to work. He was good at accounts and good at languages so perhaps he would be able to find a good position here in the Netherlands.

Carts rolled by and people laughed together as they passed him. They didn't know and they didn't care that he had just escaped with only his life and that he was drinking in freedom among them, taking it into his body as fast as he could. Gilles saw many different kinds of businesses here but none of the ale houses that dominated the other areas of the city. In no time at all he had made a circle around the block and was back in front of Dirck's house. He hadn't given much thought to the businesses that he had passed during his walk; he was too much taken with watching birds eating crumbs and how the breeze moved the leaves in the trees today, things that he ordinarily took no notice of at all. He didn't want to sit back down and he wasn't sure if he ever wanted to go back inside with Dirck so Gilles started around the block again and this time he forced himself to take notice of each and every building and business that might offer him some kind of employment. He saw no counting houses that he could identify but uppermost in his mind was the thought that he needed to find some kind of work today. A man put his hand on Gilles' sleeve, interrupting his thoughts and Gilles thought that he might want to ask for directions to somewhere but instead the man said to him, "You're Diego's visitor."

Gilles felt some pity and even some empathy for him, them both being on the same street and both being unable to find any coherency in their lives today. Gilles attempted to go around the man but he stood rudely in the way, studying Gilles, and blocking the path. The man didn't wait for a reply but spoke again.

"If you need work, I need a stable boy. You look strong enough. Mine ran off yesterday. He thinks he'll do better somewhere else. The idiot! One guilder a day, it's very good pay!"

Gilles was rendered speechless by the rapid delivery of this stream of information and could not understand what he was saying at first, especially with the odd

Nederlands accent. Stable boy? The funny little man stared at him intently, and Gilles stopped long enough to take in his long hooked nose and pointed ears. Gray hair stuck out in every direction from under a battered hat and merged with a shaggy gray beard.

"I ..." Gilles began, not knowing exactly what to say. Gilles had not expected him to *offer* money, he expected him to beg Gilles for money. The old man *was* in rather good condition for a beggar, not looking like he suffered greatly from malnutrition. He must have been one of the ones that they let out of the asylum.

"You can start tomorrow if today isn't good." The old man was very quick.

"I'm not ..."

"All right then, eight guilders a week but that's my last offer!"

This was ridiculous. Gilles couldn't talk to him so he would just have to ignore him and walk around.

"Take it or someone else will; it's a good job. I just offer it because of Jean."

"Jean?"

"Jean Durie! Come when the sun is rising. Two streets over, everyone knows Jacob's stable."

"How do you ..." Gilles started to ask but the man had already turned away and was walking up the street while Gilles stood there wondering how the man knew him and how he had come to have a job offer working in a stable. Gilles wouldn't go, of course. If the man was *really* an acquaintance of Jean's, Gilles would simply explain that he hadn't understood what he was saying due to the language barrier. With the old elf already gone from sight now though, Gilles began to think that he might have imagined the whole thing.

Returning to his canvas of the area, Gilles found a butcher shop, a dry goods shop, a surgeon and a tailor, none of which were promising for finding a job since Gilles had no experience in any of those jobs. Some of the business signs had peculiar designs on them, designs like those he had seen on the cover of the silver book in Dirck's house. Gilles wondered if the designs might be some kind of writing, although it was like nothing he had ever seen, much more unusual than even the way Italians wrote their Latin letters. He still had not seen a local counting house but he knew there were many of those nearer to the market and the water. If those businesses were too far into the mainstream of Amsterdam, he couldn't go there, not and remain safe. Perhaps any contact with people having dealings with the port would be too dangerous now, anyway. Gilles didn't see anything that looked any better in terms of work before his feet took him back to the house again. If he was going to live here, he hoped that the rest of this section of the city wasn't as dull and hopeless as this street was. Panic overtook Gilles momentarily at this thought so he sat down again outside the house and tried to regain control of his emotions.

It *was* good just to be outside and not in a prison cell, not in a closed compartment inside a boat, or stuffed inside a barrel. Gilles breathed in the smells of Amsterdam and it was good to be alive after all, even if his future was uncertain here. There were more women in the street now, traveling alone or in pairs. Almost all of them traveled empty-handed to his left and returned, loaded down with packages, as they passed by to his right. What business was it that drew such a steady stream of shoppers today? Such a business might need some help with their accounts if they had so many customers. Curiosity got the better of him and Gilles left his seat, following discreetly behind two of the women for a distance of about three blocks. They both went into a butcher shop and when they emerged loaded down with bundles, they went inside another shop next door. Gilles couldn't determine what kind of a shop it was exactly although the sign outside had a collection of items listed that seemed completely unrelated to each other including candles, books, spices and clothing. The women emerged from the store with their baskets and their arms full as they began the return journey that led them past Dirck's house again. Gilles didn't think that a job slaughtering animals would suit him and the little shop next door was too strange and intimidating for him to even think about walking inside and asking for work so he returned to the house and seated himself outside the front door again.

Food was cooking in every house in the city judging from the warm smell of peppers, onions, and various meats in the air. Gilles could smell food preparations inside Dirck's house, too, and he only hoped that Dirck would keep his promise and feed him supper tonight. He remembered that he had a little money in his pocket for food and then there were the pearls but what would he do when that was gone?

Jean walked outside the house and sat down next to Gilles. He was now dressed in clean clothes that were stylish but slightly large for him.

"So he didn't drive you off yet?" Jean asked.

"Non." Gilles didn't know what else to add so he left his reply as it was, standing alone.

"Old bastard." Jean's face had recovered its calm exterior, a glassy pond with no ripples at all, at least on the surface.

A dark young girl wearing a black fringed shawl over a black dress approached them. She carried a heavy tray of what looked and smelled like cooked meat. Jean opened the door for her and she entered without looking at Jean or Gilles or speaking to them, not even thanking Jean for opening the door.

"She helps to prepare supper for us tonight," Jean explained to Gilles.

Gilles felt reassured that he was going to eat after all and he wondered when they were going to eat. A very old man passing by the house stopped in front of them and shook hands with Jean.

"Jean! It's good to see you again! Will you be staying long?"

"No, not very long." Jean had a smile for the man.

"That's too bad. At least come by and say hello to the family. I have to hurry! Gut Shabbos!" The man tipped his hat and left, walking quickly up the street.

"Does anyone introduce anyone else here?" Gilles asked sharply, wondering what had happened to Jean Durie's normally excellent manners.

"Non. They know all about each other and each other's business. Why should they bother with introductions? Believe me, the less they know about you, too, the better."

"Do they all know about us already?" Gilles asked, aghast at Jean's revelation.

"I could stop anyone, anyone at all, on the street and prove it to you."

"That explains it!" Gilles said and he told Jean about his job offer.

"You could do worse than to work for Jacob," Jean said. "I helped him when he first came here and now he has a very good business going. Perhaps he is returning the favor by offering a job to you."

"You don't think I should *accept* it?" Gilles was incredulous.

"We need to take whatever work we can get right now, Gilles. With some money saved we can go on to Leiden in a few weeks, when traveling will be safer for us and detection less likely. New people are always coming and going at the University and they welcome anyone there, even those round heads, the English Pure Ones, as they call themselves. It will be much easier to disappear into the crowd there and it's a great place."

Gilles wondered if he *should* go to work at Jacob's in the morning. It would give him an excuse to get out of Dirck's house and a stable wouldn't be too bad for the time being. Gilles liked nothing better than being around his horses at home and he often helped to take care of them. He could use the money and certainly no one would be looking for him there.

Jean straightened his cuffs and said matter-of-factly, "It *will* work out all right, Gilles, and we will be moving on very soon. I can't stay here for long, not and stay sane. You heard him try to take the credit for our rescue? I know that it was all your father's doing,"

Gilles evaluated Jean's assessment and it made sense to him: The trial had been too soon after their arrest for word to have traveled to Amsterdam and escape plans to travel back. Gilles was surprised to think that his father could have planned and executed such an escape and now he wondered if perhaps he had underestimated the man who had sired him. Their being here at Dirck's house meant that Jean Montroville must know all about Jean Durie, all about Dirck too, and had *still* hired Durie, even sent Gilles to learn about the business from him. Jean Montroville must have held Jean Durie and his abilities in great esteem to carry on a business association with someone who could have been a major liability, and in fact had turned out to be trouble for him at the end. Whatever relationship there had been or could be salvaged between Jean Durie and Jean Montroville, Gilles didn't know, but he *was* relieved that Jean had included him in his future plans, wherever they ended up, not because he couldn't take care of himself but because Jean was now the closest thing to family that Gilles had left. He didn't want to let go of that, even knowing that a part of Jean Durie was, and probably always would remain, a stranger to him.

As twilight approached, a woman in the house across the street placed two candles in her front window and lit them. She seemed to be talking to someone as she did this and Gilles thought of his mother in France and wondered if she was lighting a candle in the church for him now, praying for her son's safety. The woman covered her eyes with her hands and Gilles wondered if she was greatly distressed about something. He noticed that every house in the city, for as far as he could see up and down the street, appeared to have two glowing candles in the front window, never less and never more than two. Gilles thought it very odd at first, then beautiful and somewhat magical: It completely altered the dark and sinister appearance of this part of the city.

The girl came to the door and motioned for Gilles and Jean to come inside. The only light from the interior was from the two candles that stood in their gleaming silver holders on the supper table. The large table was otherwise nearly empty, having no food on it, only the candles in the middle, linen covering something on a platter and one large and very ornate silver cup filled with dark wine that had been placed in front of Dirck. Gilles waited for the girl to bring the rest of the food and the other silver cups of wine but she didn't. Maybe Dirck would be the only one to get any wine tonight. The girl stood next to her chair as did Jean but Gilles removed his hat and sat down.

"Put your hat back on! You will observe our customs while you are my guest," Dirck said gruffly to Gilles. "And *you* missed candle lighting," he admonished Jean.

Gilles got to his feet again and with his face still burning in embarrassment from Dirck's upbraiding, he stood rigidly by his chair after he jammed the ugly hat back down over his head. The girl brought a pitcher and small water basin over to the table now. She set the basin on the table and poured the water from the pitcher over Dirck's hands while he muttered something in another language, half speaking and half singing as he washed his hands. When he had finished, he dried his hands on a towel that the girl carried over her arm. The girl took the pitcher to Jean who also washed his hands and dried them, muttering something that sounded like what Dirck had just said. She then brought the pitcher to Gilles. Gilles wondered why it was that with such a wealthy home as Dirck's, that there was no better washing accommodation. Gilles washed his hands in silence, not knowing what it was that he was supposed to say but Dirck repeated the prayer while Gilles washed. The girl finally washed her own hands as her lips moved silently, then took the bowl and pitcher away from the table.

When she returned, Dirck said something again in the other language as he lifted the cup of wine. It was the same sing-song voice, somehow sad, but also hopeful at the same time. The words were unintelligible but might have been invoking something. The girl and Jean stood attentively and Gilles did his best to follow their example, even standing the same way Jean stood in case he accidentally transgressed by moving his arms or standing in the wrong way. Dirck sipped the wine when the prayer was finished and then passed the cup over to Jean. It was being used as a communion cup and the rite was familiar and yet very strange as it was being performed outside of a church.

Jean sipped the wine and passed it over to Gilles. The cup seemed small now, if that was all the wine they were going to have with dinner and Gilles didn't like the idea of sharing the cup with the bearded stranger. He thought he might sip a little without thinking about it but the peculiar taste of the wine overtook his earlier thoughts of revulsion. The liquid was appallingly sweet and like nothing he had ever tasted; he resisted the urge to spit it out and forced himself to swallow, just hoping that the sticky, bitter taste would leave his mouth very soon.

"Pass it to the girl," Dirck instructed him.

She accepted the cup from Gilles, drank, and then handed it back to Dirck.

Dirck said another prayer as he lifted the linen and revealed two beautiful braided loaves of bread, then broke off a bit of it with his bare hands. He handed a small piece to each of them and Gilles once again followed Jean's lead, eating his piece when everyone else ate, only after Jean had responded to Dirck's prayer with something that sounded vaguely like "Amen".

Gilles wondered why Dirck handled all of their food. It was surely a perversion of Holy Communion with Dirck serving as a priest, not in a Catholic church but in his home, not speaking in Latin as God required, but speaking the language of the infidels. The thought came to Gilles that it might be some kind of cruel mockery, a personal test or insult directed at him and he would have believed this without a doubt if anyone had once looked at him and smiled, but none of them did and at last they were allowed to sit before the meal began.

The girl brought glasses for each of them to have more of the wine with dinner and she also brought soup, fish, chicken, beef and three kinds of vegetables before she pulled up a seat and joined them, occasionally getting up to serve the men more food or to clear the table. There was nothing unusual about the feast except for their eating with their hats on and what Gilles thought must be Spanish styles and flavorings of the food. It was the best meal that Gilles had had since the night they had taken him away from the dining room in his own home. He tried not to eat like an animal but he noticed that Jean was also eating a lot. The candles in the center of the table spluttered and dripped wax but the girl did not move them or light the chandeliers or lanterns. Gilles felt that it might be safer not to try and be helpful by pointing this out. The girl kept the wine glasses filled and Gilles would have consumed a great deal had it been the good French wine that Gilles was used to and not the sugary vinegar that was before him now. Gilles thought of Christ on the cross and of his thirst being quenched by the vinegar offered by the Roman soldiers. He wondered if this might be the very vinegar mentioned in the holy scriptures. The spicy dinner made it necessary to drink Dirck's wine though, so Gilles put only enough in his mouth to digest his food and as quickly as he could manage, he swallowed it down.

After dinner the girl cleared the table and brought the dishes over into the darkness of the kitchen where she apparently just set them down without washing them. It was no wonder that Gilles had heard that the Jews were filthy people with filthy habits. If they never cleaned, their kitchens were no doubt overrun quickly with every manner of crawling bugs. No one else left the table so Gilles continued to sit with Dirck and Jean.

"It *is* good that you are here," Dirck said to Jean.

Jean said nothing but chewed on the cuticle of one finger. Dirck spoke no more but sighed and then gazed off into the darkness of the room with his arms folded across his chest. The shadows jumped from the candles as the girl moved around the table, collecting plates and dishes.

"Someone offered me a job at their stable," Gilles offered, hoping to end the uncomfortable silence by starting conversation.

"That would be Jacob. You could do worse," Dirck said. "He is one of Jean's success stories. We won't talk of work tonight, though."

Jean had said the same thing to Gilles, *"You could do worse"*. Had they discussed his offer? *They would not have had the chance,* Gilles thought. Gilles searched his mental repertoire for other safe subjects to bring up.

"Dinner was good."

"Yes. Don't get used to it. As I said, I'm *not* feeding you." Dirck said.

Jean bit the side of another fingernail. Dirck continued to sit silently in the darkness.

"Maybe it will rain tomorrow." Gilles tried the weather.

"Maybe."

Gilles conceded defeat. They all just sat there, listening to the sounds of the girl in the kitchen. It took her just a little time to stack the dirty dishes and all of the men sat in silence around the table as the room grew continually darker. The candles grew shorter but still no other lamps were lit. When the girl had finished, she nodded at Dirck, put her shawl on and left.

The three men continued to sit, Gilles uncomfortably sitting there, wondering why they did not move, did not leave the table if they were finished eating, and weren't speaking. He couldn't help thinking about the last time his family had sat around the dinner table at home. There were candles there also, but there had been warmth and conversation, laughter and the clinking sounds of silverware and china. This dinner was too quiet, too strained, unhappy in spite of good reason to celebrate and good food.

"You should go take care of your needs if you are going tonight," Dirck said to Gilles.

Gilles was happy to accept the offer to escape the room. He had to go use the chamber pot but he went without a candle after Dirck refused to let him take one from the table.

It took him time to find it, time to go without making a mess and a little less time to find his way back to the kitchen. When he returned, Dirck directed Gilles to the alcove off the sitting room.

"Remember, you sleep there," Dirck said gesturing. "I had the girl leave a blanket there for you. Don't touch the candles!"

Dirck got up from the table and walked into the darkness toward the back of the house. Gilles heard the sound of a door closing somewhere deep inside the dwelling and then Jean rose from the table as well.

"It has been a very long day. Sleep well, Gilles."

As Jean left the room, Gilles wondered if his friend was going to get a real bed to sleep in tonight. Gilles had glimpsed a grand upper floor at the top of the hall stairs but he had not seen anyone go up the stairs since his arrival. He wondered what might be up there since apparently there were no bedrooms or guest rooms.

The candles were burning ever lower and Gilles thought that he should ready himself for sleep since there would be no other light forthcoming.

"The house of silence and darkness," Gilles thought to himself, as he made his way in to the sitting room and then the alcove before taking his shoes and pants off.

He was exhausted and had no trouble at all falling asleep, even though he only had a worn blanket along with his cape and the priest's robe to use as bedding. As he eased into sleep, he realized that although he had lost so much, there was one thing that he had gained and that was complete freedom. He could now go wherever he wanted and do whatever he wanted, all day and every day. His time was his own, his life was his own, and now his only constraints were his concern for his own personal safety and his need for money. He remembered making the wish for freedom and now he realized that that wish had been granted to him.

The floor was hard and intruded on his consciousness but still Gilles slept. His body had been drained of energy from the ordeal of prison, the trial, his escape, the strange house and worries about the future. It was an exhausted sleep that was not renewing enough as yet, still more of a temporary way of escaping reality. The room was a lighter dark than it had been when he fell asleep and he became slowly aware of someone chanting something in the sitting room, a recitation that encroached on the sanctuary of sleep that he had finally found. He didn't open his eyes right away, but slowly remembered where he was and all of the events that had led up to his being here. He opened his right eye just a little to see where the noise was coming from.

Dirck was standing in the sitting room, facing a wall with a single painting on it, bobbing back and forth and reading in a melodious but off-key sing-song from a book he held. He still had his hat on and Gilles had to wonder if Dirck slept in it as well. The hat wasn't the only thing that was peculiar about the way Dirck was attired: Over his shoulders Dirck wore a white shawl, like the kind that women wore with long fringe along the edges. He stayed facing in the same direction as he rocked and moved back and forth, sideways and forward and back, half singing, and half talking to himself. Gilles didn't move a muscle and he wondered how long he could stay there and remain motionless. One of Gilles' arms was numb from being under his head while he slept and Gilles needed to move it to start relieving the pins and needles sensation he was feeling. How much longer would Dirck be? Gilles lay quietly for a few minutes more and as he was about to pretend to roll over in his sleep, the prayers ended. Gilles saw Dirck touch the book with a corner of his shawl and then kiss the shawl, then removing the garment, he folded it quickly, sticking it inside a gold-embroidered velvet pouch before he walked over to Gilles and nudged him with his foot.

"Wake up! It is Saturday and time for you to go to work!"

With his awakening senses, Gilles was suddenly aware that he still smelled from his time in prison and on the ship. He wanted to wash himself but Dirck did not offer him any water. Gilles got to his feet, folded his bedding and placed it in the corner of the little room while Dirck waited impatiently for Gilles to finish. Dirck walked with him to the front door where he held the door open for him. Gilles felt the ache of hunger in his stomach but breakfast was not something that was going to be offered to him here. Gilles remembered the change that he still had in his pocket and being comforted with that thought, he resolved to go right away to buy some food. He also remembered the pearls that he still had and they would serve as currency too, if necessary. Gilles stumbled out of the house, still groggy from sleep, hunger, and exhaustion. He was accompanied part of the way on his journey by Dirck.

At the first cross street, Dirck gestured.

"Go that way," he said. "You can't miss it."

Dirck didn't turn but kept going straight and Gilles thought that it was not too late to keep going in another direction himself. The only difficulty was that he didn't know where he would go; to the east perhaps, on a ship to the Orient or maybe to the new world in the west. The pearls would probably be enough to get him passage there if they wouldn't hire him on as a sailor. The French soldiers would not think to look for him in *either* of those places but then Gilles thought about leaving Jean behind. It was simply the idea of never seeing Jean Durie again that kept his feet moving toward Jacob's and not turning toward the ships in the harbor.

The odd thing was that he *did* know the building when he saw it. It was a run-down old stable with a sign at the door that had both Nederlands and the same peculiar lettering or designs that he had been seeing all over this part of the city. Jacob saw Gilles coming and he walked outside to greet him, preventing Gilles from walking right on by without stopping, a brief impulse that he had and too soon lost.

"You came then? Gut, gut, well come inside."

His Nederlands had a peculiar accent to it but Gilles understood what he said. Jacob wasted no time but started a tour of the stables and how the business worked. Gilles couldn't help but think with sadness of his own horse that he had left behind in France. He hoped that someone would care for her as he had, and he hoped that his brother didn't get his horse. Charles always rode his horses too hard and paid them too little attention.

Gilles had cramps in his belly now and when his stomach made a loud noise, Jacob stopped talking.

"He didn't feed you, did he? He probably didn't even let you get cleaned up! Well, you just go in the back, there's water there and I'll bring you some food."

Gilles left the stable and found what he needed. The yard was full of chickens scurrying before him, feathers lofting up into the air as Gilles stepped carefully to avoid the chickens as well as their droppings but both seemed impossible to avoid. Gilles felt a little more settled when he returned with a clean face and hands and a stomach with some water in it. Jacob handed him some bread, the remains of a cooked chicken, and an apple. It was one of the best meals Gilles could ever remember having, at least as far as the enjoyment of it.

"Eat while I show you around; the water dipper is over there if you need a drink. It is usually a boy who thinks only of one person, *of himself*, and the grown man who thinks also of his fellow men! But perhaps Dirck is not that old yet."

Jacob winked and Gilles wasn't sure if he understood any of what Jacob had just said but he smiled at his benefactor anyway: The old man might be crazy but he seemed kind. Jacob showed Gilles where the horses and saddles were kept and explained to him what his duties would be.

"We only have five horses in today, not counting my own. No grooming! We just feed the horses and watch them until their owners come back for them. Payment first! No horses go out until we get payment, no matter what sad story they tell you! We are not responsible for injuries, broken reins or other complaints! We are not horse doctors here, either."

Jacob ran a very tight ship and he reminded Gilles a great deal of his own father in that respect.

"When it piles up out here, you shovel into the buckets and then dump them in the back, I'll show you where. The carts come around on Thursday to haul it away. You understand? If you like, you can stay here and sleep in the loft. Call me from the house if you need me today, but I know you can handle yourself. There won't be anything for you to do today but tomorrow we will collect two guilders when they come for their horses."

The thought of having to call Jacob for help with the horses made Gilles smile although he might ordinarily have taken offense at such an offer. Being paid to sit in a stable all day wouldn't be very hard work at all.

"You'll be all right." Jacob grinned and clapped him on the back. "I'm sure of it. I go now to save what is left of my Sabbath and I'll be back with your wages after the sun goes down."

"If I'm still here," Gilles thought but he just nodded. He would be there, though; he wouldn't leave before he got his money.

When Jacob had gone, Gilles finished eating his own meal before he fed the animals that Jacob had not finished feeding. It was good to be around horses again and he rubbed their shoulders and patted them as he went. A big black was nasty and mean-tempered.

"Hello, Poteet." Gilles grinned at him. "You don't scare me."

He finished the feeding and looked around for what he could do next. He expected *some* people to come by for their horses but none came. What had Jacob said? Something about a Sabbath, but it was Saturday, not Sunday. Perhaps he had misunderstood and it was some kind of a holiday in Amsterdam. Gilles walked around again and was confident that he knew where everything was kept. At home, he was not one to call the servants and have them care for *his* horse: He cared for his own, in spite of his sisters' mockery.

His sisters.

He had barely given them a thought. He pushed the thoughts of his family out of his mind and he looked around for more work that he might do or more stable that he could explore, anything that would keep him too busy to think. He looked outside the back of the stable and his eyes traveled over a well, an old shed, the privy, and the ramshackle old house just beyond the chicken coop. He was caught off guard when he saw Jacob sitting inside the house near the window, just sitting there, doing nothing except looking outside. That was most peculiar. What was he doing? Gilles ducked his head back inside the barn and he hoped that Jacob hadn't seen him wandering away from his job.

"There you are."

The voice behind him startled him.

"You're new here, aren't you?"

Like Jacob, the man had a peculiar type of accent and some of the words were different, perhaps more German than Dutch.

"The red one's mine, my saddle has initials JB on it."

Gilles found it quickly and put it on the horse's back but he didn't fasten the girth.

"Payment first," Gilles said in Nederlands, trying to speak the words firmly as he thought he had heard Jacob say them, as if he was familiar with the language and as if he had always spoken them in this way. Aside from his insecurities as to how well he used their language, Gilles was still afraid that someone would recognize him as French from the way that he spoke the words.

"It's the Sabbath. I don't carry any money," the man replied. "Jacob knows me; I always pay the next time I come in. *Next time*, you understand me, boy? *Next time.*"

"Payment first." Gilles held his ground and the man's attitude angered him.

"I'm going to tell Jacob about this! You just hand me those reins right now and I'll overlook your impertinence. I'll be back with the money in two hours."

"Payment first."

Even if he hadn't been told by Jacob to get the money first, Gilles still didn't know any more words that he could use to bargain with.

The man swore and dug into his pocket. "Een guilder, right?"

"Two."

The man practically threw it at Gilles.

"Actually four." Jacob stood at the back door, his arms crossed over his chest.

"Of course. Forgetful of me." The man smiled a patronizing smile at Jacob and handed Gilles the other two guilders.

Jacob said, "I wouldn't want to *forget* to save room for you to keep your horse here on a busy day. You'd have to pay much more down the street or take your horse with you everywhere you go." Jacob smiled back at the man but Gilles could see that it was not a sincere expression of affection.

Gilles turned back to the horse and pulled the strap across the horse's girth. He didn't bother to retighten it: If it came loose, it came loose. The man didn't seem to notice but led his horse outside and mounted there.

After he had left, Jacob sighed. "I should have warned you about *him*. He *always* does that on the Sabbath when he's here, never mind that he is breaking God's law, he tries to cheat another man on a holy day! He owes me more money than I can count but it's a game we always play."

"Why do you keep taking in his horse then?" Gilles asked.

"Oh, it's nothing *personal*; it's just something he does, so I watch for him to come back now. Someday maybe I'll just sell his horse before he returns."

Jacob winked at Gilles, then turned back toward his crooked little house. Gilles thought about this for a minute but finally shrugged it off and accepted it. Why should the Netherlanders in *this* part of the city be any less peculiar than any of the other Netherlanders?

There was no business at all for the rest of the day and Gilles noted when he looked out the front door that there was not a single horse or wagon on the street. It was eerie and he wondered how he would diplomatically ask Jacob about it. Maybe he could ask Jean Durie and Jean would know.

It was well into the afternoon when his stomach started to make noises again. Gilles tried to quiet it with water but it took less time after each drink for his hunger and the rumbles to start back up again. After so much water, he found himself going into the back to relieve himself too often. Giving in to the urge, he munched on a handful of the horse's grain, checking for bugs first of course, and found it not too bad. He hoped that Jacob would not find out about it and see this as stealing the horse's food.

The horses had plenty of hay and water now and Gilles looked around for something else to occupy his time and to keep his thoughts at bay. Perhaps there was too much manure piling up and it was time to move it to the back. He had never actually shoveled any since the servants at home did that for him, but he remembered the shovel Luc had used at home and he found one that looked like it suited the purpose. He started down the line of horses with the first one in line, the one farthest from the back door. The black horse showed the white of his eye and took a side kick at him that narrowly missed.

"Damned animal," Gilles muttered but he kept going.

His stomach hurt, his hands were blistering from carrying the buckets of water and shoveling and he was suddenly very tired. He leaned against the stall, just for a moment's rest, and unexpectedly, tears came to his eyes, not stopping there but spilling down over his cheeks and onto his sore hands that rested momentarily on the handle of the shovel. He even sobbed out loud once before he quickly stifled any further sounds, just in case Jacob or someone else coming in might hear him.

It was unthinkable, *a Montroville* shoveling out horse stalls for the Jews. His new master was a beggar of a man, of beggarly stock, sitting in a ramshackle house, resting like a king on his derriere while Gilles worked shoveling horse excrement in the stable. Gilles tried to stop the tears but they continued to fall although he tried with all his might, unsuccessfully for several minutes, to regain his composure. Anger rescued him at last, though, as he wiped the tears of self-pity away on his sleeves and made a tontine with himself that he would get Marie back, get his home back, get everything back that he had lost and more. Gilles bit the inside of his mouth to stop the last of the tears, and it was with a new determination that he picked the shovel up again and threw his body into it as he shoveled and talked to himself.

"One guilder, seven stuivers a day, then; it starts here! If I spend *none* of it and invest it well, it is a beginning and I will look for other opportunities."

Gilles' anger took him through cleaning the barn floor faster and more thoroughly than it had been done in years.

The day was long and Gilles did not think that it would ever come to an end. Not having that much work to do was harder than he thought it might be but at last the sun started to go down. Gilles washed his hands and had another drink of water. Where was Jacob? Jacob had promised to be back at sundown but there was no sign of him yet. Maybe he played a game with Gilles and was not going to pay him the pitiful sum that had been agreed upon for spending the entire miserable day here.

Gilles would just have to go to the house to look for him and demand payment. He would find some food somewhere tonight, even if he had to steal it, and he would look for other work in the morning. It was getting quite dark now and Gilles decided that he would wait no longer. He wondered now if he would be able to find his way back to Dirck's house in the darkness but maybe that didn't matter either. He started resolutely toward the back door, to the house, but there he met Jacob coming to the stable at last, a lantern in his hand.

"Still here, eh? Gut, gut. Here's your wages. Go to the inn up the street for some food. You know where the *shochet*, the butcher is? It's two doors down from there. Go up the street to the right and when you get there, knock on the side door and tell them that I sent you. They'll sell you some food for a good price and it will fill your stomach. Come back tomorrow, same time." Jacob dropped the money into Gilles' hands.

Gilles felt the unfamiliar size and weight of the Nederlands money and now he remembered that the coins in his pocket were French Louis d'Ors. He hadn't even thought about that. The money in his pocket might be useless, even dangerous, to use here. Old Hendrick had accepted his French money at his inn, though. Was it safe to go near the dam to exchange it?

Gilles decided that he couldn't take the risk. He hoped that the food Jacob recommended would be all right but he wondered why he should go to the side door and not in the front door: Only beggars went to the side doors or back doors.

"For a good price," Jacob had said.

It was late in the evening now and Gilles didn't know what other choice he had. Gilles went up the street as directed but he hesitated again outside the front door of the inn, trying to decide what he should do. If he went to the side door, it would cost him less money and people wouldn't see him there in the dark, neither to recognize him as a fugitive nor to scoff at the sorry state of his clothes. In the end, his hunger and fear were stronger than his pride. There was only one door up in the alley and it had to be the one that Jacob mentioned. With some trepidation from his last experience with an alley in Amsterdam, Gilles went into the dark passage and walked up to the door. Looking around once again, just to make certain that he was alone, he knocked and a pretty young girl answered. She was dark haired and dressed in the modest manner of the Jews.

"Yes?" she asked, scowling at him, her eyes quickly taking in the details of his soiled and ragged clothes.

"Jacob from the stable sent me. He said you would sell me food."

It was difficult for him to say that.

She closed the door halfway while he waited impatiently. When she reappeared, she had some bread and cold meat.

"Do you have any butter?" he asked her.

"Butter?! No! No butter!" She looked at him strangely, even angrily.

Gilles decided not to say anything else to her and not to ask her for anything. He held out his hand, offering her all of his wages that he still held. By the light that streamed out of the building behind her, she examined what was in his hand, selected a few florins from his palm and then closed the door in his face.

Two weeks ago a pretty girl would have smiled at him and flirted, especially if she knew who he was. Now Gilles was just another dirty stable boy of no interest at all to a girl with better prospects. Without his money even the oldest and ugliest of the prostitutes wouldn't want him now. Gilles wondered if his life was going to be completely lonely and miserable from now on. The tears of self-pity started to fall again, this time on the bread as he ate it. He wiped his nose on his sleeve and moved his tired and heavy feet in the direction of Dirck's house: It was the only place in the world that would take him in tonight.

A great feast was on the table at Dirck's house. Dirck sat alone, eating, while the servant that Gilles had seen on the first day waited patiently for Dirck to request more or request that a dish be passed closer to him. Jean was nowhere in sight. Gilles knew better than to even look at the food; he knew he would not be offered any or receive any if he should be so bold as to ask. Dirck didn't speak to him when he entered the house but Gilles bid his host a good evening as he passed by the table on the way to his alcove. Gilles' eye fell on a beautiful candle with braids of brightly-colored wax, not in a holder but lying on the table, just next to an unusual gold ornament of some kind. He was mildly curious about these two strange objects but he didn't slow a single step as any interaction with Dirck would probably not turn out well. Gilles didn't even look back in Dirck's direction but quickly spread out his blanket and with his back to the kitchen, he tried to go to sleep, ignoring the sounds of Dirck eating just a few feet away.

The morning didn't find Gilles feeling any more optimistic about his future prospects. His stomach growled and woke him up and he wished now that he had saved even a small piece of bread from the night before but he would try to remember to do that tonight. Gilles was actually looking forward to leaving Dirck's house even if he wasn't looking forward to going to the stable. He rolled over to get up but his body ached in places that he had not anticipated. He wondered briefly if this was what old age felt like and thought that this was a peculiar thought for someone his age to be thinking. His back, shoulders, and legs hurt but the pain subsided a little when he was still. Gilles rolled up the blanket and as he did so, he noted that his hands hurt too: His palms still burned and there were blisters at the bases of his fingers.

In the dim light Gilles noticed a great brown smear on his pants that hadn't been there the morning before. He hated the idea of wearing the same clothes on yet another day and he promised himself that he would find a way to bathe by day's end and to wash his clothes or to find new ones. He thought of how much he had enjoyed swimming in the river in Rouen as a child. Perhaps he could bathe in the canal later. Maybe he could ask Jean for clean clothes or maybe he could steal some. Unlike Jean, Gilles had never given clothes much thought before but strangely enough, today his main ambition in life was to clean himself and find clean clothing. He shook his head at this odd thought, put the rolled-up blanket next to the wall and walked out into the kitchen.

Jean entered the kitchen at nearly the same time and Gilles was greatly surprised to see the very stylish new clothes that he had on.

"Dirck found me a job at a counting house where I won't be seen," Jean told Gilles as he straightened one lace cuff. "I have to dress well for it."

"Congratulations," Gilles said to Jean but he thought to himself, *The old bastard couldn't find me a job as well? Would a morsel of food, some clean clothing, or a job be too much more to ask for a fellow human being? I'm sure my father has paid him well enough that he could help me out just a little more.*"

Gilles didn't feel comfortable in asking Jean for his help now. On the day that they went to trial, Gilles' clothes had been as fine as those that Jean wore now, but days of living in them and the miserable conditions that Gilles had endured recently had reduced them nearly to rags.

Gilles suddenly remembered that it was Sunday but he doubted that Jean was going to church first in his new clothes. At home Gilles would have been preparing for a day in church by putting on *his* best clothes. Here he was preparing for another day of laboring in his *only* clothes. He hoped that God would understand his transgression of the Sabbath.

Gilles bid Jean good day and found the way to Jacob's stable without any difficulty. He did not see his employer in the stable when he walked in so he started to feed the hungry horses. He was on the third one when Jacob joined him, filling another bucket with feed.

"How are you today, young fellow? What are you called again?"

"I'm called Gilles."

"Gilles. Is that like Yellas? You are not a bad worker, Gilles." Jacob was trying the name out and appeared to enjoy the sound the odd name made as it rolled over his tongue.

"We didn't speak much yesterday, it being the Sabbath, but most days I will work with you."

"I can handle the job," Gilles said defensively.

"So you proved, but a man doesn't have to work himself to death to get through life."

Gilles had nothing to say to that.

"You're French, right? Your Nederlands isn't too bad, though, I can still understand you most of the time."

"I'm good at languages," Gilles replied. It was a fact.

"Ja," Jacob smiled at him. "I can see that. Did you find everything that you needed yesterday?"

"Yes, I found everything."

"Gut, gut."

Gilles thought about it for a moment and decided that Jacob might help him. The old man really had come to his rescue with the money that Gilles needed for food. It was worth taking the risk and asking.

"There is *one thing* that you might help me with, after work."

"What would that be?" Jacob asked him.

Gilles just said it. "To bathe and to clean my clothes. Could I get some water from you?"

Jacob laughed and shook his head.

Anger and shame welled up in Gilles again. He shouldn't have asked. After all, what did Jews care about clean clothes?

"Such a simple thing! None of my stable boys *ever* asked me that before!" Jacob exclaimed. "You stay here and I'll be back soon with something *even better!*"

Jacob left and Gilles hoped that he was going to return with a bucket of water to wash in. Maybe it would even be *warm* water, but that seemed to be too much to hope for.

Jacob took a very long time before he returned. Gilles had finished feeding, watering and even cleaning up after the horses. He was wondering what to do next when Jacob finally came back. The old elf didn't come back with any water at all but he carried with him a simple linen shirt and pants.

"These will fit you and you can bathe now in the back of my house. You have to make up the time you owe me tonight but I will get you some food while you work today. You can make some repairs for me too, yes? You know how?"

Gilles nodded happily. It was probably the ugliest shirt he had ever seen but it was clean and it smelled of soap. The shirt and pants were both slightly stained, soft and well-worn, but Gilles didn't care. They looked comfortable.

Jacob said, "I'm sure *He* will not mind if you make use of it. My wife, may she find good rest forever, used it before Manasseh Ben Israel built one for the community, and my daughter would use it too, but a need is filled in many ways and many things have many uses to fill many needs, thanks be to the Creator for that! Go ahead, to the right behind the house. Climb in, wash, and come back when you are clean."

Gilles could make no sense at all of this rambling but he wasn't really listening anymore. He practically ran, afraid that he might discover it was not true and there was not really any water. Gilles turned the corner on the far side of the house and was perplexed when he discovered a crudely made wall of wood on three sides with a small opening on the fourth side, the side to the house. Inside the enclosure was a trough similar to the kind used for watering horses but it had a longer and wider shape to it. It was dark from old water and soap stains but was smooth wood on the inside. Tar between the boards waterproofed it for the most part although a great long crack in the wood allowed water to seep out in a steady stream of droplets onto the ground. It was filled nearly to the top with cool water.

"Climb in," Jacob had said and although it was an odd idea, it had great appeal to Gilles even though it would probably be cold. Gilles didn't care if it was ice, he was getting in. For the last few days, since his time in the prison, his skin had the sensation of fleas or something else crawling on it and biting him. If the water did no more than to remove this feeling, he would gladly brave the cold. Gilles also discovered some soap that Jacob had left nearby and Gilles was as happy as a child on Christmas Feast Day. He set the clean clothes down, quickly took his clothes off, and grabbing the soap, he put his feet in first, taking just a moment to enjoy the cool water on his feet. He didn't wait long, though, before he sat down quickly, plunging himself into the chill water as he caught his breath sharply, doing his utmost to ignore the cold and to celebrate the clean water. He refused to believe that he would die from the experience; instead he joyously poured the water over his arms and splashed it under his armpits, then sank lower, managing to get his entire head under the water in spite of the trough being a little short for him in length. He held his breath and kept his itchy head under the water completely as he scrubbed it with his fingers. When he surfaced he saw a dark and greasy film on the surface of the water and he cursed it.

"Allez! Be gone, black bile of France!" he exclaimed, suddenly feeling very cheerful and refreshed. It was not so much like falling into the river at home but more like the feeling of a baptism, a life renewed.

He stopped splashing when he suddenly realized that someone was standing behind him. Not believing that it was Jacob and wondering in a panic if he had been found already by French agents of the King, he tried to remain calm while he twisted his head around to see who it was. Looking over his shoulder he saw a girl who had black hair and eyes and Jacob's nose. Her arms were crossed and she had an annoyed expression on her face.

"Father sent me for your dirty clothes, to clean them. You're the new boy who kept him from coming to my home yesterday for dinner."

"I apologize."

"It's all right. He can't keep help, he treats them too well," she said disparagingly.

"My clothes are there, thank you. Does he always send his daughter to pick up men's clothing while they bathe?"

The girl shrugged, her sullen expression never changing. "It doesn't matter, I'm married." The girl seemed pleasant enough but humorless. "I'm Hannah. What do they call you?"

"My name is Gilles."

"Gilles. That's a strange name." She tried the name out in the same way her father had. She moved to reach for the discarded clothing but stopped short at the clean pile.

"It's David's shirt. Did Father give that to you?"

"Yes, who is David?"

"No one. He just worked here before."

The brief flicker of interest had already gone from her eyes as quickly as it had appeared. Her eyes traveled to Gilles' chest and she did not seem to be picking up the dirty clothing very quickly. Gilles thought of Tryntje and wondered briefly if every young woman in Amsterdam went around accosting men. If that was the case, the back yards of the city must be very busy every day here and a young man wasn't safe at all but while Tryntje made him feel uncomfortable and defensive, Jacob's daughter was having the opposite effect on him. Gilles stretched his arms out and folded them behind his head. She was older than Jean Durie, he guessed. She was thin and angular but not totally unattractive. She was still just standing there, not speaking, not moving at all.

"I'd be grateful for clean clothes. When will I get them back?" His eyes moved over her, taking all of her in.

"I'll get them to you."

She smiled at him with one side of her mouth and then finally with her full mouth and her eyes.She broke eye contact with him when they heard Jacob calling.

"Hannah! Hannah, where are you?"

"Coming!" she called back.

She picked up the dirty clothes, turned around, and was gone. Much as Gilles wanted to stay in the water forever, he quickly got out and started to dress; he wanted to get a last look at Hannah before she left. The clean clothes stuck to his wet body but fit fairly well even if they were a little short in the length of the pants and the arms. He cursed the sticking clothes out loud and jammed his boots back onto his feet before he hurried back to the stable, shivering from the cold only for a few moments before he warmed up and walked nonchalantly back inside.

"Thank you again," Gilles said to Jacob as he tried to fasten the top buttons on his shirt. He finally gave up. It was just too tight a fit around his neck.

"It's the small things that we find make life good, not the big things that we *expect* will make it so," Jacob replied as he shook loose a small bundle of hay for a horse.

While Jacob worked, he and Hannah had a brief conversation in a language that was similar to German. Gilles caught words in their language that he had heard before in the streets here and there but just when he thought he was following along in German and understanding a good deal of what they were saying, Gilles became lost among the strange words and alien expressions. Jacob waived his arms excitedly. Hannah clucked sympathetically and shook her head, saying something in a low voice. Finally they finished their conversation and then Hannah left with a bundle of clothes, Gilles' and others that were probably Jacob's. She didn't say goodbye to Gilles or look at him again but Gilles thought about her for the rest of the day.

Sunday was a busy day but Monday was even more so with many people coming and going in the stable. The customers left their horses so they could move with greater ease around the city and came back to a rested horse, one that was well fed and ready to travel home. At times it was all that Jacob and Gilles could do to keep up with the pace of arrivals and departures. Several people would come in all at once, running late and needing to drop off or get their horse right away. They would impatiently wait as Gilles and Jacob hurried to take their horses or get horses and saddles out before Gilles would run to the next horse. At one point in the early afternoon they did not have enough places to put all of the horses coming in.

"It's all right!" Jacob called over to Gilles, "Put them in the saddle area far away from each other so there is no problem. We will end up with the right number by the end of the day; the Almighty has planned for this."

Gilles had no time to stop and think about it. The pace was dizzying and he almost forgot to collect the money a few times. Jacob disappeared at lunchtime but when he returned he had food for Gilles.

"Go sit and eat."

He gestured over to a bench by the front door. Gilles thanked him and ate the food quickly, washing it down with a dipper of water before he went right back to work. Gilles decided that he had to find a way to get regular meals. He needed more than bread to keep him going and the food Jacob brought was good but not always enough to fill his stomach. Gilles wanted meat and vegetables and fruit, foods that Jacob did not seem to be very well acquainted with.

After work on Monday, Gilles discovered another inn that was just a little bit out of the way from his route back to Dirck's. He went inside and had a grand meal with wine but it cost him his entire day's wages. He couldn't do that every day, even though he greatly enjoyed the meal and had filled his stomach to capacity and beyond.

On Tuesday morning when he arrived there, Gilles met Jacob coming out of the door to the stable just as he was going in. Jacob led his old horse outside and hitched him up to a small wagon that was waiting there.

"It's my day to go to the Dam. I get the best prices I can on feed and other things I need if I buy a lot of it. I won't be back until late in the day, but you can probably handle it, I'm sure. Any other problems can wait for my return. Just put this sign out on the front door if you need to go get food or go out in the back."

Jacob showed Gilles a sign that purported to say "I will be back shortly" and Jacob told him which way was the right way to put it up since Gilles could not make out the letters, the language, or even which way was up and which way was down. Gilles wasn't so sure that he could handle it all after the extremely busy day they had had the day before, on Monday, but he said nothing about this to

Jacob. There was enough feed left for now but with too many days like the day before, it was hard to tell how many day's supply remained. Gilles noted a hole in the corner of the grain room and would try to remember to tell Jacob. It should be patched and since he hadn't seen a barn cat around, he would suggest that Jacob get one to keep the rats out.

Tuesday morning turned out to be much quieter than the previous day, and in no time at all, Gilles had finished the feed and hay for the few horses they had left over from the day before and no new customers had come in this morning to interrupt him. He was nearly finished with the water when the first customer came in.

"One day only, I'll be back at sundown," the man said throwing the reins to Gilles. "Understand?"

Gilles nodded as he set down the water bucket and led the horse into an empty stall. As he removed the saddle and bridle, Gilles noted that the horse seemed to have come a great distance already this morning. The animal limped slightly and Gilles thought that the horse may have picked up a stone but he saw nothing unusual when he examined the hoof.

"You do know something about horses then?" a voice behind him asked.

He turned to see Hannah standing there before he went back to the horse and picked up the other hoof.

"Yes, I know a little bit. Your father has gone into town today."

"I know. He goes every Tuesday."

"You need something from the house?" Gilles put the horse's foot down and straightened up.

"No. I brought your clothes back."

Hannah tipped her head toward a large basket of folded clothes that sat on the floor near the door. Gilles' clothing was on the top of the stack and it looked very good, almost like new, but it was very odd having a complete stranger who was not a servant handling his clothes.

"They are the finest clothes that I have ever seen. Who *are* you?" she asked.

Gilles decided to pretend that he didn't understand the question's meaning.

"I'm Gilles," he said.

He might have said "Thank you for cleaning my clothes" but he couldn't manage it in their language and then he remembered that Elsje and Tryntje sometimes shook hands as a gesture of gratitude. Gilles offered Hannah his hand and she looked at it for a moment before Gilles realized his mistake, that the women in this part of the city did not shake hands with men.

Before he could rescind his offer though, she put her hand in his. No person's flesh had come into contact with his in weeks. He held her hand fast and then kissed her on each cheek, a common enough gesture of thanks among both men and women in France but instead of stepping back afterwards as he expected her to do, she pulled him closer, and without warning, kissed him on the mouth, a passionate kiss that left no question as to its meaning, tradition, or custom.

"The sign," she said, walking over to it and putting it up on the door.

Hannah walked back to him and taking up his hand again, she led him outside to the small shed behind the stable. She pushed open the door with her other hand and the smell of old feed sacks and lamp oil filled the air inside. A shaft of sunlight lit up a stream of escaping grain dust particles as Hannah pulled Gilles inside the shed and then shut the door behind them. In the dim light Gilles saw her swiftly remove a gold ring from her right hand and then hang it up on a nail on the wall before she kissed him again. Gilles returned her kisses hungrily and touched her hair, glossy and black and smelling like wildflowers. It had been so long … Hannah pulled one old grain sack from the top of a great pile of sacks and tossed it onto the floor. She sat down on it, pulling Gilles down on top of her. Gilles moved over her and worked her skirts up but she pushed him back.

"Nee."

"No?" Gilles stopped, dumbfounded and wondering if this was a jest. No one had ever told him "no" before, especially when it was she who had so unexpectedly approached him and then led him on.

"Not yet."

He was puzzled but he kissed her once again, hoping to discover what was happening. He considered forcing her but he knew that no matter how much he wanted to, he could not bring himself to commit such an uncivilized act. As he continued to kiss her and wonder what she was thinking, he moved his hands over her body, something that she did not object to, until he felt her suddenly relax and say, "Now." He wasn't at all sure that he could perform on command but he decided that he would not wait for her to change her mind once again.

When she was done with him and he was done with her, he wondered what in the name of God she had just done to him but more importantly, what she had just done to herself. Perhaps it was some kind of magic that only the Jewish women had as he had never experienced anything like it before. He didn't have very long to rest, though, before she rolled him over onto his back again. This was an abomination, bestiality, and now it was beginning to make him nervous and even a bit worried for his soul: Women did not *do* such things and he was fairly certain that Christian women never, ever, acted like this.

Gilles recalled that the priests in France had warned the congregation about such things, in an abstract and obtuse sort of way of course, but the sermon and the situation seemed to fit, given that he was a Christian man having relations with a Jewish woman. Perhaps it *was* the work of the devil and he had no doubt for a moment or two that she was about to take possession of his soul. He wondered where he had left his rosary: He might wear it under his clothes if it wasn't so dangerous a thing to have here.

By the time Hannah was finally sated and was finally still, Gilles' fear had evaporated with his perspiration on this dry summer day and he smiled at her.

"I would not have believed that there were such women in the world."

"There aren't, there is only me," she replied. "I'm the only one."

"They would kill enchantresses like you in Fr ... where I come from," Gilles said. He didn't mention that they would kill adulterers and Jews too, but that was true as well.

"I'm glad I'm not there, then." Hannah sat up and pulled her skirts down.

"Wait, can't you stay with me?" He touched her warm and sweaty arm. "Just for a little while longer?"

"Nee."

She laced her bodice up in silence and then straightened her hair, pinning it up off her neck again. Gilles watched her, speechless and exhausted. He barely knew her name. He felt something peculiar in his stomach, though, something that was not so good, when she stood up and reached for her wedding ring. What kind of a relationship did she have with her husband that she was able to remove that piece of ornament so casually? She slipped her ring back onto her finger and giving Gilles a last passionate kiss, she opened the door, walked out, and was gone.

Gilles was afraid that someone would find him in this state of dishabille, so he quickly pulled his clothing back together, too. He tossed the sack from the floor back up on top of the others in the pile, hoping that Jacob would not notice anything amiss, and closed the door of the shed behind him as he left. Gilles felt a little uneasy about being with Jacob's daughter but it was really none of Jacob's business, he told himself. Besides, it was *she* who had approached him first.

Gilles returned to the stable and it appeared that he had missed nothing at all in the time that he had been gone. He took the sign down and shook his head, smiling as he looked at it. Perhaps Jacob had used it for the same thing a long time ago, back when his wife was still alive.

The afternoon went by quickly with Gilles thinking about Hannah's morning visit throughout the day. He fantasized about Hannah returning before Jacob got back but she didn't. Jacob arrived late in the day with a cart full of feed and hay for the horses as well as some food for himself

"Were there any problems while I was away?" he asked Gilles.

"No, nothing," Gilles replied.

"Gut, gut," Jacob said and they started to unload the cart together. "I see Hannah brought our clothes."

Gilles didn't know what to say that wouldn't incriminate him, either with his words or the sound of his voice so he said nothing. He did start to wonder just a little more about Hannah's husband. Was he a cruel man, a cold or unloving man, a fool that she could not love? Perhaps he was a sick old man. Gilles could not ask these questions of Jacob or the old man would certainly want to know why he was so interested.

"You seem to have something on your mind today. Keeping your thoughts captive will only make them restless," Jacob said.

"Oh, I'm only thinking about dinner and how I can save more money."

Jacob smiled. "Is that all? I will tell you what you can do: Go to the inn I sent you to and *make a bargain* with them. Tell them that you will take whatever meal they have left over each evening for half price. Tell them that they can sell their leftover food to you *every* night."

"How can I be sure there will be food left over?" Gilles asked.

"Because they will cook it *just for you*! Go and do it tonight!" Jacob urged him.

Gilles didn't think it was something that he would do, but he didn't want to be rude to Jacob so he said no more.

When the long day was over, Gilles did give a little thought to Jacob's suggestion but before he thought about it much more, Jacob grabbed him by the elbow.

"Come with me now, we will fix your food situation."

"I really don't think ..." Gilles began but before he could say any more, Jacob had closed the door and was leading him up the street. Gilles didn't want to talk to the girl. He wanted the food at the best price he could get but he didn't want to do what Jacob told him to do; it was too much like begging.

When they got to the inn, Jacob knocked on the door in the alley, then he stepped away to the side. Gilles panicked but there was nothing he could do but stammer out his request when the haughty girl opened the door.

Her response was to laugh out loud but she smiled at Jacob when she saw him and said "Done!" before she closed the door on both of them. Gilles looked over uncertainly at Jacob who only nodded at him and said, "Just wait."

After a minute or two the girl opened the door again, handed Gilles some food, and counted the money from his palm before she shut the door again.

Gilles turned to Jacob, wondering if he had managed the transaction correctly. Apparently he had not because Jacob smiled patronizingly at him, as he shook his head. "*Goyim!* Next time, leave *only* the amount you want to pay in your hand, the amount that you will agree to. Tell her that you have no more! If there is any question at all, shrug your shoulders and sigh, turn around, and walk away. She will come after you."

"What if she doesn't come after me?" Gilles asked.

"'*What if they don't agree to the bargain?*' Isn't that what you said to me before? *You* worry too much."

Jacob poked Gilles in the chest and then patted him on the shoulder before he straightened his hat and left Gilles, going back up the street toward the stable. Gilles just stood there for a moment, looking after him, holding his money in one hand and his food in the other. As Gilles walked toward Dirck's house, eating his meal as he went, he couldn't believe that it was only his fourth day at Jacob's. It seemed like he had been working there for much longer.

On Wednesday Gilles decided to move into the stable, taking Jacob up on his offer to sleep there. It was just too uncomfortable seeing Dirck every evening and every morning, his insults and his large meals always spread out before him. Although Gilles would miss seeing Jean every day, Gilles saw little enough of him due to the long hours of work. Gilles remembered his manners and thanked Dirck, as graciously as he could, for letting him stay there and told Dirck and Jean where he would be living. Jean was looking more like his former self these days with his face healing, his weight starting to return to normal and stylish clothes on his back. The only change in him was the perpetual scowl that was on his face. Gilles knew that he was jealous of Jean's position but he reminded himself that he needed to be happy for his friend, especially because Jean was not so happy for himself.

Gilles claimed a corner in the hay loft at Jacob's stable and converted it into a bedroom of sorts. "*It's certainly not home,*" he thought to himself sardonically but he shut that thought out in a hurry when he started to think of his old room, the new wing, and Marie. He used the priest's robe for a pillow and his cloak as a bedcover for the hay. Jacob also donated an old woven blanket for his use.

Gilles found a small cask of nails in the storage room and he moved the contents to another container so he could use the cask as a table and to store things inside. He used two of the nails, one to hang his pants on at night and the other to hold his French clothes. He didn't like wearing the same clothes every day for work and he didn't want to wear his old clothes; they were much too fine for stable work and as Dirck had said, they looked too French. Gilles wanted to get another change of clothes to work in.

He thought of the silks and laces that he used to wear every day, and not so long ago. He thought of the gold buttons, the ostrich feathers and the fine embroidery work that adorned all of the clothing that crowded his wardrobe at home. Even if he could afford them, even if he had someone to make these things for him and even if he could wear them where they wouldn't be covered with sweat or manure from the horses, it would be dangerous to wear such things now and to call attention to himself.

Gilles thought that perhaps he might spend just a little of his money on a change of clothes even though it was taking him much longer to save even a little money than he ever thought it would.

Jean gave Gilles a mirror and some scissors to trim his scraggly and uneven beard and Gilles kept these few possessions on one exposed wooden beam near his bedding. When he had the time, he looked often at the man who returned his gaze from the little bit of mirror. It was no longer a boy's face, but a man's face that looked back at him. The face was becoming lined and it was framed by unkempt, unadorned auburn hair and a red beard. It was a thinner face now and not without an aspect of sadness to it.

"I'd better get used to having you around," Gilles said to the mirror. "The other one isn't coming back."

For the most part Gilles enjoyed working with the horses. If someone had told him that he could do this all day long back in France, he might have thought it was a wonderful way to spend every day and his greatest wish come true. The only bad parts of his day usually occurred when the inevitable dandy, a nouveau rich, showed up. They were often very young, sometimes no older than Gilles himself. Success in the trade business had filled their pockets with money and swelled their sense of self-importance. The young men ignored Gilles or worse, treated him like a stray dog. When they came inside in a group, they often tried to outdo each other to see who could be the most rude to Gilles. They threw their reins at him, and thinking that he did not understand them or must be a mute or an idiot, they often made rude remarks about him as if he wasn't there.

At these times Gilles wanted to shout, "Do you know who I used to be?" but he didn't. Instead he sent them off with loose girths or burrs on the back of the saddle that would not touch the horse but would find their way into the men's coats and pants as they traveled and bounced along.

Hannah returned to the stable on the following Tuesday and they greeted each other with smiles as they waited for Gilles' customer to leave. She returned to Gilles every Tuesday after Jacob left for the Dam. Gilles settled into the routine and was comfortable with it: There were busy Mondays, Hannah on Tuesdays, the manure carting men on Thursdays, busy Sabbath preparations on Friday and very quiet Saturdays.

One day after work Gilles was looking in the mirror and thinking about how much his face had changed. *"My own mother wouldn't know me,"* he was thinking, and then he heard a voice from down below.

"Is anyone here?"

Who could be coming in so late? He looked over the side of the loft and saw Jean Durie standing down below. Gilles swung down from his lookout and embraced his friend in greeting.

"I brought you a present," Jean said, reaching into his pocket.

"A present?" Gilles was curious. "Why? What is it?"

"You don't remember on the ship coming over, that you kept me alive and sane?" Jean asked, handing Gilles the heavy package.

Gilles ignored the slushy sentiment and pulled the fabric off the parcel. "What is it?" Gilles asked again, looking at his gift. "It's beautiful but what is it? Do I wear it or hang it up or what?"

Jean grinned at him and Gilles liked seeing Jean smile again.

"It's called a *wampum belt* and you can do whatever you like with it. The purple and white beads are shells from the new world and they are supposed to tell some kind of story, although I have no idea what the story might be. I just thought you might like it since we promised to buy each other something when our first pay came in."

"I like it," Gilles said, although he was still not sure what he would do with it. "But I have nothing for you!"

"When you make your fortune, I'm sure you will get me something. Can you come to supper with me now? I want to buy you supper."

"Supper too? I have nothing suitable to wear ..."

Jean dismissed this and interrupted, "I just want to get away from Dirck and *enjoy* myself. I thought I might bring you along and we could find some kind of mischief to get into together."

Gilles had to smile at this. Surely they could get into no more trouble here than they had in France. He protested that he had to clean himself up first but in truth he had very little to do to get ready besides washing his face and hands, putting on his other clothes and pulling his hair back again. He left the wampum belt under his hay pillow before they set out.

They went up the street to an inn at some distance from the stable and first Jean ordered the best wine he could after he questioned the proprietor about their available selection. Gilles had not had any wine at all since he had left France unless one counted Dirck's sacramental wine on his first night after their escape. Gilles and Jean quickly finished one bottle while they decided on food and then started on a second bottle. Every dish that passed by looked good to Gilles, and Jean, perhaps seeing this in his friend's face, ordered one of everything.

When Gilles protested that he couldn't eat it all, Jean only said, "You will do your very best, I'm sure."

They drank and ate, ate and drank and were almost unable to eat any more when Jean exclaimed, "I almost forgot! I got a letter from your father and I'm sure there is some money in it for you. Dirck was going to keep the money but I intercepted it. He said it was fair compensation for the risk he took in having you stay with him for the first few days. We can probably send a letter back to your father, Gilles, but you must be careful not to mention his name or yours, or any other details when you write."

Gilles trembled when he saw his father's looping writing on the packet and he touched it, not sure if he wanted to open it there at the table. It was a connection to a life that no longer existed, like handling the clothes of the dead and then still smelling that person's scent on them. He worried that he might become too emotional in front of Jean but after bracing himself and taking another mouthful of wine, he resolutely ripped the packet open. There was indeed money inside but Gilles bypassed that and read the accompanying note silently:

> *"We are sorry that you can not come back to us again. We manage although there were some difficulties and hope only that you are well. We will try to send more and also send our wishes for your continued well-being."*

It was not signed and the note only served to make Gilles angry: It was too brief, too cold, and Gilles had nearly memorized it after reading it just twice.

"That's all?" he said out loud.

He took the money, sent in Nederland Florins, which would not have been a large sum when he lived at home but now seemed a small fortune to him, and shoved it into his pocket.

"May I?" Jean pointed to the letter and Gilles thrust it toward him. Jean took the letter from Gilles' hand and scanned it.

"He wrote to you, Gilles, this at great risk to himself."

"Mmm," Gilles replied putting his fork down amidst the dozen plates on the table.

"Gilles, you don't know, there may have been *great hardships* that he faced and all because of us."

"You defend him, and this after he abandoned *you*. He just doesn't care; it's all simply business to him."

"I know a *little* something about family," Jean said sharply, handing the letter back to Gilles. "He was *trying* to save his son. Any decent man would have done the same, would have done *anything* to that end."

Both men fell silent. Gilles tucked the letter in his pocket with the money.

"Pay attention and watch that," Jean said, leaning over the table. "There are thieves everywhere."

Gilles nodded to Jean but he didn't want to talk any more about either the money or the letter.

"Where did you get the wampum belt?" he asked Jean, changing the subject.

A servant brought dessert out. Gilles hungrily eyed the cream and the berries as well as the girl.

"A ship from the New Netherlands colony came in today with a large cargo of tobacco, beaver pelts, and some savages to be sold as slaves; dried fish too, but who needs fish here? That was a silly waste of space even if they were a *different kind* of fish. I handled the accounting for them. They will be taking back farm animals, guns, and women for the company men. Can you imagine? A boatload of women! The most interesting part of the cargo was the savages and their things: the wampum belt, some war axes or tomahawks as they call them, some arrows, and their leather clothes and decorated leather shoes. They burned the savage's clothing, of course, but one of the sailors wanted their decorated shoes and took those. The crew was a mélange of Frenchmen, Netherlanders, and some Germans. She was flying a French flag when she came in and was almost fired on and boarded by a Spanish warship just outside the harbor when she wouldn't identify herself right away. It was a good thing that they recognized her as being from this port before they touched off the powder! Anyway, I suppose they made a stop in New France and needed the flag for safe passage out to sea through the savage villages that line the St Laurent Riviere, and then they just left it up on the mast hoping pirates would think she was carrying French weapons and soldiers. Holland *exports* soldiers and weaponry but she *never* brings any back home; everyone knows that."

Gilles hung on to Jean's every word and envied his friend's having seen the excitement for himself. Not summoned by Gilles though, a memory came to him of walking with his father by the docks and a man throwing himself at their feet, pleading for help while soldiers pried the man's arms loose from Jean Montrovilles' knees before dragging him away.

"Was it safe for you to go to the Dam, Jean?"

"I don't go there too often but when I do, I try to blend in with the crowds from this part of town. With the beard and my hat pulled down over my eyes, I don't think anyone would know me at all."

Gilles knew at that moment that he had to go. He would go the very next day if he could manage it. He wanted desperately to see more of the world than what little he had seen, especially now that he was trapped inside one miserable little building, the stable, since his exile from France. He said nothing to Jean about his intentions but he listened intently, reliving the experience of visiting the square through his friend.

They embraced in farewell outside the inn and Gilles thanked his friend for the food, his gift and even for the letter from his father although he wasn't sure if his life was better for having received it or not. Gilles checked his pocket for the envelope and money, checked the streets for thieves, and made his way back to Jacob's stable as quickly as he could, avoiding the alleys and any dark areas that he passed.

Gilles didn't know why he did it, but for some reason he had carried some bread away with him, hiding it in his other pocket and guiltily nibbling on it after he left Jean. His stomach was still completely full and the bread made a mess in his pocket but it seemed a waste of food just to leave it unconsumed. Although the crumbs accumulated in his pocket and built up under his dirty fingernails when he reached in for more of it, Gilles thought that he might have the rest of it for his breakfast the next morning. He hoped that if there were thieves around they would be content to just steal the bread and not his money, although good food was almost as valuable to Gilles now as the money itself was.

Gilles paused outside the stable to listen for any thieves or anyone else that might be in the streets but all was quiet. He unlatched the door and stood on the other side after he closed it behind him, swaying back and forth a little from the effects of the wine he had consumed, and listening for just a few more moments. It was silly to be so concerned about having ventured such a short distance away. Gilles made his way through the stable and into the deeper darkness inside the building as one of the horses made a noise of acknowledgement. Gilles climbed the stable wall to go up to his bed but even after Gilles was up in the loft, he paused yet again and listened. He put his worried thoughts aside and put the bread inside the small cask before he jammed the lid on tightly to keep the bugs and rats out.

Gilles settled into his bed in the hay, thinking about all the wonderful food and wine that he had enjoyed so much that evening. A shaft of moonlight came through a broken board in the barn wall and illuminated the area near his head. Feeling the hard lump of the wampum belt under his pillow, Gilles remembered Jean's gift and pulled it out, holding it up in the moonlight to admire it. The shell beads had seemed smooth before but now he could feel, more than see, that they had a gritty texture, more like pearls than glass beads.

He got out of his bed and checked his hiding place in a corner under the hay. The pearls were still there. He wasn't sure what to do with them and so he had hidden them for the time being. He didn't want to trade them in just for food or clothes but he also did not want the daily reminder of carrying them around on his person, either. He didn't know who he could trust to give him a fair price so he just kept them, just far enough away that the reminder would not be there constantly, throughout every day. It was only at night when he closed his eyes that he thought about them at all, thought of how alone he was in the world, and thought of Marie. He always replaced his thoughts of her quickly with Hannah and summoned the thought of the next Tuesday when they would meet again.

Sometimes this trick of the mind worked and sometimes it didn't. Gilles put the pearls back under the hay and didn't bother to stand back up. He crawled on his knees over the hay to his bedding. The shaft of moonbeam had moved just a little and was in his eyes now so he shifted his pillow of hay over, out of the bright light, and looked at the wampum belt again. It had what appeared to him to be pictures of men and houses, rivers and mountains and other peculiar patterns that had no meaning to him. It danced and moved in the moonlight, pulsating the way Gilles' vision was pulsating, moving to the beat of the wine-laced blood that was moving through his veins. He put the belt down on the hay next to him and decided that he would hang it up as his first artwork, the first piece of a collection perhaps, on the wall near his bed in the morning. He was asleep before his next thought, dreaming of savages wearing wampum belts and the artists on the streets in Amsterdam making pictures with wampum designs to hang on the walls of the wealthy merchants of Amsterdam.

It was a little lighter in the barn when Gilles woke up. He wanted to sleep more but he kept dreaming about his father's letter. He finally got up, his head and stomach aching from the wine and the food, and thinking that he might have just a little bit of the salvaged bread but he finished it all, reasoning that it would be too hard to eat later on. He got some water to drink and then brought a hammer and nail up to hang the wampum belt on the wall before Jacob came in. When Jacob did walk in, he saw it right away.

"What is that thing?" he asked Gilles.

Gilles explained what little he knew about it.

"It looks like it could scare the horses!" Jacob replied, adjusting his hat on his head as he looked up at it.

"I think it's a beautiful thing," Gilles said.

Jacob shrugged and said no more.

"I need some time off," Gilles said, thinking that he would use his father's money to buy clothes.

"You just started working for me! Impossible!" Jacob picked up the water buckets and went outside to fill them.

When Jacob returned, Gilles decided to try the same tactics that Jacob had taught him for getting food at the inn.

"I just need a few hours to get some more clothes and I'll be back before it gets busy."

Jacob stood still, his bucket in mid-air. "What do you need clothes for? The *horses* don't care!"

"Today would be a good day. It's Thursday and not too busy. I could go after your lunchtime and be back in time to finish my work before dark."

"And leave me to do all the work before you get back, I suppose?"

"You could leave it for me and I could work *longer*."

"The horses need to be fed *now*! And what about the people who come in? Shall I tell them to come back when it is a better time for you?" Jacob scowled at Gilles.

"There won't be many today. I'll clean *all* of the stalls for you, every one."

"All right, all right, but feed all the horses first! You will clean *all* the stalls and I'm only paying you half a day's pay."

Jacob drove a hard bargain. Gilles hated to give up half a day's wages but he had what he needed, time off, a little money in his pocket, and not coincidently, the chance to see the Dam again. He worked faster and harder than he had since his first day. Jacob looked over at him from time to time and shook his head. Gilles had the distinct feeling that Jacob did not believe the requested time off was for buying new clothes at all.

"Just stay inside our area if you want to be safe," Jacob admonished him.

The thought did occur to Gilles that not only was Jacob at risk for giving him refuge, but Jacob could also have collected a fine reward for himself by turning Gilles in. There were many refugees in this part of the city but there were none like Gilles. Jean Durie fit in, could blend in easily, but Gilles did not.

Gilles felt a momentary urge to stay in the safety of the Jewish quarter but he knew that he could not, even if it endangered him to venture outside; so great was his need to see the outside world that he would risk even his own safety, just for the smallest taste of freedom.

"I saw Jean Durie come here last night and I saw the two of you leave together. He takes too many risks. Don't follow his example," Jacob warned. "Sometimes I think he *wants* to die."

Gilles said nothing in reply to this odd comment. He just kept working. He gathered up a length of rope and took it over to where it belonged, hanging it up on a nail near the front door. Jacob came over and set his pitch fork down against the wall. They both stood and watched in amusement as two Marrano men dragged a large table past the front door of the stable and on up the street.

"Someone should tell you. It *shouldn't* be me, but if no one else will, then it will *have* to be me, I suppose. You know I don't gossip, but Jean Durie's life is not simple. If you don't know that about him, it can be confusing," Jacob said.

"He said something like that once," Gilles said, hoping that Jacob would tell him more. Jacob obliged.

"They say that Jean's mother was a French merchant's daughter who only lived in Amsterdam for a short time. The old women all tell me that Dirck, or *Diego*, as he was called then, was a fine young man to look at, that all the young girls *did* look, and not just the Jewish girls. They probably met at the market, and young people being what they are, the two found a way to see each other more often."

"Isn't it, ah, *illegal* here for a Jewish man and a Christian woman …?" Gilles didn't know how to ask it delicately.

"If she had been a Nederlander, it would have turned out very differently for Diego," Jacob agreed, not at all put off by Gilles' inquiry, "but she was French and very soon she was shipped back to France and married off right away to a wealthy old Frenchman. Young Jean must have known something of his origins, though. He was no older than you when he came looking for Diego during his first trip to Amsterdam. Finding *our* people at the end of his search, at his own beginnings, must have been a terrible shock to him and yet he didn't turn his back on us, he always returned and always treated us like family even if *we* didn't always treat him like a long-lost son. I know that Jean was raised with a good education, money, and a fine name. I also know that he was raised a Catholic, a *Converso*, as Diego calls him. Any other man would have walked away, and it would have been so much easier, but Jean didn't do that. He got to know us, and because of that, we got to know him. Now that Jean is here for a time, Diego wants him to stay. It would seem to be a happy ending, no?"

"Why don't they get along then?" Gilles asked. "Jean can get along with anyone, can't he?"

Jacob sighed and shook his head. "Jean and Diego are *completely* different men. Diego is a typical Sephardic, conceited, miserly, selfish, and mean-spirited, the Almighty forgive me for telling the truth! Jean saw the refugee in himself, maybe, and knows in his heart what *tsadaka*, charity, is. In spite of his outward show of piety, Diego has nearly forgotten what he is although he proclaims to the world at every opportunity how much he is a religious man. His religion is *making money*, as if money can ever change what you are! The truth is that Diego *needs* Jean. He wants Jean to forget about the upbringing and the parents he had and to come be his son, to justify the way Diego has lived his life by showing the world what a fine son he has in Jean. Diego has never shared his life with *anyone*, though, not even with a woman; he is too selfish even for the convenience of regular gratification or maybe he just never found a woman with enough money for him. Diego probably thinks that he can quickly acquire an entire family, a future blood line now that the loneliness of old age is fast approaching, but all he shares with Jean Durie *is* his blood. Jean moves between the two worlds and you can't ask him to completely leave either one forever. It is the Almighty's little joke that the only place Jean could come to for protection this time was to his father's, to Diego's, know him or not, like him or not. Family is like that."

Jacob finished his story and winked at Gilles. Gilles held back a lump that was rising in his throat. His family was gone from him now, probably forever. There was no place at all, good or bad, for him to find sanctuary. There was no place at all except Jacob's stable.

"Where is his mother then? Is his father in France dead?" Gilles hoped he was not being too inquisitive by asking but he wanted to know more about Jean and to think less about his own family at the moment.

"That's about all anyone knows. Jean doesn't talk about it and neither does Diego. Jean has probably told *you* more about his family than he's told anyone else."

"He's told me nothing!" Gilles protested.

"Yes, well.... What is lost always leaves something gained, just as something gained *always* leaves something lost."

Jacob picked the fork up again and resumed his work. Gilles only puzzled over this latest rambling for a moment or two before he returned to work as well, eager to get the job done so he could leave for the square but Jacob's strange tale about Jean Durie repeated in his head while he labored.

Jacob went into his house for his midday dinner and it seemed to Gilles to take longer than the usual amount of time before he returned. Gilles waited impatiently and he cursed the old man's taking so much time. It was silly to be so excited about such a routine errand. At long last Jacob returned, bringing Gilles some food and carrying some fringed material in his other hand. The fringe looked like the kind Gilles had seen Dirck and other Jewish men wearing underneath their clothes.

"Wear this," Jacob said. "Put it on under your shirt but let it hang out just enough for others to see it. Don't take off that ugly hat that Diego gave you, either, *not ever*. The Almighty forgive *me* and protect *you*, but you are just a boy." Jacob looked up to the heavens and made a conciliatory gesture. "… and make sure you go to the *Jewish* tailors on the square!"

Gilles didn't really want to wear the thing but he didn't see that he had a choice with Jacob standing there. He pulled his shirt off and put the sweat-stained old garment on with a little help from Jacob. Gilles put his shirt back on over it, and was gone before Jacob could finish his series of warnings and admonitions.

The tailor shop was a small and shabby place just on the outskirts of the market square. It had just dawned on Gilles as he thought about clothing and the shops he had passed on his previous visits to Amsterdam that this particular one was owned by Jews although he would not have realized that as he passed by the outside of it just weeks earlier. Now he was reasonably sure that he could pick out which ones were shops owned by Jews and which were not, with almost total accuracy. With such a good location one might think that this tailor would do at least as well as the larger clothing makers who belonged to the Amsterdam guild, but that was not the case. Because it was owned by Jews, the people who walked into this shop all fell into one of three categories: Jews of all sorts, Marranos looking for work, and a few strangers to the city who wandered in by mistake and then quickly wandered back out again.

There were other tailors, prosperous men with profitable shops that made excellent clothing but Gilles neither needed the sort of clothes they made nor the attention that he might get there, even if he had the money for such extravagance. It was hard to believe that there were so many men in the city that had no wives, mothers, daughters or servants to make their clothing for them or whose women did not possess the skill needed to work with lace, silk, or beading but as a result both the guilds and the little shops had very healthy businesses going. Some of the tailors catered exclusively to the wealthy; their very stylish clothing was magnificently ornate and could only be made by professionals who had the expertise from years of apprenticeship and sufficient compensation to spend days sewing webs of pearls onto lace collars, evenly-spaced patterns of smocking on sleeves of layered fabrics, and cascades of jewels into brocades.

Gilles noted that the dreary little shop was one and the same that Jacob had mentioned as he put his hand on the door. He walked inside and saw a long table with three men and a young boy sitting there, all with hats on their heads and needles in their hands and all so similar in appearance that they could have been the same man at different ages of his life. Stacks of drab, dark material overflowed from the table onto the floor and stacks of clothes with bits of paper pinned to them were folded on another smaller table to the side. A third table had satiny white material with fringe on it along with various colors of velvet and spools of bright yellow and sky blue thread. An old man got up stiffly from his seat and limped over to Gilles, looking him over closely as if to decide for himself whether Gilles was Jewish, Marrano or the wandered-in type. He seemed at last to settle on Jewish or wandered-in, judging from his polite manner.

"I need three shirts and three pairs of pants, for work," Gilles said to him.

"When do you need them?" the tailor asked, closely inspecting Gilles' clothing and appearance without any apparent trace of embarrassment at doing so.

"When can I have them?" Gilles responded, thinking that he was beginning to sound like Jacob.

"When they are done?" the tailor tested.

"This week?" Gilles asked.

"Next week?" the tailor proposed.

"How much?"

"One guilder, three stuivers apiece," the old man replied.

"Too much!" Gilles turned around.

"One guilder, two!" the old man raised his voice and threw it after Gilles.

Gilles paused but did not turn back around to face him yet.

"One guilder each, our last offer," the old tailor bid.

"Then I can get a pocket in the pants?"

"We can make *one* pocket in each pair," the tailor shrugged.

"Simple shirts but with a button on top."

"Buttons? Buttons are extra!"

"One button on each shirt, on the top, that's all," Gilles argued.

"Three stuivers for the extra buttons!"

"One is all I can pay."

"Two, two stuivers for the three buttons."

"All right, six guilders, two stuivers total."

"Eight guilders total including our work." The tailor now added in his labor costs.

"Seven," Giles countered.

"For three shirts with buttons and three pairs of britches?! Eight guilders, no less! And only because we are slow this week!" the tailor acted as though his feelings had been hurt.

"Seven is my last offer."

"Eight." the tailor glowered at him.

Gilles turned with a louder than average sigh and started to the door. The tailor wasn't coming. Gilles reached the door and wondered what he would do next but the tailor called out just in time, "All right! Seven! But we aren't even *breaking even* on this!"

Gilles turned around and wanted to smile but he kept a scowl in place on his face.

The tailor came over to Gilles and took some measurements, writing them down on a small wooden board with something that looked like a piece of white stone. He started a little when he saw the fringes on Gilles' undergarment which he had apparently not noticed before. He smiled up at Gilles.

"They will be ready next Tuesday. I'll take the money now."

"I don't have it with me," Gilles lied.

He wasn't sure why he said that but he just did. Perhaps he simply liked the feeling of keeping the money in his pocket and the feel of having it full for a change.

"I need to buy the materials and I need to pay my help."

"I can give you half now and half when they are completed." Gilles said.

The tailor seemed to expect this and just smiled in agreement. Gilles gave him four guilders, being careful to leave the rest in his pocket and not jingle it as he pulled the money out for the tailor. He handed it over to the man and left the shop.

Next Gilles wanted to see if there was a place where he could sell his pearls. A part of him wanted to keep the pearls because they were so beautiful and as long as he had possession of them, he could hold fast to the hope that he would be with Marie and by extension, with his family in the future.

Another part of him, the realistic part, felt too much pain and sorrow every time he looked at them and wanted to be rid of them once and for all. Even if he sold them, he was not sure that he would ever be able to forget about either the pearls or Marie. When things finally settled down in France, if Gilles could go back one day, he would buy Marie other jewels when he returned.

It *did* feel good to be anonymous in his disguise and the momentary panic Gilles felt at passing some Frenchmen subsided quickly when they drew their cloaks away from him to avoid having him, a Jew, come into contact with their clothes. He remembered doing the very same thing himself, a long time ago in a different life.

He relaxed a little and started to take in the sights, sounds, and smells as he entered the Dam. He had never really noticed the artists and paintings before. Of course he saw them everywhere on the streets during his earlier visits but now he was so taken with the beauty of their paintings that he wanted to buy them all. They were very inexpensive and he thought that he might buy just one but in the end he kept his money in his pocket. Now Gilles remembered the portrait over the fireplace in his father's study. It was supposed to have gone to him when his father died but now it would certainly be Charles' picture someday.

The artists were everywhere and pictures of food, dramatic events, successful men and beautiful women filled the easels. The artists spilled over into the streets from buildings that housed great schools of art or just popped up individually like stray tulips in the spring. Less successful artists hawked their wares while the more prosperous ones looked down upon the streets from their studios. Gilles looked up and saw that the upper floor of one building had many artists busily painting away up there; all with a good view of the square and the Zuiderkirk also.

The wind had changed direction now and Gilles could smell the spices from the East India Company building. Goods were traveling back and forth from France, New France, and New Amsterdam and ships were arriving from other ports across the world. He had almost forgotten the smell of the exotic foods that lingered in the air, the ginger, the curry and the cinnamon, and he took a deep breath to take it all in. Some of the early morning street vendors were closing up, having already sold all of their wares for the day.

Gilles still could not get used to the free and easy way that the couples moved hand-in-hand in the streets; such a thing would not have been tolerated in France. Gilles made a quick circuit around the square, looking for a place to trade the pearls, keeping a careful eye out for Frenchmen, particularly the kind that might be looking to return missing prisoners and collect a reward. Gilles attempted to look as Jewish as he could, even imitating Jacob's posture and gait as much as possible.

One store on the opposite end of the square had jewelry displayed in a window along with other silver and gold objects. They might be interested in buying the pearls. Gilles walked inside and looked over the shelves of wares on display. The shopkeeper didn't come over to talk to Gilles from his place behind a table, didn't even greet him, but stood staring at him. Gilles looked around a little and then asked if he dealt in pearls at all.

"Pearls? Nee, no pearls here."

The man's manner was so unfriendly and suspicious that Gilles left without asking any further questions.

A few doors up the street a store sign declared that it sold all manner of shipping items. Gilles went inside and walked past great coils of rope, large wooden pulleys and buckets of metal hardware of every kind and discovered the shopkeeper completing the sale of a knife to a customer. Gilles wasn't even sure why he was drawn inside; perhaps just being so close to things that would end up on a ship, even if he never did set foot on board a ship again, was enough to bring his feet through the door. He might buy Jean a knife here. There were knives for cutting rope, knives for cutting into barrels, and knives that made quick work of troublesome canvas. Gilles had no idea that there could be so many different types of knives.

"What do you want it for?" the man asked Gilles as he showed him a sampling of his wares.

Sheepishly Gilles told him that his friend carved wooden things. He tried to speak quietly so the sailors in the shop wouldn't hear him. The shopkeeper just smiled and showed Gilles more knives. Gilles decided on a knife that seemed similar to the one Jean had owned before but he wondered now if two guilders was too much to pay for a knife. In the end he bought two, one for Jean and another one for himself as well. He wasn't sure why he did that, but it seemed like a good investment in his future safety as long as he was buying knives.

"We don't see many of you in here," the shopkeeper said with a kind smile as he wrapped Gilles' knives up in a bit of rag and handed them over to him. Gilles puzzled over his meaning at first but then it occurred to him that the Jews were generally not given to buying a great many sailing knives. This shopkeeper had just had the unusual experience of having one Jew walk boldly into a store that was not owned by Jews and buy not one, but *two* knives. Gilles remembered the treatment that he had received earlier from the shopkeeper with the gold and silver as realization dawned on him that he was not acting in accordance with his new persona. He was amused by these thoughts and with his adventure over, it was time to go back to Jacob's stable.

Just as he was leaving the store, he saw her. She had her basket over her arm and was standing by the vegetable stands. Seeing Elsje there was as startlingly familiar as it would have been if he had seen his own mother in the square. He had to speak to her but he wouldn't do it here, not out in the open. Gilles followed her at a safe distance as she stopped and bought some carrots and it was at that moment that he realized how tired he was of the heavy taste of garlic in every dish that the Jewish girl at the inn made for him. He wondered what wonderful dish Elsje would be making with those carrots.

She stopped at a few vendor stalls and shook her head at the produce but finally bought a great quantity of beets before she started back toward the inn with her purchases. Gilles caught up with her just before the church and after first looking around to make sure that they were alone, he grabbed her by the arm. Elsje was taken completely unawares and drew a fist back to hit him.

"Elsje, it's me! It's Gilles!"

"*It is!*" she exclaimed.

She took him by the hand to the back courtyard of the church where a secluded arbor built for mourners offered them a greater measure of privacy. She pulled him into the seat with her.

"We heard that you were *dead!*" she exclaimed. She still held his hand.

"Nee, I would have been, but I escaped from the prison."

"Look at you! What are you *wearing*? Are you living here in the city?"

Gilles turned red but he had to smile. "Ja, it's a good disguise, nee?"

"My father will be *so* pleased that you are alive and well, but you *must* be careful! There are French hunters in the city who look for fugitives, *for the reward.* We heard that you were executed for *treason!*" Elsje whispered as she peered just beyond him to be sure that they were alone.

"I think my crime was actually against the church but they weren't very clear about that."

"What do you have there in your hand?"

"Just some things that I needed to get," Gilles said.

He wasn't sure why, but he didn't want to tell her that he carried two knives on him. It felt good to know that *someone* was pleased to see him. He did not remember seeing *any* joy on his father's face when he last saw him, although the circumstances had been vastly different.

"Where are you staying?" Elsje wanted details.

"Jean and I are staying in the Jewish section. We don't come out too much."

Elsje nodded. "It's safer. I had heard that Jean had ties of some sort to the Jews. You are so thin! Are you getting enough to eat? Can I get you some food?"

"I am eating better now but I *do* miss your cooking." Gilles eyed the carrots again.

"I can meet you here tomorrow at the same time and give you some food then," Elsje offered.

"I'd like that."

Gilles wanted to throw his arms around her but he wondered how she would react if he did. If she lost her temper she might not come back and he wouldn't get the food. He didn't want to risk losing out on a great meal.

"I have to get back now but you will meet me here tomorrow at the same time?"

"Yes."

Elsje smiled and he squeezed her hand before they walked back to the street, still holding hands. A man walking by the church as they emerged from the courtyard glared at them and a magnificent coach rumbled by at a great rate of speed, almost hitting them before Gilles jumped out of the way, pulling Elsje with him.

"Van Rensselaer!" Elsje exclaimed. "He almost ran us over! There must be *very* important business somewhere for the pearl merchant to be here in town today and to be in such a hurry. Be very careful, Gilles, be safe."

Elsje shook hands with him to say good bye and then walked up the street with her loaded basket as Gilles stood and watched her for a short time. Elsje knew about everyone and everything in Amsterdam so maybe he could ask her about Van Rensselaer buying his pearls. He would ask her another time; he did not need to sell the pearls today. Gilles looked around to make sure that there were no bounty hunters or reckless coaches before he headed back up the street to the Jewish section. He thought about the plump carrots all the way back to the stable but he made sure to check behind him frequently and even zigzagged across some streets to be sure that no one followed him.

"I'm glad to see you back!" Jacob called. "It has been *busy*! It's starting early this week!"

Gilles tossed the package up into the loft and picked up a shovel.

"Did you get your clothes ordered?" Jacob asked.

"Ja."

"Hmph. He takes half the day off and has nothing much to say about it, only a smile on his face, and all for work clothes?"

Gilles did not answer as he wasn't sure if Jacob's comments were directed at him or were even meant to be heard at all but the words were too loud not to hear. He wondered what Jacob would say about his taking time off tomorrow, on a Friday.

Jacob wasn't going to like that.

Gilles would just have to find the best time to ask him for it.

A better time to approach Jacob for time off on the following day did not present itself. Business was busier than usual and Gilles was still working hard when Jacob left the stable for the night.

That night, in his hay bed, Gilles thought about Elsje. He thought first about the food but then he wondered what it would be like to kiss her, to be with her. He thought of her wearing a silk dress as he fell asleep.

The stable was very busy the next morning and a better time still did not come for Gilles to ask Jacob for time off that afternoon. Jacob got his midday dinner, a thick slice of dark bread with butter and he brought some back for Gilles. Gilles asked Jacob if it was midday already.

"Does it matter? Are you worried about observing sundown; too?" Jacob asked.

"I forgot to do something yesterday and I just have to run back to the Dam for a minute," Gilles lied.

"Not today!" Jacob said emphatically, "Not on Friday!"

"I *have* to go and it won't take me very long," Gilles said stubbornly.

"Whatever it is will wait until Monday," Jacob said, putting his food down as he grabbed the reins of two horses. The horses' owners hurried out of the stable without wasting energy on any conversation. "We already have people coming back and it will just be *worse* by the end of the day."

"I have to go *now*," Gilles said.

"Then don't come back," Jacob replied.

Not waiting to argue any more, Gilles went out the door and walked as quickly as he could toward the square. Others from the Jewish quarter were hurrying, too, hurrying to beat the sun's movement across the sky. He hoped that he did not smell too much like horses and he didn't waste any energy worrying about Jacob's threat: Gilles only thought of getting to Elsje on time and he wasn't going to think about anything else right now.

Gilles looked around the church courtyard when he got there. For a moment he panicked and worried that he was too late, wondered if he imagined yesterday, if she forgot, or if her father forbade her to come. He decided that he would go to

Hendrick's inn to see Elsje there if he had to; he would go to the back near the kitchen door and she would come outside and bring him food as she did for the Marranos. Gilles would wait in the churchyard for just a few more minutes and then he would go on to Hendrick's.

Now that Gilles had a little time to think, he worried about Jacob. What if Jacob meant what he said and found another stable worker? Gilles needed the money and if it was true that not many paid any better, where would he go and what would he do? When the sun came up this morning Gilles' life had seemed very good for the first time in a long time. Perhaps now he had lost the little he had gained back, had thrown it all away on the chance to get a basket of food. He looked up the street once again but still there was no sign of Elsje.

He went back into the churchyard and looked at the stones to pass some time. He wondered briefly what their lives had been like as he read some of the names and the dates. Had they lived their lives in peace and prosperity? They probably were born, lived and died in the same house and in the same circumstances. When they departed this life, sometimes after having been on this earth for nearly a century, they left no trace of having been here at all, nothing besides this stone and perhaps some surviving children.

Gilles' circumstances and his life had changed drastically from the time of his birth. Perhaps he had brought all of this trouble on himself by cursing his boring life in France. He wondered if he should leave Amsterdam and run away to sea. He thought he might book passage to the new world and New France was probably his first choice but there were other places that he could go. As he turned away from the stones, he saw Elsje coming into the churchyard at last with her basket.

"What are you doing all the way back here, Gilles?"

"Waiting for you."

"Waiting for my food!"

The weight of the large basket may have been what slowed her progress.

"Eat your way *down* from the top. There is chicken and some other food that will not keep for very long on the top but underneath I gave you two loaves of bread and some pastries." She smiled a special smile at him when she said the word "pastries".

"Thank you, it sounds wonderful, Elsje. How can I get your basket back to you?"

"Tomorrow?" she asked. "I can get away for a little while after dinner tomorrow but not for very long. Saturday is always a very busy ale night."

"Tomorrow it is!" Gilles took the food, gave Elsje a squeezing embrace with his left arm, and a kiss on each cheek. Before she could say anything more, he was gone with her basket.

He almost forgot to make sure that he was not being followed but he remembered at the last corner before Jacob's. Gilles prepared himself mentally before he entered the barn and faced his employer.

"You're back then." Jacob's eyes went right to the basket.

"It's food. Would you like some?"

"No, I just want someone who will work and not disappear when I need him the most."

"Yes, Jacob."

Gilles set the basket down on the table that they used sometimes for working on the horses' equipment. Gilles jumped into his work but before long the customers coming back for their mounts were lined up in the street and he was racing to catch up. Some of the dandies jingled money in their pockets impatiently or tapped their feet. Gilles didn't get to eat much at all until the sun started to go down and the customers abruptly stopped coming in. Jacob handed Gilles his pay and departed for Friday prayers without saying anything to him, which made Gilles more than happy: He didn't need a lecture tonight. The candle lights came up across the Jewish section of the city and peace settled in with the darkness.

Jacob usually let Gilles go get his dinner from the girl early on Fridays but Gilles was much later tonight. He put the basket up in his loft and took some of Elsje's chicken with him. He ate all the way to the inn and even though he already had a basket full of food, he wanted more, as much more as he could get. Being so much later, the girl had left his food outside on the stoep. He was a little surprised that the dogs in the street had not gotten to it yet but maybe she had just put it outside a few minutes before his arrival. He knocked on the door, and the girl opened it. Gilles was surprised to see her dressed in a formal-looking green dress.

"Yes? You are later tonight than usual," she observed.

"I have your money if this is my food." Gilles offered her the coins.

"*It's Sabbath*! No money today, you pay me *tomorrow*! Take your food and *go away*! You should at least learn our ways if you are going to stay here! *Idiot*!"

She muttered more complaints to herself and cursed at him in two languages as she slammed the door in his face.

Gilles didn't pay any attention to her. He would feast the night away up in his loft. He took all of the food back to the stable and ate until his stomach ached with the fullness of it all. He washed his food down with water and thought how nice some good wine would be to drink with it.

"If only I could change water into wine!" he said to himself.

He could not believe his good fortune in having plenty of good food, though; that alone was a small miracle, and enough to be thankful for, he decided. He wouldn't think about finding more food tomorrow. If *only* his financial fortunes could be what they had been before, but then he reasoned that it had happened with the food, so it *could* happen with his income.

Gilles ate so much that his stomach hurt and he found it hard to sleep. He was still feeling full the next morning but he didn't have to get up early so he stayed in his bed until he could sleep and lie there no more. His thoughts returned to Elsje and to their planned meeting later. He thought about using Jacob's tub to bathe in again when he saw Jacob leave the house in his best clothes, going to Hannah's house for dinner, no doubt.

Gilles took care of all of the horses but the day still went by too slowly and with too little to do before it was time to return Elsje's basket so Gilles passed the time by using some old bits of harness and leather to make an ugly but functional sheath and belt for his new knife, allowing him to wear it at his side underneath his outer clothes. He had never had a knife before and it did hold a certain interest for him; it was shiny, it felt comfortable in his hand and it was deadly sharp. Crafting the holder passed the time away until the sun was overhead, telling him that it was about noon-time. Gilles decided to forego the tub and just bathe using his usual bucket. He thought about wearing his new clothes, whatever they might look like, but he didn't have them yet. That was all right though, the French clothes were clean and would be more of what Elsje would expect him to wear.

It was hard to believe that she even spoke to him when he was dressed the way he had been two days before, like a shabby Jewish stable boy. Gilles' only concern now was that he might look too French in his old clothes and that they might attract the wrong kind of attention from the wrong people. Even though it was a warm day, he decided to wear his cloak to hide his clothes.

He emptied the last of the food from her basket but he wasn't sure what to do with Elsje's pastry. He finally put it in his storage keg and tapped the top down. He didn't want to just throw it out although he was quite sure that he didn't want to eat it, either. Now that he was looking and smelling acceptable to himself, and he hoped, to Elsje as well, he picked up the empty basket, put the sign up, closed the stable door behind him, and stepped outside.

The streets in the Jewish section were still quiet and it was too early for their little city within the great city to come back to life again. The entire population was still far away in their sacred world. Gilles could feel his knife in its new sheath under his clothing as he walked to the churchyard. It was a reassuring feeling but comfortable enough so that he forgot that he had it on by the time he arrived at their meeting place.

This time Elsje was already there, waiting for him. She had on a dress that was somewhat nicer than what she usually wore every day.

Gilles took her hand and kissed it in greeting. "Elsje, thank you for the food," he said. "It was magnificent." She didn't pull away so Gilles ventured, "Let's sit, I can stay awhile today." He escorted her over to the bench. He had all the time in the world to spend with her, he had until tomorrow morning.

They sat and said nothing for a few minutes. Elsje held the empty basket with one hand and looked out into the churchyard. Gilles sat looking at Elsje, holding her other hand. She really *was* a pretty girl but perhaps no one had ever noticed this because she was just Elsje, sensible, capable Elsje.

"Your food was wonderful. I have greatly missed your cooking." Gilles told her.

He brought her hand up to his lips and held it there. She made a slight attempt to pull it away but she stopped short of success.

"Did you get enough food?" She stole a glance at him and seemed almost shy today.

"Yes. I would love to have another basket sometime," he said as he pulled her hand back up to his lips.

"Your beard tickles. I can't stay long, I have to get back to the inn," Elsje said.

"Was your father pleased to hear that I was alive then?" Gilles asked, looking at her hand in his and bringing it up to his face to take in her hand's scent of soap.

"I didn't tell him," she said, her eyes avoiding his.

"Why not?"

The thought *had* crossed his mind that he might ask Elsje to check on the return on his investments but if Hendrick didn't even know that he was still alive, he might not ever see his money again. He could certainly use some of that money now.

"I … I just didn't. We had a busy day today. You look so different," Elsje said, giving Gilles a sideways look.

"Do clothes or appearance matter so much?" he asked her. He knew they did.

"I suppose not," she replied.

It was a little unnerving that she was *so* uncomfortable with him now. "We used to talk easily when I would come to the inn, Elsje."

"I thought I knew that person," Elsje said, looking out into the distance again.

"Is it because I have been in prison and have lost everything? Tell me to go away then, and I will."

Gilles half feared that he was right about this. Why should she be any different than anyone else? Everyone else avoided him after he had been cast into the gutter.

"Nee." She looked him fully in the face and smiled a half smile. "You just seem, *different*, older maybe, like you are not just a boy anymore."

"It was only weeks ago that I last saw you but perhaps my recent difficulties have aged me?"

"That must be it," she said but Elsje was still looking at him in a strange way.

"Tell me how I can repay you for your food and for your kindness."

"Repayment is not necessary. I have to go now." Elsje stood up and straightened her skirts.

"Don't go Elsje. Can't you stay for a few more minutes?"

She grabbed the basket handle. "It will be getting very busy at the inn already and they need me there. I am glad that you are well, Gilles. We will probably see each other in the market from time to time."

Gilles refused to be pushed aside though, and refused to let her go.

"Can I get some more food from you sometime? Tomorrow, maybe?"

"Nee, I don't think so."

"Next Friday then. Say you'll meet me here after sundown next Friday, Elsje."

"I don't think I can get away."

She looked out to the street, somewhat nervously, Gilles thought.

"Do I have to go to your back door after dark and beg? It would be dangerous but for your cooking, *I would*. I would go and *plead* with you for more of your cooking. I *can* pay you, if you'd like." He smiled his most charming smile for her.

There was a smile there, one that she struggled to hide, but it moved across her lips.

"All right, I can bring you another basket *next Friday*. You don't have to pay me but I'm sure that I won't be able to stay for very long then, either. God keep you safe, Gilles Montroville."

He returned to the stable that afternoon dancing up the streets and humming to himself. Life seemed good again and all because it had possibilities and hope. Having a full stomach had probably helped his outlook as well and it wasn't until much later that he realized he had forgotten to get his dinner from the girl at the inn.

Ah, well.

He got up, opened his little cask and tried a bite of the pastry. It was really no better than it had been before but in spite of this, he ate it and enjoyed the familiarity of the food if not the taste. Smiling at the memory of the first time he had tried it, he swallowed the last of it, got back into his bed, rolled over and quickly fell asleep.

In the early hours of the morning he woke suddenly after hearing a loud crash from somewhere down below him. With his heart pounding, Gilles stayed perfectly still, listening for more sounds. Whoever was down there was being very quiet now that he was awake. The horses didn't seem too disturbed although Gilles could tell that they were awake, too. His first thought was that it might be grain or horse thieves and his second thought was that it could be bounty hunters that had found him. He strained to hear any more sounds but many more minutes passed and still he could hear no noise at all from inside the barn except for the horses. Slowly Gilles reached over and took his new knife from under his pillow of hay, extricated himself from his bedding and crept slowly over to the edge of the loft. A bright moon was outside and enough of it came in through broken boards for Gilles to see that the front door was closed and that no one was standing down below him. He stayed at the edge of the loft listening for some time but hearing nothing more, he climbed down and moved quickly but quietly toward the back room where the grain was kept. If someone was hiding in the grain room, they wouldn't be able to get out without his seeing them. He crept into the room, checking on either side of the door first as he entered but he saw no one there. The only place anyone could hide was behind the sacks of grain.

Glancing over his shoulder to be sure that no one was behind him, he advanced toward the grain, his knife in his hand. Behind the sacks he saw only a pail, displaced from its usual hook and lying on its side.

"Damned rats!" Gilles muttered and noticed that the hole in the wall looked bigger than it had been before. His heart gradually stopped pounding as he dragged the pail against the hole and then anchored it there with a heavy sack of grain. "That will keep you out until morning," he said and went back up to sleep, feeling very foolish at the magnitude of his fear.

Gilles woke up when Jacob came in and called a loud good morning up to him. "Wake up! You sleep the day away! I need someone *reliable* to work for me. You can't just leave when there is work to be done, either," Jacob admonished him.

Gilles said nothing. He hoped that he would have many more chances to get out but hopefully his meetings would be more like last night's, with no urgency to return.

"You are a good worker and I would hate to have to train someone new all over again," Jacob said to him.

Gilles felt irritation at the implied threat but again he held his tongue. How hard could it be to train a stable boy?

"I myself had a good Sabbath," Jacob continued. My daughter sets a lovely table and is a wonderful cook like her mother, may my wife find eternal rest."

Gilles thought angrily that *he* never got a day of rest. Still he kept his silence.

"You *are* quiet today. You look tired and I noticed that you were not here when I arrived home last night," Jacob continued. "Were you and Jean out together again?"

Gilles skipped over the question about Jean. "I'm tired because the rats woke me up last night! You need to patch the hole in the grain room wall or get a barn cat."

"A cat? Oh no, they are evil creatures, no cat!"

"Is anyone here?" Jean Durie called out as he pushed the door open and stepped inside.

"You know we are; the horses never answer you, do they? Where is your horse, Jean?" Jacob asked. "We keep horses here."

"I need to get a horse so I can ride for two blocks just to give *you* my money?" Jean jokingly asked.

Jean made small talk with Jacob as Gilles and Jacob fed and watered the horses together. Jean asked Jacob about Hannah, making polite inquiries as to her health and then about some other people that Gilles did not know.

"Comment ca va?" Jean asked Gilles and then he spoke to Jacob. "I'm sorry, Jacob, Gilles still speaks more easily with me in French. You don't mind, do you?"

He continued to speak to Gilles in French, purposefully excluding Jacob from further conversation, Gilles was sure of it. Jacob tired of listening to the incomprehensible chatter and went to the store room to check on how much feed was left.

"What is the news here, Gilles? You haven't given me a letter to send to your father yet," Jean said.

"I didn't write one yet. What is new is that I saw Elsje."

"Where? How? You didn't go there?!"

"Non, I ran into her in the market and then she brought me some food. I feel like a charity case but I *did* enjoy it … except for the pastry of course."

Jean smiled at the mention of the pastry. "She didn't bring it *here?*"

"Non, I met her near the Dam. I was *very* careful and it was *so* good to get away from here, just for a little while. What is new in your life, Jean?"

"It's the same. Living with Dirck is driving me insane and I can't stay there. I have been thinking about living somewhere else and I wonder if I want to stay in this city at all."

"Where would you go?" Gilles could not imagine being left all alone in Amsterdam without Jean.

"Oh, I don't know. Italy maybe. Not Spain of course. England's trade is going quite well but the political situation is in too much of a mess right now and besides, *Englishmen* live there. Maybe I should go to New Amsterdam. There are many deals to be made there, many trades to make. They could use my services and it certainly wouldn't be dull."

"You? Living in New Amsterdam, among the savages? Among the traders and the criminals that live there? You know you could not live without your fine clothes and your little luxuries." Gilles pointed this out to dismiss the entire idea as a wild fantasy but Jean was not laughing and this worried Gilles a little.

"Speaking of pastimes, I have a gift for *you*," Gilles said. He climbed up into the loft and returned with the knife that he had bought for Jean. "I hope you like it. I thought of you when I saw it and remembered our bets on the ship coming over. Besides, you gave me the wampum belt."

Jean looked at it and didn't say anything at all for a few moments. It was not the reaction that Gilles was expecting.

"It's the wrong kind, not right?" Gilles asked him.

"Non, non, it's fine, it's very fine. I had thought about getting another sometime but … well, thank you." Jean tucked the knife inside his waistband.

"You won't leave and go anywhere far away without telling me first?" Gilles asked anxiously.

"Non, my friend. I have not worked out *any* of the details yet. I only know that I will be going somewhere, maybe only up the street, maybe farther. Well, tell Jacob I had to get back to my work. Write that letter to your father if you are going to."

It was going to be a very warm day and it was already getting hot inside the stable. Gilles opened the big door in the front and propped it open with the old bench that they used exclusively for this purpose since no one ever had the time to sit on the bench, not Jacob, not Gilles, and certainly not the harried customers. Gilles watched as a man in a blue suit passed by the door, looking curiously in at Gilles and at the stable. He was very finely dressed, right down to his matching blue silk garters and a blue feather and band on his hat. There were some interesting sights to see every day in Amsterdam. He stepped back inside just as Jacob came out of the store room.

"Did Jean leave already?" Jacob sounded disappointed. "He's a good man, Jean Durie, even if he talks a little too much. He helped us when we first came here with no more than a will to stay alive and the clothing we wore on our backs."

"Was it a long time ago?" Gilles asked, somewhat curious about this history.

"A very long time ago," Jacob replied, "and like it was yesterday. No one would help us except for Jean. He found us all work, even my wife, and a place for us to live."

"So you help others because of what Jean did for you?"

"Something like that," Jacob said, with traces of a smile around his eyes.

"Did you have a stable and horses where you lived before?" Gilles wondered where Jacob had come from.

Jacob smiled and shook his head. "So many questions! No, I didn't have a stable. I was a rebbeh, a teacher and a holy man, although I am given to understand that *your* God had something to do with a stable, too."

This revelation was quite unexpected. Had Jacob been a priest in his church?

"Was it just easier to find this kind of work here?" Gilles asked.

"I *chose* this kind of work when I came here. Horses are better to deal with than people sometimes," Jacob said, somewhat more forcefully than Gilles was expecting. "I thought when I bought this stable that my sons would follow me into the business and take over running it after I grew old."

"You have sons? Where are they?" Gilles had never heard of any sons.

"Some things in life don't work out exactly the way you think they will when you are young," Jacob said, "but I don't think I have to tell *you* about that."

"What made you come to Amsterdam?"

"We left a country at war and settled for a time in Zeeland but my wife had family here so we continued on to Amsterdam. You'd better start cleaning up behind the horses now. It's starting to pile up out there and will get tracked all over if we don't get to it soon."

Jacob was finished answering questions. He picked up the empty water buckets and went out to fill them at the well.

Gilles was busy enough that he didn't have much time to think about his conversation with Jean until he settled into his bed for the night. There was a smell of approaching rain in the air and the figures on the wampum belt looked as though they danced in the dim light.

What would it be like to live in the New World? He had wondered about New France once but going there now was out of the question. Aside from the obvious dangers, the magistrates' powers reached even across the Atlantic although it was asserted by some that the authorities turned a blind eye away from criminals living there for the sake of having enough French citizens there to hold the territory, to keep it from falling into the hands of the savages or the other world powers who constantly sent their envoys to the French King with ridiculous claims. Gilles certainly wasn't going to take the risk of going there though; the reward offered for his and Jean's return to French custody was probably substantial. He could not believe that Jean would even consider crossing the ocean.

No, Jean was more likely to go to Italy if he went anywhere. Italy was very much like France: The glamour, the wealth, the opportunities, the trade, the women, they were more like home but then again, perhaps the trials, the burnings and hangings were like those in France as well. Gilles remembered hearing about a man in Italy who wrote a book asserting that the world traveled around the sun. The man was either thrown in jail or executed for continuing to tell his silly stories, Gilles could not recall which. In Gilles' opinion, the Italians wasted far too much time worrying about such madmen.

Maybe Gilles and Jean would go to Malaysia together. That was the last thing he remembered thinking before Monday morning arrived with Jacob yelling up to him, "Wake up, Boy! Are you going to sleep all day?"

Monday was busy in spite of the steady rain that was falling. The streets were slick and some of the patrons were out of sorts, trying to keep bundles and parcels dry under their arms or outer garments. Gilles usually liked the sound of the rain on the roof but today he was in a foul mood as well. Another week had begun but what difference did that make? The days were all the same.

Gilles was simply tired of working all day, seven days a week. What he really wanted was for his life to go back to the way it had been on the family estate in France before everything happened. He wanted to marry Marie, to take trips to Amsterdam and to other places and then to go home to the comfort of the estate. He wanted to roam the fields and vineyards at home, to tease his sisters, yes, even to go to church and see Claude. He wanted to sit at the dinner table again and to ride his horse all day long.

He sighed. He could have none of those things, except for Amsterdam, and only a little piece of Amsterdam at that. A life of only work and poverty stretched out before him and the only journeys that he could take would be mental ones fabricated from the bits of stories overheard from those who threw their reins at him when they came in. Life was harsh with no foreseeable escape from it and the idea put him into a black mood. He envied Jean, even with his dull job and having to live with Dirck. At least Jean had a measure of comfort and a measure of freedom that Gilles did not have.

"Are you all right?" Jacob inquired anxiously mid-afternoon. "You aren't coming down with fever?"

"No, I'm well enough," Gilles replied grumpily. What did it matter that he had good health if his life was miserable?

"Naming out loud those blessings God has given us helps to remind us what good lives we have been given," Jacob said, as if reading Gilles' mind.

Gilles held his tongue but Jacob's philosophizing did nothing to improve his state of mind: If anything it angered him even more.

"God saved me from the fires to do stable work?" he asked himself. The only thing that he was grateful for was that they were much too busy for Jacob to bother him any more that afternoon. Gilles realized with a shock that it had been weeks since he had been to a church or to confession. The very idea would have been unthinkable a few months ago.

Would he ever go back to a church again?

Did he want to?

He wasn't sure. In any case, he knew there were not many Catholic churches in Amsterdam and there were none at all that he knew. Dutch law decreed that they could have no spires or outer vestiges of being a church so spotting them, even if you were passing directly in front of them, was difficult in the extreme. Venturing into a Catholic Church in this part of the Netherlands was dangerous for anyone even if they were *not* being sought for extradition. Protestants had been known to rough up or even kill priests and being a Catholic here was almost as dangerous as *not* being one in France.

That night Gilles could not fall asleep even though he was very tired from the busy day. His angry feelings wouldn't go away and there was no comfort or refuge for him to find. He finally fell asleep but slept off and on during the night, always waking with the same trapped feeling. Just before dawn, Gilles gave up and got up to get ready for work. His arms and legs were still tired, his eyes were dry and swollen but moving around was better than lying there.

The horses were already fed and watered by the time Jacob arrived at the barn. Gilles observed that Jacob was dressed rather well and then Gilles remembered that it was Tuesday.

"You will be all right?" Jacob asked. "You did not seem well yesterday."

"Yes, yes. I'm just tired," Gilles said. It was mostly true.

Jacob gave him another probing look but satisfying himself that Gilles was not coming down with the plague, he turned to get his horse and his cart. "Wish me many bargains!" he called to Gilles as he set off.

"Many bargains," Gilles mumbled.

He picked up one of Jacob's harnesses that had become hardened with age and difficult to work. If he could find some oil, Gilles could make it almost as good as new. The hard work would be good for him since he still had some angry energy to work off. He was bending down to look at an assortment of old containers of oil under the little table when Hannah's hands moved over his shoulders.

"It's Tuesday," she said moving his hair away, and kissing the back of his neck. "Maybe it's time for you to take another bath."

"Stable boys smell this way," Gilles said crossly as he straightened up.

Hannah didn't reply to his statement. "The sign is up and I have missed you." She moved to the front of him now and Gilles put his arms around her.

"What is this?" she asked in surprise as she found the new knife at his side.

"Just some personal protection."

"From me?" she laughed.

He pulled her closer and said in a low voice, "Maybe I won't wait for the shed, but I will have you right here."

"And risk my father coming back for something or a familiar customer coming in? No, you aren't so bold. Your friend Jean might stop by. What would you say to *him*?"

"That I like the benefits this job has?" Gilles smiled for the first time in a day and kissed her with an intensity that left no question as to his intentions. He picked her up and carried his prize to the shed. Laughing, she struggled to the ground and pushed him aside for a moment while she took off her ring, hung it on the nail and kicked the door shut behind them. She barely had time to get the covering on the floor before they fell to each other.

Afterwards she rested for a few moments in the crook of his arm. She had never stayed for so long before and the silence was more than a little uncomfortable. Gilles couldn't think of anything to say to her so he said, "You are a beautiful woman."

"No, I'm not," she said with a smile, "but thank you for saying so. Ani ledodi v'dodi li."

"What? What did you say?"

"I said that you are beautiful, too," she kissed his nose.

"What if I decided to live somewhere else? Could you see me more often then?"

"Getting greedy now, are you?" She shivered as he kissed her shoulder. "That would be a wonderful thing, to be with you every day but I'm afraid once a week here in the shed is all that is possible." She traced his eyebrow line with her finger and then his jaw line. "You aren't used to wearing a beard, are you? I wonder what you would look like without it ..."

"You will never know that because I'm not shaving it."

"Father said there was some trouble in France and that's why you hide among us. I've never been with a Catholic man before. There's more to you."

She smiled a mischievous smile but Gilles did not understand her meaning. He did feel a little strange to hear that he was a topic of conversation with her father.

"Yes, some trouble. I'm not a murderer or anything, though."

"Is there a very big bounty for you?"

She smiled teasingly but the question made him uneasy.

"I don't know. Were you planning to turn me in?"

He tensed a little. He really didn't know her at all, didn't know if she *was* teasing or was serious. If he needed the money enough or wanted it enough, maybe he would be tempted to turn someone in ...

"Perhaps ..." she whispered and bit his ear.

"I'd have to tell them that you were my overseas accomplice and then they would take you, too."

This statement had a different effect on her than the one that Gilles had intended. Instead of being intimidated, it seemed to arouse her and she kissed him again with a passion that created new desire in Gilles. He was about to kiss her again when he thought he heard a noise just outside the shed.

"Shhhhh!" he held her and froze.

"What is it?" she asked after a few moments of silence.

"I thought I heard someone!"

Pushing her aside, Gilles took up his knife and moved over to the door. He listened for a moment before yanking it open.

There was no one there and sheepishly he shut the door again.

"You might have waited for me to get dressed or at least to get out of the way before you opened the door!" Hannah said. "Well, I have to get going now, anyway. I leave you to deal with intruders, real or imaginary."

She pulled her sleeves back up over her shoulders and stood up, finding her bodice laces as Gilles started to pull his own clothing back together again.

Hannah was finished dressing in seconds and as she reached for her wedding ring she said, "I'll see you next week, my young French pirate. Maybe I'll give you more lessons in our language!"

She kissed him passionately again as a reminder, or maybe a promise, while holding his chin in her hand. Gathering up her skirts, she left the dusty shed and once again she was gone. Gilles kicked things back into place, put his knife back in the sheath and went outside. He brushed his loose hair back with his fingers but he couldn't shake the feeling that someone was watching him. He circled the shed and the other buildings before giving it up and re-entering the barn. It *must* have been his imagination after all, malaise brought on by lack of sleep or lack of good food, a cold coming on perhaps from sleeping out in the drafty hayloft. He took the sign down and turned back to the harness that he had started to work on but he still had not found any suitable oil to use.

"There you are."

The strange voice startled him. With his heart pounding, Gilles turned around.

"I saw your sign up earlier and you weren't around. You were in the back, eh?"

"Ja."

Gilles dropped the harness back down on the table, ready to take the man's horse from him but the man didn't hand the horse over right away.

"I have never seen you here before. Are you from around here?" the man asked, watching Gilles intently.

"Nee."

Gilles was afraid that if he said too much his accent would give him away. He refused to say any more although the man waited. Gilles could play this game and pretend he was an idiot, didn't speak the language or any other game. He had the advantage here and the patron realized it too.

"Here is my horse. I'll be back at the end of the day tomorrow." The man handed Gilles the reins and walked away, but he still looked at Gilles as he left.

Gilles went over to the door and watched the man continue down the street. Gilles had detected no trace of a French accent and the man's style of dress gave no clear indication, either. Gilles looked the horse and saddle over too. There was nothing there to identify him as a French agent. Gilles decided that his imagination was completely getting the better of him lately, perhaps due to his depressed state of mind during the last two days. What French agent would come into this part of the city and then leave his horse for two days?

Jacob arrived back somewhat earlier than he had the week before with a man he was half dragging, half pushing, into the stable. The man was handsome and very light-skinned for a Jew. He was dressed very well and Gilles noted that his pale curly hair and clean nails were well cared for. The man's green eyes darted around in search of an escape and he shifted impatiently from foot to foot as he eagerly sought a place to drop the bundles from his arms so he could run back to the open door.

"I found so many bargains that I needed help in getting them back! And *look* who I found to help me, Gilles! Do you remember meeting my daughter Hannah? This is her husband, Aaron."

Gilles was not sure whether to shake his hand or not but the man answered Gilles' question by just nodding in Gilles' direction as if it was too much trouble to talk to a stable boy, especially while he was still so desperately trying to find a way to leave. Gilles sized up his rival and concluded that unless there was something radically wrong with Aaron, something that was not apparent at first glance, Hannah must be crazy to come looking for Gilles. He was, in fact, the Jewish version of what Gilles might have been in a few years had he stayed in France: wealthy, handsome, and intelligent

"Ja, I have to get back to work, I was just helping ..." Aaron dropped the bundles in the middle of the floor and exited quickly, throwing a quick farewell over his shoulder to Jacob and ignoring Gilles completely.

"Not much on conversation, is he?" Gilles asked Jacob.

"No, but he's a *good* man, handsome and successful too! I couldn't believe what a good match I made for my daughter."

Jacob rubbed his hands together and beamed in pride. Gilles thought that if Aaron paid as much attention to his wife as he did to his father-in-law, it was probably no wonder that she searched for other companionship. Gilles suddenly realized that he probably still had Hannah's scent on his hands and his body so it was a good thing that Aaron had not taken his hand. Aaron would certainly have no idea that Jacob's stable boy knew his wife so well, right down to the mole on her rib cage ...

"All couples have their *tsouris* of course," Jacob said, "but these small things mustn't be allowed to disrupt a good marriage. Well, I have more outside in the cart that we need to get unloaded. Come and help me, Boy."

They unloaded the last of Jacob's bundles, sacks and barrels together as Gilles wondered what it could be like to have Jacob as a father-in-law. Gilles decided that he might have been jealous, not of Hannah but more of Aaron's position in life, if he didn't feel so much sympathy for Aaron's having Jacob as a father-in-law

That evening Gilles ate his dinner while he walked up the street and was seized with the urge to go to the French part of town. At first he thought that it might be too dangerous but the more he thought about Aaron's adverse reaction to him, the more he smiled and the more he thought that no one would recognize him as he looked now. It might be fun going there, passing himself off as a lost and wandering Jew.

Gilles became aware of a disturbance in the street as he approached the Huguenot area. Half a dozen burley men were dragging a kicking and screaming man down the street and Gilles was surprised that there would be so much commotion over the seizure of a pickpocket. The crowd drew back from the scuffle as though fearing that any contact with the men at all would poison them but at the same time they were drawn closer to the scene, unable to move their eyes away. Gilles stayed far from the fracas but strained to hear what was going on from the whispers of the crowd surrounding him.

"What is this?"

A newcomer speaking French rushed up to a woman who was standing next to Gilles.

"They have seized someone. He'll be bound on a ship back to the French magistrates before the night is out and hanged within a week too, or burned."

Without warning, the smell of the fires flooded back into Gilles' memory. Why had no one attempted to fight for the man's freedom? He alone had been outnumbered by his abductors but they were outnumbered by the hundreds who lived here in this enclave of French expatriates.

Gilles asked the woman next to him about it but he had the presence of mind to ask her in Nederlands. Why? Why did they not fight?

At first she looked at him blankly and did not reply. Gilles wondered if she even knew the language of her adopted country but he took the chance that she did, and asked her once again.

She understood Gilles well enough for she replied, "Stupid Jew! They would take us *too* if we fought them! At least *you* have the comfort of knowing there are no Spanish officials here who want *your* kind back!"

She picked up her skirts and went up the street muttering things to herself in French that Gilles was greatly surprised to hear coming from a woman's mouth. She obviously had no idea that Gilles understood her language and Gilles wondered if he had lost his French accent completely or had picked up an accent from Jacob. Perhaps the woman only looked as far as Gilles' clothing and did not listen to his voice at all. Gilles was comforted by the fact that he passed for one of the Jews but disquieted by what he had witnessed.

Even though it was Wednesday, a weekday morning when he should have been working, Jean Durie came into the stable early the next day.

"I just came by to tell you that I am moving out of Dirck's and into some rooms that a family has available for lease not very far from here. Your father sent you more money and I sent instructions back to him to have it sent to my work from now on, sent to *Gilles Jansen*."

Gilles pocketed the money as Jacob looked on with interest.

"*Gilles Jansen*."

Gilles tried out his new name. It would work. It was different than what he was used to, but he rather liked the sound of it.

After Jean had left, Jacob commented that Jean was a good friend to be watching so closely over Gilles.

"Like a guardian angel?" Gilles asked.

"I guess so," Jacob replied. "He protects you from Diego's greed."

Jacob returned to feeding the horses and Gilles realized that Dirck must have once again attempted to keep Gilles' money and Jean must have interceded on his friend's behalf, the incident leading to his moving out of his father's house. Jean had said nothing about this but Gilles believed that it must have been so; Jean was in fact a very good friend and protector.

The strange man who had left his horse there the day before came in later on in the afternoon. He said nothing to Gilles but he paused and spoke for a moment with Jacob.

"You have a new boy, eh?"

"That's right."

"He seems able to handle the horses all right."

"That he does."

The man seemed interested in talking more about Gilles but Jacob made himself too busy to talk any more. After he was gone, Gilles asked Jacob if the stranger was a regular customer but Jacob was sure that he had never seen the man before today.

The unsettling events of the last few days put Gilles on edge and caused him to stay very close to the stable for a few days, with the exception of going out to get his meals and the clothes that he had ordered at the tailors. Jacob grumbled about the work time lost, of course, but he let his helper go. Gilles was careful to look around him when he left the stable and as he traveled to and from the Dam. The same smell of the fabric and the same sense of gloom greeted Gilles again when he walked into the shop.

"I'm here to pick up my clothes," he told the old tailor.

"Four guilders."

"We agreed on seven *total* and I already paid you four!" Gilles protested.

"You gave me four and we *did agree* it was half."

The tailor would not budge and in the end Gilles had no choice but to give him the four guilders. He was annoyed but had learned another lesson about trade and it could have been much worse: He might have given the tailor all of his money to begin with. The clothes were worth it though, being well-made and fitting his new, more slender frame, so Gilles could not complain too much. They were plain and sturdy clothes, made for working in the stable or the fields anyway. Gilles hated to spend any money at all, especially for working clothes, but they would last him a very long time and Gilles would buy no more, at least not from that establishment.

On Friday the stable was busy as usual but Gilles thought about nothing all day except for his meeting that night with Elsje. He led the wrong horse out once and then another time he forgot who had come to ask for the horse that he had just saddled up. In spite of his excitement there was still some residual fear that he had of going out into the Dam. If the French came to seize people in the very midst of the other expatriates, how much bolder would they be in the sympathetic territory of the Dam? The Dutch would be reluctant to start an incident under the watchful eyes of any Spanish soldiers although Gilles was beginning to understand what he had originally taken to be Dutch passivity: He understood now that it was a quiet resistance and if they all went about their daily business peacefully, then Spain's young Turks would just have to find their fights elsewhere. With any luck at all, they would do just that, go elsewhere.

Jacob was barely out of the door for the evening start of the Sabbath when Gilles ran outside for a bucket of water to wash in. He changed into his new clothes which weren't stylish at all, but they were clean and new and they didn't smell of horses. He quickly closed up the stable and was happy to see that he still had some time left before complete darkness fell on the city. He was famished from the long day of hard work so he stopped by the local inn for his dinner even though Elsje would be bringing him more food than he could eat. He left his money under the basket and picked out the bread to eat on the way, leaving the other food behind. He would be feasting on Elsje's food later tonight.

Gilles wondered if Elsje was leaving her inn with her basket right now, at this very moment. He was in high spirits as he approached the church and he considered the possibility of stealing a kiss from Elsje tonight. He remembered the silk dress she wore when Peter Stuyvesant was their guest and he grinned at the memory. As he approached the church though, he did not see Elsje, but a man loitered in the nearby shadows.

With caution foremost in his mind, Gilles slowed down and then came to a full stop to study the figure in the dim light. He seemed familiar to Gilles somehow but it took a little time before he came to the realization that it was *Hendrick* who stood there. Where was Elsje?

"Montroville." Hendrick nodded a greeting to him.

"It's good to see you again, Hendrick." Gilles said, offering his hand.

The gesture was not accepted.

"It's not so good to see *you* under the circumstances. I could not believe it when my daughter told me that she saw you and spoke to you last week. You will not speak again with Elsje."

"Hendrick, we met by chance and ..."

"Save your fine words! If you had any concern for her safety or her future, you would leave her alone. It is regrettable that you lost everything in France, but I won't allow you to interfere with Elsje's marriage prospects to Pieter Stuyvesant."

"I ... We are only friends!" Gilles' words were spilling out faster than he could think them over.

There was a flashpoint of anger in Hendrick's eyes that Gilles had never seen before.

"*Friends!* I know well enough about the intentions of *your kind.* You stay away from her or I will see to it that the authorities have you trussed up like a pig and on a French ship in no time! Here's your investment money back, *with interest. I am a man of my word.*"

Hendrick threw a handful of guilders onto the ground and stamped off into the night. Gilles' mouth was still open, trying to form a response, a defense that would never be heard.

Humiliation came down on Gilles' head as he fell to his knees and gathered up the precious coins in the darkness. The old Gilles might have been too proud, have left it on the ground, but he needed it too much to walk away from it. He stuffed it into his pocket and taking a quick look around him, he sped back to the safety of the Jewish section, shaken from the confrontation. He had lost the little hope for the future that had started to take root in recent days, crushed now under the broad heel of Hendrick's boots.

Gilles didn't know what he should do so he paced around the stable until he noticed that it was just making the horses nervous and not soothing him at all.

He should talk to Jean. He would just have to escape, to go away again, maybe with Jean. This time it would not be locked away in a hidden hold but as a free man on the deck of a ship, sailing to somewhere, anywhere, to freedom. He would go someplace where he could be completely anonymous and just live his life. He touched the knife at his side and wondered if Hendrick was really angry enough to turn him in. If he didn't know it before, he knew now where Elsje got her volatile temper from. A fearsome thought of the authorities finding him and taking him away to his death came into his mind. If they did that, he would fight this time and fight with everything he had in him. He wouldn't let them take him away to jail, not this time. Life was turning out to be more painful and more complicated than he could ever have imagined just months ago.

Sanity slowly returned to him though, and a quiet reassuring voice in the back of his mind persisted, telling him that Hendrick had no idea where he was right now and would pay no attention to him as long as Elsje was nowhere around him but Gilles still thought about where he might like to live if he had to leave the city. He looked at the wampum belt and shook his head. *"No, I can't see myself there,"* he thought, although Villeneuve's praises of the wilderness crossed his mind and Gilles hoped that somehow Villeneuve had made it back there, to live among the squirrels, as Poteet had said.

Gilles considered Malaysia but that was almost as wild and savage a place as the new world. Gilles thought of the German Palatinate and about farming there. Perhaps their German wouldn't be so difficult to learn since he already knew Latin and Nederlands. Farming there would be good. It might be like living in France again. He could start vineyards and have horses.

The energy of fear finally left him and now Gilles felt very tired. He put his head down on his pillow and was asleep before he knew it, building a barn in the

Palatinate, stone by stone and board by board in a beautiful place, peace coming to him at last in his sleep.

He still felt tired in the morning but the light coming in brought him a measure of relief. No one had come for him during the night so he reasoned that he was secure in the stable if not outside on the street. Because it was Saturday, Jacob wouldn't be in today so there was really no need to get up at all. Gilles could just stay in the hay loft all day and think about what he should do next. The horses had other ideas though, and stirred impatiently until Gilles finally gave in to their demands and got up to feed them.

After he took care of the horses, Gilles sat down on the bench next to the table where he fixed the harnesses to think about where his life was taking him. There were some very good reasons to leave Amsterdam but also equally good reasons to stay. Gilles leaned forward, sitting with his elbows on his knees, his fingers laced together and his eyes staring at the floor just in front of him but his thoughts took him far away.

This place had been a safe haven for him and it was still unlikely that anyone would look for him here. If he did leave, he had nothing to pack and very few good-byes to say. Wasn't it pointless to stay here, working in the stable? This was no life for him; there was no future here. It wasn't even the work that he minded so much as the feeling of being trapped here all the time, of being tied to the physical structure of the building and being unable to go out into the wider world whenever it pleased him. He would rather go to sea and labor on a ship that moved under his feet, traveling from place to place while he did his work, arriving at someplace new each day when his work was done.

If Jean would not go away with him, perhaps the time had come for Gilles to leave him behind as well. Gilles thought about what it would be like working on the sea: It would be nothing at all like what he had been used to: It would be very hard work and very dangerous work but it might also be very exciting.

The door to the stable opened and Jean Durie walked in. He said nothing but sat down next to Gilles without saying a word.

"Why aren't you resting today?" Gilles asked his friend. "It's the Sabbath, you know."

"I'm hiding from Dirck," Jean replied.

Gilles had to smile at this. "Do you want to run away with me? I was just considering where I might go."

"Maybe I will. Italy looks better and better to me."

"I was thinking about the Palatinate."

"The land of nightmares?" Jean asked him. "I won't even tell you what they had to do to survive the wars; it would turn your stomach away from food for a week or more. Aside from that minor consideration, there is absolutely nothing *there* except for hills and empty land."

"Exactly," Gilles replied, "*farmland.*"

"What's the matter with your life here today?" Jean set aside his own concerns for the moment and looked more closely at his friend.

Gilles told him about his encounter with Hendrick.

"I don't know what harm it does to talk with Elsje and to accept her food. She feeds the Marranos, doesn't she? Am I so much *lower* than the beggars? I have only two people in the city that I can talk to, you and Elsje, and her father doesn't want me to even *speak* to her."

Gilles sighed over his own problems but then he remembered that Jean did not seem very happy this morning, either.

"So tell me, why are you hiding from Dirck?"

"He *really* surprised me this time, Gilles. He has already arranged for me to *marry* some girl and told me that I had to do it and move back in with him if I wanted to keep my position at the accountant's. They don't *know* that I am wanted in France and if he tells them, the very *least* they will do is throw me out. I should have known better! *Any* help from Dirck always comes with a price, and usually a very *large* price. I just won't accept anything more from him, not ever again! Thinking that I would take a wife of his choosing! That's the way *these people* live and that's fine for them but I just don't think I could ever *marry* one of them."

Jean stopped talking, perhaps looking for a reaction from Gilles.

"I see," was all that Gilles said.

They both sat contemplating their respective situations for a little longer before Jean spoke again.

"I was *supposed* to be in their religious services all day today with the family of this girl. What is so ridiculous is that I don't know *anything* about her at all." Jean moved a bit of hay around in front of him with his foot. "Going to services with them is as serious as a formal proposal of marriage at home and I probably wouldn't even get to see *what she looks like* before the ceremony. The women all wear veils and sit in a separate section and I would just sit all day with her male relatives and try to pretend that I know something of their language or their customs, which I don't. It is also possible that money has already changed hands and that's what *really* has me concerned. I don't know how seriously they view a breach of contract or what they might do to remedy such a situation."

"Hendrick is probably telling the authorities about me right now."

Gilles sympathized with Jean but he could only think of his own situation at the moment. Jean's trouble didn't really seem so bad to him: No one was going to turn *him* over to the French.

"No, he won't, Gilles. Hendrick is not foolish enough to start trouble, not over some minor issue with his daughter. They would start to ask *him* questions, to watch *him* and to investigate his business dealings if he did that."

"Why is it *all* so complicated?"

"It's not, really. Hendrick is only protecting his assets. He hears the musical sound of gold pouring into his pocket from distant trading posts, from suitors like Stuyvesant, the trade agreements sealed into place with marriages to his daughters. It's like this: Children are either an asset or a debit, just another commodity for a man to trade and a means to furthering his wealth or they are a liability, and this is *particularly* true of female children. I am no child though, and I never was Dirck's property to trade."

"I don't want to interfere with Hendrick's prosperity, I just want to invest my money with him and have some of Elsje's food. Maybe you could talk to Hendrick for me. You could talk to him and send my apologies."

"And what should I say? That you want to be *friends* with Elsje and promise not to get in the way of her future marriage prospects?" Jean shook his head doubtfully.

"Why not? Just let him know that he can *trust* me. Just ask him if I can reinvest my money with him."

Jean sighed. "All right, I'll ask. For you, Gilles, I'll ask. Are you sure that you don't have more of an interest in Elsje than you are telling me? It isn't the *challenge of it*, is it?" Jean peered at his friend questioningly.

"It is all just a big misunderstanding! I have always been a *perfect gentleman* when I am with Elsje."

"It's *always* a misunderstanding with you, Gilles, but I suppose that it won't hurt anything to send your apologies on to Hendrick. It *will* give me an excuse to seek him out and ask about my *own* investments although he may not be happy to see me, either."

"I'm sorry I can't help you with your situation, Jean."

Jean slapped his hands on his thighs and jumped to his feet. "There is nothing to be done! I must just say 'non' to Dirck and see what happens; I can see that plainly now. Perhaps we should both just get on the next ship to Italy, eh?"

"You are crazy to think about Italy, Jean. They would send us both back to France as soon as we got there."

"What is crazy is to think that I can even *mention* your name to Hendrick and then have a civilized conversation with him afterwards. It could be the end of the most profitable business agreement I've ever had, but what are friends for?"

Gilles didn't need Jean to remind him that marriage was a business arrangement: Thinking about the advantages of the right marriage was enough to tempt even Gilles into considering it. If Gilles married someone like Elsje, there would be business and trade connections through her father and all the good food that he could eat every day. Companionship in bed aside, marrying a Netherlander would secure much better job prospects for him and there might even be legal considerations from the Dutch government, maybe enough to block Gilles' extradition back to France if it ever came to that.

Marry Elsje?

"Maybe I should," Gilles thought, seriously considering the idea for the first time.

Tuesday morning came and Jean had not yet been back to the stable to tell Gilles if he had met with Hendrick or how it went. Jacob left early for the Dam, as usual, and Hannah arrived soon after. Before he put the sign up, Gilles looked outside the stable to make sure that no one lurked outside today.

"What are you doing?"

Hannah walked up behind him and twisted a lock of Gilles' hair around her finger.

"Just checking to make sure that your father is gone," Gilles said as he put the sign in place.

"He's gone. I always make sure of that first."

Today Gilles couldn't get enough of Hannah and she asked him teasingly what he had had for his breakfast this morning. Gilles' reply was to smile and to pull her over to him again.

"No, no more!" she laughed, but Gilles would not be put off nor would he be rushed today.

"Did I do this to you?" she asked him.

Gilles noticed for the first time that she was actually somewhat pretty when she smiled. He had probably never seen this before because her smiles were such a rare thing.

"Of course you did. I thought I knew it all until I met you," he flattered her.

"It's time to go," she told him as she kissed Gilles once again. "I'll see you next week if I can, but I may not be able to get away."

"Why not?"

He didn't think he could wait two weeks for her to come back to him.

"I just might not, that's all."

She wouldn't say anything more about it as she laced her overdress up.

"I will be here, waiting patiently for you, and missing you."

Hannah pushed her ring back onto her finger as she said, "I'll see you *soon*." She pulled him over to her by his shirt collar and kissed him good-bye.

Back inside the stable, Gilles was surprised to find someone sitting on the bench but quickly realizing that it was only Jean Durie, he relaxed and walked over to take the sign down. If Jean noticed anything amiss, he didn't mention it. Perhaps he had not seen Hannah when she left.

"Aren't you working today, Jean?" Gilles asked casually.

"I sent word to them that I wasn't feeling well and would be in later. I wanted to come here first and tell you that I saw Hendrick yesterday."

"Oui? Tell me!" Gilles was eager to hear the news.

"He won't turn you in but he has serious reservations about your character."

"And were you able to convince him otherwise?"

"Non, but he agreed to reinvest your money anyway. I don't know why it is *so* important for you to invest with *him*; there are many other good investments that you could make here. I *did* tell him that you were not seriously interested in any-one at all right now because you are just too young, but that you valued Elsje's friendship, as an older sister of course, and appreciated her culinary skills."

"Excellent! Thank you for that," Gilles cut in but Jean hadn't finished talking.

"Gilles, *why* is it that you always antagonize the people who can be the greatest help to you? I never understood why you couldn't get along better with your father and you must *know* that the stakes are higher here. People have the advan-tage of knowing that they can dispatch you easily just by calling in the authori-ties. You risk losing the good will of Hendrick and Jacob and they are the two

men here who can improve your lot in life *the most*. You risk everything for your
… *your appetites*. I *must* be a fool because I try to mend your bridges for you even
as you build more bonfires under them! I promised Hendrick that you wanted
nothing more than to continue investing with him so if I bring your money back
to him, it may smooth things over, but you will *still* have to stay *far* away from
Elsje. The less you have to do with Hendrick, the better."

Gilles was surprised by the unusual criticism as Jean had never lectured him
before; he did have the presence of mind to hold his tongue and think about what
his reply might be as he went up to the loft to get his money. He climbed down,
handed it over to Jean, and still not knowing what he could say that wouldn't
instigate another lecture, he only mumbled, "Thank you, Jean."

Jean shook his head in disbelief or perhaps in disgust, but Gilles thought that
he detected the slightest trace of a smile in Jean's eyes as he deposited Gilles'
money into his purse.

Jacob returned from the Dam earlier than usual and was not in a good mood
when he came in. He muttered and grumbled to himself and spoke sharply to
Gilles, ordering him about as they unloaded the little wagon. Following Jacob's
lead, Gilles picked up a shovel and they both proceeded to clean the stable, making one large pile of manure in the cart from the many small ones. The horses
had done an unusually efficient job in covering the floor again while Jacob was
out and Jacob insisted that this was because Gilles always fed them too much.
While they shoveled, Jacob continued to mutter and criticize the work Gilles had
done, or more precisely, what he had *not* done, while Jacob was away.

At last Gilles could stand it no longer and he threw down his shovel.

"My work was good enough for you yesterday! Why do you blame me if *you*
had a bad day at the market?"

"Because *your kind* are all alike! Friendship is only an ornament that you wear
when it goes with your outfit! Even if we embraced *every one* of your beliefs and
all of your ways, a hundred years later you would come down on our grandchil-
dren's heads after the first disagreement!"

"Then why talk to us at all? Why did you offer *me* this job if you hate us so
much?"

Gilles could see that ship, the one that would take him far away, very clearly in
his mind now. It was waiting for him at the port and all he had to do was to grab
his few belongings and go. He would make a quick stop at Hendrick's to retrieve
his investment money and then he would be gone from this manure pit and gone
from Amsterdam.

Jacob shoveled harder and faster and still mumbled under his breath but he didn't answer Gilles' questions.

After a few moments of standing in silence with clenched fists, Gilles decided that not much more than angry words would come from Jacob's ranting, so he picked his own shovel back up again. He wasn't going to leave tonight, not without talking to Jean first or knowing where he was going, so with nothing at all to lose, he made an attempt at having a rational conversation with Jacob. Waiting one more day to leave wouldn't make a difference, anyway.

"I'm sorry that you had a bad day, Jacob. While it's true that we don't understand your ways, most of the time we *do* get along. '*My own kind*', as you call them, will not let *me* live my life in peace, either."

Jacob looked beyond Gilles, not at him, as he replied.

"*When* will it stop? Is it *always* over religion or do people ever fight about other things?"

"It's not about religion at all. That's just a convenience, an excuse," Gilles offered. He put his shovel against the wall and reached for the cart to begin hauling the manure outside.

Jacob leaned on his shovel and spoke again. "Someday, and it won't be long now, we won't have to fight anymore. We will all be able to go home, to openly be who we want to be and no one will ever spit on us again. Merchants and men of learning, we will be. We will be free to fight over *just* the money, *only* the money, when we return to the land of Israel."

Gilles needed to take the cart outside right away because he didn't know if he could keep himself from laughing out loud at Jacob: The crazy old man *really believed* what he had just said. The mythical land of the Bible stories would never exist again, and Gilles seriously doubted that it had *ever* existed at all; it was just another tale in a great book that was filled with great lies, something contrived by both the Jewish and the Christian collaborating priests to keep the ignorant masses of both persuasions in line. If that golden land ever did come into being again, God certainly intended it for those who were faithful to his commandments, for the Catholics, and not for the Jews.

While the Jews daydreamed and contemplated a better future, Cardinal Richelieu labored in the present to ensure that *all* of the undesirables, most especially the Protestants, were gone from the face of the earth or at least from France, something that he was rapidly accomplishing. It was astounding to see what only one man, one powerful man, could accomplish in a few short years and Gilles had no doubt at all that one day Richelieu would succeed in clearing every Huguenot from within the borders of France.

"Imagine though, going to a place where anyone at all could just live his life in peace," Gilles mused. He tried to but he couldn't envision it.

It was the last thing that Gilles expected, but Jacob's fantasy took root in his mind. For the rest of the day, Gilles thought about what it would be like to sail away to a place where religion didn't matter, where men lived in peace. Was there no religion at all in such a place or many religions coexisting peacefully side by side? Villeneuve had hinted that such a thing existed in New France and Gilles remembered what Villeneuve had said about defending the savages and their beliefs from the invading brown-robed Jesuit priests. With sadness, Gilles thought that even the hope and promise of peaceful coexistence somewhere always seemed to require fighting those forces from without and within that refused to accept any divergence in beliefs.

If Gilles did go to sea, maybe one day he would see New France for himself and see if this peculiar idea really had seeded itself there. The voyage alone would be amazing, three months or more of living on the water with no sign of land at all, a modern day Noah's ark. Perhaps there would even be savages waiting at the port, living there in peace with the transplanted French, a sign from heaven that truly a miracle had taken place there. There would be no overcrowded cities or great prisons there, just trees, fields, and vineyards, similar to what heaven was like. Maybe it was as Villeneuve had said: Maybe it was heaven on earth.

There had been groups of people and individuals, the peculiar religious cult from the south of England for one, who had passed through the Netherlands with the original intention of staying on, but they soon found the Netherlands to be too decadent and just not to their liking at all. These people had, for whatever ill-conceived reason, made the unwise choice of relocating themselves to the liberal and free-thinking university town of Leiden and it was only a short time before the *Puritans*, as they preferred to be called, ran screaming away from the excesses of freedom and continued on to the new continent, some twenty years before. It was said in France, and rightly so Gilles thought, that these people were religious fanatics with bizarre and extreme beliefs and that most of them had eventually died out over in the Massachusetts Colony, no doubt a well-deserved punishment from God for not following the Catholic authorities' directives and for instituting among themselves strict and strange behavioral codes.

Gilles had plenty of time today to wonder exactly how they died. Did they die from the ferocious winters, the long hot summers, the great beasts that freely roamed the land, some terrible disease, or at the bloodied hands of a savage? Was New France so very different from these English, Dutch and Spanish colonies that lay just a little further to the south? It was enough to keep an imagination occupied for hours and the silence in the stable except for the scraping shovels allowed time for the earlier storm between Jacob and Gilles to blow over.

When Jacob left for the night, he didn't apologize or say anything at all to Gilles regarding his earlier outburst of anger. He did tell Gilles that he would be gone on Sunday night, Monday, and Tuesday as well as the following Wednesday but that there wouldn't be much work for him to do. Gilles remembered Hannah's mentioning that she might not be there on the following Tuesday and he wondered about their joint absence but he didn't ask Jacob directly about it: Gilles wasn't going to say or do *anything* that might put Jacob in a bad mood.

Jacob was right about there being no work. There was no one in at all on Monday and Gilles wondered where everyone was. He had seen Jacob leave early on Monday in his Sabbath finery and Hannah did not show up on Tuesday, either. Gilles waited for a customer, any customer, to show up on Tuesday, but none ever did. Boredom overtook him by early afternoon and Gilles decided that in spite of the risk, he would go to the Dam. Gilles closed up the stable, tucked his knife into his waistband under his shirt and stepped outside to freedom.

The streets in the Jewish quarter were eerily silent, as quiet as a town completely emptied by plague, but Gilles found his food ready and waiting for him on the stoep of the inn on Tuesday, just as he had on Monday, in the usual basket but under a great ceramic pot. He knew his food was in there because a few rats pushed unsuccessfully at the heavy cover and Gilles had to chase them away. His dinner was an unimaginative mix of uncooked fruits and vegetables that looked to Gilles as if it had been set out in the morning, as one would set out food for a dog. Gilles pulled the food out to take with him and left the money behind in the basket under the pot. He wasn't going to let his disappointment in the meal ruin his afternoon off, though. As he walked toward the square eating a carrot, he noticed that a few people stared at him and he nervously wondered why there were no other Jews around. Where were they all? He had all but forgotten that back in France they told tales of the Jews all disappearing like this, of yearly gatherings in the woods and hills for occasional sacrifices of children. He didn't think he believed this but *where were they?*

Gilles walked around the perimeter of the Dam. It was definitely not as busy today with all of the Jews missing. The spice stalls overflowed with wares and Gilles wondered exactly which spice it was that he smelled on the wind now. It was something sharp and peppery but with something else in it too, something sweet. The East India Company had so much wealth and so many different commodities that most people didn't even know what all of their perishable goods were, except for tea of course, the wildly popular new drink. Gilles noted as he passed by the Waag that the ground was colored red and brown and ochre in places where the spices were accidentally spilled. He saw colorful deposits on the other side as well, where the West India Company unloaded *their* commodities, tobacco, maize, chocolate, and who knew what else coming from the Americas. Artists working in the street beckoned and called out to Gilles to see their finished works for sale. Gilles nodded a greeting to them but he didn't stop; He had no extra money for luxuries like that, even as affordable as they were.

As he passed by Elsje's church, Gilles glanced in the direction of the churchyard, perhaps from habit, and came to a sudden full stop when he saw that Elsje was in there, sitting alone in the arbor seat. Looking around to make sure that Hendrick was not nearby, Gilles tossed his better judgment aside and crossed the path that led from the front of the church around the side and into the churchyard.

"Elsje, Goedenavond! What are you doing here?"

"I just came to see my mother."

"I apologize if I caused any trouble between you and your father. Can you stay and talk with me for a few minutes?"

"No, I should be getting back."

"You can't stay for just a little?"

"Nee."

She got up from her seat and straightened her skirt. She meant to move past him but Gilles would not move from the middle of the path.

"I hope he's not angry with you. I *did* appreciate your food," Gilles said to her.

"I'm glad. Goodbye, Gilles." Elsje took a step forward and attempted to move by him once again.

"Goodbye, Elsje." Gilles took a step toward her and kissed her on each cheek in farewell but when Gilles kissed her lightly on the lips, he didn't want to let her go with such a token farewell. He kissed her again, this time with more intensity and for much longer, and Gilles was pleasantly surprised when Elsje returned his passion, returned it until they were both short of breath.

Gilles took a small step back and looked into her eyes. There was so much that he wanted to say to her, mainly about her father, but he never got the chance. She looked into his eyes for just a moment before she brought her foot down hard on the top of his, drew her skirts back and moved around him, walking away to the street before he had the chance to know what had just happened, let alone to recover from it.

Gilles was dumbfounded and could only stare after her in amazement. *"She's her father's daughter,"* he thought, the breath-taking remembrance of the kiss competing in his thoughts with the rapidly intensifying pain in his foot.

His foot was still painful for the next week and he hoped that she had not broken it, although if it was broken, it seemed to be getting no worse. He wondered if he had lost all reason for continuing to think about her. She could be, as Jean had pointed out, a possible threat to his future, and there were times that Gilles believed Elsje had nothing but an outright dislike of him. Why did she bring him food then, was it only about charity?

He just wanted to talk with her for a few moments, to ask her *why*. Going to Hendrick's inn was out of the question but going to her church might be a possibility. He might find a good time to talk with her alone, in the midst of the crowds, to demand an explanation as to why she had assaulted him. He would demand an apology and would accept no less.

If he was going to go there though, he would have to make himself look more presentable. Having nothing else available to him, Gilles used his knife to try and trim his beard and hair to one length on the following Saturday. He decided that he had done about all that could be done with it when Jean Durie walked into the stable, dripping from the rain that had started, stopped, and then started again all morning.

"Should I expect to see you hiding in here every Saturday?" Gilles asked as he put the knife back into its sheath at his side.

Jean eyed the knife but made no comment, good or bad, about Gilles' efforts at grooming. He tossed his damp hat and cloak on the bench as he replied.

"For now, I suppose. We are in a stalemate, Dirck and I. Dirck is not telling the accounting house about me and I am not leaving the city but neither am I going to their services! I considered telling the girl's family that I am a *Christian* and was baptized in the Catholic Church but that would not matter to them *at all*; so many of them have had forced baptisms that they disregard it as having any meaning whatsoever."

"Maybe Dirck only wants to keep you nearby so he will have family here."

"Wanting me nearby has *nothing* to do with it, Gilles! He wants to control my life, to add me to the asset column on his ledgers. He is not my father and I *cannot* be his son."

Jean walked back over to the door with his arms folded across his chest and looked out at nothing in particular besides the morning mist. Gilles thought that

Jean might be watching for Dirck but Jean just stood there in silence for a few moments.

"My father was such a different man," Jean said at last, turning back around to Gilles. "He was *nothing* at all like Dirck. I don't know who this man is that shares my blood and looks like I will when I'm old."

"You had to know him, though, didn't you?"

Gilles could not imagine what it would be like to find out that his father was not his own.

Jean sighed as he walked back over to Gilles. "I would have been *satisfied* with shaking his hand but Dirck wouldn't let it go at that. I don't know what family *is* anymore, Gilles. I see Reformees taken from their families in France and Marranos ripped away from theirs in Spain and Portugal, men who are able to start new families here, knowing full well that they have left behind wives and children who have survived the terrors at home, living on somewhere in their shared past world, waiting patiently to this day for men who have no intention of *ever* returning. I see people bound together by vows in a church sharing a house and meals but not having much of anything else in common except perhaps keeping the family going as a business concern. Then I see truly loving and devoted families forged together of the most *unlikely* materials: Netherlander and French, Marranos and Amsterdam Jews marrying and creating new kinds of families. Did you know that some of the savages in the New World *kidnap* colonists and they consider it a legal and binding adoption among their kind? After this barbaric act they love their captives as their own and even *weep for them* if they are taken back to live among their own kind."

A well-dressed man suddenly appeared in the doorway behind Jean, sending Gilles into a momentary panic. The French could not have found them here? No one ever came to the door on a Saturday, especially not rich men. Gilles saw no others outside with him but neither did he see a horse. Gilles' fears were only dissipated after the man started to speak.

"Dirck told me that I would find you here, Jean. You *must* get me passage to New Amsterdam right away unless you can connect me with someone going further south. I have important business in the Virginia Colony that won't wait."

The man spoke in perfect French but with a Spanish accent. He didn't look or sound at all to Gilles like a Jew but Gilles had the idea that he *was* one of them.

"Do you need it today?" Jean asked him. "When do you want to leave?"

"I need to leave *right away*! This news took *over three months* to reach me and opportunity does not wait."

The gentleman was dressed in red brocade from head to toe and Gilles thought that he looked rather more like a walking armchair or a set of portieres than a man in a suit of clothes. He carried a matching purse and red lace handkerchief that he kept putting up to his nose as if to ward off a threatening cold or to protect himself from a noxious odor.

"Ferdinand, this is my friend Gilles," Jean said, by way of introduction.

"Of course," the dandy replied in a disinterested sort of way. He did not even look at Gilles but he did click his heels together, cast his eyes to the floor briefly, and tipped his head to one side in a weak acknowledgement of the introduction and of Gilles' presence. Ferdinand then continued speaking to Jean as if the interruption of the introduction had never taken place, taking Jean by the elbow and leading him further into the stable as if to tell Jean a great secret, leaving in his wake the scent of Spanish perfume.

Gilles could hear some of what Ferdinand was saying and it didn't seem to be of a very private nature. Gilles was annoyed at the insult and he decided to ignore both of them. Grumpily he got up and limped over to the work table. He picked up the harness that he had been trying to restore for so long but it had been left outside by accident and now the leather was very hard, becoming even drier and more brittle with each passing day. The brass rings were green and no longer moved freely through the leather loops of the harness. Jacob was too miserly to throw the thing out and even though Gilles was certain that it was well beyond repair, he insisted that Gilles try to salvage it. Perhaps with enough fish oil or goose fat rubbed in, it could be saved, at least for a few more weeks of use before it disintegrated totally.

Gilles picked up a rag and the corked bottle of whale oil that he had decided to try on it next while Ferdinand continued to speak to Jean.

"Quite probably the silly fop doesn't even realize that I am French," Gilles thought.

"Did you know that they have great stores of gold as well as cochineal? More even than the Incas or Aztecs? That they do not know *what it is* or have any *reasonable* use for it?" Ferdinand waved his arm in the air with his red handkerchief in hand, the banner flying like a flag during a windstorm.

Gilles suppressed a smile as he watched Jean humor the man by nodding.

"I *must* get there as soon as possible before others do or before the savages discover the value of gold! We can trade some *fabric* for it! What savage would not like a fine coat in exchange for his gold? You *must* get word back to me today. Do it soon, Jean; do it now!"

Ferdinand tapped Jean on the shoulder, as one would do to a servant, and made his exit from the stable and Jean, far from hurrying to accommodate the man and act on his demands, acted as though nothing at all had happened since he had been conversing with Gilles earlier. Jean acted, in fact, as though he had already forgotten about Ferdinand's urgent request. Jean wandered back over to the table where Gilles was working.

"Well, it looks like Dirck has found my hiding place," Jean sighed.

"Who was that annoying man? Is he one of your patrons?" Gilles asked.

Jean smiled and snorted. "Non, he is just a very demanding acquaintance with no idea at all about the trade he proposes to work at. He thinks he will go over and make a great fortune trading in tropical plants. He doesn't even know where they get the cochineal dye from!"

"Ferdinand was his name? He doesn't look like one of your Marrano friends." Gilles picked up the jug of oil again and poured more onto his rag.

"My Marrano friends?"

"Yes, the groups of men you are with sometimes." Gilles tried to move the rusty ring but it was still frozen in place.

"How do you know …?" Jean asked.

"I just know. I have known for a long time." Gilles tried twisting the ring but it still didn't move.

"Since before the trial you *knew*? And you said nothing?"

Gilles looked up at him. There was no mistaking the incredulous look on Jean's face.

"You knew that I was a Jew involved in smuggling Marranos? You could have saved yourself by telling them at your hearing and yet you said nothing?"

Disbelief, astonishment and something else, too, was there on Jean's face. "Gilles, did you not understand that *all* you had to do was to say something about it to the magistrate; that you could have just turned me in and you would have been released?"

"I understood that."

The ring turned a little in the leather now. Gilles had made some progress with it.

"All this time I have been feeling *guilty* that you did not know what the authorities knew and could not even properly defend yourself!"

"*I knew.*"

Gilles threw down the rag and the harness and looked into his friend's eyes. "I could make no other choice. Even if it would have saved me, I would *not* have told them. Besides, the choice was between the church or burning, it was not *freedom* or burning. It wasn't much of a choice."

Jean spoke softly as if not to awaken all of the memory. "You and I, we have never spoken of that time. They were going to *kill* me. They cut me with my own knife, *marked* me as they say the Jews are *all* marked, and only the need for my physical presence at *your* hearing interrupted their finishing the job by cutting my throat, too."

"You weren't guilty of anything," Gilles said stubbornly, "and neither was I. Should one innocent man die just to save another?" Gilles' voice was calm but his hands shook: He had not been prepared to hear all of the details of Jean's torture today.

Jean shook his head in perplexity. "It is hard to defend yourself when you don't *know* if you are guilty or not. What is a Jew? Is there any *one* defining characteristic? It is all *too* complicated. Just look at Ferdinand! He was a highly placed courtier in Spain and someone turned him in for having a Jewish grandfather. He *detests* Jews but he finds us useful. He lost *everything* he had in Spain, save for the fortune he managed to take out. I know he would gladly give some of it for the chance to go back to his old life. Is blood *so* important?" Jean fell silent but one slightly raised eyebrow told Gilles that Jean's anger had not completely left him.

Gilles was shaken and now he understood too well the source of the blood stains and Jean's fever after the trial, as well as his friend's cold reaction to his recent gift of the knife. What had been intended to give his friend pleasure had only hurt him by bringing back painful memories.

Jean had had enough conversation for the day. He shook his head as if to shake off the memories that he had just been reliving.

"Well, I should go find Ferdinand his transport now, or at the least go and make some inquiries. He pays well, even if he is arrogant about making his demands. Perhaps I could send Dirck and the girl he wants me to marry away *with him* to the Virginia Colonies, get rid of all of my problems at once." Jean shook some water off his hat and cloak before he put them back on.

"Why don't you just put Ferdinand on the first ship that you see in the harbor and *tell* him that it's going across the Atlantic? He won't know the difference until he gets there and he can't speak Nederlands, can he?"

This suggestion elicited a smile from Jean. "What happened to your foot?" he asked.

"It was stepped on," Gilles replied and he felt his face turning red. Nothing ever escaped Jean's notice, even when he was up to his ears in his own troubles.

"Ah, I'd think you would know enough to keep your distance from the beasts by now," Jean said.

"You would think so," Gilles answered.

Jean returned to the rainy day outside and Gilles tossed the harness aside. It was either good enough for Jacob or it wasn't, but Gilles wasn't going to spend the rest of the day on it. He sat on the bench by the door, his sore foot propped up on an overturned bucket, looking out at the drizzle leaking out of the morning skies. For the first time, he allowed himself to think about how close to death they had been in France. He made a decision on the spot not to spend so much time on fixing harnesses and to spend just a little more of his money, to invest it in his sanity, and to celebrate being alive.

There were a lot of apples in the market now with prices so good that Gilles decided to buy some apples, apple wine and maybe even a book or a painting. As he sat there thinking about the abundance of apples and the different look and taste of the Netherlands apples, Gilles realized that the days were getting shorter and there were more rainy days. Some of the leaves on the trees were taking on shades of gold and russet, too. He didn't know what date it was, but summer was definitely over.

After darkness fell, Jacob entered the barn, returning from Hannah's and carrying a large basket of food.

"Did you have a good Sabbath, Gilles?"

It was more of a habitual greeting on Saturday nights and Sunday mornings than an actual question that required a real answer.

"Yes, fine, and you, Jacob?"

"Very fine. Here, have some food!"

Gilles selected a piece of Hannah's chicken from the basket. Jacob started to move past Gilles to go into his house but Gilles decided that this might be a good time to ask him; it was certainly no worse than any other time.

"Jacob, I would like to go to Christian services tomorrow, just for a few hours."

"You have a sudden interest in the church now? I thought you were not on speaking terms with them. Will they not think it a little strange that a Jew is attending? Have you seen yourself lately? I thought they had no use for you except as firewood."

"I will go to the reformers service, of course. You are a good influence on me with your Sabbath, Jacob, and I promise you that I will be very careful and bring no trouble down on you."

Jacob shrugged. "I suppose I can manage alone for a few hours but I'm *not* paying you …"

"Agreed. Have a good night, Jacob."

The next day dawned very cool and very foggy and Gilles wondered just how cold it was going to get on winter mornings in the barn. The bricks and stones that formed the lower walls of the building already seemed to retain all of the cold of the night and none of the heat of the day. Gilles dressed as quickly as he could in his new work clothes, the ones made for him by the Jewish tailors. They were not stylish at all but they were clean, fit him well, and would not stand out in a crowd. The fabric was cold on his skin for just a few minutes until it warmed up to him. He was ready to leave long before Jacob came out to the barn but still he lingered until he heard the bells, the call to worship. It might have been only his imagination but it seemed to Gilles that Jacob stared at him today.

"It's too bad if he isn't comfortable with my attending a church, " Gilles thought as he set out for Elsje's church, hoping that the day would go well for him.

Jacob shook his head as he watched Gilles go. "Who else would *pay* to have a suit made for work in a barn?" Jacob asked the horses.

Gilles ate an apple as he walked, one that he had purchased on the street while on his way to get dinner the night before. His mother would despair if she knew about the bad habits he had picked up, eating and otherwise, but Gilles no longer cared that he ate in the streets like the common people did. He thought about nothing but Elsje this morning even though Hendrick was certain to be right next to her most of the time.

What if she didn't go to church today for some reason?

He wouldn't accept that thought. She had to be there.

"And then what?" he asked himself.

He didn't know the answer; he just knew that he wanted to see her. He tossed the apple core under a carriage in the street before he snatched off his ugly hat and went inside where the worshippers were already mostly seated and the service was already starting. Gilles eased himself into a seat next to a large family in the back corner and too late Gilles discovered that the space was open because the woman was busy with a small but very red and very fretful baby. Gilles hoped that the child would not attract attention by crying during the entire service. He considered moving away to another seat but if he did that now, the chances were good that either Hendrick or Elsje would see him. Finally giving in and heaving a loud sigh though, the woman next to Gilles opened the bodice of her dress and began to feed the child. The child rooted around for a few moments before it started to suck noisily at the breast but at least it had stopped howling.

Elsje's family was there with all of them in their usual seats and Gilles heard Heintje, Elsje's little brother, drop something onto the stone floor. Elsje glared at the boy as he bent down to retrieve whatever it was and Gilles noted that Tryntje wasn't sitting still either; she was looking all around the church. Gilles slouched down and tried to give the impression that he accompanied the nursing woman and her children. How was he going to talk to Elsje alone? How would he get by Hendrick? He didn't know but he could at least *see* Elsje from this vantage point.

Gilles was grateful that he had gone to the services with them before: At least he was not completely unfamiliar with their ritual. The clergyman began the sermon, speaking eloquently on the subject of reconciliation, moving some in his audience to tears as he urged his flock to put behind them old differences and to make amends with family and neighbors right now, today. He got Gilles' attention when he told the congregation that the Jews had one time of year that they set aside for this and that it was a wonderful thing, a very Christian thing, for them to do. Gilles gave the subject some brief thought but he decided that it didn't really apply to him because his family had cast *him* out and he was still more or less on good terms with them. Jean's situation came to mind next and Gilles wondered how *even God* could reasonably expect Jean to get along with someone as difficult as Dirck.

Over in Hendrick's pew, Tryntje had her head tilted to one side. She appeared to be listening while she rubbed the backs of her fingers up and down slowly inside the front of her dress, a dress which seemed to Gilles to be far too revealing for a church dress. Elsje turned her head once in Gilles' direction, apparently to better reach the back of her neck and to scratch there. Gilles leaned back as far as he could, behind the woman seated next to him, as Elsje scratched and scratched for what seemed like a very long time until at last she turned her face back in the direction of the pastor.

Gilles reasoned that he was seated nearer to the entrance of the church than Elsje and so he decided that he would leave right away when the service ended and watch for his chance to speak with her outside. Perhaps Hendrick would have many friends to talk with afterwards and he would be separated from Elsje for a time; Gilles could always disappear into the crowd if there was no possibility at all of talking to Elsje alone.

Impatiently Gilles waited for the service to end but it took an eternity, almost as long as a Catholic service would have taken. Hendrick's younger children must have been thinking the very same thing for they began to fidget more and more and Elsje had to give them stern looks more and more often. Tryntje's attention had wandered, too, and was now solidly fixed on a young man in the third row. Only Hendrick seemed not to move at all, but stayed motionless in one position, possibly sleeping with his eyes wide open.

When the service finally did end, Gilles bolted out of the door ahead of everyone else. He ignored the pain in his foot and dashed up the street, positioning himself behind a waiting carriage where he could watch the door to the church and everyone coming out. The family would have to walk right by him on their way home and it was Gilles' hope that Elsje would trail behind the group just enough so that he could talk briefly with her, at least long enough to demand the apology he sought. If things didn't work out as he planned, Gilles could duck behind the coach and not be seen at all when they passed by. Gilles congratulated himself on finding this spot and on coming up with such a good plan; he gambled that the carriage wouldn't drive off right away and leave him out in the open street without cover, but his alternative plan was to retreat behind one of the large Elm trees that stood nearby.

The worshippers filed out slowly at first but then there was a sudden eruption of people from the church. It was difficult for Gilles to see each and every person and he hoped that he had not missed Elsje in the surging crowd. He was relieved when he finally did see them but unfortunately Elsje was right behind her Father. Hendrick led the way through the crowd, greeting everyone. They traveled from handshake to handshake, from the church door to the street and then in Gilles' direction, networking their way from the church toward the inn. Gilles marveled at how many, many hands they shook, how many people they knew in their church.

Hendrick had made steady progress, all the way out to the people standing in front of the carriage where Gilles was hiding, where he was nervously expecting Hendrick to pass by on the other side very soon. Just as Gilles was beginning to wonder what was taking them so long, Hendrick's voice boomed out.

"What are *you* doing here, Montroville? Have you joined our church?"

"I-uh, I came to see you," Gilles stammered as he stepped forward, out from behind the coach, clutching his battered hat in his hand and unable to think of anything better to say.

Hendrick glared at him. "Hmph! It's an *odd* time to come and see me, during church! What business would you have with me on the Sabbath?"

"It's about my investments. I … I don't have any time off during the week to speak with you about them."

"I suppose not. Well, come to the inn tonight after your work then, and we will talk. If it *is* about business, then you won't have any need to talk to my daughters." He turned to the little flock that trailed him and barked, "Come along! Keep up!"

The group moved forward together, just slightly out of step with each other due to the varying lengths of their legs. Elsje glanced at Gilles briefly and he thought he saw her hiding a smile, but just in case, he made certain to keep far enough away from her to save his foot if she made another assault on it. Tryntje brought up the rear, walking behind the other children, flirting with her eyes as she approached Gilles and going out of her way to brush up against him as she passed by. She looked back at Gilles again after she passed him and giggled before she ran to keep up with the rest of the family.

It was time for Gilles to go and he hadn't had the chance to talk with Elsje but something good had come out of the morning: Gilles had an invitation to go to Hendrick's inn that night. Gilles hoped that it would be safe enough for him to go there now as many weeks had passed since his departure from France. Gilles had a lot to think about as he put his old hat back on his head and turned around toward the church and the route home.

Before he could take two steps though, someone else exiting the church caught his eye. Gilles stopped again and held his breath as he watched the man with the bushy eyebrows come down the steps. Gilles could see now that he had been mistaken about the man's age: He was far younger than Gilles had first thought, probably no older than Gilles himself. Gilles was certain now that he had seen that same face in the alley just before he was beaten. There was nothing remarkable about the man's face, really, except for his eyebrows and the suggestion of a mole or a birthmark on his left cheek. Now that Gilles had some time to observe the man, he noted that it was not really that his eyebrows were so thick, it was more the effect the man's dark eyebrows had against the high, white forehead, the determined set to his chin and the confident look in his eyes that made him seem older and more formidable than he might actually be.

Gilles had seen the man somewhere else, too, but where had it been? Was it in church when he had attended services there before or had he seen him passing by Jacob's stable? Perhaps it had been in Hendrick's tavern room. It couldn't have been in France. Gilles struggled to place him but it was only after the man swept his plumed hat up onto his head and then turned up the street in the very same direction that Gilles would have to travel, that Gilles realized where he had seen him. On his first day in Amsterdam when they arrived at the docks around night-fall, the man had been looking for work, pulling behind him a cart with mismatched wheels.

Gilles wondered how much of their crossing paths had been coincidence and how much had been by someone's design. Perhaps the man followed Gilles then and followed him *still*. Gilles was caught completely off guard when the owner of the carriage, accompanied by a much younger woman, returned at last from the church services. He looked Gilles over quickly as he escorted the girl over to the coach's door.

"Watch your pockets," Gilles thought he heard the man say to the girl. At any other time Gilles would have been greatly offended but today Gilles paid no attention to the man *or* to the remark. He surveyed the area completely first to make sure that there were no French agents around before he hurried after the man with the eyebrows, following him up several streets, traveling in the general direction of Jacob's stable. Gilles followed him right up until the man disappeared completely from sight after rounding a corner just a few blocks away from Jacob's. Gilles wondered at first if he had been led into a trap and he began to panic but after looking all around and then down all of the connecting streets, Gilles decided that the man had simply vanished into thin air. Gilles used the utmost care to make sure that no one followed him the rest of the way back.

The sign was up and Jacob was not inside the stable when Gilles returned so he quickly changed out of his clean clothes and back into his dirty ones. He was still unnerved enough by his encounter with the man with the bushy eyebrows to put his knife into the waistband of his clothes after he had changed. Gilles was pretty sure that Jacob had not seen the knife yet and Gilles didn't want him to see it: If Jacob had forgotten that he harbored a fugitive, then Gilles didn't want to be the one to remind him of that fact. Feeling a little more secure now that he was back inside, that some time had passed since his return from the church and that he now carried the knife on his person, Gilles took the sign down and checked on the horses even though Jacob surely would have taken care of everything, surely would not pay him anything for the entire day, and surely would remind Gilles of the time he had taken off for many weeks to come. Gilles noticed that one of the horses had a cut on his shoulder and dark blood ran down the length of the horse's leg, big flies buzzing all around the sticky, dark trail. Gilles would have to ask Jacob what had happened to the animal. Although Jacob refused to do anything besides feed and water the animals, no good would come of it if the horse developed an infection while it was in their care; the very least Gilles could do was to clean the wound.

Gilles was running his hand over the rest of the animal to make sure that there were no other injuries when he heard someone walk in. Gilles thought it a little odd that there were no sounds of accompanying hooves and he peered around the injured horse to see who was there. His heart started to pound wildly right away when he saw the man with the bushy eyebrows standing just inside the door of his stable. The man had not seen Gilles yet but he walked hesitantly inside, looking all around. Gilles silently pulled his knife from his belt and waited for the man to go just a little farther toward the back of the building so he could get behind him.

Jacob would be coming back in soon. What was Gilles going to say to Jacob, that agents of the French king had found him due to his carelessness? Gilles would have no choice now but to kill the man and to leave on the next ship out of Amsterdam, going to wherever it was headed, just as long as it wasn't back to France.

The man walked around looking at this and that, making his quiet way over to the table with the harness that Gilles had worked on so recently. Gilles took just enough time to look outside the front door, making certain that the man was alone before he crept out from behind the injured horse.

Gilles was exposed now, out in the open, but if he could surprise him, Gilles would be the likely winner of a fight because he was taller and had the element of surprise on his side. In spite of his advantages, Gilles was taking no chances this time. In one motion, Gilles grabbed the man around the neck with his left arm and put his knife firmly at the man's throat.

Gilles growled at the man in French.

"Before I kill you, I only want to know *who* sent you and *why* you have been trying to kill me."

The man was absolutely still as he whispered back to Gilles, not in French as Gilles expected, but in Nederlands, "I don't know what you are saying. Are you insane?"

At the same moment, Jacob entered the back door and dropped the buckets of water that he had been carrying, sending the water gushing over the stable floor while Gilles repeated the question in Nederlands, pressing the knife tighter to the man's throat and moving just enough to the side to let the man get a glimpse of Gilles' face.

Recognition and surprise came over the man's face but instead of answering the question and providing the requested information, he replied, "I've never seen you before in my life."

Gilles was in a quandary. He didn't know if he could just take a man's life, especially with Jacob watching, even to preserve his own. He was somewhat hoping that Jacob would advise him as to what he should do next. Perhaps Jacob would help Gilles tie him up, leaving the man alive while Gilles made his escape but instead Jacob called over to Gilles, "Go ahead and kill him."

In the split seconds of confusion in which Gilles considered what he should do next, the man cried out, "No, Uncle, it's me! It's *Claes!*"

"I *know* it's you. What do you want with us?" Jacob asked the man angrily.

"I just came by to say that I wish we could talk."

"All right, you came by, you said it. Does my stable boy tell the truth? Are you trying to kill him?"

"No, I swear on my mother, I don't know him!"

"Hmph. That's *not much* to swear on."

The young man swallowed the insult to the woman who gave birth to him and said nothing, possibly because of the knife still at his throat or maybe because he knew that it was a lie.

Gilles really hoped that some better idea of what he should do next would come to him: He still didn't trust the man. The man lied about knowing him but the fact that he was Jacob's nephew greatly complicated matters and Gilles couldn't just hold him there forever.

Claes spoke again. "I have been giving it some thought lately, and I wish that we could be friends, Uncle. That's all I came to say. I decided to come today and to say it to you myself. I think Johan and Willem feel the same way."

"All right, you said it, now you can leave."

"So you won't take my hand if I offer it to you?"

"Not until you come back to us. I don't hold out any hope for your father as he has been bewitched by that woman whose bed he shares, but are you ready to return?"

"To …?"

"*To the faith!*"

"I can't do that, Uncle."

Well then, be gone out of this part of town and *don't* come back. You aren't welcome here."

"I *miss* you, Uncle Jacob."

Jacob's eyes softened but the tone of his voice didn't. It was husky but still harsh as he replied, "Go tell Isaac I said 'hello' but that's *all* I say to him."

"I can't. Father died last January, the third of January, if you want to say kaddish for him or light a yarzeit."

"You still remember that much, eh? Well, you go now, we have work to do here." Jacob turned away from Claes, to the spilled water buckets and picking them up, he took them out the back door again. Claes just stood there watching him go.

"Why are you lying?" Gilles asked as he lowered the knife and put it back in his belt, all the while thinking that he might *still* have to leave right away even if he wasn't going to kill anyone today.

Claes turned to face him and now that Gilles saw him up close, he did indeed look much younger. Gilles was convinced that Claes only left the uneven stubble on his face to try to look older.

"*Please* don't tell Uncle Jacob. I made a mistake! We needed the money so much since my father died and I … it was wrong to join up with the smugglers. I didn't *know* anyone could be hurt. If there is a better way for hard-working people to get enough money for food, I haven't found it yet. I'm sorry about what happened; I *truly* am. They wanted to kill you but I stopped them. Please don't tell Uncle Jacob."

Claes' words tumbled out so quickly that Gilles didn't comprehend all that he was saying until he stopped speaking and only then was Gilles convinced that Claes had told the truth. Gilles didn't want Jacob to know about the incident either, not just because it was embarrassing, but also because it would make Gilles seem like even more of a liability, and so he agreed not to tell.

"I haven't seen my uncle since I was very small. Is he always like this?"

"Mostly," Gilles replied. "Once in a great while he's reasonable. Keep on trying, though, he's here most of the time except for Tuesdays when he is at the Dam all day and on Saturdays when he is at his daughter's."

"You won't tell Uncle Jacob?" Claes asked Gilles again.

"I won't tell your Uncle Jacob," Gilles agreed.

Claes offered Gilles his hand. As Gilles accepted it, he noticed that the young man had a ring on his smallest finger, a ring with a cross on it. Jacob's nephew was a Christian.

Gilles *did* have some curiosity as to how his accounts with Hendrick were doing and he had not really had a full accounting from Hendrick although he couldn't help noticing that the money retrieved when Hendrick had thrown it to the ground was more than he had originally invested. Gilles wondered if he had made enough money now to start over comfortably somewhere else. More and more he thought about farming in the German states, particularly in the Palatinate. He would leave life in the crowded city and start his own vineyards along the Rhine. He would build a business for himself there, an empire like his father's, and continue to invest what he could in his overseas holdings with Jacob. He would find a way to make a comfortable life.

These thoughts preoccupied him for most of the day and distracted him until Jacob said, "Go on, you're not much good to me today with your mind somewhere else; go and get your supper."

"Are we done for the day?"

"Ja, you're done for the day, not that you have done much of *anything* today."

Gilles went outside and washed his face and hands. When he returned to the barn, he climbed up into the loft and changed into the new clothes. He put a few coins in his pocket and tucked his knife into his waistband before he left. Jacob continued to do odd things down in the stable area, moving this here, doing that there, and grumbling occasionally until Gilles climbed back down.

"You changed your clothes *again*? He changes clothes more often than a prince!" Jacob shook his head in disbelief and stood his shovel up against the wall. Unbalanced, it clattered noisily down across the stone wall as it fell over.

"Have a good night Jacob," Gilles called out in farewell but Jacob stopped him.

"You have a woman outside?"

"There is no woman outside. I have some business there."

"What *business* do you have there? You have a job here with me."

"Yes, and I'm grateful for that Jacob. It's just … *business*."

"So you'll leave me soon, then?"

"No, Jacob, I have no plans to leave you. I'll need the investments for later, when I'm too old to work for you. Good night, Jacob."

Gilles knew that this was not exactly the whole truth but he wasn't ready to make any definite plans for his future without knowing how much money he had to invest in it. He stopped to get his usual supper even though he planned to buy food and ale when he got to Elsje's but until then, the usual fare would tide him over. The girl came to the door tonight and tossed his dinner to him as Gilles gave her the coins.

"Like one tosses food out to chickens," Gilles thought.

He remembered Elsje's kindness to the Marrano beggars and noted that *she* gave them her best food for free and even served it to them on a real plate. Gilles opened his mouth to thank the girl, but she had already turned away to shut the door, to shut him out. Tonight's supper was a bit of bread and some oily smoked fish that he tried not to get on his clothes. Since no napkin was ever supplied to him with his meal, Gilles pulled his handkerchief out of his pocket to use that, his greasy hand grasping at one corner of the fabric. For a few brief moments, a vision of supper at home in France flashed across his mind. Gilles saw himself seated at the table with fine linen napkins, silverware and crystal all around him, several courses of food, and several servants to serve it all and then to take the empty dishes away. It was not a fantasy; it had been reality once. Gilles had not changed so much but his world had changed completely since then.

When Gilles got there, it was dark outside already and when the lights from the inn came into sight, it filled Gilles with a sense of familiarity and warmth that he did not think he would ever feel again in his lifetime. It also filled him with sadness, though, because it was not *his* home, it was someone else's home. He stood there for a moment, trying to store the feeling in his memory for when he might need to call on it again at some future time. He looked around to be sure that no one followed him tonight before he went up to the old inn door. As he pushed it open, a wave of smoke, warmth and laughter billowed out over him and Elsje raced by the door, both hands full with plates of food, but she had an extra smile for him.

"I will tell my father that you are here, Gilles."

Gilles was surprised to smell the scent of flowers on her as she breezed by but perhaps they were expecting important guests like Pieter Stuyvesant here tonight. She set the plates down in front of two men and then went back into the kitchen. Gilles stood waiting at the front door, not daring to take a seat and he saw none open anyway, even if he wanted to sit. Elsje's father followed her back out into the dining room from the kitchen, saying something to her in a low voice before she waived her free hand in some kind of dismissal and then placed a pitcher of bier in front of a ragged-looking group of men. They laughed loudly and all looked impertinently at Elsje but she paid no attention to them. Hendrick motioned Gilles over to the usual corner table where the old Dutchman always held court, kicked two strangers out of the seats, and then settled himself back into the corner. Gilles took the other chair but moved it around so that he leaned back against the wall, too. He needed to keep his eyes on the room and he touched the handle of his hidden knife once, just to reassure himself that it was at the ready if he needed it. The room was filled with tobacco smoke and noise but far from being uncomfortable, it was very pleasant and very familiar to Gilles.

"I'll need a pen and some paper," Gilles said to Hendrick.

Hendrick looked surprised but beckoned to Elsje. She came over and was immediately dispatched for the pen, paper, two ales and Hendrick's pipe.

"So you really *did* want to talk business with me?" Hendrick asked him.

"Ja, I thought I might want to invest *more* money with you, that is, if my current investments are doing well enough."

Hendrick looked a little surprised but he said nothing until after Elsje had brought the ales over. Gilles still didn't like the taste but he took a miniscule sip, remembering that his father had always said, *"Never trust a man who won't drink with you, Gilles."* Gilles had also learned that the Netherlanders didn't trust people who didn't always have their ale in hand so he kept the handle strategically affixed to his left hand.

Elsje returned with a tray that held the pipe, straws to light it, a lit candle, paper, ink, and pen.

"Anything more?" she asked her father irritably.

"Nee, go now."

Hendrick waved her away and Gilles avoided looking at her. After spending so much time in the stables Gilles had to wonder if he would remember anything at all of his former training with finance.

"You had invested this much with me." Hendrick wrote down a number and slid the paper across the table.

"Agreed, Hendrick."

"I have invested it for you and *this* is your return. It is a very handsome return!"

Gilles wrote numbers and odd lines on the paper before he replied, "It *is* a good return ..."

Hendrick nodded at him in agreement, leaned back in his seat, smiled and lit his pipe, letting the smoke escape from his lips at its own pace.

"... but it is *not* as good a return as my friend Jean's, though. *Why* is that?"

The smile on his face faded slightly before Hendrick responded. "Well, there are different rates of return for investments at different times and for my work in managing your funds. I have paid myself a part of it for all the work that I did on your behalf."

"So you have taken a percentage?"

"Ja, exactly!" Hendrick beamed at him but Gilles started writing numbers again.

"*What percentage* did you charge me, Hendrick?"

Hendrick's smile faded a little but he maintained his relaxed demeanor.

"I don't think *two* percent is unreasonable to pay me for my efforts, do you? Especially when you have made such a *good* profit."

"*Two* percent is a reasonable fee but seven percent is *not*. You have charged me here seven percent," Gilles insisted, pointing at the paper.

"Well, I don't think it works out to *seven* percent but it's more profit than you would have had if I did not invest *any* of it for you, is that not so?"

"And does the Dutch West India Company know how much of *their* money and the money of their investors that you take?"

"It's a free market and I am sure that they would not mind, Msr. Montroville. If you don't think so, I can give you your money plus interest now and we can end this partnership."

"End it? Oh, no! I hope we have a very *long* partnership, Hendrick, *and* a very profitable one."

"Did you need some of the money *now*? Is that why you wanted to meet with me? I imagine you would, since stable jobs on that side of town don't pay very well."

Gilles turned red and wondered how much Hendrick knew about where he had been living and working; Elsje must have told him. Gilles would not be distracted or put off balance, though. His father had taught him well, had taught him never to take his eye away from the bottom line.

"We have not yet come to an agreement as to how much money I *currently* have invested with you, Hendrick. Of course if you and I are unable to agree, I could take the matter of investments and percentages up with someone else, maybe with Joseph D'Acosta."

"Do you know Joseph D'Acosta?" Hendrick's eyes widened a little.

"Well, I *have* had occasion to meet him since he lives near where I live now."

Gilles stretched the truth a little but living on the other side of town could be used to his advantage just as well as to his disadvantage. Gilles turned his mug of ale around and wiped some moisture from one side. He knew that Hendrick was wondering if Gilles *really* did know Joseph D'Acosta or if he was merely bluffing. Gilles closed his mouth and kept it closed as his father had always said, *"The man who speaks first, loses."*

Gilles took another sip of ale and resumed staring at it, trying to look as though he was lost in thought and not like he was waiting for Hendrick to say something.

Hendrick cleared his throat. "You don't *really* want to deal with those company guilder-counters, do you Montroville? They have too many middle men and your profits over time will be *much better* with me!"

"I'd rather *not* deal with them Hendrick, but now that I've made some more contacts, I *could* work directly with them. I just knew you first, and so I am giving you the opportunity to keep my business. With me, it's about *loyalty.*"

Gilles sipped his ale again. It was only down a little from the top but was starting to taste a little better now. He knew that Hendrick would like the last part, the part about loyalty.

"Gilles, Gilles! You have been a guest at my inn and we even nursed you back to health when you were so badly injured a few months ago! Let me do *this* for you, Gilles: I will look at the numbers and give you a better return if you invest *more* money with me right now or, if you are in need of the money, you can just send *other* investors to me. I will count their investment as a part of yours, percentage-wise only of course, but being a larger share holder, I could give you a *better* rate of return."

"Actually I am doing well enough now and I don't need *any* of the money. I will continue to invest more with you as long as I see a *fair* rate of return and seven percent taken from the top is *not* a fair return. *Two* percent is."

Hendrick cleared his throat again, the tobacco smoke having irritated it a bit, but he seemed to hear what Gilles was saying. "It will take me a little time to rework those numbers but I can probably have them ready for you tomorrow night."

He folded the paper and put it into his pocket as Gilles wondered if the old man was stalling, needed that much time to add a simple column of figures, was too drunk to think, or was trying another trick, but Gilles could return to the inn on the following evening. It didn't matter: Waiting one more day would do no harm.

"Tomorrow then, Hendrick. I will come back tomorrow night and if I don't like what I see, I will take all of my money then and reinvest it directly with the West India Company."

A disturbance took their attention away from the discussion of money. The table with the rough men was the center of the discord in the normally peaceful, if lively, inn. One of the men held Elsje by the wrist as she scolded him in a low but fast Nederlands. The man's eyes had an uncomprehending glazed look but he grinned at her as his dinner companions smirked. Gilles jumped up from his seat and was over at the table in an instant.

"… am not just some serving girl, and even if I was, I would not *go* anywhere with you *nor* would I let any of our *girls* go with you! I don't know how you behave or *don't* behave in England but you will be out of here right now if you don't behave any better; now take your hands *off* me!"

"Leave the girl," Gilles said in English, wondering if this was the time to pull his knife out but there were too many of them for him and his one weapon.

"You stay out of this!" the man barked at Gilles in English. "Does anyone know what this Dutch Dumpling is saying? I *like* a woman with some fight in her! Makes having her all the better!"

His companions all laughed and Gilles raised his voice to be heard above the laughter as he answered the man. "She is saying to leave her alone, that she is the owner's daughter!"

"Oooh, the owner's daughter!" the men at the table mocked Gilles and exchanged looks with each other.

"Leave her alone!" Elsje parroted Gilles' English and yanked her arm but the dirty man held fast to it.

The man's companions just sat where they were, content to let him work this one out on his own and they watched in amusement, apparently quite accustomed to such entertainment.

"And will you fight me for this prize, Plowboy?" The drunk's attention had turned to Gilles and perhaps if the pirate had a pastime that he liked better than the conquest of a woman, it was fighting with a man. "All the Dutch women are *pigs*, everyone knows that. It's always just a matter of coming to terms on their price but I do *like* the negotiation process."

"You can't fight while you hold her arm. Let her go and I will fight you then," Gilles offered.

One on one, Gilles thought that he *might* have a chance: He was taller than the other man and more sober, but the drunk was far heavier and much of his bulk was muscle from working on sailing ships. The bully considered Gilles' proposal while the other patrons at the inn looked on but being accustomed to a quieter and friendlier tavern, they were not enjoying the spectacle. Many of them were regulars who were quite fond of Elsje and were certainly wondering how the matter was going to be resolved. This question, and the question of where Hendrick had been during the exchange between Gilles, Elsje, and the freebooter, were soon answered when the old man appeared at the kitchen doorway with a gun in his hands. Gilles didn't have the time to wonder where the old man could have gotten such a thing, whether he knew how to use it, or even if he had any shot in it. Gilles did guess, and quite correctly, that it wasn't illegal to *own* one, but it *was* illegal to shoot one, in the typically nonsensical way that the Dutch wrote their laws. It would be much better for Gilles, at least in terms of avoiding contact with the authorities and so to preserve his anonymity, if Hendrick did not fire the gun.

"You freebooters leave! Go back to your ship!" Hendrick shouted in Nederlands and motioned toward the door with the gun.

The rough group didn't understand the words but they were not *so* drunk that they didn't understand the meaning.

"Go now!" Gilles roared at them.

The scruffy man looked at the gun just one more time before he decided not to accept the challenge. He released Elsje's wrist and Gilles pulled Elsje over to him and then shoved her behind him.

"But we haven't finished our dinner yet," the drunk whined as he looked sadly down at his plate that was still full of food. He didn't sit back down again and he wasn't leaving yet, either. He picked up his ale and took a long drink as he swayed back and forth. His companions were still sitting, still eating, and still waiting patiently for the outcome of the main event. Hendrick clicked back the flint hammer and this noise seemed to be the signal that they all waited for.

"Aye, we'll go," the man muttered, setting his mug back down on the table and bending over to pick up a battered hat from the floor, but not without some difficulty as he almost fell over during the effort. Gilles and Elsje moved back together, out of their path to the door.

"But your Netherlands hospitality is verra bad! You'll be *sorry* for this and I'll be back for you, my girl!"

He pointed at Gilles and winked at Elsje before he made his way to the door with every eye in the room still watching him. His companions rose to follow, some of them stuffing Elsje's bread and rolls into their pockets even as they left. Gilles noticed with a shock that one of the "men" was a woman dressed as a man, no less rough than her companions, but unmistakably female. Gilles wondered briefly about her availability or lack thereof to the amorous drunken man, what she thought of this exchange, and if she witnessed it very often, as well as how she came to be traveling with this pack of wild dogs.

The ragged bunch stumbled outside and Hendrick looked out the window to make sure that they were gone. Elsje went off to check on a table as Gilles looked after her in amazement. Any other woman might have fled, collapsed, or dissolved into tears, but she acted as though nothing at all had happened. As the room slowly returned to its former noise level, Gilles wondered if Elsje and Hendrick had very much experience with such incidents. Hendrick eased the flint on the gun back to its resting position and set the gun against the wall before he sat down again.

"Come back, Montroville! Come finish your ale."

Gilles returned to Hendrick's table from where he had been standing during the confrontation but Elsje was already into her third table since the incident and Hendrick was lighting his pipe again. Gilles thought that they either didn't understand the threats or that they just didn't take it very seriously. A few men at the tables stole glances at Gilles as they laughed and talked among themselves. Gilles received no thanks from Elsje or her father, not even any acknowledgement of the risk that he had just undertaken on her behalf.

Hendrick waved to Tryntje to bring two fresh ales over although Gilles' ale was hardly half of the way down.

Gilles stayed to drink the fresh ale, just so that he could stay at the inn a little longer. Elsje smiled at Gilles openly once and if Hendrick noticed this, he pretended not to. Gilles did not want to drink too much though, particularly if the group of men waited outside for him, but for now he used the remaining ale as an excuse to stay.

"Do you often have trouble like that in here?" Gilles asked Hendrick.

"Sometimes. This group was trouble from the start! I usually tell them that I'm full up and they should go somewhere else but they begged for food and you know Elsje, she wouldn't turn them away. Someone said they came in this afternoon on a ship flying the Spanish flag but they're no Spaniards! Pirates most likely, vrijbuiters just stopping on their way to plunder something or do some other mischief."

"They spoke English with maybe a trace of Scots."

"Well, it's not worth thinking about." Hendrick ended the discussion on that subject but he did have something else on his mind. "Gilles, I have been approached by another group of people who need investors for their venture. They say that it is time to go on to where the *real* money is, north into the wilderness beyond the pine plains and Fort Orange. It's very risky but a man with your resolve might like such a challenge."

"Did you ask for any numbers, estimates of what profit they might get out of there?" Gilles was mildly amused that the old man appeared to be asking *him* for financial advice when only a short time earlier he had been trying to shortchange Gilles.

"The numbers are incredible enough, but maybe they are *too* incredible, you know what I'm saying? The great amount of time that it takes to get goods down the Mauritius River, Hudson's River, and the exposure to dangers during the entire time increases the risk. Our traders would have to pass through no less than a dozen different tribes of savages, some friendly, but some not. The group proposing this is led by a *very* young man and his uncle who claim they are going to *live* over there."

Gilles could see that Hendrick was having difficulty in objectively weighing his desire for very large profits against the overwhelming odds that even a single attempted trip would not be successful. Across the room, Gilles saw Elsje pause to talk to a man, the ale pitcher in her hand as the patron reached out and touched her arm. Gilles stiffened, ready for another fight, but Elsje just patted the man's hand and left his table with a smile.

"Perhaps the savages can be bought off," Gilles said in response to Hendrick, but he did not take his eyes off Elsje.

"Oh they *can*, but they are cunning animals and demand more and more money all the time. Some are being stirred up by the English and the Swedes and *now* they want *guns*; beads and iron pots are just not buying them off anymore. It's a frightening thought, the woods overrun by savages with guns, firing at will at anyone who ventures there. They are terrifying enough with their primitive weapons, their spears and their stone knives, even without guns!" Hendrick was turning it over and over in his mind like a puzzle with a solution that he just could not find.

"Maybe you can pay them *after* they make it through," Gilles suggested.

"They need the investment up front so there *has* to be *some* way for me to judge the risk, to find out if even *one time* I should risk giving them the money."

"I might know some people who can check into it," Gilles suggested, thinking of Jean Durie and his many connections.

"I have made some inquiries myself and they seem to be honest men. Men! Their leader on this expedition is hardly more than a *boy* but he has such fire and conviction! He should have been a clergyman. Nee, Gilles, my *real* question is *not* their intentions, whether or not they are honest men: I am convinced of that, but *can* they do it? Is it possible? We might be able to establish trade with the savages only to have one competitor give them just a little more money and then the entire proposition falls apart."

Gilles gave Hendrick a guarded smile. "Perhaps the only way to know is to *try*, then. I would be happy to go over the numbers with you and then have my connections check into it."

Their conversation was interrupted by a gale of laughter from Elsje and a table of patrons. The noise level had not only returned to normal, it was more boisterous than ever. Gilles' and Elsje's eyes met. She turned away from him, still smiling at whatever joke had made her laugh out loud. Gilles liked her smiles, they warmed the entire inn. How could he fault the pirate for wanting to touch some of that warmth after months away at sea?

Hendrick wrote down some numbers on the paper in front of him. "This is the expected profit from just *one* trip."

Gilles looked at the figures and thought that the old man must be delirious. "How many men would it take to bring that out of the wilderness and what would we have to pay them up front for expenses and for their shares? What would we have to pay the Indians for the furs? Is that *all* in beaver or does it include mink, muskrat, and otter too?" Gilles stared at the numbers again. Hendrick had put at least one too many zeros on the end, possibly two.

"It's for six men including two Indian guides. They save money by trapping their own, not buying or trading for the furs and we split it, twenty percent to them and eighty percent to us, based on these numbers. They don't know we can get *this* price for them here in Amsterdam, they think they can only get this much." Hendrick circled two sets of numbers, dipped the pen in the ink again and drew an arrow between them. "It's mostly beaver because beaver brings the best price, but some otter and other furs could be included as well."

"But they will have to buy the land to trap on, *that* will cost some money," Gilles objected.

"Hah! That is the beauty of the new continent! The Indians have some crazy idea that land can't be bought or sold and they quickly sell their rights to anyone for next to nothing. We can just go in and *take* the furs with a very, very, small investment. The WIC has laid claim to some of the land in question, but the Netherlands can not track the use of *every* bit of the land; there is just too much land involved and it is so far into the wilderness that they only pass by maybe once every five years, but mostly they have *never even seen* what they lay claim to. The odds are very good that they would never happen across one of the traps in a hundred years."

"So our company would be like tenant farmers?"

"Something like that, I suppose ..." Hendrick didn't seem too clear on the details of how that worked but he continued talking. "Even if we had to buy them off, it would have very little effect on our profit. Others are making a good deal of money just with trading alone but they could make *much more* by going into the wilderness themselves. There just aren't many men who are willing to risk going in there, even for a much greater profit."

"They probably value their lives too much," Gilles said wryly.

"Well, check them out, see what you think. You know I have a *great* business sense; see all the money you have made through my ventures? The man's name is Van Corlaer. Let me know and soon, Gilles; others will want to be in on this if it works as well as I think it might," Hendrick said. "We'll want to be in there first."

It did sound interesting to Gilles. He didn't have that much to lose but he did have everything to gain, perhaps a fortune to gain.

"There is just one more bit of business that we have tonight," Hendrick said.

Gilles wondered if there was another trade deal that Hendrick had to offer but instead he went on to yet another subject.

"You do not follow after my daughter like an animal. You speak with her openly if you speak with her at all. You act like a man, not like a cat, sneaking and stealing things from a man's table. I don't want to waste my gunshot on you; it would bring too much trouble to us both. Do you understand me, Frenchman?"

What could Gilles say to him? It was time for him to leave before the conversation took a turn to something worse. "I understand. Goedenacht, Hendrick." Gilles gathered up his cloak, shook hands with Hendrick and left the inn.

The rains had started again and it was a very dark night. He did not relish the thought of going out with the pirates perhaps lying in wait for him but it was better to leave early while there were still people on the streets. Gilles smiled when he thought of Hendrick holding the gun even if he *had* threatened to use it on Gilles. It was a great, worthless thing: In the time that it would take him to load it, someone could carry off all of the old man's holdings as well as both daughters. Leaving it loaded was dangerous and leaving it near a fireplace could be a very risky practice, too. Gilles appreciated the portability of a knife and he touched the handle before he moved forward, quickly and silently through the streets, winding his way here, stopping in a doorway there, listening for anyone who might be following behind him in the rain.

His return was quiet enough though. The freebooters were probably too drunk to make good on their promise of revenge tonight and more likely they had found some sport somewhere else if they were still so inclined; after all, this *was* Amsterdam and the alehouses never closed here. As Gilles crawled into his loft to sleep, he thought about Hendrick's new trade proposal. The scheme sounded insane, though: How could a few Dutchmen travel through hundreds of miles of a wilderness filled with so many different varieties of savages and wild beasts as well as other hazards, dragging large quantities of fur with them and then appear days, weeks away from where they set out, with all of the goods and themselves still intact? The old man was crazy to think that it could ever work. What was his name? Van Corlaer? Van Curler? Gilles would find some excuse to decline the offer. If Gilles happened to see Jean tomorrow, though, it might be worth asking him if he knew anything about Van Curler.

The merchants and traders coming to the stable had become less numerous as the autumn days passed and winter approached. People still needed to buy flour, milk, cheese, and dried foods but there were no longer any fresh fruits or vegetables available in the market. The ships coming in from across the oceans now weathered fierce storms on nearly every voyage; some limped in with damaged or lost cargo and crew, while others that were long overdue never made it in at all, either making for port elsewhere or having been lost at sea.

This Monday morning was rainy, dark and cold. Jacob yelled up to the loft for Gilles to wake up, that it was already late. Gilles didn't respond to the call at first because he had been dreaming of savages yelling in the woods in New France but then he believed that the pirates had found him and it was only then that he woke with a start. He quickly got his bearings and realized that he was safe, but his mouth was dry and he needed to go to the privy before he could think of doing anything else. Jacob was still grumbling when Gilles returned, something about not getting a boy who worked for his pay, just a fine gentleman who stayed out all night long. Gilles had become accustomed to Jacob's grousing and accustomed to having fewer customers every day so he was surprised to see that there were men already waiting to leave their horses this morning.

"We have people coming in! Get to work!" Jacob bellowed at Gilles.

The two men stood uncertainly in the doorway with reins in hand and another man pulled up in front of the stable in a carriage with four horses.

"No! We don't do carriages! Take them elsewhere!" Jacob shooed them away.

The driver muttered a curse at Jacob and drove off, splashing mud on the other two customers who cursed the driver *and* Jacob but Gilles resolved to stay in a good mood in spite of the way the day had just started. He grabbed a horse with each hand and left Jacob to try and placate the soggy owners. It was much busier than Gilles expected with the horses coming in all morning without a break and people who might ordinarily take their animals into the city with them, people who were not their regular customers, leaving their animals with Jacob just to keep them safe and keep them out of the mud. A man could often travel faster on foot through the quagmire in the Amsterdam streets than a large animal could, and the many rain-slicked bridges in the city were injury hazards to a good horse.

Sometimes, particularly on rainy days like today, the customers didn't want to carry a stack of goods through the streets and they had their purchases delivered to the stable. Jacob irritably tried to find out who belonged to what packages and they both had to explain over and over to delivery people that they were *not* paying for *anything* that was delivered there. It was another one of those days, and Gilles' single greatest wish was for Jacob to disappear for the rest of the day because the old goat was in such a bad mood. Gilles looked forward to the next day, to Tuesday, just as much for Jacob's being away as for Hannah's visit.

He got through the day, but after work Gilles was very tired and he felt feverish. He didn't feel well enough to go to Hendrick's so he sent word through a young boy that he would meet with him when he felt better. He did not even feel well enough to go get his dinner but he managed to climb up into the loft where fell down onto his bedding and closed his eyes right away.

For the first time in his life Gilles was worried about his own health. Even after his older brother died, it had never occurred to him that *he* might die someday. If he died here in this place, who would know about it? How would Jacob dispose of his body? He shook these odd thoughts off and attributed them to the fever. He was so tired that very soon he was fast asleep, dreaming more odd dreams.

He felt a little better the next morning and felt better still when Jacob left. A pale sun had not warmed the day up very much and he moved his blanket into the shed for Hannah. If she had been expecting Gilles to be as enthusiastic he had been the previous week, she was disappointed; Gilles still had no appetite for food and he had no appetite for her either, today. For the first time since they had started meeting on Tuesdays, there was uncomfortable silence between them. Gilles' fevered brain struggled to think of something to say to alleviate the malaise and he eventually thought of several things, but none of them escaped his mouth in time. Her clothes went back on, and then the ring, a fast kiss on his lips, and then Gilles wordlessly watched her go.

He ran his fingers through his hair and then he thought about lost opportunities, including the one that had just passed. He was aware that he was in a very strange mood today but there was nothing to be done about it. He picked up the blanket, threw it over his shoulder, and carried it back inside. When he entered the barn he saw Jean Durie sitting in the very same spot where he had been the week before. Gilles tossed the blanket up to the loft and took the sign down before he spoke.

"You've been coming here a lot lately. Don't you ever have any work to do on Tuesday mornings?"

"I could ask the same of you. Aren't you happy to see me?" Jean countered.

"Of course," Gilles said and sat down next to him. "I just don't feel very well."

"I'm sorry to hear that. Do you think I come here just to bother you about Jacob's daughter?"

Gilles shrugged. Jean could scold away; it didn't make any difference. He wasn't going to listen to it, anyway. At times there didn't seem to be any age difference at all between Gilles and Jean but then there were days like today when the difference was enormous and Gilles felt like he was sitting next to his father.

"Actually I'm on my way in to work, Gilles. It's slow this time of year so they won't look for me to be in very early. I ran into Hendrick this morning in the square and he said he had some numbers for you. I hope that's all right, that he gave them to me; he didn't think you would mind."

"Non, that's fine."

"I'm very glad to see that you are investing and planning for your future, Gilles. You need to make more decisions and exercise more control over your finances. You should make up your mind about Elsje, too."

"Elsje? What is there to decide about Elsje? Hendrick told me that I could talk to her. There is no decision about Elsje that needs to be made."

"She would make you a good wife, Gilles. I can see that you like each other."

Gilles snorted. "Elsje? She is an *innkeeper's* daughter and I am a Montroville!"

"You *were* a Montroville. That world is gone and Gilles Jansen needs to go forward with his life."

"I'm not interested in marriage. I'm as interested in marriage as … as I am in raising sheep."

Gilles was more than a little irritated with Jean's topic of conversation this morning. He didn't feel well and it was really none of his business how he spent his spare time. The last thing he needed was a wife to nag him; he already had *Jean* to do that.

"What about you? You're much older than I am and you have not married, Jean."

"I am a different story, as you well know. I'm not anxious to marry any of the Jewish women I know and I'm not eager to test the Dutch legal system and see what the court's verdict would be if I had a relationship with a Christian woman. You could easily forget Marie if only you would try, Gilles. You never cared about her anyway; it was only the compensation your father promised that you were enamored of."

"How do *you* know what I wanted? Even if I *was* interested in Elsje, her father would not have me, being the lowly stable boy I am! It is quite ridiculous! At once I am too far *above* her social standing and too far *below* it. All that is left to me is to accept what comfort is offered to me."

Jean sighed. "*Comfort*, eh? Ah Gilles, your family has convinced you that you are too good for *anyone*. It will be a long, cold, and lonely life if you must wait for one of your status to arrive in your life. Maybe you are looking for a princess who works as a cleaning woman somewhere?"

"Did you come here just to annoy me this morning?"

Gilles got up and picked up a pitch fork, angrily poking at some hay that had spilled over from the loft.

"Gilles, I see a chance for you to be happy. You like Elsje, don't you? Why not ask for her?"

"I don't think you have been *paying attention* for the past six months, Jean. Hendrick hates me and has told me in no uncertain terms to stay away from her. Do you want me to risk *my* investments now?

"Gilles, if you want a thing in this life, any thing, you must *try* for it, no matter what the obstacles appear to be. That is not to say that there isn't a right way and a wrong way to go about getting what you want, of course. If you truly have no interest in her at all, then that is quite another matter."

"Thank you, Jean. Are you finished yet?"

Gilles could hear the sarcasm in his own voice and he waited for Jean to scold him some more.

"Think about what I said, Gilles, *all of it*. I think you like each other and would both benefit from an alliance."

Thank you, Jean, but I can manage my own affairs."

"So I see." Jean smirked at him as he picked up his cloak and hat. "Oh, yes. The other reason I came here: I have a letter from your father."

He handed the packet to Gilles. Gilles looked at it and put it into his pocket. Letters from his father usually put him in a bad mood and he didn't feel like reading it just now. "Jean, there is *one* thing that I would like to ask you about."

Jean seemed pleased that perhaps Gilles was finally going to ask for his advice. "Yes, Gilles?"

"Did Hendrick talk to you about a proposition in the new world with some-one named Van Curler?"

"Yes, Arent Van Corlaer, he talked to me about it."

"Are you going to invest in this venture then?"

"I'm still thinking it over and checking into what anyone knows about his integrity. He's well connected but what is *the man* like? Did you know that he is Kiliaen Van Rensselaer's great nephew and has been managing the patroonship over there for the past couple of years? That's quite impressive for such a young man! Drop that piece of information on Hendrick when you see him; I'll bet he doesn't know that."

Jean winked at Gilles, put his hat on and went out into the morning.

Gilles realized that he was feeling a little light-headed and decided that he needed some food in his stomach even if it wouldn't stay there for very long. He laboriously climbed up into the loft and took some of his money out to go and buy himself a little breakfast. He put the sign back up and as he went out to get himself some food, he realized that it had been nearly a full day since he had eaten anything.

The girl at the inn was unsympathetic, as bad-tempered as Jacob had been the day before and she told Gilles that he needed to pay for last night's supper, too, as she handed him the breakfast he had just paid for.

"But I did not get to eat it!" he objected. "I was sick!"

"A bargain is a bargain. You agreed to buy it, I agreed to make it," she said. "I *made* it so you need to *pay* me, even if you *didn't* come to get it. This isn't the first time that you haven't shown up and haven't paid me!"

"If I pay for it, then you must give my supper to me now," Gilles insisted.

"The dogs have finished it long ago," she replied haughtily.

"You want me to pay for something that I did not get?!" Gilles was getting angrier by the moment.

"That is *not* my fault. If you wish to call off our arrangement, that would suit me."

Gilles knew that he would not find a better deal so he acquiesced. "I want some food, then, for my money, for last night's money that I give to you today."

"There is an old potato root left."

She went back inside and returned with the shriveled earth apple. She held it out to him with a self-satisfied smile.

If he had to give her the money, he would take the food although it humili-ated and angered him to think of how much money she had taken from him today and how little he got in return. He waited until she went back inside and closed the door before he walked around the building and threw the rotten vegetable down at the front steps of her inn and then mashed it flat on the walk for good measure. He scraped the mess from the heel of his boot onto her stoep before he walked away, feeling just a little bit better.

He did eat the bread and cheese the girl had given him for breakfast. He still had no appetite but he ate as much as he could because he needed to keep his strength up. The walk back was not long but it was long enough for thoughts of his earlier conversation with Jean to return to him.

It was ridiculous to even consider marriage to Elsje. What would he say to Hendrick? *"I want your daughter to marry me and come live with me in my stable in the Jewish quarter"?* He could hear Elsje's peals of laughter and see her walking away, still holding her sides and laughing. *"I can offer her an old earth apple which I have just thrown away. I have some investments that might work out ... or might not. On Tuesdays, she can share me with the stable-keeper's daughter."*

Gilles was wasting his time by even *thinking* about what Jean had said. He took the sign down and was alone again in the stable with three horses and his thoughts. He thought briefly about what it would be like to take Elsje to the back shed but he pushed that thought away quickly. It was ridiculous to daydream of such things; only Hannah would consider being with Gilles without getting paid for it and would have him in an old shed, at that.

Jacob didn't stay for very long at the market today and he returned in a somewhat better frame of mind. He offered Gilles fish and dried apples, perhaps as a peace offering. Gilles had no appetite for the fish but he accepted the dried apple slices. Gilles thought about it and decided that his situation was peculiar if not humorous: A Jew harboring a Christian, keeping him safe by pretending to the rest of the world and possibly even to himself that the boy was not who he *was*, a gentleman from a great family of France, that he was just another particle of dust that had been plucked from the streets. In a strange way, Jacob and Gilles were kin and strangers at the same time, having to trust each other of necessity even though they should have been naturally mistrustful of each other due to the earliest trajectories of their lives.

Gilles chewed on the apple slice, thinking about the apples at home in Rouen. They didn't *dry* the last of the apples there; they crushed them into juices, wines and vinegar and fed the leftover skins and pulp to the animals. The pigs and cows adored the sticky remains and grew fat from them. Maybe Gilles' home *was* lost forever and maybe he *should* consider Jean's words on that subject now. If this was a new life, Gilles should go forward and live it as a new life, not wait around to regain or continue his old one.

This thought was not completely new to him but Jean's words strongly suggested *new* possibilities and for the first time in weeks, Gilles thought about what it was that he *really* wanted, not what he couldn't have. He thought about his love of the sea. He might join up with the pirates and go plunder the world. More wild ideas entered Gilles' mind and he let his thoughts go where they would, freed from the restraints of conscience or morality. When he tired of thinking about riches and women, his thoughts turned to food. He was weary of the leftovers for dinner, tired of the breads for breakfast and he longed for a *real* meal. To sit down again in a real dining room, the servants waiting nearby, the candles adding to the warmth of the fire and family, *that* was what he craved, that along with some good wine and real meat, vegetables that had not been cooked to the point of being distinguishable from each other only by shape and color, and an elaborate dessert, a *very* elaborate dessert. Gilles decided that he was going to find such a place to eat one of these meals and that he would tell Jacob that he had to go out at supper time, not after work when everyone else was already sleeping. His soul needed it and he was going to have it.

On this night though, Gilles didn't go to such a place; he wasn't feeling up to it yet. He returned to the inn up the street and then crept back to the stable when he had eaten enough supper to appease his still-recovering stomach. In the darkness of the barn he imagined that he was entering his old room at home or the new room that he was to have shared with his bride, with Marie, but Gilles' sleeping place here was not even a real room; it was open to everything, open to the elements and to passers by. What would Marie say if she could see how he lived here in the stable? His face burned with shame and anger in the darkness. It was *not* fair but he didn't know *who* to blame for his current situation. He was angry at whoever it was who had ruined his life, angry at his family and Marie for abandoning him, angry at the church for their misinformed prosecution and angry at God for allowing such a thing to happen to him.

He was cold even though he was sweating a little from the fever that he still harbored in his body. Gilles kept all of his clothes on and even put on another layer to stay warm enough through the night as he settled down in the dark. He felt something in his pocket as he rolled over and then he remembered the forgotten letter from his father. Gilles had slept a lot on the previous night and was not really so very sleepy so he decided that he would read the letter: At least it would have money in it. There was no light in the stable so Gilles put his cloak on over his clothes and went out into the street to find some light to read by. He came to a house that had a lantern inside on a table by the window and there was just enough light shining outside for Gilles to read the letter. He moved under the window, like a criminal in the night, not even owning so much as a candle or a lantern of his own, and pulled out the packet, emptying the coins into his pocket before he unfolded the letter and read it.

In the letter, his father explained that he had found a trustworthy courier and would be able to send more news as well as money and send them more often. He mentioned sickness at home but that everyone was recovering.

Gilles reread the next part, not sure if he was reading correctly but it was so; Charles had married Marie and Jean Montroville related some of the details of the wedding at the cathedral and their new married life. Gilles angrily crumpled up the letter without finishing it but he did not have the satisfaction of throwing it to the ground: He had learned too well at his trial in France that it could be dangerous if the wrong person found it. He carried the crumpled paper back to the stable in his pocket, cursing his brother, Marie, and his father all the way.

He stomped back up into his loft and it was quite some time before his anger even started to subside. His teeth chattered as he pulled the covers and more hay up over his body, all the way to his chilled shoulders and his chin. If it got any colder in the stable at night, Gilles wasn't sure if he could stand it. At long last he grew warm enough and calm enough to go to sleep. His last conscious thought was that it was time to start a new life and they could all go to hell, Marie, his brother, his father, and his father's money too.

Gilles went down to get the barn chores started and it was a beautiful sunny morning. He had never seen the sun come in so brightly and he thought that there must be more windows somewhere up high in the roof, maybe stained glass windows that Jacob had put in. He went to the back and was amazed to find his old horse from France there. She whinnied and searched his pockets.

"Hi, girl," he said to her.

Jacob would not miss him if he took a quick ride on her … He was away and in the fields before he knew it. Gilles came to a lake and urging her on into it, he felt the cool water come up over his feet in the stirrups as she pushed through. They climbed the bank on the far side and he wheeled his horse around to look back at the glade. It didn't look like the Netherlands now, it looked more like Rouen. The sunbeams slanted in and branches moved slightly in the warm breeze as he made his way along the riverbank to the fields. The morning mist was still rising and the rows were fragrant with the newly upturned earth that displayed the tiniest pale green seedlings pushing up in the rows. Gilles jumped down from his horse and stood in the fields with the reins still in his hands.

"This is beautiful. I know this place. I've missed this place ..." Gilles thought. His feet were still very cold from crossing the river and he looked down to see why but all that he could see were his boots covered with mud from the fields, beautiful, fragrant Rouen mud. The soil was *very* good in this place; it was just *perfect* for planting grapevines.

"I guess I'll have to clean these boots up before I go back inside," he thought, even as he woke up in the darkness of the stable.

He was shivering from the cold and his feet were like ice but Gilles tried to hold on to what he remembered of the wonderful dream. He had been sleeping with his boots on so he took them off and rubbed his feet with his hands until they were warm enough for him to go back to sleep. He pushed them deeper down into the hay and he hoped they would stay warm enough to let him sleep through until the morning.

Jacob woke him up by tossing two more blankets up on top of him. They landed next to his head but Jacob did not apologize for waking Gilles in this manner.

"You need a good night's sleep to do your work! These will help."

"Yes, I do need a good night's sleep to do *your* work." Gilles mumbled.

Gilles remembered the glade. He had to get back there. Something in him had changed when he had looked at his muddy boots and now it would not change back. He decided that he would wait no longer to start his new life; he would go out to supper tonight in the French quarter. He would wear the fine clothes that he had worn to his trial. He couldn't do much about his face since he had not seen a razor since he left France but he could straighten up his hair.

Gilles imagined six different menus during the day and realized that he could never eat it all but then he gave himself permission to imagine even more menus. He imagined music and lovely women to admire and then he threw in a beautiful French dining companion for himself. He would dream today, dine tonight, and he would not deny himself a few hours of heaven on earth.

"You are very dreamy today. Pay attention!" Jacob scolded him. "You put out too much feed to each horse and I will be out of money in no time!"

Gilles did not answer him but scooped some of the grain back into the bucket.

The incessant rain finally had stopped and it *did* look brighter out, although not as bright, not nearly as bright, as it had been in Gilles' dream. In spite of the sun it was still cold in the stable and Jacob gave Gilles a patched old coat of his to wear even though it was much too small for him.

"You need to buy yourself more warm clothes instead of wasting your money on *fancy* clothes and gambling on investments," Jacob chided. "Usually my stable boys waste it on a horse, a woman, or drink."

"I need none of those things," Gilles replied, thinking that Jacob would do well to look to his own finances and not bother Gilles about his.

After work Gilles washed himself and put on his French clothes. They seemed loose, wrinkled, and unfamiliar to him as they had not been worn much at all lately but had mostly been hanging on a nail in the corner since he moved into the barn. The clothing brought back bad memories, but this occasion demanded something better than his usual garments so he pushed the bad thoughts away to the back of his mind. He brushed his hair using Jacob's horse brush, tying it back with a leather tie, and then he brushed through his beard, too. It was a pity that he had no other ornamentation to wear, no gold jewelry or a good hat, but he looked fine enough.

Gilles hoped that his appearance had changed enough so that no one would recognize him but the chances of his seeing anyone that he knew were miniscule. He stuffed more than enough money into his pocket to take a woman to dinner if he should happen to be so lucky as to find one, and as he put the rest of his small savings away, he laughed at himself for thinking that being with a woman was even possible, unless, of course, she was a prostitute. Gilles' boots were badly worn and shabby looking so he darkened them with grease and dirt, being careful not to get any of the smelly stuff on his hands or his clothes. He had no mirror but seeing what he could of himself, he assured himself that it would suffice.

It was still fairly early as work nights in the autumn and winter were not as late as nights in the summer. The streets were dry but the air was chilled and Gilles' cloak did not keep the damp cold out completely. Gilles thought that perhaps he would just pretend that he was a traveler and ask for a seat by the fire if one was available.

When he entered the French section, he noticed that the air had changed. First Gilles smelled what he thought *must* have been French cooking and sadly he thought that he would have gladly given *all* of his money just to have a little of his mother's food now. He thought he smelled perfume, not just any perfume, but Marie's and he initially felt anger and sadness but then he told himself that he was only going to allow good thoughts to enter his mind this evening.

His mood continued to improve as he spied a grand inn that he had noticed on one of his few earlier jaunts through the quarter. Finely dressed ladies and gentlemen were climbing down from carriages driven right up to the front door by well-dressed servants. Some of Gilles' fellow countrymen must have done very well for themselves in Amsterdam or could they be Netherlanders who had come to appreciate the finer things in life? Gilles studied their clothing and their mannerisms for a moment, and even without hearing any words spoken by the patrons, he decided that they *had* to be French.

Two doormen stood at attention by the front door, nearly motionless except for when they moved in unison to open the doors for incoming customers. Gilles straightened his collar, drew himself up to his full height and walked in, right behind a middle-aged couple, acting and starting to feel very much as though he *belonged* here.

Inside, the noises as well as the smells were very different than those in Elsje's inn: Instead of the clank of pewter and the thuds of wood or heavy pottery, there was the higher-pitched clinking noise of contact between fine china, crystal and silver utensils coming from all corners of the room. Heavy seats did not scrape over sandy floors but more delicate wood chairs moved quietly across a polished wood floor with almost a musical quality to the sound. Gilles could hear and confirm it now: The language spoken here was almost *exclusively* French, not Nederlands. Gilles took in the sounds eagerly with his ears and he only wished that he could stand there for just a little while longer, taking in the sights, sounds and fragrances.

The one smell that he was able to separate out from all the others was onion soup and a brief wave of homesickness passed over him before he banished it from his heart. He was certain that he would start with the onion soup. A man eating alone in this place was sure to be a curious thing; what story should he tell them?

That he was a traveler in need of a good meal?

Not many travelers probably came in here.

That his fiancée had jilted him and he wanted a consoling meal?

That would be too complicated.

That he was there to meet some other gentlemen and was not sure why they were delayed?

He had half decided on the latter story when a man, who was obviously not the owner but acting as the host, came over to escort the couple that stood in front of Gilles over to their seats. The superior quality of the establishment was verified in Gilles' mind by having someone whose only job was to welcome patrons and by the obvious fact that there were no women employed here; This dining place was run strictly by men and the wives who were dining with their husbands were very few in number. No, this was mainly a gentleman's gathering place, judging from the overwhelming number of men, all of them dressed impeccably and very stylishly. Gilles could not help but think of the contrast between the two dining rooms, Hendrick's and here, both catering to the success-ful businessmen of Amsterdam but in very different ways.

As the host returned to Gilles, the man's eyes scanned him from head to toe, with a slight frown appearing on the man's face when he got to Gilles' boots. The host managed to look down his nose at Gilles, even though Gilles was much taller, and he asked Gilles in Nederlands if he was here this evening for the full supper or just for drinks. Gilles suppressed a sudden urge to laugh at him, and drawing himself up to his full height which was very nearly a foot taller than the little man, he told him in French that his intention was *exactly* that, to have a *very* complete supper, if they were *able* to provide him with one.

The aristocratic French accent as well as the polite challenge drew more than one look from those within earshot and the host's demeanor toward Gilles changed perceptibly right away, although he still looked at Gilles with a suspi-cious eye. The man must have finally concluded that Gilles was an important fugitive in exile or perhaps a stray businessman who had recently been robbed of his *good* boots, because he motioned for Gilles to follow him over to a vacant table.

"Gilles!"

Who could be calling his name *here*?

Jean Durie was waving to Gilles from across the room, beckoning him to come and join him at his table. Gilles turned to his host to inform him of the change in seating arrangements and saw a look of stunned surprise on the man's face.

"I ... I am *so* sorry, Monsieur, I did not know ..." the man stammered.

Gilles smiled patronizingly at the little man but he had no idea why the man reacted that way. Was Jean so well known here, so highly respected? Gilles waived the host off and made his own way over to Jean's table where two other men were seated with Jean.

"Gilles Montroville Jansen, let me introduce Gillaume Ste Germaine, the owner of this fine establishment, and his good friend Andre LaRue," Jean Durie introduced them.

Gilles shook hands with them and Ste Germaine gestured for Gilles to sit. His face carried a friendly smile on it and Gilles liked him immediately, thinking that the company was at least pleasant, even if it *was* all male.

Ste Germaine was very tall, taller even than Gilles, handsome, well-groomed, and at least twenty years older than Gilles or Jean. Gold thread trimmed his clothing and there was a large gold pin on his coat. His hair was beautifully curled with just a few strands of silver in it and even his hands spoke of wealth; soft and smooth, with nails polished to a shine and several exquisite gold and diamond rings adorning his fingers.

The other man was slightly younger and more conservatively dressed. He was powerfully built, as though he was an equestrian or had some other pastime that required great strength and physical conditioning. His very pale blond hair was pulled back from a face that would have been quite handsome had it not been for the pock-marks, the souvenir of a victorious childhood battle with the pox.

"What brings you here tonight, Gilles?" Jean asked, smiling at him in a peculiar sort of way. "You are *very* far from home, are you not?"

Gilles thought that it must be very good wine that put smiles on all of their faces at once and if it was truly the bottle he *thought* he recognized on the table, it was an *excellent* French wine. Gilles wondered if he could order some for himself but a waiter had already poured him a glass and set it down in front of him before Gilles could give voice to his request. He resisted the inclination to seize the glass and taste it before he answered Jean's question but he waited no longer than that.

"I needed some fine French food for my soul," Gilles replied and taking a sip of the wine, he held the liquid for as long as he could against his palate before slowly releasing it, savoring each drop before it moved down his throat. It was even *better* than he remembered and for someone who had had nothing but Amsterdam ale to drink lately, it was like eating the finest cake after only having the coarsest of bread to eat, riding a fine horse after months of riding on an ox. He inadvertently closed his eyes briefly, so great was his pleasure in the drink.

"We have *only* the best here. What would you like to start your meal with?" Msr. Ste Germaine asked Gilles.

Gilles did not hesitate. "I believe I smelled some onion soup. I would like to start with that."

The three men laughed out loud and Gilles wondered what the joke was. He looked at Jean in puzzlement and Jean smiled that strange smile at him again.

"Do you remember the last time you told me about smelling onion soup, Gilles?"

Gilles remembered only too clearly waking up after the incident in the alley where he had very nearly lost his life. He did not want to share this memory with everyone at the table so he just nodded at Jean.

Jean leaned across the table and said, "Msr. Ste Germaine and Msr. LaRue are your guardian angels, Gilles. It was *they* who brought you back to Hendrick's inn that day." Jean's voice was conspiratorially low but the two gentlemen had no trouble at all hearing his words.

Gilles stole a glance at them and wondered if Jean was joking. Ste Germaine and LaRue were certainly big enough men to lift him from the street, but it didn't seem very likely that French gentlemen would be wandering around in dark alleys and dragging robbery victims across town to safe havens.

"Oh," Gilles said politely, but he did not believe it.

Ste Germaine must have seen this skepticism because he added, "They had left you for dead. We could tell from your clothes that you *must* be French and the coins in your pocket *proved* it. We did not recognize you as being from the French quarter so we surmised that you had to be in town on business. We loaded you into our empty wine cart, made a few inquiries at the docks, and voila! It was a simple matter to return you to the inn where you were staying. We regret that we could only confirm that you belonged there before we had to leave you, as the authorities had been alerted and were on the way: People were starting to realize that you were injured and not drunk. It's generally safer for us to stay over here in *this* part of town and stray no farther than the warehouses.

Anyway, we must have carried the scent of the onion soup that we made that morning on our clothes and your sense of smell must be *so* excellent that you picked it up and took it with you into your dreams. We have only recently come to know Jean and piece the whole story together with him. I must confess to you that it has provided us with a hearty laugh, not to mention the very good feeling of knowing that we saved a fellow countryman!"

"Then I *do* owe you my life." Gilles offered his hand to Ste Germaine again but the older man just shook his head.

"It was nothing but simple human decency. When I was a boy, I had a younger brother that I *always* had to watch over and you brought him back to me although he has been gone these many years; Anyway, we enjoyed the brief bit of intrigue that it brought into our lives, didn't we Andre?"

Andre LaRue said nothing but just nodded unconvincingly.

The waiters buzzed around the table bringing samples of food to each of the four men. In addition, Ste Germaine ordered a very large meal for Gilles and he told them to bring some onion soup out for him right away.

"Please enjoy your meal, it is our gift to you tonight as you have given *us* a gift," Ste Germaine said to Gilles as he waived his hand to dismiss the waiter.

"*Just as my father used to do,*" Gilles thought when he saw the gesture, but he rather liked Ste Germaine all the same.

"Why did you not tell me the whole story before?" Gilles asked Jean.

"I only just found out the rest of it myself!" Jean explained as he picked up a fork and took a taste of what looked like a game bird in cream sauce.

Ste Germaine tasted his food and called the waiter over. He sent word to the kitchen that the sauce was not as good as it could be and that the chef should look into the reason for this shortcoming. "Not served quickly enough, I suppose," he commented. "My cook is generally excellent, though."

Gilles could have eaten the onion soup all night and it made him feel almost like he was back at home again. He reluctantly went on to the other courses and each one was better than the last. If the sauce was a little cool, it was close enough to perfection and the familiarity of the taste was what he had missed the most. He was happy to be speaking French again and eating excellent French food; the good company only added to Gilles' enjoyment of the entire evening.

"I did not mean to interrupt your dinner," Gilles apologized as he rested his fork between courses. He hadn't said much at all to his supper companions but had been eating non-stop and finishing everything on his plates since he sat down. It was the only thing that he could think of to say other than to bring up the cooling weather.

"We had finished discussing our business before your arrival, Gilles. I am just pleased to see that you have had no permanent ill effects from your encounter with trouble and a new friend from a good French family is *always* welcomed here. What do you do now that you live here in Amsterdam?" Ste Germaine pushed one full plate away and pulled a different plate of food over to him.

"A little of this, a little of that." Gilles hoped that Ste Germaine would not ask him for any more details so he would not have to lie in front of Jean.

"He is looking for a better position, doing accounts as I do, but he needs a position with a low profile," Jean interceded for him.

"He should definitely come to work among the French here, then; no one asks questions of anyone else here. I will have to ask around, make some inquiries for you," Ste Germaine offered, nodding understandingly. "Surely someone is in need of a good man with refined tastes to help with their accounts." He started to cut up some beef on his plate but interrupted the process to motion impatiently for more wine although his glass was not yet half empty.

Gilles was trying very hard not to appear too greedy or to get too drunk but he could not stay away from the food or the wine. He wished that he could stay here forever but eventually he would be too full to eat any more, Ste Germaine would leave, or some other event would bring an end to the wonderful evening.

"Gilles, have some more wine! I *do* enjoy watching people who love good food and drink; that's why I started this establishment! The Netherlanders have no taste for fine things, you know. They are good people, don't misunderstand me, but they only excel at three things: sailing, painting, and drinking ale." Ste Germaine waived a fork toward the wall and Gilles took a closer look at the gold-framed oil paintings, including one portrait of Ste Germaine and a second portrait that seemed to be of him, his wife and a small daughter. The other pictures were of landscapes and room scenes, many of them with food featured prominently in them. Gilles wondered where Ste Germaine's family was tonight. Perhaps they were at home now, while he conducted business with Jean and LaRue.

"I have admired the art here," Gilles said. "I see it in the streets but I have not had the opportunity to see as much of it as I would like."

"Some of it is quite good and it's not very expensive. Unless the artist has found himself a patron, it is a meager living for most of them but that makes it all the more affordable! I don't care for the mass-produced work of someone like Rembrandt van Rijn, and most definitely *not* for his ugly little pictures of the beggars. He did that one over there but the *miller's son* puts on too many airs. He's a common and irritating man, even when one tries to take into consideration his personal troubles of late, just too difficult to deal with, and he thinks he has *much* more talent than he really has." Ste Germaine leaned over and whispered a secret. "He uses *lenses*, you know; I doubt that he has enough of an artist's eye for *any* freehand work! That picture is good enough, if you like that sort of thing, but if I had it to do over, I would have commissioned his young protégé, Flinck, to do it, as he's *much* more of a natural talent than his teacher. Andre has no interest in such things, do you Andre, but I'll bet that *you* do. I could take you to see some of the very best art in private homes, art that the public will never see. Would you like that, Gilles?"

"I'd like that a great deal," Gilles answered honestly, thinking what a wonderful opportunity it would be but wondering how he would be able to get away and how he would avoid revealing to Ste Germaine his other life in the stable.

"One must *take* the time each day to see the art and beauty that is all around us. Each day is a *gift*! We are surrounded with so much art today that it is virtually lying unappreciated out in the streets. One day though, the opportunity could be gone from us."

Ste Germaine pushed another still-full plate aside and reached for a plate containing some type of pudding. He tasted it and took his time, moving it all around in his mouth. Gilles noticed the waiters behind him all eyeing Ste Germaine like nervous horses at the start of a race, all waiting for the pronouncement of his verdict. Ste Germaine motioned them over again.

"Very good, tell the cook, very good today."

One waiter continued to stand by the table after the other had hurried back to the kitchen to relay the good news.

"*Go* over there!" Ste Germaine waived him off. "*Don't* hover over the table! See what that fellow is doing there, that's how to act."

The man moved off and Ste Germaine sighed.

"It's *so* hard training new people and you would think the others would train him so that I don't have to do that *as well*, but they don't. I have to do *everything*."

Ste Germaine moved on to the dessert course. The waiters brought out a concoction of cake and cream sauce. Ste Germaine tasted it and again motioned the waiter over.

"Are there no fresh fruits of *any* kind in the market now?" he asked the man.

"Non, Monsieur, the season ..." the man began.

"Yes, yes. This sticky stuff is all well and good but I would *love* some berries or even some apples to finish my dinner. *Surely* they must have apples? Well, go on!"

Ste Germaine waived the waiter away and turned back to Gilles. "Well, I must see to the kitchen now. Take your time in finishing your meal, ask for anything else you would like, anything at all, just call Robert over, and *do* come again, both of you."

Ste Germaine embraced Jean and Gilles after they stood up to acknowledge his leaving but LaRue remained seated and continued to eat. The waiters remained in position until Ste Germaine was gone and then on Robert's signal, they moved forward to take away all of the sampled dishes. Unlike Ste Germaine, who had barely finished any of his food but had tasted everything, LaRue finished most of the offerings in front of him with the exception of the ones that Ste Germaine had told him to try. He excused himself too, saying that the hour was late and that he needed some sleep. Jean and Gilles stood up to shake his hand as he left and Gilles hoped that he would see both men again.

"Ste Germaine's not really so difficult," Jean appeared to read Gilles' mind. "He keeps his standards very high and it pays off handsomely for him but he is truly one of the kindest, most generous souls I know."

"I suppose he must get back to his wife and child," Gilles said.

"He has no family left," Jean replied. "Oh, the portrait! They were taken by the plague many years ago."

Gilles was feeling the effects of the wine but he could not stop himself from drinking even more. A waiter emptied the bottle of wine into his glass and when Gilles finished that, another bottle quickly appeared.

"They will bring it out to you all night long, Gilles," Jean smiled at him. "For as long as you drink it, they will bring it; such is Msr. Ste Germaine's hospitality."

Gilles was grateful to have had this incredible night. He would remember it always, he told himself but then he thought about returning to the stable. Perhaps it was the wine that made Gilles suddenly confess his thoughts and feelings to Jean.

"Jean, I have to find a way to leave Jacob's; I can't stand it anymore."

"Your pride? Pride doesn't pay for food, Gilles."

"No, it's not just that. I can't stay *inside* working all the time, it's killing me."

"You would be inside anyway if you were doing accounts."

"I don't think I can do that, either."

"Gilles, people who work *outside* do not often earn a good living! Your circumstances have changed and I do not think that you fully understand this."

"I understand it, Jean. This is my *life*, though. I need to live it while I can."

"Do you want me to continue to look for a better position for you?"

"Yes, thank you, Jean, but I have the feeling ... I need to be somewhere else."

"You aren't hearing voices too?" Jean joked but he might have been half serious.

"It's time. I just have to leave Jacob's and I have to go soon before I go mad."

"All right, Gilles. To new things then!" Jean toasted him.

Gilles had the distinct feeling that Jean had just had too much wine and was humoring him, avoiding a discussion that might ruin the evening so he dropped the subject as well.

"To new things," Gilles agreed, "To better things!"

When he left Ste Germaine's establishment at last, Gilles could think of nothing more that he could ask for, except perhaps a good night's sleep in a real bed, a warm bed. He did not want the evening to end at all but he knew that it would be very hard to wake up tomorrow if he stayed for too long and it would make for a very, very long day. He bid Jean good night and stepped outside from the warmth of Ste Germaine's. The air was so cold and crisp tonight that it hurt his lungs to breathe too deeply. He pulled his thin cloak around him tighter and gave thanks to the heavens that there was no wind or rain to make the cold even worse.

"Montroville!"

A strange voice called out from behind him.

A shock of adrenaline went through Gilles leaving a taste of quicksilver in his mouth. He had not brought his knife with him tonight and he could not run back inside because Jean was still in there and doing so could endanger Jean as well. Who else in this city knew his real name?

"I *thought* that was you! Some of us have done very well after leaving France and others have *not* done as well," the voice said.

A man with a silver-headed cane stepped from the shadows and Gilles recognized the man from Rouen. His name was Botte and he had fled with his family just before the soldiers had arrived to take them away. Botte's family had been wealthy, too, but the man standing before Gilles now was ragged and gaunt looking. From the looks of him, the silver-headed cane that he leaned on must have been the last vestige of his former life.

"Surprised at my appearance, Montroville? Life here has been *painful*! I could not *believe* it when I saw *you* here!" he rasped.

Gilles could say nothing. He was too shocked at the man's appearance.

"I need money, Montroville. Perhaps you could help me, my old friend?"

"I am sorry, Msr. Botte. I have been unable to find a good position for myself."

"You look to be doing all right, good food here, very nice clothes. You will not help a fellow countryman?"

"I told you that I am not able ... appearances are not always ..."

"Fine!" the man snarled. He shook the cane at Gilles. You can't even spare a few coins since I am reduced to begging!"

"Amsterdam has food and shelter for those who need it ..." Gilles began.

"You would have me live as a charity case?" The man's eyes flashed anger in the moonlight.

"I only meant to say ... that it is against the law and dangerous to be caught begging when there is food and shelter enough ..."

"You *bastard*! You *selfish* bastard! Out on the town at night in the most expensive place in *all* of Amsterdam and you can't spare a few coins for a starving man!"

Gilles remembered the money in his pocket and he pulled out some coins. It might be easier to just give him the money and leave than to try and reason with him. Gilles handed the money over to Botte who looked down at it, moving his thumb over it, counting and feeling the quantity of it in his hand. Far from being grateful though, the man growled at Gilles again.

"You *must* have more than this!" He gestured at Gilles with his closed fist as he leaned on the cane on his other side. "If I was able to work, I *would*, but I cannot! For God's sake, have some Christian charity, you son of a bitch!"

Gilles remembered what Botte had been like before. He had been a pleasant man, a refined man. This creature was more like a wild beast, a starving street-dog, and Gilles could not believe that he could be the same person, but the cane proved it.

It had been a riding accident, a fine spirited horse that had made Botte lame and he was extremely lucky not to have been killed outright by the large animal. Botte was known to have liberal tendencies and the family had escaped France right after the accident, even before his leg had completely healed. Apparently Botte had no connections at all here in Amsterdam and any money that he might have brought with him was already gone.

"I have very little I can spare, I'm afraid," Gilles informed him.

Gilles felt an emotion that was somewhere between disgust and fear although pity was in the mix, too; his prevailing wish at the moment was to get away from this man but what he *really* wished was that he had never run into him at all.

"There are those that would pay me well for news of your whereabouts, Montroville. *They know that you are here* and they have *not* stopped looking for you. I would not tell them if you gave me a few more coins. My family is hungry, Montroville."

Gilles stood there, not knowing what to say to him. Before he could say anything at all though, Botte spoke again.

"Your friends here might want to know that they just dined with a *papist*, a Catholic. It might be worth some more coins for you to buy my silence on that matter, too."

Gilles pulled his cloak around him and walked away. He was angry now and *wasn't* going to be blackmailed. Instead of walking in the direction of the stable though, Gilles took a quick turn in the opposite direction, just in case the deranged man attempted to follow him home.

"You'll be sorry for this Montroville! You will regret this!" Botte called after him.

Gilles kept walking but he could sense Botte standing there, shaking his cane in the air at him. His being drunk did nothing to ease Gilles' fears; if anything it made things *worse*, for Gilles knew that his senses and his ability to defend himself were not at their best, even though his fears were at their apex. His heart pounded in his chest for a long time, until he had wandered the streets long enough to know with certainty that a crippled man couldn't have followed him that far, until he had made enough turns to go around the back way into the Jewish section of the city. Only when he was inside the sanctuary of the Hebrews did he pause to listen for a few minutes for anyone who might have been following him.

Later on he curled up in his hay bed but in spite of all of the wine that he had consumed during the evening, Gilles found that he could not get to sleep. He did not for a minute regret going out to enjoy the night that he had just had and he refused to let that good memory be spoiled by the evening's final events in the French quarter. Jacob's two extra blankets helped assuage his physical discomfort from the cold but Gilles could find no balm for his worries concerning Botte's threats: French soldiers could well be covering the city and looking for Gilles in a matter of hours. Gilles was probably safe as long as he stayed inside Jacob's stable but how long would he have to live like that, like a cockroach, a blatte afraid of the light?

The morning light arrived before sleep came to him. Jacob threw a bridle up into the loft to wake him and Gilles leapt into full consciousness, back from where he had been lost in a half sleep. Dragging himself out of his bed, he picked bits of hay from his hair and his clothes, the same clothes that he had been wearing the night before. Gilles took a few minutes to change into his work clothing and to try to get his mind functioning while Jacob groused around below. Gilles fumbled with the fastenings on his clothing, his arms and legs fatigued from lack of sleep and his fingers numb with the cold; it didn't help that he could still feel the effects of the wine, but he managed to climb down from the loft without losing his tenuous hold on the stable wall.

Several times during the day Gilles dozed off while he was standing upright, lurching back into consciousness just as he started to topple over. When Jacob observed these episodes, he didn't say anything but he made small clucking noises of disapproval. Gilles had much more to worry about today than his employer's disapproval, though. He wouldn't say anything to Jacob but he would have to talk with Jean as soon as possible and look into arranging safe passage out of the city.

There were people who died every day in the city of Amsterdam from all kinds of things. There were those who died of old age in their beds of course, and then there were the old men who hung around the breweries and drinking establishments, sometimes found the next morning with blissful smiles on their faces, dead from exposure in the winter or unknown causes in the summer. There were the very poor who retained the identifying marks of some recent epidemic on them, and occasionally there were whole families, their bodies sometimes still huddled together, just as they had been in their last earthly moments. Very rarely there were women found in an alley or behind a barn, some of them certainly prostitutes, with torn or missing clothing.

To the city's great credit and unlike the rest of the world, there were very few deaths of men who had been robbed, men who perhaps started home a little too drunk, a little too late at night and looking a little too prosperous, like pigeons ripe for the plucking. The perpetrators of these crimes were quickly apprehended by the authorities and just as quickly tried and executed. On the whole in the city of Amsterdam, the people were very law abiding and there were not that many deaths by another's hand.

There were almost never any deaths of that kind in the Jewish quarter: The Jewish men stayed closer to home and seemed to have less of a liking for strong drink than their Christian counterparts. If a Jewish woman pursued a livelihood as a prostitute, she generally found business to be much more profitable in other parts of the city where the citizens were more fiercely intent on having a good time.

The French quarter was generally peaceful as well: It was not that they did not also like a good time, strong drink, or prostitutes, but because so many of them were in hiding, there was a collective dread of any kind of attention being drawn to them, especially the official kind.

This death was different: The man's body was found sprawled in the street just a few blocks from Ste Germaine's with a little bit of money still clutched in his hand, the same battered hand that had been raised in a futile effort to shield his head from the many blows that had killed him.

Gilles was taken aback by the horrific news when Jean came in late in the day and told him about it.

"One would think that Amsterdam's thieves would do a better job of finding *all* of the money on their victims or it could just be that the murderer was surprised by someone before he could finish the job. Crime here is *definitely* getting worse because it wasn't so very long ago that they assaulted you, Gilles. It must have happened after we left Ste Germaine's because I saw nothing unusual, did you?"

"Well, I think I *did* see a beggar ... Do you know what he looked like?"

Jean described Botte's appearance fairly well. "He was clubbed to death with *his own* silver-topped cane, a grisly way for an old man to go. So you *did* see him?"

"I saw a man," Gilles replied, "but whether it was the same man or no, who can say? The man that I saw was alive and well when I left him."

Gilles decided not to tell Jean about his encounter with Botte or that he had known him in France: It would serve no purpose now. Gilles *was* relieved that Botte could no longer tell anyone anything but he did wonder how Botte's family was going to survive now that he was dead. Perhaps Botte's wife and three teenage daughters were living under a bridge or in a field somewhere near Ste Germaine's.

"Well, it happens. Don't let it upset you, Gilles. I can see by your face that you are taking it to heart too much; just use some caution when you are out in the streets at night. Another letter came for you today," Jean said, changing the subject and handing Gilles a packet that was thicker than usual.

The letter was addressed to Yellis Jansen, the Nederlands version of "Jean's son Gilles". Gilles was still distracted by Jean's news, still thinking about Botte, as he absent-mindedly ripped the letter open, moving his eyes over the writing before he consciously remembered how much he hated reading his father's letters. With Jean standing right there though, Gilles decided to finish reading the letter in spite of the fact that he still had the last one that he had received, lying crumpled up and unread somewhere in his loft.

Gilles' father had enclosed money and told Gilles that he would probably be able to send more to "Yellis Jansen" from now on. The letter also related an incident that had taken place on board one of Jean Montroville's ships.

A young sailor working with a vagabond crew at Havre was loading a shipment of gunpowder out of Brouage onto the Montroville ship that would then transport the cargo, supplies for the King's muskets, into Rouen and then Paris. The young man had acquired a taste for tobacco somewhere and had a pipe going as he worked. This careless stupidity was thought to be the cause of the explosion and fire that swept the ship, trapping the youth down in the ship's hold and burning him to death there, the crew unable to reach him through the heat of the flames in spite of his heart-wrenching screams for help. The rest of the ragtag crew and their free-agent captain were so shaken by the incident that they quickly deposited the remainder of the volatile cargo on the docks, accepted pay for the portion of it left undamaged, and instead of returning to Brouage, they headed out to sea to seek safer work, possibly in the French colonies overseas. The captain's parting words to Jean Montroville were that he believed the young sailor to be an orphan and that he was free to dispose of the body in any way that he wished.

Msr. Montroville sent word out to his associates in Havre that upon closer inspection, he saw that it was no ordinary sailor that had been killed; it was his son Gilles who had been attempting to secret himself onto his father's ship.

Jean Montroville brought the charred body back to Rouen on another one of his ships, along with the undamaged portion of the cargo. Upon his arrival in his home town with the corpse, the entire family went into mourning. The body, or what was left of it, was prepared and laid out in the small family chapel behind the manse house. After requesting that the priest Claude preside over a funeral mass and after the church refused the request due to Gilles' questionable salvation status, a private ceremony was held. Words of tribute were spoken for the deceased by Jean Montroville himself and then the body was buried just outside the hallowed ground of the family plot although a magnificent monument was commissioned, as befitted any member of the Montroville family.

The letter also mentioned that the damaged ship was probably not salvageable, and all of the cargo, with the exception of what was on the dock, had been lost, but luckily Jean Montroville was found to be blameless in the loss of the King's powder; this ruling perhaps arrived at in part due to sympathetic feelings for the poor man who was in so much obvious grief over the loss of his son's life in such a tragic way.

Gilles thought that his father's role in the entire episode was not only cold but absolutely unconscionable, an offense to God himself to use a grave in that way even if Jean Montroville was, as always, able to use any misfortune to his own advantage. What was even worse was his father's small but cheerful notation at the end of the letter that Charles and Marie had been setting up housekeeping in the refurbished wing of the house.

"What is it?" Jean asked, seeing the look of disgust and anger on Gilles' face. There was nothing really personal in the letter, so Gilles handed it over to Jean.

Jean's face registered only some surprise as he read it.

"Your father is a clever and creative man: These qualities have served him well to expand and increase his fortune as well as to protect his family," Jean said as he handed the letter back to Gilles.

"I cannot believe that my father could do such a thing! A body! With *my* name!"

"You might be surprised ..." Jean's voice trailed off and Gilles did not pursue the subject. He didn't *want* to know.

Jean changed the subject again: He had some better news for Gilles.

"Msr. Ste Germaine was in *very* good spirits when I left there last night. He thought that you were *marvelous* and wants to offer you a position working for him."

"What?" Gilles couldn't believe his ears. "I hardly spoke two words to him! I just ate all of his food and drank all of his wine."

"Apparently your enthusiasm for his food and drink was sufficient. He wants you to run the business for him and to keep accounts there. He's *very* demanding but it is a very good position. I don't know if I would accept it if I were you, although he *will* pay you two guilders a day for six days of work. It's a good bit of money."

Gilles was taken aback by the offer. There was just too much happening, too quickly: bodies and marriages and better jobs far away from the smell of manure. Was providence restoring things or taking them away? It could have been either, it was both.

And Botte had still not left Gilles' mind. Who had killed him and why? Botte said that others knew of Gilles' presence in Amsterdam and had insinuated that there was a substantial reward being offered. Who was looking for Gilles and where were they looking? Would his father's grand staging of Gilles' death change any of that? Would France finally call off her hounds?

If Gilles left the Jewish quarter to work for Ste Germaine in his public house, he would be more out in the open, more exposed, and if Botte had recognized him in spite of his changed appearance, others might recognize him, too.

"What do you think, Jean? Is it too dangerous?" Gilles asked.

"Life is *always* a risk but would you be happy to stay in the shadows just to remain safe? Only *you* can say if the risk is worth it to you. I will only tell you this: if you want a thing, *truly* want a thing, then you must *try* for it, *ask* for it, and *expect* to get it."

"Maybe you are right about that," Gilles said slowly, another thought occurring to him now. "When does he need my answer?"

"Ste Germaine is not a man that likes to be kept waiting. I do not believe that he was actually *looking* for someone but as I said, he liked you and you could be of great benefit to each other. I'm going to have dinner with him again on Saturday night so a reply then would probably be all right."

At that moment, two men ran into the stable to get their horses. Gilles handed them the already-saddled and bridled horses, swiftly collecting their money with some extra in the bargain because Gilles had been expecting them, had been ready for them.

"You see what an asset you are to any business?" Jean smiled at him. "Come and join me at Ste Germaine's on Friday night, Gilles. I have no appointment with Ste Germaine and I do not know if he will be there or be too busy to talk, but he will be pleased that we patronize his establishment. You could at least tell him that you accept his offer, if that is your choice. Anyway, there is *always* good wine and food there."

"Thank you, but I might have something else that I need to do then," Gilles replied as he pocketed the money and stuffed the letter from his father inside his shirt.

"A musical performance? A play? Other entertainment?" Jean teased his friend. "What could be more important than a fine evening out with a friend?"

Gilles ignored the sarcasm. "I just need some time alone, to think about the offer," Gilles said, "but I will let you know my decision before Saturday night."

Gilles just wanted to be left alone. His brother and Marie were married and living in the wing of the house that should have been *his*. Somehow it had not been real to him before but it was real now, it was final, it was done. He would not be going back home and he didn't want to talk to anyone today, not even Jean.

He had felt crushed at first, weak, but then anger overtook his pain, seeping through his being like a keg of wine spreading across the ground, turning everything red in its path. They would all have danced and feasted at the wedding in France and now even Marie would have a larger share of the Montroville fortune than Gilles *ever* would.

Perhaps all she had ever wanted was the family money and perhaps one Montroville brother was completely interchangeable with the other. He could see them laughing and eating, drinking fine wine in the warm house, rolling naked in

Gilles' bed together. Perhaps they went together to the burial grounds and giggled over the new grave as well. His entire family had killed even the memory of Gilles off, once and for all.

A small part of Gilles whispered that it was not his family's fault but he quickly silenced that part of himself with a fiery blast of temper. He would accept Ste Germaine's job offer. It did not matter if he was captured and killed within a week's time: At least he would live his last week with good wine, excellent food and plenty of warmth, the way he was *meant* to live his life for however long he was able to live it out.

It *might* not be so hazardous, though. It was just possible that there could be some protection afforded to Gilles as a result of working for Ste Germaine. The man seemed to have very little fear of being seized inside the French quarter and he was probably rich enough that he could buy off any threats if necessary. Living a good life would be Gilles' revenge and with Jean's advice still echoing in his ears, there was just one more thing that Gilles was going to do before he told Jean that he was definitely going to accept the job.

He slept badly that night but it was too cold to sleep well, anyway. He was awake on time in the morning and he did everything that Jacob asked of him without a single word of question or argument. Sundown on Friday came early at this time of the year and Jacob was gone for the Sabbath not long after midday. Not very long after Jacob's departure, Gilles went out into the back and returned with a bucket of water to wash his face and hands. He didn't spend too much time in the icy liquid but he did run some water through his hair before he bound it up again with his leather tie. He wished that he had some ribbon or other ornament but the plain tie would have to do. He went up into his loft and quickly changed into his French clothes, shivering as he did so, with anticipation as much as with the cold. He put the sign up before he left although there was not much point to it; no one else would be coming into the stable today. He closed up the doors and set out on his mission.

Preparations were being made for the evening crowds that would soon fill the room and Elsje was busy as usual. Gilles' eyes met hers as soon as he walked in the door. He smiled at her, said good afternoon, and asked if her father was there. Elsje smiled back, possibly remembering the incident with the pirates, and pointed to a table other than his usual one. Hendrick was leaning back in his chair with his arms folded across his great chest, his long white clay pipe firmly clamped in his teeth as usual. Mugs and a pitcher of ale had been pushed to one side of the table as Hendrick and another man listened intently to a young man who was about Gilles' age. The young man was tracing something out on the tabletop as he spoke and he had Hendrick's full and rapt attention. Gilles wasn't sure whether to join them or not, but Hendrick, perhaps seeing someone just standing there in the middle of the room, looked up briefly and beckoned to Gilles to come over and join them.

"Gilles! Excellent timing!" Hendrick called and motioned for Elsje to bring another chair. "The Van Curlers are here and they can explain their proposition to you in person."

The two men stood up and shook hands as Hendrick made introductions and Elsje brought the chair and an empty mug over for Gilles.

Young Van Curler's eyes were a deep, hypnotic blue, and he turned his steady gaze on Gilles. The expression was friendly, if it was also a little formal and reserved. He gave Gilles the impression of great intelligence and Gilles thought that he was the most Gallic Dutchman that he had ever met.

"What can I explain *better* so that *you* can make a good decision?"

It was an excellent question. Was this the boy that ran the greatest patroonship in the new world? Gilles was impressed and yes, even perhaps a little in awe of him. Van Curler's rich great-uncle's trust had not been misplaced.

"Hendrick has told me the basic premise of your venture. What do you think the chances *really* are of being able to get *more* fur, *better* fur, than we are able to get now by obtaining it directly from the savages and bypassing the usual trade conduits?"

Van Curler smiled a practiced smile at Gilles. "If I did not believe that we would succeed in this venture, I would not even attempt it. I have been living on the outskirts of the territory for several years and have met with all of the Wilden's tribal representatives who can secure our route. As you may know, Rensselaerwyck is just north of Fort Orange, halfway to New France up the North River from New Amsterdam. Not far to the west of Fort Orange on the Maqua Kill is the place they call Shenahtade, The Place Beyond the Pines. There have been experienced trappers making a very good living there for years, bringing out the very best quality skins. We have much better relationships with our Indian neighbors than those self-important bureaucrats that huddle together down in New Amsterdam. There are *vast* lands to the north, east and west of Rensselaerwyck that haven't even been *explored* yet. The great mountains to the north and east have kept out most of the faint-hearted flatlanders but what they don't realize is that the great river and its tributaries can quickly bring furs from the entire region down to our waiting ships in a matter of *days*. The land to the south of Rensselaerwyck could well be trapped out in a few years but we could never empty the northern lands of beaver if we worked day and night for the rest of our lives. We only need to get there *first* and extend our hands to receive the bounty that is there."

Van Curler lifted his ale to his lips when he finished talking, but he never once removed his eyes from Gilles'.

Gilles admired Arent Van Curler but he was keenly aware that he felt some jealousy as well. *Gilles* should have been living these adventures in New France, handling large land and trade concerns, negotiating contracts for his own father. Jean Montroville was wealthier by far than Van Rensselaer but he had had no interest at all in the exciting happenings of the new continent and truth be told, little power to direct his own destiny, anyway. In spite of his envy, Gilles liked Van Curler. The plan itself was logical, well thought out, well presented, and made complete sense to him. Gilles nodded, understanding how it would work, although he was not yet convinced that all of the alliances would hold with the savages and if one fell, the entire route, the entire plan could be in danger of col-lapse. Van Curler seemed trustworthy, the trappers would do what they did well, and the ships were there to transport the goods, but Gilles had no reliable infor-mation or experience regarding the integrity of the heathens and their inclination to uphold agreements. Gilles had worked too hard to lose the little money that he had saved on a flawed plan.

"I can write you a receipt right now and we can get started just as soon as I go back," Van Curler offered. "I am only here for a short time to make a personal report to Kiliaen Rensselaer's accountants."

"To your great-uncle, you mean," Gilles thought but aloud he said, "I like the sound of your offer but would like some time to more fully consider it. I never make investment decisions on the spot."

"A very wise thing," Van Curler nodded, "but let me tell you this: The Van Rensselaer reputation is beyond reproach, as anyone can tell you. When you invest with us, your profit is *assured*. We could write the agreement today and give you, let's say a half percentage higher than any subsequent investors. I won't be able to make that offer again later."

"That is very tempting, but as I said, I want to fully consider it. Hasn't Kiliaen Van Rensselaer fully backed this venture himself?"

Gilles had been wondering why one of the richest men in the Netherlands would need a stable boy's savings. He thought he saw Van Curler squirm slightly in his chair but he had a ready reply for Gilles.

"This is *my* venture, not Van Rensselaer's. I have invested all of my money into it but to do a proper job of it and to ensure our success I need just a little more capital than I have managed to save. I will even buy you out in two years' time if you are not satisfied with the return."

A well-informed man with such certainty of success that he would invest his entire life's savings, even if it was a young life, was a good recommendation and the guarantee of profit was reassuring too if Van Curler would consent to put it into writing. Collecting on it later might be a little more difficult but the Amsterdam courts would probably uphold such an agreement if enough witnesses signed.

Gilles had pretty much decided that he *would* invest in this venture but he was not going to sign today. Van Curler had respected his decision to think it over and Gilles would retain that respect as well as a measure of control over both Van Curler and Hendrick by delaying the final signing of an agreement.

Hendrick and Gilles shook hands with the Van Curlers and bid them good evening as the two visitors left.

"You handle yourself well in negotiations, Montroville. What do you think of the Van Curlers?" Hendrick asked as he filled his pipe with tobacco again.

"It sounds good, Hendrick but I'll get back to you on my final decision before they leave. Will that be all right?"

"I guess it will have to be. Ah, to be honest, Montroville, I have no other takers! They are all afraid that the risk is too great. They have no vision, no sense of the great opportunities that sometimes come your way." Hendrick shook his head in disbelief at the slow-wittedness of all of the nonbelievers. "Well, on to other matters! Have we come to an agreement on percentages and your current balance in our other investment?"

"I believe we have, and we might write up an agreement on that too, just so that we understand each other *completely*. If you would like, we could do that at the same time that we write up the Van Curler's contract."

"We could," Hendrick agreed, his face brightening up at the implied acceptance of both deals.

Gilles offered his hand and Hendrick shook it, then Gilles folded his hands together so they would not shake as he leaned forward across the table and started to speak.

"Hendrick, I have been offered a good position running a fine establishment in town. I have started to make some investments and I will invest even more as my fortunes improve. Whatever you may have thought of me, I am *sincere*, I can tell you that."

Hendrick waived his hand in Gilles' direction as if to dismiss any misunderstandings or discord that might have previously existed between them. So jovial was his mood that Gilles had to wonder if this was Hendrick's first pitcher of ale tonight.

"That's all right, Montroville. Investments will come and go. You and I will work together again in the future, even if you decide not to invest in this one, but you are usually quick to spot an opportunity; it would surprise me if you didn't jump on this one."

Perhaps because there were no servants or daughters in sight to call over, Hendrick got up and retrieved a candle from a nearby table to light his pipe. Gilles waited impatiently, watching the peculiar ritual as Hendrick held the pipe bowl next to the flame and sucked on the pipe stem until the flame bent over and then leapt back up from the lighted bowl. It was a very peculiar substance and the method of tobacco consumption was a strange one.

Hendrick leaned back in his chair, perhaps wondering what conversation to start next, but Gilles had not yet finished with the topic that he was trying to start.

"I want to marry Elsje," Gilles blurted out.

Hendrick looked as though he would choke on his tobacco for a moment and a jumble of emotions crossed the old man's face. In the short time that it took Hendrick to recover, Gilles took some hope that not all of the emotions appeared to be bad ones.

"You want to take her away?" Hendrick asked at last. "She's very young. We don't generally allow our children to marry until they are at least twenty five ..."

"No, she would stay with you during the day, as always, and live with me in the French quarter at night." Gilles hoped this arrangement would appeal to the old man; they could both have what they wanted.

"You would allow your wife to work, to be a woman of the world? Perhaps you would not be much of a husband then."

The old man' pipe was clamped firmly between his lips. Gilles would let him have his say: It was the only way he was going to find out all of Hendrick's objections and overcome them. Hendrick suddenly looked over at Gilles again as if another thought had just occurred to him.

"It's not much of a secret, I guess, that I have not thought of you or *any* of your kind as suitable husbands for my girls. You people put on too many airs, think yourselves superior, and think our women are too free. You conspire with the other Catholics in Spain to keep us an occupied country and are only here as long as there is money to be made. You probably want to marry a Netherlander woman to help you out of your legal difficulties, isn't that right, Montroville? Well, perhaps then we *could* reach an agreement. You can have Tryntje as a wife. She will make you a good gentleman's wife and she would not have to work."

Gilles had not expected this at all. He was not sure what he would say besides "no". He took a deep breath to gain some time to think and to come up with what he hoped were the right words before he answered Hendrick.

"Hendrick, I do not *need* a wife. I want *Elsje* for my wife. I would not ordinarily consider allowing my wife to work, but I know that Elsje is not like French women; I like her just the way she is and that is why I want her, and *only* her, for my wife."

Gilles hoped that he was skilled enough in trade negotiations to secure the outcome that he wanted in this transaction but Hendrick didn't answer him right away; he seemed so lost in thought that Gilles wondered if he should prod him for a response. There was silence for such a long time that Gilles thought Hendrick might not have heard him or was going to just ignore him for the rest of the night. Gilles considered repeating some of what he had just said but he decided to give Hendrick a little more time: After all, it was the old man's daughter, the mainstay of his life, in the balance. Finally Hendrick inhaled from his pipe again and then exhaled a cloud of gray smoke in Gilles' direction.

"You have already spoken with her about this?"

"No, I wanted to ask you first."

A smile spread slowly over Hendricks face. "Then you do not know if she will even accept you?"

"No ..." Gilles began to get a sick feeling. The old man *knew* that she would reject him.

"Elsje!" Hendrick called out to her.

Gilles dreaded what was surely going to happen next: He had intended to secure Hendrick's permission to woo Elsje, to take the time to win her over, but now he would be driven away like a defeated dog that had come to beg at the door. This humiliation would be yet another painful rejection and it came too soon after the letter from France.

It was more than Gilles could bear and it was small consolation that he had not yet given Van Curler a final answer. He would simply move on to Ste Germaine's and Jean could retrieve his investment money for him so Gilles wouldn't have to see Hendrick or Elsje ever again. Gilles straightened his spine up in his chair and took a firm hold on his dignity. He might be facing defeat but he would maintain his composure and his dignity.

"Elsje, finish your business there! We have business to discuss with you here," Hendrick said. She looked from Hendrick's happy face to Gilles' grave and ashen face and was obviously puzzled. She nodded to her father and called one of the servant girls over, explaining something quickly to her and pointing to a table in another part of the room.

"You will not accept my Tryntje then? There is something wrong with her?" Hendrick almost glared at Gilles but underneath the expression, Gilles could see that his mood was jubilant.

"No, I only want Elsje," Gilles said as he tried not to let his voice shake.

Elsje came over and sat rigidly upright in one of the chairs recently vacated by the Van Curlers, hands folded and palms up in her lap, waiting expectantly.

Gilles' heart sank even further; He should have asked her first. She looked again from face to face and then concentrated on her father's face, her eyes narrowing with her focus of attention. Gilles steeled himself and waited for the final blow to fall. Of course there was a chance that Elsje might say yes, but he would have liked to ask her when they were alone, in his own time, in his own way, *after* he had secured Hendrick's permission: That was the way it was done in France. Gilles hoped that the rejection would not be too loud in this terribly public place and he silently berated himself. This had been a *very* bad idea and he should have waited until Sunday to find the family alone in their apartment upstairs.

Hendrick wasted no time or words. "Gilles Montroville wants to marry you." A puff of smoke escaped his pipe again and his eyes twinkled.

Elsje sat quietly looking at her father. She seemed to be looking for something more or expecting something else completely. She did not speak and her expression did not change.

"Well?" Hendrick asked her.

"Are you asking me if I want to marry him?"

"You probably don't get many proposals and if you do, none that I know would bother to ask *my* permission first," Hendrick said gruffly. Then Hendrick smiled a cat-like smile, waiting for the rejection that he knew was coming.

"Yes."

Elsje moved her eyes from her father to Gilles now. There was no warmth, no emotion, just decision. Both men were taken aback by her short reply.

"I will marry Msr. Montroville but continue to live here and run the inn. He will live here, too, if he wants to live with me."

Hendrick started to say something but stopped. Gilles didn't know what to say and so he remained silent, trying to comprehend what Elsje was saying.

"If you are finished with me, the kitchen is behind tonight. I leave you both to make arrangements since it appears that I am the *last* to be consulted on this matter."

She rose abruptly, roughly shoving her chair in before she turned and strode back to her work but Gilles thought that he saw light in her eyes as they briefly swept by his. Gilles knew that his life with her was not always going to be an easy one but it was what he wanted: He felt comfortable when he was with Elsje. She had said "yes", but more importantly, Hendrick did not say "no".

Could Hendrick *still* say no? Gilles could never determine who had the final say in the complex relationship between Elsje and her father. As the Netherlanders were so fond of saying in matters of marriage, "the man is the head but the woman is the neck". At times it seemed to Gilles that Elsje respected her father's every decision and at other times, Hendrick appeared to be afraid of his own child. In the Netherlands there were the courts, of course, and Gilles could petition to marry her without her father's permission, but he didn't want to deal with the courts if he didn't have to, especially with the outstanding difficulties of his legal status; they were even less likely to rule in his favor due to Gilles' not being a citizen and being of minority age.

The two men sat in silence for a short time, each preoccupied with his respective thoughts. Hendrick tried to puff on his pipe but it had gone out.

Finally he said to Gilles, "You will have to give up the Jewish woman."

Gilles was stunned by the statement and said nothing in response. How did Hendrick know?

Hendrick wasn't looking for excuses or explanations, though. "I told Elsje about her but she does not believe me. If she *does* find out about her, it will not go well for you *or* the woman. I don't know what she would do, but it is not good to make Elsje angry: She has a *very* bad temper.

Gilles couldn't imagine what Elsje's reaction might be.

"Perhaps you should come and run this inn for me," Hendrick said.

"No, Hendrick, you and Elsje already run the inn well enough without *my* help and besides, too much time together might not be such a good thing for us."

Gilles was surprised by the offer but he didn't consider it for a second: He knew with absolute certainty that he could *never* work for Hendrick. Contemplation of the upcoming changes in his life was overwhelming but Gilles *did* want the thing done, and he wanted it done quickly; before Elsje or Hendrick had the time to change their minds. It would not have been done that way in France.

"Too much time together? You talk nonsense!" The old man rolled his eyes and sighed as if to say, "Providence sends me a husband for her and just look at what is sent!"

"Hendrick, I understand that we have to publish the banns first, because of our ages and my, ah, situation. How soon can we get them published? Can someone else, like Jean Durie, act as my guardian? Do the courts have to appoint him? I want us to be married as soon as possible."

"Go and talk with Elsje about it; she will probably handle everything."

Hendrick stared out into the room at nothing in particular beyond his pipe smoke, perhaps more disbelieving of the evening's events than Gilles, or perhaps he had just had too much to drink. He didn't move at all and might not have even heard Gilles when he bid him "Good Evening" and went off to find Elsje.

It was difficult to find any time to be alone with her when she wasn't racing to a table or asking a patron for his order, but Gilles caught up with her at last in the kitchen as she dished up more food.

"Would you not consider staying at home, afterwards?" he asked.

"Nee."

"Why didn't you give me any indication that you would consider marrying me?"

"You did not ask," she said simply.

"Then why did you step on my foot at the churchyard?"

Elsje didn't reply to this but threw back her head and laughed out loud as she pushed past Gilles to bring the two dishes out to her customers. Gilles just watched her go, wondering if all of their married life would be her working, rushing from table to table, from before the sunrise until well after midnight. Gilles decided on the spot that tonight his luck had finally turned for the better. From now on he was going to have whatever he wanted and what he wanted was for Elsje to stop working. She didn't know it yet, but Tryntje was going to help him accomplish this.

Gilles was bursting with the news and he had to tell someone so he went to Jean Durie's new home after he left Hendrick's inn. Gilles had never been there before but from Jean's description, Gilles found it without any great difficulty. Jean greeted Gilles heartily and invited him inside.

"Welcome, welcome! I was wondering how long it would take for you to get word back to me. You are dressed *very* nicely this evening! You have already made the decision to accept Ste Germaine's offer, then?"

"I have," Gilles said.

"Come in and sit down, then, this requires a drink!" Jean seized a decanter filled with a dark red liquid and two glasses.

"We have *two* things to drink to tonight, Jean. I am accepting Ste Germaine's offer *and* marrying Elsje Hendricks."

Jean just laughed and poured the two drinks. He handed one of them to Gilles before he settled into the other chair with his glass.

"You don't believe me," Gilles pouted.

"All right then, when will you ask her?"

"I already *did*."

"Really? You asked? She *agreed* and so did Hendrick?"

"Yes, just like that!"

"Then I hope that you both will be *very* happy although you might have a more peaceful life if you married a wildcat. Excuse me, I *shouldn't* say that. Just let me say simply, 'Congratulations'. So you will join me for dinner at Ste Germaine's tomorrow?"

"Of course I will."

"I'll send word to Ste Germaine and we can celebrate again tomorrow night. You know, I never had any doubt at all that things were going to work out for you eventually, Gilles."

The next stop that Gilles made on the way home was to get his dinner. Gilles felt around for his food in the darkness and left his coins for the girl as a silent glee started slowly in his stomach and then spread throughout him, even down into his fingertips and his toes. Very soon he would be dining elsewhere and he would never have to see the girl again, eat her peasant food, or take his meals on the doorstep like a wild animal.

He savored these thoughts as he had savored the wine at Ste Germaine's, slowly and deliberately, using all of his senses to imprint his surroundings permanently on his memory. He wanted to remember every detail of the doorway, the stoop, and the miserable girl forever, just so that he could pleasure himself with the knowledge that he would never again have to come back here. He made a pledge to himself that he would become as successful as his father and would *never* allow himself to be dragged into the pit of poverty that had claimed that poor creature, Botte.

It was quite late when he returned to the stable and climbed into the hay.

A real bed.

He had not slept in one, nor even dared to think about one, for quite some time now and it was going to be wonderful, especially since he was going to be sharing that bed with Elsje. Gilles perked up his ears at a noise down below but it was a small noise, probably just the rats returning. His worries over French spies finding him here had been unfounded after all: It had been *Hendrick* who had been spying on him all along and only God and Hendrick knew why because Gilles was never going to ask Hendrick directly. Asking would only invite more barbed comments and bad feelings. Gilles shut Hendrick out of his thoughts but he let Elsje in. It was a nice to think about her as he fell asleep.

On Saturday morning his mind was already crowded with thoughts before he even woke up. He didn't want to get up out of his warm bed but he had little choice in the matter. It probably wasn't going to get very much warmer during the day and he would have to get up to relieve himself eventually, but first he took a few minutes for himself, to luxuriate in his daydreams of the future.

His life was about to change completely and strangely enough, Gilles discovered that he was not altogether comfortable with that thought, as good as those changes were going to be. What if the new job did not work out? If Ste Germaine pressed him the way he did all of his other employees, it could be hard to suffer through that all day, every day.

Gilles would have a wife to support now, though. He could not imagine what he would do if the position at Ste Germaine's vanished, if he had to go beg Hendrick to work for him or ask Jacob for his old job back. No, Gilles decided that he would *not* leave Ste Germaine's, no matter how bad things might get, but he *could* always be dismissed.

It accomplished nothing to worry about the future though, and Gilles realized that he just had to go forward and live his life each day, making the best decisions that he could at each moment. Then a new determination settled into his bones, that he *would* be successful, he *would* be happy, and things *would* work out well for him at Ste Germaine's. He would help to grow his new employer's business into the finest in Amsterdam, if it had not already attained this status, and Ste Germaine would, of course, be grateful and treat him very well.

Elsje would be proud of him, too. Gilles didn't think he could stand it if anyone found out that his wife worked in her father's tavern *after* their marriage; it was shameful enough that he was *marrying* a woman who had worked in an ale house before the ceremony but having children would keep Elsje at home. They would be an added burden, of course, but Gilles would pass his French culture on to them. Gilles did appreciate Elsje's finer qualities, but it had not escaped Gilles' notice that she was incredibly ignorant when it came to what made a fine wine, good cuisine, or the correct etiquette in certain social situations.

Gilles wished that he had just a little more reassurance that he was doing the right thing, but except for Jean Durie, he was now completely alone in making his life's decisions. His parents had always known, and without hesitation, *exactly* what was to be done in every situation and never had any doubts at all on such matters. Gilles thought that he might send word to his family after the wedding, after he had time to think about what he was going to say to them and how he would say it.

Gilles wasn't sure what he would do: A part of him wanted to tell Charles, Marie, and his father that he, too, had good things happening in his life, things that he had chosen for himself, things that they were not included in, but another part of him didn't want to share any part of his life with them at all.

Gilles thought briefly about Hannah, too, and he remembered the remark that Hendrick had made:

"You have to give up the Jewish woman."

For a secret meeting in an out-of-the-way place that lasted for less than an hour once a week, it seemed as if a good many people knew about it. Gilles would have to leave her without saying anything at all; it was just easier that way and he did feel a little guilty about it, but what else could he do? Maybe he would give her something, a souvenir, a gift, a token of his thanks on Tuesday. If arrangements for the wedding went quickly enough, it might very well be the last time he would ever see Hannah again.

Gilles decided to get out of bed and start his day so he could get started on the rest of his life. As he tried to open a new sack of grain though, his numb fingers fumbled in the cold, maladroit at loosening the knotted strings. He wondered if his toes and fingers would finally be warm at Ste Germaine's or if they would be stuck in his past, staying stiff and cold for the rest of his life.

That night Gilles met Jean Durie at his house and together they walked to Ste Germaine's. Gilles couldn't help but think of his confrontation with Botte as the front of the building came into view. He wondered where Botte had actually met his end but Gilles saw no traces of blood on the street even though he looked. He shook off the chill that ran through him for the moment, set his shoulders back and left the ghost behind as he walked into Ste Germaine's with Jean.

The evening was as pleasant as it had been before but this time Ste Germaine talked incessantly about the right way to do things in the hospitality business and the mistakes that were so frequently made by the uninformed. LaRue was there again and said nothing for most of the evening but found recreation in his consumption of drink. Jean focused his attention on the food and Gilles soaked up as much of the food, the wine and the tutorial as he could.

On Sunday morning, Gilles decided that he would tell Jacob early in the day, just as soon as Gilles set eyes on him. This afternoon would not be good for any conversation, as it would surely be too busy.

Jacob did not come into the stable right away and Gilles grew impatient: He just wanted to get it over with. It felt odd and not quite real to him yet that he would be leaving this familiar place. What if there really was no job at all or if there was some kind of misunderstanding about the compensation?

"You could do worse," Jean had told him of Jacob's job offer so long ago. It was not yet too late to stay here in the safety of the Jewish quarter barn.

Gilles *had* to go forward, though. He had already told Hendrick about his new position and it was the height of insanity to even *consider* staying here: It was cowardly and ridiculous. There was Jacob's disrespectful treatment of him, the ever-present smell of the horses on his clothes and hair, the freezing cold, and the shame of living in a barn, not to mention having to eat leftover food on a back stoep. After mentally recounting *all* of his grievances, Gilles was more than ready when Jacob finally came in.

"It is not so bad in here this morning," he smiled at Gilles. "You slept well?"

"Yes, thank you, Jacob.

"Hannah has offered to make you some warmer clothes for the winter but I told her that you probably have enough clothes now and don't need any more."

Jacob's teasing did not bother Gilles today. There were times when it had a hard edge to it but this morning it did not, perhaps because it had been tempered by Jacob's day off and Sabbath visit to his daughter or maybe it no longer bothered Gilles.

"Jacob, I have accepted the offer of another job, in the French quarter."

"Hmm. Well, get your things then, and go." Jacob didn't hesitate for a moment but went out to the storeroom to check on the feed.

"I ..." Gilles began, ready to offer the explanation that was never requested.

"Your decision has been made, so *go!*" Jacob called over his shoulder. He was not interested in hearing anything more that Gilles had to say to him.

Gilles climbed up into the loft to get his things. It felt odd, almost like a rejection, but what did he expect, that Jacob would try to talk him out of it, maybe embrace him and then wish him well?

It didn't take Gilles very long to gather up his few belongings. He carefully wrapped the wampum belt, the pearls, and his money in the priest's robe first and then put the entire bundle inside his cloak: Carrying a priest's robe openly through the streets of Amsterdam would not be a smart thing to do. The blankets were still spread out on the hay, still a little warm and still turned back the way they had been when Gilles climbed out of them a short time earlier. Gilles suddenly realized that he was wearing Jacob's old coat. He climbed down from the loft using his free arm, the other full of his possessions.

"Jacob, your coat and the bed coverings ..." Gilles began.

"Take the coat, leave the covers." Jacob continued to work. He didn't even look up when Gilles paused at the door.

"Goodbye, Jacob," Gilles called back to him.

"Yes, yes, goodbye."

Amsterdam was quiet and peaceful this morning: It was, after all, very early on a Sunday and it *was* wintertime. A slight breeze was blowing, an icy cold breeze that carried sounds over to him from near the water. Gilles felt very strange, though, as if he was forgetting something, or doing something that he shouldn't, but he knew that it was simply his mind's inability to comprehend that the day and indeed the *moment* had finally come when his life was changing for the better. As peculiar as their goodbye was, Gilles had no time now to think about Jacob now. Changes were pouring into his life and his excitement grew with each step that he took toward his future.

He would have to go to Jean's first: There was simply nowhere else for him to go at this hour of the morning. Gilles passed the inn where he had taken his meals for the last few months and he grinned. He would never again have to stop there for food, and would not bother to tell the girl that the arrangement was finished. Perhaps she would leave some food out today and wonder what had happened to him or perhaps she would hear the news from someone and know that he had gone. It wasn't even so much a small act of revenge, his not telling her, but more that he hoped never to set eyes on her supercilious face again.

Both households were quiet and everyone appeared to be asleep when Gilles arrived at Jean's home. Being the first time that he was there in daylight, Gilles had a chance to look it over on the outside. The building was at the very edge of the bulging and expanding Jewish quarter, and Gilles noted that it appeared to have both Gentile and Jewish architectural characteristics, either because the Gentile trappings had not been completely eradicated yet or perhaps because the neighborhood was rapidly taking on a unique character of its own, a mixture of both cultures, with financiers, diamond dealers and traders of both persuasions living in very close proximity to each other, at first for the ease of conducting business, but now more and more because they had come to accept each other. Gilles didn't want to disturb anyone except Jean so he avoided the front door and went around the house, tapping on the window in Jean's sitting room. It took

Gilles several tries before Jean eventually came out of his bedroom to see what caused the noise and then opened the door to let Gilles in.

"Gilles! What's wrong? What brings you here so early?"

"I told Jacob that I would be leaving him and he told me to leave *now*. I didn't want to wake anyone else so I tapped at your window."

This struck Jean as amusing. "How very considerate of you! Well, come in, come in, we'll have some tea." He yawned and scratched his stomach as he led the way inside.

"I've brought all my things."

"I can see that. Put them over there, in the corner. We have much to do today, my friend, so it is probably just as well that you came early."

Gilles looked at him in puzzlement.

"Your hair! Your clothes! Your beard!" Jean exclaimed in mock exasperation at what he thought should have been obvious.

Gilles was a little embarrassed at his friend's open and acute appraisal and it hadn't occurred to him before that his appearance would need some work.

Jean continued in a more kindly tone, "You don't look *really* bad but for this position you must look ... ah, *better*. Yes, better."

He cocked his head to one side and squinted at Gilles. The gesture worried Gilles and he hoped that Jean didn't have some vision of turning him into some sort of fop like the ones who came into the stable, like the dandy that *he* used to be back in France. There was a knock on the door and a maid brought in hot tea and some biscuits, not the hard kind that they had on the ship coming over from France, but sweet, buttery, soft biscuits with jam and cream. She set the tray down on a small table and left.

"Eh? Eh?" Jean asked when she had left. "Is life good here?" He grinned at Gilles.

They sat down to enjoy their breakfast together and the luxuriant food was all that Gilles had on his mind for the moment, but it seemed to him that Jean continued to look at him too much over his tea cup, as though Gilles might have been a new acquisition to his art collection.

Jean put his cup down after a few minutes and excused himself. He went out of the door, and disappeared across the hall into the main house for a few minutes. Gilles could hear him speaking with other people on the other side but he couldn't make out what was being said. When Jean returned, he picked up his teacup again and resumed sipping his tea so Gilles thought that perhaps it was a private matter having to do with the household and not about him at all.

Gilles had almost finished eating and was beginning to feel totally relaxed when there was one knock on the door and then three servants bustled into the room loaded down with a variety of items including a pincushion, scissors, a razor, and a washbasin. Jean waved them over to Gilles and the man servant went first, telling Gilles to move his chair over just a little. Gilles obeyed but he wondered what the production was all about. The manservant laid a great cloth on the floor all around Gilles and put a smaller cloth around his shoulders which he fastened with a heavy pin. It had been so long since Gilles had someone else do his hair that he felt self-conscious, even in front of a servant. The man poured water into the wash basin from Jean's pitcher and set to work with his comb, having some difficulty in getting it all wet as water dripped down Gilles' nose and neck. The man never said a word but finally had the hair dampened and had worked his comb through the snarls in Gilles' thick, curly, hair to his satisfaction. He tipped Gilles' head this way and that, looking it over before finally taking up scissors and working quickly but expertly with them. Gilles was happy to have his hair trimmed neatly and he was relieved to see that it was left to beyond shoulder length, still long enough to tie back, but when the man started closely trimming his beard, Gilles protested.

"I need to keep my beard!" he cried out. *What if someone recognized him?*

"So you shall," Jean laughed, "but you will be a *different* man with a *different* beard!"

The servant barely paused at this exchange but kept trimming, closer on the sides, *too* close to Gilles' skin for him to be working so fast, Gilles thought. The servant trimmed less tightly at the bottom but pulled a little comb out of his pocket and trimmed the moustache and beard. Gilles' nose tickled with hair clippings but he dared not move, so fast was the man with the scissors. At last the man set the scissors down and Gilles snorted several times to remove the loose hair from his face and nose. The servant quickly brushed Gilles' face with a small brush, then proceeded to dip the brush into the basin of water and then into a small cup that he had with him. Lather came out of the cup and went onto Gilles' face from his ears down his jaw line. A razor was then produced and Gilles held absolutely still: If the servant was frightening with scissors, he was absolutely terrifying with a razor in his hands. The long blade was quickly sharpened on a hand stone and then put to work. The servant worked quickly and painlessly, though, across Gilles' face and neck, and it was obvious that he was very skilled and had been doing this for a great many years. Finally, the servant splashed great quantities of perfumed oil on Gilles' beard and head, rubbing it into his hair.

"What are you doing?" Gilles cried. "I smell like a prostitute!"

"For the fleas and lice, it gets rid of the bugs," the man said matter-of-factly. He stood back, admired his work and grunted, picked up all of his equipment, and without waiting for any thanks or money, he left. Gilles' face was red and burning from the assault but Jean seemed pleased and led his young friend over to a wall mirror.

"La voila!" he said to Gilles. "Monsieur Jansen!"

"A mustache and goatee!" Gilles exclaimed. He liked the appearance of the young man who looked back at him, even if he was unfamiliar.

Jean looked satisfied, too. "*Very* distinguished. He can cut your hair and beard every week for you, if you'd like. Now the women will get your measurements for some clothes. Ste Germaine mentioned twelve guilders a week to me, did he tell you that? He feels that you should be *very* pleased with such good compensation as well as being privileged to work for him. We'll hold him to it so be sure to show your gratitude every time he mentions compensation, as I'm sure he will."

The women approached Gilles now and the first one took his coat from him, Hendrick's old coat.

"You can throw that out," Jean said to her.

Gilles was going to argue with him but he changed his mind. Why keep it?

Both women bustled around Gilles, measuring and sticking him occasionally with pins. They put pins into the clothes that he had on and he wondered why they did it as he had *no* intention of taking those off. They ignored his protests and questions and they moved his arms out like a windmill. They told him to stand on a chair and all the while Jean said nothing, just sipped his tea and watched in amusement. Unlike the silent man servant, these two women were full of chatter and strange references to things that Gilles did not understand except that they had to do with fitting his clothes to him. He grew uncomfortable and nervous when they moved to take measurements of his crotch but they just giggled and put two pins on the outside of his thigh. It was bizarre to feel strange women touching him on his legs but far from being embarrassed, they didn't seem to give any thought to it all and hurried on, marking, pinning, and chattering in Nederlands to each other. The older woman nodded in approval at last and then she ordered Gilles to go into Jean's bedroom and remove his clothes, being careful not to dislodge any of her pins. Gilles turned red and the younger one laughed out loud before she stifled it with the back of her hand.

At Jean's insistence, Gilles did as he was told, and went into the bedroom with his bundle of clothes that he had brought along with him. After he had removed his pinned clothes and put his French clothing on, reluctantly and very self-consciously he went back out and handed the pinned clothes to the women, noticing as he did so that they smelled of oats and manure and were covered with stains of various types. He hadn't noticed that they looked so bad before and he was suddenly ashamed.

Had his appearance deteriorated that much? He couldn't believe that Elsje had said "yes" to him when his appearance was so shabby.

After the servants left with his pinned clothes and Jacob's coat, Gilles moved to the mirror again and regarded his new reflection. He had to admit that he *had* become a little lax in his personal habits but maybe not as much as he had initially thought; he had made an attempt to keep his beard trimmed and his clothing presentable but his parents would definitely have been ashamed of his old appearance. The thought occurred to him now though, that perhaps his unkempt appearance was what had kept him safe. He dismissed further ruminations on his appearance as they were a waste of time and besides, Jean was moving too fast to let him dwell on anything for very long.

"You need to get yourself some better shoes. We can clean those boots up for now but you *must* have new ones." Jean appraised the completed work on Gilles over his teacup and seemed satisfied. "The clothes that the girls are making will tide you over until you can get to a *real* tailor and have better clothes made. Don't go back to the tailor that you went to before, though. They did a good enough job on stable clothing but you will need a *gentleman's* clothing now. I'll give you the name of my tailor who is a member of the Amsterdam Guild."

Jean sipped more tea as the servant girl came in to remove the breakfast dishes. Gilles watched her gather up the cups, thinking about how completely different this world was from his old one. Gilles was accustomed to starting work right away, every morning, and most of the time Gilles did not get any breakfast at all. Here there was a servant, serving him all that he could eat. Gilles grabbed a last leftover biscuit from the tray before she removed it and she looked at him with wide eyes but said nothing.

"I should talk with Elsje today," Gilles mumbled to Jean as he put the whole biscuit into his mouth.

"You *should* have gone to church with her this morning, but it is probably too late for that now," Jean replied. "Go over, have midday dinner with them. Make sure all is well with her so that you can keep your mind on your work tomorrow."

Gilles' thoughts had been entirely on his new job and leaving Jacob's stable but now he remembered that a wedding was about to take place and it was his wedding. Very soon he would have a warm place to live and good food *all* the time and he was grateful for that, too. He wondered if he and Elsje would sleep in the same bed that he had recovered in or if there was a better room, a more private room, for them to occupy. The choices seemed pretty limited in the family's tiny apartment.

"You will write to your family, of course," Jean said. "The *Bon Chance* sails for home tomorrow but you have time to write a letter today and send word of your news."

Gilles didn't say anything to that. He had too much that he needed to do to take any time out to write his father. "Is it too early to go to Elsje's now?" Gilles asked Jean.

"I'm sure it's not but wash yourself before you go. We'll get you a fresh basin of water and towels. Do I have to tell you everything?" Jean teased Gilles.

The servant girl brought the water and towels and Gilles obediently washed while Jean busied himself nearby with a book. Gilles' face still stung from the razor and the perfume but there were no bleeding cuts on his face so Gilles took heart that it would feel better soon. He put his cloak on and set out for Hendrick's inn, hoping even as he went that nothing had changed with Hendrick or Elsje, including their hearts, and that he would still be welcomed when he got there.

Gilles arrived just after Elsje and the family returned from the morning church services. Elsje led him upstairs to the family's living quarters where there was a good deal of exclamation from everyone over his new appearance, everyone except Elsje, who just looked at him a little more than usual.

"My future son-in-law!" Hendrick greeted him. "You could not make it in time for church? Maybe you took too long in getting dressed? What kind of man will my neighbors think my daughter marries? A sweet-smelling man I suppose …" There was good humor in his tone, though.

"I apologize, Hendrick, and I will make it to church services *every* Sunday from this day on, I promise."

Hendrick knew that Gilles used to be a Catholic; had he come to the conclusion that Gilles was now one of the Reformees? Both men avoided further discussion of the subject. The idea of getting Elsje married and still keeping her with him at the same time must have appealed greatly to Hendrick as the old man was friendly to Gilles, even without a drink in his hand, and in very good spirits. If Hendrick had reconciled himself to the marriage, then perhaps Gilles could also reconcile himself to sharing Elsje with her father. At least Gilles could now smile openly at Elsje and she smiled back at him.

"Can you stay for dinner with us?" Hendrick asked him.

"I can," Gilles answered, trying to make it sound as though it was an unexpected invitation.

Elsje and Tryntje set the table and a place was made for Gilles next to Elsje at the other end of the table from Hendrick. It was an odd setup but it seemed the most agreeable way: Elsje would not be moved from her end of the table and putting Gilles at a side seat would certainly be a bad omen for the marriage.

"It might also be too close to Tryntje," Gilles thought, although Elsje's younger sister seemed to be better behaved today, showing him a little more respect and deference. The family's upstairs room was cozy and familiar to him although Gilles had only been there twice before, once to eat another Sunday dinner with the family and then to recover from his injuries, but he had been unconscious much of the time during that stay.

The three little ones poked each other and whispered among themselves, being a little diffident and saying little out loud, but kicking and poking each other under the table and replying with shy smiles whenever Gilles spoke to them. Elsje and her father were more tolerant of this behavior than they had been the last time Gilles took a meal there. Today they dined on an unusual chicken stew that was bright yellow, with dots of bright red and some kind of beans in it. Gilles thought briefly of Jacob who seemed forever to be eating chicken.

"How soon do we have the wedding?" Hendrick asked. Gilles was taken aback by the directness of this question. He felt that he needed to say something even though he had no idea.

"I-I am not good at these matters. I had someone who handled matters like these for me in France ..." Gilles' voice trailed off and he felt his face starting to turn red.

The smallest children laughed, not so much at understanding the joke but at his discomfort. Even Tryntje suppressed a giggle in her napkin. Elsje gave them all a silencing sharp look but turned back to Gilles with a confident smile.

"Cousin Vroutje and I will make *all* the arrangements and make arrangements with the church. Father is worried that if we don't do it quickly, then it will not happen at all so I hope that this is agreeable to you, Gilles."

Gilles was grateful for her rescue and said, "Of course. Soon is good."

He *had* meant it at the time when he told Hendrick the very same thing but now he was getting the dizzying feeling that things were happening too fast for him. If only he could be alone with Elsje without having to marry her first, just to reassure himself ...

Elsje continued talking. "A few weeks will be enough time if Cousin Vroutje can help me make a dress and if the banns are published. We can't publish them under *Gilles Montroville*, though."

Gilles was glad to see that Elsje was concerned with his safety more than any legal technicalities that needed straightening out and Hendrick said nothing to acknowledge the fact that his future son-in-law was a fugitive. The subject and meaning of the present discussion had completely bored and eluded the youngest members of the family.

"Yellas Jansen will work," Hendrick said, "there are more than enough Jansens in the city to confuse anyone."

"We have no busy times expected for this month?" Elsje asked her father. "No companies asking for use of the party room?"

Gilles wondered if she was always going to think of the business first. He had nothing to contribute to the conversation so he just sat there, trying to look happy and interested, but now he was feeling more than just a little bit frightened. He was certainly old enough to be married, at least in France, but inside he still felt that he was too young for this change in his life. He had faced death, prison, assaults, even untamed horses with mean streaks, but nothing scared him as much as the prospect of being married, of being tied to one woman, one place, for life and the certainty of the children that would follow.

With Marie it had been different: His parents had arranged it and they would have made certain that the new couple was protected from any reverses of fortune. Gilles would have, at least in theory, been able to leave his wife in his father's care and travel. Elsje had no great social position but as Jean had pointed out to him, Hendrick *did* have many business contacts. Gilles had also heard it said around Amsterdam, and from more than one source, that Hendrick had a great deal of money although you couldn't tell that from the way the inn looked or the way the family dressed every day but *all* of the Netherlanders were like that, modest and temperate to a man, except when it came to ale consumption, wedding celebrations, and having one's portrait painted.

When dinner was over, Gilles was ready to leave. He needed some time alone to think and he felt like walking in the Dam to clear his head. He wondered how he should say "goodnight" to Elsje. Was he expected to embrace her? He had seen couples embracing and kissing on the street here. Gilles was initially shocked to see it because this behavior in public was unthinkable in France. He finally decided to kiss her on the cheek and then kiss her hand. When he did this, these gestures of affection elicited giggles from the other children but from Hendrick there was a look of absolute approval. Elsje seemed pleased with it too, and so Gilles decided that he had made the correct choice to err on the side of modesty.

"This must be a dream," Gilles thought, as he reviewed all of the events of the very long day and then he wondered where he might be in reality if this was so?

Perhaps he was really at home in France in his own comfortable bed and none of it had ever happened. Was he still in the hay in the stable, dreaming of this miraculous escape from poverty? Gilles hoped that the marriage would turn out all right and the job would bring him prosperity; at the very least he hoped that both wouldn't end in disaster.

Gilles had seen a group of gypsies in the Dam from time to time, dancing and telling fortunes until the authorities drove them out, escorting them to the edge of the city after branding their forearms with hot irons to mark them for future reference if they ever decided to return. Gilles did not ordinarily believe in *the Sight* but if he could just have a *small* glimpse of the future now, to reassure him that it would be well with them, then maybe he could relax a little. He had a definite feeling of malaise when he thought about times to come but he could not say exactly why; perhaps it was just a case of nerves, all of the changes, that so unsettled him.

"How did it go?" Jean asked him on his return.

"It was all right." Gilles didn't want to share any of his insecurities with Jean.

"Are you hungry? Do you want any supper?"

"No, we had a very large dinner and I'm more tired than hungry. I think I need some sleep. Can you go with me to Ste Germaine's tomorrow?"

"I can take you over on my way into work. I am sorry that I do not have an extra bed but I do have a small sitting room that will make a nice private room for you."

"Do you have a place here where I can keep some valuables?" Gilles asked, pulling the pearls and his savings out of his belongings.

"What is this?" Jean opened the box and was greatly surprised by the contents. "They are very beautiful, Gilles! Are they what she likes?"

"She? Oh, you mean 'are they too much for a girl who works at an inn?' Perhaps. I don't know."

Gilles could see Jean puzzling inwardly as he closed the box but he didn't ask any more questions and Gilles offered no answers.

"I will keep them safe for you, Gilles. You did not give them to her today?"

"No, I guess I forgot about them."

"Well, you *did* have rather a big day."

Jean provided Gilles with blankets and Gilles used his cloak and the priest's robe for a pillow. The warmth of the fire, even coming from as far away as the next room, was a wonderful change for Gilles from the murderous and penetrating cold of the stable.

Jean had his collections in this room and Gilles looked around at everything in the tiny room before he blew out the lamp for the night. In one corner a round brass lantern with punched out designs hung from the ceiling, suspended by three small chains. Inside was a candle that had never been used. A small table underneath the lantern was made with a wood darker than any Gilles had ever seen before and ugly carvings of long faces with distorted features adorned it. A painted wooden mask and a crude wooden flute were casually placed on top of the dark table.

Carvings and inlaid wood with mother-of-pearl added to another small table's more attractive design in a second corner. It held a glass vase and a few smoothly-polished rocks that were brilliant blue, pink and green.

The third corner's table had a leather top, embossed in a gold design. This table held things of more interest to Gilles. There was a smaller version of his wampum belt, similar, but not as intricate in design, and a stone hatchet that took up much of the tabletop, or at least divided it in half diagonally. There were carvings on the top part of the handle that looked like hawks and other birds. The wood appeared to be lighter and smoother than oak but with a finer grain. It had a polish and smoothness on the handle that testified to much use by whoever the owner had been. Gilles wondered if this small thing had been used to fell trees. He had heard there were many trees in the new world, but they must all be very small and very sturdy trees to use an axe such as this on them. Woven designs of some sort of bead-type material were attached top and bottom to the ax handle with a waxy-looking but hard cord that had also been wound around the neck of the handle where it met and held the blade, lashing it firmly to the wood. A bright blue, white and black feather was attached to the top with the same cord in such a way that it moved freely in any direction. The blade was surprisingly sharp for being made of stone and only had a few nicks in it. Where the blade was attached to the handle there was a brown dye of some sort, darkest where the two materials met.

On the table top just below the ax was a small turtle's shell affixed to a carved wooden handle and decorated with a string of shell beads. Gilles picked that up too, but it made a noise when he lifted it. Stones or something else inside the turtle shell announced loudly that Gilles was picking it up. Gilles wondered if Jean had heard the noise as he quickly put it down and turned to the last corner of the tiny room.

A small chair, of a similar size to the one in his mother's boudoir, was draped in a red and gold material so strikingly beautiful that Gilles was drawn to touch it. It had the signature sticky texture to it of silk and it smelled strongly of sweet but pungent spices that he was not familiar with. A tall urn adorned with dragons and large golden birds stood next to the chair and spread open across the top of the urn was the most elaborately carved white fan that Gilles had ever seen. He could have spent the entire night looking at the detail in the fan alone but then there were the walls.

Unlike the precise arrangement and grouping of the artifacts into categories of the four corners of the world, the paintings were mainly of Amsterdam and Gilles counted no less than twenty of them crowding the walls in what seemed like no particular arrangement. A scene of Amsterdam under the first rays of the morning sun filled the smallest frame on the smallest wall. A laughing young blond girl in a pink dress with a little white dog in her arms looked down on the savage's artifacts and a kitchen scene with a large and smiling family seated at the table took up most of the large wall. Gilles thought that the kitchen portrait, even though it was nice enough, was an odd thing to have at all but the colors were repeated in the silk drapery and upholstered chair so Gilles supposed that this was the reason Jean would have such a picture here.

"I would not have any ugly Dutch kitchen scenes in my home," Gilles thought.

The floor space left in the little room was barely enough for Gilles to sleep in so he moved the chair back a little more to have room for stretching his legs out when he slept. The blond girl with the dog was going to look down at him all night long but there was nothing to be done about that except to roll over and face the other way. Gilles blew the lamp out and crawled under his covers. He was unaccustomed to the hard floor but Gilles gladly exchanged the hard floor and warmth for the cold of Jacob's hay loft.

Jean and Gilles set out early the next morning for Ste Germaine's, right after breakfast. It was the first morning with a real frost and the city was exceptionally quiet except for the crunch of the frozen ground under their feet.

"We have arrived!" Jean called out when they entered the front door at Ste Germaine's. "You will be fine, Gilles, do not worry!" Jean whispered in his ear as if reading his thoughts.

Gilles nodded.

"Come here and let me look at you!" Ste Germaine looked Gilles over with almost fatherly pride. "Very nice," he said as he straightened Gilles' collar.

"You approve then?" Jean smiled at him.

"Ah yes, very nice," Ste Germaine repeated. "Thank you for bringing him but you can go away now, Jean, we will be fine together."

Jean nodded and smiled at Gilles. "You can come and get your things any time you want."

"Oh, you did not bring them?" Ste Germaine asked. "You will live here, of course. The hours in this business are so long that you must use most of your time off to sleep. I will show you to your accommodations later, but first, the tour!"

Ste Germaine left Jean to find his own way out and took Gilles by the elbow, leading him through the dining room, the storerooms, the kitchen and the reception area, pointing out minute details and explaining procedures on everything from how to open the door the proper way to what side he wanted Gilles to stand on when he had to approach a patron. Gilles wondered how he was going to remember everything: Some procedures made sense to him but others did not and just seemed to be things that Ste Germaine had made up for no reason in particular.

Ste Germaine made no introductions to other staff but Gilles nodded greetings to the cook, the host, and even to the kitchen servants as they made their way through the entire business. One of the most interesting features of the place was the wine cave, which was not really a cave at all, but a structure in the back lot that had been covered with dirt to imitate an actual cave and was constructed especially for the wines. The great mound of dirt was entered through a doorway, complete with a locking door, and inside the wooden walls there was a framework that permitted bottle upon bottle of wine to be stacked up to the ceiling.

"The temperature is almost *exactly* right all year," Ste Germaine boasted. "Only sometimes do I need to put warmed bricks inside in the winter or to pour water over the dirt in the summer to adjust the temperature. The wine will be no good if it is not stored properly so always keep the door closed *tightly*," Ste Germaine admonished him. "It is critical to the survival of the wine, but you knew that, n'est-ce pas?"

The "Necessity Facilities", as Ste Germaine called them, were likewise an engineering marvel. The facilities were not located outside but down a hall, *inside* the building, and were quite warm. There were even separate facilities for women, although Gilles doubted that the women's had ever actually been used by anyone.

Ste Germaine proudly explained the workings of the thing to Gilles. "A system of clay pipes carries the waste away to the gutter after buckets of water are poured through it. I have the Flusher Boy clean the glazed tiles around the opening every single night. Outside on the street, even the gutter has an enclosed pipe to keep the odors from assaulting people as they pass by."

Gilles thought that it was quite possibly the most bizarre thing that he had ever seen but apparently the patrons had become accustomed to using it and he would have to get used to using it as well. In many ways, being with Ste Germaine reminded Gilles of his apprenticeship with his father but he resolved to work harder with Ste Germaine than he had with his father. Perhaps he *had* learned some things from his father and from Charles, after all, chiefly, patience and how to get along with people.

"Don't worry," Ste Germaine said to him for the twentieth time that morning, "You *will* catch on. Just *try*, if you can, to hold the plates *this way* when you serve ... "

Gilles' sleeping quarters were upstairs and across the hall from Ste Germaine's. The room was small but well appointed and had every comfort that he had been missing since he had left France. There was a great comfortable bed, a fireplace of his own, and two windows with curtains. Every detail had been given the greatest consideration and even the basin and pitcher were works of art with painted flowers decorating the usually plain porcelain. Linen towels with fine Netherlands lace worked into them hung next to the basin on a small wooden stand. The large canopied bed had heavy coverings that would certainly keep out the morning chill and there was even a desk in the room for Gilles to keep the accounts there. Gilles' private fireplace was lined with delicate blue on white tiles and the design of the fireplace was repeated on the tiled floor underneath carpets that had been imported from the east. Above the fireplace was a large painting of a gentleman mounted on a fine horse in front of a country estate. Gilles wondered if the man in the painting was supposed to be Ste Germaine but he didn't ask.

Ste Germaine put him to work right away and Gilles worked hard all day and all night. When Ste Germaine asked if he needed to go get his clothing from Jean Durie's, Gilles made the excuse that his clothing was all being washed and had probably not dried as yet in the cold weather. He didn't want Ste Germaine to know that he had no other suitable clothes to wear at the moment. Gilles went to bed after midnight on the first night and he wondered if every day would be so long. He took all of his clothes off and pushed his legs down between the smoothest bed coverings that he had ever experienced. He drifted quickly off to sleep, feeling the smoothness of the sheets with his hands one more time to reassure himself that they were real and that he was really here.

Unlike the stables, Gilles' days at Ste Germaine's would be very much alike except for Sundays, when only a late dinner was served in deference to the Sabbath, and on Wednesdays, Gilles' one day off. Ste Germaine told him that there were generally not busy days and quiet days here, that every day was busy and to Gilles' astonishment, the late suppers were even busier than dinners. Gilles worked until the early hours of the morning when the last customers left and then supervised the clean up efforts by the kitchen and dining room staff for another hour or two. He was up again at midmorning to set the dining room up before the midday dinner crowds arrived and in between he entered the credits and debits on Ste Germaine's books. It seemed to Gilles that Ste Germaine never slept. He was there when Gilles arrived in the morning and still there when he went to bed at night. Gilles wondered if Ste Germaine believed that his new employee was lazy and slept too much.

With the diamond rings on all of his fingers flashing in the light, Ste Germaine always gestured in the air as he corrected everything that Gilles did. The corrections were always done in a kindly manner with an added, "That's all right, you will learn", but nothing Gilles did ever seemed to be right.

By the end of the second day, Gilles was depressed and discouraged. He even thought wistfully of the stable and his life back there; at least he had worked alone there most of the time and Jacob didn't watch the way he did everything. Gilles remembered that today was Tuesday and it would have been the day for Hannah's visit. He wondered if she would miss him very much.

Gilles did have all day off on Wednesday, every Wednesday. This day off was not paid nor due to the generous nature of Ste Germaine but was due to the fact that Ste Germaine wanted to observe all there was to observe about the place alone, without Gilles there to present everything to him in the best possible light, as a sort of check on the progress of his new employee's work. Gilles only came to understand this much later though, and he spent his first day off blissfully unaware of his employer's motives.

Gilles decided that he would go to Hendrick's on this Wednesday morning to draw up and sign the final trade agreements with him and with Van Curler. After the commitment of that hour or so of time, Gilles was free for the day and had twenty three more hours to do whatever he wanted.

Gilles walked through the Dam on his way over to Hendrick's, just taking in the sights at the docks. The docks were as interesting as ever even if they were not nearly as busy at this time of year: Only the more adventurous entrepreneurs' ships still followed the trade routes in the wintertime. Silks and spices were being unloaded from one ship today, perfuming the cold breeze as they emerged from the hold of a ship which probably now smelled as good as its cargo and would probably continue to smell wonderful through the next several voyages.

A savage wrapped in a blanket stood looking out over the harbor from the deck of one of the ships. It had been some weeks now since the last ship had come in from the new world and it was very unusual for this one to be arriving at this time of year. The Gilded Beaver must have had some very important cargo to deliver to risk making a run so late in the season.

Gilles saw a ship of his father's, *The Normandie*, and he ducked out of sight, just in case one of the sailors might recognize him and be inclined to turn him in to make a quick reward. He cut across the side streets and was at Hendrick's inn in no time at all.

He looked around for Elsje first after he pushed the door open and saw her standing at a table, taking a customer's order. Patiently he waited for her to finish; Ste Germaine had at least taught him that much. He waited no longer, though, and took her warm hand in his cold one, kissing her cheek in greeting. Elsje kissed him back on both cheeks, and then his mouth, before she went on to the kitchen to fill the order.

Some of the patrons smiled and winked at Gilles, murmuring something to their companions but Gilles paid them no attention: It probably *was* unusual for someone, a male someone, to be there just to see Elsje. Gilles took a seat by the fire to warm up and Hendrick came out from the kitchen carrying a mug of ale and his pipe.

"Don't you work today? Have they fired you already?" he asked, but he smiled as he said it.

"I have Wednesdays off, *every* Wednesday," Gilles said, proud of the excellent terms of his new employment. "Are the Van Curlers here yet?"

"They won't be here today, but I have the agreements all written up for you to read. I'll make sure they get them before they sail."

"And you have made three copies, one for each of us on the Van Curler's agreement and two copies for our other one?"

"Yes, yes," Hendrick said. "It shouldn't take you too long to read them over and sign."

"Well, if they are all in order, then afterwards I can see Elsje," Gilles said, thinking that this might please Hendrick.

"She's too busy to talk to you; she has work to do." Hendrick tapped his pipe upside down into a porcelain dish to empty the spent tobacco ash out.

"Maybe she's too busy to marry me," Gilles said, only half in jest. Compared to Ste Germaine's, Hendrick's inn did not look at all busy to Gilles, especially at this time of year.

"The sooner you two are married, the better," Hendrick said gruffly and Gilles heard determination in his voice. "We'll just work around St. Nicolaas' Day and the other celebrations."

Gilles had forgotten completely about St. Nicolaas' Day. He had forgotten about most of the Christian holidays while he had been working at Jacob's because he never had any holidays or days when he attended church. There had been no cycles of feast or fast days for him there, just endless weeks of oats, water buckets, and shoveling manure, broken up only by Hannah on Tuesdays, busy Fridays and Mondays, and quiet Saturdays.

Thinking about those Tuesdays now, Gilles was not sure if he could wait another few weeks to be with Elsje. Gilles looked across the room and studied the outline of Elsje's blouse as she leaned over and delivered the plate of food to her customer. He knew that he would have to wait for her, but it wasn't going to be easy. Elsje brought Gilles an ale and sat down next to him.

"Cousin Vroutje and I have it all planned," she said. "We will have the ceremony two Saturdays after St. Nicolaas' Day. That *is* what you men were discussing, was it not?"

"Yes, yes, Elsje. Don't burden your future husband with all the details, just let him know where, when, and what to wear." Hendrick's good humor persisted. "If he remembers that much, it's enough."

"You *will* remember, won't you, Gilles?" Elsje looked at him with a critical eye.

"I'll remember. It can't be soon enough for me," he said truthfully.

Elsje gave him a warm smile but Hendrick seemed to have a disapproving look on his face. Perhaps Gilles only imagined it.

"Until then we have church and Sunday dinners to get to know each other," Elsje said, placing her hand over Gilles'.

Gilles *did* want to get to know her better and not just over dinner. "I won't be able to stay very long at Sunday dinners," Gilles explained. "Ste Germaine told me that Sundays are very busy days. He opens at one o'clock."

"He opens according to a *clock*?" Hendrick couldn't believe his ears.

"Yes, he has one in the foyer." Gilles needed to change the subject. Although Hendrick and Ste Germaine were in the same line of work, they couldn't exactly be considered competitors; the differences in their operations and clientele were enormous.

"I have today off, Elsje. Are you *very* busy? Can't Tryntje take over for just for a little while so we can go for a walk or sit somewhere together?"

Hendrick pounced on this suggestion. "That's a good idea! Elsje, go put on a nice dress and take a walk with your future husband."

Elsje snorted. "I have too much to do! Put on a nice dress! Walk! Haven't you noticed? It's cold outside!" She got up and walked away to the kitchen to join the cleaning that was in progress there, the hand towel that she carried flapping as she went.

Gilles put his mind back on the business at hand and took up the agreements, reading them over very slowly and very carefully. He only changed a few things and clarified others before he signed the contracts, making doubly sure that the numbers and terms had been carefully copied onto each copy to match the others. He didn't ask who had drawn them up but Gilles was fairly certain that the Van Curlers had a professional draw up their contract; he could tell by the neat appearance of the document, almost as if it had been printed on a press, and by the very precise speech in the agreement.

When Gilles finished signing, he had another glass of ale with Hendrick to cement the agreements in place. They were halfway through the glass when Hendrick exclaimed, "We should drink some good wine to celebrate the wedding. You like wine best, don't you?"

Gilles acknowledged that he *did* like wine and before he knew it, Hendrick had gone to the back and returned with a bottle of wine that was better than his usual but still not a quality that Gilles would consider *good*. Hendrick poured them each large glasses and Gilles was obliged to drink it.

"To your marriage!"

"To my daughter!"

"To health and long life!"

Too many glasses followed. Even with Gilles cutting his toasting drinks to sips, Hendrick was refilling the glasses at an alarming rate.

"To the inn!"

"To your friend Jean!"

"To your new job!"

Snow flurries started to drift by the window and soon they were coming down as quickly as the wine was *going* down. Before Gilles knew it, Hendrick had disappeared to get a third bottle. Gilles tried to come up with an excuse to leave the table and the inn but now Hendrick wasn't hearing any of it.

"To many healthy children!" Hendrick toasted before his mood suddenly became somber. He grabbed Gilles' sleeve, pulling him closer.

"Oh no, he's completely drunk!" Gilles thought. *"Elsje won't like this."* Gilles was feeling the effects of too much wine himself and he wasn't sure if he was still completely in control of his mental and physical functions.

"I have to talk with you, Montroville." Hendrick leaned over and grabbed Gilles' collar, his elbow knocking his pipe onto the floor where it broke in half. The old man slid his seat over the gritty floor and bent over in an attempt to retrieve the pieces even though he nearly fell out of his chair in doing so.

"*This is important,*" he said when he straightened up again. The old man's tobacco and wine breath was in his face and Gilles tried not to breathe it in.

"I'm listening." Gilles said, wondering what he had to say. Something about the wedding, perhaps?

"Montroville, be *careful* with my daughter on your wedding night. She has not had any experience with men. She acts worldly but she is not *like* the women that you are used to! Please be careful with her."

"I will." Gilles colored in spite of his greatly relaxed state. He longed to say something to Hendrick about Tryntje but he shook his head and clamped his mouth tightly shut so he wouldn't be tempted.

Hendrick leaned over and pulled Gilles closer to him, his foul breath coming again into Gilles' face. "And promise me *one more thing*, Montroville."

"What is that?" Gilles asked, feeling suddenly very dizzy as he tried to back away from the fetid breeze.

"Promise me that you will wait a week after the wedding night to go to her again."

"*What?*" Gilles asked sharply and sobriety coursed through his brain for a brief moment.

"*Shhh, shhh!*" Hendrick gestured toward the kitchen. He pulled Gilles over to him again although both men were sitting very close together and there was no one nearby to hear: the inn was now nearly empty. Gilles' neck was starting to hurt from the old man's constant pulling on his collar.

"Just promise me! She *needs* the time to recover! *Promise me!*"

"All right, all right."

"*Really.* Promise me." The old man was pleading now.

"I promise, Hendrick, I promise!"

"And you won't forget?"

"No, I won't forget." Unfortunately Gilles rarely did forget things when he had too much wine. He would have *liked* to forget, as some men did, especially when he did something foolish after consuming too much drink, but his memory never failed him, although his judgment sometimes did.

"Goed, goed." Hendrick released him just as Elsje came back into the room from the kitchen.

She had her hands on her hips and she glared at both of them. "This is *not* good! Both of you are drunk! It's bad enough that I have my father to watch after sometimes but it seems I have picked a very sorry husband too! What is going on here?" She eyed their unusually friendly manner toward each other suspiciously.

Gilles tried to show Hendrick that he could handle Elsje. "We were just talking, Elsje. We were drinking to celebrate our wedding."

"Then I should have a drink too!" Elsje cried, seizing the wine bottle by the neck. Both men looked at her wide-eyed, and Gilles wondered if she would tip the bottle up and drink but instead she shook her finger at them and took the bottle with her into the kitchen. Gilles got up halfway from his seat to follow her but Hendrick stopped him.

"Let her go, don't even argue with her, Montroville! I've learned that. Not that she isn't a wonderful girl! But I don't have to tell you about her many *good* qualities!"

"Was her mother like that?" Gilles sat down again and looked after her, somewhat helplessly, as he took another sip from his glass but in truth he was somewhat relieved that the bottle was gone.

"Oh no! Her mother was a sweet and quiet thing. She *looks* like her mother but I don't know *where* she gets her personality from."

Gilles just smiled at Hendrick; he had *a very good idea* as to where Elsje got her temperament: She was just as stubborn and volatile as her father.

Hendrick took another opportunity to close the sale again. "She *will* make you a good wife, Montroville."

"Jansen."

"What?"

"I go by Jansen now."

"Oh ja, I'll try to remember that."

Elsje reappeared from the kitchen without the bottle. She had her cloak on and picking up Gilles' cloak from the chair next to him, she tossed it to him. "Come husband! I will walk with you outside in the cold air. Do not make a habit of this; I don't have time for it and if it happens again I may just leave you outside in an alley with your old acquaintances to help you recover your sobriety!"

She dragged Gilles through the kitchen and outside into the gathering darkness in the back, probably because she did not want the entire city to see Gilles in the front of the house in his present state. There were no Marranos outside today and even the chickens stayed in their pens to avoid the cold. Elsje took Gilles inside the animal's shelter to get out of the great wet snowflakes that were still coming down from the sky.

The animals and the hay brought the stable and Hannah back into Gilles' alcohol-clouded mind and he put his arms around Elsje's waist, pulling her over to him. He took a deep draught of the scent of her hair and kissed her temple. Pulling a lock of hair from her cap, he ran it along his lips before he kissed her temple once again. He kissed her cheekbone, her cheek and then her lips. He moved in front of her and shifted his weight, pulling her closer to him.

"I can't wait until we are married, Elsje."

It occurred to Gilles now that even if Elsje was willing, he might have had too much wine and that would make for a very inauspicious start to their married life. "... But I need to show the proper respect for you and return you to your father now."

After Elsje served him a late supper, Gilles insisted that he was all right to walk back to Ste Germaine's alone. The snow had stopped falling, the streets were quiet, and so was Ste Germaine's, there being no customers there either. Ste Germaine and LaRue sat at a table with a bottle of wine, perhaps just enjoying the peaceful solitude of the winter night. Gilles asked Ste Germaine if he had had a good night.

"It was not bad for being close to Christmastime, Gilles. Come sit down and have a glass of wine with us."

Ste Germaine pulled out a chair. Gilles was still feeling the effects of the wine from Hendrick's but felt that he should not refuse his employer. He nodded and sat down, pushing his cloak back off his shoulders. He could have one glass.

Ste Germaine excused himself to go get another bottle of wine.

LaRue appeared to be inebriated and Gilles wondered if LaRue could tell that Gilles was drunk as well.

LaRue spoke slowly and carefully. "How are things going so far, Gilles?"

Gilles spoke slowly also, trying not to slur or mispronounce words although forming them was an effort for his alcohol-saturated brain.

"Very well, so far. This is a wonderful eshtablishment, ishn't it?"

LaRue smiled at him and said, "Oui. He thinks of you as a son, you know. Since he lost his only child, he has been empty but you have brought new life back to him."

Gilles was taken aback. He would not have expected this, or known what to say, even if he *had* been sober.

LaRue continued, "If you have *any* other difficulties, *any at all*, just let me know and I will personally take care of it for you."

Gilles didn't know what to say besides "Merci, Monsieur."

LaRue winked at Gilles as Ste Germaine returned to the dining room with the new bottle. Gilles noticed that it was a good wine, not quite as good as what he had on his first visit, but it was still a very good one. If Ste Germaine was drunk as well, it was not apparent.

"So many people do not understand about wine," Ste Germaine mused, "even the French people who should *all* be educated in such matters very early, even before they start formal schooling. Each vineyard is so individual that I can taste the difference even if they were to come in *identical* bottles." He poured the glasses and held his up to the lantern light. "Each year is different, to taste the hot dry summers and the cold rainy ones again, the bad springs and the good ones. Every bottle is different too, like every man, just slightly different from his fellow, though they might come from the very same place at the same time."

"He must be drunk," Gilles thought, although Ste Germaine's words had truth to them. "Msr. Ste Germaine, I am *very* tired. May I excuse myself after this glass and go to sleep?"

Neither man appeared to have heard what Gilles said or at least they did not acknowledge it, as LaRue nodded thoughtfully at Ste Germaine's philosophy, nodded his head a few too many times, and Ste Germaine just fell silent, still looking into his glass as if to divine the future in the red liquid, or perhaps the past.

Gilles finished his glass in three large gulps and said, "I need to rise early tomorrow so I will just...."

"But non! You were thirsty! Sit and have another!" Ste Germaine caught his sleeve and motioned for Gilles to sit. Gilles sat back down, somewhat unhappily, but he made the attempt to smile at his employer anyway. On any other night, with any *less* wine already consumed, he would have loved to sit with them but he had already had way too much to drink. Ste Germaine refilled the glass and Gilles resignedly sat back in his chair.

"How did you spend your day today, Gilles? Was it a good day off?" LaRue turned to Gilles.

Gilles suddenly needed more air and he took a deep breath with his open mouth but he also tried to answer the question. "I went to see my fiancée and her family." Gilles continued to breathe deeply, still looking for more air than there was available in the room.

"Wonderful! A fiancée! Will she come here to live with you?" LaRue asked.

Ste Germaine, who had been looking on with interest, had remained silent but now he spoke. "This *is* news. She a French woman, yes?"

"Ah ... non. She is a Netherlander and her father wants me to live with them after the wedding."

A hot, prickly chill traveled across the back of Gilles' neck and settled into his armpits and stomach. It seemed to be getting much warmer in the room all of a sudden and now his neck and forehead were hot, too.

Ste Germaine still contemplated his glass of wine but with less intensity. "When I was young, I too, felt that I had to perform my duty and marry; my father left no question as to that! It is no longer necessary to marry if one does not wish it, though. Msr. Durie is a good example of that."

Gilles replied before he realized that he was speaking. "Jean? He still mourns for a woman he lost in France." Gilles' stomach felt hot and sour now. It was far too warm and the room began to tilt to one side. "I ... I need some fresh air!"

Gilles left the table and ran to the necessary facilities as he started to retch. His stomach heaved several times before it started giving up all the wine, the good years and places and the not-so-good years and places. The burning in his stomach was replaced by what felt like a pulled muscle just under his ribcage. At last there was no more wine coming up and he spit into the hole to clear his mouth. He was still shaking as he poured the bucket of water down the hole to flush it away. Gilles wondered if Ste Germaine and LaRue knew why he had left so suddenly or if they thought that he just had a sudden need to relieve his bladder.

"Surely they know," Gilles thought. *"I will just go back to get my cloak before I go up to sleep."* He straightened up and the air was suddenly heavy again on his head and shoulders. A hot flush spread across his forehead and then the rest of his face but Gilles' hands were like ice. He knew that he had to get to the sanctuary of his bedroom.

"I am not going to be sick again," he told himself. He straightened up and as calmly as he could, Gilles rejoined the men but he did not sit down with them.

"Let me offer my apologies but I am *very* tired. I *must* sleep or I will not be able to work tomorrow," Gilles said, grabbing at his cloak and missing once before his hand closed on it successfully on the second attempt.

"I will see you up the stairs, Gilles," Ste Germaine said, picking up a candle and lighting it from the table's lamp. They both climbed the stairs slowly and heavily, Gilles going first with Ste Germaine's hand on his back. Gilles was surprised, but not feeling well enough to think much about it when Ste Germaine followed him into his room and removed his boots and pants. Ste Germaine pulled back the covers and helped Gilles inside them, cool covers with a faint scent of roses that brought Marie and his mother to mind. Ste Germaine smoothed back the hair on Gilles' forehead and put the basin on the floor next to the bed before he picked up the candle and went out, shutting the door behind him.

Gilles' dreams were vivid but he could not remember them all afterwards. It seemed to Gilles that someone was in the room stoking the fire in the fireplace or perhaps it was just a log settling. He was alternately cold and then hot, kicking off covers and later struggling to find them and pull them up to his chin again as he shivered. He heard voices across the way in Ste Germaine's room, whispers at first, then louder, then softer again. He heard the creak of the bed across the hall as it was occupied and then he dreamed on to other places.

He dreamed of his home in France because he thought his mother was in his room but he woke with a start to see that it was Ste Germaine's kitchen boy with a tray of tea and dry bread.

"It's after noon," the boy explained. "Monsieur thought you might be getting hungry by now."

Gilles *was* hungry and except for the remaining headache, a slightly sore and sour stomach and being as dry as an old attic, he was surprised to find that he was none the worse for his consumption of wine the night before. He pulled himself up to a sitting position and had his first chance to wonder if he had made a complete fool of himself the night before with Hendrick and Elsje as well as with Ste Germaine and LaRue. He berated himself for drinking too much and for walking home in such a state: It was not only undignified, it was dangerous. *Anyone* could have accosted him, from a robber to the men in the alley or even French bounty hunters. Instead of waking up in a nice bed, he might have come to his senses in chains or locked away in a ship's hold on his way back to France. He swore to himself that he would be much more careful in the future.

Gilles ate the toasted bread and drank the tea, pulled his clothes on and went down the stairs to face his employer. He only hoped that he wouldn't be fired or lose favor in Ste Germaine's eyes for his intemperance. When Gilles walked into the dining room though, Ste Germaine barely noticed him: He was too busy with his staff rearranging the layout of the tables. The man who acted as Ste Germaine's host looked very unhappy about having to do manual labor; after all, his job was to stand and direct everyone else and he obviously felt that it was beneath him to be moving tables. Ste Germaine had either not noticed the man's attitude or pretended not to notice it but he himself seized one end of the table and barked at the man, "Go! Take the other end so that we can move this over here. Quickly! Quickly!"

"What are we doing?" Gilles asked.

"Ah, Gilles! Are you feeling better now? I am going to have some musicians in for the next three nights and perhaps even longer. The music brings in more customers and it worked very well last year except for that minor difficulty I had with the city's licensing authorities. If you are hungry, get yourself something to eat from the kitchen."

Ste Germaine barked out orders as his employees scurried about, an avalanche of directions and orders coming from him faster than they could react to them, although they all did their best to comply.

Gilles left the frenzied scene and went to use the necessary facilities first before getting some water and looking for food. There was not much to find because unlike Hendrick's, Ste Germaine insisted that the meals be freshly prepared for each customer, with the exception of the soups and some of the desserts. Gilles did find a pot of soup on the hearth and thought he might try some of that. He was happy to discover that it was an oxtail soup and not a bouillabaisse or onion soup. He was not sure if his stomach wanted any fish just yet and he didn't want to ruin his love of the onion soup by having it when he did not feel well. Gilles ate a very small bowl of the soup before he went back out to the dining room. The host and a waiter were still moving the tables back and forth with Ste Germaine directing the activity. Gilles hadn't missed a thing.

"Non, out from the wall more! How can they sit like that? To the left a little. No, forward! Forward! We already tried it that way!" Ste Germaine sighed and scratched his head with one finger. "Why do I always have to do everything myself?"

The host and cook's helper said nothing in response but both of them smiled a grimacing, ingratiating sort of smile at Ste Germaine.

"That's all right, you don't know...."

With several more minor adjustments the arrangement was finally where it suited Ste Germaine. Having achieved what looked like their employer's satisfaction, the employees all tried to disappear from the room but Ste Germaine called the head waiter back to straighten up all of the paintings on the wall. Gilles wondered if Ste Germaine did this on purpose because this request seemed to infuriate the man to the very limits of his endurance. Surely Ste Germaine could see this as well.

Two patrons walked in, the first of the day from the looks of things, shaking drops of melted snowflakes from their cloaks and inquiring about an early supper.

Ste Germaine fumed under his breath to Gilles that he had guests in the door and the musicians who were supposed to be here already had not shown up yet but Gilles was *more* concerned that he had not seen the cook anywhere.

"I told them three o'clock and it is almost that now!" Ste Germaine checked out the window and Gilles followed behind him, looking over his shoulder. In the distance a lone man trudged up the slippery street carrying a lute under his arm. They watched until he turned in at the entrance to Ste Germaine's and climbed the icy steps. He was greeted at the door by Ste Germaine who hustled him quickly into the dining room, barely allowing the man to get his coat off first.

Gilles' stomach still wasn't quite right yet but he wanted to prove to Ste Germaine that he was back on his feet and ready to work. The host had seated the two customers and a bottle of wine was brought over to the table. Gilles wondered what they were going to do about the missing cook and whether they could stall the men until he returned.

The rest of the musicians arrived in a group and the lute player was joined by two violinists and a flutist. It seemed to Gilles an odd combination of instruments but he was not surprised that Ste Germaine had such a production going; he wondered why Ste Germaine had not ordered a harpsichord to be brought in as well.

Ste Germaine said to Gilles, "This is a good group but if *only* there was enough room in here for a harpsichord ..."

The musicians started to move chairs, re-arranging the furniture that Ste Germaine had just put in place to his own satisfaction. A lively debate followed between the head of the musicians and Ste Germaine while the rest of the assembly, the armies under both generals, tuned their instruments or attended to their dining room duties.

Ste Germaine insisted that he had set up the room in the best possible way and the head of the musicians group argued that one of the musicians was left-handed and the arrangement would not work for them at all. The stand-off was finally resolved with some minor changes to the seating arrangements, and finally the musicians took their seats and started to play. Pleasant music, if not peaceful thoughts, filled the room at last.

The next tune they played was very fast and very loud and Ste Germaine went over to the musicians. He made a motion for them to stop.

"What *is* that?" he hissed at them.

"A lively tune I learned in Italy," one of the violinists replied indignantly. "This establishment could use some energy."

"Non, non, non! Elegant, French, sophisticated, is what I want!"

The musician shrugged, nodded, and they started a song that was very similar to the first one they played but a little more like a funeral dirge.

The two customers summoned the host to their table and Gilles knew that they were looking for their food. As of yet, none at all had come out to them and they only had the wine. Ste Germaine looked unhappy as he surveyed the situation from across the room and Gilles, not wanting him to start thinking about bad things, in particular his own intemperance the night before, rushed over to try and placate the men.

"Can I start you with a wonderful soup?"

"We don't want soup; we have already given our order!"

"Yes, and it *is* coming, but the soup comes with your meal at no additional charge," Gilles said quickly, thinking that even if Ste Germaine forced him to pay for it out of his own pocket, it was worth it to keep the patrons there and his employer happy.

The customers smiled at Gilles and at each other, the host was flustered and the waiters whispered among themselves. From the actions of his coworkers, Gilles ascertained that there was *still* no sign of the cook anywhere. Gilles went into the kitchen, pulling one of the waiters in with him, and together they searched the shelves and cabinets until they found a ladle and the right bowls. Gilles dished up two bowls and handed them to the waiter.

"Take this out and tell them that their dinner is coming soon," Gilles told him.

"But the cook ..." the man protested.

"Then we'll just have to cook it ourselves, won't we?" Gilles lashed out at him.

"But Msr., *no one* touches the cook's ..."

At that moment, the cook and Ste Germaine both arrived in the kitchen, Ste Germaine from the dining room door and the cook from the back door.

"Take the soup out, now!" Gilles waived at the waiter to keep him moving.

"Merci, Gilles," Ste Germaine smiled his gratitude at him.

"Oui, merci," the cook said amiably, picking up his apron and moving back to his fire as if there had never been any question at all that he would arrive in time.

Ste Germaine talked about ending the music after only two days to save on the expense since it did not appear to be increasing his business at all. Every business was very slow and Gilles was a little surprised that he himself was still employed there when Ste Germaine still seemed to either correct or re-do all of his work for him. Winter had a firm grip on the Netherlands and the cold and gray of the skies did little to lift Gilles' spirits. He missed France and he missed the food that they had during the holidays at home. Even though the French quarter had many of the same treats available in the shops, when he bought them and ate them alone, it did nothing but increase his homesickness and loneliness. The only bright spot was spending a little time with Elsje on Sunday and looking forward to spending more time with her.

On his next day off, Gilles woke earlier than usual and he couldn't get back to sleep. He wanted to go somewhere. He didn't feel like sitting with Hendrick and watching Elsje work all day and there was nothing much to see at the Dam. As he pulled on his pants, he decided that he would go to Jean Durie's house and have breakfast with him. Jean would probably like to see how he looked in his new clothes that had been made just for Gilles and recently delivered to Ste Germaine's.

Gilles knocked quietly on Jean's door, just in case he slept late but Jean called out for him to enter. Jean was sitting at a desk, a new addition to the main room, and he gestured for Gilles to take a seat. A young man who looked like an apprentice bookkeeper shifted nervously from foot to foot in front of Jean Durie, turning his hat around and around in his hands. Jean appeared to be busy going over some accounting books for the youth and was in an agitated state.

"What a mess!" Jean declared. "I can't tell who bought what, who stored what, and who sold what!" Jean closed the book with a slam and thrust it at the youth. "Tell him that I am a *bookkeeper*, not a magician or a mind-reader! If he wants to come in and try to reconstruct what happened with these books, tell him to make an appointment with me. It will probably take a week *or longer* and I will be sure to charge him every stuiver I deserve for my expertise and my time!"

The trembling boy took the book and left quickly.

"Bad day already, Jean?" Gilles went over to warm his hands in front of the fire.

"Non, it's just this time of year. It's a slow time for business so they try to reconcile their accounts from the previous year. The way some of them keep records is not to be believed! If they kept their records as they went, they might have *some* idea of what they spent their money on. They need capital for new ventures in a few weeks when business picks up again. Fools! And they wonder why they get into trouble with the taxing authorities. Surely it is worth avoiding fines, jail time, or worse to hire someone to do the job right the first time?"

"If they kept their accounts the right way, you would have no work to do." Gilles grinned at him.

Jean shook his head. "I could do very well *without* work that is this troublesome. Why do the worst thieves and thickest heads go into finance? It's art and science and yet so simple that *anyone* who puts a modicum of effort into it could do a very good job! But non! They come up with new schemes and shortcuts to line their own pockets and they *all* end up making a mess of it. It's time that I started my own business: A man *never* gets rich working for someone else and besides, if Dirck talks to the firm and I am forced to leave there, I will at least have another business going already."

Jean finished his rant and turned his mind away from business. "What fine clothes you have on, Gilles! What are you doing wandering around here this morning, enjoying your last few weeks of freedom as a single man?"

"It's my usual day off."

"Why aren't you with Elsje then? You aren't having any misgivings about her?"

"Non, but I do wonder if my life will always be the same from now on, will never be any different."

"What did you want? To hop on a ship and travel whenever you like? I suppose you could run away to sea and become a buccaneer."

Gilles let the subject drop. Even if he knew exactly what he was feeling, he was not sure that he could communicate it in the right words to Jean. The feeling was a vague one of loss or of being in prison again.

"It's all right, Gilles, I have heard that *every* man feels that way just before his wedding about his betrothed."

"Did you?" Gilles asked.

"Non."

Jean changed the subject again. "I see that you have the same old boots on. Did you never get new shoes? Come on then, I'll take you to a good shoemaker right now. It's a good time of year to go; they aren't busy and neither are we; besides, they charge less."

Jean took up his cloak and pushed Gilles out the door ahead of him, into the cold wind driving down across the city from the north.

"I understand that St. Nicolaas Day is *the* big celebration day here. I should probably buy a present for Elsje," Gilles said, "is that right?"

"For Elsje *and* for her family too, Gilles! I have been meaning to ask you about that. Those pearls you bought Elsje were nice but the box is worn. Did you get them in trade for something?"

"Non, I bought them new," Gilles answered, hoping that Jean would not ask any more questions.

You've been carrying them around? Have you thought to marry Elsje for so long, then?"

"I suppose so," Gilles lied. "Should I get a new box for them?"

"Absolutely, and I know a good place for that, too."

They came to the shop for the pearl box first. The shop's primary inventory was material for making clothing, draperies, and upholstered furniture but in one corner a young woman sat with needle and thread, making small containers out of the leftover scraps of fabric. A sturdy table in front of her held finished masterpieces as well as a bucket of water, a pot of glue, a large block of wood covered with dents and holes, a small anvil, tacks, and a little hammer. On inquiry, the woman directed Gilles to some boxes that she had already finished while she spoke with another customer regarding a purchase. After completing that transaction, she turned her attention back to Gilles and smiled at him.

"St. Nicolaas Day gift boxes?" she inquired.

"Ja," Gilles replied, "for a necklace."

Gilles looked over all of the boxes she had made. There was a little cylindrical green velvet box with a gold cord attached to it that first formed decorative trim and then wound around to become a delicate handle. The box had a pale green lining inside and fabric hinges kept the top half attached to the bottom half. A tiny little latch made of braided thread looped over a small green bead and kept the lid closed.

Seeing Gilles' interest in the little box, she asked "How large is your necklace? This box was made for a ring."

"It is a large necklace," Gilles replied and he moved his attention to some of her other creations. The woman kept working as Gilles looked over her wares. She had a very thin strip of wood, almost as thin as a shaving, that she dipped into the water and curled around in a circle. She carefully tacked the sides together on the wood block and then bent the end of the tack over on the anvil. She cut out a new piece of fabric and proceeded to cover the box with it after she had applied the glue to the frame.

There were many boxes; some trimmed with lace and cording and others plain. There were large hatboxes and boxes big enough to hold a woman's dress or fur coat, tiny ring boxes, and every imaginable shape, size, and color in between. There were bright colors, somber colors, prints and plain colors. Gilles liked the plain ones best: they just looked more dignified to him.

Gilles examined the green box again, turning it around and looking inside.

"I forgot about a ring!" he whispered to Jean.

Jean rolled his eyes good-naturedly at Gilles and shook his head in disbelief.

A blue box was just the right size for the pearls. It was rectangular with a fitted top and the lining of pale blue satin would show off the warm glow of the pearls.

"That's a good choice," Jean said, approving of Gilles' taste.

"I'll take the little green box *and* the blue box," Gilles told the woman.

"Two guilders," she said as she tied the two together with a piece of fabric. It was more than Gilles expected but he decided that it was worth it.

"You have no ring yet, Gilles? I can see that I will need to walk you through everything," Jean said once they were outside again.

"I never had a wedding before!"

"For the man, it's not so hard. Get permission, wear good clothes, bring a ring, and show up on time. Your bride will take care of the rest." Jean laughed but Gilles didn't feel very cheerful. He felt overwhelmed.

There were no other customers in the shop and the shoemaker was obviously pleased to have the business. The shop had a good smell to it, a smell of leather and wood. The shoemaker stood up from his stool behind the iron shoe form and removed several tacks from between his lips. Jean immediately ordered three pairs of shoes for Gilles as Gilles gasped.

"I don't need *four* pairs of shoes! *One* new pair is all that I need."

"Nonsense! One for your job, one for church, and one for you for everyday. A gentleman needs shoes, isn't that right, Msr. LaFountaine?"

"Of course! A gentleman needs shoes!"

"Do you need some more money, Gilles?" Jean asked as he prepared to open his purse.

"Non, non, I *have* the money; it's not the money …"

"Did you not have four pairs of shoes in France?"

"I had *more* but …"

"Well, then, it's settled, three pairs of fine shoes. When can they be ready?" Jean asked the schoenmaker.

"I could have them done by Monday," he offered.

"Gilles can pick them up on Wednesday. You should get yourself some new boots, too, Gilles."

Gilles thought that if he went anywhere else with Jean Durie he would have no money left at all. Gilles stood still while the shoemaker made tracings of his feet with charcoal on a thin piece of wood that was placed on the floor for that purpose.

"Why do you do both feet?" Gilles asked. "Can't you just take a measurement and make both shoes, the same way everyone else does?"

"*I* don't do just *any* general fitting," the man replied. "*I* am an artisan and my shoes will *never* cause you any pain. They are the best, especially if you have any bunions or are missing any toes; each shoe is made *just* for you." He smiled up at Gilles with obvious pride.

"A true artist!" Jean exclaimed.

Gilles wondered how much this was going to cost him.

Jean dropped a coin into the shoemaker's hand. "For our good faith, for you to keep. We will pay you in full, as always, when they are done." The shoemaker thanked him as Jean held the door for Gilles and they walked out.

"I just wish this wedding was over with," Gilles said to Jean.

"Is that a good sentiment about the biggest, most important event in your life," Jean asked him, "other than your new position, of course?"

Gilles shrugged. Nothing would really change afterwards except that he would have a license to be with Elsje, permission from her father and their church to lie with her. The ceremony was simply a nuisance, a delay. *"Damn all the churches for the strings that they are forever attaching to my life,"* Gilles thought.

Jean interrupted his thoughts. "You aren't just bringing your hungry self to the St. Nicolaas Day feast at Hendrick's, are you? I would suggest bringing them a goose. Let them know that you will be bringing this gift so they won't order another one and be sure you bring it the day before so Elsje has time to cook it! Order one from the butcher in plenty of time, too, in fact, do it today. Bring some little gifts for all of the children, too. And don't mention Christmas Mass in front of them or their Protestant friends, either!"

Gilles sighed. "This is *too* much work, Jean. Will it be any easier after the wedding?"

"If you want the marriage to be a happy one, non. Women *always* have these expectations."

"I should probably go to see her today."

"Yes, go to her. Is her father still happy to see you there?"

"He is *overjoyed* to see me but she is always too busy for me!"

"Hah!" Jean laughed. "Elsje is Elsje. You knew she was like that when you asked her to marry you, Gilles."

"Can't the city run without her for one night, our wedding night?" Gilles shook his head, discouraged now that he would ever be able to get her away from her work.

"I guess we will see if she takes the time off. You know, Gilles, it's an embarrassment, unthinkable, for these Netherlanders to have wedding feasts that last *less* than three days but I would be surprised if anything could get Elsje to stop working for more than just *one* day. Maybe you and I should have a wager on it, eh? I'll bet the entire city would like to be in on that one! Just don't have *too* much to drink and go easy on the girl the first night."

"That's what her father said," Gilles muttered.

"What?!"

"That's what her father said. He told me to wait a week afterwards as well."

"I don't think I want to hear this, Gilles. It is not going to be an easy living arrangement afterwards, I'm sure. Are you certain that you can all live under the same roof? Is there at least a separate room for you and Elsje?"

"Hendrick has his own room."

"You *can't* start a marriage off like that, Gilles. I'll talk to Hendrick."

"*What?* What will you talk to Hendrick about?" Gilles worried that there might be severe repercussions if anyone said *anything* to Hendrick.

"Don't worry, Gilles! I will get you out of the old man's house for the wedding night; you just leave it to me. Now you should go spend some time with her before she changes her mind. You don't want to be guilty of laches."

"She will be starting their supper soon and I won't get to talk with her unless I go with her into the kitchen."

"Nonsense! There's no one around to cook for Gilles; it's wintertime! The ale houses are all empty except for the regulars and they don't go in there to *eat*."

"I suppose."

"What you need to do is to put her to work on your needs *before* the wedding," Jean added. "That is the best way to start a marriage. She needs to get used to the idea of working for you, so have her start by making you some new stockings and a new cloak."

"What's wrong with this cloak?" Gilles looked down. He saw no holes or stains.

Jean sighed. "Maybe I'm moving too fast for you. Just go and see Elsje, Gilles."

Jean was right about the inn. There was no one there even though Gilles could smell that the cooking had not been neglected on the off chance that someone other than the five men who were usually there drinking, might come in, desperate for a good meal. Gilles took a seat with Hendrick at Hendrick's usual table.

"It's good that the girls get a chance to catch up on cleaning but I worry when there is no money coming in, especially at the feast time," Hendrick confided to Gilles. Elsje and Tryntje were busy cleaning corners with a broom and cloth and wiping down the undersides of tables and chairs.

"Do the floors later, just in case someone comes in!" Hendrick called over to them and Elsje nodded assent to her father. "Your business is busy now, ja?" Hendrick asked.

"Not as busy as we were, but some businessmen come in to meet there every day."

"That's good. We should open the back room for that here, at least in the winter."

"We should just close the inn until spring," Tryntje muttered.

"And how would we pay for all the dress material that you always want?" Hendrick sighed. "*Children!* But you will know, soon enough!"

Tryntje gave her father a disdainful look before she turned back to her bucket of water and a cobweb that hung from the corner of one of the windows.

"Will you close the inn for our wedding day?" Gilles asked Hendrick.

"Close? Oh, no! We'll just serve everyone who comes in; they can join the feast!"

Gilles couldn't help thinking about what his wedding to Marie would have been like, in point of fact, what Marie's wedding to Charles must have *been* like a few months earlier. The great ballroom would have been decorated for days in advance and music would have been playing continuously. The food would be rich enough to kill anyone with a weak liver, and the drink! The drink would have been only the best, any kind, non, *every* kind imaginable. Dignitaries would come and go and an army of extra servants would have been hired just for the day. Perhaps the King himself would have put in an appearance. Not just *anyone* would be able to attend but everyone in the province would *want* to come, would wish that they had been privileged enough to receive an invitation. One entire corner of the gold and blue room would have been piled nearly to the twenty-foot ceiling with gifts and the celebration would have gone on into the night. The stables would have been a constant fury of guest transportation coming and going and some stable boy, like the one Gilles had been just weeks ago, would pin his hopes for the year on the generosity of just a few of them.

But that wedding was not to be, not for Gilles.

For just a moment he felt ashamed that he looked at his own upcoming wedding with an accountant's eyes, noting a meager credit column and a large debit column when he compared it to the other ledger that he had just been thinking of.

He felt cheated: He *deserved* more.

He had expected and looked forward to a large increase in his own personal wealth on his wedding day since he was a small child.

"These stables will be yours, Gilles." "These vineyards." "This house." "A ship of your own." "You can change the color of this room when it is yours." "When you marry." It was always when, they had never said "*if*" and Gilles had never for a moment doubted that it would be so.

"Your future husband daydreams a lot," Hendrick observed loudly, a puff of smoke rising from his pipe's bowl, covering his face and slowly floating upwards toward the ceiling.

"I've noticed that," Elsje called over. "Perhaps he is just busy planning some very important detail of our wedding." Elsje smiled teasingly at Gilles.

"Perhaps he is just letting his future wife and her father do all the talking, as they usually do," Gilles replied, with as much good nature as he could find within himself.

Gilles realized that Jean was right about the wedding night; that something would have to be done. Gilles had a great deal of faith in Jean's ability to handle the delicate situation but still Gilles worried. Why had Gilles agreed to live under his father-in-law's roof?

It would have been different in France with a suite of rooms, an entire wing just for the newlyweds, far away from the rest of the family.

Gilles was still brooding when Elsje brought him some supper. There was no one else to feed with all of the food that she had just prepared. Gilles knew that he was not good company this evening and should probably have left the inn earlier but there was no immediate graceful exit that presented itself or any pretext of getting back to work, either. After he finished his meal and when the wind started to come up outside, rattling the windows in their frames, Gilles excused himself, telling Elsje that he needed to get back, just in case the incoming storm was a bad one.

"I'll return on Sunday," he assured her, and kissed Elsje as he took his leave.

Gilles worried more and more that Ste Germaine really did not need his help at all, did not need to pay him to just stand there and preside over an empty dining room or add up four accounts a day in his room. Ste Germaine's other staff had all been given time off, without pay of course, until after the holidays. When they were out of earshot of Ste Germaine and on their way out the door, Gilles heard the men grumbling to each other about the lack of income that this would mean for them. Gilles was given the following Wednesday and Thursday off, "for a St. Nicolaas Day holiday" but Gilles knew very well that it was not a gesture of generosity, only a cost saving measure on Ste Germaine's part. Gilles did not complain though; he was relieved that he was not given any *more* time off or encouraged to find other employment altogether.

On Wednesday morning, Gilles went to Hendrick's inn again but this time he was in a better frame of mind than he had been on his last visit.

"Does my future wife never take time off work?" he asked Elsje. "Come with me to the Dam, just for a walk. Tryntje can handle the inn for a time."

Gilles hoped that if he gave Tryntje every opportunity to run the inn on her own that Elsje's younger sister would rise to the occasion so Elsje could be eased completely out of the business.

"Why do you want to go there? There is no one there at this time of year but pickpockets looking for silly people like you! There are no vegetables to buy."

"Go *somewhere*," Hendrick said to her, taking Gilles' side for once. "Go out with your future husband for a little while. You've cleaned the same lamp four times."

Elsje made a pretense of having work to do around the inn but there really wasn't any as she had already cleaned everything at least once that week. At last she could find no more excuses and gave in to Gilles' request. She grabbed her cloak from the kitchen pausing on the way out to give a few instructions to Tryntje who appeared to be intently ignoring them.

Gilles let Elsje take the lead up the street and they didn't walk to the square at all but walked to the church yard instead.

"You love this place, don't you?" Gilles asked her.

He didn't understand why she liked to come here so often. It was macabre, peculiar for her to be just sitting there among the dead all the time.

"Sometimes I come here to think, to ask my mother for her advice. We *all* got sick that winter but she was the only one who died. She seemed to be getting better but then she started coughing more and more and then one day she just died."

"And your Cousin Vroutje took over caring for your younger sisters and brother?"

"Ja, she was my mother's cousin and took care of *her* when she was a baby. Vroutje has the time for the little ones; her son is grown and she does not keep an inn."

"Should I get to know Vroutje then, to see if she approves of me?" Gilles asked Elsje with a teasing smile.

"It's a little late for that!" Elsje laughed, "You have already asked and Father and I have already accepted! But I think Mother would have liked you."

"Are you afraid to marry me?" Gilles asked, hoping that she would admit to being a little afraid too, just as he was, or to reassure him that their life together would be good.

"I'm afraid of *nothing*, Gilles, except that my life will change. I have thought about living other kinds of lives, of course, of being at home all day with children, or being the wife of a rich man, but the truth is that I *like* my life the way it is. I have my father and the inn, and all of our family together for dinner on Sundays. I can't *imagine* any other kind of life. If I could have any wish, *any wish at all*, it would only be for my mother to be back with us and the whole family to live together again but if I can't have those things, then I would change very little about my life as it is now."

"And is that all that you would change?"

"Ja, except for being with you." She smiled at Gilles and he hoped that it wasn't a perfunctory statement, an obligatory compliment. Then she asked, "What would you change about *your* life?"

A brief flash of memory crossed his consciousness like a sudden gust of winter wind. Even if he *could* tell her the truth, he could never explain adequately to her all that it was about his old life that he missed so much, not so that she would be able to understand it and not take offense at what he said. It wasn't *just* the money. *"You can never understand what you have never known,"* he thought sadly but he plunged in gamely and tried to rationally consider his life as it was now, in this framework, and how it might be improved.

"I would make my job just a little easier, my investments a little more profitable. I would be able to spend some time on the ships, like I did when I lived in France. I would travel a little and have unlimited time to spend with *you*."

Elsje smiled at this but she cut their conversation short. "Well, we should be getting back to the inn now."

"But we just got here! There is no one there, no reason to hurry back."

"I can't leave the inn for very long with no one running it."

"Tryntje's there."

Elsje removed a dried leaf from her cape and stood up to go, leaving Gilles with little choice in the matter. He added one more thought to their conversation though, a seed planted and a wedge in the door of her closed mind, in the hopes that she would someday come around to his way of thinking and stop working at the inn.

"Things *can* and *do* change sometimes, Elsje, even when you may not want them to change at first. It isn't *always* a bad thing, though, once you decide that you can get used to it."

Elsje didn't answer him.

St Nicolaas' Day was celebrated with cakes and little gifts. Gilles didn't ask, didn't even try to figure out why the family was celebrating a saint's feast day when they were not Catholic and when he had so often heard Hendrick's vitriolic comments on papists in general. Gilles gave Elsje the pearls, her father some tobacco, and had little gifts for the rest of the family. Cousin Vroutje came over early in the morning with her husband, son, and Hendrick's three other children. Vroutje was warm and friendly, much more relaxed and laissez faire than either Hendrick or Elsje even though it might have been the occasion that put her in such good spirits. She welcomed Gilles into the family with hug and a kiss.

Everyone exclaimed too much over the pearls, though, so much so that Gilles was sorry that he gave them to Elsje at all. It was not simply that they were much more expensive than the small gifts that everyone else exchanged, but every mention of the cursed things reminded Gilles of Marie and of France. He should have just sold the horrid souvenir of his past and bought Elsje some other token of his affections. Elsje took them out of the box and put them on right away, wearing them all afternoon, even as she cooked and cleaned and washed the dishes. The effort of being cheerful and on his best behavior for the duration of the day, in addition to the strange foods and strange customs, was just too taxing for him so Gilles took his leave immediately after dinner, claiming that he had a headache and needed to go home and sleep.

He returned to Ste Germaine's loaded down with gifts and little cakes and he thought about either taking a nap or having a drink when he got there but when he opened the front door at Ste Germaine's, he could hear LaRue and the cook fighting, even before he put his first foot inside the door. The two had had occasional shouting matches before, usually in the morning before any guests arrived, and Gilles thought that they might stop if they heard the front door, but they did not, not even after Gilles loudly banged the front door closed.

Perhaps they had not heard him. Gilles still thought that they might break it up when he walked into the kitchen to ask where Ste Germaine was, but when he got there, Gilles suddenly realized that the dispute was far more serious than any of their previous altercations.

The cook got along well with Gilles, at first only because Gilles dearly loved the man's onion soup, and then later because the two talked about places they had both been to in France, chiefly Havre, Rouen and Paris. Gilles couldn't explain *why* he got along so well with LaRue though; he just did. He didn't try very hard, didn't feel any particular warmth toward him, and truth be told, there *was* something about LaRue that made Gilles uncomfortable, something that he couldn't quite put his finger on, but if Andre LaRue noticed this malaise on Gilles' part or was concerned about it, he never indicated as much. Gilles didn't spend much time thinking about LaRue as he reasoned that being on good terms with Ste Germaine's best friend could not hurt his future employment prospects.

Why the two men hated each other so much was a complete mystery to Gilles and he had no idea what might have passed between the two before he came to live and work at Ste Germaine's. Perhaps there was a reason why the cook and LaRue had come to dislike each other so much, or perhaps there was none at all: Gilles knew very little of either man's history.

The cook had traveled throughout Europe, following the French wars and fighting with the King's army, and, employee rumor had it, had fled the unceasing violence when he could no longer stomach the misery of war any longer, the missing arms, legs and faces of those he had come to know, even from the relative safety of the back lines. Like so many others in that time and place, the cook was in hiding in the great anonymity that was Amsterdam, in hiding from those who would take him back to finish his incomplete service to the French military and in hiding from his own memories.

Gilles knew nothing of LaRue's past at all so he could not even make a guess as to what had started the friction or what kept it going. On some days low-level shots were traded between the two adversaries or there was general grumbling from one about the other, but today it had erupted into all-out warfare, possibly only because Ste Germaine was not around. Apparently LaRue had been in the kitchen this morning and had made some passing comment about the quality of the food and the cook had responded by grabbing a large kitchen knife just seconds before Gilles walked in.

The cook moved to circle LaRue with his knife in hand, a cat with a bird in his sights, and the look in his eyes told Gilles that he was ready; he had found enough of an excuse to follow through with his threat of murder. Gilles could see that LaRue *was* frightened but so far he had not fled the kitchen.

"You put one hand on me and I will see to it that the authorities know your whereabouts!" LaRue threatened.

"I could say the same to you but don't worry about my hands! I'm going to spitchcock you with my knife!" the cook countered.

LaRue cast a quick glance backwards for anything with which he might defend himself as he inched backwards toward Gilles and the dining room door. He was bigger than the cook but LaRue had foolishly entered into enemy territory unarmed, while the cook was surrounded by his own knives and cleavers, completely at his ease and in his own element.

"*Stop this now!*" Gilles demanded but neither man took his eyes from the other.

Gilles wondered whether he should move slowly away from them, drop his gifts to the floor and run, or try to intervene. He didn't feel particularly brave or lucky today and he certainly didn't want to be in the way of the cook's long knife when it so eagerly sought a target.

"Stay back! This is not *your* fight," the cook called out to Gilles as he continued to advance on LaRue.

The kitchen boy who peeled the vegetables and carried the water in had entered from the back door and now he paused there to see if he would have to be the one to mop up LaRue's blood from the kitchen floor.

"*Stop it! Stop it right now!*"

Gilles used his father's voice but it still made no difference at all. The distance narrowed between the two men.

"*Tous les deux! Arrete!*" Ste Germaine roared at them as he entered the kitchen from the dining room to find out what the disturbance was.

The cook's arm slowly started to come down but his eyes never left LaRue. He stood his ground, refusing to retreat, but neither did LaRue.

"Jacques! Out! Out of my kitchen *now!*" Ste Germaine ordered LaRue away and into the dining room.

"*Avec plaisir.* His cooking smells like dead rats anyway."

"You wouldn't *know* the difference between dead rats and good food," the cook retorted. "I *will* serve you rats next time and we will see if you can tell me whether it is beef or chicken!"

LaRue was about to reply to this insult but Ste Germaine stepped between the two men and with his back to the cook, he said to LaRue, "You will leave my kitchen, *right now.*" His voice was quiet but it was stern.

LaRue took his leave but not before he flashed a threatening glare at the cook from the safety of his position behind Ste Germaine.

Gilles was relieved, of course, that there was no serious injury to either of the men but very quickly behind that sentiment he was overcome with feelings of insecurity. He wondered *why* Ste Germaine would keep him on as the manager of his establishment when Gilles seemed unable to resolve any problems, establish any discipline, in short, unable to do *anything* to manage the place properly. Gilles had generally commanded the respect of his father's sailors but here in this place he seemed unable to do this and he was not sure why. Had it only been his familial relationship to his father that commanded the deference of the sailors? Perhaps Gilles really had no management abilities at all.

Gilles recovered his composure before he left the kitchen and went out into the dining room where Ste Germaine was standing with LaRue, completing a quiet lecture to an uninterested audience of one.

"Do not bait him, Jacques! He is the best cook I have had *in years* and I need him!"

"He's not so good, *I* could do better." LaRue cast his arm out in the direction of the kitchen. "He's *insubordinate*. You need to get rid of him!"

"Once and for all, I say, stay out of *my* kitchen. This is *not* your business," Ste Germaine said.

"Yes, my lord."

LaRue made a grand sweeping bow to Ste Germaine and left by the front door just as the musicians made their entrance for the day, completely unaware of the scene they had just missed. The first musician and his instrument were nearly knocked down by LaRue as the two men attempted to use the same door at the same time going in opposite directions.

Ste Germaine sighed and said in a low voice to Gilles, "I forgot to tell them *not* to come today but I thought it would have been *obvious* because it is a holiday and business will be very slow. It's not enough that I must spend my day keeping those two away from each other! It *must* be a punishment or a penance from the heavens: I have no choice but to keep both of them, and now I have these irritating musicians who bring in *no* new customers and frighten our old ones away. If I am to get rid of *anyone*, it will be them."

Ste Germaine went back to the kitchen to check on the cook as Gilles took his armload of gifts up to his room. He couldn't remember now what it was that he had wanted to talk to Ste Germaine about.

At last the day before the wedding came. Still Gilles worked at his job with no change at all to his daily routine.

"You must take some time to prepare yourself," Ste Germaine told him. "It's not every day that one gets married."

"There are no preparations for me to make!" Gilles protested but Ste Germaine sent him away from the dining room anyway and Gilles went upstairs to his room. He stared at his own reflection in the mirror. Was he really going to do this? He was alone in a strange land and now was he really going to marry a foreign woman? He looked at his own face in the gold-framed mirror but the face and eyes looking back at him and the life he saw stretched out ahead of him were not familiar to him at all.

Everyone else made great preparations for Gilles' wedding; Ste Germaine was even going to close his business for a few hours to attend the wedding and feast, at least for the first day of the event, a great honor in and of itself. Gilles wondered if Ste Germaine just did not want to leave the running of his business to someone else who might not run it exactly in the way that Ste Germaine would have wanted. Of course there was no one else besides Gilles, and even if there was, Ste Germaine probably believed that if he abandoned his business to less capable hands, his reputation could be completely ruined in the few hours that he was going to be away.

Ste Germaine insisted that the cook make food for Gilles' wedding feast as well, perhaps as much out of a desire to have good French cuisine there and to give the cook some extra practice as out of any innate generosity. That evening after supper, Jean Durie appeared at the door to Gilles' chamber with a bundle that turned out to be Gilles' new shoes.

"Where have you been, Gilles? Why did you not pick up your shoes? I just thought to stop by on my way back from my office and there they were! The wedding night is all set, though, don't worry about that: You and your bride will spend your first night at my home to give you some privacy."

"Thank you, Jean. Do I owe you money? For the shoes?"

"Non. What other preparations do you need to make? You bought a ring didn't you? Let me see it." Jean stood there with his hand out, waiting to inspect it.

Gilles pulled out the ring and handed it over.

"That *is* nice. Interesting design. Why did she pick *this* one?"

Gilles' puzzled look gave Jean the answer he sought.

"She didn't go with you? What if it doesn't fit?! *Gilles!*"

But then in a more kindly tone, Jean added, "It's all right. The jeweler can fix it … probably. I can see now that I will have to stay right by your side throughout this entire production. Let me see your clothes. Go on, show me what you will wear!"

Gilles obediently brought his new clothes out from the chest. He had gone to Jean's tailor and the fit was good but Gilles did not feel completely comfortable in them: He doubted that he was ever going to wear them after the ceremony as there was too much stiff lace on the collar and the sleeves were so ornate with their elaborately sewn smocking and beading that it hurt his skin just to rest his arm on a table. Jean scrutinized every detail and made only minor suggestions.

"I think a gold chain there and a pin? Non, no pin ..."

"Jean, stop! You are making me nervous! I only need to go there and go through with this."

"You do not want to marry Elsje?"

"Yes, yes. It's just ... *all these preparations.*"

"There would have been more in Rouen."

"Yes."

"Ah, I see. Gilles, you and Elsje *will* have a good life together."

"Yes, yes, I know that but ..."

"Let's have some wine, then."

"All right, but not too much. I don't want to be feeling drunk or sick for this."

Jean went downstairs for a bottle and Gilles sat on the tapestry-covered chair waiting for his friend to come back up. It was really so much fuss for nothing. He was more than ready for this wedding, no dukes or other royalty would be coming, just the local burgers. What preparations were needed for *them*? Who cared?

Jean reappeared with a bottle and two glasses. "Ste Germaine is coming, oui?" Then under his breath, "Not LaRue, I hope."

Jean's tone changed and he spoke more decisively to Gilles. "Tomorrow you *will* be happy and you *will* be charming. You will solidify our trade opportunities, not just with Hendrick, but with *all* of his important and even his not-so-important guests, because you can *never* tell when someone is about to become very rich and powerful *and* you never know what connections they might already have. *No one* celebrates a wedding or makes business connections like these Netherlanders! Your father would be proud, Gilles. He would believe that you have made a very good match, a very good choice."

At this comment Gilles could at last smile a sincere smile. "Thank you for saying that, Jean. It is not the way that I ever thought it would be ..."

"Non, it is not, but the world is changing and we need to recognize that, change with it, and quickly take advantage of these changes. The old money can no longer hold it; the adventurer will become rich while the old families sit idly by, watching their fortunes trickle away. You must understand that we have the advantage, Gilles! We know how to keep our money and what it can best be used for, but we have opportunities that your father would be far too hesitant to take advantage of. He is too comfortable in his old life, too comfortable in what will soon be past."

Gilles considered Jean's statement but he rejected the validity of it. Maybe his friend was simply trying to make him feel better. "I hadn't thought of it as opportunity, just as needless pain. I would much rather be sitting at home in Rouen counting the money I inherited."

"Making great fortunes sometimes requires taking great risk, I have seen this," Jean stated emphatically as he finished off his first glass of wine.

"Like marriage, I suppose."

"Exactly! You have to know what you want *first* and then you must go forward. Too often, even when people know what they want, they are either afraid to wade out into the unknown alone or else they blame someone else for their own choices. Of course, you will have no one at all to blame if you are unhappy, since it was you and not your parents who chose Elsje, but I hope that you can find contentment with such a … ah, *spirited* woman."

"Do you think I will ever again be able to restore my fortunes?"

"I'm certain of it! We will *both* be rich someday, Gilles. These setbacks are only temporary and we mustn't forget that we do quite well now, considering that there are those who used to dine with us who now dine at the garbage heaps."

Gilles thought of Botte and gave an involuntary shudder. Gilles' finances *had* improved but he wondered if the threat of having to return to the stable would always be there in the shadows, driving him forward and obfuscating his ability to see his true financial worth.

Jean clapped him on the arm. "I have to go now but I will be back tomorrow morning to protect my trade interests with Hendrick by ensuring that *you* show up looking presentable enough to marry his oldest daughter. Have some wine tomorrow morning; keep this bottle here but have it *before* you dress so you don't spill it on your good clothes. And get some sleep, Gilles! You will need it for four days of celebrating."

Jean left before Gilles could ask him to stay longer. It was not so much because he needed the emotional support as that he needed something to do to help him pass the time. There really was nothing much for Gilles to do in the next twelve hours except sleep, be there on time, be impeccably dressed, and bring the ring.

Gilles wasn't sleepy so he crossed the hall and went into Ste Germaine's room to get a book to read. He had often glimpsed the wall of books next to the bed as he passed by the open chamber door and he was sure that Ste Germaine wouldn't mind. Gilles had missed books as much as he missed Calvados: He hadn't had the money, time, or the energy to do any reading at Jacob's, even if he had ever found himself with enough daylight left after he finished his work.

Gilles located a Latin Bible, and thinking that it was appropriate reading before a wedding, he pulled the large volume down from the shelf. He had just turned to leave the room when he spotted something gold and silver on the Oriental rug, just peeking out from under the edge of the great bed. Gilles picked it up, recognizing it as a gold and silver jeweled pin, a favorite of LaRue's, and on closer inspection he saw that it had the initials J.R. on it.

That was peculiar: "Jacques" was what Ste Germaine had called Andre LaRue during the skirmish with the cook. Gilles had thought nothing about the misnomer at the time and simply thought that the emotionally charged atmosphere had gotten the better of Ste Germaine, just as it sometimes had with his father when his angry words came out, directed at Gilles, but with the name of one of his brothers attached. Was it a nickname, a disdained Christian name long ago abandoned by LaRue, or was there some other reason for the name change, a better reason why the cook believed the authorities might be interested in Andre LaRue?

Gilles decided that it was none of his business; LaRue might have a story just as Gilles did, a very good reason to use another name. But how did the pin get in here?

Gilles would never know. Shrugging, Gilles tossed the pin back onto the floor and returned to his room with the heavy book.

He read for some time, skipping around from book to book but he found no inspiration anywhere, only long dry pages of genealogy and admonitions not to do this or that, not to sin. Gilles finally extinguished the lamp, deciding to follow Jean's advice to get some sleep, mainly because there was nothing more interesting for him to do.

After a few minutes of lying there in the dark he heard Ste Germaine ascending the stairs with someone. It had probably been a very slow night for business, as every night had been since St. Nicolaas' Day. Gilles could not determine whose low voices they were but Gilles recognized Ste Germaine's step on the landing. The door to Ste Germaine's bedroom across the hall closed and there were muted sounds and rustles. Eventually there were low murmurs and the noises of physical consummation.

Gilles smiled to himself.

He had only one more night to wait; tomorrow he would be with Elsje. Perhaps Ste Germaine's life was not so terribly lonely after all. The loss of a wife could be a very hard thing on some men if they found no outlet for their affections. What had Ste Germaine said once? That his father had expected him to do his duty and marry? Gilles wondered briefly if he would ever find himself in that position, with his wife gone on to her heavenly rest before him and his having to seek out new companionship.

No, Elsje was strong, and in all probability she would bear children easily and outlive him. Gilles wondered who the woman could be who was in Ste Germaine's arms on this night. Was it one of Ste Germaine's married guest's wives? A wealthy young woman with good social and business connections? A naïve young girl or a sophisticated woman who knew something of life? Knowing Ste Germaine's impeccable and definite tastes, Gilles doubted seriously that it would be a Netherlander or a prostitute.

Now that Gilles' door was closed and the fire on the hearth had passed beyond its hottest point, Gilles rolled himself over into the bed covers to keep himself warm in the rapidly cooling room. The down comforter, pillows and featherbed crackled cozily around him until he found just the right position and very soon he was almost fast asleep.

At first he thought he dreamed it when he heard the voices across the hall rising.

"You must not tease him so!" from Ste Germaine.

A low voice responded, too low for Gilles to hear the individual words.

"You *do*! How would I ever find another?"

Was she flirting with another man? Was it Gilles' job they were discussing? Gilles was awake again, trying to make sense of the conversation.

The other voice rose slightly but still remained too low for Gilles to hear clearly.

"Do I have to refuse you access to my *entire* establishment?" Ste Germaine asked.

"*Damn* your kitchen, *damn* your cook, *damn* your establishment, and *damn you!*" LaRue's voice was unmistakable.

Gilles next heard the sound of someone sharply pulling on clothes and then the door across the hall slamming as LaRue exited, his staccato steps descending to the first floor before the front door, too, opened and then was slammed shut.

Gilles' heart pounded in his chest. The shock was almost too much for him to bear and he would *never* have anticipated this: La Rue was always there with Ste Germaine but Gilles had thought that the two men were simply good friends, just as he and Jean Durie were friends. If Jean knew about this bestiality, this sin, it would explain why Jean disliked LaRue so much but why, then, didn't Jean feel the same way about Ste Germaine?

Gilles' ruminations were cut short when another set of footsteps, Ste Germaine's, crossed the hall and Gilles' door opened. Now Gilles feared that Ste Germaine would come to him as a woman would, in the dark of the night, seeking solace from Gilles after his lover's quarrel. Gilles stayed very still with his eyes closed while his heart continued to beat wildly against the cage of his ribs. He would defend himself from any advances or assaults on his person and Gilles tried to remember if there was anything near at hand that he might use as a weapon.

There was the lamp. It might burn his hand but that might be preferable to ...

Gilles wondered if the heat of the lamp's glass and the smell of the recently extinguished lamp would give away the fact that Gilles' room had not been darkened for very long. Ste Germaine was as large a man as Gilles was, even larger perhaps, and the idea of having to defend himself against the advances of the older man from the disadvantageous position of the bed gave Gilles some pause.

These turned out to be unnecessary thoughts, though, as his door closed quietly with Ste Germaine retiring back across the hall, never having entered Gilles' room at all: He had apparently only been checking to see if Gilles had heard the argument. Gilles heard Ste Germaine's door close again and he listened keenly to all the sounds in the room across the hall until he heard familiar soft snoring sounds and only then did Gilles relax enough to regain his presence of mind and move. He got out of his warm bed and slowly, as quietly as he could, he pulled his heavy armchair across the tile floor and the Oriental rug before pushing it up against his chamber door. It wouldn't *stop* Ste Germaine from coming in but the noise would give Gilles some warning and he would be able to sleep better knowing that it was there.

As Gilles returned to his bed on numb and icy feet, he worried next about his job, his income. Was there something more that Ste Germaine expected of him? He would not give up his position voluntarily and he was certainly not going to submit to any improprieties. There were laws in place in Amsterdam and if he had to, he just might hold revelation of Ste Germaine's secret over him in order to keep his job and his income.

Gilles did not want to spend another night here, though, not under this roof. He would miss the beautiful room and he was a little sad knowing that he would never again feel the same way about working into the early hours of the morning with Ste Germaine at his side. His privileged position at such a young age and Ste Germaine's infrequent praise gave him a feeling of pride that he had not felt since he had left his school lessons.

He made the conscious decision that he could not afford to worry about Ste Germaine right now though; he had a big day tomorrow and he would just have to keep working at Ste Germaine's and pretend that he did not know his secret. If it came to that, Gilles could always work at Elsje's father's inn. She was his insurance and as good as in his hand already with only hours to go until the signed alliance of the wedding.

In spite of the previous evening's events, Gilles slept well enough and when he climbed out of bed very early the next morning, he had a fortifying glass of wine and dressed himself fully before he pulled the armchair away from the door and returned it to its usual place. The sounds of passion from the night before clung to his memory though, in spite of his conscious efforts to shake them off.

Jean Durie arrived early and they had some breakfast together when it was sent up from the kitchen. Gilles thought about ways that he might bring up the subject of Ste Germaine and LaRue but no tactful ideas came to him and he wondered if he should say anything at all: Jean might think that he only *imagined* such a bizarre thing and even if he did believe Gilles, it would change nothing of reality.

Jean gave Gilles a little more wine, cautioning him each time not to spill it on his clothes, until Gilles worried that he would have to leave the ceremony for the outhouse if he drank any more.

Ste Germaine knocked on the door and Jean invited him in.

"Are you ready, Gilles?" he asked, a fatherly smile on his face.

"I'm ready," Gilles replied, wondering if the smile was sincere and if his voice sounded normal to Ste Germaine's ears.

They all set off for the church in Ste Germaine's fine carriage. LaRue was nowhere in sight today and no one mentioned his name. Memories of the evening before still refused to leave Gilles, even though he was on the way to his own wedding and under any other circumstances would have had more than enough other things to think about.

When they arrived at the church, Ste Germaine went inside after embracing Gilles. Ordinarily it would have been a nice gesture, but today it made Gilles uncomfortable and he had to wonder if Ste Germaine sensed his malaise. Perhaps Jean knew or perhaps not, but after Ste Germaine was gone, Jean made a brief comment to Gilles that it was a good thing that LaRue was not there.

Jean and Gilles walked to the front of the church and the clergyman smiled at Gilles. There would be no long church service first, no Latin, no incense, no attendants, and no crowds other than the good neighbors of Amsterdam. There was no sign of Elsje or her family either, and for a few panicked moments, Gilles worried that he had been rejected by a prospective bride once again. The last time that happened, the soldiers came and took him away and now he nervously looked over his shoulder at the front door and wondered where the door behind the clergyman led if he and Jean had to find an escape route again.

Jean leaned over and whispered, "It's all right; we *are* a little early. You aren't thinking of running from Elsje already, are you?"

Gilles gave Jean a weak smile but the anxious feeling wouldn't leave him. More people entered the church now, filling it up row by row, cutting off any escape through the front door. Gilles was starting to feel faint when at last he heard the family entering at the door.

Hendrick came in first, barking commands over his shoulder, followed by Tryntje and then Cousin Vroutje shepherding the noisy little ones in front of her. Cousin Vroutje's husband, grown son, and daughter-in-law followed with their own two small children. They all took their seats quickly, except for Hendrick, who went back to the front door and returned with Elsje. She was breathtakingly beautiful in a blue silk dress with lace trim at the neck and sleeves, her hair up on top of her head and not just pulled back severely under an old cap. Her hair had a jeweled pin in it and a bit of lace and in her hands she carried a small, worn book of prayers.

"You are mine," Gilles thought breathlessly, and his panic left him but not the shaky feeling. He took Elsje's hand when Hendrick handed it to him and Elsje smiled up at Gilles. Although the church was cool, even with the fire going, his hand was damp with perspiration so he gripped her hand tighter to steady himself. He wished now that he had taken just a little bit more of the wine although he wasn't sure if he needed to use the outhouse or not. He ignored the contradictory signals from his bladder and tried to focus on what the clergyman was saying but he could not seem to hear the words although the minister had been talking now for several minutes about the sanctity of marriage and the blessings of children.

Gilles was grateful now that Elsje was not a Calvinist. The severity of the sect and the rigidity of their strange rituals would have been too much for him to suffer. He reminded himself that a good Calvinist would not want one such as him anyway, someone with a history of Catholicism but no reformation fervor to convert others.

The clergyman paused for a moment before he went on in a slightly louder voice, reading several sections of the Bible in Nederlands. Gilles began to feel light-headed again but he caught a glimpse of Jean's face and his friend's visage bolstered and reassured him. There was a trace of a smile on Jean's lips and Gilles thought that Jean must be either smiling in amusement or contentedly counting up the dollars of some future profit. Hendrick looked pleased, too, and after what seemed like too long, when Gilles thought he must either sit down or fall down, the minister changed the tone of his voice again and went into the vows. Gilles wondered if he still had the ring and checked his pocket surreptitiously. He felt it there and consequently, he relaxed a little, but while his concentration was on finding the ring, he almost missed the part of his vows that he needed to hear and respond to.

"Do you?" the clergyman asked Gilles again.

"Ja," Gilles answered.

"Yes, he does," the clergyman repeated as if to correct him and to ensure that the ceremony was valid. He continued, turning to Elsje, and Gilles wondered how she had the fortitude to go on with all of this.

"I do and I will," Elsje spoke loudly, obviously familiar with this service. She looked at Gilles, with certainty of her answer but at the same time, almost shyly, Gilles thought with some surprise.

At this point in the ceremony though, the proceedings were interrupted by five Spanish soldiers who clanked their way noisily into the church.

"What goes on here?" The captain shouted in peculiarly accented Nederlands.

"What does it look like? It's a wedding!" the clergyman said indignantly.

"We are looking for enemies of the state and we saw one run in here for sanctuary." The soldiers apprised all of the guests as well as the wedding party. "Pretty bride," the captain said, leering at Elsje.

Gilles stepped between the captain and Elsje and Jean stepped forward as well.

"Whatever escaped undesirables you seek, I assure you, they are *not* here among Amsterdam's *finest* citizens," Jean said to the Spanish captain. Jean's manner took the captain aback and after glaring for a moment at Jean, the Spaniard swept the assemblage one more time with his eyes.

"It had *better* be so," he said in his thick accent, "or the happy couple won't live long enough to create any more Netherlander vermin!"

The captain turned to his small company of men and jerked his head toward the door, sheathing his sword as he led the way out.

The clergyman resumed the ceremony, never losing his place or saying a word about the interruption. Gilles' trembling fingers placed the ring without incident and the requirements having been met, the minister then finished the ceremony.

"This couple has now been joined in the church before God and country. Let this union be sealed now by a token ring, a kiss, and your witness, in person and on the marriage document. And let all of us now go forward and create as many

Netherlander vermin as we can, to throw off the repression of the ever-present Spanish bastards. Amen."

An eruption of snickering approval, guffaws, and a few shocked whispers took attention away from Gilles' tentative kiss on Elsje's cheeks and lips. There was an atmosphere of celebration but also of general relief from the spectators, especially from Elsje's family group. Her father raced over to be the first to witness the wedding document and he gathered the other witnesses as quickly as he could, not even allowing them time to congratulate the couple first. Hendrick was so intent upon completing the legal requirements that the bottom of the page forever after showed the ink stains repeating the witnesses' signatures backwards on the opposite side where Hendrick had grabbed it up too quickly after the signing, folded it in half, and put it into his pocket without giving it sufficient time to dry.

"Msr. Hendricks!" Ste Germaine called out to him. "Allow Gilles and his bride to return to the reception in my carriage and Msr. Durie and I will ride there with you." His heavy French accent echoed through the church.

"All right, thank you Msr., ah, Ste Germaine is it?" Hendrick agreed, smiling his great missing-toothed smile at him. Hendrick led the way over to the old wagon. "It's not grand like yours, Msr. Ste Germaine. I borrowed it from my neighbor and sometimes use it for getting supplies when I need them."

"I am sure that it will get us there all right." Ste Germaine assured him but Gilles wasn't too sure that the one old horse could carry the great load of family members.

The group all fit themselves into the wagon, more like eggs in a pail than people in a conveyance; Jean Durie, Ste Germaine, and Hendrick squeezed into the front seat and everyone else, Hendrick's children, Cousin Vroutje and her family all in the back on the wagon bed. Gilles could not get over the sight of Ste Germaine sitting in the driver's seat of the decrepit old wagon and had to suppress what might otherwise have turned quickly into uncontrollable laughter. The boards in the back of the wagon sagged with the weight and perhaps sensing this, Cousin Vroutje's insisted that she, her husband, and her son would walk to Hendrick's, even refusing the offer from Gilles and Elsje to ride in Ste Germaine's coach.

Before the overloaded wagon pulled away though, Hendrick delayed their departure for a moment as he ran back into the church. When he returned, Ste Germaine asked him if he had forgotten something.

"Ja!" Hendrick replied. "I forgot to ask the fugitive hiding there to our reception; he declined though."

Ste Germaine laughed heartily and clapped him on the shoulder saying, "A rascal after my own heart, you are Hendrick!"

Gilles helped Elsje inside after the driver opened the door to Ste Germaine's fine carriage, climbing in after her as he tried to assimilate the new reality that he now had a *wife*. When Gilles sat down next to her, he could feel her thigh through the blue dress and he moved even closer. Elsje seemed not to notice this intimacy but was looking over all the accoutrements of the cab interior as the coach was probably much grander than anything Elsje had ever seen up close. There were leather straps to hang onto during rough journeys and footstools that pulled out from under the seats on leather hinges. The seats were made of leather and everywhere there was brass ornamentation, polished to a golden shine. Real glass windows, not just roll-down blinds, afforded a view as they rolled along and here and there were little compartments for storage of whatever one desired to store there. Small lanterns attached to the walls could be lit after dark and red velvet and damask upholstered the walls, ceiling and curtains at the windows. The conveyance was even grander than Gilles' father's best coach at home and he was greatly amused to see his new wife's astonishment as she took it all in.

As the carriage moved forward, Gilles asked, "Would you like me to buy you one of these?" He smiled at Elsje, taking her hand in his and pressing it to his lips.

"What would I do with one of these other than ride it home from a wedding? Perhaps if you die and I marry again I would need such a carriage for *that* ceremony."

Gilles pulled her hand up and placed it on his breast. "Now you have wounded me with this sad vision of the future! What makes you think anyone would have you but me? Ah, but I *do* want you for my wife! Can you feel my heart beating faster?"

Elsje pulled her hand away. "We have a reception to go to *first*, Gilles."

"And then?" Gilles took her hand up again and pressed it to his lips. He pressed his lips to her wrist.

"Stop! Behave now! I will have to always treat you as a child, I can see that now." She said this sternly but she smiled as she spoke.

"This child is impatient and wants time *alone* with you." Gilles moved his face close to hers and then kissed her.

She pushed him away after a brief kiss. "What will my father and our guests think? Stop, Gilles!"

"They will think that we are married and that it is a *happy* marriage."

"I should have known that you were like this," Elsje said sternly but a thinly disguised smile moved across her mouth. "One kiss then, to satisfy you for the moment, but you must behave yourself until we are alone again! We are almost there."

They kissed a short but passionate kiss and Gilles wondered again how she knew to kiss him that way. He wished now that she had not agreed to kiss him at all as it was not satisfying him but making the waiting for her all the more difficult.

The back room of the inn had been opened up for the feast and it looked more like a large meeting of the Dutch India Companies than a wedding reception. Ste Germaine had cornered one of the West India officers and another was standing with Jean Durie and Hendrick, part of a circle including five men that Gilles did not know very well, all talking about trade. Elsje's sisters and other women circled around her with much giggling and the two kitchen girls employed at Hendrick's brought trays of food out containing pineapple, marzipan, cakes and cheese, much of the food courtesy of Ste Germaine. Wine and ale were being consumed in great quantity too, even before Gilles and Elsje walked in. Elsje left Gilles to go giggle with Cousin Vroutje and Gilles stood alone at first, wondering whether he should join his wife or take part in the conversation with one of the groups of men. Jean took leave of the group he was in and walked over to Gilles, deciding the matter for him.

"Congratulations! Long and happy life, prosperity and many healthy heirs!" Jean handed him a glass of wine. "It is all set with Hendrick and Ste Germaine. You spend tonight at my home, in my bed, but tomorrow you are on your own, back at Hendrick's house. Did you tell Elsje yet?"

Gilles paled slightly but replied, "I ... I'll tell her soon."

Gilles thought that Elsje might be surprised, wonder at the change of venue or have already made other plans but she would surely appreciate some privacy for her on her wedding night, as long as Gilles could explain it to her in a delicate enough way that would not be offensive.

Four more men arrived that Gilles had not seen at the church and joined the trade discussion circle. Gilles wondered just how many people Hendrick had invited but he supposed that it did not really matter because he was not paying for it.

"All of these Nederlanders here! When they talk it sounds like a bundle of sticks stuck in a wagon wheel!" Jean laughed in Gilles' ear.

"Does anyone here speak French," Gilles asked, "besides the three of us and Elsje?"

"I have some *very* bad news for you, my friend. Unless you teach her, Elsje really knows very little and has a very hard time even following it. She has practiced a few phrases, and *that's all*. She fooled you about that, too?" Jean laughed heartily.

"Mmph," Gilles said over his wine.

"Don't worry; I'm sure you will be able to communicate well enough!"

Jean laughed out loud again and went off in search of another wine bottle to replace the empty one he held. Gilles was wondering how much wine Jean had consumed already to make him so convivial when Elsje came over and linked her arm in his.

"Husband, we have many gifts to open."

"*You* open the gifts, I will come and watch."

Gilles was happy to see that she was in such a good humor, but he still could not help but think of the great pile that there would have been in France. What were they going to give him, ale tankards? Elsje took his hand and led him over to the table where the great a variety of gifts had been placed: There were gifts of wine that were obviously last-minute thoughts and there were gifts that were very large and indicated much advance planning. There were plain packets that surely held money and elaborate wrappings that might have compensated for less than exciting gifts.

As each gift was opened, every gift giver was thanked with a kiss from Elsje and a handshake from Gilles. Hendrick gave the couple five hundred guilders and Elsje gave her father a big hug and kiss after she got over the shock of the large sum.

"It's just a bribe so your new husband won't run away from you in the first week!" Hendrick laughed, flush with the wine and the joy of pleasant company but Gilles wondered if he wasn't speaking the truth. Ste Germaine handed Gilles an envelope and Gilles found horsehair inside as well as one hundred guilders.

"Your new horse," Ste Germaine said with a flourish. "You can come to my country home and ride whenever you wish or keep it here in the city if you would prefer."

Everyone in the room oohed and aahed. A fine horse!

Although Gilles was thrilled with the present, he had to wonder how Elsje felt about it: A horse was something that she would *never* use, unless it pulled a wagon, and Gilles wasn't feeling much inclined to go alone to Ste Germaine's country house with him for *any* reason.

Ste Germaine was not finished though: He handed Elsje a small package which she opened after she smiled her thanks at him. A small silver and gold cream pitcher was inside the wrappings, a gift at the same time totally practical but too ostentatious to use and Gilles *knew* what Elsje was thinking: When would she *ever* use such a thing? Gilles could see that she was less than impressed with it but she thanked Ste Germaine graciously with kisses on both cheeks. Gilles studied Ste Germaine's face as she did so, but he detected no revulsion on his employer's features from the touch of a woman.

"Open Christian's! He gives the *best* gifts!" one of the crowd called out and the cry was taken up by the others. "Open Christian's! Open Christian's!"

Christian the trader smiled a secret smile, took a breath of tobacco smoke from the stem of his pipe, and pointed over to a package wrapped in leather. A large, heavy, square object reaching almost to Gilles' knees was pulled out of the pile and placed at Elsje's feet. She untied the bright fabric ribbon and Gilles wondered, even after it was unwrapped, what the piece might be. It was a dark and beautiful wooden box, the height and width being close in their dimensions although it was slightly less deep. A square of richly polished wood on the face of it was ornamented by an inlaid hexagon of lighter wood and small lock and key secured the hinged front of it. The small piece of furniture had feet on the bottom and Gilles still couldn't guess what the item's purpose was. It was too small for a desk and it probably wasn't a jewelry box. Starting with Elsje first and then moving through the spectators from front to back, everyone noticed that it had a scent to it as well and when Elsje opened the little door, rows of little drawers were revealed. Several people gasped in awe of the fine carpentry work and then a few in the front row took the scent in again, an assortment of fragrances eddying around them.

"There is no star in the east and no baby *yet*," one man joked at the extravagance.

Elsje pulled one drawer open and exclaimed, "Oh, it's a *spice box*! It's wonderful! I will have so many new recipes to try!"

Elsje threw her arms around Christian's neck as Hendrick moaned, "And all of them will be tried on *me,* as well as her new husband!" This elicited inebriated laughter from the crowd

"Elsje's reputation as a cook is known throughout the *country*, if you don't know it yet," one man said authoritatively to Gilles. "She hasn't had a bad recipe *yet* and I'll be the *first* to volunteer to try any new ones."

Gilles thought doubtfully of the pastry and spicy clam dish but he said nothing in reply to this resounding endorsement of his wife's cooking. He *was* slightly worried at Hendrick's comment but he guessed that he would survive her experiments until the spices ran out. Elsje kissed the volunteer taster too, as well as Christian once again and Gilles wondered if she was getting a little too liberal with the kisses and partaking of too much wine. Elsje had nearly finished an entire glass in spite of being busy with gifts and Gilles could not recall ever seeing her drink anything more than a few sips of ale at one time, and that was with dinner.

Jean Durie held up a newly-opened bottle of wine and as he filled his own glass and the glasses of several men around him he called out, "Open my present next! It's the pink one."

Jean's gift was the one gift that Gilles had been most looking forward to; Elsje opened the fabric box, the pretty packaging no doubt from the shop where Gilles had bought the cases for Elsje's ring and pearls, and primarily selected to appeal to Elsje. Inside was a beautiful glass vase with silver overlay.

"It's lovely, Jean!" Elsje seemed truly taken with the delicate vase and she kissed him, then set it down very carefully on the table with the other opened gifts.

"The very finest from Amsterdam's finest glass makers but that's not all," Jean smiled a mysterious smile at her.

"No?" She smiled back at him uncertainly.

Jean picked up the vase and handed it to Gilles. "No. I charge your new husband with keeping this vase *always* filled with flowers or gifts for you and your home always filled with loving thoughts of you."

"Ooooh!" Several of the women sighed and more than a few of them were looking at Jean Durie with renewed interest.

"I will, Jean, and thank you," Gilles said in Nederlands for the room's benefit and he embraced Jean in thanks, after which he placed the vase back on the table, a little disappointed and puzzled but ready to move on.

"That's not *all*." Jean continued to smile at Gilles.

"No?" Gilles wondered what could be next.

"There is a piece of paper inside the vase, and it needs to be read."

Gilles carefully pulled out the document and unfolded it. Puzzlement covered his face followed by enlightenment. "It's a deed! A deed in ... *New Amsterdam*?" Gilles made the effort to look happily surprised and he hoped that it was not already too late.

"Yes. A plot of land for you with a house already on it. You can have it farmed, rent it out, whatever you like."

Now the men of both India Companies oohed and aahed and pushed forward, in front of the women who had formerly occupied the first rows of the celebrants.

"It's *good* land!" one cried. "I know the plot right next to it and it is wonderful farmland!"

"It's right on the main trail to the northern trade lands!"

"The Savage's trail? Really?!" The men nearly crowded Gilles out in their effort to see it. "Is there a map somewhere?"

"It is! It's on Heere Street, the broad way, next to the stream!"

Jean smiled a self-satisfied smile but Gilles wondered what on earth he was going to do with a piece of land a world away that he was never going to see.

"Jean always gives me the *most* unusual gifts, like the wampum belt," Gilles said good-naturedly.

"*You* have a wampum belt? Zewant?" One man gazed pop-eyed at him.

"I've been trying to get one for years!"

"Will you sell it? How much do you want?"

Their reaction shocked and surprised Gilles who thought these men must not have a very good grasp of reality, even without the dubious benefits of the wine and ale that flowed so freely today. He made a mental note to see how much he might sell it for, just out of curiosity, but for Jean's benefit he said, "Of course I would *never* consider selling my friend's gift to me."

The men resumed reading the deed again, word by word, passing it around among themselves and pointing out interesting parts as Elsje went over to Jean to deliver another thank you kiss.

"That is *very* nice, Jean."

Gilles embraced his friend again, too. "Thank you, Jean."

Gilles' dark mood, which had dispersed for a short time with the festivities, had now returned. He thought of the land that he *should* have had deeded to him on this day, his wedding day. He should have had fields and vineyards in France and perhaps would have had *several* horses as well as many, many, more gifts. When everyone had turned their attention to the next gift, he swallowed the next glass of wine in a single gulp, hoping to bolster his flagging mood.

"Is anything the matter, Husband?" Elsje whispered to him, taking notice of something amiss.

"Nee, it has just been a long day." His lips brushed her hair and he did feel better.

Jean joined Gilles at his other side.

"Stop sulking!" Jean whispered in his other ear. "Your life could have been *much* worse; you might not have lived to see this day at all!"

Gilles nodded. Jean was right, of course. Gilles was acting like a spoiled and ungrateful child. Gilles took control of his emotions, poured himself another glass of wine and after he put his hand on Elsje's back, his mood *did* start to improve.

It took some time but finally all the gifts were opened and Gilles and Elsje went in to the wedding feast which had in reality already been going on for some time with the guests helping themselves to the fruits and cheeses without waiting for the bride and groom.

If Gilles thought that the French easily claimed first place in their ability to consume food and drink, he discovered now that he was greatly mistaken: Between Elsje's kitchen, Cousin Vroutje's kitchen, and Ste Germaine's kitchen, it was nearly impossible to have just a taste of every dish, let alone to eat any great quantities of it and then have room left for anything more, but they did have several days to go, days in which they could attempt this feat. Most of the Dutch guests gravitated toward the Netherland dishes but a few sampled Ste Germaine's food out of curiosity and there were now enough French expatriates in the room to make sure that none of the food was going to go to waste. They continued to eat and drink and talk and joke throughout the day and Gilles was surprised again and again at the amounts that even the thinnest or the youngest of the guests could consume.

Gilles avoided all of the pastries and desserts at first because he was not sure who had prepared them, but Ste Germaine had ordered his cook to make some, and even supplemented those with some he had ordered from the French bakeries in the city, which he had pronounced "acceptable". When Gilles was at last assured of their origins, he happily indulged himself in the sweets. He really had very little choice in his diet today as he was set upon by guests whenever his plate or his glass even *approached* empty and if he set his drink down even for a moment, someone always picked it up and handed it back to him, scolding that he wouldn't want anyone to think that he couldn't drink any more. Indeed, if Gilles wanted to *drink* less, he had little choice but to *eat* more. Most of the celebrants were going to stay for as long as there was more to drink and Hendrick had put in supplies above and beyond the usual, calculated to last for at least four days. Ste Germaine had also contributed many bottles of wine to the cause as well, even though bier and ale were the drinks of choice for most of the guests.

"It *is* good wine but not *quite* what I need for my customers," Ste Germaine had confided to Gilles when Gilles had exclaimed over yet another gift from him. "It's the perfect occasion to donate my wine to less sensitive palates, even more so because they have already consumed so much. *You* make sure that you drink from that case over there though; it's better."

It wasn't until hours after darkness had fallen on the first day of the wedding feast that a few of the guests finally began to leave the inn to go and get some rest. The wives of the East and West India Company men had taken advantage of the occasion to show off the latest styles in their new dresses and hats and in order to showcase both the costume and the performance, each attempted as dramatic an exit as possible. The India Companies' men stayed on though, well after their wives had already left alone, lingering over the drink and talk of business propositions for the coming year. Those guests who had left to attend to pressing duties at home for a time were not leaving for good though; they would return sooner or later for more revelry. The little inn overflowed with guests but the turnout was to be expected considering the Netherlanders' love of celebration and the fact that everyone in the city seemed to know either Elsje or Hendrick's inn.

Ste Germaine was one of the first to leave, and after embracing Gilles and Jean, and announcing loudly to Gilles that the same wonderful food could be had *every* day at *his* eating establishment, he was gone, rushing to salvage what was left of his business that had no doubt been reduced to complete ruin during his short absence.

The Netherlanders looked askance at each other, surprised at the groom's employer's leaving so early, but probably concluded that, being French, his rude behavior was not at all surprising, and in fact, was to be expected.

Gilles' disposition was better now than it had been: There was the drink of course and then, looking over at the waistline of Elsje's blue dress, he remembered that he was about to get the only gift that he *really* wanted from this entire production. He crossed the crowded room and kissed Elsje on the back of her neck even though he was very much aware that Hendrick was watching him. Ordinarily this scrutiny would have made him uncomfortable in the extreme, but now it only served to make him more impatient to take Elsje away with him to Jean Durie's. The quantity of drink he had consumed combined with the boisterous crowd had put Gilles in a belligerent and confrontational mood. He left Elsje momentarily and strode over to Hendrick.

"You have our money gifts and our marriage document?" Gilles asked him.

"Yes, I have them and I can keep them safe for you," the old man offered.

"The document is mine and I will have it now."

Gilles held out his hand. He would just feel better having it in his possession: It was not only a license to the country's benefits to which he was now entitled, it was also his claim to Elsje. The part of Gilles that no longer trusted in the intentions of men irrationally worried that the old man could misplace it, either accidentally or intentionally, make an accusation of rape and then turn Gilles over to the authorities just to keep the wedding gifts and his daughter for himself. Although this was unlikely in the extreme, if only due to the many witnesses alone, Gilles would just feel better if he had the paper in his own pocket.

Hendrick did not argue, though. He shrugged and handed the document over to his new son-in-law. Gilles tucked it into the inside breast pocket of his coat and looked around for Elsje but before he found her again, Jean found him.

"Go to my place whenever you are ready, Gilles; I already brought my things over to Ste Germaine's."

"You are a true friend, Jean."

"It's nothing. You would do the same for me, I'm certain of it."

Jean joined Hendrick who was standing a few feet away, the targeted audience of a drunken man expounding on his belief that the quality of Ming china no longer justified paying the escalating prices in the marketplace.

Hendrick seized upon the distraction of Jean's arrival to turn in Gilles' direction and silently mouth the words *"Remember your promise!"*

Gilles had already waited so long now, and a week afterwards wouldn't be *too* bad. He had always waited a week between visits from Hannah. Gilles said nothing in reply but took another drink as he turned away. Gaining no further satisfaction or argument, Hendrick reluctantly returned his attention to Jean and the drunk.

Gilles had decided that the time had definitely come to leave and he didn't much care anymore if anyone thought he was rude. He found Elsje in a circle of women, and holding her fast by her upper arm, he moved his lips over her hair, feeling the softness of it before he whispered to her.

"I want to get acquainted with my new wife now," he whispered to her.

Elsje blushed. "It's so early ..." she began.

"Do you want me to go away and come back?" he asked her.

"Nee. Just let me clean some of this up."

"Let someone *else* clean it up, just for this *one* day."

Elsje shook her head though, smiling up at him as she picked up a few plates and carried them out to the kitchen where Cousin Vroutje, Tryntje, and a few other women washed the dishes and attempted to stay ahead of the constantly accumulating mess. Gilles watched from a safe distance as Jean led a distracted Hendrick away, still trying to talk to the old man about trade but all the while Hendrick kept his eyes fixed on Gilles.

Gilles made a note to himself to get a full accounting of the cash gifts later and to make sure that none of it got lost in Hendrick's pockets, even if Gilles had to personally thank each donor himself, mentioning the guilder amounts as he did so. Hendrick would know by now, though, that Gilles was no fool with accounts and it would not be wise to forget to turn over any portion of it.

Jean had dragged Hendrick over to another group of men that was heatedly discussing the current situation with the savages and what percentage of the WIC's profit was being lost in the ongoing attacks on the New Amsterdam colony. Gilles listened in from a distance as he waited for Elsje to return from the kitchen.

"We need to reach an agreement," Jean declared, "To get them to work *with* us."

"Bah! They have no loyalty, they are *animals!*" Hendrick declared. "Their loyalty is to the highest bidder, us today, the English tomorrow, and the Swedes next week! Governor Kieft is right to exterminate as many of the heathens as possible. They just get in the way of our expansion, our cultivating the land and getting our just profit!"

"*Every* man has his price. They *know* the land and they can help us with mapping it out and finding the *best* beaver and fur. Do you not think they could *increase* our profits if we offered them sufficient compensation?" Jean asked.

"That's crazy! Why should we pay them *anything* for land that we have already made claim to *and* purchased from them? We have the document, we paid them the money! Besides, the fur is not that difficult to find; it is everywhere, there for the taking!"

Elsje returned from the kitchen and a stop upstairs as well. She was carrying with her a bundle of clothing, her cloak, and Gilles' cloak.

"Are you *finally* ready?" Gilles asked her but he smiled as he said it.

He took her elbow, hopeful that Jean's presence would distract Hendrick long enough for them to make their escape but her father had noticed Elsje, surmised their intentions, and called across the room to his daughter.

"It's rude to leave so early, Elsje!" Hendrick admonished her. He had had too much to drink to care about the laughter and rude remarks his comment educed from his drunken guests.

"I'm *tired*, Father! It's been a long day and I'm going to rest with my husband. I'll see you in the morning." Elsje kissed her father's forehead as she and Gilles passed him on their way to the door. "Take care of him for me, Jean!"

"I will. Don't worry, we'll be just fine," Jean replied. He nodded encouragement at Gilles and motioned behind Hendrick's back for Gilles to keep going out of the door.

Gilles pushed through the crowd of well-wishers, helping Elsje on with her cloak and putting his own on while they walked. Once they were both bundled up against the cold night, he took the clothes from Elsje. They both ignored the good-natured cheers and rowdy taunts of the guests as they closed the door to the inn behind them. Bits of ice came down through the air, stinging their faces as they traveled up the street toward Jean Durie's house.

"Does the ring fit you?" he asked, thinking that he should say *something* to her.

"Well enough, Gilles. It is beautiful."

"I can have it fixed."

"It fits."

Gilles was impatient now and he took her hand with his free one in an attempt to hurry her up the slippery street. Elsje thanked him for helping her.

When they reached Jean's house, Gilles opened the door to the dark apartment and was surprised to find that now he felt a little bit nervous. Elsje seemed to be her calm and confident self but Gilles noticed that her hand shook as she fumbled at her cloak strings. A knock came at the door immediately after they entered and Gilles went to see who it was.

"Msr. Gilles, shall I light the lamps and fix the fire?" the servant girl asked. "I hadn't expected you back so soon."

"Yes, that will be fine."

Gilles was impatient with the interruption but it *was* cold in the room. His feet were chilled and Elsje's probably were, too.

"I'll be back right away then," the girl said.

Gilles had a few moments now to decide how he was going to approach his wife. He had never before been with a woman who had *no* experience with men and it *was* a little awkward: After all, Elsje had been his friend long before she became his wife and being with her was going to be different from now on. In a way, approaching her would be more difficult than approaching any other woman: He would have to have some consideration of her feelings, for one thing.

"I've never stayed anywhere else overnight before," Elsje confided to Gilles. "This is Jean's home? It's nice here."

The servant girl returned from across the hall, carrying a lamp and a scuttle with hot coals in it. She lit two lamps from hers before she searched the hearth for remaining embers and then shoveled a few of her own into the front room fireplace, quickly building a fire for them. She soon had a blaze going and while Elsje and Gilles warmed themselves and made small talk about the wedding and feast, the servant started the fire for them in the bedroom fireplace.

After she had finished with her work, the girl said to Gilles, "This should do for the night. You can call for me later if you need me; otherwise I won't be back until after you leave tomorrow."

As she said this, she blushed and averted her eyes and Gilles knew then that Jean had taken care of *every* detail, including her instructions. The girl picked up her lamp and scuttle and hurried out of the room.

Gilles latched the door after her and took off his confining new shoes. He noticed that Jean had left out two bottles of good wine and two glasses, for which Gilles was very grateful. He opened the wine up and poured two glasses but Elsje shook her head at the offer so Gilles set her glass down on the table. He wanted, needed, just one more drink as the effects of the earlier drinks had completely worn off with the passage of time, the great quantity of food he had consumed, and the walk in the cold. Gilles wanted Elsje to have at least one drink with him too, but he wouldn't bother her about drinking it right away.

Elsje was exploring the little sitting room, as curious about Jean's collection as Gilles had been on his first visit. Gilles knew that she probably needed a little time and space to get comfortable with the idea of being alone in a room with a man that she was about to …

Gilles came up behind her and put his arms around her waist. He kissed her cheek and pulled her closer to him.

"Are you cold?" he asked her. "The heat hasn't come over into this room yet."

"Nee," she said but her voice shook a little.

"I'll warm you."

He held her for a short time and then started pulling pins out of her hair, setting them down on a table.

"So many pins …" he mused.

He pulled a stray lock of her hair out of place and ran it through his fingers before he kissed her forehead and her cheek, then her lips. Elsje was trembling slightly and he could feel this as he took her by the hand and led her into the bedroom.

He kissed her once again.

"*You* smell like wine." She giggled a little.

"Then we must both have some more!"

Gilles went out to the other room and returned with the two full glasses. "Drink!" he said to her as he handed Elsje the glass. She had a sip but she was still giggling and it was hard for her to drink any more without spilling it or choking.

"Am I *that* comical then?" He straightened up in mock injury.

"I … I can't help it! I just start laughing sometimes when I'm …" Elsje giggled harder than ever after a gulp of the wine. Gilles took his glass and hers and set them both down on the bedside table, then turned back to her, putting his arms around her.

"There is only one cure for that."

"W-what? Mmmphm!" Elsje tried even harder to stifle her giggles.

"I will see if you are ticklish. Maybe I can tire you out so much that you won't be able to laugh any more."

He reached around her with one arm, pinning both of her arms in the process and tickled her on other side with his free hand. Elsje squirmed and jumped, fending him off as she continued to laugh.

"You are so foolish!" she said. "That's what comes of marrying one so young."

"Ah, perhaps you are right."

He was wounded in pride only slightly but he removed his hands and paused to take another sip of wine. He offered his new wife some but she shook her head.

"Hmm. I guess the more time we spend on wine, the less time we have for other things. Maybe I will just finish this glass and be done with any more wine for tonight."

As if in response to his statement, Elsje picked up her glass of wine.

"Ah-ah! Don't spill my wine!" she said teasingly to him.

"Not on that beautiful dress. You look *so* good in it," Gilles complimented her.

She *did* look wonderful in it and Gilles was glad that he would be able to take her out of this particular dress and was glad that it would be tonight, glad that he would not have to wait any longer. Gilles took a last sip of his wine and put it down on the table. He took Elsje's glass from her without protest and set that down as well.

"Are your feet cold?"

Gilles led her over to the arm chair next to the bed and knelt in front of her, removing her wet shoes.

"They must be frozen!" he exclaimed. He ran his hands over her feet, rubbing them for a short time until he asked with a mischievous grin, "What else is ticklish?"

She braced herself, waiting for him to start tickling her feet but instead he ran his hands up over her ankles, calves, and knees

"I don't know," Elsje whispered and now she seemed a little breathless.

She was just sitting, looking at Gilles with very wide eyes. He had never seen her eyes so wide or her hair down before and he liked the way it looked in the lamplight. He reminded himself that she was probably nervous and that he mustn't move too fast for her.

"I'm afraid I'll do something to your dress, tear it or spill wine on it. May I take it off now?" he asked her.

Elsje didn't answer him. She suddenly stood up and walked away, standing with her back to him, facing a painting of a woman in a garden. She just stood there with her arms crossed over her chest, rubbing her upper arms as if to warm them.

Gilles wasn't sure what to do next so he waited for a few moments, trying to discern what the best course of action would be. Did she need encouragement, time, or persuasion?

"I feel ... strange."

She took a few deep breaths but then she turned back to Gilles. "I *like* you, Gilles Montroville. Don't take it as my *not* liking you. I just ..." her voice fell away with her eyes.

Gilles walked over to her and took her hand firmly in his. "We have been friends, ja?"

"Ja." She looked up at him and smiled. There was no question about that.

"You *did* agree to marry me?"

"Ja."

"And you don't find me ... repulsive in any way?"

"Nee." She smiled at him but her eyes still had difficulty in meeting his.

Gilles took both of her hands in his and put them behind his own back. He moved his hands around her waist and pulled her close to him again. He touched her lips with his briefly and then kissed her with a more serious kiss. Elsje's response was to take his forearms in her hands and step back a step, holding him at arm's length away from her.

She smiled up at him, an obligatory kind of smile. "Gilles, I ..."

She didn't finish the sentence though, so Gilles decided to give her a little more time. He reached into his breast pocket, wondering what he was going to do if she was not going to come willingly to him. He brought out the marriage contract and set it down on the table next to the wine glasses. Her eyes fell to it briefly before she looked back at Gilles. Still she said nothing.

He took off his coat while he waited for her to say something to him. He unbuttoned his vest slowly, a button at a time so as not to frighten her, removed it and put it on the chair with his coat. He picked up his glass of wine once again and offered her hers. This time she accepted, drank deeply and then put her glass down.

Elsje stepped up to Gilles and kissed him, a slow kiss that gained momentum. After the kiss, she moved a step back again and took the pearls off, depositing them carefully on the table beside the bed before she started to undo the buttons on her dress. Gilles helped her and kissed her again, reminding himself not to go too fast for her. After all, she was not Hannah; thank God she was not Hannah. He had some difficulty with the fastenings at her cuffs due to the small fabric loops that held the tiny buttons. When the sleeves were undone at last, Elsje slipped her dress off, putting it on the chair over Gilles' vest. She was quiet and serious now. She kissed Gilles as he puzzled over the fastenings on her undergarments. He had never seen so many undergarments on a woman before but knowing that there were just a finite number of ways that they *could* be fastened, he solved the puzzles in the dim light and removed everything down to Elsje's chemise. Elsje still kissed him but seemed more uncomfortable than ever now.

"Are you all right with me so far?" Gilles asked.

"I just, no one has ever seen me, without … it's silly. We're *married*."

"No, it isn't silly. Do you want the lamps out?"

"Some of them?" she asked.

Gilles extinguished the lamp in the bedroom. He did understand that the quality of their future relationship could very well depend largely on how she would remember this night. He was glad that he had the patience and restraint that he had needed so far but it was getting more and more difficult to be patient with her with each passing minute. Gilles took the rest of his clothes off except for his shirt and dropped them onto the chair.

"Elsje, come into the bed with me. It's cold out there."

He slid under the covers, holding her hand and pulling her along with him as the featherbed billowed up around them. He pulled off his shirt, his last item of clothing, and tossed it over to the chair before he slid the last of her clothing off. Elsje was as still as a stone statue.

"I want to lie next to you and hold you," Gilles said as he moved closer to her.

Elsje said nothing but he heard her take a few deep breaths.

Gilles held her for a time so she could get used to him and Gilles thought briefly of the horses that he had tamed in the past. She was like a wild thing, too, and he found that thought not unappealing. He kissed her as much as he wanted to now and they were both short of air when Gilles proceeded to satisfy the curiosity that had been building in him for the past few months. Gilles was as patient as he could be and at last when he finally went to Elsje, it was not so very difficult for him.

He believed that he was completely spent when he finally rolled over in exhaustion afterwards. Gilles tugged at the covers, pulling them up over her shoulders.

"Keep warm!" he said as he kissed her. "I don't want my wife to get sick."

"Was it all right then?" she asked.

"Mmmm. More than all right." Gilles closed his eyes, smiling in sweet memory, as he moved his fingers across her shoulder, feeling the smoothness of her skin. She was no Hannah, though, and now he asked her, "Did you like it, even a little, Elsje?"

"Satisfactory then?" she asked.

"Satisfactory?" Gilles opened his eyes, rolled up on his elbow, and looked into her face to see what she meant.

"You think we don't know what the French say about Netherlanders?"

"*What?*"

"You say we make many agreements and then never live up to them."

He hoisted himself up into a full sitting position. There was enough light from the fire for him to see her face but he still couldn't fathom what her meaning was.

"You thought that I wouldn't honor the contract and that's why you pulled it out of your pocket, to show it to me," she said.

"I pulled the contract out of my pocket so it would not get crumpled when I took my coat and vest off. I took my coat and vest off because the fire was making it too warm to wear them any longer."

Elsje said nothing more. She settled back on the pillow, clutching the covers to her neck and staring up at the ceiling. She didn't seem angry. She didn't seem anything at all, except cadaverous.

Gilles couldn't believe what his ears had just heard. "You just ... because you thought I had the contract out to ... to ..."

It was Gilles' turn to be short of breath, not in excitement, but in anger laced with panic. "You came to me because of the contract, not because you *wanted* to? So you were just honoring an agreement?"

Gilles lowered himself back down on his pillow, stunned, and the thought occurred to him that the scene was more reminiscent of two statues lying in eternal repose in some great marble cathedral than of a happy wedding bed. He shut his new wife out, a barrage of unhappy feelings and thoughts traveling as rapidly through his mind as the blood coursed through his veins. Hannah's teasing face passed through his mind briefly and Gilles had to wonder now if he had just made a terrible mistake in marrying Elsje, a mistake that he would have to live with for the rest of his life.

"Was there some trade bargain with my father, then?" Elsje spoke to him in a sharp tone. "I know it is easier to get better jobs and benefits if you marry one of us. They won't make you leave the country if you take a Netherlander for a wife."

Gilles reined in his emotions for the moment but in order to keep from losing his temper completely, he was only able to respond to her with a few terse sentences.

"There *was* no bargain. I asked for you, your father offered me Tryntje, and I insisted on you. I wanted to be with my wife tonight and I *thought* that you wanted to be with me, tonight, and *every* night."

"You made that up! He wouldn't offer you Tryntje, she's still a baby! We usually marry *much* later but Father despaired of *ever* finding a husband for me so you made a bargain, didn't you? It all happened on the *same* night: He got you the position at Ste Germaine's in exchange for marrying me."

Elsje still seemed calm enough, even cold. Gilles couldn't believe what she was saying and what he was hearing.

"As far as I know, they never even *met* each other until today!"

Exasperated and miserable, Gilles got out of bed and pulled his pants on. Far from wanting to celebrate now, he just wanted to drink for a good, long time. He only hoped that there was enough wine to get him thoroughly drunk so he wouldn't have to go into Jean's stock of other spirits. Gilles took up his half-empty glass, walked over to the fire, and stood looking into the flames, trying to control his feelings and gather his thoughts.

All was not lost: There *were* the advantages that Elsje had named, and of course there were always many more unhappy marriages in the world than happy ones. He could find other outlets for himself. Finally he spoke to her but he still didn't turn his face from the fire. He didn't want to look at her.

"I'm sorry you think that, Elsje; I wanted *you*. I didn't know that you were just fulfilling a contract out of some sense of obligation. I thought that you wanted me, too."

Sadness gathered over Gilles, a long line of clouds that reached at once forward into the future and at the same time back into France as well. He remembered that he had promised to fulfill a wedding contract once long ago but he had looked forward to it eagerly, not with a sense of obligation or doom. He had hoped that *this* wedding night, the one that had become a reality and not the great imagined one that had never come to pass, would finally drive away all of the old ghosts that had been following after him for so long.

Now Gilles realized that he had been wanting something that he craved above and beyond mere physical gratification: He wanted to feel the fullness of family again, to fill the empty spaces in his life with others, at the very least *one* other person to share his life and his future memories with him. Of course there was Jean Durie, but Gilles was not satisfied and wanted *more*, to build a new empire, starting on the foundation of a marriage and taking first a wife, then adding sons, eventually filling up a whole dining room.

The act of consummation, that brief moment of knowing that kind of joining, belonging, and fulfillment, of not being completely alone in the world, if it had passed through his being at all tonight, had been so fleeting that Gilles had not had the opportunity to take notice of it and now it was gone, lost to him forever. Gilles took another long drink from his glass and the only noise in the room now was from the popping of the fire.

The flames might have been his fate once. The fires had drawn a line, had separated his old, good, life from his miserable new one. This current existence seemed to offer no comfort to him and no permanent peace. Trapped in these thoughts, Gilles didn't even hear Elsje, not as she was leaving their bed, not when she was standing right next to him, not until she finally spoke.

"The French marry sometimes for money, isn't that right?" she asked. "We see that as an offense against God. But you wanted *me*?"

"Nee, I was just fulfilling my contractual obligation but I had hoped that I was enthusiastic enough in the execution of my duties," Gilles replied sullenly and sarcastically, not bothering to look at her as he took another gulp of the wine, his glass now completely empty.

Her hand slid around his waist to his chest and Gilles' heart leapt at the gentle touch. Putting the glass down on the mantle, he covered her hand with his, then turned around to face her, still holding her hand against his heart. She had only a thin bed covering around her, clutched to her neck with her other hand and she shivered as she stood there, searching his eyes for his true feelings or perhaps just more reassurance for herself.

"I just want to know," he asked, "how do you act when you are not simply fulfilling your legal obligations, when you really *do* want to be with someone?"

"Like this," she said and she kissed him the way she had in the churchyard.

After the kiss Gilles asked, "Could we ratify this contract again, then, just one more time?"

"I think it's our *duty*," she said and she kissed him once again.

Gilles was surprised to wake up during the night with a renewed craving for Elsje. He ran his hand over Elsje's arm and the curve of her body. Elsje sighed and turned over to face him, even though she was still more asleep than awake. He kissed both of her cheeks and joined with her again until she moaned a soft moan that made him stop.

"Am I hurting you?" he whispered.

"It's all right," she replied but she held onto him very tightly.

Gilles tried to slow himself and be gentle but in the end he could not. When he had finished he held her close to him.

She kissed his nose that was damp with sweat in spite of the frosty cold of the room. The fire was only embers now, no longer warming anything else in the room besides the grate. Elsje took up Gilles' hand and kissed the palm of it.

"Your hands are so different now: I remember looking at your hands when I first met you," she murmured.

Gilles felt his face redden in the dark and he thought about the calluses on his hands and the dirt under his fingernails that had not yet gone away. Maybe they would never go away, like the memories he had of prison, like the smell of the fires in France and the pervasive stink of working in the stable. He said nothing in reply but took up her hand and kissed it, a returning of affection. Her hands had calluses too, and he had never really taken notice of them before. He was not at all sure how he felt about that: Women were supposed to have *women's* hands, not laborer's hands, but Elsje's hands were not showpieces; they were strong and useful. He thought of his sisters briefly and then he thought of Marie and the tiny gold ring that she wore on her little finger. Gilles moved closer to Elsje, for warmth and to ward off these unwanted thoughts. At last he was able to drive the other faces from his mind and fall asleep again.

The next time he woke up it was lighter in the room. Elsje was moving slowly toward the edge of the bed.

"Where is my wife going?" he asked her.

"She goes back to the celebration and back to her work." Elsje replied.

"Work? Oh, no! We have *at least* two more days of feast, don't we?"

"Yes, that too, but I have to check on the inn also, Gilles."

Gilles panicked at the thought of her leaving so soon. If he had to wait an entire week before being with her again, he would need to take advantage of his time left before the wedding night officially ended.

"One kiss first, Elsje. Just one!"

She complied with his request but what started out as a friendly kiss turned into much more.

"Husband." Elsje spoke softly from beneath him.

There was no answer.

"Gilles, I *have* to go and check on the inn! I need to check on my father and the girls won't do *any* work at all if I am not there. *Gilles!*" She punched him in the arm.

Gilles groaned and rolled away from her. "All right! You don't have to hit me."

"Go and get my clean clothes."

"I can't. I need to rest for a moment."

"Gilles!"

"Elsje, we've been together all night long. I promise I won't look at you."

"You probably *will*; it's lighter now."

"You don't trust your husband not to look?"

"*Gilles!*"

The last "Gilles" had a tonal quality that Gilles knew only too well. He sighed and threw the covers aside, racing to get her clothing and return to the warm bed before he had a chance to feel much of the cold. Elsje had a strange look on her face when he returned and he realized that she had been watching him. Her lack of familiarity with the adult male form amused Gilles and he gleefully kissed her on the cheek.

"Anything for my new wife! Shall I get up again and get the fire going for you?"

He had no serious intention of standing out in the cold for very long with no clothing on but he thoroughly enjoyed the look on her face, the way that he had wrenched that calm self-control from her grasp for the moment.

"There is no need for that: I'm leaving here right now and *you* need to come back to the feast too, that is, if you want to stay on good terms with my father."

Elsje endeavored to dress herself completely under the covers but finding this too slow and difficult a process with her long skirts, she pushed the covers aside to finish dressing after her undergarments were in place. She dragged herself over to the edge of the bed and Gilles realized by her slow movements that she was in some pain from the night before. He didn't concern himself with this for very long though, and he stayed where he was with his arms tucked under his head, taking in and enjoying every line of her body while she finished dressing. Elsje couldn't help but notice his interest.

"I thought that you weren't going to look," she reminded him.

"That was only if you got out of bed with *no* clothes on," he smiled at her.

"You are a *wicked* man!"

Gilles replied with a Latin phrase from the Bible.

"What did you say? What language is that?" Elsje twisted her dress around into place and straightened the bodice.

"I was quoting the Bible, in Latin."

His sly smile told her that she might not want to venture into this territory. "Good, then you are ready to go to church with us this morning after we see to my father and the inn. I would *hate* to think that I married a man without *any* religious convictions." She pulled one stocking on.

Gilles grinned and threw the bedcovers back the rest of the way before he rolled out of bed again and ran over to his clothes. His rumpled clothes compared poorly to Elsje's fresh ones and Jean had been right about one thing: Gilles needed to get Elsje used to the idea of taking care of her new husband's needs.

"These clothes have some wine stains on them and I don't want to wear them to church. I'll go to Ste Germaine's to change but I'll meet you at the inn before it is time for services. Do we start drinking again *before* or *after* church?"

Elsje shook her head in mock vexation at him, already resigning herself to the fact that Gilles was Gilles, and it would be difficult to change him.

Wet snow had fallen during the night and the paving stones were covered with an icy glaze. The bushes and trees still had ice clinging to them and as the sun's early rays touched the icing, they were refracted, touching everything with tiny rainbow prisms of sparkling light. Gilles could not remember the earth looking any better or more magical to him: The world was a diamond-encrusted gem today and for a few moments, he was ashamed of the greedy and mundane thoughts that he had previously harbored regarding expected benefits from his wedding. He was not just lucky; he was privileged to live in this sacred space today, grateful to the heavens for the very simplest of things in his life this morning, the cold air in his lungs and his wife on his arm.

They made their way slowly over the treacherous streets with Elsje holding fast to Gilles. He was aware that she walked stiffly, as if recovering from an injury, and he felt a little remorse that he was the one to have caused her this pain, but then, strangely enough, these thoughts brought on an unexpected surge of desire in him once again. It was surely not very Christian to have these feelings and Gilles wondered if they might be the devil's doing, but whatever it was and wherever it came from, this morning his insatiable desire for Elsje would not leave him.

When they reached the inn, Gilles didn't enter but left Elsje at the front door, giving her a brief kiss and continuing on to Ste Germaine's where he found Jean Durie awake and fully dressed, preparing to leave.

"What are you doing up so early, Gilles? I would have thought that you would be in bed until noon." Jean winked at him.

"Elsje *insisted* on getting up. She thought they needed her at the inn."

"So they probably do!" Jean laughed. "You are still a happy man this morning?"

"Oui," Gilles answered with a smile and a wave of passion from the previous night echoed through him again. "Did you sleep all right here, Jean?"

"Non, but the night is over now. I trust that you left something of my bed?"

"Well, it *will* need some changing. How was Hendrick last night?"

"The man is obsessed with his daughter! He kept on saying, 'I should *not* have given my permission, I should *never* have given my permission.'"

"Really?" Gilles briefly considered not returning to the inn at all until later on in the day but he *had* promised Elsje that they would attend church together.

"Don't worry Gilles, it was just the drink talking. He can't believe that she is married, that's all. She's the first one of his children to be wed but he'll get used to it after he sits through four more weddings."

"Where is Ste Germaine this morning?"

"Still asleep in bed, I suppose." Jean tipped his head in the direction of the bedroom across the hall.

Gilles quickly changed into clean pants and a shirt and together he and Jean left Ste Germaine's to start their day. The pale sun had just started to come up and soften the icy streets and the walking was a little bit easier now. They trudged up the street until Gilles and Jean parted company at the intersection of the Jewish and Christian quarters. On his way back to the inn alone, Gilles thought

about Hendrick, hoped that the ale would be flowing, and that the old man
would be in a good mood.

Gilles needn't have worried though: When he arrived at the inn he found that
Hendrick was too preoccupied with Elsje to talk to anyone else at all, being overly
solicitous of his daughter and attempting to help her with everything she did
until she shooed him away like a persistent chicken in the pen.

Celebrants were still crowded into the inn's dining room and had either stayed
on their feet all night, slept for a few hours in the chairs, or left and then come
back very early, Gilles couldn't tell which. As long as the abundant supply of ale
and wine held out, the guests would be there, and would continue to fill their
tankards, thump Gilles on the back, and shake his hand in congratulations. In
their generally inebriated condition, Gilles wondered how anyone was going to
make it to the church, let alone stay awake and cognizant during the services.

Cousin Vroutje brought the younger children over to the inn for Elsje to take
them to worship but Vroutje poured a mug of ale for herself and then waded into
the crowd of celebrants. The guests all cajoled Elsje to skip church services this
one morning but she laughingly shook her head, not even considering it for a
moment. It occurred to Gilles now, that with the exception of the wedding ceremony, he had never seen Vroutje in church at all and he wondered briefly about
this. Maybe she belonged to another church or perhaps it was not a sin to miss
attending Protestant services. If attendance was not a requirement though, then
all of the people Gilles saw in Elsje's church went because they *wanted* to be
there. This was a very novel and alien idea to him.

Gilles was happy enough to take any excuse to get away from the inn, and not
just because of Hendrick, but also because he was running out of things to talk
about with the wedding guests. He had been cornered by a few women who were
probably a little curious about the foreigner Elsje had married, or perhaps they
were just trying to make him feel more welcome and at his ease. Gilles didn't
think he imagined it that Hendrick glared at him when the women were under
the age of forty, and the older women all seemed strangely interested in discussing childcare with him, a subject in which they should have known that Gilles
would have absolutely no interest at all.

The men had completely exhausted the subjects of weather, slow trade, and
the overseas colonies in the first few hours of the previous day, before they had
moved on to the incompetence of the councilmen at Leiden and heads of state in
general, their own exploits on their wedding nights, and what might be done
about the growing problem of outsiders and undesirables coming to live in the
city. With inhibitions being lowered to new depths from twenty-four hours of

drinking, they all seemed oblivious to the fact that Gilles might be a little uncomfortable discussing the latter subjects for obvious reasons. Gilles could see that even this early in the day, many of them were completely drunk and he did not believe that they could stay on their feet for even another *few* hours, but when he whispered this to Elsje, she just laughed and assured him that another three or four days of drinking would require no effort at all on the part of these seasoned veterans of so many other wedding feasts.

Elsje's little group walked slowly to church this morning and once they were all inside, Gilles slid into his seat, noting as he did so the many empty seats around them. *"Half of the town is probably still over at Hendrick's inn or else recovering,"* he thought.

Many in the congregation came over to congratulate Elsje and Gilles before services started, assuring them that they, too, would be going along to the inn afterwards to help them celebrate. The fireplaces warmed the air in the church but the hard wooden seats under them were icy cold on their backsides, so they kept their cloaks around them this morning. Gilles still found it difficult to get comfortable on the seats in Elsje's church: The wealthier families in Rouen all sat on velvet cushions in their reserved pews but in this church every seat was available to every man and every man was treated like one of the poor, to a plain, hard, wooden seat.

Occasionally the boy who tended the fire came forward to poke at it or to add some more peat. The boy's duties gave the less attentive worshippers one more way to gauge the service's progress and how soon it might be over: one stoking, two, three. The clergyman spoke this morning about the childhood of Jesus, as was customary at this time of year, but he seemed to be wholly uninspired by this subject and quickly transitioned to another biblical story in his sermon. This deviation from the liturgical calendar would not have been permitted in Gilles' church at home. When the man of God started talking about Jacob and Rachel, Gilles was certain that a smile was aimed in his direction.

"Laban told him that it was not their custom to give the younger daughter first, but Jacob *only* had eyes for Rachel. He might have married Laban's older daughter and said nothing at all, just to improve his lot in life, but he did not do that; Jacob was a man who was *honest* with other men as well as with himself. We don't know if Laban's plan was to discourage Jacob from marrying *any* of Laban's daughters at all; you see it was not their custom to intermarry. Jacob worked hard for his new father-in-law in spite of the unfairness of the situation and eventually all was well with them. If Laban had *only* informed Jacob as to their customs, they might have had a better understanding of each other from the very beginning."

Gilles remembered the night he had asked Hendrick for his permission to marry Elsje and wondered how the clergyman came to use this particular story today. Did the whole city know the details of Gilles' short and unusual courtship of Elsje?

The clergyman continued, "… where we see again the reference of a *stranger in a strange land*. Likewise we must deal fairly with *all* of the strangers among us, even those with whom no intermarriage is permitted."

Gilles wondered why the governors of Holland felt that it was necessary to pass such laws in the first place: Surely the Christian girls had no interest in the peculiar, unfashionable, and unkempt Jewish men. But then Gilles thought about Dirck and Jean Durie, both handsome, both elegant, both successful. Gilles was not at all sure that he liked being put into the same category with the Jews although he was fairly certain that the pastor meant no slight to him with his words.

After the clergyman had concluded the service he greeted the new couple warmly at the door as they left.

"God bless you both!" he cried before he kissed Elsje and wrung Gilles' hand.

Elsje beamed and Gilles had to smile too, so enthusiastic was his greeting.

"The Almighty had to look very far to find a match for two such *special* people, but he found a good union in the two of you, I am *certain* of this. Your father must be *so* pleased to have found such a good man for you, Elsje. It's just too bad that he was not here with us this morning. I trust he is well?"

Gilles found it difficult to suppress his laughter. He liked the minister; he was warmer and more human than any clergyman he had ever known, with the exceptions of Father Jogues and Claude, but Claude had been completely removed from the rest of humanity and now Gilles' friend could talk only to God.

"You will come to celebrate with us?" Elsje asked the minister of the church.

"Of course! I'll be over as soon as I bid my flock 'Goedemiddag'", he assured her.

"Congratulations on your wedding," said a voice behind them.

Gilles turned around to see Claes, Jacob's nephew, standing there.

"Thank you," Gilles said simply. He didn't know what else to say to him and he hoped that Claes wouldn't mention either Jacob or the stable in front of Elsje.

"You haven't introduced me, Gilles. Is this a friend of yours?" Elsje asked, looking the young man over with keen interest.

Claes held out his hand. "Claes," he offered.

"*Just* Claes?" Elsje asked him with a smile. "I'm Elsje Hendricks."

Claes smiled back at her. "You can call me Claes."

"Gilles, you did not tell me that you had friends who should have been invited to the wedding!" Elsje looked a little uncomfortable, even abashed.

"I, uh ..."

Claes replied quickly, "I could not have attended the ceremony, anyway."

"But you are free today to join us at the feast! You *will* come along with us now, ja?" Elsje already had linked her arm through Claes'.

Gilles had no great objection to Claes' coming along, although he was still not sure how he felt about Jacob's nephew. For too long Claes had been someone that Gilles feared and Gilles *still* wasn't convinced that he could trust him.

Claes was more than willing to go along with Elsje, probably for the food, and Gilles rationalized that he couldn't get into very much trouble with the motley crowd of villains and scoundrels they already had there. In fact, maybe it would be a *good* thing for Claes to accompany them: He might be able to make some excellent contacts with the power brokers at the feast and work his way into a good job so he wouldn't have to badger people all day at the docks to haul their goods or have dealings with smugglers in dark alleyways. If Claes was able to work himself into a position with one of the big companies, and Gilles had no doubt that he could, he might fit in quite well with the shylocks and thieves that were so liberally sprinkled throughout every level of both of the India Companies' corporations.

Outside the church, Elsje and Gilles were congratulated again and again by the other congregants while Tryntje flirted with Claes and the three smallest children wandered off into the crowd. When every hand had been shaken, Elsje rounded up the three younger children and berated Tryntje for not watching them more closely. Gilles and Elsje led the way home and the entire family group, Claes included, set off to the inn and the second day of the feast. The temperature had not gone up very much during the morning and the little ones complained about freezing feet and hands but hurrying back was out of the question this morning due to the slick city streets. Gilles helped his new wife by holding her elbow but Tryntje had difficulty in managing the three little ones who tried to keep up but frequently lost their footing.

Progress stopped completely for a time when Corretje fell down and started to cry. Her tears were dried and she was comforted by Elsje who glared at Tryntje over the little girl's head for not helping their littlest sister enough. Claes stepped into the breach and offered to take Jennetje up the street so that Tryntje could better manage Heintje and Corretje.

Gilles could see that Claes was one very astute person: He was very quick to offer his services and quick to seize an opportunity. Gilles had no doubt at all that Claes' fortunes in life could improve very quickly if he was just introduced into the right milieu.

When the church goers made it back to the inn, they went immediately to the fireplace to warm their hands and feet. Elsje didn't linger there for very long, though, before she left to oversee food preparations. Corretje and Heintje, for all their complaints and tears on the way home, thawed out very quickly and ran off into the throngs that were engaged in inebriated badinage, laughingly chasing other children and causing disturbances here and there as they bumped into people and knocked over plates of unattended food and mugs of ale. Tryntje left the warmth of the fire to bring an East India Company captain a fresh mug of ale as soon as she spied him across the room. Jennetje and Claes had found something to talk about while they continued to warm their hands and Gilles wondered if it was time to go find Hendrick and mend some bridges. Gilles reasoned that he might get on better terms with him if he approached his new father-in-law when he had a drink in one hand and a full plate of food in the other. Hendrick found Gilles first, though.

"Gilles, you are back! Who is your friend here?" he asked.

"This is Claes. You might know him from your church," Gilles said, not offering Hendrick any more information than that. He didn't *know* anything more about Claes, nothing that he cared to share with his father-in-law anyway.

"Good to meet you, young fellow. Come over here, Gilles, I want you to meet the pearl importing specialist for the Westindisch Huis over in the Haarlemmerstraat. He taught Van Rensselaer everything he knows about pearls and I told him that you had something of an interest in pearls yourself with the ones you gave Elsje. Bring young Claes over, too. I have never met any of your other friends besides Durie."

Gilles didn't know much about pearls at all and was uncomfortable when the expert questioned him about their particulars. The pearl connoisseur had of course seen and admired Elsje's pearls, which she now wore to church every Sunday and in between whenever she found an excuse to put them on. She had worn them at the wedding and she still had them on.

Where had these pearls come from? Who was the artist who had fashioned them? Where had the gold come from? Gilles was as honest as he could be and told the man that, as far as he knew, they were created by a jewelry maker in France from materials either from France or her colonies. The subject of France and the subject of the pearls both made Gilles ill at ease and as Hendrick listened in to their conversation, Gilles wondered how many more questions he would be asked about the necklace.

When Elsje came out of the kitchen with more food, Gilles excused himself and took the opportunity to escape Hendrick and the pearl merchant. It probably was a good idea to put something in his stomach besides the wine that he had been drinking, anyway. Before he even tasted the fish, Gilles could see by the unusual yellow and orange color that the dish had more spices covering it than Gilles had ever seen on a plate before. He wondered if Elsje had seasoned it herself and if anyone had bothered to taste it first before they sent it out of the kitchen. Maybe they had tried it, but with the consumption of too much ale, maybe they had not realized what they had done to the poor fish.

"Too much of my new spices?" Elsje asked Gilles anxiously when she returned to Gilles a few moments later and saw him standing with an older woman, his full plate of fish still in his hand.

"It's very good, Elsje Dear," the old woman said, patting Elsje on the shoulder. "I've just been telling your husband all about how to train children to the chamber pot."

Gilles noticed that the woman had only tried one bite of her fish as well.

"It's *very* good," Gilles said, cutting off a piece so that he could take another big bite in front of Elsje.

It wasn't only the spices that had kept Gilles from eating more, though; his mind just wasn't on food. All Gilles could think about since this morning when he had been sitting with his thigh touching Elsje's at church for two hours, since the sermon about Jacob's two wives, was that it would be another six days before he could be with Elsje again. He tried to reason with himself that he had *always* waited a week for Hannah, every week, and it was not *really* so difficult, but his body was not accepting the rational argument.

Gilles put the fish into his mouth and started to chew but suddenly the thought popped into his head that Hannah had never missed a week with him except for that Tuesday when the Jews had mysteriously disappeared from the streets and the entire city. In the several months that she had been his lover, she had never missed a week at all. He drew his breath in sharply at the realization, wondering how this could be so and Elsje looked at him questioningly.

"Oh, it *is* just a *little* spicy!" he said as he quickly took a sip of his wine. He hoped that the lie was convincing.

"I'll fix it for you, Gilles." Elsje kissed his cheek and took his full plate with her to the kitchen.

The old woman picked up where she had left off on the subject of toilet train-ing as Gilles continued to wonder *how* it could be possible. In France, Catherine the kitchen maid would send him away and say "Ooooh, come back in a few days, Lover, I'll be ready for you then …"

He had noticed nothing unusual the last time he was with Hannah, no change in her belly. Maybe there was something wrong with her, some abnormality, something about Jewish women? He had heard tales of such things. He certainly could not ask Jean to help him out on this matter; he could not even confide in him about his fears.

The question had at first simply surprised him, then piqued his interest, but soon it began to gnaw at him. The last thing in the world that he needed was for Hendrick to find any loose ends from his previous life.

Gilles did his duty and stayed at the feast all day, talking with everyone in attendance, even with Brant Schaghen who had brought his dog and then laughed in hysterics after the animal relieved itself on one of the table legs, until there was no one sober enough to talk to anymore. Jean Durie had slipped away early in the evening and even Claes had left in the company of two of the WIC men. Still Gilles put off going upstairs. It was dark outside and too cold to con-sider going anywhere out there, even if he *could* think up some excuse, and Gilles was too tired to stay on his feet any longer so reluctantly he went up the stairs to the family apartment.

Elsje was already there, directing Corretje, Heintje and Jennetje to wash up for their return to Cousin Vroutje's for the night.

"I *am* sorry, Gilles!" Elsje said as she pushed Corretje over to the wash basin.

Gilles wondered what she was sorry about until he realized that she was speak-ing to him about the spicy fish that he had forgotten about hours earlier.

"… and you probably aren't used to all this celebration and you have to go to work the day after tomorrow," she added sympathetically.

"We *do* celebrate weddings in France, too, Elsje but I *should* probably check in with Ste Germaine tomorrow, just for a short time and get the rest of my things."

Gilles needed a little time to get away and possibly during that time he would think of what he could do about Hannah. Where was Hannah on Mondays? He had never thought to ask her.

"Go and get some rest, Gilles, this is our bedroom now." Elsje kissed his fore-head and pointed toward the bedroom that until today had been her father's. "Come along children! Jennetje! Heintje! Corretje!" Elsje clapped her hands together. "We are all going out in back *first*."

There was general moaning and complaining about this but Elsje rejected all the protests and arguments that it was only a short distance to Vroutje's house.

"I want *no* accidents tonight! Cousin Vroutje told me about what happened last week!"

There was still some grumbling about the cold seats but the futile arguments finally ceased. Elsje kissed Gilles' cheek again. "I'll be back shortly husband, keep the bed warm for me!" She smiled at him shyly.

After she was gone, Gilles went into the dark bedroom, shut the door, took off his shoes and got into bed with his pants still on. He rolled to the far side near the wall and thumped the lumpy straw bedding a few times to even it out. He pulled the down comforter over his head and tried to go to sleep but he found that he could not: It was a strange bed and it smelled like Hendrick, like old man's sweat and pipe smoke. Gilles stuck his face outside the covers for some fresh, cold air.

Gilles heard Elsje return, heard her pause for a minute outside, probably to hang up her cloak, before she entered the bedroom with a lamp and closed the door. He kept his eyes tightly closed as he heard her remove her dress and her undergarments, before she blew out the lamp and climbed into bed next to him.

She moved closer to Gilles but he did not move at all; he pretended to be sound asleep. His heart thumped in his chest and he hoped that she would not hear the loud noise it made. It seemed to be a very long time before Elsje finally said softly, "You *are* tired, husband. Sleep well." She stroked the back of his head and rolled over to her own side.

Although it was still dark on this Monday morning, the cook was already at his work by lamplight in Ste Germaine's kitchen but today he had a bloody bandage wrapped around his head. He leaned over the preparation table that was covered with piles of shriveled vegetables brought up from the root cellar and a dozen pans, each one containing raw fish, chicken, or some bloody meat. He banged pots and utensils and grumbled something under his breath before he selected a knife from the drawer and angrily started to chop onions on a wooden block, pausing only briefly to smash two eggs into a bowl, swearing as he picked out pieces of eggshell.

Gilles paused in the doorway for a moment, the heat from the cook's fireplace drifting slowly past his face, out through the open door and into the cooler dining room. Gilles was taken aback by the bandage and the demeanor of the usually docile cook.

"Salaud!" the cook exclaimed to no one in particular before he looked up for a moment and noticed Gilles standing there.

"Excuse me, Gilles, I did not know that you were here. Are you not still celebrating?" he asked. He was pleasant enough, but he continued to chop away furiously.

"I just came to get my things and to see if I was needed back at work yet."

Ste Germaine came into the kitchen just after Gilles, straightening his collar.

"What is the noise in here this morning and what has happened to you?" he asked.

"I was attacked last night, Monsieur."

"That is terrible! Did the authorities get him? We will find out who did this thing and be sure that he gets his deserved punishment!"

"I know the man. He tried to kill me and when I see him again, I will most certainly kill *him*!" He chopped carrots fiercely now, applying his anger to his work.

"We will seek justice together ..." Ste Germaine began a new speech but stopped abruptly when LaRue entered the kitchen and the cook made for him with his knife, tiny orange pieces of carrot still clinging to the blade.

"I will kill him, cut his heart out, and serve it up for dinner!"

Ste Germaine put himself between the two men, holding fast to LaRue's sleeve as he addressed the cook.

"You think it was Msr. LaRue who attacked you? You *must* be mistaken...."

The cook was careful not to inflict injury on Gilles or Ste Germaine but he still attempted to get at LaRue with the knife, even though he would have to go around both men to reach his quarry.

"I am *not* mistaken! Check his left arm!"

The cook tried once again to advance beyond Gilles and Ste Germaine as LaRue drew himself up in obvious indignation.

"Don't be *ridiculous*. He's a *madman*, Gillaume; *all* soldiers are, you know. It's the fighting that makes them crazy. Let me do you this *one* favor, and turn him in to the bounty hunters. It will save you from any future trouble just as long as you don't hire any more like him."

The cook made another attempt to get around Gilles but Gilles grabbed the cook's wrist and held him back with the full weight of his body.

"For your own sake, don't do it!" Gilles whispered to the cook.

Far from the situation diffusing now, though, LaRue angered the cook even more with his response to this action. "Of *course* he would like to fight me here with a crowd of witnesses; he's a *coward*. He makes wild accusations in front of an audience and that justifies attacking and killing an unarmed man! If he had *any* honor at all and if there was *any* substance to these allegations, he would challenge me openly so that we could both get our weapons and meet at an appointed time on a field of honor."

The cook struggled all the harder to get at LaRue but he still refrained from injuring Gilles in these attempts. Gilles had no doubt at all that if anyone else had been attempting to restrain him, the cook would have done whatever was needed to make good on his threat without concerning himself as to who was in the way.

Gilles still held the cook's wrist but over his shoulder Gilles yelled to Ste Germaine, "Please, Monsieur, just look at his arm!"

"Don't be *stupid*, Gillaume," LaRue said, pulling away from Ste Germaine and straightening his sleeve. "I'm not coming back here *at all* if you insist on hiring all these criminals and surrounding yourself with them. *Quality establishment!*"

He turned toward the door but Gilles, angry now at LaRue's slander, called out to Ste Germaine once again.

"Msr. Ste Germaine! Let us settle this once and for all by inspecting his arm!"

Ste Germaine grabbed LaRue's sleeve and yanked it up, revealing a long red scratch on it.

"Explain this to me!" Ste Germaine looked at LaRue in surprise.

"Explain what?" LaRue jerked his arm away and pulled his sleeve down again. "I scraped it on a nail in the stable getting my horse out the other day. Obviously the cook noticed it and now he uses it to support these imagined attacks of his; there is nothing more for me to explain. He probably fell down, hit his head and dreamed the whole thing while he was drunk!"

LaRue wheeled around and walked out of the kitchen.

Ste Germaine turned his attention to the cook. "You must not make such wild accusations or people *will* think that you are mad. Are you sure that it was him? You saw him clearly?"

"Nooo," the man admitted. "But when I was attacked I was close enough to scratch him and to hear him."

"He spoke? What did he say?" Ste Germaine continued his questioning.

"He made grunting sounds as we struggled."

"Grunting sounds and a scratch. That is *not* much evidence. You would be wise *not* to make accusations that you cannot support. Now get back to work."

Ste Germaine dismissed the man's charges and turned to follow LaRue out into the dining room as Gilles released the cook's arm.

"If this was not the best job in the city, I would be gone by now!" the cook fumed.

"Are you *certain* that it was LaRue?" Gilles asked, still not wanting to believe it. The cook *did* drink occasionally and from time to time he had blamed others for taking his pans or utensils, items that were generally located later where the cook had left them. Still, the man had never accused anyone of attempted murder before, and there *was* the visible scratch on LaRue's arm.

"I am as sure as you stand here! Don't you believe me?"

The cook glowered at Gilles and there was a hardness in his eyes that Gilles had never seen there before.

"I believe that you *think* it was him."

The cook turned away from Gilles with renewed anger. "Allez-vous! Leave my kitchen, too, if you think I'm a liar or a crazy person! Just watch out for yourself! He does not scare me, though. I have had to fight for my life and kill before, and I will do it again if I have to!" The cook banged the pots together once more.

Gilles decided that the man *was* raving. Perhaps LaRue was right; perhaps it was a case of Soldier's Madness but the cook *was* an excellent chef and it would be terrible if the establishment lost his considerable talents. Gilles tried one last time to calm the man.

"Listen to me: You are safe here. Just keep to your work and keep your job."

The cook was not to be placated though, so Gilles thought it best to leave him to chop his vegetables and eventually to find his own peace. Gilles went out into the dining room where LaRue sat at a table that held a lighted lamp, an empty bottle, and a glass of wine, leaning back in one chair with his feet up on another, chewing unconcernedly at a piece of loose fingernail as Ste Germaine lectured him.

"I have asked you to stay away from him! Do not upset the man! Just leave him alone to do his work! *Why* can't you do that, follow this simple directive?"

LaRue looked over his hands through the shadows at Ste Germaine. "He's *completely* insane as well as a drunk and you *know* it. I can't believe that there isn't anyone else in the city who knows how to cook a decent meal. Hire a woman."

"*A woman?* Be serious! Just stay out of the kitchen. I have told you that before. And get your boots off my good chairs."

"I simply went into the kitchen to get another bottle of wine. Can't I get some wine if I'm thirsty?" LaRue ignored Ste Germaine's request to remove his feet.

"We need *harmony* here, we need *peaceful* surroundings," Ste Germaine implored him. "Serenity, tranquility, is what we need!"

LaRue acted as though he hadn't heard a word. "It has come to the point where I hate to even come in here anymore! All of your other *former* patrons do, too, from the empty looks of the place. If you fired that cook you'd have *much* more business, Gillaume."

LaRue put his feet on the floor, scraped the chair back away from the table and rose to leave. Grabbing his cloak on the way, he stalked out the door, leaving the chairs behind him in disarray.

Ste Germaine sighed a deep sigh and ran his hands through his hair. "I don't have *enough* other troubles! I have *him* to deal with!"

He visibly relaxed his shoulders, though, and smiled at Gilles. "You look tired. Is that good? Why aren't you celebrating with your new wife? Why are you back here?"

"I just came to get my things and see when you needed me back," Gilles answered, but then another idea occurred to him. "Would it be possible for me to have some time off on this coming Friday, to have dinner with my new wife?"

"You can take the rest of this week, since we are not busy at all and because it's your wedding week; I'll see you on Saturday. Oh, Mon Dieu, where *are* all the customers?" Ste Germaine implored the heavens.

"It is only the time of year; they will be back soon," Gilles tried to reassure him.

"Yes, yes, of course they will. Can you just straighten these chairs up for me before you go, Gilles?"

Ste Germaine went back into the kitchen, probably to make sure that his cook had not quit or committed some act of angry reprisal there. Gilles fixed the table arrangement and turned to go up the stairs to get his belongings.

As if in immediate answer to Ste Germaine's prayer though, a few patrons *did* come in at just that moment, and even though Gilles wasn't there to work, he seated the first group at Ste Germaine's best table. Gilles decided that they were businessmen who were looking for a warm place to meet together in neutral territory. Gilles returned to the entrance to seat the other man who had walked in behind the others and was alone.

It was too early for midday dinner and Gilles looked the man over to determine why he was here. One of the aspects of his job that Gilles liked the least was trying to determine who was a *real* customer and who was only trying to get a meal for free. He had already learned during his short tenure in Ste Germaine's employment that it had a lot more to do with what their shoes or boots looked like and less to do with how much jewelry they wore or how wealthy they appeared to be. Jean had been right about appearance being important: Good shoes, good customer, poor shoes, poor customer. The man waiting at the door had medium shoes on.

"What can we do for you today, Monsieur?" Gilles asked as he tried to discern which type of customer he was.

"I am in need of a good meal and I heard that your establishment was the best in all of Amsterdam." The man's speech had been polished to a shine but his French accent was curious.

"Are you looking for the full meal or just a small one?" Gilles asked him.

"I hadn't decided yet. I suppose if the food is really that good.... Didn't you have musicians in here yesterday?" The man looked over Gilles' shoulder.

"Yes, we did have musicians. Did you come for the music, too?"

Gilles wondered what this one was up to: The music wasn't *that* good that it would induce someone to return just to hear it again.

Sometimes, when they weren't too certain about a customer's ability to pay, Ste Germaine had his host ask for the money before the customer was even seated, before the cook prepared the food. It saved everyone the embarrassment later on, Ste Germaine had explained, and anyone who did not have more than enough to pay for the culinary experience should not even bother to come in the front door. Gilles felt that this was one of those times when the situation called for upfront payment but before he could make the request, the stranger made another comment.

"Music makes dinner *so* much more pleasant...." The stranger smiled at Gilles, but Gilles thought that it was rather a snaky sort of a smile.

"Gilles! May I see you over here for a moment?"

Ste Germaine beckoned him over to the kitchen door. Gilles excused himself, said that he would be right back to seat him, and went over to his employer while the stranger examined a table nearby, examined it very closely in much the same way Ste Germaine did when he was not at all sure if some item was acceptable.

"Oui, Monsieur?"

"Gilles, *what* are you doing? With business this slow, we cannot afford to make good customers uncomfortable!"

"I was just trying ..."

"Tut, tut! Show the man to a table and bring him some food!"

"Oui, Monsieur."

Gilles complied with his employer's request but he kept his eyes on the stranger. The man was surveying the establishment with an air of curiosity about every detail, perhaps to see if it was clean enough, or perhaps with the intent to rob it. The man smiled a broad smile at Ste Germaine and then just briefly, a look of recognition crossed his face. The look was fleeting and the bland smile quickly returned to his visage but Gilles did not think that he had imagined it;

Gilles led the man over to a good table and as he did so, he wondered what had just transpired. If they already knew each other, why didn't the man say anything more and why didn't Ste Germaine greet him as an old friend?

The cook was still banging things around when Gilles entered the kitchen and relayed the menu requests to him from their guests.

"It makes you sick, doesn't it? I saw it, I saw it! What is this one after? They are more trouble than women with their moods!"

The cook ranted on as Gilles peered outside the door and out into the dining room. Ste Germaine was attending to the stranger and they both seemed very friendly, like they were old friends, but they still did not appear to be as comfortable as old acquaintances might be. Gilles noticed, for the first time, the stranger's sky blue eyes, the strong jaw line, and light blond hair. Realization dawned on him and Gilles resolved to stay out of this one. He would bring the food out, drop it on the table, and then simply tell Ste Germaine that he had to leave, that he had to get back to the feast.

The thought occurred to Gilles, though, that if LaRue were to come back in unexpectedly, there could be trouble and he could find himself out of a job if all four men, Ste Germaine, LaRue, the cook, and the stranger, fought to someone's death across the battleground of the dining room. Even if no one was killed, the authorities might shut the business down if Ste Germaine was involved in a fracas and if there were people who were badly injured. If Gilles stayed on in the dining room for a time, his presence might be enough of a deterrent to keep such an incident from happening.

Ste Germaine passed through the kitchen and continued on out the back door. He returned in a few minutes with a bottle from the wine cave and Gilles noticed that it was a bottle of his very best wine.

"Is Monsieur MacEwen's food ready yet?" Ste Germaine asked Gilles as he paused to pick up a bottle opener and two glasses. He didn't inquire as to the progress of his other customer's meals.

"I just brought the request in …" Gilles said as the cook banged another pot onto the preparation table from the overhead shelf.

"It will be right out," Ste Germaine called to MacEwen in musical tones as he left the kitchen and walked back into the dining room.

"Here, this goes out to the three men." The cook loaded up the tray with three simple dishes of croissants, butter, tea and preserves.

Gilles had had very little practice in serving but he managed to carry the tray out successfully. The sun was now coming up over Amsterdam and after he had served the food to the businessmen, now involved in a spirited discussion about the iron ore trade, Gilles opened the dining room curtains to let in some of the morning light before he returned to the kitchen with his empty tray. He avoided looking directly at Ste Germaine and MacEwen as he passed by.

"His damned food is ready," the cook announced after a few more minutes. He slopped the main course into a dish, wiped the edge with a cloth, and set it on the tray in front of Gilles with a variety of other dishes of bread and vegetables. In fact, there were more dishes going out to MacEwen alone than went to the three businessmen combined.

The cook wiped his hands on his apron and put his hands on his hips as he watched Gilles rearrange the dishes on the serving tray to better balance them on the way out. The cook, knowing that Gilles was not very experienced at handling a tray, opened the kitchen door for him and Gilles was relieved when he made it safely to the stranger's table without mishap. Gilles prayed that he would not drop anything now in front of Ste Germaine and he only stopped holding his breath when he was finally able to pick up the empty tray and go back into the kitchen.

The cook had removed his apron and was putting on his hat and cloak.

"Where are you going?" Gilles asked in a panic.

"I'm going to find LaRue and kill him," the cook answered calmly.

"You can't leave now, what if we have more customers? What if MacEwen wants dessert?" Gilles asked, more concerned with whether Ste Germaine would be angry at the cook's absence than with any mere infractions of the law or biblical commandments.

"Then either Msr. Ste Germaine or you will have to make it for him. It will not take me very long, though. I will break his neck quickly and be back before supper time." The cook flashed Gilles a humorless smile before he walked out through the back door, leaving a blast of icy air to take his place.

For a moment Gilles was worried that perhaps the cook *really* was going out to find and kill LaRue but then he dismissed the idea as ridiculous and told himself that the cook would surely be back after he had a few drinks. If business was as slow as it had been all week, it was quite possible that Ste Germaine would not notice the absence at all, but this scenario was unlikely given the way that Ste Germaine ran his business. There was really nothing Gilles could do to stop the cook short of wrestling him to the floor and tying him up, so Gilles decided to just return to the dining room and pretend that he did not know that the cook had just left. Maybe it was better though: The cook would not be there to fight with if LaRue returned.

Gilles adjusted the curtains and straightened up everything in the dining room, even though the tables did not need straightening. He added another piece of wood to the fire and hoped that his employer would not think that he was wasting the firewood. Ste Germaine refused to use peat even though it was cheaper; he insisted on using only wood in the guest dining room, preferably apple or cherry wood, even though it generated less heat and more sparks.

The musicians walked in through the front door, sending a wave of cold into the dining room before them. Ste Germaine excused himself from MacEwen's table and invited the head musician to a far corner of the room. After a short time the musician returned to his group, grumpily collected his men and their instruments, and they were gone, probably for good.

"Oh, are they leaving?" MacEwen asked Ste Germaine.

"Oui, for now."

"That *is* a pity. I am a musician myself and I would have loved to play with them," MacEwen said.

"I could call them back for you," Ste Germaine offered. He started to get up from the table.

"That's all right." The Scotsman smiled at him and patted Ste Germaine's hand.

"What do you play?" Ste Germaine asked his new acquaintance.

"I just play a little flute when I want to relax." MacEwen produced a very small flute out of his breast pocket and handed it to Ste Germaine.

Gilles noticed that MacEwen had not stopped eating or drinking during the entire time that Ste Germaine was there, nor had MacEwen produced any money yet to pay for this meal.

"I would like to hear it sometime. Would you play for me, after your meal?"

"I would be *happy* to."

MacEwen returned to his food in a leisurely but thorough manner. He ate until every morsel was gone and only then, after wiping his mouth daintily with Ste Germaine's white linen napkin, did he take up his flute.

When he finished his first tune, Ste Germaine applauded and said, "What wonderful lively music! So much better than the dreary songs the musicians played!"

Gilles sighed. There was no comparison between professional musicians and one self-taught flute player but Ste Germaine, usually so discerning in all of his tastes, appeared to be quite blind to this at the moment.

Ste Germaine touched MacEwen's sleeve, "I wonder if I could impose on you, would you even consider, playing for us here? We would pay you of course, if it would not offend your sensibilities to accept money in return for your talents. A talent such as yours would add so much to our little establishment."

"As it happens," said MacEwen, taking another sip of his wine, "I find myself between business engagements and so I would be happy to play for you for an hour or two a day. I could play at dinner time and again at supper time. This would be just for a short time, though, since I have other business obligations to which I will soon have to return."

Gilles rolled his eyes at this. He just hoped that MacEwen would not rob all of the patrons in one single night. Now he would have to add to his list of daily duties watching this "musician" too.

Gilles listened in on the conversation and discovered that MacEwen was not finished yet with further terms of his employment, though.

"Three guilders a day would be all I would ask and I *won't* take a stuiver more since I would be only too happy to bring music to your fine establishment for a time."

Gilles nearly choked. Not only was MacEwen *not* worth three guilders a day, it was *more* than Gilles was paid.

"All meals and drinks of my choice will be included of course? I just *cannot* perform on an empty stomach." MacEwen rested his hand on Ste Germaine's wrist.

Ste Germaine had always made the other musicians pay for *everything* they consumed and Gilles couldn't believe it when his employer murmured in the affirmative.

"Then we have a deal." McEwen smiled broadly and offered his hand. Ste Germaine accepted and Gilles felt that the handclasp lasted for a little longer than was absolutely necessary.

"I will start tomorrow, then." MacEwen smiled and picked up his cloak, patting Ste Germaine's arm as he left.

Gilles shook his head as he cleared the table. Ste Germaine had not held the new musician to his usual rigorous scrutiny and unreasonably high standards and Gilles suddenly realized as well that no money at all had been collected for this meal. He was not about to bring that subject up to Ste Germaine though, who was now bustling around, humming to himself. It was several minutes more before Ste Germaine went into the kitchen and then returned to the dining room. He was still humming but he paused briefly as he passed Gilles to ask the question that Gilles knew was coming:

"Oh Gilles, where is the cook?"

"I'm not sure. Perhaps he went out to get some supplies."

Gilles did not even know where that lie came from, it just escaped from him before he had the opportunity to think about it. Perhaps it was because that was where the cook *always* said he was going when he left, even when he came back with no supplies at all hours later and smelling of wine.

"I have *never* seen business this slow! By all means, spend some time with your wife, Gilles, take her to see the new Joost van den Vondel's work that is just opening."

"That sounds good, Monsieur," Gilles replied, but he would rather have had the money from working and he doubted seriously that he could ever interest Elsje in such things, even if he succeeded in getting her to leave the inn for a few hours.

Gilles climbed Ste Germaine's stairs to collect the last of his belongings from his room. He wrapped everything that he owned in the priest's robe and then stuffed the entire bundle under his arm. Gilles took one last look around his comfortable room before he shut that door behind him for good.

By the time he arrived back at Hendrick's, it was after noon and Gilles was in an angry mood. He was just not inclined to drink with Hendrick any more and he was tired of talking with drunks and old women who asked him stupid questions, often about their misconceptions of France. Time off from work was not really what Gilles wanted right now even though it was something that he would have dreamed about when he worked at the stable. He had to count his blessings though, that he had the rest of the week off with enough money to enjoy it and a woman to spend the time with, but he had five days left before he could touch Elsje again.

"Surely heaven and hell are two sides of the same coin," Gilles thought.

He considered taking her away somewhere to be alone with her but if he suggested such a thing, she would wonder why. There was no privacy for them at the inn; Hendrick was *always* there. Perhaps he should just be with his wife, her father and the promise be damned. The church had sanctioned it. Even the Catholic Church made no such outrageous demands on new husbands.

The party raged on at Hendrick's, even if it was at a lower noise level than it had been previously and Gilles could hear it from up the street, even before he opened the front door. Hendrick chided Gilles for missing his own celebration and Elsje, ale in hand and herself a little tipsy, made a point of brushing up against Gilles. At that particular moment he thought that he might go mad if he had to wait another five days to be with her and Gilles thought that he did very well to manage a begrudging smile at the guests as he made his way over to the stairs with his bundle of clothing and belongings. Elsje followed him up to their living quarters.

"Do you have a place for me to keep my things?" he asked her as he dumped the load onto their bed.

"Father said you would have a lot of clothes, so I emptied a whole chest for you to put your things in."

The chest was exactly that, a trunk, and not a real chest made specifically to hang clothes inside. Gilles shrugged and picked the pile up again, dumping every- thing into the container: his savings, the knife, the wampum belt, the priest's robe, his French clothing and the three ugly dark suits of clothes from the Jewish tailors. Gilles surveyed this odd collection of things, his only worldly possessions, and thought about what a strange year it had been for him and what a strange life he was *still* living. He closed the lid on that thought after he pulled out his French clothes, laying those out on the top of the trunk.

"I'll need more hooks on the wall to hang my good clothes up," he told Elsje, knowing that a real chest for his clothes would be too much to ask for. "They will be too badly wrinkled to wear again if I don't."

"Wrinkled? Well, I guess we can do that for you," she smiled at him. "Will you come down with me to our guests now?"

"I don't feel well," Gilles complained. *"I don't feel like it,"* was what he wanted to say to her.

"Do you have a headache again?" Elsje asked anxiously.

"I'll be all right. I just need some more sleep," he replied.

"I'll stay with you then." Elsje smiled at him.

Gilles tried to put some distance between them, to send her away.

"No, you go down and make my apologies for me. I just don't feel well."

He removed only his shoes and rolled into the bed, moving over to the wall and shutting his eyes. He heard a small sigh from Elsje and her hand touched his shoulder.

"Sleep well, Husband. Feel better soon."

Gilles did fall asleep, and he must have been more tired than he knew. It was true that he had not had a lot of sleep during the last few days. He woke later when it was dark outside and very dark in the bedroom. He felt his way over to his shoes and, for lack of anything better to do, he joined the celebration down- stairs where he found enough food to fill his stomach and a bottle of wine to go with it. Gilles circulated through the room once, finishing the bottle by himself and then, not having seen Jean Durie anywhere and only speaking with Elsje briefly to assure her that he felt much better, he slipped back up the stairs to his bed where he fell asleep again from the effects of the wine, not waking up at all until the following morning when Elsje shook his shoulder and told him that he would be late for work if he didn't get up soon.

Gilles started to tell her that he had the week off from work but then he decided that pretending to go to work all week might not be such a bad idea. He would not have to lie; he just wouldn't tell her that he had been given the time off. He could go to the French quarter, hang around the docks or perhaps visit Jean today. Gilles got up, dressed in his good work clothes, and from the trunk he retrieved his knife and some money from his savings before he joined Elsje and her father downstairs.

"Sit, Gilles! I have breakfast all ready for you. Are you feeling better today?"

"A little, yes."

"You aren't getting sick with the fevers?" she asked, looking at him more closely.

Gilles remembered then that she had lost her mother to an epidemic and he smiled what he hoped was a reassuring smile at her.

"No, Elsje, I am fine. I am just … tired. It has been a *very* long week."

Elsje felt his forehead anyway. "Are you sure you are not a little warm?"

"Nee, I'm not warm."

Gilles took her hand and put it to his face. It was cool and it felt good. There were four days left after today, four days that he had to wait to be with her again.

Gilles ate his food quickly and finished before Hendrick did, although Hendrick had been well into his breakfast of bread and smoked fish by the time Gilles came down.

"You eat too fast," Hendrick chided him with a grin.

Gilles thought briefly about rising from his seat and going to the other end of the table to choke the old man but he said nothing. He just had to get outside quickly though, before he lost control of his temper.

"I'll be back later," Gilles said as he picked up his cloak on his way out. Elsje cornered him and kissed both of his cheeks. Gilles kissed her back obediently.

Outside the morning air was cold and it hurt his lungs. He breathed in deeply, though, enjoying the momentary distraction of the pain. He would not think about Elsje or her father now; he had the whole day to himself before he had to go back. Unfortunately the French quarter was depressingly quiet and gray today so he continued on to Jean's house.

"Jean is not here," the servant girl told him. "He's probably at work already and I don't know when he will return."

Gilles decided to go to Jacob's stable even though it was Tuesday and Jacob probably wouldn't be there. Would Hannah be busy there with the new stable boy? Maybe the closed and empty stable was a place where Hannah might go to be alone until her father returned from the Dam. Gilles might get a chance to see her there.

The stable door was closed when Gilles got there but no sign was up so Gilles removed his hat and walked inside. The smell came back to him first, the manure and the hay, followed by the oats and the leather. The oily smell was only slightly in evidence but it was there, too. Jacob's old horse whinnied at Gilles in recognition.

Jacob and a very young Jewish boy, no more than a child really, stepped out from behind the horse.

"Hello Gilles, how is life with you?" Jacob seemed reserved but friendly enough.

"Good, and yourself, Jacob?"

Gilles had already forgotten that they *always* wore their hats here, both inside and outside, and he quickly put his hat back on after he saw them standing there with theirs still on their heads.

The young boy eyed the Christian visitor with suspicion and said nothing.

"You look very nice, very nice. Is the job going well then?"

"Yes. I just came by to say 'hello', to see how you were doing."

"We are fine, fine without you, if that is what you are asking. I've found a good, hard-working boy in Yossi here, isn't that right, Yossi?"

The boy looked up at Jacob and then back at Gilles, still saying nothing. Gilles wondered if he was a mute.

"We have work to do now. Good-bye, Gilles."

Jacob and Yossi turned to go back to their work and Gilles had no choice but to leave before he could think of a way to ask Jacob about Hannah, to make a polite general inquiry about her. Coming here had been a mistake and as he left the stable, Gilles knew with certainty that he would never come back to this place again.

Gilles decided to walk and drink the rest of the week away. If Hendrick and the other celebrants could drink for three days, then Gilles could certainly drink for four. He walked away from the center of the city until the buildings no longer stood shoulder to shoulder, walked until there were larger and larger patches of land between the houses, and then he walked on some more until there were more plots of open and tilled land than there were structures covering the plots.

There, on the outskirts of the city, he found a poor tavern by the side of the road, wreathed in weeds and neglect, where it was less likely that they would have sailors for patrons and, Gilles hoped, less likely that they would know Elsje.

The tavern was very quiet on this frosty morning but Gilles walked up the rickety steps and pushed his way inside the squeaking door anyway. Places like these were never closed to paying customers. Two drunks anchored tables on either side of the fireplace and Gilles guessed from their dirt-saturated attire that they claimed to be farmers. He wondered what condition their farms must be in if they were already in the tavern drinking at this hour of the morning, but then again, it *was* wintertime and there wouldn't be any fields to tend to, only the animals.

Gilles removed his hat as he entered and crunched across the sand-covered floor, picking out one of the cleaner tables, ignoring the smell of stale beer and spoiled food as well as the stares of the farmers. He was definitely dressed too well to be in this part of town but it was too late for him to walk back out now.

The owner shuffled over to ask Gilles what he wanted and Gilles noted the man's swollen feet, swollen belly, and runny red eyes as the man stood there, waiting to find out what he could sell the traveler. Gilles hoped that the old man's malady wasn't contagious.

While Gilles waited for his ale and some food, he thought about Jacob and the indifferent reception that he had received at the stable. Hannah wasn't likely to be visiting young Yossi on Tuesdays and Gilles wondered if Jacob had hired the child chiefly for that reason. Gilles was more than ready to forget about the stable and that entire part of his life and his intention was to do so, just as soon as he ascertained that Hannah did not have a child on the way, at least not *his* child on the way.

Gilles might knock on her door and make up some excuse, possibly even say that he was at her door by accident, that is, if he could find out where she lived. Just a glimpse of her was *all* that Gilles needed, but he didn't know where he could find her. He did know that Jacob would be leaving for her house late in the afternoon on Friday, as he did every week. This thought had passed over his mind swiftly once before, at Ste Germaine's, like the wisp of a stray cloud on a breezy summer day, that he just might follow Jacob to her house this week at the start of their Sabbath. The drink that Gilles was consuming made this seem more and more like a plausible plan and then a tentative plan. By the end of his third ale, it was a definite plan.

Gilles imagined every possible scenario and outcome: Hannah declaring that she carried Gilles' child, throwing her arms around him, declaring feelings for him and threatening to tell Elsje unless there was some kind of financial settlement, Hannah with child coolly telling him that she had planned to end the relationship anyway because the child was her husband's, and Hannah thinner than ever, laughing in his face, mocking him for his worries.

When there were no more scenarios to run in his head regarding Hannah, Gilles continued to avoid thinking about how much he wanted to be with Elsje by thinking about Ste Germaine. Gilles wondered if any other eating establishment *ever* had as much insanity to deal with on a daily basis. Even at Elsje's inn, the worst crises, aside from the requisite stray drunks and troublemakers, usually consisted of running out of food or drink and the heated discussions between Elsje and Tryntje on how best to hang the laundry up outside.

Gilles had already finished three ales by the time his food was brought to his table. He tasted the greasy, gray sausage and the taste might have been all right but the hard bits of bone and hair that he found in every bite were enough to keep him from finishing it. Gilles just ordered another drink and followed that order with another. Perhaps if he stayed drunk enough for long enough, all of his problems, including his hunger, would eventually work themselves out and be gone.

When the tavern keeper started to light the lamps, Gilles decided that it was probably time to go home. He followed his ears back to the city's sounds until he was close enough to find some familiar landmarks and the rest of the way home in the dark. He took a deep breath and braced himself before he pushed open the door to the inn.

The party seemed like it had almost come to an end and the inn was almost back to its normal level of activity. Only a few dozen leftover guests remained there, the residue of the previous three days of celebration. One of the girls who worked in the kitchen greeted Gilles with a wave of her hand.

"The family is upstairs eating," she called out to him.

Gilles straightened his clothes before he climbed the stairs, thinking of various things that he might tell them if they asked questions about his day. Elsje, Hendrick and Tryntje were seated at the table but they had not yet started eating. Gilles could feel all of their eyes on him as he slid into his chair. He realized that he had not eaten all day except for the bad food he had at the tavern and now he was very hungry.

It was quiet at the table during dinner and to his great relief, nobody asked Gilles anything, except to pass this or that dish. Hendrick said nothing at all and seemed to be in a bad mood but Gilles was far from feeling any sympathy for him. Even Tryntje and Elsje had nothing much to say to each other for a change, not a single item to dispute or to argue over. When Hendrick finished his supper, he left the table and went down the stairs to check on the inn and to use the privy.

"How was work today?" Elsje asked Gilles for the first time. Tryntje was looking intently at him now, too.

"It was all right," Gilles lied.

"Jean stopped over today," Elsje said, as she got up and started to clear the table.

"I wonder why he didn't come to Ste Germaine's?" Gilles asked.

"He did. He said it was closed."

Gilles noticed now that Elsje's mouth had that angry set to it and her eyes had that glint that they always got just before she lost her temper.

"Yes, well, we will be taking more time between opening hours for each meal due to business being so slow. Ste Germaine cancelled supper tonight altogether! We will just have to see how business goes for the rest of the week."

Gilles didn't look at her; he hoped that his explanation sounded all right.

Elsje said nothing in reply and neither did Tryntje.

Gilles pushed his empty plate away. "I need some sleep now," he said. "The wedding feast has worn me out."

He pushed his chair back and got up, losing his balance slightly as he rose but he recovered it quickly. He couldn't help but notice that Elsje looked so good tonight, even in her simple dress, that he wanted to reach out and touch her cheek. Even with her temper smoldering, there was nothing that he wanted more than to touch her. He wouldn't allow those thoughts, though; tonight and the rest of the week would be too long if he started to think about that. Gilles went into the bedroom, took his pants off, and crawled into bed.

Outside he heard Hendrick return upstairs and there were angry whispered exchanges between father and daughter before Elsje came into the bedroom with a lamp and closed the door behind her.

"Husband, wake up," she said, sweeping the covers off him.

Gilles grunted as if he could not be awakened.

Elsje shook him. "*Wake up!*"

Gilles rolled over to face her, trying to look sleepy.

"What has happened to you? You are not the man I thought I married! Do you drink all day now?"

Gilles didn't know what to say. Any conciliatory gesture would bring him into contact with her and he didn't think he could hold himself back once that happened.

"I am tired, Elsje, please let me sleep." Gilles rolled back over, listening for her to do whatever she was going to do but for a long time he heard only silence. He lay there for what seemed like many minutes before she finally left, slamming the bedroom door behind her.

It was a very difficult week but Gilles had no other choice than to live his way through it, a few minutes at a time. He left very early in the mornings and returned to Hendrick's very late at night, hoping that everyone would be asleep when he returned. When he came face to face with Elsje or with anyone else, he spoke as little as possible to them; this was not really so difficult because Elsje was angry and all of the others were aloof. It was not hard to leave well before the sun was up, either, because he didn't sleep much at all now when he was next to Elsje. He hoped that no one checked up on him any more at Ste Germaine's but there was really nothing he could do about that. He didn't want to think about asking for his old room back at Ste Germaine's or asking Jean if he could sleep on his floor again, but if it came to that, he would at least have a warm place to sleep for the winter.

Gilles slept during the day in the country tavern with an ale and food on the table in front of him. He only lived for two things now: for the seventh day after his wedding when he could try to get his wife back and reconcile with her, and for Friday night when he would follow Jacob to Hannah's house and dismiss the worries from his mind permsnently. Gilles had no idea what he would do if the consequences of his past indiscretions threatened his future. He could only imagine the West India wives' gossip at the next wedding feast if his worst fears were realized. The humiliation to Elsje would be too much for her to bear and Gilles really didn't want her to be hurt. He could hear the gossip now, "… a *Fransman*, you know … and with a *Jewish* girl!"

Even if everything worked out all right with Hannah, and Gilles was reasonably sure that it would, he wondered how he was ever going to work things out with Elsje. Gilles hoped that there had not been irreparable damage done to his relationship with her and he cursed Hendrick again. Either the old man was not aware of it or perhaps he did not care that the promise he had extracted from Gilles was destroying his own daughter's marriage just as it had barely started.

Gilles was in such a state of mind from his turmoil and from his constant state of inebriation and lack of sleep, that he didn't quite believe it when Friday really did come at last and things could start to be made right again in the world. He spent the day in the country tavern, as he had all of the previous days, but today he ate more, drank less, and spent most of the day planning. He measured the shadows outside the grimy window as the daylight came, stayed for a few winter hours, and then retreated behind the shadows.

When the sun started its descent in the west, Gilles settled his bill and walked up the road, back to the dusty streets in the Jewish section of Amsterdam so that he would be there in plenty of time. He pulled his cloak up over his chin, more to hide his changed appearance than to obscure his true identity or to keep out the cold. He took up his post down the street, fixed his eyes on Jacob's stable door and waited.

A few of his former neighbors did recognize him and they exchanged brief greetings with Gilles. He stood openly and cheerfully, making it look as though he was waiting to meet up with someone at the corner, not lurking there on some surreptitious errand. Passers-by probably thought that there was nothing strange about this at all except for his lack of haste in getting ready for sundown, but they were certainly too preoccupied with their own Sabbath preparations to give it very much thought.

At last Gilles saw Jacob leaving. Gilles followed quietly behind him at a safe distance but the old man never stopped, slowed, or turned around until he reached his destination. Jacob stopped at a large stone home in the newly prosperous Sephardic area of the city. Diamond-leaded glass casement windows looked down onto the street from up above Jacob as he climbed the long flight of stone steps leading up to the massive front door. Gilles watched as Hannah let her father in then quickly shut the door against the cold and darkening night. Gilles could not see well enough in the twilight at this distance to know absolutely, but from what he could see of her profile, she did not look any larger to him.

A noise behind him broke into his thoughts and Gilles nearly jumped as he turned around to see who it was who stood so near to him.

Elsje was the last person in the world that he expected to see standing there in the dark but she was not an apparition. She spoke angrily to Gilles.

"What is she to you that you cannot let her go, even though we are wed? Is she married? Is that why you would not marry her or is it because she is a Jew? I can see that she is rich, so maybe she wouldn't have *you*! My father was *right*!"

Elsje turned to flee but Gilles caught her arm and held fast to it.

"I followed Jacob, just to see where he was going, and he ended up here."

Although parts of what he said were true, panic engulfed Gilles and then anger at Hendrick. Had he sent his own daughter here to find her husband, letting her get hurt by what she would surely see with her own eyes? How did Hendrick *know*? Perhaps Gilles' father-in-law still sought to find a way out of the marriage contract. Gilles cared a great deal about Elsje's feelings but even if he didn't, it would be impossible for him to end the marriage now: It would be a sin.

"Do you deny that you are interested in that woman?" Elsje snarled.

Her voice was as angry as he had ever heard it before but Gilles took hope in the fact that he could see tears of pain in her eyes.

"Yes, I do! I want *you*, Elsje!"

Elsje stopped suddenly and looked at him as if she had been struck across the face. A sob broke from her lips and she struggled to free herself from his grip. "Leave me now, you bastard! You are a liar, too, as well as a drunk!"

"Nee! This has been a *terrible* thing, a *terrible* week, and I blame *your father* for everything!"

Gilles held her arm very tightly, as tightly as he had ever held the reins of a fighting horse. She was the closest thing that he had to family now and he was suddenly afraid that if he let her go now, that he would never see her again. He was not going to release his grip on her, no matter what happened next.

"*My father?!* Don't blame my father for *my* poor choice of a husband! I have only myself to blame! You are a drunk who chases other women and cares *nothing* for me, only for the legal benefits and security you got when we signed the marriage contract!"

"You must listen to me Elsje!" Gilles pleaded.

"Of course! Tell me more lies about why you come here every day when you have no work and why you don't feel it is important to mention this to me?"

"I leave every day because your father *ordered* me to stay away from you. It is *he* who kept us apart for the past week! He made me promise not to touch you again for a week after our wedding night and like a complete idiot *I agreed!* It's been too difficult for me to be around you!"

"Why would he do that?"

"He had some idea about your needing to recover from the wedding night. Is it important now *why* he made me promise? What is important is that this must stop, now! I want my wife back!"

His grip had slid down her arm to her wrist now and he held her more tightly than ever, hoping that he wasn't crushing any of her bones. His intention was not to hurt her, but to keep her. He thought that she might strike him but he resisted the urge to put his other hand up to protect himself, hoping that his being somewhat open and unprotected would encourage the return of some small measure of trust between them. Gilles could see Elsje struggling mentally with her confusion, trying to reconcile what the two men in her life had each told her, two very different juxtaposed stories. What Gilles wanted, more than anything else in the world at this moment, was to kiss her, here and now, in the street if he had to, and this made no sense at all to his rational mind, but there it was.

Elsje's chest still heaved from her recent bout of anger and confusion still ruled her face but she had stopped pulling away from Gilles. She looked from the closed front door of Hannah's house back to Gilles' face.

"You promised him? And you didn't tell me this?" Her eyes narrowed as she searched her husband's face for the truth.

"In France we respect our parents and we honor their wishes, no matter what they ask of us," Gilles said, somewhat abashedly.

He felt stupid. He felt like he had been taken advantage of by Hendrick. He wouldn't have let the old Dutchman dictate terms of trade to him in this way so why had he allowed him to dictate the terms of his own marriage?

"And of course you were raised to be *honorable*, to keep your promises?" There was sarcasm in Elsje's voice.

"Yes." Gilles relaxed his grip just a little, but he had learned the hard way that he should not relax too much; she might pull away at any moment or stamp on his foot again. "Yes, I was."

"You would break your vow to my father now, though, just to be with me?"

Gilles wasn't sure how to answer but he opened his mouth and the truth came out.

"I'm having a hard time keeping my word. I don't think it is reasonable for one man to tell another *not* to be with his wife when he wants to."

Elsje was somewhat calmer now and she regarded him with a stare that he had no idea how to interpret. He wasn't sure if she believed *any* of what he had just said to her although it was the truth, all of it.

Elsje took a deep breath before she spoke again. "If what you are telling me is true, then we need to start our lives over again, but on our *own* terms. We'll go home now and we'll straighten this out, off the streets where we can talk privately."

She turned in the direction of the inn and started to walk with Gilles still gripping her wrist. They walked faster as they went and at some point during their return, her hand slid into his. They said nothing to each other at all but hurried home together through the darkening streets, faster and faster until Gilles could feel her running at his side, as fast as he was running, and now the feeling came over him that together they could run faster than any other person in the world, that together they could vanquish anything or anyone that might stand in their way.

As they opened the front door to the inn, a man stood at the doorway adjusting his hat, preparing to leave. Elsje, her face red and flushed from running in the cold, moved aside to let the customer pass but Gilles recognized him as the man from Jacob's stable, the man who had asked Jacob all the questions about him and had been waiting for him on the day Gilles heard noises outside the shed when he was with Hannah. The man touched the brim of his hat in greeting, grinned at Gilles and jingled a pocket full of coins as he left the inn. Now Gilles had a pretty good idea as to how Hendrick knew about Hannah. He seethed in anger but said nothing to the man, just followed Elsje over to the stairs that led up to the apartment. They found Hendrick upstairs, sitting at the table.

"Ah, you are home, Elsje," Hendrick said, "You need to get our supper started." He looked a little surprised to see Gilles and even more startled to see Gilles take his wife's cloak from her shoulders.

"Tryntje can get your supper tonight," Elsje shot back immediately.

"Tryntje? You joke! She can't cook. What are we having? They have been serving leftover food from the feast down in the dining room until you could get back to cook."

"I don't know, you can make something yourself if you don't like *her* cooking," Elsje said, barely slowing down on the way to the bedroom with her husband's hand in hers, pulling him along behind her.

Elsje pulled Gilles into the bedroom and shut the door behind them but Hendrick knocked and then, without waiting for an invitation, he walked inside.

"I need a word with your husband," he said sternly to Elsje.

"He's busy now. Whatever it is, it can wait until afterwards, so please leave."

"I need to talk with him *now!*" Hendrick roared, glaring at Gilles.

Again Gilles opened his mouth to speak and again his wife spoke before he got the chance to answer his father-in-law.

"You will stay *out* of our bedroom and *out* of our bed! I will not have it! You are my father but you have no claim over me in matters that now relate to my husband. Get out now or we will move out this very night!" she said angrily.

Hendrick grumbled loudly and stormed out of the bedroom, kicking the door as he left, not seeming to be at all regretful of his intrusion. They could hear him stomping down the stairs as Elsje led Gilles over and sat him down on the bed. Gilles started to kiss her but Elsje held him off at arm's length.

"We have no difficulties *there*, Husband, so do not confuse the issue!"

Gilles pulled his hands away and wondered what Elsje needed to say first. It was very difficult to be patient when she was so close to him.

Elsje scolded Gilles as she would one of her younger siblings. "I would *never* have believed that he would do such a thing and *you* should never have made such a bargain but then, even if you did, you should have *told* me."

"It is not done so in France. A father's word is law."

"And it is not discussed with the women? Are they just property then?"

"Oh, no! It is our great respect for women that requires us to shield them from the world's concerns as much as possible."

"Hmph. Well, I want *no* such respect! I want you to talk with me. We have no regard here for those who do not take their wives' opinions into consideration. We always say it, the man is the head but the woman is the neck. One can't work *without* the other. Do I have your word on this?" She stretched her hand out to Gilles, a serious and determined look on her face.

Gilles accepted her hand and her terms, and as they shook on the agreement, Gilles felt a remnant of what he had felt before, on their way back to the inn. It was an odd thing, this feeling of trust and camaraderie, something rare enough by itself to share with another man but absolutely strange to feel in conjunction with a feminine body. It was a good feeling, though, one of the best of feelings, but he couldn't stop himself from asking her the other question.

"Could we confuse the issue *now?*"

Elsje threw back her head and laughed.

978-0-595-44349-
0-595-44349-4

LaVergne, TN USA
03 November 2009
162963LV00001B/85/A